ReGenesis

ReGenesis

An Alternative Future

To Nikki
You're just the
type of gal to
enjoy an adventure
to the stars!
Ben Lightfoot

Benjamin Lightfoot

To order additional copies of this book, contact:
Xlibris Corporation
1-888-795-4274
www.Xlibris.com
Orders@Xlibris.com
56643

Dedication

For my lovely wife, Linda, whose inspiring encouragement made *ReGenesis* possible.

Prologue

 B y the year 2025, the world situation on planet Earth had become critical. Terrorists had citizens of many countries on edge. In the United States, subway bombings in New York and Boston and airport bombings in several cities had national security teams on the alert everywhere. Even the Mall of America in Minneapolis had endured an explosion that destroyed a third of that facility, killing 485 people and injuring another 250. In Houston, Texas, a bomb exploded at the Johnson Spaceflight Center, destroying half of that facility. A deranged former astronaut was suspected.

That event and threats of bombings in cities all over the nation was causing the populace to stay at home. Most states had passed laws allowing the carrying of concealed weapons for self-defense, and handguns were as common as cell phones—especially in large cities. Gunfights in the street were becoming almost routine. People were afraid to use populated public and private facilities. The economy was really feeling the impact of widespread fear throughout the general public.

As a result of the devastation to the manned spaceflight center facility in Houston, NASA rebuilt the facility at Cape Canaveral, combining it with the launch facility there under the name Kennedy Spaceflight Center.

In the Middle East, little had really changed since the year 2008. Israel was still an island in a sea of Muslim nations all hating the Jews. Iran had become the dominant military power in the area with many weapons, including long-range nuclear missiles. It had not yet used such weapons, but it seemed to be only a matter of time. The United States had been forced to discontinue its efforts to create a solid democratic Iraq. It had withdrawn the last of its military forces in 2015. The Sunnis and the Shiites continued their civil conflict for control of the country. Iraq remained in chaos—far worse off than it had been before the United States invaded the country and ousted Saddam Hussein.

Civil wars were common around the globe, and conflicts between nations were rapidly increasing in number. Eight countries of the world were boasting nuclear weapons capability with another half-dozen countries expecting to come on line by 2030.

In the United States, crime was on the increase, prisons could not hold all those who should be incarcerated, and the streets in large areas of major cities were unsafe at night. Homes in affluent neighborhoods were being broken into on a regular basis, with many break-ins resulting in injuries and deaths. Drug trafficking was totally out of control, requiring a major application of law enforcement personnel. Because of overcrowded prisons and soft sentences, criminals of all types moved through the justice system like a revolving door. Punishment for crimes committed seemed totally ineffective.

With each new generation came an increasing disrespect for the law. Evil was winning over good. The antiquated system of justice in the United States and all democratic countries was proving to be totally inadequate in coping with deteriorating morals. The world seemed to be following the pattern of moral decay demonstrated by ancient Rome. Laws intended to protect the innocent were in fact protecting and shielding the guilty. Soft prisons and mild sentences for the guilty fueled the fires of crime rather than serve as a deterrent.

Because of the Middle East conflicts and the continued depletion of world oil reserves, the cost of oil-based fuel had skyrocketed. The pump price of gasoline had reached a crippling level, with the result that the average American family greatly curtailed its travel. The cost of oil and gas had a snowballing impact on almost all the economy in the United States and in other countries. Plastics, manufacturing, public and commercial transportation, and shipping costs were heavily affected. The price of oil was inflating the price of most goods and services across the nation. The countries of the world had failed miserably in their efforts to develop alternative fuels and were stuck with a dependency on far-too-expensive oil.

In addition, the widespread and continued burning of fossil fuels beginning in the twentieth century had resulted in extensive damage to the ozone layer and serious global warming of the planet. Glaciers began melting and the oceans of the world were rising, beginning in the 1990s and continuing into the twenty-first century. A special panel had been convened to study the effect of glacial melting. This panel estimated that by the year 2100, sea levels of the world will have risen by two feet. The projected impact of such a sea level rise would be devastating to all coastal cities.

All the adverse trends in war, terrorism, crime, and social and ecological decay were increasing at an increasing rate. The governments of the world were totally ineffective in taking actions to reverse the trends that were literally destroying the planet.

In spite of the badly deteriorating world situation, NASA continued its mission to venture beyond the bounds of Earth, exploring and utilizing other bodies in the solar system. The United States also continued its efforts to probe the galaxy in search of extraterrestrial intelligence. SETI had constructed and installed even more sophisticated equipment to reach out to the stars. One of the most advanced facilities in use by SETI was the Arecibo Observatory in Puerto Rico constructed in the early twenty-first century. Arecibo boasted the world's largest and most sensitive radio telescope. Built primarily to track asteroids that might impact Earth, its great power was also used to scan the stars in search of intelligent life.

1

Kennedy Spaceflight Center – 2025

The Earth rotated on its axis as usual during the night, revealing the sun in the east at dawn. It looked to be an absolutely perfect day at the Cape. A gentle breeze caressed the thousands of onlookers camping and waiting patiently across the dunes as far as the eye could see. A shout was heard from someone positioned on a large dune.

Then the shouts began increasing in number and in volume as each spectator began to see what the first one saw. During the night, the *Revelation* had been rolled from its hangar "nest" onto the pad only a few hundred yards from the end of the runway. Its white hull glistened in the early-morning sun. Onlookers had read all there was to read about the huge spacecraft and watched all the TV specials and news items. But looking at the real thing for the first time was overwhelming, even to the sturdiest of souls in the mass of humanity.

It seemed, to most, impossible to believe that the sleek craft standing majestically before them was preparing to charge through space as fast as light comes to Earth from the sun. Could it really be that this spaceship will travel 1300 years and trillions of miles to finally arrive on a distant world? Could it be that its crew, now all well known to the citizens of Earth, would age only a *year* during this spectacular voyage?

The numbers were too overwhelming for the average person to grasp. *Is the government lying to us again?* thought some.

But the throng was mesmerized. People were shooting pictures from hundreds of yards away and, as they often do at football games, using camera flashes and expecting the flashes to light the *Revelation* in the faint early-morning light.

The USAF Marching Band, positioned now by the open hangar doors, began its task at hand with "God Bless America." It had never sounded better in the clear morning air. Soon, all the thousands of spectators were singing with the band. Some voices were even in the right key.

A van rolled up near the stairs positioned at the crew flight deck door. The stairs had a Delta Air Lines logo on the side. It appeared that NASA had saved some of its budgeted funds by borrowing a 747-sized set of passenger stairs from an airline. The huge crowd cheered wildly as each of the astronauts exited the van, waving to the crowd and climbing the stairs toward the open flight deck door. At the top of the stairs, the six all turned and waved together. Camera flashes could be seen from hundreds of yards away. For a moment, as the band played the last verse of the music, it seemed as though time stood still. The astronauts wanted to enter the ship, but they seemed locked in a common bond with all the onlookers. It was the last time they would *ever stand on Earth*. The music stopped. The crew turned silently and entered the ship. The door closed behind them.

Inside the spacecraft, Colonel Dante Washington took the captain's left seat. First Officer Susan Chen locked herself firmly into the right seat. Jake Loneghan took the seat directly between and behind Dante and Susan. David and Ellen Marks and Maria Rodriguez locked themselves into their designated seats behind and slightly above the level of the seats of the pilots and Jake.

Dante initiated the engine-start sequence. As the mighty HD engines began to turn under their own power, the sound from them was clearly different from any the crowd had ever heard before. Some likened the noise to that of huge electrical dynamos. Onlookers could feel the enormous power of the engines in their bones as they watched in awe. The strength of the sound gave witness to the mega-power of these engines of the future.

David turned to scan all the instrumentation on the flight engineer's panel. Dante called for the removal of chocks and initiated the short taxi to the end of the 14,000 foot runway.

Dante prepared to advance power as he, Susan, Jake, and David once again scanned all instrumentation. Maria had been calling checklist items after the pre—takeoff procedure had been initiated. Ellen was monitoring all the vital signs of the crew on her panel.

Dante called out, "All systems go?" In predetermined sequence, each crew member responded, "All systems go."

Susan contacted Mission Control with, "Mission Control, this is *Revelation*. We are all systems in the green and prepared to launch."

"Roger, *Revelation*. We have all greens here. You are cleared for launch," came back over the flight deck intercom.

Dante clicked off the communication with Mission Control and said, "Now if we can just get this big SOB off the ground . . ."

Susan looked with raised eyebrows at Jake who was practically doubled over. Dante advanced the power levers to takeoff position as the *Revelation* started to roll.

None of the crew had ever felt anything like the acceleration resulting from the two HD engines. They had been conditioned somewhat by centrifuge training for the compressive pain they were now experiencing as the *Revelation* moved faster than a drag racer to its rotation point. The engine noise was now reaching *120 dB*! After about a four-second run and about five hundred feet down the runway, Dante rotated the ship for liftoff. Unlike any spacecraft flown off the

Earth before, rotation continued to the vertical as the *Revelation* shot off the runway into a vertical climb! Within seconds, the ship was a tiny dot overhead as the crowd strained to follow it. The *Revelation* had disappeared, not into the clouds, but *into the upper reaches of the atmosphere.*

Not a soul in the crowd had ever seen or heard anything like the departure of this machine—the powerful, unfamiliar sound of the engines; the liftoff after only five hundred feet of runway; and the vertical climb at unbelievable speed. The huge spacecraft had been right there in front of them; a few seconds later, it was *gone.*

Reaching orbital altitude, approximately one hundred miles above sea level, Dante pulled back on the column for insertion into orbit at about eighteen thousand miles per hour. As the ship completed insertion, Dante rolled the *Revelation* on its longitudinal axis to the same position as it had been on the runway—with the bottom of the ship facing Earth.

As Dante rolled the ship, Susan reduced engine power to idle, and all was absolutely quiet and still. All accelerations were now zero as the ship floated in orbit. Everything in the ship was weightless.

Ellen broke the silence. "My instruments say that you are all still alive!"

Everyone sighed and welcomed the relief. None had ever felt *anything* like that takeoff. Even the TransMars missions were using a single HD engine to attain orbit, then escape orbit, and launch for Mars. Dante was overwhelmed as were the others, but he tried to act nonchalant as though the whole thing was old hat to him.

But this trip was *something else.*

Jake, having never experienced a launch into space, was speechless.

Dante, sensing that the *Revelation* had finally gotten Jake's attention, was laughing. "So you had done everything there was to do on Earth, huh, Jake? Welcome to NASA and the world of space!"

"OK, boys," piped Maria. She had almost lost it during the launch but was now completely recovered. "We have work to do. In less than one hour, we reach the tangent point for our *real* launch and the jump to light-speed. There is plenty to do, so I suggest you guys quit marveling at our past accomplishments and *get busy.*"

Dante took a long look at Maria and said with a grin, "Those are *my* lines. OK, guys, let's hop on it!"

David was already deep into system checkout, reading and noting all system parameters. So far, so good. Susan was doing something with the landing gear lights and acting not too happy. "What's wrong?" asked Jake and Dante almost simultaneously.

"Nothing, I hope," said Susan. "I thought I saw a flicker on the nose gear door light after we were in vertical climb. Dante, did you notice anything abnormal with control as we approached orbit?"

"Seemed normal to me," said Dante. "David, what is the computer showing on the nose gear?"

"No indication of anomalies. The gear shows 'up and locked.' It's probably just an indicator glitch. We'll check it again before we go downtown."

Maria got everyone's attention with, "Should we *consider going out and taking a look?*"

Dante and Jake looked at each other with expressions that said *Oh crap! Why did she even say that?*

Dante responded, "Maria, there is a *lot wrong* with going for a space walk at this point. First, we only saw one flicker of the light. Secondly, the computer does not show a problem. And thirdly, we will have to take at least one extra rotation in orbit to give us enough time for a walk."

Susan offered, "I agree. If we had more flickers or a steady light, then maybe we should consider taking a look. What's the worst case on this?"

David heard his cue. "Worst case, since the gear shows 'up and locked,' is that the *gear door* is not closed properly. If that is the case, it will not cause a problem in flight. There will be no drag in space. The only risk I see would be a possible gear door malfunction on our arrival at Nyvar. I say check the lights and the computer again before we leave Earth, then after we reach orbit at Nyvar. If we need to, we can do a walk then before our approach to land. We need to keep in mind that Nyvar *may not be advanced enough to even have runways*. Longitudinal runway landing might *not even be possible*. In that case, we will be landing vertically from a hover position and attempting to set all three gears on the ground at once. There is nothing that has given us any indication of a *gear* problem, only a *possible* gear *door* problem.

"If the problem is still with us when we prepare to land, the worst case then would be that the door might jam the extension of the gear. In that case, one of us—probably me—will crawl down into the nose gear well and mechanically dislodge the strut from whatever is holding it on the door. Failing that, the ship will land *without the nose gear* in the vertical mode. Dante, in that case, you will just have to either set her down with the two mains and the nose structure *on the ground* or just land with all gear retracted—on the belly!"

"That," said Jake, "will be kinda messy because we may not be able to get the cargo doors open!"

"I agree," said Dante. "In case the nose gear will not come down, I will leave the main gear down. We might even be able to find a rock or a mound of dirt to set the nose on and keep the ship fairly level . . . who knows?"

"*All* we *had* was a caution light flicker on the nose gear door," said David. "Let's worry about it later."

The ladies weren't so sure about the men's rationale, but they didn't want to risk the space walk either—especially if the problem could be solved otherwise.

Susan said, "David, tell me again how you know that it is only the gear door."

After a more detailed explanation of how the nose gear and gear door worked, Susan was in agreement with the men. They would worry about the problem on arrival at Nyvar.

Thirty-five minutes later, all checks of systems and instrumentation had been completed. Ellen had completed her required medical checks of the crew, and no problems were found. The computer showed no anomalies. The nose gear lights and all other indicators were green.

Susan said, "Are we ready to call Mission Control?"

"Could we just do one more thing before we call?" asked Maria.

"What is that?" said Dante. "Did we miss something?"

"No," continued Maria. "But I, for one, would just like to take one last look at the magnificent blue planet before we leave it forever."

"I vote for that!" said Ellen.

"Me too," chimed in Susan.

David offered, "Do we have time?"

"Yes," said Jake.

"OK," said Dante. "Let's do it!" With that, Dante rolled the *Revelation* once again with the control thrusters. The entire flight deck window, below them now, was filled with the image of Earth. Gorgeous blue oceans and white clouds. The major continental landmasses were easily distinguishable. They were passing over China, and Maria said, "There's the Great Wall!" They were all in awe. Dante and Susan had seen this view before, but the others had not. They all just stared and soaked it up.

Finally, Jake broke everyone's trance with, "I see Donald Trump's hair!"

That did it. It brought them all back to reality.

Susan said, "OK, guys, back to work."

Each crew member was separately doing a gut check on their decisions to leave Earth. At least two of the crew were thinking, *I think I would change my mind now—If I could . . .*

But it was too late. They had given up their rights to life on Earth. They hoped that *maybe Nyvar would be a better place.*

Dante didn't want to hog all the fun. He said, "Susan, roll 'er back over for us!"

Susan eagerly took the controls and applied the needed pressures. The massive ship again rolled smoothly over like a big whale enjoying a still ocean. Dante made the call to base.

"Mission Control, this is *Revelation*. All Earth orbit checks have been completed, and all systems are go. Do you confirm our findings on your screens?"

Over the intercom came, "We concur, *Revelation*. We show all green. You are go to turn the ship over to the computer and move to your hibernation capsules. And . . . er . . . good luck and have a *great life*, you guys!"

"Roger," responded Dante, "and thanks!"

The bunk room was directly behind the flight deck. Here, the six hibernation capsules were arranged—two on each side and two in the rear of the compartment, bunk bed style. Dante and Susan were assigned the lower bunks, left and right; Jake and Maria the upper bunks, left and right; and David and Ellen Marks the rear bunks. Procedure required that Dante as mission commander be the last to enter his capsule. He would make one final check of all indicators and instruments before nap time. The computer was now in full command of the ship, holding orbit until the time to execute the command for orbit exit and JLS.

The six all exchanged pleasantries with one another. Even the men seemed a little wet—eyed. Jake asked not to be disturbed if there were any calls for him, and they promised to one another, "See you at Nyvar." The five climbed into their assigned berths and, using the internal controls for their separate capsules, initiated the hibernation, or sleep sequence, for each. The capsules closed and locked, and each occupant was administered the required drug. The atmosphere and temperature in each capsule were automatically altered consistent with the requirements for extended suspended animation. The Accel-Safe modules protected them from the accelerations to come.

Dante was still in the command left seat and again looked carefully at each and every indicator. He turned and scanned the flight engineer's panel to the right of David's chair. Everything looked A-OK. He looked at the time. Five minutes to go before the big trip would be initiated. He looked at his fellow crew members lying in their respective capsules and thought, *They look pretty dead to me.*

Dante climbed into his berth and initiated the sleep sequence. He thought, *I just* feel *like there's something I forgot to do, but I can't think of what it is.*

The capsule closed and Dante quickly looked as "dead" as the five other brave souls.

All was still. Two minutes to go.

2

At the Main Gate—Kennedy Spaceflight Center

The guard was calling in to the main security post. "Sir, this is Adams at the gate. We have a person here with no credentials for entry to the base . . . but he does have an FBI ID."

The officer of the day responded, "What's he want, Henry?"

"He says he needs to see a Jakob Loneghan. Say, isn't that one of the six astronauts we just launched on the *Revelation* this morning?"

"You are correct. Let me speak with the man."

The gate guard turned to the FBI man and said, "Our OD wants to speak with you."

The agent took the phone. "This is Archie Bloomster, special agent for the FBI. I have a warrant here for the arrest of one Jakob Loneghan, who I understand now works for NASA. It seems he is wanted on tax-evasion charges."

The officer of the day turned white and gulped. He regained his composure and said firmly, "Well, I'm sorry, but you *just missed him*."

"Where is he?"

"That would be impossible for me to say with any accuracy. I can tell you that at this very moment, he is somewhere in orbit around the Earth." He glanced at his watch. "And in just a few minutes, that information will be old."

"Look here, sir," said the agent. "I do not *have time for games*. When exactly will Mr. Loneghan be back here so I can serve him with this warrant?"

"I am not playing games with you, sir, and the answer to your question is *never!*"

"What is that supposed to mean?" retorted the agent.

The OD continued, "I'm not sure where you are getting your information from, but let me be completely clear. Jake Loneghan is one of the six astronauts now aboard the *Revelation* spaceship en route to a planet called Nyvar. The crew will never return to Earth. I thought everybody knew that."

"Don't get snide with me, bud. I am just doing my job. I need to talk with your superior!"

The OD had had quite enough of Mr. Bloomster and said, "Sir, I will do better than that. I will arrange for you to see the director of the space center, and I will send a car down to the gate to pick you up. Just park your vehicle and wait. Someone will be there in five minutes."

The NASA vehicle arrived on time and took agent Bloomster to the elevator door that would deliver him directly to the tenth floor and to the office of the Director of Kennedy Spaceflight Center, Dr. Aaron Soderberg. Erica, the director's secretary, met the FBI agent at the elevator door.

"Right this way, sir," she said and led agent Bloomster into Director Soderberg's office.

Aaron rose from behind his desk, greeted the agent, and offered him a chair. As Archie took the chair, Aaron said, "There must be some mistake on this, mister . . . er . . . Bloomster, is it?"

"Bloomster is correct, and there is no mistake," asserted the agent.

Aaron was instantly annoyed with the agent's manner. "I'll tell you *why* there is some mistake. May I call you Archie?" Archie nodded, and Aaron continued, "Here is why there *has to be a mistake*. Your agency, the Federal Bureau of Investigation, conducted your top-level investigation of all our six astronauts selected for our *Revelation* mission, Archie . . . You *have* heard of the *Revelation* mission, have you not?" Archie shuffled a bit and said that he had been pretty busy of late and wasn't real sure whether he had heard about the mission.

Aaron could not believe his ears. "Oh, I see. Well, no matter. Either *you* are making a mistake with your warrant, or your agency had made a *colossal blunder* in granting the top secret clearance to our astronaut Mr. Loneghan. And either way, it doesn't matter now because Jake Loneghan and the rest of the *Revelation* crew are moments away from leaving Earth's orbit for travel to a distant star system—*never to return to Earth*!"

Aaron continued—he was hot!—"So I suggest that you go right back to Washington and explain things to the director of the FBI. Furthermore, you might want to keep this *huge snafu* under wraps and just hope that the media doesn't get wind of it."

Dr. Soderberg added as he arose from his chair and buzzed for Erica, "We will do our best here at NASA to keep the matter quiet although I make no guarantees." He looked at Erica, saying, "Erica, please see that Mr. Bloomster is returned to the main gate and to his vehicle."

After the two left the room, Aaron put in a call for Doctor Ben Javitz, director of NASA, in Washington. He wanted to be the very first to let Ben in on the news. As Ben's phone was ringing, Aaron turned again to the monitor that was giving him the latest from the *Revelation*. They were now only *two minutes from Earth departure*. The crew was in hibernation, and all instruments and sensors were green. The director put down the phone and headed for Mission Control—he could always talk to Ben Javitz. Besides, he just remembered that Ben and all his headquarters staff were receiving all the same data from the ship that Mission

Control was. They would all be in a conclave in the main conference room at headquarters in Washington.

As Aaron entered Mission Control, all controllers were gazing intently on their individually assigned screens. The *ten-second countdown had begun*. Three large screens at the front of the room displayed images of the Earth on the left and right screens. These were being transmitted from cameras mounted in the nose and at the rear of the *Revelation*. An image showing the top of the *Revelation* was being shot from a wide-angle camera atop the vertical fin of the spacecraft and was being presented on center screen.

All instrumentation and sensors were still green. All systems were go. The countdown continued, "Eight . . . seven . . . six . . . five . . . four . . . three . . . two . . . one."

"WE HAVE JLS!" called the chief of Mission Control.

On the *Revelation*, the ship's computer engaged the immense power of the HD engines. *The spacecraft exited orbit faster than a cannon shot!* The *Revelation* was on its way. Its speed was rapidly increasing—50,000 miles per second, 100,000 mps, now 150,000 mps—rapidly approaching light-speed. The camera on the rear of the ship transmitted a magnificent view of the receding Earth. Within two seconds, while continuing to accelerate, the ship passed directly above the moon, casting its shadow on the small NASA lunar outpost station constructed in the last three years.

Back in Mission Control, cheering and shouting permeated the center. Everyone was congratulating everyone!

Exactly at JLS and while there were still images and data being received by Mission Control, a *single red light* glowed on one of the controllers' panels and also appeared at the bottom of the main center screen. The cheering and shouts instantly ceased as if all voice boxes suddenly went inop. Cigars fell to the floor.

Director Soderberg shouted to a nearby controller, "*What is that light?*"

By the time the controller identified the light and said, "That's *the nose gear door light*, sir," all the screens and panels were blank! The *Revelation* was moving away at almost light—speed, and communication with the ship was no longer possible.

The *Revelation* had now achieved the required mission cruise speed. No additional acceleration was needed, and the ship's computer reduced power to that required to maintain cruise speed and enable the shield around the ship. The protective shield would cause most space debris to bounce off and away from the ship's hull. If anything large was detected to be approaching on a collision track, the computer would then maneuver the ship and deal with it as required.

Aboard the *Revelation*, its valuable crew rested comfortably. The massive acceleration accomplished by the HD engines caused them no harm in their suspended state. They would not have survived the acceleration sequence had they not been safely in their capsules. The HD engines were at constant power now, having achieved near light-speed; and a low-pitched hum was audible, emanating from the equipment powering the capsules. Too bad the crew couldn't see the magnificent view outside the *Revelation*. The aft camera dutifully recorded what it saw.

Five hours after JLS, the *Revelation* crossed the orbit of Pluto, once classified as the ninth planet of the solar system.

The planets of the solar system first grew small, then began to fade from the camera's view. Now only the sun could be seen by the rear camera of the ship—only a tiny star in the heavens, but a bright one. All the ship's eight cameras continued to photograph beautiful, unimpaired views of the heavens. Ahead over four hundred light-years from the sun was the Orion constellation of stars, including Betelgeuse, the largest star within one thousand light-years. The Pleiades, the Lagoon Nebula of Sagittarius, and thousands of other celestial sights were being filmed and photographed with crystal clarity in the absence of atmosphere. Photographs even the Keck and Hubble telescopes had never captured were being recorded as the *Revelation* raced across the Milky Way galaxy.

Straight ahead, the Setarian star system—home of Nyvar—could be seen by the ship's nose camera.

3

Six Months Earlier—at NASA Headquarters, Washington DC

"Fred!" called Armond with a loud whisper. "Let's go. We'll be late!"

"For what?"

"The director's staff meeting. You know *what*!"

"Are we invited? I thought it was just his direct reports."

"Today is a special meeting! Where *have you been*, in orbit?"

Fred took no offense to the friendly poke. "I've been right here, working very hard, unlike some of us who have our noses in everyone else's business," he returned the jab. Armond ignored the comment.

"Director Javitz is supposedly going to make a very special announcement this morning."

"Any idea about what?" Fred queried as he looked at his watch and picked up the pace toward the main conference room.

By this time, the two had been joined by several others heading in the same direction. Someone said, "I'll bet this meeting is about the *Revelation*! I heard a rumor!"

"Naw," said another. "That project is on indefinite hold."

"Five bucks says Javitz is going to announce a 'go' for *Revelation*."

"You're on!" said Armond.

By this time, the group reached the main doors of the conference room and entered. Already seated around the large conference table in the center of the room were all the project managers and team leaders, those who reported to the director. The only seats open were the "peon" seats around the wall.

Fred, Armond, and the others, arriving a tad on the late side, quickly sought and slid into available seats, waiting to be chided for their tardiness. The director did not disappoint them. Speaking from a simple lectern at the head of the table, he began, "Now that we are *all here*," he voiced with half-smiling glance in the direction of the latecomers, "I hope all of you are prepared for some exciting news."

Fred nudged Armond and exhibited a slight smirk.

The director continued, "As you all know, our *Revelation* mission has been on hold for almost a year now as we have been busy sorting out and selecting the best possible destination for the mission. Some of you are new to the division and may not be aware of the mission we have planned for the finest ship we have ever constructed. I will give you all a quick review.

"Ten years ago, the General Electric Company, working with Pratt & Whitney Aircraft Engines, announced to the world that their team had successfully built and tested a hyperdrive engine capable of propelling a spacecraft at near light-speed. As a result of that achievement, we have successfully built a ship with those engines and flown two of our round-trip missions to Mars. About eight years ago, we proposed to Congress a plan to build a starship capable of attaining the speed of light and with a range of two thousand light-years' flight time."

One of the recent additions to the space research staff dropped his coffee cup.

The director pretended not to notice and continued, "The mission proposed for this magnificent technical achievement is to transport explorers and astronauts to a distant planet somewhere within the range of the vehicle. The purpose of the mission is to have our team *join* whatever life there is on the target planet or if there *is no intelligent life there*, to *become* the human life on the planet and begin a new civilization.

"As most of you know, after considerable debate, Congress approved the plan and the funds to develop the ship and send it on its mission. Since that approval and authorization eight years ago, we have accomplished much. The *Revelation* has been designed and built and is now housed in hangar 7 at the Kennedy Spaceflight Center in Florida. It is virtually ready to launch."

He continued, "The good news is that we have sorted through several candidate planets and selected one. A planet in the Setarian star system about 1300 light-years from our Earth. We have named the planet Nyvar, a word taken from two Swedish words, *ny* and *varld*, meaning 'new world.'"

A gasp of excitement rippled through the conference room!

Director Javitz continued, "Our Deep Space Research Team has done an excellent job over the past eighteen months in examining and studying planets in several systems within the range of *Revelation*. Our criteria has been to find a planet as *much like Earth as possible* and as near the *age* of Earth as possible. We believe that such a planet would have the best possible chance of supporting life as we know it. We hope that Nyvar is home to intelligent life. Unfortunately, our radio, optical, and sensor capabilities cannot actually detect from this distance whether or not life exists on the planet but our devices *have told* us that the temperature range of the planet and its atmospheric conditions are conducive to life as we know it. We have also determined the *presence of water* and the percentage of water on its surface. Trust me when I tell you that Nyvar is enough like Earth in the parameters we can measure to be its twin!"

A murmur of awe and excitement rippled through the room. Director Javitz continued, "And now for the biggest news of the day. Just ten days ago, as we were preparing a proposal for President Buchard's approval to launch the *Revelation* on a mission to Nyvar, SETI's observatory in Arecibo, Puerto Rico, contacted us with a startling report. They had received electronic signals from the vicinity of the Setarian star system. The data appears to have been transmitted from an intelligent life source!"

The crowd gasped in awe! *Finally*, after hundreds of years of searching and probing, a message from *extraterrestrial intelligence.*

Director Javitz continued, "So far, we only know that the signals received are transmitted messages—we have no idea as to the message content. From the characteristics of the signals, we believe them to be the transmission of a *woman's voice*. The receipt of this data has served to support our earlier findings about the nature of the planet Nyvar and our belief that the planet supports intelligent life. Needless to say, we immediately submitted our proposal for the *Revelation* mission to the president along with the report from Arecibo. President Buchard has enthusiastically given us a green light to *proceed with the mission.*"

A cheer went up from the audience, requiring Director Javitz to raise his arms for silence. "We have more to share with you," he said. "Director Edmunds has headed up the Deep Space Research Team and will give you more details about Nyvar. Doctor Edmunds?"

"Sir!" ventured a voice from among the "peon" ranks on the back wall.

"Please stand and identify yourself," said Director Javitz as Carl Edmunds made his way to the podium.

The young man stood. "I just joined your staff, coming from a research position at MIT, and I have only been here two weeks. My name is Jason Mauer. Can I interrupt and ask a question?"

"You have already interrupted, Mr. Mauer, and you have already asked a question. Now please take your seat and wait until our presentation is finished. We will try to answer all questions at that time."

A murmur of amusement trickled about as Doctor Edmunds prepared to speak.

"Nyvar is approximately 1300 light-years from Earth, taking into account its orbit about its star. As near as we can determine, the Setarian system has eight planets orbiting its star, and the system is amazingly similar to our solar system and our sun. The planet we are calling Nyvar is roughly the same distance from its star as we are from our sun."

He continued, "As Director Javitz stated, the size of Nyvar, the condition of its surface, and the content of its atmosphere appear to be very similar to ours. Our ability to estimate the age of the Setarian system is limited, but we believe the system probably was formed about 4.7 billion years ago, putting it in roughly at the same time of formation as that of our Earth. Of course, we all know that modern man has only been on Earth for some four thousand to thirty thousand years, an instant of time when we consider our estimated lifetime of the universe and that of our galaxy—somewhere around twenty to thirty billion years."

"We looked at twelve other systems and planets within the range of the *Revelation*, searching for a target planet to explore. Nyvar is the *closest match* to Earth and *our best bet*. We are confident of that!"

Looking at the director, Director Edmunds said, "That's all I planned to say at this time unless you want more detail."

"No, that's fine," said Director Javitz, retaking the lectern. "Now, Mr. Mauer, what is your question?"

Jason Mauer had been nursing his wounds and was startled by the sudden word from the director and by the stares in his direction. Not to be deterred, however, he stood up straight and cleared his throat.

"Sorry for the earlier interruption, sir. I was not familiar with the protocol in this meeting forum."

"No problem, Mr. Mauer. Now PLEASE, we are all in suspense. What is your question?"

More laughter dotted the room. Jason summoned his courage.

"Why are we sending an astronaut team on a mission that will take 1300 years to complete? There is no way they can report back what they find, and everything that is now on this Earth will probably be long gone before they reach their destination."

The room suddenly became so silent one could have heard a pin drop on the carpet. Director Javitz stared at the young scientist for what seemed like a lifetime and finally said, "That is an excellent question, Mr. Mauer. Who would like to answer it?"

No one dared to move or even breathe.

"No brave souls among us?" said Ben Javitz. "Then I will answer it."

Everyone began to breathe again, and Jason Mauer sat down. He really wanted to be somewhere else at that moment, but he thought his mother might be proud of him for his bravery in asking the question.

"Why, indeed?" started Director Javitz. "Why does NASA exist? Why have we ventured into space? Why do we have orbiting space stations? Why have we returned to the moon? Why have we successfully completed three missions now to Mars?

"Because we MUST, Jason. Because we *must*! It is in man's nature to go beyond what he knows. What else is out there? He must find out! If Christopher Columbus had not looked for and found the new world, where would we be now? Still in Europe, wondering how far away the edge of the Earth was . . .

"The only thing new and different about the *Revelation* mission is that we—you and I and indeed no one alive today—will ever *know what our explorers find*. But *our astronauts* will know! The six brave, adventurous souls that volunteer their very lives and souls to this mission will, hopefully, in only about a year's time of their lives, have traveled almost eight thousand *trillion* miles through space and arrived at a new world—at least *new to them.* They will have moved through not only space but *time.* The physical conditions or civilization they find on Nyvar will not be the one that is there now. It will be the civilization on that planet *1300 years from now.*"

He continued, "If they find *no civilization,* they will begin one. We are confident that there will be some forms of life there—there *has* to be. Hopefully, they will be wise enough to develop a civilization on their new home, avoiding the problems we have created on this Earth—problems that essentially began when Cain killed Abel . . .

"If there *is* intelligent life on Nyvar, let us hope that the beings on that planet embrace our pioneers as I am sure our brave adventurers will embrace them. Maybe our team will find a greatly advanced society with technologies far more sophisticated than ours now on Earth. Maybe this advanced society will have solved all the social and degenerative problems we have that are beginning to destroy our Earth and its people. And just *maybe* the society on Nyvar will be far enough advanced to have developed spacecraft that can even *exceed* the speed of light! Perhaps they will have even developed a *time machine* which would let our representatives return to Earth in our present time with solutions for us that might just save Earth from possible destruction. I am sure that our six astronauts will, if it is possible to do so, find a way to return to us with great knowledge and technology from the future. They could possibly bring information and capabilities that can greatly benefit our Earth and its people."

Director Javitz continued, "But if we don't send our brave astronauts to explore this new world, we will *never know what might have been,* will we?"

The room was still and hushed. Everyone was overwhelmed by the director's words. Some felt sympathy for Jason, others felt disdain, and still others were very proud of him. *But all were glad he asked his question.* They all remembered *why they were there.*

4

Director Javitz was excited beyond words. His pet project was going to fly! Not just fly, mind you, but fly to the far reaches of the galaxy. The *Revelation* had been Javitz's baby since before the "child" was conceived. When the engine builders found the key to a propulsion system capable of moving a ship at near the speed of light, Ben Javitz began to dream of the possibilities. The first applications of the HD engine were the previously planned missions to Mars. The engine was capable of reducing the travel time from Earth to Mars from over two days to a *few hours*. The ship was so fast that from Earth to Mars, it was operated at *much less* than its light-speed capability. The mission usually took three days. The HD engine had proven to be so successful in powering the Mars and lunar missions that the mining of valuable ores from those bodies had become both practical and economical. HD-powered ships were now returning several times each month with minerals now in short supply on Earth. The HD engine was ready for the ultimate challenge—the mission to Nyvar *and to the future*.

Ben had no worries about the hardware, but he had substantial concerns about the selection of the crew. After all, NASA would be selecting a team who would represent either the Adams and Eves of another world or our ambassadors from Earth to the civilization of a world new to us. In either case, the choices for the six-person crew must be the *right choices* as far as humanly possible.

The director put out the notice to all astronauts on staff both in Washington and at the Cape and gave them one week to apply for any of the positions they were interested in.

Notice to All Astronaut Personnel
Mission Volunteers Requested

Background. The *Revelation* mission to a distant planet has been approved. The target is the planet Nyvar in the Setarian system, approximately 1300 light-years from Earth. Those volunteering for this mission will be part of the crew traveling at very close to light-speed for 1300 Earth years. Because of the cruise speed of this mission, members of the crew will only age about one year by the time the Revelation reaches Nyvar.

A little about Nyvar. The planet and its system are strikingly similar to Earth. This is why Nyvar was selected. We have determined that Nyvar is about the same size as Earth, has a very similar atmospheric content, and has about the same amount of water on its surface as does Earth. The temperature range of the planet is slightly warmer than that of Earth.

What we are not able to determine is whether the planet has intelligent life. Since we think that Nyvar is about the same age as Earth and because of its other similarities to our planet, we believe that it must have life and may well have an intelligent civilization. Voice transmissions recently detected by the Arecibo Observatory appear to have originated from the vicinity of the Setarian star system. This reinforces our belief that Nyvar has intelligent life. However, we cannot be sure. On the other hand, the planet may not have any form of life. The crew of six going on this mission must be prepared for either eventuality as well as others.

This is a one-way mission. As stated, the Earth will have aged 1300 years by the time the crew of the Revelation reaches Nyvar. Because of the speed of the ship and the distances involved, there will be no way for the crew to communicate with us during the mission or, so far as we know, after arrival at Nyvar. The Revelation will be stocked with all the food, supplies, tools, and equipment you will need to begin life on the new planet. Beyond that, you will be on your own. This is the most personally demanding mission ever undertaken by NASA astronauts.

Crew Requirements. With guidance from Congress and the administration, NASA has set the crew size at six members—three male and three female. The age range for the mission is twenty-five to thirty-five; and all members of the crew must be single, heterosexual, fertile, and able to father or conceive children. All applicants must have at least one college degree. We have also established hard specifications for the six positions to be filled. The following lists the crew positions and minimum qualifications required.

Medical Doctor—Internist preferred, others will be considered. Specialties that will be helpful include orthopedics and work in artificial organ and/or limb development.

Lawyer and Expert in Government—Background in contracts and torts desirable. Experience in elected office at state or federal level very desirable.

CEO—Experience in directing a successful company most desirable. Knowledge of business and accounting practices a must.

Engineer/Designer—Degree in electrical or mechanical engineering highly desirable. Experience in designing and developing electromechanical devices and/or computers a plus.

Military Leader—Officer with command experience required. The larger the scope of command, the better. Combat experience a plus. Officers with no command experience need not apply.

Humanitarian/Theologian/Consumer Advocate—Persons with experience in any of these fields will be considered.

Application Procedure. There is only one of each of the above positions available. If you are qualified and have a sincere interest in this mission, please complete the back of this form and submit it to the assistant director of personnel located at DNP@NASA. gov. All applications, to be considered, must be submitted by Friday, June 6.

Two Months Later—in Director Javitz's Office

At the time the notice went out to the astronaut corps, Ben Javitz had selected three of his most trusted staff members to receive and evaluate all applications for the *Revelation* mission. The three had subsequently reported to Director Javitz that they were not going to be able to fill two of the slots from within the NASA ranks—they would need to look outside for the CEO and the consumer advocate. They were given the OK to do this and now had solid candidates for all six positions. They were ready to present their recommendations to Director Javitz.

Adam Gray and Emile Johansson had arrived and were seated. Ed Ray was just entering the room as Director Javitz's secretary, Diane, was asking if anyone would like coffee.

Ben Javitz said, "Diane, you better take some lunch orders while you are at it. We're going to be in this one a long time."

Diane took everyone's sandwich order while Javitz finished the phone call he was on and took his seat at the table. He opened the discussion.

"Gentlemen, I understand you have recommendations for all six of our *Revelation* mission crew. Am I correct?"

Adam responded, "You are correct, sir, but all of our recommendations are not exactly in line with the strict specifications we were told to follow for each of the crew positions."

"Why not?" asked Javitz.

"We think the choices we have to recommend are better than our available choices if we must stick to the script," said Ed Ray.

"I trust the judgment of you three," said Javitz. "But even if you convince me that we should go with your choices, which don't all follow the rules, how about Congress? Do you guys realize what a can of worms that will be? It could delay the mission weeks, maybe months, before the clowns get through their act and finally approve what we want to do. And they may *not* approve any deviation from the specs that we were given!"

"Wait!" said Emile. "Out of the six positions, four of our recommendations meet the specifications we were given. Only two don't, but they meet the intent!"

Ben Javitz felt some degree of relief. "Which positions are OK, and which are not OK? Maybe this won't be as bad as I had thought."

Emile continued, "The positions of CEO, military officer, legal expert, and consumer advocate are covered. No problems with those, but—"

"Now *wait* a minute!" Javitz voice was raised to a tone unfamiliar to the group. "You are telling me that you have a problem with the doctor and the engineer? We had four doctors on staff and thirty—how many—engineers, and you have a problem finding TWO that will meet our requirements for these two positions?"

Adam jumped in, "Relax, Ben, we aren't presenting this properly. Let me quickly tell you that we *have* alternates that meet our specs *exactly* for both of these slots, but we are *recommending* two people on staff that don't *exactly* meet the specs."

"Then we will go with the two that meet the specs!" said Javitz. "Why screw around? Now you are telling me that we have our crew. We have six volunteers that meet the specs approved by NASA and Congress! I don't see a problem."

Adam, Ed, and Emile looked at one another.

"*What*?" said Javitz. "What am I missing? What do you guys know that I don't?"

"Sir, just let us tell you *why* we recommend a doctor and an engineer that don't meet the specs."

"Well, I will be *overjoyed* to hear this! Please tell me!" Javitz almost hissed at the three.

Ed took the floor. "The *doctor and the engineer we recommend are married—to each other . . .*"

Director Javitz was speechless. He just looked at them.

Ed continued, "This couple is outstanding. Ellen Marks and David Marks are the best in their fields in our entire astronaut corps. Let us just review their accomplishments and their capabilities."

Javitz was frozen. He *knew* both Ellen and David personally and had been most impressed with them each time he spoke with them or worked with them. He said, "You three have put on a Three Stooges act for the last ten minutes, and my blood pressure is up thirty-five points! Why didn't you tell me you were talking about David and Ellen in the first place?"

"Well . . . er . . . we . . . er . . . ," stammered Emile.

Adam slumped into his chair, and Ed started to laugh.

The laugh caught on, and everyone laughed.

Javitz, regaining his composure, said, "So you are telling me that each person you are recommending *individually* meets our requirements?"

"Outstandingly!" Adam injected.

Javitz continued, "But two of them are married to each other."

The three just sat and smiled at Ben Javitz. No one spoke for what seemed like forever. Director Javitz got up and walked to the window, looking out. "Do any of your recommended candidates have any family alive?"

Adam spoke, "Some do . . . mothers, sisters, cousins, etc. None feel that their relatives will be of any concern in their volunteering for the mission, however."

"How about David and Ellen?" said Javitz.

Emile flipped a couple of papers. "Her mother is alive. His parents are both deceased. There are no children."

"OK, let's leave David and Ellen in the mix, but I will review your second choices for those two slots as well. Let's take five, then go into the details of each astronaut. By the way, are those you recommend for the CEO slot and the consumer advocate on our staff?"

"No, sir," said Ed.

The break lasted fifteen minutes rather than five, and the four reconvened at the table.

"Who do you want first, sir? Any preference?" said Emile.

"Nope." said Ben. "Your show . . . proceed."

By prior agreement, Adam was to present two—the military officer and the CEO. Ed was taking the lawyer and the consumer advocate, and Emile was to cover the doctor/engineer couple and, if required, the alternates for those two. Adam began.

"Dante Washington is our choice for the military officer. He is thirty-five years old, African American, holds the rank of bird colonel USAF, and has eight years experience in administration as squadron commander. He is a veteran of our space programs, having completed three missions thus far—two shuttle missions and one round-trip to Mars. He is a graduate of the Air Force Academy with top honors. Dante is divorced and has no children. He maintains himself in excellent physical condition and is a black belt in karate. We believe that Colonel Washington is an outstanding candidate for our crew."

"Do all of you agree with that assessment?" Javitz looked at each around the table.

All nodded and said, "Yes, sir."

"Next," said Javitz.

Ed took a turn. "Susan Chen was an attorney before becoming an astronaut. She is twenty-eight years old and obtained a degree in engineering before she studied law. She specialized in corporate law and considers herself somewhat of an expert in that field. Susan also studied law enforcement and our judicial system. Both of these studies came after she received her law degree and while she was practicing. She has also done some volunteer work for the Republican Party. Susan has been a crew member on two shuttle flights. We were limited in our choice for an attorney. Both of the two on staff applied for the mission. Susan seems to be the best qualified and is eager to be a part of the *Revelation* team. She is not married and has one brother living in Denver. She has not seen her parents since they returned to China while she was in college. We think she has the right skills and personality to be an excellent crew member."

"All agree?" said Javitz. All indicated agreement, and the director said, "Next . . ."

Adam presented the next applicant. "Our CEO applicant is quite the guy. Jake Loneghan made his first money with his own golf equipment business. He started small with a web site and was successful. He kept expanding and now has over 250 retail outlets nationwide. His company employs about 7,300 people and does about $850 million annually. Nobody can quite figure how he has done so well in a field that is so competitive. Anyway, he is now wealthy and bored. Two years ago, he built his own yacht, sailed in the America's Cup, and won. He now owns a professional basketball team and a movie company, with both apparently doing well. Last year, he flew around the world nonstop in a single-engine Bert Rutan Corporation plane. Jakob saw our ad in the *Journal* and immediately responded. His comment to me was 'This sounds like a real blast!' We think he meets all our requirements."

"I'm wary of this guy already, and I haven't even met him," said Javitz softly.

"That was my initial reaction too," said Emile. "But after I interviewed him, I changed my mind. Jake has such a high IQ, so much talent, and so much energy that everything he tries seems easy to him. He's bored and wants a real challenge."

"Does he realize that he will basically be a passenger on a computer-controlled flight for the most part and will be sleeping almost the *entire thirteen centuries* he is in space?" Javitz queried.

"He totally understands the mission. I think it's the unknown that intrigues him, together with the boredom he is experiencing on this Earth."

"You have other good applicants for this position?" asked the director.

"Yes," said Adam, "several."

"Good! I will interview this hotshot and see what my one-to-one reaction is. Let's go to the next one."

Emile started to go with the doctor/engineer couple, but Javitz said, "Let's take the consumer advocate next and save the fun 'til last."

Ed jumped on that statement. "I think you are going to have fun with this one!"

He continued, "Maria Rodriguez has been opposed to almost everything the big government and U.S. industry have ever tried to do. She is a member of Greenpeace, about as far left as you can get. And wherever you find protesters, you will find Maria."

"Just stop right there!" Javitz snorted. "How can such a person function successfully as a member of a team?"

"I understand your reaction, but just let me tell you her long list of qualifications."

"I'll listen, but I won't put anyone on this crew that cannot work as a team member!" said Javitz. "Why the hell did she volunteer, and how did we find her?"

Ed continued, "Myron in Personnel did some spot advertising on TV. I don't know what the ads looked like, but he sure got a response. We have thirty-five candidate volunteers!"

"And this Maria is the best one?"

Ed ignored the question and said, "Here is her picture." He showed it to Javitz.

"You are kidding!" said Javitz. "This is a gorgeous woman! This is no protester."

"She's both," said Ed. "Just listen. She won the Miss America crown in 2013. She graduated magna cum laude from Vassar in 2017. She started and ran her own business for several years and accumulated some wealth. Now she models when she feels like it for *very nice fees*."

"She's doing great. Why would she want to volunteer to go away forever to a distant planet?"

"She's bored and wants to do something really important with her life."

"We've got one bored person. I'm not sure we can stand another." Javitz did not like what these two wealthy outsiders might do to his mission. "I will talk with her, but you better have some other good choices!"

"We do," countered Ed. "But Maria is of Mexican descent and, we think, the best!"

"Would you guys feel the same if this gal wasn't such a knockout?" He paused for effect and then continued, "Let's finish this meeting. Emile, let's talk about our doctor/engineer couple, David and Ellen Marks."

Emile began, "David is one of our top engineer-scientists." He received his bachelor's in electromechanical engineering at Caltech in 2014 and went on to MIT for a master's in aerospace. After two years at MIT's astrophysical Dryden Labs, he joined us here. At NASA, he has held a number of assignments including a lead design position on the TransMars spacecraft and most recently was the lead design integrator on the *Revelation* ship, taking personal charge of the engine-airframe development and integration. He knows the *Revelation* like no other scientist on our staff."

"I would hate to lose such talent," injected Javitz. "Continue."

"David's wife of six months, the former Ellen Eichmann, is one of the most talented physicians I have ever been aware of. Ellen finished her premed at the University of Alabama and transferred to the University of Virginia Medical School. Her initial degree was in general medicine, and she went on to specialize in orthopedics and artificial limbs. After that, learning of an exciting program in artificial organ design at John's Hopkins, she entered that program. While she was doing all of this, in her spare time, she became a very serious astronomer and has worked closely with our Deep Space Research Team. Ellen, in fact, discovered the planet Nyvar in the Setarian system."

"So you want me to approve sending the engineer/designer most responsible for the success of the *Revelation* development and his wife, who discovered the planet the ship is going to, on the ship as crew members?"

"Who better?" said Emile.

"I agree," said Adam. "An absolutely outstanding choice!"

"But there is so much more they can do for Earth by staying here." said Ed.

A long silence ensued while Ben Javitz went to the window and just stared at the sky. It was one of those days when you could see the full moon in broad daylight. He returned to the table.

"Let's get some lunch in here," said Director Javitz. He buzzed for Diane.

5

Director Javitz interviewed all the recommended candidates for the *Revelation* mission, including the alternates proposed for the CEO position and the consumer advocate position. After much soul-searching, he came to the same conclusion that his three-man team had. The slate of six proposed by his staff represented the best choices available for the mission. Director Javitz had persuaded the Senate Space Exploration Oversight Committee to approve, including a married couple on the astronaut team, but only because of the outstanding abilities the Marks pair possessed. He lamented the loss of both David and Ellen from the staff at NASA because of the significant contributions they had both made to the agency programs. Ben rationalized, however, that they would both be extremely valuable members of the astronaut team, both during the journey and after the arrival of the *Revelation* on Nyvar. Particularly so if any unforeseen problems should arise during the journey. David's knowledge of the *Revelation* would be invaluable.

Director Javitz also selected Dante Washington as the mission commander because of his command and administration experience, his space mission experience, and his skills as a pilot.

Letters went out to the members of the *Revelation* crew to notify them of their selection to the team. They were to be given two weeks to put their earthly affairs in order and report to Kennedy Spaceflight Center at Cape Canaveral.

Maria Rodriguez was at her condo in Georgetown packing a few things for a weekend on the beach when the postman came. She had a fun time planned with her latest "friend." Finally, Maria had found a guy that understood her. Her hectic schedule and involvement in so many protests and other political and social efforts had left little time for her own social life. Even so, it had always been so easy for her to meet new men. With her striking good looks, all she had to do was smile at a hunk and reel him in.

But her relationships had all been short-lived. Most of the men she met had turned out to be not only macho, but also conservative in their politics. Each one had assured her that their widely divergent political views wouldn't matter. Then after the two had spent some time doing fun things together, tried every possible way of making love, and reached the point where their friendship should become the most important thing in their relationship, they found that their philosophical differences were too great. All her previous "significant others" could not abide Maria's ultra-left politics no matter how fantastic her tacos were.

But this time, it was different. Enrico Valdez understood her. He basically was not interested in politics, only in his business, which seemed to be doing quite well. Rico had a beautiful home, several expensive cars, and a yacht. The two of them enjoyed speaking to each other in a mixture of English and Spanish, often switching languages in midsentence if they needed a special word to express a thought. They had moved past the point where the newness of each other was the glue that kept them together, and they were genuine friends. Maria still lived separately from Rico and devoted an unreasonable amount of time to her many political and humanitarian interests. But when she was with Rico, she was his, spending most weekends at his palatial home.

She went to the door to pick up her morning mail. *Why would I be getting a letter from the director of the National Aeronautics and Space Administration?* she thought. Then as she began to open the letter, the light came on. She said, "Oh. Now I remember. I applied for *that space trip. This is from that Javitz gentleman I interviewed with.*" She thought, *Who knows why I applied, but this is no doubt my letter of rejection.* She read the letter. She read the letter again. "There must be some mistake! He *wants* me on his *spaceship*! They can't be *serious.*"

Maria had applied for the mission on the *Revelation* at a time when she and Eddie had just broken up. At the same time, she had a number of setbacks with political projects she was working on. She was depressed and discouraged about everything. The idea of leaving her old life behind had a certain appeal to her.

She dug around in her desk, looking for the ad she had seen that requested specific volunteers with special abilities for the *Revelation* mission. She had also seen ads on TV about it. There was one particular position that seemed scripted just for her. But all that was before she met Rico.

After rereading the ad and replaying the disc she had made of the NASA TV ad, she remembered why the mission had appealed to her. During her interviews with the NASA people, she had thought that it was the most exciting thing she had ever heard of: Going millions of miles into space to a distant planet! Traveling there at near light-speed. After one year in transit and in hibernation, arriving 1300 years in the future. Talk about a trip! But she was not an astronaut. Why did they want a consumer advocate and protester on such a trip? She had done the interviews mainly to learn more about the mission. She never thought they would want her on the crew. Maria thought of Rico and how much she enjoyed his company. She needed to talk to him. She needed to talk to Director Javitz again. After all, he had *interviewed her* at their first meeting. Now she needed to interview *him.*

Jake Loneghan was going through papers on his desk in his Philadelphia office. He was on one phone call and had two on hold. "How many shares do I have? I *know* it's down . . . Look!" Jake was becoming a little heated. "*You told me this stock would be a barn burner*. You were wrong! I don't care . . . *Sell it*!" He considered smashing the phone on the desk. "I said SELL IT. Sell it NOW. Call me back when it's done and have a BETTER recommendation next time."

He punched off that line on to another. "This is Jake . . . Phil! How are you? Fine, just fine . . . What's up? . . . Tomorrow? . . . 'round noon? I'll *be* there. Bring plenty of money!" He laughed as he punched off that line and took the last one. "This is Jake . . . Yes . . . Yes . . . OK, then *do* it!" He hung up.

He noticed that the morning mail was still on the corner of the desk unopened. He reached for it, expecting to see the usual statements, solicitations, and applications when one envelope caught his eye. *Ah*, he thought, *my letter of rejection from NASA . . . Guess I never did interview very well. Good thing I am usually the interviewer instead of the other way around.* He almost tossed it to save time but decided to open it. *Let's see how they worded my rejection. Overqualified, probably.* He chuckled to himself.

He opened the envelope and read the letter. He read it again. "My god! I'm in!" he yelped.

Two of his staff rushed in two doors leading to outer offices. "Sir? Did you call?" they both said at the same time.

"*I'm going to the planet Nyvar!*" he practically shouted to them.

"Sir?" they both said in unison again.

"Gentlemen, you are going to have a new boss!" he announced to the dismayed pair.

"Frank," he said to one. "Let's do a letter . . . In fact, *several letters*."

6

Diane spoke to Director Javitz on the intercom. "Sir, Miss Rodriquez is here."

Ben Javitz automatically glanced at his watch. He didn't need to; he always knew what time it was. He was more accurate than a watch. It was uncanny. "Show her in, Diane. Ask her if she would like coffee."

Diane had already asked her about coffee, and she knew Director Javitz would have some. She showed Maria into the director's office.

"Ah, Miss Rodriguez. Good to see you again! I trust you received my letter."

"Yes, Director Javitz, I did. And that is why I am here."

"Is there a problem, Miss Rodriguez?" Ben could sense that there was. Her demeanor and composure were entirely different from the day of her original interview with him.

"Maybe, maybe not," Maria said cautiously. "I need to convince myself again that I am right for this *Revelation* mission. I need you to help me do that."

For a moment, Ben Javitz said nothing. He just looked at her.

"We don't need anyone on this mission that is not convinced she should be there. Why are you now unsure? When we met before, you seemed very sure that this is what you want to do."

"I fully realize, Dr. Javitz, that each of your six crew members must feel *positive* that they are 100 percent dedicated to this mission. If *I* am not, I will not go. I need you to help me be sure."

"How can I—," Javitz started, and Maria interrupted.

"Just convince me that I am needed, that my skills are needed. I want to know that I will have a meaningful part of the mission and will be valuable to the rest of the crew. Look at who you have other than me. You have a medical doctor, highly skilled in her field and already a member of your staff at NASA. You have an engineer who, I understand, practically built the spacecraft we are to travel in. You have an experienced USAF colonel who is good enough to be your ship's commander. You have a lawyer who is quite capable in her field and who is also already on your staff. And finally, you have a billionaire entrepreneur who is a brilliant and talented man, who is a pilot, and who has excelled in many fields, many of which have direct application to the *Revelation* mission."

She paused. "And then there is me."

"You make an excellent point, Miss Rodriguez, and you deserve a good answer. I guess I was under the impression that my staff properly explained to you when they first interviewed you why *we need you* on this mission."

Just the way he said that made Maria feel much better. She thought, *He is convinced he needs me. I am the one that must be convinced.*

Diane brought in the coffee. Maria thanked her with a very nice smile.

Director Javitz continued, "Much thought and deliberation were given to the type of crew members we need for this mission. We only have room for six. We decided long ago that the six have to be just the right six. Let me tell exactly why we need you."

He continued, "We know a lot about the planet Nyvar, your destination. But there is a lot we *do not know*. We know that the planet is enough like Earth in terms of its distance from its star, its temperature, the composition of its landmasses, and the amount of water on the planet. We know that its atmosphere is like ours. You should be able to walk about on Nyvar without space suits. The only reason to send suits with you is in case there are biological organisms in the planet's atmosphere that your immune systems cannot initially handle. Now let's talk about what we *don't* know about your destination."

Maria interrupted, "Excuse me, I am not a scientist as you well know, but how can you know *so much* about the planet and yet not know some of the *key things you need to know*?"

"That is a very long story, and we cannot cover it now. I promise you that during your training before the flight, you will be taught all we know about Nyvar and how we know it. You will also be taught why we cannot, at our distance from Nyvar, know things about it that we would like to know. Let me go on.

"The main thing we do not know about Nyvar is whether or not there is life there as we know life. Millions of years ago, there was no life on Earth. Later, still millions of years ago, there was abundant plant life and animal life, but no intelligent life here on Earth. It is believed that man first appeared on the Earth at about fifteen million BC. Man, as we now think of modern man, has only been around for about four thousand to thirty thousand years, depending on just who you define as modern man. The Earth has been here for over four and a half billion years. We believe that Nyvar is about the same age as the Earth. Considering the relative age of the planet to that of Earth and considering all the similarities between the two planets, we are hoping your team will find intelligent life on Nyvar when you arrive there."

"I still am not seeing how I fit into this game plan . . ."

"This way," said Director Javitz, "if you and the crew of the *Revelation* arrive on Nyvar and there is no intelligent life, then you will be the *only* intelligent life on that planet. You will *begin a civilization on that planet*. This is why we are sending boys and girls . . . not just boys."

She started to interrupt him again by saying, *Well, if you just need someone to get pregnant . . .* But she thought better and remained quiet.

Director Javitz continued, "If your team finds no intelligent life there and no civilization, we want the best cross section of minds, knowledge, abilities, and philosophies that we can have in only six people." He continued, "In this scenario, we hope that you six will build a new civilization that avoids all the flaws and ills which have taken Earth down its ever-worsening path. This is why you will be so important to the team. Who knows better what is *wrong* with our civilization than you do, Maria? I think that you might be just the most *important player* on the team that builds a new civilization."

At this moment, Maria was feeling very good. She said, "I see. Now I am beginning to understand."

Director Javitz continued, "There are many possible scenarios the *Revelation* team might find on Nyvar, Maria. This is just one of them—virtually a clean sheet of paper."

"Now let's talk of two other possibilities," said Director Javitz. "Another possibility is that you find a young civilization similar to that of our Earth when man first made his appearance. The Old Testament of the Bible purports to tell of the ancient history of our Earth and the beginnings of civilization on this planet. If the Bible is accurate as a historical document, then the first crime was committed when Eve took a bite of the apple and she and Adam were tossed out of Eden. This was followed shortly by the first recorded murder when Cain killed Abel."

"Are you saying that we may find a civilization that has already started down the wrong path?" Maria injected.

"Absolutely! It is *entirely* possible. We don't know *what* kind of civilization you might find. In case you find a savage and hostile environment, the team will be prepared for that. Your jobs will be much more difficult, however, but at least you will have a jump on fixing the ills of society before they have gone as far toward hell as we have on our Earth in the twenty-first century."

Maria was in deep thought. *Do I want to go to a planet of the apes?*

She said hesitantly, "You were going to mention a third possible scenario?"

"Yes. Remember, it will take the *Revelation* roughly 1300 years to reach Nyvar, Earth time. Even if *today* there is a *young civilization* on Nyvar, in 1300 years, they should be quite advanced."

"Something like ours is today?" said Maria in a caustic tone.

"Touché!" said Ben Javitz. "What I *am saying* is that we have no way of knowing what civilization, if any, you will find. Regardless, we want to put Earth's best foot forward with six of our best, most talented, and most diverse people. We consider you a key player for the team!"

Maria rose from her chair and walked slowly to the window, looking out over the city and the distant hills beyond. After a few moments, she spoke. "One thing I have to do before I can make my final decision on this. When I applied for this ride, there was no one of the opposite sex that I really cared for. Now there is. Strangely enough, until about the time I interviewed with your staff, I had had little success in finding a good relationship with a man. The week after I first interviewed with NASA, I met a wonderful man. Before I give you a yes, I need to talk with him. You DO have other candidates for the humanitarian position, I trust?"

"We do," said Director Javitz, "but we want you. We have given all of those who have firmly committed to the mission two weeks to clean up their private affairs and report for training. Do *you* need more time?"

"No. I will see Rico tonight. I will make my decision and tell you tomorrow."

What Maria did not tell Director Javitz about herself was *something only she and one other person knew.* She was certain that NASA officials would *not allow her to go* on the mission if they knew her secret. Not even Rico knew.

That night, Maria and Rico worked together in Rico's kitchen, preparing one of their very favorite dishes, lamb and rice. It was a beautiful night, and they had decided to dine on the patio overlooking the Potomac. Once the meal itself was ready, they turned the serving chores over to Donna and Miguel, two of Rico's house staff. They sat at the elegantly set patio table, and service began with glasses of Bodega Noemia wine from Argentina, a favorite of Rico's. He spoke, "You seem far, far away tonight, my dear. Is something troubling you?"

Maria thought, *Far, far away? How appropriate that he chose those words.* She said, "My dear, I am right here, only a table length away."

"True," said Rico. "But you have something *very important* on your mind."

Maria lacked the courage she needed. She could not bring herself to tell her new and now very good friend the awesome thing that she was contemplating doing. She talked her way around the issue.

"I am just overwhelmed at this point with several projects I am very interested in, and I can't be everywhere at once. The ACLU wants me to fly down to Cleveland tomorrow for a rally, the Democrats for a Better World wants me to come to Philly for a convention next week and . . . oh, it just goes on and on!"

"I see. Maybe you are taking on too much. That can happen, you know."

"I probably am. I always have. When I see something happening that is unfair to people, I have to get involved. That's just me. I will put it all aside tonight and concentrate on you and *you alone.*"

"I will have to see this to believe it!" chided Rico.

She smiled and said, "All right. You will see."

They raised their glasses simultaneously and sipped the wine. Maria was true to her word. The evening was wonderful. After the sumptuous meal, they put on some of their favorite music. It was more beautiful than ever—maybe something about the night air.

They danced to an old Guy Lombardo tune, now on CD. As they danced, he held her gracefully in his arms, allowing their bodies to flow together with the music. The moment was perfect, and as he drew her closer into his muscular body, he could feel her firm breasts against his chest. They kept swaying to the music even while the CD changed from one piece to the next. She felt so safe in his arms and kissed him on the neck. Rico's desire for her filled his whole body as they smiled at each other. He was lost in her beautiful brown eyes. Their lips met.

Rico motioned to Manuel, and he brought out another bottle; this time, it was Capo Salina, an excellent dessert wine and Maria's absolute favorite.

The evening went perfectly and progressed finally to the master suite, lavishly appointed yet warm and inviting—perfect for the intimacy ahead. Maria had put the *Revelation* out of her mind. Rico was slim and powerful, but so gentle. His kisses were better than the wine. Their bodies melted together into one.

Rico had risen first, dressed, and slipped out without waking Maria. Maria woke—at first, forgetting where she was, then quickly remembering. She heard below, through the open window, the glasses tinkling as breakfast was being set up near the pool.

"Rico!" she called softly, not expecting a response. He was not in the suite. She *must* tell him this morning of what she was thinking of doing. The timing of this whole thing could *not* be worse. Rico was the first man that she had ever had such strong feelings for. And what of all the worthwhile efforts she was involved in? Could they be sustained without her? What is the more important thing for her to do with her life? Go to a distant planet and help begin a new civilization, or stay here on Earth and try to help fix the *mess* humans have made of this one?

At any rate, she must tell Rico. Maybe what he has to say will help her decide.

She stepped onto the deck that surrounded the pool, dressed in white shorts with a matching top and a powder blue sweater over her shoulders. The morning air was chilled, but *oh so fresh*, she thought. Rico was dressed in a tee shirt and shorts, sipping coffee and reading the morning paper. He looked up and said,

"Did you hear of the amazing thing NASA is about to do? They are going to send six astronauts to a planet 1300 *light-years away*!"

"And good morning to you too, my dear," she said sarcastically. Maria could not believe that he had focused on the one thing she must talk to him about. *A coincidence?* She wondered.

"Sorry, dear," he said, "I just read about this NASA thing and found it so exciting. I forgot to say, 'Good morning, my lovely angel! How are you this wonderful morning?'"

She wasn't finished with his oversight quite yet. "I would have thought that your memories of last night would still be so powerful that you would not have room in your mind for any other thoughts."

"You were *wonderful* my dear, as always. I have been thinking of you up to the moment I saw this unusual news item." He was hoping *that* would get him off the hook.

She flipped the conversation on him, ignoring his attempts to recover, and said, "Tell me about this NASA mission you have discovered. What do you think of it?" She *had* him. But now he was free to talk about the Nyvar mission, which had apparently really impressed him.

Rico eagerly looked again at the article as he began speaking, "They are going to send a crew of six astronauts on an amazing mission. NASA has built this spaceship that travels at near light-speed and they are going to try to establish a colony on a planet some 7,627 *trillion miles* from Earth! This article says that it will take the ship 1300 Earth years to make the trip, but the astronauts will have only aged *about a year* during the trip. Don't ask me how *that* works. It's apparently something Albert Einstein figured out a couple of centuries ago. Isn't that incredible?"

"They want me to go as one of the crew," Maria blurted out. She hadn't planned to be so brutal, but Rico's enthusiasm had taken her by surprise. Maybe he would understand her interest in being part of this monumental undertaking.

"*What?* What did you say?"

"I said they want me to be one of the crew members on the *Revelation* mission."

Rico was frozen. He seemed to be in shock. She became concerned about him.

"Are you OK?" she said.

Rico found his voice—and his composure. He calmly, with his usual aplomb, said, "You are not an astronaut. Why would they want you on this mission?" Rico was hurt. He could not believe that Maria would even consider going away for the rest of her life, never to see him again. He decided to be cool, however, and hear what she had to say.

"They want a cross section of talents, abilities, and interests," Maria started.

"But you are not an astronaut!" Rico was having trouble containing his emotions.

"They will train me—thoroughly—before we launch. There is another of the six that is not an astronaut."

"Then you have decided to go?" he said in a harsh tone.

"*No!*" she retorted. "I have *not* decided to go! I told them that I had to discuss the whole thing with you. I want your opinion. They are waiting for my answer."

Rico regained his composure. *Why am I acting this way?* he thought. *I have everything in the world. There are many beautiful women who would die to be with me! I have never felt this way about a woman! Damn me!* Then he calmly said, "Tell me why you want to go."

"Oh, Rico. I don't know why I put in an application for the mission."

"You APPLIED FOR THE MISSION?" He could not believe his ears.

"I applied *before I met you.* I think that this is a very worthwhile thing for six people to do with their lives. I interviewed with NASA people, including the director of the agency. If I had met you before . . ." She hesitated, then continued, "I probably would not have applied. But I *did* put my application in, and they *have chosen me* out of many other applicants."

He just looked at her. He thought about what she said. *"This is a very worthwhile thing for six people to do with their lives."* Those were her exact words, and she is right. But why does Maria have to be one of the six? "Maria," he said, "most paths we choose in our lives have forks in the road. We can make choices and change directions. If you choose the path that leads to this mission, there are *no other forks* in the road for you. If you launch with the crew of the *Revelation*, there is no turning back. You will *never see Earth again*, and none of us here on Earth will ever see you again. This is an overwhelming decision you must make."

He continued, "Maria, I do not want to lose you. But I understand what you are thinking. I am trying to be objective—but I am in love with you."

She wasn't ready for that. "Oh, Rico! I . . ." She paused. "I care so much for you also. I think I love you . . . but it's so soon . . . We *need more time.*"

"How much time do you have? When must you report for training?"

"They must know *now.* Training starts Monday week at the Kennedy Spaceflight Center in Florida."

"Then there *is* no time," he said with detectable sadness in his voice.

"Help me, Rico," she pleaded. Maria had always been strong and able to make all her own decisions. But this time, it was different.

"How can I help you?" Rico was defeated. He felt that he knew what she would ultimately do, no matter what he said.

"Is this mission a worthwhile thing for me to do with my life?"

He took her in his arms and held her. She sobbed softly. Rico said, "Tell me all you know about the mission. We will see if it is worth *as much* as my beautiful Maria."

7

Kennedy Spaceflight Center—Cape Canaveral, Florida

"Good morning, ladies and gentlemen. I am Aaron Soderberg, director of the center here at Kennedy. Welcome! Congratulations on your selection to the crew of the most advanced spaceship that has ever been constructed—at least on *this* planet! Your training class will be a mixed bag for us since some of you already work here at NASA, and some of those that do have spaceflight experience. Others don't. Others of you have not worked for NASA and do not have any spaceflight experience."

Seated in the front row of the astronaut briefing room were the future crew members of the *Revelation*: David Marks, Dr. Ellen Marks, Col. Dante Washington, Susan Chen, Jake Loneghan, and Maria Rodriguez.

Director Soderberg continued, "Therefore, for each of you six very special crew members, we will have a personalized curriculum. Those of you that have flown may get some time off while others receive the training you have already had. Or if you choose, you can stick around and act as advisors to your future team members. Others such as Miss Maria Rodriguez will receive the full treatment.

"Additionally, we will conduct the specific mission training—the training that has only to do with your mission to Nyvar—last in the program. That way, all of you will be up to speed on the basics of spaceflight and will hopefully understand how our previous and current missions are conducted. You will have gone through all the physical testing and skills development, will have received training in all our operational routines, will have become familiar with all the instrumentations and flight computers common to our flight hardware, and will therefore be on *somewhat* equal footing. That is, except for actual flight experience. For those of you who *have not flown* an actual mission into space, you will have all the training routines we offer, designed to closely simulate the space environment, including several 0 g suborbital trips.

"The program I just summarized will take approximately six weeks. As I said, some of you will have some time off during that six weeks because of prior training and experience but may stay in the sessions if you so desire."

Director Soderberg continued, "In the seventh week, we will introduce you to the *Revelation*, the ship that will take you to the Setarian system and to the planet we now call Nyvar. You will learn everything *we* know about the ship.

45

After the seventh week of initial hardware, skills, and systems training, we will move to instructional sessions on the Setarian system and Nyvar, the destination of the *Revelation* mission. We will share with you all we know about the planet and how we know it.

"Finally, we will go through several of the possible scenarios you may find yourself in on your arrival on the planet Nyvar. We will tell you why *we do not know* what manner of life or civilization you will find on your arrival.

"We will acquaint you with all the tools, equipment, supplies, weapons, and safety devices you will have on board your spacecraft. You will learn how to survive and live on Nyvar, *no matter what life or what civilization you find there*. The complete training program will cover ten weeks. During that time, it is our desire that you minimize contact with those outside our complex and work as closely as possible with the team that is training you and your fellow crew members. This protocol will provide you an opportunity to *test yourselves on your decisions to leave your life on Earth behind*. If you should decide during the course of your ten weeks with us that you *made a mistake* in becoming a part of the *Revelation* crew, *you must tell us*. It will be unfair to all concerned for you to go on this mission if you are not *fully 100 percent committed*!"

The director paused and then continued, "A few more facts about your mission: When you reach Earth's orbit at the first stage of your journey, you will have about one hour to check out all systems and then, after clearance from Mission Control, place yourselves in suspended animation, or hibernation. Each of you will be assigned a special compartment or capsule that will maintain your sleep state until you reach proximity with your destination. That will occur about twenty hours before you enter orbit around Nyvar. Your individual capsules will do one other very important thing for you. They are each equipped with a very special electromagnetic device that protects your internal organs against extreme acceleration forces. When the *Revelation* jumps to light-speed, or at JLS, the ship and all aboard will be subjected to immense accelerations. Were it not for your special capsules, your body would not be able to stand the g-forces as the ship jumps to light-speed. In other words, JLS would be fatal for you." Aaron paused to let that sink in.

"When you are awakened prior to arrival at Nyvar, you will exit your capsules to prepare for entry into orbit about the planet and for your eventual landing. You will be very weak after your long sleep and very hungry. Your ship's stores will include frozen meals that, once heated, will be quite tasty. On any other NASA missions, including TransMars, at this stage of the journey, you would be able to communicate with Earth base here at Kennedy. But because of your extreme distance from Earth, that will not be possible. It would take your communications 1300 years to return to us. Also, during your flight at near light-speed, no communications or telemetery from the ship will be possible.

"By the time you reach Nyvar, you and your ship will have aged approximately one year, 1304 years of Earth time will have passed, and you will have covered a distance of roughly 7,627 *trillion miles*. Beginning with the works of Albert Einstein, scientists have proven mathematically that nothing can exceed the speed of light. As a moving object approaches the speed of light, time passes much slower for the object. *Exactly at* the speed of light, time *stands still*. During your 1300 years of flight, you and your ship will only age approximately one year."

Susan raised her hand. "Director Soderberg, please excuse me for interrupting. This phenomenon about aging as it relates to the speed of light has me totally baffled. I realize that its origin comes from Einstein's work, but I cannot grasp how this can possibly be true. Can you help me understand it?"

The others gazed with blank stares at Susan as she spoke and then at the director.

Aaron remained silent for a time, then said, "Susan, that is a tall order. David, would you like to take this one?"

David smiled slyly and said, "Sir, I'm sure you can do a much better job than I!"

Aaron knew he had been had. His look at David could be interpreted as "Thanks a lot!" He said, "I can share with you the Einstein formula that defines the relation of time of a stationary object with respect to the time measured on a moving object. Maybe that will help. Beyond that, I can refer you to several books that try to explain why the time dilation equation works.

"Here is the equation." He wrote on a wallboard with a marker.

$$t_e = \frac{t_s}{\sqrt{1 - \dfrac{v^2}{c^2}}}$$

t_e is the time as measured on Earth,
t_s is the time as measured on the ship,
v is the speed of the ship, and
c is the speed of light, roughly 186,000 miles per second.

"If you plug some numbers into the equation, you will see that there is not significant dilation of time until you are almost *at* the speed of light. Then the effect becomes quite large. *It is this relationship that makes the* Revelation *mission possible*."

Looking at Susan, he said, "See me after this meeting, and I will give you references you may like to explore. For the time being, you just *have to trust me*!" He smiled. "Now let us go on.

"When you arrive at your destination, Earth, as you know it today, will exist only in history books. Hopefully, our planet will have *survived* through the 1300 years you will have been en route. And hopefully, we on Earth will have been able to solve our many problems and evolved to a better society and civilization.

"I think I will close with this point: once you leave Earth's orbit on the *Revelation*, there *is no way to get any further assistance* from us. This is why you *must learn all you can* in the next ten weeks. You must know your ship thoroughly, and you must know how to survive as a people once you arrive at your destination. You must be able to handle *whatever* you find at your new home . . ."

The response of each of the six crew members, as measured by their facial expressions and body language, was interesting and varied. Some appeared quite confident and even showed the hint of a smile as the *Revelation* mission was summarized. Others showed concern and trepidation. With one or two, the look in their eyes reflected fear—not to a great degree—but it was clearly there. And Director Soderberg saw it.

The director continued, "All of you are to report to classroom 35E at 0800 tomorrow. Are there any questions before we break today?"

Jake Loneghan stood and said, "I have one. Any chance we could have a look at the *Revelation* today? It's still early."

Aaron looked at his watch and glanced over at two others who were with him. He said something to them, and they answered. One left the room. He turned back to the six future crew members. "We don't see why not. Follow me."

The Revelation

The new *Revelation* crew entered the mammoth hangar following the director. What they saw left them awestruck! That is, all except for David Marks. He had practically lived with the *Revelation* since the first design curves were put on paper. Ellen had seen drawings and photos that David brought home, but never the actual ship.

The huge all-white craft seemed to fill the entire hangar. In actuality, it wasn't much larger than a 747 aircraft, but it resembled an enlarged Concorde SST. The spacecraft had a very sharp nose and delta-shaped flying surfaces. You could not identify the engine locations from the front quarter position off the ship where the group was standing. Under what appeared to be the fuselage was an elongated pod. Although the ship was most impressive, it was hard to believe that it was capable of near light-speed! Its secret was well hidden within the confines of its handsomely sculptured shape.

"Can we go inside?" said Colonel Washington.

"I'm sorry, but not yet," responded Director Soderberg. "There is a lot of work still going on inside with the control panels and crew accommodations. There will be plenty of time for you all to be inside her as you progress through your training."

"She's standing on her own gear," commented Jake. "Will our launch be from a vertical stack or a conventional runway takeoff?" He quickly continued, "I guess a better question is, 'Are the hyperdrive engines capable of powering the ship from zero start through the mission until landing, or will a booster rocket be needed for launch?'"

"Excellent question," said Director Soderberg. "Why don't you take that one, David?" He turned to David Marks.

"Fine, sir," said David. "The hyperdrive engines are all we will need. And there are two of them in the design. Each one is capable of powering the *Revelation* from a standing start using a runway or a *vertical* takeoff through the atmosphere to deep space cruise flight. Landing on Nyvar will be a conventional shuttle-type landing with braking and reverse thrust—IF there is a civilization on Nyvar that has airports and runways."

"And if there are *no runways*?" commented Dante.

"Then we will use a vertical descent from a hover position above the ground, touching down on all three gears simultaneously—exactly as we have on missions to Mars, Colonel."

All the crew except David was in total awe. Ellen Marks was looking proudly at David, Maria's mouth was hanging open, and the other three were all gazing at the ship and smiling. Colonel Washington said, "Well, I don't know about anyone else, but I surely am *damn well impressed*!"

The others turned toward the colonel, and Jake said, "I understand that you will be the mission commander, Colonel. Think you can handle this bird?"

Dante was still gazing at the ship. "No problem," he said. "If I can't, then I'll bet you can!" Dante slowly turned, and he and Jake locked in a power gaze.

"No problem," said Jake, exuding confidence as well as cockiness.

While this chatter was going on, Maria was carefully reviewing her reasoning for being there at all. *I don't even like roller coasters*, she thought.

"OK, gentlemen and ladies," said the director, "enough drooling! Let's call it a day. Have a good evening, and we will see you tomorrow at 0800 sharp in classroom 35E. By the way, the Coach and Six, just off the base, has excellent beef and fresh seafood. You might want to check it out."

As they walked out, all thought the Coach and Six sounded great and would be a good opportunity for them to get acquainted. They agreed to meet there that evening.

The Coach and Six

Jake Loneghan arrived at the restaurant early, at least earlier than they had all agreed upon. Jake was always early, no matter where he was going or what he was doing. He spoke to the hostess and asked her to hold a table for six in a good spot by the small dance floor. It appeared that a combo would be entertaining later in the evening. Jake took a spot at the bar, requested a light beer, and began surveying the clientele.

It was pretty obvious that most of the customers were either astronauts or employees of the spaceflight center. After all, the Coach and Six was just outside the main gate of the base, in a great spot to lure everyone leaving after their shift. The spaceflight center operated three shifts, but 'swing' and 'graveyard' were lightly staffed, being mostly involved with preparation of flights to be launched.

The crowd was average for a Monday night, he thought. Monday Night Football would be kicking off at eight, and the Broncos were playing Seattle.

Maria was the next to arrive and spotted Jake at the bar. She came over.

"Hi, I guess we are early." she said, "Is this seat saved for me?"

"Absolutely." smiled Jake, admiring Maria's beauty from top to bottom. "We have a table being held for us over by the dance floor."

"What'll it be, ma'am?" said the bartender, who looked to be young for the job.

Maria glanced at what Jake was drinking and said, "A glass of Chardonnay will be fine. Do you have Kendall Jackson?"

"No problem," said the bartender as he stepped away.

Jake wasted no time. He, at least at the moment, had the prettiest girl in the place all to himself. "You are gorgeous," he said, "and obviously smart. What makes you want to leave this life and trade it in for the vast unknown?"

"Maybe the same reasons you want to." she parried, smiling and looking into the very depth of his eyes.

"And what are those?"

"Don't *you* know?" she said and laughed.

Jake, realizing that this line of conversation was not working, surprised Maria by saying, "Tell me about yourself. I know you are quite lovely and obviously very smart, or you wouldn't have been selected. The info we were given refers to you as a humanitarian and consumer advocate. What exactly do you do?"

Maria took a sip of her wine, looking at the glass and thinking. Jake waited.

"I am in training for a most exciting and scary trip. I feel lucky that you will be along." She nailed him with that one. He had not expected it.

"Are we eating at the bar?" said Colonel Washington who appeared, arriving with Susan Chen. Jake and Maria were so intent on each other they hadn't noticed Dante and Susan entering.

Jake laughed. "No, I arranged for a table. Why don't we move over to it?"

As the others proceeded to the table, Dante said, "I'll put orders in for drinks. What would you all like?"

"I'm fine," echoed both Jake and Maria while Susan selected a Riesling.

"I'll be right over," said Dante, turning for the bar.

At this moment, the Marks were entering; and Dante stopped them, pointing out the table and taking a drink order from them.

"Just bottled water," said Ellen.

"Me too," said David. "Thanks."

With all comfortably seated and drinks all around, Jake proposed a toast. "To the *Revelation* and a successful journey!" he said, then added, "*What are we all thinking?*"

Jake's remark was intended to be funny but fell absolutely flat. Everyone at the table seemed to be in a very somber and serious mood, and the timing was just not right for Jake's comment. If he had stopped with the toast, things would have gotten off to a much better beginning.

Maria, in just a few brief moments at the bar with Jake, had begun to understand him. She jumped in to put things back on track. "Why don't we all look at the menus and get our orders going? We will be off to an early start tomorrow morning."

The waiter came over on a signal from Dante and took dinner orders.

The mood at the table remained quite awkward.

Susan Chen broke the ice. "Not that anyone is particularly interested, but I will tell you all why I volunteered for the *Revelation* mission." Since there were no objections, she continued, "I am an attorney, and I work for NASA here at the spaceflight center. I have been trained as an astronaut and have flown as a crewman on two shuttle flights. That aside, my work here has been mostly on legal matters—contracts with suppliers and that sort of thing.

"I do have experience in other than corporate and contract law, however. I have training in criminal justice and experience in our court system. Along the way, I have been a prosecuting attorney for the State of Virginia and have done some volunteer work for the Republican Party."

She continued, "When I learned about the *Revelation* mission and the fact that a person of my background and expertise was needed on the crew, I jumped at the chance! My only hesitation was that this mission is *one-way*. None of us will ever see this Earth again . . ."

"Well, *that's just it*, isn't it?" said Dante. "I came to grips with that fact *long ago*, but I'm not sure *all at this table have*." He looked into the eyes of each of the other five crew members as he made this statement. "See, I have been on many military missions in my life—*combat missions*. When a military man goes on a combat mission, *he never knows if he is coming back*. But he must be prepared *not to come back*.

"The *Revelation* mission is the same as any other mission for me, except that this is as dangerous and hazardous a mission *as I can conceive of*. We will be on a ship that has never been test-flown. We will be attempting to fly at speeds never before remotely approached by humans. We will be heading for a planet that is over 1300 light-years from this Earth—a planet that our best NASA scientists *think* is like our Earth. We don't know what we will find on Nyvar—maybe no life, maybe primitive life, maybe an advanced civilization. We will have *no contact* with Earth from the time we reach light-speed. And no contact with Earth after we land. We six people will be on our lonesome—no matter what we find on Nyvar."

"Hear, *hear!*" exclaimed Jake. "Now *that's my kind of trip*. I don't have to tell you why I am on this mission. Our good colonel *just did it for me*."

Dante looked at Jake with an expression that said, "*That's mighty brave talk for a person who has never been in combat*." Dante had recognized, however, from reading Jake's resume that Loneghan *had* put his life on the line, many times, in things he had accomplished and situations he had been in. He respected that. *But what about David? And what about the three ladies? How will they hold up*? thought Dante.

Again, the table grew silent. The awkwardness had returned.

David Marks spoke softly. "My heart and my mind have been in space since I was a small boy," he started. "This ship we will travel on represents the culmination of all my dreams. Ellen will have to speak for herself, but I could not choose a better use for the balance of my life than to go on this mission." David looked into each face around the table. "I will tell you all something else. The mission profile does not require that the designer of this ship be on board. It does require that an engineer and technical expert be a part of the mission. I don't mean to blow my own horn, but if we have any unforeseen technical issues arise in our journey, I expect to be able to solve them." His expression changed from a stern look to a smile. Then he said, "So just be nice to me."

David's comment finally loosened up the group. Everyone laughed at his remark.

Ellen chimed in after David and said, "And I am your doctor, whether you like it or not! So maybe you macho guys had just better not get sick. You'll have to take off all your clothes and see me in my office."

This really brought the laughs, and everyone was feeling much better.

"What about you, Maria?" Jake was back to his original question that Maria had skirted at the bar. This time, she was the only one who had not shared her thoughts.

"That is a *good question*," she started. "I am here *because NASA wants me to be here*. As Director Javitz put it, in case our crew of six has to begin a new civilization, he wants me to be there to represent the interests of the people."

At first, no one said anything. Then Dante jumped in with, "Well, I am the mission commander, so the people consists of you five sitting with me at this table."

Everyone found that funny, except Maria. She retorted with, "You just wait, Colonel. I intend to keep our new civilization on track. Strictly a government by the people and for the people. We can't let the new civilization make the same mistakes we have on Earth. We *have* to do a better job on Nyvar!" The others gave that some thought. Ellen thought deeply, *Earth, our wonderful war-ravaged, crime-laden, polluted planet. How did man let this happen to the beautiful blue planet, which may truly be one of a kind?*

Maria's comment had sobered the group temporarily. But the ice among the crew members had been broken, and each found it easy to talk to the others.

The rest of the evening went smoothly with the little band of six coming to know and appreciate one another and what each had to offer to the whole.

8

The final two weeks of training and preparation seemed to fly by. The crew had been given many training hours in the *Revelation* FDS (flight deck simulator). The simulator was almost a perfect replica of the spaceship's flight deck with six degrees of motion freedom and a cockpit window-screen visualization that was so realistic the crew members felt they were *already in space*. It had been decided that Jake, Dante, and Susan would be given the training required for them to qualify as pilots for the ship. Both Dante and Jake had logged thousands of hours as pilots of aircraft, and Dante and Susan had both been trained as shuttle pilots having several such missions under their belts. Dante, of course, had commanded and flown one of the TransMars missions in the spacecraft specifically designed for that mission. David, the most knowledgeable member of the team on the design and systems of the *Revelation*, had logged many hours in operating the FDS but had not been officially trained as a pilot of the ship. He was assigned as flight engineer for the mission.

Dante would command the ship in the left seat, and Susan would serve as first officer for the flight. Jake would back up both of them in case he was needed.

Ellen Marks, as a physician, was assigned as medical officer and had primary responsibility for all medical equipment and for all drugs, serums, and medical supplies that might conceivably be needed for the mission en route and after arrival at their destination.

Dante, because of his military and combat background, was designated as the weapons officer in addition to his duties as mission commander. The large payload capacity of the *Revelation* allowed for some heavy weapons devices and ordinance. Dante had selected those that would be most useful should they find themselves in a hostile environment.

Susan was also assigned as equipment officer and had the duty to ensure that all non-weapons equipment, tools, portable generators, lighting, breakdown shelters, and a wide range of other items were being properly stowed aboard for possible use on the ground at their destination. Susan also was assigned to ensure that the one-year food supply planned for the mission was adequately packaged and stored aboard the ship.

Maria was assigned as quality assurance officer with the duty of ensuring that all designated assignments of other crew members were in fact carried out *perfectly*. This turned out to be an excellent assignment for Maria, who, at times, almost drove the others nuts with her insistence on perfection.

The crew was tired. Six ten-hour days per week were taking their toll. Each crew member looked forward to Sunday to crash. On a personal basis, Dante, Jake, and Susan spent most of the hours after dinner break each day flying the simulator. They practiced all types of landings—sidehill, downhill, just about any way they could imagine that they might be required to land on rough terrain.

Maria worked with Ellen testing and operating all the medical and other portable equipment that might possibly be needed once they were on the surface of Nyvar.

David spent the evening hours going over the ship's systems details, simulating faults and using his manuals to trace the faults and correct them.

There was little or no sign of fun and games, parties, or romance. Maria still thought of Rico when her mind was not otherwise fully occupied.

All in all, the crew seemed to enjoy the work and effort required of them as the last days marched by in preparation for the launch. They all worked well together. At times, Dante and Jake locked horns over some procedural matter, but this was not surprising considering their strong type A personalities. In the advent of questions or confusion regarding any design or systems issue, all deferred to David without hesitation.

The NASA training officers, generally very pleased with the progress and response of the crew members, had some concern at times that the five others were placing too much reliance on David with his knowledge of the ship. Although the training program imparted all the knowledge that the crew members would need for operation of the ship, David was the only member of the crew that would be able to go *beyond* the systems diagnosis capability of the computer. That is to say, if systems malfunctions occurred that could not be resolved by the ship's computer using built-in routines and redundancies, David would then be the only resource capable of detail system repair or alteration. The NASA instructors would have preferred that at least one other crew member be an engineer. After all, what if David became incapacitated and a serious system malfunction arose? To attempt to backstop such an occurrence, NASA gave both Jake and Dante additional detailed systems training.

The *Revelation* was ready. During the last week before launch—while all items of equipment, tools, supplies, and weapons were being loaded by NASA personnel with Ellen and Maria riding herd—Dante, Jake, Susan, and David were running "failure simulations" and "surprise scenarios" and combinations of the two types of situations. One example was the "unforeseen asteroid event." At light-speed, if the ship impacted even a baseball-sized object, this would then probably result in the total destruction of the ship and its crew.

In normal cruise, the *Revelation*'s computer sees objects over a million miles ahead in the ship's intended path and makes slight adjustments in the ship's track to avoid such objects. One added plus of the HD engine is that during its operation, in addition to generating power to propel the ship, the engine also creates a shield surrounding the ship. This shield is resilient enough to cause smaller objects to be deflected away from the ship and result in no impact and no damage to the hull. However, objects such as large asteroids coming at the *Revelation* at high speed and within a certain window would penetrate the shield and most certainly destroy the spacecraft if allowed to impact it.

In the "unforeseen asteroid event," or UAE, an asteroid appears out of nowhere on a collision course with the *Revelation*. The ship is at near light-speed, and the asteroid is coming in from about two o'clock in the horizontal plane and one o'clock in the vertical plane at a relative speed of about fifty thousand miles per second. The *Revelation* is in cruise mode (i.e., the engines are in idle mode using only enough power to enable the shields), and the crew is in hibernation. The drill is to ensure that the ship's computer responds correctly to avoid a hit from the asteroid. The first design requirement for this scenario was to ensure that the *Revelation*'s computer senses the incoming object early enough to allow time for evasive action. The second requirement was to ensure that a burst from the main engines occurs soon enough to cause the ship to jump ahead and allow the asteroid to pass behind the spacecraft.

This simulation and many others were run more than once to verify each time that the ship's computer and its engines performed flawlessly.

A typical "failure simulation" might be some failure within the ship's computer or other systems that would jeopardize the safety of the crew and perhaps that of the ship if the problem was not addressed and solved quickly enough. For example, one such "failure simulation" is where both the main and standby temperature and oxygen control units for the crew capsules might fail. There are additional standby control units, and the ship's computer must immediately sense the failure and reroute signals to a backup unit. Even though all the systems and components of the *Revelation* had been designed and tested to be fail-safe to a "one in one billion" level, additionally, the systems were designed with multiple backups where crew or ship safety was involved.

As the last week before launch whizzed by, the members of the *Revelation*'s crew had become so engrossed in their training and special assignments they hardly knew that anything else existed. For the most part, they were sleeping well—although by choice, their days were very long. As Jake once put it, "What the hell! In about a week, I'll be able to sleep for a year!"

The rest of the world became more excited with the *Revelation* mission as each day passed. The story was on every front-page daily. The countdown 'til launch was printed in the lower right-hand corner of the front page, just like the days until Christmas. Hats, tee shirts, and all manner of items with the *Revelation* name and logo were everywhere. Kids and adults could not get enough of them. The press still clamored for more, *more*, MORE info from NASA on how things were going. The media was willing to interview anyone even close to the project. But NASA stuck to their guns regarding the crew. Each member of the crew was free to read newspapers or watch TV on their own time, but none of the astronauts did. They were LIVING the *Revelation* mission. What could they possibly get from the media that they didn't already know? And they sure as heck were not interested in outside expert opinions.

Outside the gates of Kennedy Spaceflight Center, mobile homes, campers, and tents were packed like sardines as far as the eye could see. Two of the NASA maintenance specialists were working atop of the Vertical Assembly Building on the day before the launch, and one commented to the other, "You know, Joe, I've been working here at the center since before the first moon shot. And I have never seen so many people." He waved his arm pointing at all the land in view. There was *no* land in view! From that lofty observation point, every inch of land seemed covered with vehicles and people.

"Yeah," the other commented. "Guess we might as well sleep in the bunk rooms here again tonight. We'll never get home. The roads are all clogged." They both stopped working and just stared at the mass of humanity.

Finally, the first mechanic said, "How'd you like to be going on the *Revelation* tomorrow?" The other took a long time pondering the question.

"Life ain't so bad here. We got problems, sure, but life ain't so bad."

"You think they got baseball on this Nyvar planet?"

9

Enrico Valdez was alone at breakfast on his patio. The morning air was still. A light fog drifted just above the Potomac as he picked up the *Post* and stared at the headlines:

REVELATION SUCCESSFULLY LAUNCHES FOR THE STARS!

He thought of Maria. How he already missed her. They had not spoken even once since she made the decision to go to Nyvar. Rico understood her choice, and at the time, she had discussed it with him. He honestly believed that he could put her out of his mind. Alas, he was quite wrong. Never had he felt about a woman the way he cared for Maria! He missed her so very much.

In the early light, the moon was still quite visible, and he could *just* see a morning star. *Is that the direction my Maria is flying?* he thought.

Manuel came onto the deck. "Sir, this just arrived in the morning mail." He handed a letter to Rico. It was from Maria!

Rico hesitated, not sure that he even wanted to open it. The silence between them after Maria's decision was by her choice. She had said that it would be too hard for her to go through with the training and the mission if she continued to stoke the love she felt for him. He understood and had agreed not to contact her. Why had she now chosen to torture him with a note after it was too late, after she had left his life forever? He set the letter aside, unopened.

The article about the launch and the voyage of the *Revelation* offered little new information. After all, the mission had been front-page for weeks. *What new could they find to write?* he thought.

But suddenly, he realized that the front page emblazoned a picture of the spaceship! NASA had in the past released only *simulated sequences* of the *Revelation* and its mission, but this was the first time he had seen actual photos. The front-page shot showed the ship climbing vertically straight above the runway. A note under the liftoff shot said to turn to page 5 for more photographs.

He turned the pages; and *there was Maria*, standing with the crew at the top of the stairs, boarding the ship. He studied the photo. *Nice-looking group*, he thought. *Three women and three men. My Maria is the star of the crew.*

Oh, Maria, he thought, *find a way to come back to me. I refuse to believe that I will never see you again.* He picked up the letter and was about to open it.

Manuel was again at the door. "Sir, I am so sorry to interrupt your breakfast again."

"It's all right, Manuel, what is it now?" said Rico in a somewhat annoyed tone.

"You have a phone call, sir. *President Buchard is calling.*"

At FBI headquarters, things were heating up. The director was holding a meeting that included the chief of Personnel Clearances Section and the chief of Tax Fraud Investigations. A few others were present. The only one that had spoken so far was the director.

"I will ask you, gentlemen, the *same question one more time*. This time, I would like someone to *answer* my question. *How can we grant a top secret clearance to a person we are planning to indict on tax-evasion charges?*

"Now who would like to be the *lucky one* to give me the *correct answer* for my question?" he demanded.

"That *cannot* happen!" volunteered the chief of Tax Fraud Investigations.

"*I agree with you, Harvey, 100 percent!*" yelled the director. "But it DID happen! And now one Mr. Jakob Loneghan is on his way *to another planet* for chrissakes, never to return to Earth. So help me God. If the press gets hold to this, I will be fired. But *not before I fire every one of you in this room, plus a few others*!

The director continued, "Don't you guys ever *talk to each other*? Don't you read the goddam *papers*?

"I did some checking on my own this morning, and Jake Loneghan's name has been in almost every paper in this country, every day for the last month. This guy owes about $52 *million* in back taxes, and WE HELPED HIM GET AWAY!

"You guys get out of here. Wait, no, here's what I want you to do. Harvey, I want to know the date that your people knew that Jakob Loneghan owed back taxes. I want the *name of the person that knew it first*. Then find out *who else knew it and when they found out.*"

Turning to the other chief, the director said, "Delwood, I want the name of your guy that ran the clearance check and the date the clearance was granted. I want the names of all that knew about his clearance. I want all of this info by this time tomorrow. Now all of you *get out of here*! And you better hope the press *doesn't learn about Loneghan.*"

At NASA headquarters, Ben Javitz and Aaron Soderberg were celebrating the successful launch of the mission to Nyvar. They were having a laugh about the FBI and their screw-up with Jake.

Aaron was saying, "This thing makes me worry, not about Jake—he's going to be an excellent astronaut and crew member. But I worry about how the FBI let this happen. What does this say about other clearances granted? In this case, the guy that knew about the tax thing was just down the hall from the guy running the clearance. It really makes me think . . ."

"In Jake's case," said Ben, "this tax thing could have influenced his decision to volunteer for the *Revelation*. After all, if he had been convicted of the charges, we are talking a *big fine* and considerable *time in jail*."

"You might be right. I guess he was sweating out the days 'til launch."

"He must have felt relieved when he went into the sleep sequence, figuring that he had it made." Ben continued, "What would it have done to the *Revelation* mission if the FBI had arrived at your office the day before the launch?"

Aaron had been thinking a lot about that question. "Well, I'm sure the FBI would have blocked the departure. And we would not have flown with just five. The whole mission was built around the six members with specific qualifications. We did have backup crew being trained."

"But they were pilots and engineers, male and female, weren't they?"

"That's correct," said Aaron. "We couldn't really look outside our astronaut corps for people to give up their lives for backup positions and then maybe *not go* on the mission. We have many well-qualified astronauts, both male or female that would have, I think, been satisfactory as crew members."

"I'm just very glad that we didn't lose Jake. I don't care if he did owe fifty million in taxes. None of his money will ever do him any good anymore. Better that he be on a worthwhile mission than sitting in jail."

Ben continued, "Aaron, tell me about the *nose gear door light*. How did that get by us?"

"Good question. We had no malfunction lights of any kind during the orbital checkout sequence. The damn light popped on just at JLS."

"Are you concerned about it? Do you think the gear is unsafe?"

"No and no," said Aaron. "Here's why. The gear was obviously stowed, or we would have had other warning lights, and the computer would have indicated a problem. We *had* a nose *gear 'up and locked' light*. We believe that the nose gear *door* was not closed tightly enough to activate the switch, a micro switch-type device. This would have been a 'rigging' problem. Either the switch was not aligned properly or it failed after checking 'good' many times."

"If the door is in fact not closed tight enough, won't that cause problems in flight?"

"No, not in space. There is no air and, therefore, no drag. The condition of the door will remain as it was at JLS. If there is really a mechanical problem with the door, which results in causing the gear to hang up when it is commanded to extend, *then* they might have a problem."

"If that is the case, what do they do?"

"There is more than one way to get the gear down, and then there is also a manual extension crank. Here's another consideration. They can always land vertically by hovering over their touchdown point and setting her down real easy. If they can't get the nose gear down, they can let the nose structure of the ship settle onto the surface.

"Then an inop nose gear would not really be *critical* unless they were doing a high-speed rollout landing?"

Aaron nodded, "That's correct. I believe they will be fine. In the first place, I don't think there *is* anything wrong with the door or the nose gear. In the second place, they have *vertical landing* they can use. And finally, if there is *anything wrong at all*, I am confident that David Marks will *find a solution* to the problem."

"I guess we will never know what happens."

"I agree with that. You want some more coffee?"

Across the country and around the world, the *Revelation* mission was the talk. It had been two weeks now since the ship departed. The media had dropped it and moved on, but the citizens had not. Everywhere, people were still talking about the launch and about the mission. There had never before been anything that captured the public's imagination like the *Revelation*. The members of the crew were like gods.

At the *New York Times*, Sally Northrop, a staff reporter well known for digging a little deeper was in the city editor's office. Sally was saying, "I've got a source that tells me we should look more into the backgrounds of the *Revelation* astronauts. My source is saying that there are a couple of the crew members who have, shall we say, *secrets*—things that just might have *kept them off the mission*."

"That so? It would have been very nice if your 'source' had come forward earlier—like *before* the launch. All it will do now is sell a few more papers."

"*Well*?" said Sally. They grinned at each other.

Perry paused. "OK, take some time and look into it. Keep me up-to-date and don't print anything without talking to me first."

"Right, boss." Sally left the room.

10

The *Revelation* had been streaking across the galaxy for just over 325 years Earth time, only three months ship time. While the crew slept, the ship's cameras were dutifully recording the images of the heavens. The cameras off the portside were photographing unbelievably sharp images of the constellation Orion and its foremost star Betelgeuse, the brightest star within one thousand light-years from the sun. The stars that make up Orion vary from three hundred light-years to over 1300 light-years from our sun.

The journey continued on course as programmed into the ship's computer. After 650 years Earth time, the nose camera was recording a magnificent view of the Eagle Nebula some six thousand light-years from the sun. The computer didn't question its own program, *but the crew would have questioned the relative location of the Eagle Nebula.*

As far as the ship and its valuable cargo were concerned, just over six months had gone by. The crew was still sleeping comfortably, and the ship's computer was dodging space rocks and debris that were too large to be deflected by the shield surrounding the ship. Additionally, the computer was babysitting the crew, monitoring vital signs and ensuring that the capsules' environmental equipment was functioning properly.

This blissful state was about to be interrupted, however, as an asteroid was coming in from high and to the right on a track *that would impact the ship in about forty seconds*! The relative speed of the asteroid was about sixteen thousand miles per second, and the computer had not yet picked it up on scan.

Time until impact was now thirty-seven seconds, thirty-five seconds, now thirty.

At twenty-five seconds, the computer identified the threat, commanded full available power from the engines, and caused the ship to jump ahead just as the asteroid passed directly behind and slightly below the ship. Sensors read the proximity of the two objects at about 312 *feet* at the closest point. The engines were returned to cruise power instantly after the event, and the ship returned to its normal cruise mode. The ship's brain had performed flawlessly.

Now 975 light-years into the mission, the *Revelation* was on the programmed course and without any serious technical problems. The nose gear warning light was still showing red, and there had been some insignificant system malfunctions, but each had been handled quickly and satisfactorily by the computer. Some signal rerouting had been accomplished, and some alternate equipment had been called into service; but all in all, the mission was going extremely well. The ship was now about 325 light-years from its intended destination. The portside cameras were obtaining beautiful shots of the Lagoon Nebula, located some 4,500 light-years from Earth's sun.

Had the crew been awake and observing the sky, they would have realized that *something was definitely amiss*. According to the original mission plan, at this stage in the journey, the nose camera should have been looking almost directly at the Crab Nebula some 6,000 light-years from the sun *but on the opposite side of the sun from the Lagoon Nebula*.

As far as the ship's computer was concerned, the *Revelation* was now three-quarters of its way toward its programmed destination—Nyvar.

11

The *Revelation* was nearing its planned destination—the planet that had been named Nyvar by NASA in the year 2025. The ship's display clocks now read:

Earth year: 3339
Ship year: 2026

The spacecraft, still moving at near light-speed, was now only *about twenty seconds* from entering orbit around Nyvar. The program called for deceleration by exactly *ten seconds out* to a speed of about one hundred thousand miles per hour, thus putting the ship a little less than nineteen *hours* from orbit. This would give the crew plenty of time to recover from hibernation, get some food, and conduct a complete checkout of all ship systems before entering orbit. This would also allow time for the *Revelation* crew to make voice contact with the planet—if there was anyone there to talk to.

Since the ship was still in space, there was no atmosphere and, therefore, no drag. To slow the ship to 100,000 miles per hour from 186,000 *miles per second* required almost as much power from the hyperdrive engines as had been needed for the *JLS* when the ship left Earth's orbit. This time, the HD power would be applied in the reverse direction, decelerating the ship—the opposite of the jump to light-speed.

The engines roared to life on point and accomplished the *RJLS*, or reverse jump from light-speed, exactly as they were programmed to do.

When the computer had confirmed that the *Revelation*'s speed was now stable at 100,000 miles per hour and still on track, its next task was to arouse the crew.

The computer began the process of bringing the crew out of their suspended states. Monitors were showing acceptable values displayed on each of the six capsules. Vital signs were returning to normal, and the atmosphere in each capsule was stabilizing at a temperature of seventy degrees and a content of 80% nitrogen and 20% oxygen. The crew members were beginning to show slight movement, and groans were audible.

The latches on the transparent covers on each of the capsules were unlatched automatically, and the covers were slowly raised to fully open positions.

Jake was the first to sit up and look around. He was followed by David, then Dante. The ladies appeared to be slowly waking. Susan said, without sitting up, "Would someone call me when breakfast is ready?"

Ellen yawned, stretched, and added, "Yeah, me too! Seems like a nice day for sleeping in!"

Maria said, "Are we there yet?"

Before anyone realized what was happening, Dante was out of his berth and floating wildly across the cabin. He tried to grab something for control, but his arms were weak from no use. Ellen said, "Take it easy, everyone . . . We are all *very weak*."

Dante mumbled from his inverted position on the ceiling. "Tell me about it."

After that, everyone moved cautiously until they began to get some strength.

"Hey!" said Jake. "Am I *the only hungry one*?"

Maria chimed in with, "Well, I am *starved*. I'll fix the meals while you guys start checking things out." She donned her magnetic boots and proceeded to the small galley in the rear of the bunk room.

Jake said, "I'll help you, Maria, unless the others need me."

"Go ahead and help her," said Dante. "We have plenty of help up here." By this time, Dante was in the left seat, Susan in the right, and David in his chair, checking the engineer's panel. Ellen was checking the medical panel, reviewing the scans of their vitals over the last year.

Dante, glancing over the forward and overhead panels, said, "Looks like we are right on track according to what I'm seeing. We are slow cruising now at one hundred thousand miles per hour. That will put us at our orbit entry point in just over eighteen hours. Nyvar should be dead ahead."

Susan said, "I think I can see Nyvar . . . There! Isn't that a *planet*?"

David squinted, looking ahead. "It's still pretty far, but it looks like a planet." He continued, "And there is Setar, the mother star of the Setarian system!"

"Looks a whole lot like our sun," said Ellen, "or what our sun looked like 1300 years ago. Can we magnify the image of Nyvar and bring it up on screen?"

"We can try," said David as he began working with a control pad. The large monitor viewscreen came alive.

Before them on screen was a beautiful planet! It was blue like Earth with landmasses and oceans and white clouds. They were in awe with what they saw. Susan called to Jake and Maria who were still in the galley getting the meals thawed out and heated. "Hey, guys! Come take a look at our new home!"

"We're coming up with four meals if you guys are ready," said Maria.

"I've been ready to eat for a year!" shouted Dante.

"Bring 'em on!" said Susan and David at the same time.

Ellen said, "OK, people, remember our training. Eat slowly. Your stomachs have forgotten what food is."

Jake and Maria brought up two trays each and then went back for the last two. They all silently dug in and really tried to eat slowly. After a couple of swallows felt like pieces of lead in their stomachs, they slowed down. They now understood why they must eat slowly.

Jake had been gazing at the viewscreen and wondering just what this new world would be like. The magnified image was blurred, and no details of the planet's surface could be identified.

As David finished his meal, he set it aside and said, "I'll start some sensor checks on the atmospheric content of the planet."

Susan said, "We're still too far out for communications, aren't we?"

"Well, let's do some quick math," said David. "What did you say our speed is, Dante?"

"One hundred thousand miles per hour. We're just poking along now."

"OK," said David, "and at this speed, the computer tells us we are now about seventeen hours from orbit entry. That means we are about 1,700,000 miles from Nyvar or about seven times the distance from the Earth to the moon."

Susan said, "That's too far for clear transmissions. Let's wait until we are about 250,000 miles out. That'll be another fourteen hours or so."

Dante said, "If we are going too slow, I can fix that . . ." and reached for the power levers.

"No!" said David. "We have a lot of things to do, and we need the time."

"Just pulling your chain, David. I thought you might squawk." A couple of snickers were heard. David didn't think it was funny.

Jake helped Maria trash the breakfast trays, and they discovered some coffee.

Jake yelled up to the front. "Coffee coming, guys. How do you take it?" He and Maria again served the others. The year-old coffee was pretty good even through these special straws.

All systems checks seemed OK except for the gear door light. The computer was used to check and recheck the light and its switch, but nothing changed.

The crew began to discuss their options. Finally, a plan emerged. Dante stated, "If this planet has runways, we will go for a normal longitudinal wheels-down landing. If, on final approach, when we extend the gear, if we fail to get a 'down and locked' green light on the nose gear, we'll try a g pull up and free fall. If that doesn't work, we'll go around and try to crank it down."

He continued, "If all efforts fail to get a green on the nose gear, we will go for a vertical landing—we will have no choice. If there are no runways, we look for the flattest spot we can find.

"Are we all agreed?"

Nobody said anything at first. They really hoped to make a normal landing. They wanted to make a good impression on the natives, whoever they are, and a conventional touchdown and rollout landing seemed the more professional way.

Finally, Jake said, "Sounds like a plan!" Everyone seemed to agree. So that was finally settled. Jake offered to make side bets on the nose gear, but no one took him up on it.

Susan asked David, "How's our fuel? Do we have any concern there?"

David didn't even have to look. He said, "I checked it already, and we have enough to fly another year—ship time. Anybody have suggestions for an alternate if we don't like the looks of Nyvar?" Everyone was mildly stunned. That kind of comment sounded more like Jake or Dante than David.

Ellen said, "I will consult my star charts and let you know."

For the next few hours, the crew took turns in the "gym" just below the bunk room. The compartment had stationary bikes, treadmills, and strength machines. The exercise felt good to everyone. The facility also had a small shower and a toilet area. The women seemed to need more time downstairs than the men, but for once, there was plenty of time. Nobody had any concert or ball game tickets to worry about. They would land when they were ready to land. After all, they had the rest of their lives ahead of them.

Maria and Ellen were the last ones in the gym area. Maria looked like she wasn't too happy.

"What's wrong, Maria? Do you feel OK?" queried Ellen.

"I feel fine physically, but I've got a burden on my mind that I would like to share with someone. Will you keep a secret?"

"Of course. What is it?"

"I am *not a U.S. citizen*. I'm an illegal alien." She looked deep into Ellen's eyes. Maria's beautiful dark brown eyes reflected her concern and sadness.

"Well, that *is* a surprise! But you hold a degree from a U.S. college, and haven't you lived for most of your life in the States?"

"Yes, since I was three years old. My parents brought me with them through a tunnel from Mexico into San Diego. Neither of them are legal citizens either although my father is a very successful businessman now."

"How did you sneak through the FBI screening and receive your clearance to join the *Revelation* team?"

"When I was sixteen and took my first job—a part-time position at Wal-Mart—*somehow* my father got me a *valid social security card*. After that, I had no trouble getting jobs or even competing in the *Miss America contest*, which I *won* in 2013. I had no trouble in gaining entrance to Vassar, where I graduated from in 2017. But I have never been a legal American citizen!"

Ellen thought for a moment. "You know," she said, chuckling, "there is something really funny about this."

"Funny?" said Maria. "I don't see . . ."

Ellen was laughing. "You have lived in the USA since you were three, graduated from one of the premier women's colleges in the country, and won the *Miss America* crown! And you are not even an American citizen! At least, not strictly speaking."

Ellen continued, "And the real kicker in this is that the FBI investigated you and awarded you a *top secret clearance* to join the *Revelation* team. I think it's a *riot*."

Finally, Maria saw the irony and the humor and began to smile, then laugh! Then Ellen laughed more. She gave Maria a big hug and said, "You are A-OK in my book. Let's just keep this between the two of us. Besides, we'll *all be aliens* when we land on Nyvar."

Maria smiled. She was a lot happier now. They both finished donning their *Revelation* jumpsuits with the NASA logo, the *Revelation* logo, and the *American flag*.

They climbed the stairs and entered the flight deck. The others were all strapped in.

Susan said, "Two and a half hours to go, guys. We are about 250,000 miles out. Think I'll see if *anyone is home* . . . What do you think Mr. Mission Commander?" addressing Dante.

"Let's do it!" said Dante. "Jake, you want to make any bets on this phone call?"

"Man, I will bet on anything!" said Jake. "I will say that we get an intelligent response. But I'm not betting on what language our new friends speak."

"OK," said Dante, "you're on for five bucks. I say there is *nobody home with a radio transmitter*."

Susan announced, "Here goes, guys. Make your wishes and hope they come true." She turned to Dante. "Any suggestion on what frequency I should try first?"

"Try the one that is already set in our transmitter—the frequency we used when we last talked to Mission Control at the Cape. That's as good a place to start as any."

"Here goes!" said Susan. She had the full attention of the crew. All were in their seats looking out the forward cockpit window. Nyvar was dead ahead—a beautiful blue planet.

"Calling anyone!" transmitted Susan. "This is *Revelation*, NASA tail number N2025R, calling from 250,000 miles out. Do you read me?" There was no response . . . not a sound.

Then someone said, "Look! To the port! There is a natural satellite of this planet!" Everyone looked, and there it was—a bright body that looked to be covered with white dust and craters. "Wow!" said Jake. "That's pretty *big*, and the ship *didn't react to it*!"

"Too far away," said David, "and it's just sitting there in orbit." The object was now behind them.

"I'll try again," said Susan. "Calling anyone. This is *Revelation*, calling from about 235,000 miles out from your planet. Do you read me?"

Everyone was silent, straining for a sound . . . *any sound.*

"Whoa!" said Dante suddenly. "*We're being scanned!*"

"What? How do you know that?" said Maria.

"That's what this little instrument tells me." Dante pointed at a device on the overhead panel, now with an indicator glowing red. Everyone focused on the instrument—an electronic wave sensor.

"What type of transmission is it sensitive to?" asked Ellen.

David responded, "We installed that specifically to pick up infrared or laser-based beams that might be coming our way. A good guess is that someone is *aiming a weapon at us.*"

"A *weapon*?" said Maria.

"Ground based or airborne?" said Jake.

"Either from the ground or from something in orbit," said Dante. "Or possibly from a spacecraft. It's coming from the vicinity of Nyvar." They all began searching the expanse of space ahead.

"Anybody see anything?" called Dante. There was no response. "We have to put this in the proper perspective. We are over two hundred thousand miles from Nyvar, moving at one hundred thousand miles per hour, and something *we can't even see* has locked on to this ship with either an infrared or a laser beam. Further, that something is holding its lock on, steady and unwavering!"

"Should we change course or speed and try to lose it?" said Jake.

"Probably would do no good," said David. "I have a hunch that a more sophisticated technology than we have ever seen is making our acquaintance."

"Our best bet is to continue our efforts to communicate with them," said Dante. "Susan, transmit on all voice-range frequencies simultaneously—*we have to make contact now*!"

And on the World Below

At GCC, the Global Conflict Control headquarters for the planet, things were *heating up*! Deep underground and extremely well fortified was a huge command center. The center controlled, through use of viewscreens and all manner of electronics, a matrix of very powerful satellite laser weapons—in stationary orbits at about twenty-five thousand miles in space above the surface of the planet.

"What the hell is that?" the duty commander was saying, pointing to the master control screen.

"Dunno, sir," said a controller on duty. It's something that weighs about a million pounds moving directly at us at a speed of about *one hundred thousand miles per hour*! It's over two hundred thousand miles out right now."

"Call GSA and see if they have anything that big coming in from space! I don't recall that we have any spacecraft outside of orbit at this time. Did the International Space Station report anything on this?"

"We have received no message from ISS on this, sir," said another controller.

The GCC controller made the call to GSA and said, "Mission Control says they are tracking the same object and have just *received a call* from the craft!"

"Then scramble some SR40s NOW! Best we send 'em some company in case we need to give 'em a proper welcome!"

"Sir, we already have the satellite magna-lasers tracking them. If they are not friendly, they are history with a touch of this key."

"OK, belay the scramble," said the duty commander. "Let's see what GSA wants to do. We've got them well covered."

On the *Revelation*, suddenly a voice came over the flight deck overhead speaker. *"Who is this calling, and how did you get this frequency?"* The voice was in *English*!

There was not a whisper on the flight deck.

Again, the voice came on, *"Who are you? Who is calling? Identify yourselves!"*

Dante recovered first. He keyed his mike and said, "This is the starship *Revelation*. I am the mission commander, Col. Dante Washington. We are from the planet *Earth* on a mission to visit your planet. What do you call your planet, and to whom am I speaking?'

Silence. Then, "Would you give me that again? Are you saying you are an *Earth* ship? What country are you from? I'm not sure I heard you correctly."

Dante obliged and added, "Our National Aeronautics and Space Administration launched our mission over *1300 years ago* Earth time from Kennedy Spaceflight Center, and we have about one hour to go before we reach an orbit insertion point around your planet. Who are you, and how is it that you speak an Earth language?"

Again, silence. Then, "This is the duty chief of Mission Control at the Kennedy Spaceflight Center in Florida *on planet Earth*! We're havin' big trouble with your story, Colonel. You say you left Earth, traveled for *1300 years*, and now you are arriving back to Earth? You folks better just reduce your speed and wait until I can clear this. Stay on this frequency and hold for further instructions."

The *Revelation* crew was frozen. All they could do was stare at the beautiful blue planet in front of them.

Dante again keyed his mike. "chief," he said, "what year is it?"

The answer came back. "colonel, the year is 3339. Just hold your . . . course! I'm trying to confirm your story and will be back to you soon."

Dante turned and looked at Susan and then the others. Everyone was just blankly gazing at one another and at the blue planet straight ahead. Dante said to David, "Dave, you are supposed to be our emergency go-to guy. Well, I don't think we have an emergency—yet. But I sure would like someone to tell me *how we got back to Earth*."

"This can't be possible!" whined Susan.

"But apparently, it is," said Jake.

David ventured, "I can think of only one possibility that would take us on a 1300-year, seven-thousand-trillion-mile trip in a *circle*." He continued, "None of us had any responsibility for the navigational program input to the computer. I didn't check it. Not that I should have or even *could* have. Did any of you?"

No one spoke up. Finally, Ellen said, "They asked me to verify the location of Nyvar based on all of the astrological data and observations. I did that, and the planet is located between the constellation Orion and the Crab Nebula, not far from the Orion Nebula. Nyvar is *supposed to be* slightly over 1300 light-years from Earth."

They all listened intently to Ellen. No one had a good answer.

Then Dante said, "Then something must have gone wrong with the program."

"Or," said David, "the path that we observed from Earth to Nyvar wasn't *straight* as we assumed. Maybe the navigational program *was wrong*. Even though NASA programmers put in the path projected, the *actual* path brought us right back where we started. Maybe *Nyvar is Earth*!"

"I can't buy that," said Susan. "NASA has never made a mistake like this before."

"No one has ever flown out of the solar system before," said Maria.

They just sat in a kind of a trance.

Suddenly, Dante laughed. Then the others looked at him and also began to laugh almost hysterically. They all laughed and cried at the same time and couldn't stop.

Maria said with tearing eyes, "Well, at least we got the *year* right!" This started everyone laughing again.

Jake ventured, "OK, Dante, I win five bucks! These guys speak English!" He continued with, "This takes the cake for *government boondoggles*. NASA spent sixty-five billion to send us on a very long trip to where we started from." Again, the laughter was rekindled.

Dante, being a former combat officer, was accustomed to handling surprises of the large variety. He sobered up the quickest and keyed his mike. "Chief? Are you still there?"

"Go ahead," came over the speaker.

"Do you have approval for us to land, chief?" said Dante.

"Not yet. I'm still trying to convince GCC *not* to *disintegrate your ship*. I *will* stick my neck way out and give you approval to enter orbit, but *that's it* until I get further OKs from the top. On the chance that we get approval for you to land—give me your ETA for orbit entry."

Susan came on with, "We now have 1025 hours, universal time constant. Our ETA at REP, reentry point, is 1102 UTC."

"Roger," responded Mission Control. "For your reference, we are showing 1023 UTC. You might want to reset your clock. Just sit tight until I get back to you."

The *Revelation* crew was *spent*—the anxiety, the information that they were back on Earth after thirteen centuries, and the uncontrollable laughter had taken its toll. But now they were all deep in thought. *What will this world be like after 1300 years? All we ever knew is now long gone.*

Jake, as usual, had a comment. "At least the Earth is *still here*. And we don't have to worry about testing our field weapons on dinosaurs." Then he remembered his little tax problem with the IRS. *What is the interest on $59 million for 1300 years?* he thought.

"I always did like history," mused Susan. "I have one heck of a lot of reading to do."

Dante could think only of the laser weapon aimed at the ship. He hoped GSA could soon find the records of the *Revelation* mission.

Maria thought only of Rico, now dead for over *twelve hundred* years.

Then they all became quiet with their personal thoughts.

12

It was five twenty-five AM EST at Kennedy; and the duty chief, Jason Smits, was initiating a call on the hotcom to the director of the center, Klaus Stoll. "Sir, I apologize, but we have a situation here that I thought you should be aware of."

Stoll responded sleepily, "Jason, this better be a good one, or you are in deep manure."

Jason was not intimidated. "Sir, we have a large spacecraft with a crew of six people coming *in from the general direction of the moon*. They claim to have been launched by NASA from Earth over 1300 years ago with an intended destination to another planet. They refer to their ship as the *Revelation* and are *requesting permission to enter Earth's orbit and then to land.*"

"*What*?" said Klaus, springing to a sitting position in bed.

"Yes, sir. They called in a few minutes ago on an old seldom-used frequency that we still monitor. They are moving at about 100,000 mph and are less than an hour from their orbit entry point. I instructed them to hold their present course."

"You are telling me that we have an *unidentified spacecraft* approaching from the general direction of the moon?" Director Stoll was fully awake now. "And you are further stating that this ship—what did you call it?"

"The *Revelation*, sir."

"This *Revelation* was supposedly launched by NASA some 1300 YEARS AGO as a mission to another planet, and now *it ends up back here*?"

"I know it sounds unreal, sir. But that is what the ship's commander, a Colonel Washington, is telling me. As I said, they made the initial call on an old unused frequency, which is still monitored by our AFMS. They claim that this was *the launch frequency used by NASA in 2025.*"

The director thought that he must be having a dream. He told Jason to hold on. By now, Mrs. Stoll was awake. Klaus said to her, "Am I awake or just dreaming?"

Mrs. Stoll squinted at him and said, "Dear, we are both awake, and it's only 5:35 AM."

Finally, Director Stoll said to the chief, "Did it occur to you that the ship might *not* be what they say it is, that they might not be travelers from Earth that have been lost in space for 1300 years, and that they *might be hostile aliens from who knows where*?"

The duty chief shuffled his feet, nervously looking at the tracking on screen. Finally, he said, "We have scanned the ship carefully, and it does not appear that it is equipped with weapons of any kind. The total crew is only six people, three women and three men—hardly a war party. The GCC has the ship covered with satellite magna-lasers." Klaus considered the words of his chief.

"Sir," continued the duty chief, "I have a call coming in from GCC. Can I take that and get right back with you?"

The director was in deep thought. "Chief, we have no ships in space at this time from this base. Am I correct on that?"

"That is correct, sir, other than the International Space Station—"

"That is NOT a ship, Chief."

"Right, sir." The chief was sorry he mentioned that.

"And is GCC telling you that except for the maser umbrella, *they* have no ships in space—is THAT right?"

"They said that they know nothing of the ship incoming from the moon . . . If I could just take their call, sir—"

"Take it! But you can tell the GCC that we have no knowledge of the incoming ship except that they speak English and claim to have been launched from Earth thirteen centuries ago. I will wait for you to get back to me."

"GCC, this is Chief Smits at KSC. What do you have?"

"Chief, this is Captain Mason, controller at GCC. I have spoken with our duty commander who just talked to General Whitcomb, and we are preparing *to take out the ship* unless someone can positively identify it as friendly. We have been ordered to *initiate* in ten minutes unless someone comes up with a good reason not to."

"All I can tell you from here," said Chief Smits, "is that GSA has *no ships off the planet* at this time. My personal view is that the commander of the incoming ship is telling the truth—but I have no substantiating evidence. If we come up with anything else, I will contact you. Please keep this frequency open."

"Roger out, chief," said the controller.

At KSC, Klaus Stoll picked up his red AMec. "Mr. President, This is Klaus Stoll, GSA. I am very sorry to bother you at this hour, but we have a situation . . ."

At GCC, the controller briefed his staff. "We are on standby to initiate—the countdown is now at eight minutes and counting. In the absence of countermanding orders, we will fire ML4 and ML5 in less than eight minutes."

At KSC Mission Control, Chief Smits had dispatched a young airman to the basement archives to look for records of a launch in 2025 of a light-speed ship to a destination called Nyvar. He advised Director Stoll of this action. Airman Kenny was busy at his task searching through vaults of ancient CDs.

Klaus Stoll was speaking to the president. "Mr. President, our Chief Smits strongly believes that the commander of the incoming ship, a Col. Dante Washington, sounds like he is telling the truth. However, without an order from you, General Whitcomb plans *to take the ship out*. GCC is on countdown now at six minutes and counting."

"Then is it your recommendation, Director Stoll, that we give it more time? Do you have people searching the archives on this?"

"We do, sir, but we only have one staffer on duty that we can free for this purpose."

The president pondered the situation. "We are talking about *centuries*, Stoll. How could this story be true? How could these astronauts still be alive? This is the most preposterous tale I have *ever* heard."

Airman Kenny was still busy at his task. The countdown at GCC was now at *four* minutes and counting.

The president was still on the line with Klaus Stoll. The countdown was now at two minutes.

"All right, Stoll. I will *give you more time*. Call me the *instant* you find corroborative data on this ship." The president contacted General Whitcomb. "George, on this incoming ship. Stoll and his people at KSC are looking through the archives. They believe this Commander Washington is the real thing."

"Mr. President, I can't believe that a ship is arriving back on Earth after thirteen centuries in space!"

"Where is your countdown, George?"

"Forty-five seconds, sir. We will be firing with both ML4 and ML5."

"Stand down, George. NOW! I'll wait . . . We need to discuss this further."

General Whitcomb gave the order to GCC to stand down to and returned to the president. "The boys are standing by, sir. The masers still have the ship locked-on."

"Good. George, I want you to maintain the lock-on until I advise you otherwise. You are clear on this?"

"Yes, Mr. President. I just hope we aren't making a big mistake."

"If we are, it's *my* mistake, General. Stand by. I'll contact you as soon as things change. Obviously, if the ship makes any hostile move, do what you have to." The president clicked off on the call. He contacted Klaus Stoll at KSC. "Stoll, I'm giving you some more time. General Whitcomb has ordered a stand-down at GCC. Let me know the instant you have more information."

At Mission Control, airman Kenny was running up to the duty controller's position.

"Chief Smits—I found a record! There *was* a launch of a light-speed ship from this very base in 2025. Its destination was a planet called Nyvar!" He handed the chief a few pages.

Chief Smits contacted Director Stoll. "Sir, good news! There *was* a launch of a ship called the *Revelation* from this very base in 2025. *Its intended destination was a planet they referred to as Nyvar. The ship had JLS capability.*"

The director stared out the window at the sky, now beginning to lighten with the coming dawn. The chief continued, "*They must be who they say they are, sir.* Their ship will need to enter Earth's orbit within the hour. I have instructed them to hold course until I could speak with you and determine what action you wish us to take."

Klaus Stoll was out of bed by now and extended himself to his full height of six foot four. Bridget Stoll had gone downstairs to make some coffee.

"I will tell you *what you will do the instant we end this call.*" said Klaus. "I want you to stay in close contact with GCC. I want at least two fully armed space fighters launched to rendezvous with this *Revelation*, and I want this base put on alert status. GCC is to maintain a magna-laser lock on the ship. I will call the president and advise him of our find and will be in my office in twenty minutes. This ship may enter orbit, but *do not give them permission to land until you receive the order from me.*" He paused to breathe. "Are you absolutely clear on this?"

"Crystal clear, sir," said the chief. The director punched off the call and again inserted the special code into his all-media communicator. "Mr. President, this is Klaus Stoll at KSC. Here is what we know . . ."

Nearing the orbit insertion point, the *Revelation* crew was making a final check on the flight deck. The deceleration from one hundred thousand miles per hour to eighteen thousand miles per hour would be substantial although not nearly so much as the previous decel from light—speed down to slow cruise of one hundred thousand miles per hour. As with *JLS* and *RJLS*, because of the stress on the human body and internal organs, crew members had to again take their positions in the capsules. As before, the Accel-Safe units would protect their bodies from the extreme deceleration of the ship. Slowing from one hundred thousand miles per hour to about eighteen thousand miles per hour in two minutes would result in over a 30 g deceleration force, much more than human bodies can normally stand.

Dante stayed behind to make a last scan of the instruments as the other five entered their individual capsules. Dante was satisfied that all was in readiness; then he too took his reclined position in the designated capsule. Each crew member closed and locked their bunk. They were not placed in hibernation; there was no need for that. Only the Accel-Safe anti-acceleration units were needed to protect their bodies.

The countdown was initiated by the ship's computer. "Five . . . four . . . three . . . two . . . one—mark!"

Again, the engines growled—this time, more like pussycats than lions. The ship began slowing—thirty seconds, one minute, one minute and thirty seconds, two minutes passed. The speed now read just over eighteen thousand miles per hour. The transition had been smooth. The revelation had entered tangent to the intended orbit at the precise speed required. Orbit was now achieved. The power was reduced to near zero as the ship floated in orbit over and around the Earth.

When the *Revelation* was stable, the computer unlocked the capsule covers and raised them to their open positions. The crew members felt no ill effects and immediately returned to their seats on the flight deck.

"That was easy!" said Ellen.

"This is really some machine," said Jake. "I'll bet everybody on Earth has one of their own in 3339."

"We are *still being tracked* by a laser beam," said Dante. All focused on the red indicator.

"Look! Look there to our port!" said Susan. Barely visible was an odd object shaped like a gigantic motorcycle wheel with five heavy spokes.

"What thuh . . . ?" mumbled Dante.

"I think we are seeing a space station!" said Jake.

"It looks *huge*," said Susan. "Appears to be rotating slowly."

"Let's refocus, guys," said Dante. "Lucky for us that station, or whatever it is, was not directly on *our track*. We've got work to do . . . Check all equipment indicators for problems."

Dante and Susan checked all instrumentation on the forward panels, and David scanned the flight engineer's panel for any anomalies. Dante spoke, "Everything is 'go.' I'll call MC." He keyed the mike.

"Mission Control, this is *Revelation*. We have achieved orbit and are currently about forty-five minutes from our reentry point for descent to your runway. Do we have clearance to proceed with landing when we reach REP?"

There was no response.

"Do you read me, Mission Control?" called Dante.

"We read you, *Revelation*, but we have another hang-up down here. GCC is sending out a 'greeting party' to check you folks out. You should be seeing them momentarily."

Dante looked left, and Susan looked right, scanning all the sky they could see.

Jake said, "Guess they don't trust us, guys. Can't say that I blame them. Most normal people would have trouble *believing* people over 1300 years old."

Ellen said, "If they don't believe us, they surely can look up the records of our mission in the archives."

"If they have records *that* old," said David.

"Look!" said Maria. "There are two small spacecraft on our starboard side!" The two craft looked more like high-powered sports cars than spacecraft. They were small—obviously one-seated craft with abbreviated delta wings and single vertical fins.

"Whoa!" said Dante. "Never seen ships like these before. Must be short-range fighters."

The pilots of the SR40 short-range space fighters had orders to positively identify the *Revelation*. They had been launched from Eglin AFB, Florida, with full authority to *destroy* the intruder unless they could establish that the *Revelation* was the friendly spacecraft they claimed to be. The first pilot was calling the second on a secure frequency.

"Well, it's got NASA markings and a tail number. Looks like N2025R to me. Can you confirm that?"

"Roger. That's what I'm seeing," responded the second fighter pilot. Do you see anything that looks like weapons ports?"

"Nothing. She looks docile to me. I'll call base." He switched frequency and called. "Base, this is UAF4801, come in."

"This is base, 4801. Whatcha got?"

"Er . . . roger, we're up here lookin' over this vis'tin' bird. It's got a number on the tail, N2025R, and we see no evidence of weapons anywhere. It's shaped like one of our USIC class ships—I'd put its takeoff weight at about a million pounds."

"You think she's safe to let land?" came back from base.

"What frequency is she using to talk to Kennedy? I'd like to chat with the pilot."

"They're using an old Mission Control launch frequency—transmitting it to you now."

"Roger, got it. Thanks. Stand by, I'll call them and be right back at you."

"Roger."

Switching to the old MC frequency, UAF4801 called the *Revelation*. "*Revelation,* this is UAF4801 on your right wing. How're things goin' over there?"

The voice came over the flight deck overhead speaker. Dante thought it sounded like sweet music! "Roger 4801, we are doing A-OK over here. This is Col. Dante Washington, USAF. If we could get permission to land this bird, everything would be absolutely perfect."

"Well, colonel, this is Maj. Daniel Jackson, USAF. And it's good talkin' to you. I understand that you folks have been ridin' around in that whale for a *while.*"

"Major, if I told you how long, you wouldn't believe me. Are you boys going to escort us down?"

"No, colonel, I'll let you and KSC work that out. Our orders are to make sure that you folks are *friendly.* My buddy and I will be going on back to base now. Y'all have a good ride down now, y'hear?"

"Thanks, major. I'll be calling MC now. Over and out."

UAF4801 called back to his base as he and UAF4652 pulled away and used reverse power to brake for reentry. "Base, this is UAF4801 again, come in."

"Roger, 4801, this is base."

"These folks in their antique spaceship look OK." He related his observations to the GCC controller. "I just had a chat with the pilot, and I see no problem with letting them come home."

"Roger, 4801, I'll pass the word. Come on down."

"We're on our way. Over and out."

With that, the two SR40s dropped through the atmosphere and disappeared from view. From the ground, they looked like a couple of meteors falling.

Back on the *Revelation*, Jake said, "Well, some things sure haven't changed. I'll bet money that guy's from Alabama! He talks just like everybody else from Alabama."

That brought laughs around, which were quickly stifled when Dante said, "We're OK *now,* but that country boy had orders to *shoot us down* if he didn't like us." Dante glanced up and saw that they were still being tracked by a laser beam.

Jake knew that was true, but the others just stared at Dante in amazement. They could not comprehend what he just said. Dante continued, "I'll give it a few more minutes, then call MC. We are still twenty-five minutes from our REP."

"Would somebody tell me why they are threatening to shoot us down?" said Ellen.

"National security," said Dante. "Just consider the possibility that we and our ship might be hostile, *posing* as visitors from Earth's distant past. Just consider the possibility that we have weapons on board that could *annihilate* large areas of a planet and just consider that we only contacted this planet in order to gain their confidence until we could select our targets at close range."

"Isn't that a little far-fetched?" said David.

"Maybe," said Dante, "but not out of the realm of possibility."

Susan added, "I agree with Dante. We are now in the year 3339. In this age, interplanetary travel might be commonplace. The Earth's civilization may now be able to *exceed the speed of light* even though in 2025, we believed that to be impossible."

Jake joined in. "If interplanetary travel at greater than light-speed is now possible, that could mean that the Earth has alien enemies from other planets. I can see why they must be cautious with any unidentified spacecraft."

"Are you telling me that just based on those two jet jockeys checking us out that the U.S. military is now satisfied to let us continue our descent to land?" said Maria.

"I doubt that," said Dante. "They probably found our records. But let's examine what the pilots learned by their contact with us. First, the *Revelation* matches the identity of the ship that left Earth in 2025, and they have those records on disc. Then Major Jackson and his buddy got a pretty good look at us from close range. We all look human—except maybe Jake! Finally, any serious firepower we might have would require external ports for firing. Our fighter friends didn't see any such because there are none."

"And I wouldn't rule out the confidence they gained by just talking to you, Dante," said Jake. "That was as natural exchange between two jet jockeys as I have ever heard—and you guys are at least 1300 years apart in age!"

"They still are not 100 percent convinced about who we are," said Dante. "You can bet they will keep weapons tracking us all the way down."

At the Global Conflict Control Center Somewhere in the Western United States

"Kennedy MC, this is Duty Chief Abernathy at GCC. Our boys have checked out your visitor and think it's OK to let them descend from orbit for landing."

"GCC, this is Chief Smits at KSC. I hear you but need some details. Got to make our boss happy down here."

"Right, MC. Well, here's what we've got. Ship is estimated at about a million pounds give or take, delta design, painted white with engine pods under. Tail number identifies her as N2025R. She's got no apparent weapons ports and a crew of six. At this time, she's holding orbit, and we estimate about fifteen minutes from her optimum REP."

"Sounds like she's OK. But you are keeping your masers focused until the ship lands, and we have things under control on the ground?"

"We are under orders to do that and will scramble two more SR40s out of Eglin to add to the two that are still up to keep her company on the way down. How'd that be?"

"Perfect, Chief! Thanks for your help. Over and out."

At Kennedy, Chief Smits again called Klaus Stoll at his home. He was having some breakfast when the AMec toned with "Stars and Stripes Forever."

"This is Stoll, Chief. Anything new on our visitor?"

"Sir, GCC has checked out the *Revelation* and has given us an OK to let them come on down."

"They have, have they? What tabs did they say they are keeping on them?"

"Plenty, sir. They have two magna-lasers locked on the ship, and there will be four SR40s escorting them all the way down."

"OK. Alert our base ground personnel, the usual emergency vehicles and that sort of thing. We will handle it logistically like any other of our returns from space. We'll keep the extra security on ready status until all is judged to be under control. I will be leaving here in five minutes and will check in with you when I arrive there."

"Right, sir. See you then."

"*Revelation*, this is KSC Mission Control. Come in."

Susan responded, "KSC, this is *Revelation*."

"*Revelation*, you have permission to descend from orbit and land—runway 33. Can you give me your ETA?"

"Roger, KSC. We read you, clear to land. We are at eight minutes from REP—thanks for your help."

"No problem, *Revelation*. Stay safe, and we'll see you on the ground. Over and out."

Susan turned to Dante and the rest of the crew. "We're going home, guys!" There were huge smiles and sighs of relief.

Dante said, "Now if the nose gear just doesn't embarrass us."

The smiles all faded, and everyone returned to their work and their thoughts.

"We are two minutes from our REP for reentry and final approach to Kennedy," announced Susan.

"OK, gang, let's look sharp and make our final checks," said Dante.

David had already been doing that and had found nothing amiss but the nose gear door light. "Still have an unhappy nose gear door light," he said.

"I see it," said Dante. "We will just have to hope for a good 'down and locked' indication on final. If we don't get it, we'll recycle and try to jerk it down with g-forces. We will follow our agreed plan. As a last resort, we'll do a vertical descent landing. This will be less hazardous than a conventional landing with a questionable nose gear."

"Just guessing," said Jake, "but I'll bet vertical landings are common around here in 3339."

"We are at REP," announced Dante. "Here we go." With that, he engaged reverse power on the engines; the speed dropped like a rock, and so did the *Revelation*. The heat build up outside from the atmospheric drag was impressive. The ship's speed was now at ten thousand miles per hour and continuing to reduce very quickly. Five thousand, now one thousand, now two hundred fifty miles per hour approach speed. After a few short minutes, an old friend was now in sight, dead ahead—the 14,000 foot runway at Kennedy Spaceflight Center.

Dante called, "Gear down," as Susan reached for the handle. Everyone was holding their breath, waiting for three greens . . .

A green light came on for the left main, then for the right main. Still red on the nose gear. Everyone continued to hold their breaths.

Suddenly, there it was! A beautiful shade of green on the nose gear, *down and locked*.

A cheer went up on the flight deck, which sounded like fifteen people. Everyone was ecstatic! Smiles and congratulations permeated the flight deck. Dante had the *Revelation* right on glide slope for touchdown at five hundred feet from the approach end of the runway.

All eyes were glued to the runway, and no one even noticed the four fighter escorts descending with them on the right and on the left. They knew that some weapons still had the ship locked in, but they had no way of knowing the awesome power of the magna-lasers. A single command to the satellites and the *Revelation* would have disappeared in a blinding flash with only particle remains floating to Earth.

With the skill of a highly decorated pilot, Dante greased the *Revelation* onto the runway exactly on point. The *Revelation* was *home*!

Klaus Stoll was watching from his observation deck two hundred yards off the side of the runway. A rather large crowd of KSC employees of GSA had gathered in a designated viewing area. There were no outsiders and no press. GSA PR people were filming and photographing the event. As the *Revelation* continued on its landing roll, the nose gear touched down—safely—and Dante began to brake. Reverse engine power provided most of the deceleration force required. The ship came to a halt after using only 2,500 feet of the almost three-mile-long runway. The KSC/GSA staff that attended the landing had been treated to as professional a touchdown as they had witnessed in a while. They were impressed.

Klaus made a call; and immediately, Humvee-type security trucks with considerable firepower were dispatched to the *Revelation*, stopping around the flight deck entry door. The fire trucks that had attended the landing were still on hand.

Stoll and all the GSA personnel present were quite anxious and quite careful. No one had been totally convinced that the crew members on this ship were who they said they were.

On board the *Revelation*, everybody was breathing normally and quite relaxed.

Susan called for after-landing check, and Ellen was scanning her panel for any abnormal vital signs for any of the crew.

Jake said, "Not bad, Dante! Just think of what kind of landing you could have made with some practice flights!" Dante smiled but didn't appreciate the humor.

David reported that all systems had been shut down with normal readings.

Susan was giving Dante a big hug and telling him he was the best pilot she had ever flown with.

Maria was out of her chair and looking down at the tarmac. She said, "Our reception committee has weapons I have never seen before."

Dante and Jake looked down. Jake said, "I've seen weapons like that. I think it was in the first *Star Wars* movie."

"OK, guys, everything is shut down. We can't stay in here forever. Let's go meet the greeters. Ground personnel have just brought up a set of stairs."

With that, David opened the entry door. Dante came forward to exit first. He stepped out onto the stairs and started down. The others—Susan, Jake, Maria, David, then Ellen—filed out and followed.

One of the military police stepped forward, saluted Dante, and said, "Welcome back to Earth, colonel. I am Maj. Samuel Carr." Dante returned the salute and offered his hand. They shook. Major Carr met and greeted each of the crew and said, "We have a limo here for you all. Director Stoll will receive you inside the headquarters building." The limo appeared to be made of reflective molded material. There were no headlights visible. The car looked more like a stretched short-range fighter than it did an automobile. The doors had no handles and opened to the touch. It was impossible to see in to the vehicle through what otherwise appeared to be the windows.

The rest of the military police stood at attention in tight-fitting gray uniforms with weapons drawn as the *Revelation* crew entered the limo. A senior master sergeant was at the wheel. Major Carr took the right front seat. As all were comfortably seated, Carr said OK to the driver, and a low-pitched hum was heard.

The vehicle lifted slightly, retracted its wheels, and rotated at its center. Now it was headed in the opposite direction. As steady as a rock, it accelerated forward and headed for the headquarters building. The ride was as smooth as silk.

As the limo departed the area, a large tug pulled up to the nose gear of the *Revelation*, and its driver began looking for a spot to hook up.

The crew, now able to see *out* the windows, were seated, three facing forward and three facing aft. A transparent panel separated the passenger section from the forward section of the vehicle. Between the seats was a low table with what appeared to be a pitcher of water and six glasses. Jake was the first to reach for the pitcher, but David stopped him by placing his hand on Jake's arm. "I wouldn't," said David.

Jake said, "It smells OK. It's just water," and poured himself a glass. He held it up to the light and looked at it carefully. "Looks like water to me."

"So do a lot of other things," cautioned Ellen. "Could I see it?"

Jake handed her the glass. Ellen smelled it, then put the tip of her finger in it. She put a drop on her tongue. Everyone stared at her and waited.

"It's water," she said

"Do you guarantee it?" said Jake, now showing some concern with what it might be.

"No," said Ellen. "Without a lab test, who can be sure?"

Jake said, "I'll take the chance. I'm thirsty." With that, he took a big swallow. Everyone watched with great interest to see his reaction.

Suddenly, Jake grabbed at his throat and gasped. His face was turning red, then blue! Ellen reached for her emergency kit and withdrew a syringe! She was swabbing an area on Jake's arm with a small cloth as she prepared to inject a chemical.

Jake suddenly withdrew his arm from Ellen, let go his hands from his throat, and started laughing. He said, "It's just water."

They all were PO'd at Jake, and Dante threatened to throw him out of the limo. The only one that laughed at Jake was Maria. She had expected him to do just as he did. The others tried the water. They individually decided that it was OK.

In Washington DC

At the White House, the president had called a special meeting of several key players. Present were the president's chief of staff, the chairman of the Joint Chiefs, the director of the CIA, the director of the FBI, the secretary of state, and the secretary of defense, plus others on the president's staff. President Thornhill was speaking, "Ladies and gentlemen, some of you already know this. We have some visitors from space. They claim to be from Earth, having launched their mission in the year 2025."

Sounds of disbelief and surprise rippled through the group in the Oval Office.

President Thornhill continued, "They say that their ship, the *Revelation*, traveled at near light-speed and that they themselves have only aged only about a year in the over 1300 years they have been en route."

"You say, sir, that they launched from Earth that long ago *en route* to Earth?" asked General Selvage, chairman of the Joint Chiefs.

"Not exactly, Rich," said the president. "That's the strange part of this thing. They say they launched on a mission to a planet we know as Nyvar, in the Setarian Star System. They never intended to ever see the Earth again."

Carl Kirsh, CIA, said, "Then they have actually traveled in a circle for over 1300 years?"

"Odd, isn't it?" said the president.

"Damned odd! I would say," commented the secretary of defense, Barbara Bakkus. "Where is their ship at this moment?"

"It's on the ground at Kennedy Spaceflight Center."

"We let them land?" said General Selvage. "Why on earth—"

The president interrupted. "Now just hold on, everyone, and let me finish. When their ship was about two hundred thousand miles out, we picked them up on scanners and input their coordinates into the magna-laser units. Two of the satellite masers locked on to them at that point. Our scanners told us that the *Revelation* weighed about a million pounds and was traveling at about one hundred thousand miles per hour. It was then that the *Revelation* crew called in on an old unused frequency, one that we still monitor, trying to establish communications with ground. Our controller on duty responded to the call from the ship."

"We still monitor a frequency from thirteen centuries past?" exclaimed General Selvage.

"Yes," said the president. "We monitor *all* communications frequencies, just in case a situation such as this arises. This crew said they were calling in on the launch frequency that Kennedy Spaceflight Center used in the year 2025 when they *departed* Earth. But here is the real kicker, ladies and gentlemen: KSC Dir.

Klaus Stoll was able to find a record in the archives from the year 2025 when a ship called the *Revelation was launched from Kennedy Spaceflight Center* on November 18, 2025! Its mission was a *one-way* journey to the planet called Nyvar, which we know to be located between Betelgeuse and the Crab Nebula about 1300 light-years away from Earth."

By now, the group in the Oval Office was mesmerized. The president continued, "We gave them permission to enter orbit at about one hundred miles. And, general, your boys at GCC ordered two SR40s out of Eglin to go up and check them out. The SR40 pilots reported that the *Revelation* had no weapons ports, and the crew looked and talked like ordinary U.S. citizens. They recommended we keep them in the sights of satellite masers and let them land at Kennedy. We also escorted them down with four SR40s."

President Thornhill continued, "I would like you, Rich, and you, Barbara, to stay behind for a short discussion after we end this meeting." He was addressing Gen. Richard Selvage, chairman of the Joint Chiefs, and Barbara Bakkus, the secretary of defense. Turning to all, he said, "That'll be all right now. I just wanted you to know what's cooking. Do *not* share what we just discussed with *anyone*." The president stood from behind his desk; that was the signal that the meeting was over. He walked over to a coffee table surrounded by seating for six and took a chair. General Selvage and Mrs. Bakkus joined him. The others left the room.

"I want to tell you two that I have *serious reservations* about these people from the twenty-first century. I know nothing about them except that they *are from the past,* an ancient past that shares very little in common with our Earth of 3339. I don't know how much you both have read about the twenty-first century, but I have read a lot. The Earth in that era was moving rapidly toward disaster. Civilization, even in the United States, was spinning out of control. Wars, conflicts, terrorism, crime, starvation, moral decay, awful social problems, and contamination of the atmosphere and the oceans were all intensifying at increasing rates. The governments of the nations of Earth, including the United States, seemed incapable of taking actions to reverse the trends.

"I won't go into the whole story, but if you haven't read about it, you should. The reason I bring it up now is that these six astronauts who have come to us quite by accident are from the old Earth of what I speak. Our society of today is as different from that of the Earth of 2025 as night is from day. I am not sure that these strangers from the twenty-first century *can be allowed to live in our wonderful society* we have developed and almost perfected during the last thirteen centuries."

"Excuse me, Mr. President," injected General Selvage. "Excuse me from interrupting you, but are you saying that we should send these people on their way back into space on the journey they intended . . . or . . . just what are you suggesting?"

"I'm not sure, Rich. That's why I wanted to talk with the two of you. Our choices are limited. As I see it, we have three options. One, we can attempt to retrain them and teach them about our life in the thirty-fourth century. Maybe they can make the transition. We can try that option—and it may work for some of them, but not for all. Their ship is still spaceworthy, and as a second choice, we can send those that are unfit for our society on their way. Finally, the third choice is that we treat them as we do with any unacceptable members of our society. What is your thinking, Barbara?"

Mrs. Bakkus was quite thoughtful. Finally, she said, "Mr. President, I think we should let them each prove to us whether they can live with us or not. They should all have our understanding and the best training and indoctrination we can give them."

"I agree," said the general, "except we must keep them under close surveillance—certainly in the initial stages of their indoctrination. We must keep foremost in our minds that they are from a *very different place*, and they may have very different values from those of our citizens."

"I agree with both of you," said the president. "We will give them every opportunity to become members of our society."

"How is their indoctrination to be conducted? Where?" said the general.

"Good questions, Rich. I have discussed this with Klaus Stoll, and he feels that his staff at KSC can take it on. They have a number of quite learned PhD's, and I am very confident they can do a good job. Besides, as you both know, we are keeping the arrival of these astronauts a secret. Quartering and training them at KSC keeps the wraps on the whole thing. We don't need the *media complicating our task*, especially since we aren't *sure of the outcome*."

And Back at Canaveral

At the spaceflight center, the limo bearing the *Revelation* crew was arriving at the headquarters building. The building looked like none the crew had ever seen. It appeared to be made totally of glass or transparent plastic and had no sharp corners. It tapered from the ground up such that what appeared to be the top floor was only about half as large as the first floor. On the top of the building was a dome so shiny it appeared to have a mirrored surface.

They exited the vehicle, and as they did, David bent over and looked underneath the limo. The wheels were apparently retracted! In fact, the vehicle had no contact with the pavement at all!

Ooookaaay! thought David.

Major Carr said to the driver, "Advise them that we are on our way up." He turned to the crew and said, "They are waiting for us in the tenth-floor conference room. Please follow me."

The group approached the large transparent lobby doors, which automatically swung wide as they neared them. They proceeded through what seemed to be a scanning tunnel as a security guard, seated to the right, monitored a screen. They were carrying no weapons, but the guard asked Ellen to stop and hand him her emergency kit. He spent a few moments with the kit and returned it to Ellen. The guard said, "Please proceed."

The entry area was impressive. As they walked through the lobby, their every move was being photographed by tiny hidden cameras as were the actions of every citizen in any government or public place throughout the United States and most of the world. The lobby ceiling was over twenty feet high, and hanging from that ceiling were models of spacecraft, presumably models of craft that had been launched and operated by NASA and now GSA in the past. They recognized the original lunar-landing module, and other models looked familiar to the *Revelation* crew. But most were models of ships that they had never seen. They moved across the floor to the center bank of four elevators and entered the one indicated by Major Carr.

What they had *not seen behind them* hanging directly over the main entrance was a model of an all-white craft shaped something like the Concorde SST. *It was the Revelation*! It even had the number N2025R painted on the tail.

13

The elevator doors closed and, within two seconds, reopened. The *Revelation* crew expected to see someone standing at the door who had just missed boarding when it closed. There was no one there. Major Carr motioned for them to exit and said, "Here we are!"

The elevator had risen from the ground floor to the tenth floor in two seconds, and they had felt *no acceleration*. They stepped out of the elevator into a large foyer and faced tall double doors opposite the elevator doors.

"Here's our main conference room," said Sam Carr. "Please go in."

Susan reached to push the large doors, and they opened smoothly and noiselessly without her touch. The crew filed into the room, followed by the major.

The room looked like most conference rooms they were familiar with. A large conference table in the center of the room flanked by straight but comfortable-looking chairs, ten on a side with two larger chairs at each end. The walls were lined with additional chairs.

A large presentation monitor or screen was built into the wall above one of the end chairs.

But the room was empty. Dante ventured, "I thought they were waiting on us?"

"They were, and they are," said Major Carr. "Please take seats on the center of the left side of the table." Confused, the crew obliged and sat down, leaving one chair on one end and three chairs on the other end of the row.

Major Carr said, "I'm sorry, but would you please shift down one seat that way?" pointing to the right. He explained, "There is someone already occupying the seat you are in, ma'am," addressing Ellen, seated in the second chair from the left end. Puzzled, the group obliged, and each shifted one chair to the right.

Major Carr said, speaking toward the dome-shaped device at the center of the conference table, "We are ready, sir. You can go ahead."

With that, holographic images of several people appeared seated in chairs at the conference table and in some of the chairs along the wall. The images were so sharp they looked as though the real people were seated there. The hologram of Dir. Klaus Stoll was seated at the end of the table facing the large monitor on the wall at the other end.

Director Stoll spoke from his holographic image, "Welcome to the Kennedy Spaceflight Center of the Global Space Administration. I am Klaus Stoll, the director of this facility. I would like our guests from the twenty-first century to each identify yourself. After that, I would like our GSA people to introduce yourselves to our guests, beginning on my left. Now, Colonel Washington, would you be the first from your crew?"

Dante arose and said, "Certainly, sir. I am Dante Washington, colonel, United States Air Force, and the mission commander for our *Revelation* mission."

Next, Susan stood and introduced herself as the first officer of the *Revelation*. Jake, Maria, David, and finally Ellen stood and introduced themselves.

Then each hologram of GSA staff members stood and introduced himself or herself one by one. The introductions were finally complete.

The director again spoke, "The record of this meeting, both verbal and visual, will be on disc by the time the meeting adjourns. And you will each receive a copy. Therefore, the notepads in front of you are only for doodling." The holograms all chuckled at the director's humor. He continued, "Let me again say welcome. It is an honor for us to meet you, and I speak for all when I say congratulations on completing a safe journey encompassing over 1300 years and over seven thousand trillion miles through space. The fact that you ended up here on Earth where you started from is a mystery we will try to sort out later.

"Now without further ado, I would like to show all of you a visual record that, until an hour ago, I had not seen myself. Please direct your attention to the large monitor at the end of the room."

The lights dimmed, and an image began to form on the screen. A van with NASA painted on the side was pulling up to a large aircraft. Only the undercarriage of the aircraft could be seen in the shot. From out of the van came Dante, followed by Susan, then Jake, then Maria, and finally David and Ellen. The shot pulled back, and behind the crew was not an aircraft, but the *Revelation*.

At the table, the crew was mesmerized. This must have been the video shot in 2025 when they began the mission to Nyvar. Even Jake was speechless.

The next shot showed the crew standing at the top of the Delta Air Lines entry stairs, waving to the crowd. The crew entered the ship, and the door was closed.

"Before we stop and consider what we are seeing," said Director Stoll, "I would like to show one more strip." He worked with a control in his hand. On screen came a view of the *Revelation* poised for takeoff. As the disc continued, the *Revelation* started its takeoff roll. The spacecraft disappeared off the left of the screen. The image looked as though the camera had been jerked to the left, next catching the tail of the *Revelation* climbing straight up. Again, the camera bobbed up and down and finally found a speck disappearing into the sky. The screen went blank.

"And that, my friends, unfortunately, is the only pictorial record we have of your launch in 2025!"

First, the room roared with laughter at the cameraman, now long dead, who couldn't keep the camera on the hurtling aircraft. Then all the holographs stood and applauded with *great enthusiasm.*

The director's hologram again spoke, "Now if you six icons of space history will please exit this room at the double doors directly behind you, our guys would all like to meet you in person and shake your hands. We have a reception laid out for you." The holograms faded from view.

The brave crew members from the *Revelation* were overwhelmed. They stood, each with tears in their eyes, and turned and hugged one another. They did a group hug and didn't want to stop. Susan said, "We're home, guys, really home!"

Finally, they wiped their eyes and braced up. As they approached the big doors behind them, the doors opened, and a small band started "America the Beautiful!" This time, there were no holograms, but real people. They were GSA staff members and astronauts. And they were beaming with pride and respect for the crew of the *Revelation.* Hors d'oeuvres had been laid out, and there was a refreshment bar. Klaus asked the *Revelation* team to split up so they could talk to more of the attendees. Everyone began really enjoying the celebration.

The director's AMec was signaling. In 3339, cell phones—now AMecs, or all-media communicators—could handle any form of communication available on the planet, including live TV and phone calls from Mars. People often referred to these devices as "mecs." Only the director could hear his mec's ringtone. He stepped away from the crowd and answered. "Yes?" he said. "Who did you say? Well, put him on by all means . . . Yes, sir, we are honoring them as we speak. You will? You are? OK, here are the coordinates." He keyed numbers into the mec pad.

The director turned to the noisy crowd and said, "May I have your attention, please." No one heard him. He waved his arms and yelled, "COULD I HAVE YOUR ATTENTION, PLEASE!"

This time, the room went quiet, and all looked his way. He stated in a raised voice, "We have a special guest coming. He will be here momentarily."

Someone said, "LOOK!" and pointed to the end of the room. A holographic image was materializing. It took form.

"It's the president of the United States," said Major Carr. All courteously applauded.

The president's hologram stepped forward more toward the center of the room. "I would certainly like to meet our very *old* travelers," he said with a smile.

"Greetings, Mr. President. Nice of you to drop in!" said Klaus.

"I am Edward Thornhill, and you are?" the president said to Susan, who had stepped forward. The crowd backed away and gave the *Revelation* crew and the president room to move. "I am Susan Chen. I served as first officer for the *Revelation*. Nice to meet you, Mr. President."

One by one, each crew member, ending with Dante, introduced themselves to the president. When he learned that Dante was the mission commander, he leaned over and whispered a question in Dante's ear.

Dante stepped back and said with a smile, "We didn't have one, sir."

The president let out a big laugh and then said, "Aha! I suspected as much." He continued speaking to the *Revelation* crew members, "I doubt that you have been advised, but Director Stoll here is putting together a program for the six of you. You, of course, don't know it yet, but our society in this century, and indeed for many centuries, has been radically different from the one you left in the twenty-first century. The GSA staff will undertake to teach you of our life in the thirty-fourth century. We don't know how *you will react* to what you learn. We hope, *for your sakes*, that your response will be favorable."

The president paused, looking intently into the eyes—from one to the next—of each *Revelation* crew member. Then he said, "Be open-minded—and study hard."

Then turning to Director Stoll, he said, "Now I must run. But before I go, however, I would like to sample the white wine you are serving, Director Stoll." With that, the president's hologram reached over and picked up a glass of previously poured wine and tasted it. "Ah, delicious! *I will take it along.* I'll return the glass."

The director said, "No problem, sir, you can keep the glass," as the president's hologram, *along with the glass*, disappeared.

Ellen approached the director and said, "Sir, we are overwhelmed at this reception and your kindness. I want to thank you. But you had us worried when we first arrived."

"Dr. Marks," said Klaus, "you had *us* worried—until we found that disc in our archives!"

Susan said, "Are you going to help us understand why we ended up back on Earth?"

"Absolutely. I hope we can explain that in the first indoctrination session we have planned for you. There are several people working on the program for you folks that the president referred to. You will learn of all the changes that have taken place on this planet since you left. Believe me, *there are many*."

Jake spoke up with a comment to Director Stoll, "I sensed a rather strange tone in the president's voice as he talked of how we may react to what we learn of the ways of this century. Could you comment on that?"

Stoll was taken aback and appeared to be a little nervous. He said, "Oh, I wouldn't worry about that. I think President Thornhill may be unnecessarily cautious. You folks will do fine." He changed the subject.

"First, we must assign you quarters and get you properly checked in. All of you are on the GSA's payroll until you decide what else you might want to do. For the moment, just enjoy talking with those of our staff. They are in awe of you!"

The socializing continued for a time; then the GSA staffers began to leave and drift back to their offices. The crew said good-bye to those that remained, thanked Director Stoll again, and followed Major Carr to the elevator. As they walked, Susan said to Dante, "What did the president whisper to you?"

Dante smiled and said, "He asked, 'Which one of your crew was the navigator?'"

14

As the president's hologram left the celebration at KSC, it appeared in a meeting at CIA headquarters in Virginia. Director Kirsch was chairing the meeting. "Ah, Mr. President, glad you could image-in!"

"Thanks, Carl. I'm not going to take over your meeting. I just want to impart one thought to you and your staff. While I am convinced that this crew from old Earth is who they say they are, I want us to watch them and their actions carefully. Our philosophy of government and our concept of human rights differs greatly from those ideals that these people from the twenty-first century most probably hold dear. When they begin to learn about thirty-fourth century civilization, I am not sure how they will react."

"Sir," said Director Kirsch, "we'll put our best people on the job. And as you know, they are under constant electronic surveillance even now."

"Good work, people!" President Thornhill said to the group. "I'll be going now, but keep me advised. Would you see that Director Stoll gets this back?" He sat the wine glass down and dematerialized.

Back at the Cape

Waiting for the *Revelation* crew outside the headquarters building at KSC was another limo, this time driven by a Mr. Daugherty. Mr. D., as he was known to all, was assigned to check the crew in and make them comfortable. He introduced himself to each crew member as the manager and custodian of the base personnel quarters. Mr. D. was perfectly groomed, of medium height and build, and wore the same type of rather close-fitting gray jumpsuits that the military personnel had been wearing.

After they were all comfortably seated, Mr. D. drove them to the BPQ, overlooking the Atlantic Ocean. The architecture of the eight-story building was very similar to the KSC headquarters building, also with a highly reflective dome on its roof. The BPQ contained, for the most part, extremely modern apartment-type units.

At the lobby desk, Mr. D. assigned each of the *Revelation* crew private quarters with David and Ellen getting a slightly nicer unit large enough for two. Each crew member was asked to pass their right index finger over a reader, recording their DNA. They would later learn that their individual DNAs would be the key factor for many uses requiring IDs in the thirty-fourth century. For the present purpose, their index fingers would serve as the key to their apartment units.

Jake found that amusing and commented, "Guess we better not misplace our index fingers."

No one laughed.

Mr. Daugherty also advised the crew members that GSA was providing for each of them, in addition to the complementary quarters, an interim monthly salary of three thousand credits. David asked, "How much is a credit worth?"

Mr. D. started to try to answer that but finally said, "Sir, there is not a simple answer to that. An explanation of our monetary system will be included in your indoctrination program."

Jake suddenly remembered that he had left a *sizable bank account* at the Chase Washington Bank in the twenty-first century. He had intended to do something with it before he left but never got around to it. He wondered if the account was still there. In fact, he wondered if the *bank* was still there. He thought, *How many credits is a 2025 dollar worth?*

Mr. D. continued, "You will also each receive, at no cost to you, the loan of a personal transportation vehicle referred to as a PMU, or personal mobility unit." Mr. Daugherty advised that most people called the vehicles "pumas."

"Now if you will just follow me, we will find your assigned units," directed Mr. Daugherty.

Mr. D. led them to the elevator and to the eighth floor. They arrived at the first unit, and Mr. D. said to Dante, "Try your key, sir. Touch that red pad there." Dante complied; the red pad turned green, and the door unlocked.

The unit was all painted in whites with light pastel accents. It was nicely furnished and appointed and had large windows and a small kitchenette. Mr. D. took the opportunity to take the crew through Dante's unit and instruct all of them on the operation of the environmental-control unit, the kitchen cooking, and refrigeration units, as well as other devices installed.

Dante was playing with a control near the large window overlooking the ocean and said, "Hey, guys, watch this!" As he adjusted the control, the window went from clear and transparent to completely opaque, in fact, black. He then changed it to a smoky partially opaque. They all were impressed.

Mr. D. apologized. "I always seem to forget the window-control unit."

Leaving Dante behind to get acquainted with his unit, the group continued with Mr. D. until all were into their assigned quarters. They all considered these quarters to be temporary and, in that sense, found them to be entirely satisfactory.

On the way up in the elevator, the crew had agreed to meet in the lobby of the building at six PM, find their pumas, and proceed to the hangar where the

Revelation was parked. Susan was the first to arrive in the lobby. Maria then arrived, followed by David and Ellen, and last came Dante, directly behind Jake. It seemed that Dante and Jake had found a pool table in the eighth-floor rec room and lost track of the time. They apologized for arriving late, and Jake announced, "Dante owes me three credits, whatever *they* are worth!"

Mr. Daugherty, on seeing that everyone had arrived, stepped out of his office and said, "OK, ladies and gentlemen, if you will follow me, I will take you to your pumas."

The group took the elevator to the basement garage where they were introduced to each of their PMUs. All the vehicles were exactly alike, parked side by side. Each parking slot had a name inserted in a spot in front of the pumas, and the names of the *Revelation* crew members had each been placed on their designated slots.

Maria said, "Why are they all the same ugly color? I prefer a red one!"

"We can take care of that," said Mr. D. He touched the driver's door, and it swung up and out DeLorean-like. He sat in the driver's seat and accessed a keypad. He turned to Maria and said, "What shade of red do you want?"

Maria said, "How about scarlet? I like that!"

Mr. D. punched in some numbers. The PMU slowly changed color to a beautiful scarlet red.

Everyone's jaw dropped. Jake said, "Whoa! How the hell?"

Mr. D. smiled and said, "The material used in manufacturing not only vehicles but many other products allows color selection after the item has been completed. The skin of this puma is made of what is basically a *transparent aluminum polymer*. The factory just assigns a gray shade and lets the customer pick the exact color they want. Much of this building is made of a similar material. The windows of your quarters are made of almost the same material as these vehicles.

"As you can see, if you want another shade of red or some other color, we can do that too." He made the red a little deeper. This puma is assigned to you, Miss Rodriguez, but it is registered in the name of GSA with the State. We *must* however *report* to the DMV your name, the plate number, the VIN, and the color of the PMU you are driving. Later, if you purchase your own PMU, perhaps a more stylish and powerful unit, you are required to select and install your color choice within two days and register that color when you register the vehicle in your name. The color you select becomes locked in."

Mr. Daugherty continued, "Why don't we just check you all out on Miss Rodriguez's unit? Then we can worry about changing the other colors." He touched the keypad again, putting in a code. Then he grasped the steering wheel, and a low-pitched hum became audible. The PMU rose slowly to about eight inches off the pavement as the wheels retracted. Jake pushed down on the front of the puma, and it was rock solid. He jumped and sat down on what should be the hood, and again, the vehicle did not budge.

Mr. D. got out and offered the driver's seat to Maria. Maria said, "Could I ask you something before I get in?"

"Certainly," said Mr. D.

"Do these things just hover over the ground, or do they fly higher also?"

Mr. D. said, "These six are basic models and can only fly as high as flight level A1, no more than two thousand feet AGL. They are limited to 300 mph. You can purchase any of several models including expensive ones that not only fly, but travel at higher flight levels and much higher speeds. Traffic rules govern how fast drivers can go, and speed limits are generally a function of the altitude you are operating at. There are traffic zones and corridors up to five-thousand-feet altitude for personal PMUs and public transportation. Airspace above five thousand feet is reserved for aircraft and spacecraft."

"Wow!" said Jake. "This place sure beats old Earth!"

"Let's get everyone checked out," suggested Dante. "We need to get to the ship." He looked into Maria's puma and saw four seats. The vehicle had a small trunk. "Any chance you have a van we could borrow?" he asked, directing his question to Mr. D. "That way, we can just get one of us checked out now on the puma, preferably me, then all together take the van to the ship to get our things." He continued, "Then after we return, I can check everyone out on these PMUs when we have more time."

Jake pitched in and said, "Yeah, let's do that. It'll save you time, Mr. D., and us too."

The rest agreed, but David said, "Can you just answer one question for me before you begin Dante's checkout?"

"Sure," said Daugherty. "Proceed."

"What powers these machines, and how can they hover?"

Everyone, including Mr. D., smiled. He said, "That's two questions. The power is nuclear fusion. The drive is electrical. The antigravity feature was developed centuries ago. It's a derivative of the HD engines, like those in your ship. The fusion power enables smaller practical applications of the antigravity generators. I'm certain that the indoctrination program will bring you up to speed on all the technological and other changes that have occurred to Earth since you lived here."

Mr. Daugherty checked Dante out on PMU operation. Then he left and shortly returned with a van. He said to Dante, "This operates just like the little one. Bring it back to this same location when you are finished with it."

"Roger," said Dante. "And thanks!"

"No problem," said Mr. D. "You'll be seeing a lot of me."

The crew piled in, and Dante gently spun the van on its axis and headed out the garage door.

Mr. Daugherty entered the garage office, sat down, and shut off his own android power unit. His head nodded. A Unit at Rest light glowed in amber.

The *Revelation* had been towed and parked in a large hangar and remained locked as Dante had left it. No one could get access to the ship without the code that only the crew members knew. Some decisions were needed as to what should be done with all the stores, equipment, medical, and other provisions and weaponry that was stored in the ship. Right now, the crew members only needed their personal items and clothing.

The ship also contained enough frozen food to last the crew a year. The plan had been to use just enough of the ship's power to supply the refrigeration units. Before they exited the *Revelation*, David had left the ship on battery power for this purpose. Now either external power should be supplied to the ship, or the stored foods must be removed.

The *Revelation* looked the same as when they left it. A portable stair had been placed next to the forward cargo compartment door where the bags and containers of personal items were stowed. Susan punched in the code, and the access door displayed a green light. David opened the door. Everything was just the way it had been packed—back in 2025. Each crew member had basically two large duffels and one toiletry kit.

David handed each their bags. They placed them in the waiting van.

"Anything else we need now?" asked Ellen.

"What about weapons?" posed Dante. "Everything here seems to be as it appears. I guess we don't need them."

"I think we can forget those," ventured Jake. "I'll give you ten to one, we wouldn't be allowed to keep them anyway. Something is telling me that we are going to find Earth a *lot different* than it was when we left it."

"We should treat them as courteously as they are treating us," said Ellen. "So far, they have been perfect hosts."

"Say!" said Dante. "I've got an idea. Let's remove the flight recorder and take it along. It will be a big help in trying to make sense of the navigational track we followed."

"Excellent idea," said David. "Let's move this stair back to the rear avionics bay."

They moved the stair and climbed to the door. Again, they used the code for the door and opened it. David entered and was inside for a few minutes. He stuck his head out and exclaimed, "It's *gone*! The flight recorder and flight deck voice recorder have been removed!"

The crew was stunned.

"What was that about the hospitality, Ellen?" commented Dante.

For a few moments, they were all silent. Then Susan said, "Well, I guess I'm not really surprised. We have to admit, even *we* don't believe what has happened to us."

"Questions," said Dante. "One, how did they break our access code? Two, why didn't they just ask us for the recorders? We would have been eager to share the data with them. And three, how do we handle this with them?"

"They certainly have all the cards," said Jake. "We better play the game by their rules—at least now."

"I say go directly to Director Stoll with it," said Maria. "There is a chance that the ground handling personnel have standing instructions to remove the flight data and voice recorder from any ship returning from space."

"Good point," said Jake. "Why don't we leave it alone for tonight? Our readout equipment is deep in storage somewhere anyway. It will be easier to use theirs, assuming theirs *can* read such old technology."

"The part that galls me is how they broke our code so easily and gained access," complained Dante. "Is everything we need from the ship loaded in the PMU van?"

"Yep, we are ready to roll," said Susan. "Let's dump this stuff in our units and go down and play with the new pumas. Maybe we can go to the Coach and Six for dinner!"

Everyone got a laugh out of that.

15

After Dante checked everyone out on their PMUs, they were all famished. The breakfast they had in the *Revelation* had long since been absorbed, leaving empty stomachs.

"Let's ask Mr. D. if there's a good restaurant nearby," said Jake.

"I think he is sleeping," said Maria.

David said, "He's not sleeping. He's just reading."

"Hey, Mr. Daugherty," said Dante, "where's a good restaurant?"

Mr. D. recognized the calling of his name and reactivated all his circuits. He said, "Ah yes, a restaurant. There is a good one just outside the base called the Coach and Six. I hear they have excellent steak and seafood."

Needless to say, the group could not believe their ears. The Coach and Six! *After 1300 years?* They were sure that Mr. D. was pulling their legs.

Jake tried again. "What is the name of the restaurant?"

By this time, Mr. D. was out of his office at their side. "The *Coach and Six* is its name, and everyone says it's very good."

"What about you?" said Maria. "Do you like it?"

"Well, I have never tried it. In fact, I don't eat at—" He was going to say "eat at all" but was interrupted.

"Too expensive, huh?" said Jake. "How many credits is a good dinner there?"

"I hear that five credits will buy the best in the house, sir," advised Mr. D.

They all piled in two of the pumas and headed for the Coach and Six. It turned out to be a totally new extremely modern structure, nothing but the name and the steaks were like the old Coach and Six. The crew was amazed that the name had endured.

They enjoyed delicious meals and a quiet but short evening. Their stomachs were still not quite up to par. All six returned to their units and collapsed. It had been a very long day.

The sun was up by six AM, and so was each of the crew. Wonderfully, their refrigerators had been well stocked—they assumed by Mr. D. He was the only person they had seen around. David and Ellen fixed some cereal with fruit, showered, and donned clean *Revelation* flight suits.

Dante and Jake dressed, met in the hall, and went to the main level of the building, looking for breakfast where they had seen a small cafeteria. They found it, and it was totally automated. They just verbalized what they wanted, and it appeared in a delivery bin. The cost was 0.50 credits for each item, which they paid for with their right forefingers. A voice said to Dante, "Your balance is now 2,993 credits." He had used six and a half credits the night before. Jake's balance was 2,993.25 credits. He hadn't had as much wine as Dante at the Coach.

Maria and Susan had fixed some eggs in Susan's unit and found cooking to be quite amazing. Food preparation required only that you put the ingredients into a special Instant Chef unit and verbally tell it how you wanted the meal prepared. In seconds, the meal was ready. The ladies couldn't figure out what happened to the eggshells. They placed the dishes into the compartment labeled CleanzAll and went to the lobby.

The morning debriefing and indoctrination was scheduled to begin at 8:00 AM.

David and Ellen took one of their pumas, Dante and Jake pulled out in Jake's, and Susan gave Maria a lift. Susan backed out and bumped directly into Dante's puma! All got out to inspect the damage, and there was none. Not even a scratch!

"Women drivers," chided Jake as all got back in their vehicles.

Susan ignored the comment and, flooring it, *dug off.*

"Wow!" exclaimed Maria. "These little *diablos* are *hot!*"

The group all found parking spots at the headquarters building. They were early and decided to mosey about the building to kill time. Someone said that there was also a cafeteria in the building at the basement level. They decided to go there for coffee.

Again, the cafeteria was automated with no sign of attendants. They filed in line for coffee and tea and paid credits at the end of the line. Jake decided to test the system and *not pay for his coffee.* He sat down with the others, and they all waited to see what would happen.

After about two minutes, a voice came over a speaker and said, "Mr. Loneghan, you forgot to pay." Everybody laughed, including Jake. He decided to just sit tight. In about three minutes, the voice came on again and said, "Mr. Loneghan, this is your final notice. You have not paid."

Jake continued to sit tight. They all were laughing at Jake now, not thinking that he would get in any serious trouble for a debt of 0.2 credits. Momentarily, someone appeared coming toward their table. It was Mr. D. Ellen said, "Good morning, Mr. D. Would you have some coffee with us?"

The android said, "I am not Mr. D. I am Mr. Beauchamp, or Mr. B. if you prefer. I do not drink coffee." The android faced Jake and said, "Sir, please come with me."

Jake looked up and said, "But *you are* Mr. D.! And I am having my coffee just now. Either join us or leave us, please."

Mr. B. placed his hand on Jake's shoulder and applied pressure. A very sharp pain went through Jake's shoulder and his entire arm.

"Ow!" yelled Jake. He tried to get up but could not move. It was as if a huge machine had clamped down on his arm. "Ow!" he moaned again.

Mr. B. said very calmly, "You did not pay for your item. You are required to pay for your item. You will now go to the payment point and *pay for your purchase.*" Mr. B. released Jake's arm. Jake rubbed his shoulder and looked at the others. "Guess I better pay for the coffee," he said and got up to go pay. He went to the payment unit and put his index finger at the proper spot. The machine hummed, and the screen presented a notice. "Payment of 0.2 credits for coffee from Jake Loneghan received. Also assessed is penalty payment of five credits. Your balance is now 2,988.05 credits."

Jake said, "What? A penalty of *five* credits! That is *absurd*. I just forgot to pay!"

Mr. B. was behind Jake and said, "Sir, you did *not* forget to pay. You were reminded twice, and you *refused to pay*. That negligence is not allowed. Your penalty is just. You may appeal this penalty under Penal Code Section 436p. I am required to advise you that your penalty can be increased if you fail to convince the hearing panel."

Jake was furious! First, at Mr. B. as he called himself, and then at the system that docked him five credits for not paying. For a fleeting moment, he considered to take care of Mr. B. but decided against it.

Jake returned to the table. "Did you guys see all of that? They fined me five credits for not paying for the damned coffee! What kind of deal is this?"

The others were stunned, and they all started chatting about it.

Jake said, "I was ready to deck the SOB but decided not to."

"Why didn't you?" said Dante. "I probably would have."

"Three reasons," said Jake. "One, I was in the wrong. Two, we are guests at this facility. And three, I have never felt strength like that from any human being. He was crushing my shoulder! It still hurts like hell."

"Move it around," said Ellen. "See if that increases the pain."

Jake moved the arm all about and reported that there were no additional sharp pains.

Ellen said, "Then it's probably not broken."

"We need to find out the playing rules around here," said Maria. "I think you did the smart thing, Jake—*nothing*!"

Another patron had observed the entire incident and came over to the table where the *Revelation* crew was seated. He said, "Please allow me to introduce myself. I am Mikhal Hadid, a GSA scientist. I just observed your little problem with Mr. B. and the payment." He pulled up a chair and sat down. "I believe you are the crew from the *Revelation* that landed just yesterday. Am I correct?"

They all nodded, and Dante said, "You are correct. I am Dante Washington, mission commander of the *Revelation*, and these are the crew members." Dante introduced them around.

Mikhal said, "I understand that you are to be debriefed and indoctrinated this morning and that you presently are not familiar with the ways of thirty-fourth-century Earth."

Jake said, "Well, Mr. Hadid, things were going well—in fact, quite well until I didn't pay immediately for a cup of coffee a few minutes ago."

"I saw that," said Mikhal. "You were treated rather harshly, but after your indoctrination has been completed, you will have a much better understanding of what our society is like and why our actions sometimes are harsh. As a matter of fact, I am on the program this morning for your session. I have many things to share with you."

No one could think of anything to say, least of all, Jake.

Susan looked at her watch and said, "It's ten 'til. We'd better go to the conference room."

"I am headed there too," said Mikhal. "I would be honored to walk with you."

Mr. B. was still standing over to the side as if to make sure that Jake caused no more trouble. The group of seven left the cafeteria and headed for the elevators.

The *Revelation* crew all had similar thoughts. *The ship was broken into, and now Jake is roughed up over a cup of coffee. And Mr. D. looks exactly like Mr. B. I hope we can get good explanations for all of this.*

They arrived at the tenth-floor conference room, the place where just yesterday, they had met many GSA staffers and their holograms. It was also the place where the reception was held in their honor.

This morning, the room was set up differently. It didn't even look like the same room. There was a dais at one end of the room with several chairs along the rear and a speaker's lectern. The same large screen was on the wall behind the dais. There were six chairs at floor level in front and facing the raised platform, and the rest of the room was set up like a classroom with rows of chairs and an aisle down the center of the room.

Four people were seated on the dais, including Dir. Klaus Stoll. Dr. Hadid joined the seated four and took a chair.

The *Revelation* crew members suspected that the six chairs on the front row were reserved for them but were not sure. They stood off to the side awaiting instructions. A few other seats were occupied throughout the conference room. Susan heard steps to her left and turned to see Mr. D.—or was it Mr. B.?—coming toward the crew members. The android said, "Good morning. I am Mr. Kapsten, or Mr. K. Please take your seats on the front row."

Jake looked askance at yet another person that *looked exactly like* Mr. D. and Mr. B. The group, as sheep, complied and sat in the front row. By now, it was exactly 8:00 AM.

Mr. K. had retreated to the rear of the room and stood by the door.

Klaus Stoll rose and walked to the lectern. "Good morning, everyone," he said. "And a special good morning to the crew from the *Revelation*."

Everyone in the room, almost as one, responded, "Good morning to you, sir."

The crew followed suit and said, "Good morning," but not in unison.

Klaus spoke, "I trust the *Revelation* team had a good dinner and a good rest last night. This was your first time in regular beds for over 1300 years!" He was obviously trying to lighten the mood. The director was well aware of the crew's concerns about the ship's recorders and the incident with Mr. B.

He continued, "This morning, our program will consist of two parts. Firstly, we would like to debrief you. That is, we would like for you to tell us about your mission on the *Revelation*, which ultimately brought you back to us—where you started from centuries ago. Secondly, we will attempt today, and for the next two weeks, to indoctrinate you regarding the differences between our society on Earth today and the society you left in the twenty-first century. Believe me when I tell you that *there are very few similarities between the two.*

"I should tell you that we have, in the thirty-fourth century, the capability to *brainwash* you—I believe that is a term you are familiar with. We could brainwash you so that in one session your individual brains will be imparted with the entire scope of knowledge you need to understand thirty-fourth-century Earth. We prefer however that you acquire this knowledge naturally. With the brainwashing approach, your mind is made to accept our society and its rules, and you *lose all knowledge* of your past life on Earth. If we *teach* you, as students and as individuals, you will retain your knowledge of the twenty-first century and of your past, and you will hopefully come to understand the *reasons* why Earth's society has been changed to what it is today."

The director continued, "You pose a unique and special problem for us. All other people who today live on this planet were born into either the thirty-third or thirty-fourth centuries. There have been few significant changes to our civilization since the twenty-fifth century."

Klaus noticed expressions of surprise on the faces in the front row. He continued, "So you six individuals are indeed quite unique. I don't know your individual reasons for volunteering to join a 1300-year journey from which you never expected to return to Earth, but that *is what you did*. I'm sure you must all have had good reasons.

"You expected to be arriving at a planet you named Nyvar, located 1300 light-years from Earth. You had no idea what that planet would be like, but you were prepared to take the risks. That is most admirable and courageous. We can definitely use strong people like you. But first, you must learn to live in our society as we do."

Klaus then said, "I will now yield the podium to Dr. Howard Ottinger, who will ask you to tell us more about the mission that brought you here and about the reasons why NASA in 2025 sent you. Dr. Ottinger?"

A rather stout, little bespectacled man stood and walked forward. What began as mild applause from the audience became larger as Dr. Ottinger took the lectern.

Dr. Ottinger spoke, "Good morning to all. Since you know who I am, I will get on with it." He looked at the *Revelation* team. "I understand that you have already bumped into a couple of concerns. Before we begin debriefing you, we can address those concerns if you like."

Jake raised his hand, and Dr. Ottinger acknowledged him. "Yes, Mr. Loneghan?"

"I was manhandled by a Mr. B. this morning in your cafeteria. What is the story on that, and who are these Messrs. D., B., and now K. who all look amazingly alike?"

"Good question, Mr. Loneghan. We would have covered that in our program, but since it is occupying your mind, it's best we address it now." He glanced at Director Stoll, who nodded concurrence.

Dr. Ottinger continued, "Mr. Daugherty, Mr. Beauchamp, and Mr. Kapsten are *androids*."

The six in the front row were amazed! Ottinger went on, "These units are programmed to do many routine, menial, and other tasks, many of which require round-the-clock presence at their jobs. One task they all perform is to ensure that laws, ordinances, and general rules of our society are not broken. For example, Mr. Beauchamp, who spoke with you this morning in the cafeteria, Mr. Loneghan, is charged with the management and supervision of the cafeteria. His job includes all functions related to the cafeteria from filling up the coffee urns to ensuring that patrons of the cafeteria pay for their food."

Jake and the rest of the crew were in awe. *Androids?* they thought. *No wonder Mr. B. was so strong.* The crew was astonished at how *human* the droids appeared to be.

Dr. Ottinger continued, "If the director has no objection, I would like to put on a little demonstration." He glanced at Klaus who again nodded consent. Dr. Ottinger looked to the back of the room and said, "Mr. K., would you please step up here for a moment?"

"Certainly, sir," said Mr. K. as he made his way to the front of the room and onto the dais.

Dr. Ottinger was now facing Mr. K. He said to Mr. K., "This is just a demonstration. Do not be concerned."

Mr. K. responded, "I understand, sir."

Ottinger reached into the back of the lectern and withdrew a *baseball bat*. He then took his best swing right at the head of Mr. K.! The impact jarred off Dr. Ottinger's glasses but had absolutely no effect on Mr. K. There was no damage to the android, and he did not budge at the impact of the bat. Dr. Ottinger then handed the bat to Mr. K. and said, "Break the bat."

Mr. K. held the bat in both hands out in front of him and snapped it like a matchstick! The audience applauded.

The *Revelation* crew could *not believe* what they had just seen.

After a moment, Dr. Ottinger said, "Any further questions regarding our androids?"

Dante raised his hand and said, "Yes, I have one. Other than the internal programs of these androids, what commands will they obey, from whom, and under what circumstances?"

"Excellent question, Colonel Washington. They will obey any human command any time so long as the command does *not involve breaking the law* or the command given them is not in conflict with their built-in program."

"Will they kill a human being?" asked Jake.

"No, they will not," responded Dr. Ottinger.

Jake continued, "Well, this Mr. B. nearly broke my arm this morning over a trivial matter of 0.2 credits! What if I had physically attacked Mr. B.?"

"Again, a good question Mr. Loneghan. Mr. B. would have restrained you and communicated with law enforcement personnel. He would have only used enough force as was required to restrain you until authorities arrived. I might add that these Mister Series Androids are quite powerful as you have seen and are practically invulnerable to any weapons that might be in the hands of criminals. You will find that we have an extremely low tolerance for any type of crime in the thirty-fourth century."

Director Stoll interrupted with, "I think that's enough on androids for the time being. See if they have other questions we can address before going on."

"Right, sir," said Dr. Ottinger. Seeing Dante's hand, he said, "Colonel, you have a question?"

Dante stood and said, "Yes. Your ground personnel broke into our ship sometime yesterday and took the flight recorder and voice recorder. Why did that occur, and where are the units now?"

"First, let's examine *whose* ship the *Revelation* is," said Dr. Ottinger. "You refer to it as 'our ship.' That ship was financed by the U.S. government, designed and constructed under contract to NASA, and launched by NASA. How is it 'your' ship?"

Dante nor any of the crew had thought about it that way. When they left the Earth with the *Revelation*, they considered it to be "their ship." After all, they were never coming back to Earth.

"Before you strain your brain on that question, Colonel, let me continue. The Global Space Agency is the successor to the National Aeronautics and Space Administration. Since you have brought the *Revelation* back to Earth, it belongs to the GSA. Wouldn't you agree with that?"

You could have pushed Dante over with a feather! *Of course, the man was right!* thought Dante, and the rest of the crew seemed to agree.

Dante said, "Doctor, you are absolutely right. We have been thinking we would be landing on a new world and, in that sense, considered the *Revelation* to be our ship. Of course the ship belongs to the GSA!" Dante continued, "But how did your people bypass the security code on the ship?"

"That was easy. All the records related to the ship and its launch are on discs in our archives. We just consulted those and found the codes. The only thing we don't know about the *Revelation* is where you people have *been with it* for the last 1300 years."

Everyone in the room laughed, including the crew—though not as heartily as the others.

Dr. Ottinger continued, "The recorders are now being analyzed in the lab. You are welcome to join in that analysis when this session is over."

Looking at Director Stoll, Dr. Ottinger said, "Is this a good time for a break, or should I go on?"

"Let's keep going," said Klaus. "I'm really starting to have *fun*." That brought a laugh from the audience.

"Fine," said the doctor. "Assuming there are no more questions at this time from the crew, we will begin asking *you* some questions. Colonel Washington, would you take the lectern, please." As Dante stood, Dr. Ottinger said, "OR you could stay at your seat. That might be easier since we will be asking all of you questions as we go. Please stand when you answer each question."

Howard Ottinger remained at the podium and said, "I'll ask the burning question in everyone's mind first, the one that I alluded to a moment ago: Colonel, where have you been with *our ship* for the last 1300 years?"

Everyone, including the crew, laughed again.

Dante cleared his throat and said, "It appears that ever since we left Earth, we have been on our way back to Earth. As you know by now, once we were ready to jump to light-speed, we all entered our capsules to take naps." This was intended to get a chuckle but didn't. The staff seated on the dais and the audience were now *serious*. They had had fun with some humor, but they now wanted serious answers from the crew.

Dante sensed the change in mood and continued, "We placed ourselves in hibernation and stayed there until we were within hours from this planet. During our suspended animation, the ship's computer, preprogrammed in our NASA labs, directed the path of the ship. The ship's master computer initiated the RJLS and brought the ship's speed down to one hundred thousand miles per hour. When we were roused from our sleep and manned the flight deck, the *Revelation* appeared to be on course as planned. As we got close enough to initiate contact with this planet, not having any idea what frequencies to try, we simply used, for starters, the primary launch frequency in use at Kennedy in 2025. We got the shock of our lives when your chief of Mission Control answered in *English*."

The people on the dais and the audience were silent. Dante sat down. He didn't know what else to say.

The director stood and said, "I've got a question that I would like for any one of you to answer. Why did NASA undertake this mission, knowing full well that they would *never know* the outcome? What possible benefit would the mission be to the people of Earth?"

David stood and said, "Sir, I would like to answer that. Almost that exact question was asked of the director of NASA in 2025 by a young graduate of MIT, the Massachusetts Institute of Technology. I will give you the answer that Director Benjamin Javitz gave the top-level NASA staffers and the younger staff members at that time.

"His answer was 'Because we MUST. It is man's nature to go beyond what he knows. What else is out there? He must find out! If Christopher Columbus had not looked for and found the new world, *where would we be now*? Still in Europe, wondering how far away the edge of the Earth was. The only thing different about the *Revelation* mission is that we—you and I and indeed no one alive today—will *ever know what our explorers find*. But our astronauts will know! The six brave, adventurous souls that volunteer their very lives and souls to this mission will, hopefully, in only about a year's time of their lives have traveled almost eight thousand trillion miles through space and arrived at a new world—at least new to them. They will have moved through not only space *but through time*. The physical conditions or civilization they find on Nyvar will not be the one that is there now. It will be the civilization on that planet *1300 years from now*!'"

David continued from his memorization of Director Javitz's words. "'If they find no civilization, they will begin one. We are confident that there *will be* some forms of life there—there *has to be*. Hopefully, our crew will be wise enough to develop a civilization on their new home, avoiding the problems we have created on this Earth—problems that essentially began when Cain killed Abel.

"'If there is intelligent life on Nyvar, let us hope that the beings on that planet embrace our pioneers as I am sure our brave adventurers will embrace them. Maybe our team will find a greatly advanced society with technologies far more sophisticated than ours now on Earth. Maybe this advanced society will have *solved* all the social and degenerative problems we have that are beginning to destroy our Earth and its people. And just *maybe* the society on Nyvar will be far enough advanced to have developed spacecraft that can even *exceed* the speed of light. Perhaps our team will even find that they can communicate back with thirty-fourth-century Earth.

"'But if we don't send our brave astronauts to explore this new world, *we will never know what might have been*, will we?'"

David was drained. It had been over a year since he read those words so many times and even memorized them. He added, "I may not have remembered exactly what Director Javitz's words were, but I think I am pretty close. *His words* are why *I* came on this journey."

First, there was complete silence. Then the room erupted with not only applause but with shouts of "Hear, hear!" The response went on for several minutes.

Finally, Director Stoll walked to the podium and said to Dr. Ottinger, "I'll take it now."

Director Stoll then raised his arms, symbolically asking for quiet. He said, "We now know why you brave earthlings came to visit us." The cheers and applause resumed.

Klaus raised his arms again. "Unless any of you six want to add to what David Marks has so eloquently delivered, I suggest we break for coffee and tea. And there are some scones in the back also."

No one spoke, and Director Stoll said, "Let's take ten. Please be back by nine."

People rushed out of the room, and others were madly making calls on their mecs. By nine AM, the room was *filled* with people. Everyone wanted to hear the upcoming indoctrination segment to be led by Dr. Mikhal Hadid. The crew had all gone back for tea and coffee and had been mobbed by members of the audience. They particularly focused on David. Somehow it had leaked out that he was one of the principal designers of the *Revelation*, if not *the* designer. All the crew members had their hands full with questions by those crowding around. Some were asking Jake about his encounter with Mr. B.

History is one thing, but how often can you *speak* to people of the distant past? People that *lived 1300 years ago*.

Finally, Klaus Stoll again took the lectern and asked for all to be seated. He advised those who did not have seats to stand in the rear of the room. When all was finally still, people were standing two-deep around the walls. Klaus directed Mr. K. to close the doors and not let anyone else in.

Director Stoll spoke, "The debriefing went faster than normal primarily because the crew was in hibernation during the vast majority of the mission and, therefore, were not in position to question the heading of the ship nor to make any on-course corrections. Any further analysis of the path taken by the *Revelation* that returned it to Earth will have to be made through examination of the flight data recorder, the ship's computer, *and the pictures and videos from onboard cameras* that were focused on all views of space. These cameras were *operating during the entire journey*."

The crowd gasped. No one had known of the cameras until this moment!

Klaus continued, "We did not know of the cameras until someone examining the records found a single mention of them in data deep into the records discs. About fifteen minutes ago, the photographic and video films and tapes were retrieved from the ship and are now being analyzed in the lab."

Dante and the crew, even David, *had not remembered the cameras*. They had, during training and prior to launch, considered the cameras to be nonessential equipment producing not necessary, but "nice to have" information. Now in view of the unplanned path taken by the ship, the information recorded by the cameras might just be the most valuable data GSA now had to help them in their analysis of the *Revelation*'s journey.

"After this next portion of our session, I would like the crew of the *Revelation* to join me in the lab," said Klaus. "I think we may have answers to our puzzle."

Several people left the room, including Dr. Ottinger. He was headed straight for the lab and the camera images.

"Now," said the director, "I would like to introduce Dr. Mikhal Hadid, who will lead our indoctrination presentation. Dr. Hadid, the podium is yours."

"Good morning to you all," said Dr. Hadid. A hearty round of applause greeted him. "I have the 'impossible' task of summarizing for our six new citizens of Earth what has changed about our planet in the last 1300 or so years."

This brought a genuine laugh from the audience and a mild applause. Dr. Hadid continued, "Who would like to guess how many changes there have been in such a span of time?" A moan rippled through the room. "Just kidding, of course. I don't know the answer to that one myself." Another laugh. "Let us just say thousands. Or maybe it is hundreds of thousands. But what if I ask you, how many *truly significant changes* have been made the last 1300 years?" He paused for effect. "Now there is an answerable question! Would anyone like to hazard a guess?"

Several hands went up. Dr. Hadid said, "Ah, we have some brave souls in our own midst." That got a hearty laugh! "It's always easy to laugh when you are not the risk taker. OK, let's hear some attempts at the answer." He pointed to one woman seated just behind the *Revelation* crew.

"Two hundred and thirty-six," she said cautiously.

"I said truly significant," said Dr. Hadid. "I will give you a hint. The answer is less than one hundred."

Only one other hand now remained held high—a young man standing on the back wall. "Eighty-five!" said the gentleman.

"That is a better guess, but again, way too high. The answer is *twelve*. Only *twelve* truly significant changes have morphed the civilization of 2025 to the civilization of 3339!"

He paused to let all consider what he had just said.

"Twelve changes have been the driving force behind the transition from the twenty-first century to the thirty-fourth century. And most of the discoveries and changes in governmental policies that make up these twelve *occurred before the twenty-fifth century*."

Again, Dr. Hadid paused to let the audience completely absorb his last statement.

He continued, "Yes, we have made many thousands of new discoveries and invented thousands of new products to make our lives better since the twenty-fifth century. But the twelve things that have resulted in the new world we enjoy today happened centuries before any, except six, in this room were born. If I challenge each of you in this room to come up with the twelve items I am referring to, I would wager that none of you, except the *Revelation* crew, would have the faintest chance to get even *one* of them right."

Dr. Hadid looked directly at Dante, Jake, Susan, Ellen, David, and Maria, gazing into their eyes one at a time.

"You six are the only ones in the room that have lived in the twenty-first century. You know *firsthand* the major worldwide problems that existed in those years. Now I may have been wrong about some of the rest of you if you have taken the time to study the history of the twentieth through the twenty-fourth centuries. And to anyone in the room that has done that, please see me in my office after this meeting. I probably can arrange a nice promotion for you."

Again, a hearty laugh and a murmur throughout the room.

Dr. Hadid focused on the six in the front row. "Now which of you would like to tell me and our audience about the *major world problems* of the twenty-first century?"

At first, no one seemed to be eager to volunteer. They looked at one another.

"I will take a shot at it!" said Maria bravely.

Everyone focused his or her attention on Maria. Even her crewmates admired her courage. You could have heard a pin drop on the carpet.

"Please proceed," said Dr. Hadid.

16

Dr. Hadid addressed Maria, "Would you like to come up to the podium and address everyone, Miss Rodriguez? I'm sure they could hear you better and would appreciate that."

Maria stood. She stepped onto the dais and behind the lectern. Even wearing her flight suit, she still looked like Miss America 2013. She cleared her throat and said, "I will give you my summary of what I considered the major problems of the twenty-first century. These will not be in priority order. They were *all* very serious in 2025, the year we left Earth. Before I begin, let me plead for help from my five very able associates. If I stumble and leave anything out or if you want to add anything, please jump in and help me."

She continued, "To you of the thirty-fourth century, let me say that I sincerely hope that you have solved these problems I am about to list."

She began to speak, "Humankind's propensity for conflict with one another—between sects, between countries, and, indeed, on a global scale—was a devastating problem in the twenty-first century. Terrorism had become almost commonplace in many countries of the world especially in the United States and in Britain.

"World conflicts had increased in number and in intensity such that the safety of the entire planet was in jeopardy! When we left Earth in 2025, eight nations had nuclear weapons and the means to deliver them.

"Somehow you must have solved the problem of wars and conflicts—Earth is still here!"

Hearing no comments, she continued, "Next, I would list excessive personal wealth, contrasted with dire poverty and social disparities between citizens as a serious worldwide problem. A major driver of crime in the twenty-first century came from the children of poverty. Having inadequate housing, not enough food, and a lack of family structure helped drive the children into crime and into drug use and trafficking. While the wealthy enjoyed wonderful lives, clearly separated from the middle classes and the poor, those in the lower social structures struggled to earn enough to survive. What was still referred to as the 'middle class' of citizens in the United States was gradually morphing into the 'poor class.' Earnings failed to keep pace with rising costs of housing, food, clothing, energy, medical care, prescription drugs, and insurance. Every member of the 'average' household in America had to work to provide for the needs of the family.

"Next, I would list crime—especially capital crime—as a major problem for society as a whole in the twenty-first century. The punishment and prison system was a 'revolving door' for career criminals who continued to inflict pain and death on others all of their lives. The prison system did not rehabilitate. It only served as a training ground to make criminals harder and more expert at plying their trade. A very pervasive problem was that the rich often bought their freedom from punishment by using expensive clever attorneys. While the poor, with inept representation, were punished. The system of trial by either judge or jury was lengthy and expensive. Justice was slow, ineffective, and very expensive. There were cases where horribly evil serial killers were allowed to live and languish in soft prisons for years at taxpayers' expense. I hope you will tell me that this system has been totally changed."

Maria turned to Dr. Hadid. "Am I going too far? Is this what you wanted?"

Dr. Hadid said, "Please continue, Maria, you are doing very well!"

She continued, "Medical costs—including doctors fees, hospital charges, diagnostic procedures, and prescription drug costs—were totally out of control in the twenty-first century. The doctors and hospitals tried to blame high costs on malpractice suits, which resulted in high insurance premiums, on the need for expensive research, on the requirement to provide free medical care to anyone who walked in with no money, and on a host of other contestable excuses. The truth was that the doctors, clinics, hospitals, drug companies, lawyers, and providers of medical supplies and equipment were growing very rich off Medicare payments, payments from individuals who could afford to pay, and from insurance payments. The insurance companies simply raised premiums to cover their costs, and the government recovered the Medicare costs through taxation.

"Businesses paid less and less for workers' insurance coverage and simply reduced the compensation they would have otherwise paid to their employees to cover insurance premium costs. The bottom line, therefore, was that the citizens—the public—one way or another were really shouldering all the exorbitant costs of anything related to medical services and prescription drugs.

"The underlying problem that there was *no control* over physicians' fees or medical facility charges. For example, in 2025, a heart bypass operation could cost between $500,000 and $750,000! A hip replacement was billed at between $50,000 and $100,000. Just the cost of staying a night in a hospital was from $3,000 to $5,000. The daily cost of being in intensive care was $25,000 to $50,000 a day! A five-minute visit to your family physician was billed at $225 to $375. Specialists charged many times those fees. Medical costs represented a major portion of the average family's cost of living whether or not anyone in the family was sick.

"Another subject: Environmental deterioration has to be high on the list. The level of pollution of the atmosphere, the land, and the waters of this planet was rising alarmingly fast. The burning of fossil fuels and the dumping of manufacturing wastes into the air, into dumpsites, and into the waters was driving this horrible problem. The government did little to curb or control this. The rich manufacturers had effective lobbyists. They also donated heavily to the political campaigns of elected officials.

"Destruction of the ozone layer was resulting in serious global warming and melting of the glaciers and polar ice caps. The waters of the world were rising, threatening coastal cities all over the planet."

Maria again stopped and addressed Dr. Hadid, "Should I continue?"

"Have you completed your list?" said Hadid.

"No, I have just a few more."

"You are doing wonderfully, my dear. I see in our audience many intently interested faces and somewhat incredulous expressions. Please continue."

The *Revelation* crew members were looking at Maria with surprise and admiration. They had no idea she could express herself so well and to the point.

"Thank you," said Maria as she continued. "The use of drugs and alcohol has to be on the list. Drug use was illegal, and that drove the illicit drug trade. This, of course, led to more serious crimes between drug lords, between gangs on the street, and, in fact, between nations. For example, at one time, 90 percent of the economy of Afghanistan was based on drug trade. Several South American countries considered drugs their primary export. Government officials of those countries did nothing to stop the trade—they grew wealthy by allowing it. Addiction was a rapidly growing cancer that was eating the heart out of many countries. The high cost of illegal drugs was, as I mentioned before, driving much of the crime in many countries.

"Alcohol use was not as big a problem in the world in that it was legal and socially acceptable. It was the abusers that created the problems from alcohol. Use of it contributed to many other crimes, traffic accidents, and deaths."

Mr. K. had just approached Maria with a glass of water. "Oh, thank you, Mr. K.! You read my mind." She turned and looked at Dr. Hadid. "I just have two more. Should I continue?"

Mikhal Hadid addressed the audience, "Should she continue?"

The loud response was almost unanimous. They *had never heard of such problems* and such a sorry situation for a society. "*Continue!*" they said almost in unison. Maria beamed. She was very proud of herself. People seemed sincerely interested in what she had to say.

She continued, "Depletion of wildlife and sea life had reached a very serious stage. The causes were pollution—as we have touched on—poaching and overkilling for sport or profit and, of course, for food. Many species of animal life were very nearly extinct as a result of human disregard for the impact of their activities as I listed.

"Finally, I would list ineffective, corrupt, and extremely expensive government as a major problem of the twenty-first century. Needless to say, big government only got bigger and more costly. And the larger the government got, the more ensnarled it got, and the less effective it became. We were paying extremely large salaries and benefits to hundreds of thousands of government employees and getting very little for our money. I am *especially including* members of the three branches of government and their staffs.

"Senators, representatives, and members of the administration were much more concerned with their own personal enrichment, their own salaries, their benefits, and retirement packages than they were about the people who elected them to office. Practically, every piece of legislation passed resulted in under-the-table enrichments of our representatives in government—in all three branches."

She looked at Dr. Hadid. Maria said softly, "I think my tank is dry."

Dr. Hadid stood and said, "Thank you, Miss Rodriguez. I could not have said it better myself." The room *erupted in applause* led by the *Revelation* crew. They were all hugging Maria and shaking her hand. They had not ever heard such a summary on the problems of twenty-first-century Earth until just now. What a wonderful job Maria had done! Jake, however, recognized that he and his companies had been part of the problems that Maria described. But Jake loved the capitalist system that allowed the smartest businessmen and professionals to become the wealthiest citizens. He hoped that the society of the thirty-fourth century still allowed that to happen.

Dr. Hadid took the lectern and thanked Maria again. She took her seat with the rest of the *Revelation* crew. The doctor addressed the crowd, now buzzing in discussions with one another. "Please . . . *please*, could I have your attention."

The crowd began to silence themselves. Dr. Hadid spoke, "Did you all think that the wonderful civilization and society we now have on Earth just *happened*? Did you think that it was always like we now have it on this planet? How many of you have spent any time in studying the early centuries? Specifically the twentieth through the twenty-fifth?"

A few hands were cautiously raised. They thought he might ask them a tough question.

"I have an exercise for you. *Not for the* Revelation *crew, but for you GSA staffers.* As Miss Rodriguez spoke, her words were being transcribed and printed into handouts for you all. You will receive your copy as you exit. Mr. K. will have the transcripts for you when you exit.

"Here is what I would like you to do. As you know, thirty-fourth-century Earth is practically devoid of the twenty-first-century problems Miss Rodriguez has so eloquently briefed us on. Most were eliminated by the twenty-fifth century."

The *Revelation* crew looked at one another in bewilderment. *What did he just say?* they thought.

Dr. Hadid continued, "I would like you all to take on a challenge if you want to. I would like you to individually list *all of the actions taken by the governments and the citizens of Earth* to solve the twenty-first-century problems. In other words, those eight problems discussed by Maria didn't just go away—by *no means*. People just like you and me that lived on Earth from the twenty-first through the twenty-fourth centuries did things to solve these terrible problems that were in fact destroying Earth and its civilization. We mentioned earlier the twelve major changes in our society that morphed the twenty-first century into the twenty-fifth century. Those twelve are key to your response to this challenge. There are of course other things that contributed to the creation of our society today—cover as many of those as you want. But there are *twelve* that made the largest impact.

"Now the assignment I have given you will require a lot of work on your part—and on *your own time*. Director Stoll has authorized me to offer you two prizes if you choose to compete for them. For the best paper that describes what the people of Earth have done to rid the Earth of those *eight* problems Maria listed, we will award fifteen thousand bonus credits. For the second best paper, we will award a prize of ten thousand bonus credits. You will have five days from today to work, on your own time, on your papers. You will *not help each other* because that makes no sense. You want the prizes offered, and you want to show that *you are the brightest* at GSA. Besides, I have asked the Mister Androids to tell me if anyone cheats. Anyone who cheats will automatically be disqualified.

"Again, your participation is voluntary. But if you do play, play by the rules."

Dr. Hadid addressed the director of the center, "Director Stoll, I believe you wanted to take it from here."

Klaus Stoll took the podium again. "Except for the *Revelation* crew and the staff members behind me on the dais, all others are dismissed. Mr. K., please open the doors." The crowd quietly filed out of the conference room.

The director addressed the crew, "We will break for lunch and then at one PM will meet in the lab to review what our staff and Dr. Ottinger have come up with. I think, between the data supplied by your ship's recorders and the ship's cameras and with the knowledge we now have concerning deep space flight, we can figure out what caused your ship to return to Earth.

"After that exercise, we will reconvene in this room where we will begin to tell you about life in the thirty-fourth century. These sessions will probably take five to seven days, depending on how fast you, as a group, learn and how many questions you have as we go.

"We will see you in room 16A of the lab located in the lower level of this building at one PM."

Jake whispered to the others, "Let's go to the Coach. We have time, and I don't want to *tangle with Mr. B. again.*" The others laughed and nodded in agreement. They headed for the parking lot and their pumas. They exited the main gate and headed for the Coach and Six. No one noticed the two men who exited the parking lot in one vehicle right behind them. They also parked at the Coach and Six.

The crew arrived a little earlier than the usual lunch crowd and was able to find a nice table for six in the corner. They ordered tea and coffee and began studying the menu. Jake made a quick decision as usual and looked up. The others were still reading. Jake noticed the two men who had come in behind them and taken a small table near them but thought nothing of it. Finally, the others looked up as the waiter brought their drink orders. He said, "Is everyone ready to order, or do you need more time?"

Jake glanced from face-to-face and said, "I think we are ready."

The ladies ordered first, then the guys ordered, and the waiter went on his way.

Susan could hold it no longer and said, "Did everyone hear what I think I heard Director Stoll say?"

"You mean that they have solved all the problems of the twenty-first century?" said Susan.

"I did," said Ellen. "But we must have *misheard* him! That *can't* be the case, can it?"

"I agree with Ellen," said Dante. "For starters, you are never going to eliminate wars and conflicts. That is born into the nature of man. And how are you going to eliminate crime?"

"I don't think he said that all our twenty-first-century problems had been completely solved, did he?" asked Maria. "Didn't he say 'almost' or 'practically solved' or something like that?"

"I don't remember his exact words," said Susan. "But the implication was that those eight problems as characterized by Maria have basically been solved."

"'And were *solved by the twenty-fifth century*' is what I heard," said Jake.

The waiter was setting up the serving stand, and Susan said, "Let's hold up until the meals are served."

The others seemed to agree, and Dante said, "Have you guys noticed how clear and fresh the outside air is? I cannot smell any whiff of salt or dead fish or any of the usual pollutants."

"Now that you mention it," said David, "I think you are right."

"And the sky is deep blue with occasional clouds. It looks more like an airbrush painting than the actual sky!" said Ellen.

The waiter was placing the last of the meals on the table and asked if there would be anything else for now. Hearing no requests, he withdrew.

"On the subject of the world's problems being solved," said Dante, "we may as well wait to hear what they *have done* and *how they did it*. It should be *verrry interesting*."

Everyone seemed to agree with Dante's proposal and started eating. The food was very good as usual. Then Jake said, "Say, what do you guys think about the robots? I sure know what *I* think!"

"Amazing!" said David. "Although I am not surprised, we were quite far along with robotics even in the twenty-first century. I would be very interested to see how they have designed their brains—they seem very humanistic."

"I can't believe their strength!" said Jake. "You should see the color of my shoulder and all down my upper arm. I think I will avoid making enemies of these 'Mister' Guys."

Maria commented, "You know they seem very helpful and very courteous normally. I guess we need to get a briefing on all the things that set them off."

"Make sure you *pay for everything*!" said Jake. That brought a laugh from the group.

The two men who had followed them were sitting and hardly talking. They had only ordered coffee and really weren't drinking that.

Now back at the base, the *Revelation* crew had found the laboratory building without difficulty and located lab no. 16A. It was exactly 1:00 PM when they entered the room.

The two agents had watched them enter the headquarters building but stayed outside. The surveillance cameras would watch the six carefully while they were inside the building.

Director Stoll and Dr. Ottinger were there, along with lab staff and a couple of others. Director Stoll introduced the crew members to everyone present and said, "Well, have we found out where the *Revelation* has been for the last 1300 years or so?"

Barbara Quinn was the senior lab associate assigned to the readout of all data and film from the ship. She said, "Well, sir, we know *where* they were during their journey—there is no question about that. But we don't yet know *why* they were *where* they were."

"OK," said Dr. Ottinger, "let's start with *where* they were."

Barbara pointed to a chart she had prepared and began, "The ship's cameras were the best source for our understanding of the path taken by the ship. The path taken by the *Revelation* was not a circle and was not an ellipse—although it was more akin to an ellipse than any other geometric shape. The ship took a clockwise ovate path, which started basically in the direction of the Orion Nebula and passed to the right of the Orion constellation. At that point, the ship was turning with Betelgeuse visible on its portside. It executed a slow turn from about the 300th year of its travel to the 350th year and took up a heading generally toward the Eagle Nebula as you can see here." Barbara pointed to a chart she had prepared. "Then it began another wide turn from about the 925th year to the 1,050th year of travel.

"Here is the turn illustrated. At about the midpoint of the turn, the Lagoon Nebula was photographed on the ship's portside. After completing this turn, the *Revelation* was now generally heading the same direction it was just after it executed the original JLS maneuver toward the Orion and Crab Nebula and now *toward* the sun. It was on its final leg to arrive *back at Earth* at about its 1300th year of travel. At no time in the journey of the *Revelation* was the ship heading on a straight path. As you can see here, its track had some degree of curvature at all times."

"Amazing," commented the director. "Thinking of the path the ship took as an ellipse, what would the length of the major and minor diameters be—roughly?"

"We haven't tried to determine the diameters, but I would estimate the major diameter of its ovate path was about five hundred light-years and the minor diameter about two hundred sixty light-years," responded Mrs. Quinn.

"And the center of the path?" asked Dr. Ottinger.

"The centroid of the path transcribed by the ship was about one hundred thirty light-years from our sun in the direction of the Pleiades constellation."

"What is at that location?" queried David.

The two doctors looked at David as if to say "Who gave you permission to ask questions?"

But Barbara said, "*Nothing*. There is nothing there of any consequence."

All were silent for what seemed like forever.

Barbara Quinn broke the silence by adding, "Little of value was available from the voice recorder, but the flight recorder path record agreed exactly with the path we constructed from the photographic images recorded by the ship's cameras. Watch as I overlay the two diagrams." She placed one transparent chart over the other.

"What about the computer itself?" asked Director Stoll. "Have you taken a look at the disc drive from the ship's computer?"

"We are doing that now, and I should have the results of that momentarily," said Mrs. Quinn.

"That will be the key piece of the puzzle," said Dr. Ottinger. "If the ship was *programmed* to fly an elliptical course bringing it back home, then we will know the answer. NASA *wanted the ship to return to Earth.*"

David interjected, "Excuse me, Dr. Ottinger, but I think that conclusion is premature for two reasons."

"And what are those?" responded Howard Ottinger, mildly annoyed.

"The first question I have is," said David, "was the navigational program entered into the computer *manually* by a technician, or was it transferred directly by computer link *from the lab computer* controlling the observation of Nyvar? If the latter is true, then the coordinates of the planet and the navigational path to it should have been programmed according to plan. If *that* is the case and the ship *followed* the programmed navigational path, then we are looking at a problem of *curved space!*"

"Good observation, David," said Klaus. "And the second reason?"

"The second reason is that if the program was manually entered and it is *not* the *correct path* to Nyvar, I would submit that we are looking at *sabotage* rather than *subterfuge* by NASA!" said David.

"I have a hard time believing that NASA entered an *incorrect path*," said Dante. "First, if NASA had lied to the U.S. government and the whole world about where they were sending the *Revelation*, then someone in NASA—and there are many possibilities here—would have squealed. Someone would have surely leaked this to the press."

"I agree," said Susan. "And secondly, what possible motive would *anyone* have had for sabotaging the mission?"

"Perhaps someone who volunteered but was not selected on our team could have been angry enough to do it," said Jake. "Stranger things were happening in the twenty-first century!"

As Jake spoke, a young lab assistant entered the room and handed Barbara a chart. She looked at it for a second and said, "Well, the *Revelation* flew almost exactly the course programmed into its computer. Comparing the three separate sources, the computer program, the flight recorder track, and the image record of the cameras, there is little difference in the three."

"Then there is only one other thing we can do. And that is to observe, using Hubble IX, this planet you refer to as Nyvar," said Dr. Ottinger. "We have more sophisticated equipment and techniques than you had in the twenty-first century. We can pinpoint the exact spatial location of the planet without error."

"And if we verify that it *is* where we thought it *was*," said Ellen, "then we know that the navigational route programmed into the *Revelation*'s computer did *not come from* NASA's lab computer."

"And it had to have been entered manually by someone," added David.

Dr. Ottinger said, "Mrs. Quinn, would you and Dr. Marks go now and locate Nyvar and allow us to tie up this *rather large loose end*?"

"I will be happy to, sir. Dr. Marks, please come with me."

Barbara and Ellen left to utilize the Hubble IX and other astronomical observation devices used by GSA to examine bodies in deep space.

"Coffee or tea, anyone?" said Dr. Ottinger.

The remaining group moved to a lounge area to await the results of Barbara and Ellen's work. The lounge dispenser provided *free* exotic blends of coffee and select teas. Susan quipped, "Free gourmet coffee and my favorite green tea are *definitely* improvements over twenty-first-century NASA!"

17

The two CIA types were sitting in their PMU outside the GSA headquarters building, cooling their heels.

"If you ask me," said Arte, "this is a real waste of time! These dudes are not going anywhere, and they don't even know their asses from teakettles. They just arrived in town from the twenty-first century for chrissakes!"

"I think yer right. The GSA's got 'em wrapped up in meetings every day and in the evenings. Where's to go? There *is* nothing but the Coach and Six for several miles around this joint."

"What if they decide to go into Orlando at ten PM? Whose gonna be watchin' them on that excursion?"

"Well, nobody, I guess, if we don't."

"Besides, we got no choice, and you know it. The prez himself ordered this one."

"Yeah, you're right. Seen any good movies lately?"

Back in the GSA laboratory, Ellen went with Barbara into the Astronomical Observatory Section where they could access the Hubble IX orbiting space telescope. They both viewed the screen as Barbara adjusted the controls. Ellen, from using them so many times, had no trouble remembering the coordinates of Nyvar. "There it is!" she said to Barbara. "Exactly where it was when we studied it in 2025."

Barbara studied the image on screen being transmitted from Hubble. She reviewed other data being printed below the image. "You are right, Dr. Marks. It looks enough like Earth to be its twin. And the distance is showing at 1,308 light-years. Now for the coup de grâce!"

She turned to Ellen. "I just asked for the *navigational path* to this planet. The print will come out over there." She pointed.

Ellen went over and picked up the print. It was basically a *straight line*. There were small nuances accounting for the gravitational effects of stars and objects lying near the intended straight line path, but no elliptical path. Certainly no *curved space*. Ellen exclaimed, "Then if this information had been *used properly* and entered into the *Revelation* computer, we would now be on Nyvar and not back on Earth.

The two women rushed into the lounge area where the group was awaiting word.

Barbara said to Ellen, "You tell them, Doctor!"

"Someone put an *incorrect navigational path* into our ship's computer that sent us on a long round-trip *back to Earth*! Nyvar is still where we thought it was!

"What?" said the others of the crew almost in unison.

Ellen handed the charts to the others. There was no question about it. The ship had followed exactly the track entered into its memory, and someone had *sabotaged* the mission.

"Who would do that and why?" said Dante, shaking his head. "A $65-billion program completely wasted by someone in the lab at NASA!"

"Now long dead," said Jake with the tiniest hint of a smirk, which no one noticed.

"I cannot believe that anyone would do such a thing!" exclaimed Maria.

All were quiet for several minutes—longer it seemed.

"I will say it again to you all. *Welcome home*," said Director Stoll. "And I might add that there are *much worse* places to be. We still have not identified *intelligent life* on any other planets in our galaxy—*and that includes Nyvar*."

The crew was struggling individually and as a team. There was no recourse now. There were no punishments to be assessed. All people from twenty-first-century Earth were long dead. They all wondered who and why. Everything NASA had done in those years was checked, rechecked, and triple-checked—always by more than one staffer. How did this incorrect program get entered into the *Revelation*'s brain?

"Whoever did this obviously wasn't trying to destroy the *Revelation* and kill us," said Dante. "That would have been *easy* to do. Referring to our earlier discussion, was there anyone we can think of who wanted to come on the mission but was not included?"

No one volunteered any ideas.

"Just let me say this," said Jake. "We accomplished our mission in a sense. We were sent to a new world. We had no idea what we would find. It could have been dinosaurs, or it could have been comparable to the civilization we left, or it could have been a highly advanced civilization. From what I have seen so far, *we got the best of both worlds*. We are home! We have discovered a highly advanced civilization! We are being told that Earth in 3339 has none of the old problems of twenty-first-century Earth. I don't think we could have had a more successful trip than this!"

Everyone thought hard about Jake's words. You can always use an optimist in a group effort.

"Now we must learn all we can about this new world and try to become productive citizens," said Maria.

"And we are committed to helping you do that," said Klaus. "Now that our 'little' navigational problem has been solved, why don't we drop by the cafeteria for some refreshments? After that, we can proceed back upstairs for more discussion with Dr. Hadid. I'll call and advise him that we will be up in about thirty minutes."

18

It was about three PM now—still time to make some good progress in an afternoon session. Dr. Mikhal Hadid was at the head of the table. The conference room was different again. At the center of the room was the large original conference table and chairs and, on the sides, the same additional chairs along the walls. The large screen was still in place behind Dr. Hadid. He asked the crew to take seats at the far end of the table with Dante seated in the middle at the opposite end, facing him.

"I hear that you have learned why, or is it *"how"*, you arrived back on Earth instead of your intended destination," said Dr. Hadid. "Congratulations, and again, welcome to the thirty-fourth century!"

"We have not included a large audience this afternoon," said Dr. Hadid. "In the first place, I have given them all a challenge. They will be working hard to come up with the twelve significant changes that separate the society of the thirty-fourth-century Earth from that of the twenty-first-century Earth. Starting in a few seconds, we will begin to speak of these. Why should we help them with their assignments?"

Chuckles were heard from others on the GSA staff and from the *Revelation* crew.

Dr. Hadid continued, "Secondly, all of our GSA staff, hopefully, have meaningful work to do." He paused for another laugh but hearing none proceeded, "I do have with me today two members of my staff who will help me with my discussion with you, our new friends from the twenty-first century. With me on my left is Mr. George Coulson, and on my right is Mr. Lamarr Lightman. Both of these gentlemen are experts on the social and scientific history of the world."

Speaking again to the *Revelation* crew, he said, "Would each of you please introduce yourselves to Mr. Coulson and Mr. Lightman and include just a brief comment on what your particular specialty was in the twenty-first century."

The *Revelation* crew complied with his request and introduced themselves. Then Dr. Hadid began the session. "We will begin this session by discussing the first significant problem of the twenty-first century that Maria listed for us this morning. Does everyone remember what she said about war, conflict, and terrorism?"

Seeing nods of agreement, he said, "Good. Mr. Coulson, would you like to tell our friends what was done about that—back in the twenty-second and twenty-third centuries, I believe?"

"Certainly, sir, I would be happy to," said Mr. Coulson. "In the twenty-first and into the twenty-second century, conflicts and terrorism had become a way of life. Things you always had enjoyed in your lives, such as going to a library or a museum or just to a nice restaurant, had become a matter of taking risks. One never knew when any public place might be bombed—often by suicide bombers, but also by others who had, unnoticed, placed explosives in inconspicuous spots. The terrorists were not always from other countries—many were *homegrown*."

He continued, "Wars and conflicts between countries and tribes or sects within a country were commonplace. At any one time, there might have been as many as *fifty* such armed military actions ongoing throughout the world at the same time. The United States, as you know, began in the twentieth century to try to be the world's policeman. Working under the auspices of NATO and the United Nations, the U.S., with some help from a few other countries, sent peacekeeping forces all over the globe in an effort to stem and contain conflicts. The United States also began in the twentieth and twenty-first centuries to try to spread democracy around the globe. This effort was extremely costly, in terms of both dollars and lives, and found little success.

"The driving forces for this international mayhem seemed to be several. Religious differences, believe it or not, seemed to be the biggest driver. Some religions and fascist sects, as you may know, even espoused furthering their cause by eliminating whole religions. I believe the role model for this fanaticism began with Adolf Hitler in the twentieth century. Other driving forces were jealousy and hatred of a country by other countries for any of a variety of reasons. In some cases, the warlike ways of a nation were simply a product of the dictator ruling that country. As you know, North Korea and Iran were such countries in the early twenty-first century.

"Unfortunately, one by one, other countries such as the United Kingdom began reducing their support for the peacekeeping efforts spearheaded by the United States. They were hoping that by distancing themselves from the U.S., it would lessen others' hatred for them and, therefore, reduce terrorism in their country. The withdrawals of these countries from international peacekeeping left only the United States *trying to do it alone*!

"Additionally, the U.S. and the United Nations organization were unable to stop the proliferation of nuclear power. By 2030, there were fifteen countries around the world not just with nuclear power, but with *nuclear bombs* and with the capability to deliver these weapons at *very long range*. The proliferation of nonnuclear weapons and explosives was perhaps even a bigger driver of armed conflict and terrorism than nuclear devices. Everybody seemed to have powerful and deadly weapons, *and the killing of anyone different from one's own people* was escalating in an alarming spiral.

"By the end of the twenty-first century, the world situation had come to the point that the United States could no longer offer its help to countries that were being attacked and overrun by their neighbors. The primary concern of every country in the world became civil defense. A country never knew who might be attacking them almost at any time! As powerful militarily as the United States was, it could not hope to contain or control the lunacy of the entire world. The U.S. withdrew to a position of semi-isolationism. The military and the defense systems of the U.S. were restructured to concentrate on defense of *this country*. The borders were completely sealed. No immigration was allowed, and foreign travel by any U.S. citizen was at his or her own risk! Some foreign trade continued, but on a very select basis."

Mr. Coulson paused for a breath and could see the incredulous expressions on the faces of the six astronauts from the twenty-first century. He decided he had painted enough of a picture of the late twenty-first century. It was time to switch gears.

Dr. Hadid said with tongue in cheek, "I thought you were going to tell them what we *did* about the world situation."

"I am, sir. I just wanted to be sure they had a good foundation for what I am about to tell them. Otherwise, they might have considered our actions harsh."

"I fully agree with you, George. Good idea. Proceed."

Mr. Coulson continued, "So far, all I have done is expand on what Maria touched on in her excellent summary of the situation in 2025. Now I am going to tell you what we, the United States, did about the world situation. We did *what we had to do*!

"The president in about 2107, I believe it was one Evelyn Robinson, called her cabinet together one day along with the principal leaders in Congress and laid it out on the table. I am going to paraphrase here. She said, in essence, that the *end of the world*, she felt, was very near. *Armageddon was at hand*. President Robinson had directed her staff, working with others in the administration and in Congress, to prepare charts that showed trends of several variables. The charts displayed things like the number of terrorist bombings, the number of active armed conflicts, wars, and others. Also presented were the estimated totals of various types of bombs and military weapons that existed and were being produced around the world. One chart also presented 'death from conflicts' rates from all countries. All the charts were plotted against time—and ALL the charts showed the numbers increasing at *exponential rates*.

"The president said to the assembly, '*Are we going to sit around and wait for the world to destroy itself?* Are we just going to keep passing meaningless bills, collecting and increasing taxes to fund our ever-increasing deficit spending, and trying to maintain a stronghold against the rest of the world? We have already become *an island in a world gone mad*! Our world trade has shrunk to a shadow of what it once was. We spend billions each year just maintaining a strong defense posture. We spend billions more, ensuring that materials entering our country are safe. The stronger nations of the world are overrunning the weaker nations. They are fighting with each other over how to slice up the 'world pie.' Do we think they will *leave us alone* as much as they hate us?'"

Mr. Coulson continued, "I can relate to you the rest of the transcript of that meeting because I have read it so many times. But I will not. The essence of what came out of that meeting can be summarized as follows.

"At that very meeting, the secretary of defense, Gerhard Neumann, took the lead and convinced President Robinson and the rest that there was *one hope for the world*. And that hope could be implemented as long as the United States could maintain the security and integrity of its borders long enough to implement the plan. He said to the assembly, '*To save the world, we must control the world!*' He went on to explain in detail what he and the joint chiefs had been working on for several months.

"Their plan was based on an idea first proposed by President Ronald Reagan in 1987. At that time, it was called the Strategic Defense Initiative, or SDI. The detractors, led by the *New York Times*, referred to the proposed program as *Star Wars*. Some of you may remember reading about it.

"The new plan by Neumann and his staff, after considerable deliberation, was ultimately approved by the president and Congress and implemented. The implementation of the plan was done in *complete secrecy* and accomplished for the most part by NASA and its contractors. The final product of the plan initiated under President Robinson called the Global Conflict Control system is *what we have today*, and it works like this."

He turned to Dr. Hadid and said, "I would like to use the large monitor to run a clip, if I may."

"By all means—it's *your* show." said Hadid.

The large screen brightened. It showed four men loading a missile onto a truck and getting into the truck. The location looked to be in a jungle area. The images seemed old and deteriorated. As the truck drove off, a blinding shaft of light entered the picture from the upper left. The missile, the truck, and its occupants glowed bright red orange. The shaft of light disappeared; and all that was left of the truck, its occupants, and the missile was a small pile of *white ash*.

The *Revelation* crew was struck immediately with quite varied emotions. Dante and Jake both felt like standing and applauding, David was enthralled by the technology, Susan did not believe what she just saw, and Ellen and Maria were incensed at the images they had just seen.

Ellen was the first to speak, "Is this film a real clip? Were those four people reduced to ash?"

"Yes and yes," said George. "The film was shot in the year 2123. The men were members of a militia working for a drug lord in El Salvador. The missile was nuclear, bought from the black market, and about to be employed in a strike aimed at a target in Panama."

"What was the blinding shaft of light, and where did it come from?" said David.

"That was a magna-laser beam, referred to as a maser strike, fired from a Global Conflict Control satellite orbiting Earth at roughly 22,300 miles out."

The *Revelation* team was speechless. Dante could hardly contain himself! David said "cool" and immediately drew glares from Ellen and Maria.

Susan said, "How were they sure of their target and the identity and intentions of the four men?"

David said, "How was the targeting accomplished?"

"What a weapon!" said Dante.

"Let's take your questions one at a time," said Coulson. "First, the target was located and determined to be hostile by the CIA. The targeting was accomplished through the ability of the magna-laser, or maser, to find and lock on most large bombs and military-type weapons. It uses the materials' signatures of the explosives used in constructing the bomb or weapons ammunition."

George continued, "There are enough GCC satellites in orbit to cover the Earth, and they overlap coverage to back each other up in case of a malfunction."

Dante asked, "How do the satellites defend *themselves* from attacks?"

"The same way I just described," said George. "Nowadays, it is very rare for any weapon to be launched with a GCC satellite as its target because the weapon can be detected and destroyed before launch. If a magna-laser satellite is fired on from a source beyond Earth's orbit, it locks on the missile and the source and destroys both."

"Are the satellites automatic and autonomous, or are they controlled by GCC?" said Jake.

"Both," said George. "Normally, they operate autonomously and, using surveillance techniques I have not explained, locate and destroy targets without any control from GCC on the ground. In the case of your arrival recently, neither the masers nor the GCC command considered you a threat, and you were not destroyed. To be cautious, two masers were diverted from their normal duties to target and track your ship."

They were stunned! They had had no idea of the destructive power aimed at them.

Dante said, "But we had large weapons and ammunition on our ship. Why didn't the satellites consider us a threat?"

"You were a special case—that is, not on the surface of the Earth, not in flight below orbital altitude, and were not targeting or firing at any maser or ground target. In your case, the masers were targeted manually by GCC. They do not fire unless commanded to. After you were ID'd as a potential target, they locked on your ship and stayed on it until we gave the OK to release you when you came to a stop on our runway."

The *Revelation* crew members were overwhelmed. They had not imagined that the laser beams focused on the *Revelation* were from such powerful weapons *ready to annihilate them*.

Dante pushed ahead. "Are you telling us that the GCC maser system has eliminated world conflicts and terrorism?"

"Not altogether—and not just the one system. But the maser umbrella is the *muscle*. There are three components to the total GCC conflict control system. The satellite magna-lasers, or masers; the sniffer satellites, or snats, in low earth orbit; and the sniffer utility units, or snuts, in ground locations. We will explain the snats and snuts later.

"Today, it is *rare* for a maser to fire and destroy a target—*any target*. The entire world knows if they break the Rules of Conflict, they are *history*!

"I will say one more thing on this subject so you can think about it after our session. You are all no doubt all familiar with the bomb-sniffing capability of canines. I will just say that the designs of the snats and snuts were *developed from a technology derived from the capability of dogs*. A group of scientists at Caltech worked long and hard on the study of the ability of dogs, and that work bore fruit in the early twenty-second century, in time to be integrated with the magna-lasers. These sniffing devices were linked to the GCC masers such that weapons stashes and explosive devices are sniffed out by snats in orbit or snuts on the ground. The information is relayed to the satellites, and the strike is initiated.

"I have loaded you with much—too much—on all of this for one session," said Mr. Coulson. "We have summary manuals for each of you to become more familiar with the Global Conflict Control system. What do you think, Dr. Hadid? Should we call it a day or move on to something else?"

Maria could no longer contain herself. "Please don't shoot me on the spot, but I have very real problems with what you are telling us. It sounds to me like the United States has established a global military *dictatorship*. May I ask some questions?"

"By all means," said Dr. Hadid, "Ask away."

"Do you consider the United States to be a world dictatorship?"

"Do you want me to answer that one question, or do you have more, such that I may answer all of them at the same time?" responded Dr. Hadid.

Maria was *boiling*. "Let me just relate what I have heard since we started this session and tell you what I think about it. If I may do that, then I would appreciate your comments on all that I am about to say."

"Please go ahead and tell us exactly what you think," said Hadid. "One of the primary reasons for the indoctrination we are presenting for you is to get the reaction of twenty-first-century people to what we are telling you about our civilization."

"I will start by commenting that the term *civilization* might be off target and that *fascist regime* might be closer on point!"

Maria's partners gasped. The *Revelation* crew was in no position to become adversaries with the thirty-fourth-century United States, especially if they are a fascist regime. She was going too far, too fast!

Dante quickly said, "Maria does not speak for all of us."

Maria gave Dante a dirty look and turned back to Dr. Hadid, saying, "I apologize if you are offended. But to me, it just sounds like the United States now rules the world with its power from space. No doubt all other nations are now subservient to the U.S. because of its overwhelming military strength. Am I misunderstanding what I heard?"

"Are you ready for me to address your concerns, Miss Rodriguez? Or do you have more to say first?"

"I have said how I feel about what I have heard. Please speak to my concerns."

"Fine," said Dr. Hadid. "Mr. Coulson did a good job of summarizing for you the serious world problems that existed in the twenty-first and twenty-second centuries. He told you what the president and her administration decided they *had to do*. Remember, Miss Rodriguez, we are talking about what happened in this country and in the world in the twenty-second century, over *twelve centuries ago*. If you can, look back at what the world was like twelve centuries *before* your crew left Earth on your mission. That would have been in the *ninth* century.

"I and everyone now living on Earth—*except, of course, you six*—were born into a peaceful, wonderful world on this Earth. There are almost no dictatorships, there is no oppression, there are no wars, no conflicts, and virtually no terrorism. We haven't talked about crime yet, but there is *almost no crime in the U.S. today*. People the world over are free! They can operate any kind of business they like, they can have families, they can go to public places without fear. They are free to do whatever they want to do—*with one major exception*. They are *not free to kill or seriously injure other people*—and they are *not free* to commit other capital crimes. On the international level, countries *are not free to make war*. They are not free to enslave other people, and they are not free to commit genocide. On the national level in the U.S., citizens and others will only commit a capital crime once, *never again after they are caught*! And because of other things we have done, the homicides are almost nonexistent."

Dr. Hadid continued, "The United States of America has made *into reality* worldwide freedom from wars, conflicts, enslavement, and mostly, terrorism. And we have done it with our *umbrella of conflict control*, the Global Conflict Control system and center. The only additional military force that exists today is that of the United States. That military force exists to pick up the loose ends on the ground and in the air that cannot be completely controlled from space.

"I *will* say that history tells us that the early years were not easy. The fifteen nations that held nuclear weapons and delivery capability were of course not willing to *voluntarily* give up their arms and their armies. The history books imply that if the U.S. had waited just a few more years, it would have been *too late*. But it is lucky for you and lucky for us and *lucky for this lonesome planet* that our twenty-second-century leaders stepped up to the plate!

"I want you to be aware of and remember one thing from today as you relax for your evening. It is *rare*, in the present, for the masers to make *any strikes*. The reason is this: The entire world is well aware of what happens if they build or use a bomb or large weapon. They respect the *power that will be unleashed on them*. Use of military or destructive weapons of any sort has *faded from the minds of people* the world over. They have accepted that *it must not be done*." Dr. Hadid paused and then said, "I could go further, but my plea to you *to understand* is premature. You six just have to *believe me* for the time being that our world today *is good*. Give us time to take you through the entire program we have planned, and I think we can prove it to you.

"It's been a stressful day for you folks and a long one. Please try not to judge your brethren of the thirty-fourth century until we have presented our entire case.

"Get good rest and let Mr. D. know if you need anything. We will see you here tomorrow at 8:00 AM sharp. It will be another long day."

19

The crew arrived at their parking spots, and Mr. D. was there, waiting to see if they needed anything. Dante and Jake arrived first, and Jake made sure he steered clear of Mr. D. Dante was chiding him about that.

"Hey, Jake, you not worried about that little robot, are you?" said Dante with a wry smile.

"You damn right I am! Just let them latch on to your shoulder once, and you'll understand."

Dante laughed.

Ellen and David parked, followed by Susan and Maria, who seemed to be having a few words. As they got out of their puma, Susan was saying, "Look, Maria, I didn't say that I supported the way they operate their satellite weapons. I just said I wanted to hear more before I make a judgment." Just as she finished her comment to Maria, David and Ellen pulled in. Mr. D. had walked over to see if anything was needed. There were several other PMUs in the garage area. There was a gray one down at the other end. They noticed it because it was gray—the original factory color. *Who would want that color? They couldn't see anyone in the vehicle.*

Mr. D. said to the group, "Is there anything I can get for anyone?"

Dante said, "Yeah, Mr. D., Jake here wants to arm wrestle! You interested?"

Mr. D. responded, "I will try, sir, but I've never played that game."

Jake glared at Dante and said under his breath, "You think it's OK *to kill a robot?*"

Everyone but Mr. D. heard that one and laughed. Ellen was out of her puma and said, "Say, Dave and I were talking on the way back and thought we all might have a drink at our place, do some steaks, and just unwind. I feel pretty stressed, and I'm sure you all do, but it might do us good to talk about some of the things that came up today."

Susan and Maria said almost in unison, "Sure! Sounds like a plan!"

Jake said, "Well, Dante and I had thought about going into Orlando and see how the 'natives' live. So far, all we've seen is more space center—from the one we left to the one we found yesterday."

Dante said, "Anybody interested in that?"

They all looked at one another and were silent for a moment.

Then David said, "We might be smarter to get a little further along in our training before we venture out. They may have some more *serious offenses we shouldn't commit*—not just homicide!"

Dante jumped on that. He said to the others, "Dave makes a very good point. Let's go with David and Ellen's invitation."

Jake agreed and bravely turned to Mr. D., still awaiting instructions, and said, "Mr. D., can you find some steaks, some wine, and some beer?"

"Already in the Marks' unit," said Mr. D. "Mrs. Marks mentioned it to me earlier."

Everyone looked at one another, and Jake said, "Ellen, you are on the ball!"

Ellen smiled and said, "Give us thirty minutes and come on over."

Susan turned and said to Mr. D., "I think we all have what we need for the evening, Mr. D., but thanks for asking."

"No problem, ma'am, just call if you need anything."

Everyone arrived at Marks' unit at about the same time, and David made sure they all had beer or wine. He said, "I got the first one. They're in the fridge—help yourself!"

Jake walked with Maria over to the big window and said thoughtfully as they gazed out the window together, "Say, how long do you think they are going to furnish us free room and board?"

"Who said it was free?" said Maria. "I bet we get a bill when training's over, and we check out."

"Check out?" said Jake. "Where are we gonna go?" Then he said, "I know! We have tents stored in the *Revelation*." He quickly added, "Oh shi . . . oot! We didn't remove the frozen food! I'll bet that is starting to smell great."

Ellen overheard the remark by Jake and said, "I took care of it, Jake. Mr. D. took it to the cafeteria kitchen this morning."

Jake yelled over to David, "Hey, Dave, you've got a special woman there! Hope you are treating her right!" Then he turned and held his glass toward Maria. He said sincerely, "Here's to our new life in the thirty-fourth century."

Maria touched her glass to Jake's and said, "Here's to us . . . I'm not so sure about the thirty-fourth century."

Dante and Susan had taken seats on a cornering pair of beautiful and comfortable white leather sofas. They were chatting in low tones.

David was inserting the salad ingredients into the AutoChef while Ellen was marinating the T-bones. Some elevator music that no one recognized was playing softly. The music seemed to be everywhere, but there were no speakers in view.

"Does anyone know how to change the music?" said Jake. "I don't believe that Mr. D. mentioned that, did he?" He got no answer.

Everyone did seem to be unwinding and didn't talk much about the happenings of a very long day. The scene might have been the same as in the twenty-first century but for the very modern and different furnishings and kitchen equipment.

The conversation went on in pairs as Ellen and David prepared the food. Once they all sat down at the transparent single-post dining table, they began playing what-if. They were all pretty much wondering about their individual futures on this new Earth. Dante talked of possibilities in the military for him. David seemed strongly interested in a position with GSA, and Ellen talked of going into some field of advanced medicine.

Susan stated that she hadn't really heard enough to even imagine how she might fit in. Jake seemed pretty excited by all the possibilities in the futuristic new civilization and said that personally, he would like to get his hands on one of those high-powered PMUs that would go five hundred miles per hour!

Maria was very quiet and never voiced how she thought she might fit in.

The crew members had all become good friends in the weeks of training before the launch and during the journey. They all realized how quite different they all were from one another, not only in their fields of endeavor, but in the nuances of their personalities. On that point, Maria said, "We don't want to forget that we six are brothers from another time and really from *another world*. We may have to rely on each other more than we ever imagined."

The evening went smoothly with much cross-conversation on many topics, but they were all tired. It was quite early when everyone thanked David and Ellen for their hospitality and bid them good night.

Jake and Maria were chatting outside Maria's door when Dante and Susan disappeared into Dante's unit for a nightcap.

20

On their third day in a new world, the *Revelation* crew decided to take advantage of Mr. D.'s generosity and willingness to be helpful. After a light breakfast in the first-floor AutoServe, they had Mr. D. drive them to the headquarters building in a PMU van. As they were entering the building, Dante was eyeing the impressive models of spacecraft and spaceships hanging from the ceiling. For the first time, he saw *it*.

"Hey, guys! Look above the front entry door! There is the *Revelation*!"

They all stopped and looked up. There it *was* with N2025R on the tail!

"That's a prominent spot when one is leaving the building. I wonder why none of us saw it before," remarked David.

"Seeing that," said Susan, "makes me wonder why they had any trouble whatsoever in identifying us and giving us the go-ahead to approach the space center and land. Apparently, there are some people here at GSA that have *always been aware* of the *Revelation* and its mission."

"I guess the space historians here just figured that our ship hopefully landed over 1300 light-years away, and they pretty much forgot about it since they would never have any answers," said Ellen.

"That's a beautiful ship!" said David, admiring the model.

The tenth-floor conference room looked the same as the day before, but Director Stoll wasn't there. Mr. Lightman, whom they had met the day before, was there waiting when they entered the room.

"*Gouda morghan!*" said Mr. Lightman, "Please be seated. Neither Dr. Hadid or the director will be with us today. They asked me to lead today's session on what's new in the thirty-fourth century."

The crew all took the same chairs they had the day before. Notepads and pens had been placed at each seating location. Mr. Lightman reminded them that printed notes and discs covering the material discussed that session would be passed out each day.

He began, "Maria's second area of major concern from the twenty-first century was poverty, famine, and uneven wealth distribution between strata, or classes of people—not only in the United States, but around the world. Am I correct, Maria?" Seeing a nod and hearing a yes from Maria, Lamarr Lightman continued, "There have been many changes in the United States and over the world addressing the twenty-first into the twenty-third-century problems related to poverty and wealth. I will talk to you first about what has been done in this country.

"I will simply list a number of things as line items. Some require more explanation than others. We will be able to discuss any and all of these changes after I have completed presenting the list. Observe the large screen there."

The screen brightened, and the following information was presented as Mr. Lightman read from the material:

- The minimum wage paid to any working person is sufficient to pay for decent housing, transportation, food, and other basic needs for individuals and couples with up to two children. The number of children *allowed* per family will be discussed later.
- Taxes on an individual or family are based on a flat rate and is progressive based on family income. Individuals and families earning below a certain threshold level pay *no taxes*. There is no filing of taxes, no deductions, etc. There is only the *one tax*. That is, all local, county, state, and federal taxes are taken in each year no later than the end of the tax year and based on the income of the family for that year. All levels of government receive their allocated portions of the tax pie from the one-time payment from each citizen. The *only exception* to the one-tax system is the taxing of tobacco, alcohol, and mind-altering drugs. These items are taxed just in order to support rehabilitation facilities and medical costs resulting from the use of these degenerating substances.
- There are no social security payments (i.e., as stated above). There is *only one tax* the government takes from the people—the flat-rate progressive income tax.
- All able people *must work*. That is, none in our society lives off transfer payments from the government if he or she is able to hold a job—any job. If a person or couple is wealthy enough, they *may retire and not work*. If a person is too ill or sick to work, then they may receive government assistance for the period when they cannot work, even if their situation is a permanent one. People that cannot physically work to pay for their livelihood also have the option of going into government-operated facilities that will attend to their needs until they die.
- The government provides for medical and drug needs, and no one is required to carry medical insurance. Also, individuals may not bring lawsuits against doctors or medical facilities. When mistakes are made in treating patients, the doctors and clinics and drug companies may be required to pay huge fines and perhaps lose licenses, but the families of the injured party and lawyers cannot bring suit and become wealthy because of someone's medical mistakes.

- Schools and colleges are free to all regardless of age. Qualification to attend schools of choice is based on IQ and entrance testing. In other words, the best brains get to be trained in the most advanced and highly regarded schools. However, all children get at least twelve years of education.
- There is a limitation to wealth. It applies to everyone and to every family. When a person or family reaches that ceiling, then the excess monies must be donated to a variety of designated recipients. There are no Bill Gates or Warren Buffets or Oprah Winfreys in the thirty-fourth century. Yet the allowed ceiling on wealth is indeed high and worth the incentive, hard work, and drive required to reach that ceiling. In the United States today, no one is allowed to become obscenely wealthy. This same logic and law applies to corporation executives who, in your century, got filthy rich with salaries, stock options, and bonuses while many of the corporation workers struggled to make ends meet.

Mr. Lightman continued without visual charts. "I mentioned a limit to family size. A family can have as many children as they can *afford to care for* and rear. A family may always *have at least two* children. If, however, parents give birth to more children than they can afford based on the government formula, the excess children must either be given up for adoption or placed in a government child domicile. They will then live there until they are of age to go out, get a job, and support themselves. This mandated procedure, as regard children, is in place to avoid the situations of the early centuries. Those times wherein both couples and single parents often could not afford the size of their families result in their children not being cared for properly, becoming severely undernourished, and, in many cases, turning to gangs and/or lives of crime."

By this time, the brains of our six astronauts from the twenty-first century were astir with emotions—some positive, but some quite negative. There was just too much to comprehend! *How different things were from the world they had all known*. They all had many questions; some wondered if they could contain their anger relative to certain points.

Mr. Lightman continued, "You have been very patient and very attentive. I can imagine that you are harboring many thoughts about what we just covered. I will let you air those thoughts momentarily. Let me caution you, however, that what I just described to you is a system and set of rules that *have been in place for centuries*. It is your responsibility to learn and understand *how it works* and perhaps *why* it works as well as it does. It would be most productive for all of us if you would refrain from challenging how we do things in the thirty-fourth century, at least until you fully understand *why* we do things this way.

"I am ready for your comments and questions."

Jake was first up with his hand. "How the blazes can the United States government PAY for all the *free* things you mentioned? I believe I heard about *free* medicine and drugs, *free* college, *free* homes for the disabled, and perhaps a few more. Yet you say you only collect the *one tax*! You collect no property tax, no social security tax, no gasoline tax, no state tax, no sales tax, and no local taxes? My question is, how on earth can the government afford all the *free stuff* without any tax revenue?"

"I can help you understand that a little better, Mr. Loneghan," said Mr. Lightman. "Most of the things your government was spending billions for in 2025 are not significant expenditures today. For example, we are not fighting wars like you did, and we are not rebuilding nations as you were after tearing them down when you fought those wars. We have greatly reduced the size of government. For example, there is only one senator and one representative from each state now on Capitol Hill, and the staff each congressperson may have is *severely limited*. The postal department is now a private operation and is run with much more efficiency than it was in your time. On a comparative basis, taking into account inflation over the centuries, it costs about a *third* today to post a package than it did in 2025.

"In the twenty-first century, a citizen had to pay taxes to fund multiple levels of heavily staffed government entities—city, county, state, and federal. City and county governments have been consolidated, and the size of these is greatly reduced. State governments have been reduced similarly to the manner in which federal government has been reduced.

"The reduction of crime, which we shall talk at length about later, is another of the big reasons that government expenditures are down. Just let me say now that the U.S. government's cost of crime prevention and punishment is a pittance compared with what it spent in your century, again on an equivalent monetary basis."

Mr. Lightman continued, "In summary, and so as not to belabor the first question, Mr. Loneghan, government costs today are so low that we pay for all the free services I mentioned and more and have money left over in the treasury each year. We *more than balance the government's annual budget because we have little waste!* We more than balance the budget because there are *no wars, and the cost of fighting crime and punishment is extremely low*. There is more in your manual. Let's go on to another question."

"I have one," said Ellen, raising her hand. "It sounds like doctors can't earn much money. Don't you have trouble getting enough of them to go into the profession to handle the workload? And a follow-up question, if I may. Don't you find their skills and the quality of their work wanting since the high-income motive has been taken away?"

Lamarr Lightman responded, "Quite the contrary, Dr. Marks. In the first place, young men and women who want to study medicine aren't excluded from study because they might not have the funds. Secondly, only the best practitioners graduate and become doctors. And thirdly, they still make *plenty of money* for their work, they all reach within the top-ten percentile of the wealth ceiling we spoke of earlier, and many are *at* the wealth ceiling. Again, your printed material will have more on this."

Maria raised her hand. "What about this limitation on children?" she said with a certain degree of anger in her tone. "Talk about curtailment of freedoms! You are telling a couple that wants five children that they can only have TWO!"

"A couple can have five or *ten* . . . if they can afford it!" said Mr. Lightman.

"And whether they can afford it is by government formula?" said Maria.

"That is correct," said Mr. Lightman. "Many centuries ago, it was decided to address the fact that women obviously were not considering whether or not they could *afford to* when they decided to get pregnant. Since they would not conduct their lives like responsible people, then the government had to do it for them."

"What happens if a mother conceives and bears an extra baby, one over the government-mandated limit?" growled Maria.

"She has several options," said Lamarr. "One, she may put the child up for adoption before the birth. Two, she may terminate the pregnancy. Three, she may put the child up for adoption after the birth. And four, she may enter the child into a government CDC home for children. If she refuses to choose, the *child goes into the Child Development Center*. At this point, the birth parents lose all rights to the child. In such homes, the children are well cared for and encouraged to develop to their full potentials.

"Children in the CDC homes may be adopted by eligible families. If, at some point as a child in a CDC home ages and matures, the birth parents become financially able to retrieve the child they lost, they may do so—if he or she is still in the CDC home—and bring the child home to live with the family. However, depending on its age, the *child* may be allowed to make the final determination of *whether to stay in the government facility or return to its parents*."

"Wow!" said Susan as she looked at both Maria and Ellen. "This *is* a very different new world!" All the women showed shock but a certain degree of understanding. They thought of all the terribly mistreated, neglected, and abused children in the twenty-first century. They thought of all the poor families that tried but simply could not support the number of children they produced. They thought of the unmarried poor working mothers that seemed to have child after child, many of whom ended up on paths of crime.

"Why don't we take a break?" said Mr. Lightman. "We are covering a lot here. Maybe we should slow down. Please be back in fifteen."

No one challenged that suggestion. The crew eagerly got up and headed for the elevator. All were silent on the way down. They arrived at the cafeteria level and got in line for something to drink. Still, there was no conversation.

The men took their drinks, chose a table big enough for six, and sat; the women bypassed the men, took their soft drinks, and walked out on the deck.

Maria was the first to speak. "This is not *freedom*!" she said angrily. "When the government tells you how to live your life, how much money you can earn, and how many children you may have, that is *dictatorship*. Not democracy and freedom!" She looked at Ellen and Susan for support.

Ellen had a different view. "Perhaps we had *too much freedom* in the twenty-first century," she mused softly.

Susan joined in the discussion. "If we just take *one point* and look at it, think first of a child living with a poor parent or parents, who, even though they worked hard, could not support *eight* children. Their children had insufficient food, clothes, and other necessities. Because the family was so poor, the child began working at a young age and never had the opportunities to develop into the adult he or she could have been. It takes an exceptional child to emerge from that background. Now consider the child of selfish parents who really didn't want the child in the first place. They already had three. They beat the new child, deprived the child, abused the child, and, in general, made the child's life a living hell.

"Now finally, consider the child who was forced to go to a good, controlled environment, but without parents or parental love. In the Child Development Center, the children do not want or need basic necessities. The child has a wide-open opportunity to learn and develop into whoever or whatever they want to be. If such a center is operated properly, children will not be subjected to any sort of intimidation. I assume that the goal and assignment of the CDCs is to produce the finest citizens possible."

Maria could not listen anymore! "How do you know what it's like in these *orphanages*?" Her eyes were full of fire as she glared at Susan.

"I don't," said Susan, "but I know how they *should* be. And I don't see how we can judge them until we know the details of how they are operated."

"If it's as Susan describes, then I would think a child *could be* better off in a CDC than in a poor home with too many children and not enough of anything including love," said Ellen.

At the men's table, the discussion was focused almost entirely on the limited wealth and tax issues. Jake was pretty much leading that discussion. "In the world we came from, a man was only limited by how smart he was and how hard he was willing to work. Here in 3339, no matter how hard you work or how brilliant you are, you can't earn more than the *ceiling*—whatever *that* is."

"Suppose it's more than you can spend?" said David.

"I dunno," said Jake. "I can *spend* an awful lot! I wonder if there is a Chase Washington Bank in this century. Anyone know?"

"Just how would we know that, Jake? We haven't been farther than the Coach and Six!" said Dante.

"You can find that out in your room, Jake. We all have ultra-high-speed internet connections. I was playing with ours last night," said David. "Just type in or speak the name of the bank."

"Where is the computer console? I didn't see it," asked Jake

"Oh, it's just that little silver thing by the pen on the desk. It looks like a small silver box. Press the top, and it projects a flat screen on the wall and the image of a keyboard on to the desk. Use it like any other computer. Its connection to the Internet is electronic via satellite—no wires."

"So far, I don't have any problems with what I've heard about the thirty-fourth century," said David. "I'm just waiting to hear about all the tech changes—they must be *wild*."

"Let's get the girls and go back up," said Dante. "It has already been fifteen minutes."

They looked toward the deck, and the ladies were just coming in.

When the crew returned to the conference room, Director Stoll had arrived. "How is the indoctrination going?" he said generally and pleasantly to the group.

David popped out with, "Good—so far!"

This was followed by Jake saying, "The thirty-fourth century is certainly very different."

"*Radical* is a better word," said Maria in a tone that Director Stoll did not mistake.

"Good," said Stoll. "I came over to tell all of you that President Thornhill hasn't forgotten you. He is definitely planning a Washington reception for the six of you, perhaps even at the White House. We discussed timing and agreed that *after your indoctrination* has been completed would be better than now." He waited a few moments for a response, which did not come, and said, "Well, fine! Then it's settled." Then turning to Mr. Lightman, the director said, "Can you venture a guess when this program will be completed?"

Mr. Lightman gave a small laugh and said, "I don't mean to be disrespectful, sir. But this is the *first time* this particular program has been put on, and this is *the most inexperienced class* we have ever taught—period. Nevertheless, I will hazard a guess and say a week to ten days."

"I suppose it will depend largely on the number of questions raised and the amount of time spent in discussions," said Stoll.

"Absolutely right, sir," said Lightman.

"Tell you what," said Director Stoll, "I will advise the president that he can set up his party for two weeks from now. We will just have to get it done, and that should be plenty of time."

The crew listened as this went back and forth, wondering if there was a way to completely avoid the big show in Washington. Not one of the six, except perhaps Dante, had any interest in the hoopla in Washington. And none of them wanted to deal with the press corps. But they knew that would be unavoidable.

Director Stoll bid them good-bye and wished them well in moving along rapidly in their learning process. He departed the room.

Jake said, "He could have made that trip with his hologram." The others laughed, and Mr. Lightman said, "True, but his office is just down the hall."

Mr. Lightman continued, "Well, now that we are behind schedule, let's see if we can make it up. The third area of concern Maria had from the twenty-first century was *crime*. And this is an extremely important topic for us to explore today." As he projected a chart on screen, he began, "There are two acronyms that you should become very familiar with at the outset of this discussion. They are TVU and UFS. TVU stands for Truth Validation Unit, and UFS stands for Unfit for Society. Let's acquaint you with the TVU first." He pressed the lobe of his right ear and said to no one, "Would you bring in the TVU, please. Thank you."

The door swung open, and Mr. K. came in pushing a device on wheels. Mr. K. placed the equipment at the front of the room just under the large screen. "Will that be all, sir?" he said.

"Why don't you stay for a few minutes just to see if we need you," said Mr. Lightman.

Mr. Lightman then turned to the class and said, "Can we have a volunteer to demonstrate the TVU unit?"

The astronauts all looked at one another. Clearly, no one wanted to be the guinea pig. No one moved. Lamarr waited, then said, "It will not harm you. I promise that."

Finally, Jake got up and said, "What the hell . . . I'm brave!" He went up and took a chair by the unit.

Mr. Lightman said to Jake as he reached to put an electronic headpiece on Jake's head, "This will not hurt. It just senses brain wave transmissions." Jake flinched slightly, but seeing Mr. K.'s arm move slightly toward him, he decided to allow himself to be crowned with the dome-shaped device. Then Mr. Lightman put a device around Jake's left arm that looked like a blood pressure test cuff.

Mr. Lightman then turned to a console on the side of the machine. He invited the other five crew members to come up by them so they could have a better look at the screen. With everyone in place, Mr. Lightman said, "OK. I will now ask Jake to answer a few questions. When he answers the questions, you will see printed out across the screen *what his mind is thinking* as he answers each question."

This got everyone's interest in a hurry. Could they possibly have a device that can *read minds*?

Lamarr said to Jake, "Here we go. Here is your first question. In what state were you born?"

Jake responded, "In New York."

Across the screen was printed "new york."

"Another question," said Lamarr. "Were you ever married?"

Jake responded, "I have never been married."

The screen presented "never been married."

"One more question," said Lightman. "Have you ever broken the law?"

Jake hesitated, looked at Mr. Lightman, then at Mr. K., and said, "Of course not. I have never broken the law."

On the screen was printed "once failed to pay income tax owed."

Jake couldn't see the screen but saw the surprised expressions of his team members. Mr. Lightman's expression had not changed. Jake said, "What does the screen say?"

"It says you evaded paying income tax, Jake," said Lightman.

"Well, that is not true. There is something wrong with your machine," averred Jake.

Mr. K. and Mr. Lightman removed the arm cuff and the headpiece from Jake and Lightman said, "Don't worry about that, Jake. It was a long time ago."

Jake got out of the chair and said, "I don't care what this fancy machine says. I never evaded income tax!"

"Please return to your seat, Jake, and let me tell you folks all about the TVU," said Mr. Lightman.

Jake was obviously unnerved as he took his seat at the table. Dante was eyeing Jake and smiling, and the others were looking at the TVU and wondering.

"The Truth Validation Unit was developed not long after your team left the Earth in 2025. I think the first unit was operational by 2035," said Mr. Lightman. "The TVU reads and prints out in whatever language you want what the brain is thinking when a question is asked. The brain response may not be phrased correctly or grammatically correct unless the brain attends to such details. The important point is that the brain gives the *true answer* to a question, whether the person wants to or not and regardless of what the person says."

Jake started to object but decided to stay quiet and let it ride. *Besides,* he thought, *there is no way they can prove anything on me about the taxes. It's been too long!*

Lightman continued, "You may be thinking that no machine is without faults and errors. That is true. However, the reliability of the TVU is ten to the minus ninth. That is to say, that it might malfunction one time out of a *billion*. And even if that does happen, this machine will *tell its user that it is malfunctioning* and advise the user to bring in another machine.

"Let me tell you how important this machine is. The TVU has *revolutionized* our system of trials by judge and by jury. It has practically eliminated the need for criminal lawyers in the United States and in any country that uses it. Think of the vast power of this machine! A murder is committed. A suspect is brought in for questioning. The TVU is present at the interrogation. The suspect is asked if he committed the murder described. The suspect says, 'No, I was with my girlfriend that night. She will tell you!'

"But the TVU says, '*yes, i killed him, but you will never know*.'"

Lightman continued, "The man is guilty of the crime. To be doubly sure in capital cases, we use two TVUs just so there will be no complaints. Just think, *no judge, no jury, no lawyers, no court costs of any kind*. The sentencing manual is quite clear on the punishment to be meted out. Once the complete truth of the murder has been revealed by querying the suspect's mind, it is a simple matter to reference the punishment the law prescribes."

Lightman continued, "In your century and earlier, the purpose of trials in criminal cases was to determine guilt. There were endless questions by lawyers and endless testimonies by witnesses. Juries had to listen sometimes for weeks just to try to get at the truth. The whole system was built around *learning the truth*! 'Beyond the shadow of a doubt' was the phrase, I believe. When we can find the TRUTH by having the suspect's mind *tell us the truth,* then we don't need to try to guess the truth after listening to silver-tongued lawyers question endless witnesses for endless days.

"Would any of you like to react to what you have just been exposed to?"

"I'll comment," said David. "If this TVU machine works as you say it does, and from what I am hearing it has been working since the mid-twenty-first century, it is a fabulous invention. I can well imagine the time and the money it has saved, but the important point is that it has brought swift justice to the guilty and exonerated the innocent. I, for one, could not be more impressed."

"Other comments?" said Lightman.

"I am with David," said Ellen.

One by one, the others joined in, *even Jake*. He decided that now was not the time or the place to pursue his own problem as exposed by the machine. In fact, he rather hoped that everyone would kind of let it lie.

Lamarr continued, "While the greatest use of the TVU is by far the establishing of guilt or innocence, the machine is also used in civil law. Truth is also the cornerstone to issues between people. And in your century, judges, juries, witnesses, and lawyers were also required to get at the truth in civil cases.

There was a classic case in my studies. I'm sure the name was O. J. Simpson. You may remember it. He was accused of murdering two people in cold blood. The criminal trial went on for weeks. And although there was ample evidence to convict, the ineptness of the state lawyers, the prejudices of the jury, and the cleverness of the defense lawyers *got him off*. In an unprecedented fast deliberation, a Los Angeles jury found Simpson *not guilty*. Later, Simpson was tried in a civil case brought by the families of the persons he was alleged to have killed. The families again asserted that he killed the two people and sued him for damages. In this case, tried in Brentwood, California, the city the crime was committed in, Simpson was *found guilty* by the jury and was ordered to pay very large sums of money to the families.

"If the State of California had been in possession of a TVU, the entire affair would have been over in a couple of days after the unit established positively the guilt or innocence of Mr. Simpson.

"You can imagine how wonderful this device has been for law enforcement."

Dante spoke up and said, "And I'll bet that this machine has served as a very strong deterrent to crime as well."

Lamarr added, "An excellent point, Colonel Washington. I think you can make your own judgment on that when you look at these figures." He posted on screen the crime rates through the years and through the centuries. All crime was down dramatically from the early centuries on Earth. "Let me hasten to add that there are other factors which have directly affected crime rates. You will hear of these this afternoon. Right now is a good time for us to break for lunch. We will begin again at one."

The crew decided to take their cafeteria trays outside to the patio; it was a *gorgeous* day.

All were seated and just breathing in the delightful air. Again, there were no bad smells at all—just clear fresh air.

They started with their soups or salads and avoided one another's eyes at first, like they had been maxed out. Jake was really hoping no one would bring up the income tax thing. *If they do*, he thought, *how am I going to tell them the damn machine must be wrong? Crud! They have been using it now for over twelve centuries, and the thing even tells them if it's not working properly! Think I'll just lie low and hope it will all go away.* Then he thought, *Wait! I haven't got a chance! Both Mr. Lightman and that Mr. K. witnessed the readout! And they sure won't keep still.*

David said, "Well, you guys know what I think of the Truth Validation Unit. What do you think?"

"I like it," said Maria.

They all looked at her as if to say "Am I hearing what I thought I heard?"

She continued, "In our century, too much was spent by wealthy people buying expensive slick lawyers. Just like Simpson did. Many times, they got off without the punishment they deserved. On the other side of the coin, many times, the poor, often penniless suspects got some inept and marginally qualified person acting as their no-fee defense attorney. They often got slammed away for long stretches. Some got out on parole, and some stayed for life. A lot depended on the jury, the judge, and the state the trial was held in. We haven't heard the whole story yet, but so far, I vote for the TVU!"

"I agree," said Susan. "And I would also agree, as Dante suggested, that such swift and accurate justice is quite a deterrent."

Not much else was said. The six just ate and pondered their own thoughts until it was time to return to the conference room. No one mentioned Jake's tax evasion.

Meanwhile, Lamarr Lightman had just had a brief chat with Director Stoll in his office. Jake was the subject.

21

The two CIA agents in the gray PMU were really getting bored. This twenty-first-century group was up to *nothing*. They went back and forth to school and only went to the Coach and Six a couple of times. The stakeouts were *really restless*. Then Arte's mec toned.

"Yeah? What you got? *Oh yes, sir*!" He sat up straight. "Yes, sir! Right! I see, sir . . . No problem. We'll get right on it!"

He closed his mec and turned to the other agent. "One of the group has admitted to tax evasion back in 2025. They introduced him to a TVU!" He smiled.

"Tax evasion?" said the other incredulously. "How'd he get a clearance to be on the spaceflight if he was wanted?"

"The FBI didn't figure it out 'til after the ship was outta town!"

"Whew!" said the other. "Somebody's gonna get whacked good over that mistake!"

"Guess they did already—about thirteen hundred years ago!"

With a very surprised look, the agent said, "Ooooohhh yeeeaaah! What about the perp, though? Should we take him in?"

"No, that's what the call was about. We are to concentrate on Jake Loneghan, the person of interest, if the group splits up. We do nothin'. Just watch him until we get further word."

"Well, this is just more of the same. At least we only have to worry about one now!"

"Yeah. Guess they've got somebody workin' on *ancient* records to get the whole story."

"I'll bet Mr. Loneghan has to pay Uncle what he failed to pay!"

"Probably."

The crew entered the conference room after lunch, and Director Stoll was in the room. He greeted them and said, "This afternoon's session may be the toughest one of the bunch for you people to handle. Thought I'd cover it with you myself. Mr. Lightman has some other business he needs to attend to anyway. And Mr. K. can help me if the need arises." Jake cut his eyes at Mr. K. without turning his head. He really was wary of that particular android.

"And one other point before we get started," continued Director Stoll. "I have asked a special guest to come down from Washington this afternoon to be with us. She won't really be here, just her hologram."

"I'm sorry," said Maria, "I didn't catch her name."

"Maybe I forgot to say it, Maria, thank you. Our guest will be the Honorable Margaret Webster, *chief justice of the Supreme Court.*"

Wow, thought everyone, *this must really be a heavy session coming up!*

"OK, we've got some ground to cover before she gets here, so let's do it!"

He continued, "Does anyone remember the other acronym Mr. Lightman mentioned this morning?"

Susan raised her hand and said, "Wasn't it UFS or something like that?"

"That's exactly correct," said Director Stoll. "And do you or anyone remember what the acronym stands for?"

"I remember very well," said Maria. "It stands for Unfit for Society. What does that mean?"

"That is exactly what I am going to tell you this afternoon, and Justice Webster will be on hand at three PM or so to answer any questions you may have. Let me start with a story—a true story of a serial killer. The time of this story was in the early twenty-second century in the southwestern part of the United States.

"Over a period of three or four years, a number of young girls were found raped and brutally murdered. Similar clues were always left as if the murderer wanted the authorities to know it was he who committed the horrible crimes. The murders were spread across several states—Texas, New Mexico, Colorado, Kansas, and Iowa. Finally, after the tenth murder and over four years since the original murder, a suspect was brought in. Authorities felt that there was enough evidence to convict, and he went to trial in the State of Iowa where there was no death penalty on the books. It seems that the last three of the ten murders were committed in Iowa and that state insisted that they be allowed to try the suspect because of the public clamor across the state."

Director Stoll continued, "I will try to shorten this. The suspect, one Willy Graven, was convicted after a lengthy trial and received the maximum allowable penalty in Iowa. He was committed to the Iowa State Penitentiary, a maximum-security prison with a sentence of *life without parole.* It was later reported that he died of wounds sustained in a prison fight some two years into his sentence.

"A year after Willy died in prison, a young girl was brutally raped and murdered, this time in Mississippi. The corpse of the young girl showed evidence reminiscent of the Willy Graven murders. Then another body of a young woman was found—again with similar markings and similar handling to the Graven murders of the past.

"In the next eighteen months, seven more young girls were killed Graven style. Finally, a policeman in a small town in Louisiana just happened to be walking by the mouth of a dark dead-end alley when he heard scuffling and a muffled cry from deep in the alley. He yelled, 'Hey! Who's in there? *Come out with your hands high*!' Before the officer realized what was happening, a figure butted headlong into him and ran to get away. But the man wasn't fast enough to outrun the one shot fired by the officer lying on the ground. The bullet hit Willy Graven in the right thigh and downed him. The officer had called for backup before he approached the alley. They captured a dead man.

"The body of the man in prison that was *buried as Willy Graven* turned out to be the body of a laundry worker who regularly came and went from the prison. The laundry service man had the misfortune of resembling Graven. Willy cornered the man in the laundry storage room and killed him. He managed to take the body, using a laundry bag, to his assigned cell where he mutilated it. Graven, wearing the man's clothes, left the dead man in his cell and escaped the prison using the laundry truck. Prison officials, happy to see Graven dead, obviously didn't properly verify his identity.

"Just a little more to the story," said the director. "This time, Willy was captured and tried in Louisiana. He received the death penalty and was finally executed on August 8, 2125."

"Willy Graven would be *Unfit for Society* today," said Director Stoll.

Klaus waited to let the story sink in before he continued. Then he said, "If a person is deemed UFS, he may *no longer live in our society on Earth*. We will not give him additional chances to change his ways. He may not live in prison. He may not, in fact, live on planet Earth! A person designated UFS may choose how he will terminate his life—from several choices—or the authorities will choose for him. A UFS person has thirty-six hours to live after he is marked as such or after he is in custody."

He continued, "I have given you a perfect example of a UFS person and told you what must happen to such people. Now I will give you a *detailed definition* of a person that is UFS. There are people in our world that are *evil*. Some are born evil, and it just gets worse as they grow older. Some are not born evil, but the circumstances they find themselves in cause them to become evil—irrevocably evil. *Rehabilitation does not help these people*. The process of attempting rehabilitation only serves to contaminate other criminals exposed to the truly evil ones.

"Let me give you an example of a child born evil. Did you ever know of a child that delighted in bringing pain to others and to animals? A child who enjoys dousing a cat with kerosene and setting it afire? A child that cuts off a dog's leg and laughs at it trying to get around on three legs? Such a child will grow to inflict such pain on people—even people who try to love the person."

Director Stoll paused. "This is heavy. I know that. I will try to get through it as fast as I can, but you must have the foundation before the chief justice arrives.

"UFS members of our society on Earth are those who continue to physically harm and kill others, who cannot be rehabilitated, and who enjoy seeing others in pain. They do not contribute to the good life of Earth—only to the horror and evil in the world.

"Willy Graven raped, tortured, and murdered nineteen women and one man before he received what he deserved—to be deprived of his right to live in our society. In the present century and for many centuries before, since the establishment of the UFS laws and program, we *do not allow people who are Unfit for Society to live in our world.* And we will not pay for them to live in prisons when we know that they will never do anything positive for Earth's civilization. *By their actions, these people forfeit their right to live.*

"I see that it is now a few minutes before three. Would you like to take a break now and be back before Mrs. Webster's arrival?"

They didn't need any coaxing. The crew zoomed out of the room led by Jake. They all hit the restrooms and then the elevator to the cafeteria.

As they flopped at a table, Maria said, "I've only got one question. Well, it's a two-part question. Who decides who must be labeled UFS, and how can they be sure they are right?"

"I've got another one," said Ellen. "If a person deliberately kills another person in an unpremeditated murder . . . or even in a premeditated murder, does that automatically make them UFS?"

Comments and questions came fast and furious.

David said, "I can see where there are criminal types who are always evil and will always harm and kill others. But it seems that if someone commits a capital crime, either intentionally or unintentionally, they deserve some rehabilitation and a second chance. Are they saying that some people do *not* get a second chance because they somehow know it's no use?"

"Maybe that's it," said Dante. "Maybe they use the TVU to learn the person's real thoughts."

"And combining that readout with the deeds the person has committed, they can make a correct decision," said Susan.

"Well, so far, I'm saying I don't like it," said Maria. "Come on, let's go. We're going to be late."

They looked at their watches and dashed for the elevators. As they rode up, Jake said, "Tomorrow, I'm sending my hologram to class and sleeping in." That brought chuckles around.

They entered the conference room, and the director was chatting with a distinguished older but attractive and trim woman. Both smiled and turned toward the group coming in the door. Director Stoll said, "But I told Her Honor that you twenty-first-century people are prompt!"

"Sorry, sir and Your Honor," said Dante. "But we've become somewhat insensitive to time since we lost 1300 years."

That brought a smile to the chief justice—at least to *her hologram.*

"Please introduce yourselves and state your specialty to Her Honor," said the director. Ellen stepped forward followed by Dante, Maria, David, Jake, and Susan.

Although the chief justice was appearing as a hologram, they could feel her hand! Not like a real handshake, but there was definitely something there.

"At least enough to hold a glass of wine," quipped Jake later.

Mrs. Webster was quite charming and gracious and made the crew feel welcome. They appreciated that. Director Stoll said after the introductions, "Please be seated at the table, and we will continue the session." Mrs. Webster seated herself on the right of the director after refusing the offer of his chair.

All were seated, and all were quiet. "Who has the first comment or question about the people who are Unfit for Society?" said Director Stoll.

Maria glanced first at the others, and seeing no particular eagerness, she said, "I have one. Exactly how are people determined to be UFS, and who makes the determination?"

Mrs. Webster glanced over to the director and said, "I will take that if you like."

"By all means," said Klaus.

"The determination of who gets classified is done by a panel of physicians in Washington DC under the auspices of the Department of Justice. Requests for classification to UFS come in from the state governments and are acted on in the order they are received. Each request must be accompanied by all the candidate's background data and criminal record. In every case, before a request is submitted to the state level, both a primary and a secondary TVU exam must be conducted, using a pre-prepared set of questions. The results of the two TVU exams must be included with the request for classification. Each request must be screened by the state panel before being submitted to the federal panel. The signature of each member of the state panel must appear on the RCUFS. Any and all photographs of the candidate and of victims that have suffered injuries or death by the candidate are to be included with the request. Let me add this to what I have just said. No one involved in the process of declaring people UFS takes his or her responsibility lightly."

"Then," said Maria, "if I may go on with a follow-up question."

"Please do," said the chief justice.

"Then is it fair to say that a category of people have been defined that *are not suitable to live among the rest of us*? That is to say, that because they have little or no compunction against raping, injuring, torturing, and killing of others, we say to them, '*You may not live among us*?'"

"Maria, that was extremely well put," said Mrs. Webster. "Don't you think so, Director Stoll?"

"Absolutely," said Director Stoll.

The chief justice continued, "The people of Earth have learned through experience that there are certain types of individuals who fit the UFS profile. We have become so good at applying testing and logic with even *children* who fit in this category that we are able to identify the UFS personalities when they are very young. When we identify children who we believe will mature into UFS personalities, we put them under surveillance. If these marked children commit acts of serious violence on other children or adults, they are taken from their parents and placed in special divisions of the CDC. They undergo extensive testing with the TVU and with other devices to positively determine *if they are UFS*. When we have determined that a child definitely has a UFS mind, there are techniques that we can employ to try to *reform* its mind to eliminate the evil while retaining all its personality and functionality."

"Is this process ever successful?" said Susan.

"We have managed to turn a few from the dark side and mold them into people who can be allowed to live with us. In the successful cases, we have used brain-therapy devices and drugs to accomplish this. In most cases, however, our efforts fail."

Maria said, "Can the techniques work on adults?"

"Efforts on adults have *always failed*, and the younger the child, the better the chance of success," said Mrs. Webster.

"You must try to understand the overview of what we are doing here. Before the UFS system of crime control was put in place, historical crime records clearly showed that the truly evil personalities in the United States seriously harmed, raped, or killed, on average, *twenty-eight* people each during the course of their lives. The average number of *deaths alone* attributable to UFS-type individuals was a shocking *five per person*! These figures do not include mass deaths by terrorists' bombs or armed conflicts. These are statistics for *individuals acting against individuals in peacetime situations*.

"In the process of implementing the UFS laws and procedures, a task force assigned by Congress and the Supreme Court completed abundant research into the records of crimes through the centuries. In preparation for this session with you six from the twenty-first century, I researched some of the task force records for your century.

"You may remember several instances where students of educational institutions—both high school and college—went on shooting rampages killing many fellow students. I noted a case in particular where an obviously very sick Asian student murdered over thirty fellow students at a college in Virginia.

"A characteristic of this case, as in all the massacres at educational facilities, was that the deranged student had provided many clues over a period of time that he was mentally ill. He often gave clues that he was contemplating killing others. Unfortunately, school officials, parents of the ill student, and law enforcement did nothing to halt the path this student was going down. Then it was too late. Other cases followed the same pattern. In each and every case, the ill students committed suicide after murdering many innocent people.

"In each case, if your justice system had employed use of the TVU and with the UFS procedures in place, I am quite confident that the sick students would have been identified, possibly at early ages, and taken into custody for examination and treatment. The tragedies would have been avoided.

"In some of the cases, it may have been possible, using the techniques we have available today, to reform those ill minds and make the young people acceptable to live in our society. In the cases where treatment was not successful, they would have been permanently removed from society. Many innocent lives would have been saved."

She continued, "The basis for the establishment of the UFS laws and procedures is the recognition that humans with criminal minds can be born to any woman at any time. We must identify humans with such minds as soon as possible and either reform them or eliminate them to minimize their negative impact on society. Rogues can be born into any animal kingdom—even humans. *Just because people are born on to our Earth doesn't automatically give them the right to live among us.*"

The chief justice paused. It was very draining for her to speak on this subject. However, she and the president felt that it was extremely important and only fair that these six people from Earth's distant past be helped to understand about those who are deemed Unfit for Society.

Mrs. Webster had become quiet with her own thoughts. Director Stoll said, "Are there other questions?"

"I have one," said David. "Would either of you talk about how crimes of passion by non-UFS persons and accidental manslaughter situations are handled in this century?"

The director turned and said softly to the chief justice, "I will handle this one if you are tired, but if you could stay on just a while longer, I would appreciate it."

Mrs. Webster said, "You handle this one. Something has come up in my office that I must attend to, but I will be back here momentarily." As she finished the sentence, her image faded and disappeared.

"She is coming right back," said Klaus. "Meanwhile, I will take a shot at your question, David. Any crime committed by a non-UFS citizen is handled similarly to the way such a crime was dealt with in your century—with some significant differences.

"The similarities are that when a crime is committed, an investigation is undertaken, suspects are apprehended, charges are filed. Depending on the evidence the suspect or suspects are either found guilty or found not guilty. If found guilty, the suspects are sentenced and punished."

He continued, "I believe that what I just said applies to the twenty-first century, the thirty-fourth century, and all centuries in between. Would you all agree?

Jake said, "It fits for the twenty-first century—that's all *we* can speak for."

"Of course." said the director. "Now here are the differences. First, our methods of crime detection are much more sophisticated than you can probably imagine. There are surveillance cameras virtually *everywhere*. That is, in public places, in businesses, on streets and highways, etc. The only places where there are no surveillance cameras are in private residences. And surveillance equipment may be *put into private residences*, by the government, *if the owner requests such*.

"So that is one point. There are many, many more visual records of *all activities* than there were in the twenty-first century. Secondly, with the TVU, once a suspect has been apprehended, we can immediately determine his or her guilt or innocence. There is no longer a need for criminal trials. Next, once guilt has been established, the United States Penal Code 3330 contains the prescribed punishment for the crime committed. The code is published in many forms, but the application of the code is best accomplished in the computer version. The code has flexibilities in that, for example, a first-degree murder may not be just *any* first-degree murder. There may be entirely different circumstances involved. For example, if one person is blackmailing another and is killed by the person he is blackmailing, that is one thing. If a person murders another because he didn't like what the other said to his wife, then that is another thing. The punishment meted out will most likely be different in the above two cases. The computer, armed with the complete code, can handle all the subtleties provided that all the facts are entered.

"There are many other differences in the way crime is handled in our century. Jails and prisons are not comfortable and soft as the history books tell us *that twenty-first-century prisons had become*. We understand that the prisons of the twentieth and twenty-first centuries had become almost complete cities within themselves with all manner of jobs, shopping, recreational activities, and pretty good food. We also understand that inmates, in many ways, had better lives in stir than they did outside. Hence, when they were again on the outside, they *continued their criminal ways*, knowing that if they got caught, the prison they were destined for most probably would be an OK place to be.

"When we read now about the total criminal system of the twenty-first century—the justice system and the punishment system and the ineffectiveness of the total—we shake our heads in disbelief. Can any of you speak firsthand to what it was like in those years? I assume that none of you have ever been in prison, but you must be somewhat familiar with the trial and justice system."

Susan raised her hand. "I am a lawyer and have also studied the justice and punishment systems of our century and have practiced as a prosecuting attorney."

At that moment, Chief Justice Webster materialized in the chair she had been sitting in.

"Ah, you have returned!" said Director Stoll. "And at a good time too! Susan was just telling me that she was an attorney in the twenty-first century and also has experience in the criminal justice system and punishment system of that time."

"Wonderful!" said Justice Webster. "Please give us *your thoughts* on how your system worked. What was good about it, and what was not?"

"Well, I am certainly not the expert you are, Justice Webster. But I will give you my thoughts and impressions," said Susan. "First, I agree that your history books tell the truth—to an extent. Our justice system was flawed. Evidence was often tainted. Trials were extremely expensive and often lengthy. On occasion, the guilty went free on a technicality. Money bought sharp, glib lawyers who often persuaded juries to let the guilty go free. As for the prison system, the emphasis was on rehabilitation. A great deal of money was spent to provide all manner of training and education for inmates with the hope that they would find jobs and meaningful lives once they were released from prison. In a small percentage of cases, this elaborate and very expensive system worked. But in most cases, the prisons, as Director Stoll said a few moments ago, only served as havens for those convicted and provided them free better living standards and conditions than they provided for themselves when outside the prisons."

Susan continued, "Further, the real effective training the inmates got was that which made them into more *expert crooks*. Take, for example, a young first timer in prison with all the pros. Being in prison was better than being sent to a college for criminals. By the time the first timer was released back into the free world, he or she knew all the tricks and all the ropes!"

Susan went on, "Our justice and punishment systems had one thing, I think, your system lacks, however. And that is *compassion*. The twenty-first-century system was terribly flawed and ineffective, but it erred on the compassionate side. I would say that the number of guilty that went free or that received lighter sentences than they should have *far* exceeded the number that received punishment when they didn't deserve it."

"That is a point well taken, Susan," said the chief justice. "However, I firmly believe that the laxness of your system and its tendency toward compassion resulted in *far more crimes being committed*, including capital crimes, than does our system here today. Would you not agree?"

Susan thought about that and finally said, "Yes, I would agree. The system still in place in the United States when our mission departed was based on a very old system of English law. It was totally outdated and in no way could it cope with modern criminals and modern crime. Just the jury system alone was terribly flawed. The idea was to select a jury of peers. In actuality, this never really happened. Juries were selected by opposing attorneys for various reasons, none of which had anything to do with being a peer of the person on trial. The attorneys selected juries of pliable minds. They wanted juries that could be easily influenced by their rhetoric. They wanted to be able to mesmerize the jury into believing what they, the attorneys, wanted them to believe—not necessarily the truth."

Susan continued, "If I may, just let me say this: I believe that the best system of law, justice, and punishment is one that does the following: First, it rapidly apprehends the suspected guilty party. And secondly, it proves as quickly as possible whether or not the party is in fact guilty. Thirdly, the system must, in a timely manner, begin the punishment of those proven guilty. And fourthly, the guilty must be punished in an appropriate manner so that they, hopefully, will not leave jail and commit the same or other crimes again."

"Your fourth one is, by far, the most difficult challenge of any justice system," said Mrs. Webster.

"I certainly agree with you, Your Honor," said Susan. "If I may continue, are we agreed that the objectives of punishment must be first that it is appropriate to fit the crime, and secondly, that it is severe enough so the criminal does not want to have to endure that punishment again? Are we together on this point?"

Director Stoll nodded immediately and looked at the chief justice. Mrs. Webster pondered the point for some time. The crew was impressed by Susan and quite proud of her. Finally, Mrs. Webster looked up.

"I'm not sure that our society has yet achieved the goal you so eloquently stated, Susan," she said. "I think that we in this century get it more right than your century did, but it is still not a perfect system. Our approach is a *fast resolution to guilt or innocence* followed by *harsh punishment under unpleasant conditions*. You see, we believe that by having a prisoner *dislike every minute* of his or her stay in prison, it ultimately results in more incentive for the criminal to *not return* to prison and, therefore, more incentive to *not do what got him into prison in the first place*. The opposite is what law enforcement did in your century. Your prisons were soft to our thinking, and they *did not work*. As far as we can tell, they *did not punish*, and they *did not rehabilitate*. To simply put offenders in soft prisons temporarily relieved society of the burden of having them free but did not in any way change the thinking of the criminal mind."

Mrs. Webster continued, "Another thing we do to discourage crime is that we publicize everything about the justice process *after* the trial is over and while he or she is incarcerated in their assigned prison or receives the death penalty. In your century, the murder and the trial were highly publicized, but once the criminal was found guilty and sent off to prison, no one ever knew what happened. What I am getting at here is that we publicize the punishment and the unpleasantness of it. We believe this helps push people away from crime. The public needs to be keenly aware of how unpleasant prison life is.

"Unless I am wrong, in the twenty-first century, a murder, for example, particularly of a celebrity or of a child, got front page for days and sometimes weeks after the event. Then the trial made a *celebrity* out of the murderer. Consequently, those of the general public with weak minds and miserable lives saw a way to be in the headlines. They could be celebrities—just like movie stars. They thought they might go free or, at worst, go to a soft prison they had heard about. It is doubtful that they even considered the finality of being executed until the day their execution arrived.

"I read one case in your twentieth-century history. A Charles Manson was responsible for several hideous and senseless murders. He was convicted and sentenced to death. But this happened in California, and Manson was *never executed*. He lived the rest of his life in a soft prison doing as he pleased. The cost of keeping this worthless, heinous killer was a burden on the California taxpayers, and for what reason? This serves as a type of *incentive* rather than *deterrent* for those with criminal minds. A person like Charles Manson never did anything worthwhile for the people of the Earth. Letting him live served no useful purpose.

"Today, in the thirty-fourth century, we make sure that the fast and harsh justice assigned to criminals found guilty is publicized—including their execution, if there is one." She paused on that thought before continuing.

"I think that you citizens from the twenty-first century will find that we have *a very low tolerance* for crime in any form, and we deal swiftly and harshly with it. I know you haven't discussed it yet, but the United States also has a very low tolerance for international crime, including terrorism."

The chief justice concluded her visit with, "I feel that I have sounded more adamant than I really am. I am sorry for that, but I am strongly opposed to crime in any form. That is one reason I have this job. Now I really have to get back to my office. I trust that Director Stoll can help you with other questions you may have. Susan, I really would like to talk to you more sometime. Let's see if we can work that out when you finish your indoctrination."

Mrs. Webster's image was fading as Susan said, "I would welcome the opportunity, Your Honor."

"Well!" said Director Stoll. "That went well, I thought . . . Let's see if you have any more questions on crime and punishment, and if not, we can call it a day. It has seemed quite long."

Dante tentatively raised his hand while glancing to see what the others were doing. He said, "I do have one more, if I may." Seeing no objection, he continued, "We have talked today about poverty and wealth and about crime and punishment in the United States. Could I ask you to comment just briefly on how much of what we have discussed applies to other countries of the world?"

The director tried to glance at his watch surreptitiously as he said, "After your indoctrination is complete regarding life in the U.S., we will spend some time trying to relate all that you have learned to the world situation. However, since you have asked, I will make a couple of comments on the two subjects of today and how they relate to the world of nations.

"Generally, the major nations of the globe are lined up with us on the two subjects of today. As it was in the twenty-first century, the United States is ahead of the others, but all of the more modern industrialized nations are attempting to match us stride for stride.

"Now then, the other countries of the world fall generally into two categories: One, those that have a vast gulf between the rich and the poor, and the vast majority of their populations are poor. These countries are trying to develop industry and encourage free enterprise. They are trying to raise the standards of their poor.

"The countries of the second group are not modern and not industrialized and are run by strongmen and ruling tribes. Even this second group is trying to make progress on the standard of living of their poor. I am happy to report that almost all nations of the world are making significant efforts in controlling the number of childbirths.

"The interesting but maddening thing about the lower-tier countries is that religion still controls their minds, and their rulers rule by employing both religion and strong-arm tactics. America is sensitive to situations where dictators or strongmen abuse or mistreat the people of their country. *We step in when it is deemed appropriate.*

"Most of the countries of the world are making genuine efforts on three fronts: raising the standard of living of their people and trying to eliminate the really poor; secondly, getting control of crime; and finally, as I mentioned, population control."

The director stood and apologized. "I am sorry, but I must run. I have not given you a very good answer to your question, Dante, but you must realize how truly broad and varied the answer will be when you have it all. It is a little bit like me asking one of you to describe all the governments of the twenty-first-century Earth!"

He started toward the door as the crew members were rising to their feet. "Tomorrow at eight in this room, we will cover aging, health, and new medical technologies. *Don't call in sick*!" He disappeared out the conference room door.

"Whew!" said everyone and slumped into his or her chair.

Maria turned to Jake and said, "Let's *all* send our holograms here tomorrow! Think we can figure out how to do it?" Jake smiled.

David said, "Let's go to Paddy's Pub tonight! Anybody game?"

Susan was already headed for the door and announcing, "Last one there buys the first round of drinks!"

They all scrambled for the door and headed for the elevator. Dante was last and taking his time. As the elevator door was closing, leaving Dante outside, he said, "I told Mr. D. not to leave with the van until we all were seated." The others looked at one another wide-eyed. They had forgotten that Mr. D. gave them a ride to the headquarters building.

22

Two young staffers were reporting to Director Hoover.

"Sir, we completed our search of the archives for one Jakob Loneghan."

"Well?" said Director Hoover, a Danny DeVito type. "Let's have it!"

The first staffer continued, "Mr. Loneghan was a very successful businessman with several companies and many personal interests and hobbies. There is nothing of a criminal nature in his file at all."

"Except the $52 mil he owed in back income taxes, you mean," corrected the director.

"Weeell, *that*," said the second staffer. "When he left Earth on the *Revelation* mission, he had about $59 million in the Chase Washington Bank."

"The one just down the street?" The director walked over and looked down at the Chase Bank.

"The same one, sir," said the first staffer.

"Well, I'll be damned!" said Director Hoover, still looking at the bank.

Both the staffers waited for the director to say something.

"AND?" said the director.

"Oh," said the first staffer. "Well, it seems that the then director of the FBI, one Elmer Meester, was pretttyyy hot about his boys letting Mr. Loneghan fly the coop . . . hehehe."

The director gave him a real dirty look and said, "Just the facts, Horace, *just the facts.*"

"Well, sir, Director Meester chopped a few heads in the bureau over that one, managed to keep the snafu under wraps—from the press, I mean—and get this. He pulled some documents together and *took $52 million from the Loneghan account to satisfy the indebtedness to Uncle Sam.*"

"Leaving about $7 million still in the bank," said Hoover.

The second staffer said, "Er . . . I guess so, sir," Looking at the first staffer, he added, "We hadn't thought about that, sir."

The director continued to look at the bank. "Any idea how much interest seven million bucks would earn at, say, three percent interest in 1300 years?"

Both of the staffers looked at each other and said together, "No, sir."

"A lot!" said the director. "But don't worry about that. It's none of our concern."

"What about the tax-evasion criminal charges?" said the director.

"We found no evidence of any warrant," said the first staffer. "And no outstanding charges. Looks like they all disappeared."

The second staffer said, "I guess the charges were dropped since the bureau got the money owed, and Mr. Loneghan had left on a permanent trip to deep space."

"Thanks, boys. You did a good job. You can drop it now. Make me a disc of what you found and then go on to something else."

The two staffers retreated, leaving the director still looking at the bank. *I'll bet Loneghan is wondering how many credits $59 million is worth after 1300 years*, he thought.

He picked up his AMec. "Mildred, please put me in touch with the president."

Back at Kennedy Space Center

Mr. D. chauffeured the *Revelation* crew safely back to the BPQ where they collected their pumas and headed for Paddy's Pub. Dante and David rode with Jake, and the ladies piled into Maria's PMU. They headed out the main gate, followed again by the gray puma with two men in the front seat.

Dante noticed the gray puma first and said, "There is no doubt about it. Those guys are tailing us. I think I have seen them every time we leave the BPQ."

"You're right, Dante," said David. "It's the same puma I've noticed on occasion. I'll bet those guys are feds."

"Most likely," said Jake. "Our hosts are two-faced. On the one hand, they treat us with every courtesy. And on the other hand, they put a stakeout on us. Let's just ignore them. Their orders are to watch us, so let 'em watch."

"Now when we decide to rob a bank, we'll have to lose them," said Dante, laughing.

"Right!" said David and Jake in unison.

The girls beat them to Paddy's and found a table. When the guys walked in, the women said in unison, "OK! *Which one of you is buying the first round*?"

Dante volunteered, and everyone ordered something cool.

The waiter disappeared with the orders, and Jake said, "Say, isn't that our waiter on the other side of the room?" Everyone looked, and Jake said, "Oh no, that's not him, it's just his hologram." For some reason, the group thought that one was funny. Then the hologram wisecracks came—one after another. David reasoned that one waiter alone might work four or five restaurants utilizing his holograms. That one got a big laugh!

Then the waiter returned with the drinks, and Jake put his hand on the waiter's arm. Jake said to the others, "He's real." The waiter gave Jake kind of a funny look, and the laughter started up again.

After a few snickers and giggles, the laughter subsided, and thoughts turned to the events of the day. Maria could hold it no longer and said, "Our thirty-fourth-century brethren think they are God." *That* squelched the laughter.

"Why do you say that, Maria?" said David.

"*Why?*" said Maria in a louder tone. "Because they blow away anyone that pulls out a weapon, and they decide who can live or die based on the opinion of a *machine*." No one responded. They all looked down at the table or at their glasses.

Jake said, "I don't think you are being fair, Maria."

"I am calling 'em like I see 'em!" said Maria. "Tell you all one thing! We better stay on their good side, or we won't spend much time in this thirty-fourth century."

"Now hold on," said David. "Let's be rational and reasonable about this. If whatever Earth's people did has succeeded in getting control of conflicts around the world, curbed terrorism, eliminated poverty and greatly reduced crime, how can it not be good?"

"Because it all has been done at the cost of freedom," admonished Maria.

Ellen elbowed her way into the conversation. "Let's take a good look at that word *freedom*. Does freedom include the right to injure, kill, or maim? Does freedom include the right to attack another nation because you *think* that nation did something that jeopardizes the safety of your country? Does freedom include a right to life if you use that life to consistently and repeatedly do harm to others? Should freedom include a person's right to drive a vehicle carelessly and/or recklessly and, in doing so, cause injury and death to others? Freedom cannot be *totally free and unrestrained*. There have to be limits to freedom!"

Everyone just looked at Ellen, including some people at other tables.

Ellen continued, "Let's look back at the world we left. The freedoms that we and our forefathers all fought and died for were precious. In the nineteenth through the twenty-first century, Americans fought for freedom from tyranny and dictatorships. They fought for the freedom to live in a free society. We all benefited from the blood that was shed to gain our freedoms." She paused.

"But when freedoms *come to be misused and abused* and people are given too much latitude to do as they will, then good people begin to suffer because of *that unrestricted freedom*. Does the execution of a serial killer who raped, mutilated, and killed nineteen women make up to those women or their families what they lost? Does the incarceration for six years of a person who was free to fleece sixty-five families out of their life's savings make up for their losses?"

The others at the table were beginning to get Ellen's point. Ellen went on, "The problem is that when people have too much freedom to do as they will, they often do *far more damage* than can be compensated for by the relatively small penalty that is imposed on those guilty of crimes. Our so-called justice system in the twenty-first century did not administer *adequate justice*. A system that allows *too much freedom* so that people are free to do *exactly as they will* and then *punishes* them if they break the law in doing as they will *just does not get it done!*"

The waiter had arrived and saw an opening.

"Would you folks like to order now?"

Ellen turned on the waiter with fire in her eyes and said loudly, "NO! Thank you."

Jake jumped up and stopped the waiter who was practically running away from the table. "Bring us another round, please. She didn't mean to be rude."

Ellen calmly continued, *"All I am saying is* that allowing too much freedom can result in crimes, injuries, deaths that are in no way avenged or compensated for by the act of punishing the perpetrator of the crime. What good does it do for a mother whose daughter was brutally raped and murdered if the killer is put in prison for life? Or even if the killer is executed? Her daughter is gone—forever. What has the punishment accomplished? Nothing! The criminal is not rehabilitated, and in the case of life imprisonment, the taxpayers have to bear the cost of *keeping the slimeball alive* for the rest of his life. The system of crime and justice in the twenty-first *century left much to be desired*!

"I will say one thing more and then be quiet," said Ellen as David looked at her like "WHO ARE YOU?" She continued, "If the people of the thirty-fourth century have found ways to eliminate those people *unfit to live among us* and have found ways to stop crime before it happens, then I am *with them 100 percent*. I am sick and tired of extending *compassion to sorry excuses for humanity!*"

Dante, Jake, David, and Susan looked in awe at Ellen for a moment, then clinked their glasses together, and said, "Hear, hear!"

Maria just looked at Ellen, then said, "Too much freedom? I have never thought that a society could have *too much freedom.*"

"The dichotomy is this," said Susan, *"good people cannot have too much freedom—evil people should have no freedom.* The problem is that on the surface, you cannot distinguish those that are good from those that are evil."

"But people are not either good or evil—they are a mixture of both," said Maria.

"That is largely true," said Susan. "But people who are mostly good, have a *conscience*. They are not comfortable doing evil. Those that are basically evil are largely *devoid of conscience.*"

"You see this in that child that cuts off the leg of an animal and laughs when the animal tries to get around on three legs," said Ellen. "There is a fault built into that child's brain."

"As far as I am concerned," injected Jake, "harsh punishment and elimination of those found to be Unfit for Society is the way to go."

Suddenly, no one spoke. Each picked up the menu and began looking it over. The people at the surrounding tables went back to their eating and chatting. Our six astronauts had heard enough and thought and talked enough about good and evil. They were hungry. Everyone ordered and then sat pretty quietly. Five of them knew that they were in fair agreement about the ways of the thirty-fourth century. They weren't sure about Maria.

Their discussions continued for a time after dinner. Soon, everyone felt mentally exhausted from all the talk of the day.

The Twenty First Century Six, as they were coming to be referred to by others at GSA, had a short night at Paddy's and hit the sack early. Tomorrow would be another long day.

Jake and Dante again met downstairs for some breakfast. It was their fourth day in the thirty-fourth century, and they had made up their minds. Tonight, they were going into Orlando to see what some of the rest of the new USA looked like. They agreed to take Maria and Susan if they wanted to go, and of course, David and Ellen were welcomed; but regardless, they *would be going in* after the afternoon session.

They were finishing their second cup, and Jake said, "If the girls don't go tonight, maybe we should ask Mr. D. to go."

"Mr. D.!" said Dante with a chuckle, "I didn't think you liked the Mr. droids."

"I don't. But I was just thinking as long as we don't break any laws, he won't bother us, and he might be a big asset."

"How's that?"

"Well," said Jake, smiling, "he knows a lot about the present that we don't know. He's strong as an ox if we need muscle, and he can drive us home if we need a designated driver." Jake winked on that last point.

"Jake, you are *devious*. But I like your thinking. Tell you what, my first choice is to take Susan and Maria. But if they aren't interested, we can ask Mr. D. I wonder if he can take off from his garage job, though."

Dante looked at his Casio and said, "Better move it. We've got five minutes."

They hurried down to the garage and decided to take Jake's yellow puma. As they entered the garage, they saw the van leaving with the others inside.

Jake and Dante entered the tenth-floor conference room at one minute after eight, and the ladies and David were already seated. Mikhal Hadid was at the head of the conference table.

"You boys are late," said Maria. "We waited as long as we could."

"Sorry," said Jake. "We decided at the last minute that we needed a puma after the session today. Forgot to tell you guys."

"Good morning," said Dr. Hadid. "I hear you folks had an interesting session yesterday—particularly in the afternoon."

"Very interesting!" said Susan.

"And we continued it at Paddy's last night," said Maria.

"That's where it really *revved up*," said Jake.

Dr. Hadid waited for the comments to subside and said, "You will find our session today *very interesting*. We will talk about health, aging, and the miraculous strides medicine has made in the last few centuries."

He continued, "I would like to kick it off with a demonstration. I have asked a friend and colleague of mine, Edward Steiger, to join us for a demonstration." He spoke toward his watch, and the conference room doors opened. A tall man, about six four and dressed in a flight suit of sorts, strode in toward Dr. Hadid's chair. As he got closer to the table, it appeared that he was an older gentleman, perhaps in his eighties or so. His facial skin was wrinkled; and his hair, only on the sides of his head, was gray. His eyes looked old; but his torso appeared very solid, upright, and strong. Something looked incongruous about the man.

Dr. Hadid said, "Thank you for joining us, Edward. How old are you?"

Edward smiled and said in a rather odd-sounding voice, "Which answer do you want, Mikhal?"

Dr. Hadid laughed and said, "Both. When were you born?"

"I was born in 3238," said Mr. Steiger.

"Then that makes you 101 years old, correct?" said Hadid.

"That is how old my *head* is, Dr. Hadid. My *body is only thirty-one years old.*"

The crew members did not understand. *How could he be 101 years old and look that healthy? And what is he talking about that his body is only thirty-one years old?*

"Do you mind doing a little demonstration for us, Ed?"

"Not at all, doctor. I am quite proud of what I can do."

"Fine, Mr. Steiger. Please lift this table."

Mr. Steiger reached over and grasped the side of the conference table, which weighed at least four hundred pounds, and picked it up at arm's length above the laps of the *Revelation* crew. Before they could jump or move out of the way, Edward returned the table to its original position.

Dr. Hadid said, "Thank you, Mr. Steiger. Now if you would just do one other physical demonstration before you sit down and join our discussion. Please jump up and touch the ceiling. It is about twenty feet above you."

Edward crouched slightly and pushed off the floor with his legs, rising quickly to a spot very near the ceiling, touching it, and then returning to the floor—fairly gently. He then took a seat next to Dr. Hadid.

All of our Twenty First Century Six were stunned. First, the man *looked old in the face*. Maybe he *looked* over one hundred. But then he obviously had a very powerful body. Everyone except Dr. Hadid was confused.

"When Mr. Steiger was seventy years old, he gave up on his failing natural body and replaced it with a new one."

Our crew was overwhelmed! They were looking at a *full-body replacement*!

Dr. Hadid continued, "Edward's new body is totally man-made. There are no human body parts at all. It is 100 percent android. It is attached to the nerves coming from the cerebellum of the brain and takes all of its commands from his brain. The android body supplies the blood needed by his head and brain. The other way to look at him is that he is an android with a human brain."

Edward Steiger spoke, "By the time I was seventy, my original natural body was ravaged by cancer, osteoporosis, anemia, muscular dystrophy, and diabetes. I had lost parts of two limbs because of diabetes and had been given all the treatments that were available at that time. I had about two months to live and was offered the alternative of an android body by the Mayo Clinic in Orlando. They have done worlds of research and development with artificial limbs, artificial organs, and complete android torsos. They had never attempted a full-body replacement with a human though it had been successfully accomplished with animals."

He continued, "I thought, 'Well, *what the hell*, might as well give it a try!' That was thirty-one years ago. Mayo has really fought an uphill battle to keep my brain alive and working, and any day that I live now is of course a bonus day in a long and fruitful life."

"May I ask you a couple of questions, sir?" said Ellen.

"Of course, anything you like, my dear."

"Well, I am a physician, and I think I speak for the six of us when I say we could not be more amazed than we are at what you and science have apparently accomplished. My first question is, what does it *feel like* living in an android body?"

Steiger thought a minute and then said, "You cannot imagine how strange it was at first. My mind commanded any movement of my body that I wanted, but I had control problems. I had to look at the limb I was moving to be sure of what it was doing. I had no feedback of limb position. I would do things like reach for a glass of water and crush the glass! Balance was another problem. My mind would sense that I was leaning or falling, and I would try to correct but would overcorrect and go crashing toward the opposite side. Mayo Biolab discovered after a few days that my touch-sense circuit was not working properly. That was the reason I had no touch feedback. After that system was properly tuned, I did much better. The matter of balance and control just took practice. I was not accustomed to the strength of this body."

"Do you eat or drink, and do you sleep?" said Jake.

"I certainly sleep," said Edward, "probably more than I used to. My brain seems to work harder with this body than it did with the old one. As far as eating and drinking, the answer may surprise you. I enjoy both. Once I taste, chew, and swallow food, it goes into a disposal system much like the disposal in a sink. When the garbage container is full, I throw it into a real garbage system and insert another liner. It's quite simple really. My body does not need the food, but I enjoy eating it."

"What about the blood needed by your brain and head?" said Ellen.

"That system is separate from all the rest," said Edward. "The blood used by my brain is an artificial blood that supplies all the nutrients my head needs in order to live. From the neck up, except for the fact that the blood is a special fluid, I function just like I did with the natural body."

"I imagine that you have many more questions for Mr. Steiger, but we need to move on," said Dr. Hadid.

"Just one more, if I may," said Dante. "Are there any major *disadvantages* to living with an android body?"

"A couple," said Edward. "This body is too good! I used to enjoy playing golf when I was younger. Now when I hit the ball, it's always a near-perfect shot. I can drive the green every time on a par five 575-yard hole. And I usually make the putt."

"This is a problem?" said Jake.

"Nobody will play with me!" wailed Edward. "It's the same in every sport I try."

"I know someone that might take you on," said Jake. "In fact, you could get up a foursome. You and Mr. D. and Mr. B. and Mr. K."

Everyone got a good laugh out of that comment.

Dr. Hadid said, "OK, ladies and gentlemen, enough of this. We must move on." He addressed Mr. Steiger, "Thank you so much, Edward, for coming over from Orlando to help us out with our new friends from the twenty-first century. I hope to see you again soon."

Edward Steiger arose and said as he left the room, "Don't wait too long. My brain is getting very tired . . . Nice meeting all of you."

"All right—you have seen one of the great scientific advances of our time," said Dr. Hadid. "But we have much more to show you and to talk about."

"Most types of cancer are history and have been for many centuries. Edward mentioned his cancer before the transplant. He had one that we have not found a cure for yet. Science has developed cures for most other cancers and for most diseases that plagued the people of your century. Because of this progress, the average life span of individuals is now ninety-two instead of seventy-three as it was in 2025.

"Sometime in the twenty-fifth century, I believe it was, a cure was found for AIDS. Unfortunately we have not eliminated the occurrence of new infections, although now the majority of cases can be cured—at least upon the initial infection of the disease. Another medical breakthrough occurred in the twenty-seventh century. We discovered a drug that would clear up a common cold. Nowadays, as soon as a person feels a cold coming on, they pop a single orange pill. And the problem virus is history!

"With the progress in artificial limbs and artificial organs, the quality of older-age life is much improved. Many people are quite active up to and past one hundred nowadays. Edward Steiger just had more than his share of problems, and the treatment of those problems overtime had taken its toll on his natural body. As you heard him say, he has already lived thirty-one extra years with his new body. He would have probably been happier with a less powerful one—something like the bodies of the Mister Series Androids."

"I have a question, Dr. Hadid," said Ellen. "In 2025, diagnosis of human ailments was quite a challenge. There were many tests and many special devices used to examine the human body, depending on the specific symptoms a patient might have. There were x-rays, MRIs, CT scans, ultrasounds, colonoscopies, and many more specialized procedures used, depending on symptoms. Has there been any improvement in the field of diagnostics through the centuries?"

"Excellent point, Ellen," said Dr. Hadid. "Diagnosis of human ailments is extremely simple and fast. We have only one device today that is used for all diagnosis. It is called a TotalScan. In practice, it works similarly to the way MRIs or CT scans were performed centuries ago. Only with the TotalScan, no prep is needed, and you do not have to be inserted into a narrow tube. You walk into a booth, and in fifteen seconds, you walk out. The machine completely evaluates every part of your body and the functioning of every system of your body. The data is transcribed to disc and may be viewed by your physician on computer. Imaging is in 3-D, and the viewer can change the camera position to view a spot from all sides. The user can also zoom down to as detailed as individual cells. It is really quite amazing!"

"Unbelievable!" said Ellen.

"Now then," said Mikhal, "how about a fifteen-minute break? And we will move on to drugs, addiction, and drug trafficking. Be back, please, by ten fifteen."

The *Revelation* crew was living in a world of constant and continuous amazement. They hit the restrooms, dropped to the first floor, grabbed a roll and coffee, and headed for the deck overlooking the Atlantic. There was a pleasant cool breeze moving in off the surf. Seagulls were lazily doing their thing, occasionally diving from twenty or thirty feet into the surf and climbing out with a small fish. The group just leaned over the rail and soaked up the sunshine. *Not a bad place to be—and maybe not a bad time to be here*, thought Susan.

Maria broke the silence. "This view has been the same for thousands of years."

"And hopefully for thousands more," said Dante.

Nothing more was said for a couple of minutes, and then they heard a huge engine roar to their left. Climbing skyward was a sleek white spacecraft carrying a large external pod, accelerating very fast. In what seemed like only a moment, the ship had disappeared straight up.

"Makes me want to go somewhere," said Dante.

"Me too," said Jake. "Where do you suppose that bird was headed? Anybody hear of a launch today?"

No one responded. Everyone was quiet again.

Finally, David said, "We better go. Can't be late after *every* break."

The crew filed into the building and to the elevators.

Dr. Hadid was chatting with a well-groomed tall thin man when they entered the conference room and took their seats. Mikhal turned and said, "You're back on time! I shall make a note of that." He smiled as he said, "We have another guest for this next bit. He is Dr. Louis Nevelson, administrator of the centers for drug rehabilitation of the Department of Health and Human Services. I have asked him to tell you what goes on with drugs in the thirty-fourth century."

"Good morning to you of the twenty-first century!" said Dr. Nevelson. "I don't know how many shocking things you have heard about our life in the thirty-fourth century so far, but I can promise you that *my story* will certainly surprise you. And by the way, this is *really me* standing here. I was on my way back to Washington, having been visiting in Miami, when Dr. Hadid managed to contact me.

"Let's get this off on the right foot by telling you that *drugs are legal* in the United States—and in most other countries. I believe that it was in about the twenty-third century that our government finally decided to make drugs legal. Up to that point, the trafficking of drugs had become *the* major domestic crime in the country, resulting in the employment of some 255,000 enforcement officers nationwide at a cost of thirteen billion annually. It was estimated at that time that roughly nine million deaths were caused each year by the use of drugs and by the trafficking of drugs in the U.S. alone. Illegal drugs were the major export of some twelve countries by the year 2235.

"It appears that our government in the twenty-third century finally realized that as long as the customer base for illegal drugs kept growing at an increasing rate, as long as someone would grow the plants to make the drugs, and as long as traffickers would bring them from the farms to the marketplace, *the business would never fail*. No matter how many drug enforcement officers were assigned to the problem and no matter how much money was spent to try to control the problem, the business would continue to prosper. The main thing they finally realized was that the *illegality of drugs was the principal driver in the equation*.

"Many people in government and outside government had been saying exactly that for years, but the religious right and do-good organizations would never let Congress or the administration even sponsor a bill to legalize drugs.

"Anyhow, and I don't know how it happened, but in 2236, a bill was sponsored. And it was *passed*. After all the damage drugs had done, after all the cost in lives and the cost in dollars over the years, suddenly, one day—DRUGS WERE LEGAL!"

He paused, popped two pills, and continued, "And guess what happened? No, don't guess. I want to tell you. The price of drugs plummeted! The illegal traffickers went out of business, and *drug usage dropped*! That is correct. DRUG USAGE DROPPED. The same thing had happened in the 1920s with alcohol and prohibition. When alcohol was made legal again, alcohol *usage went down*. Why was everyone so surprised when the *same thing happened with drugs*?"

He continued, "Fast-forward today in the thirty-fourth century, drugs are stocked and sold like liquor. I'll bet you folks didn't think to ask for a joint at Paddy's Pub, did you? You could have gotten one—for less than you paid for your drink. You could have gotten *cocaine* at the same bar. That would have cost you *more* than the drink. But guess what? There is very little call for either pot or coke or crack anywhere. People had rather have a martini.

"Here is what has happened. People realized that they cannot control their minds after taking the powerful drugs. They realized that such drugs put them in a place they really don't want to be. They can take a drink or two without significant impairment to their thought processes and judgment. After dinner, the drinks have worn off, and their minds return to normal. But not with some of the powerful drugs. With those, you may be wasted for the night and into the next day. And people, of course, become hooked on some of the addictive drugs. They have no choice but to continue using them. Many users realized that when drugs became legal and cheap, it was *no big deal* to use them! Too easy—not exciting enough."

He paused and had a drink of water. The crew was engrossed in Dr. Nevelson's presentation.

"So here is what happened centuries ago. The public began to reject drugs and turn away from their use. The price of drugs began to drop and continued to drop. Now a farmer in Afghanistan can earn more off his land growing *corn* than he can producing *opium*!

"Unfortunately, there are still weak people who become addicts. My job is to operate government facilities dedicated to the recovery and rehabilitation of drug addicts. There are twenty six government-owned and operated clinics across the country. There are also private facilities that do the same thing and are funded by the government. These facilities are supported primarily from taxes from the legal sale of drugs, tobacco, and alcohol.

"The cost of all the treatment ongoing in the country is a small fraction on a per capita basis of the money the government was spending to fight illegal drugs, prosecute illegal drug cases, and incarcerate offenders in your century.

"I cannot tell you that hallucinatory drugs are going completely away. That will not happen—and weak people will continue to use them. But we can and do help these people. Further, because drugs are sold at drugstores and not by pushers, we have a fighting chance to help anyone recover that wants to kick his or her habit.

"Any questions?"

"Let me make sure I understand the situation as you have described it," said Dante. "You have put drugs in the category of tobacco and alcohol. As a result, drug pushing and trafficking has disappeared, the cost of drugs has dropped dramatically, and usage of drugs has decreased. Further, these three categories *are taxed* in order to pay for rehabilitation facilities and medical problems resulting from the use of these debilitating chemicals."

"And don't forget the elimination of all the costs associated with dealing with illegal drugs," said Dr. Nevelson.

Dr. Hadid stood and said, "We believe that the situation we now have in the United States—with respect to tobacco, alcohol, and drugs—is as good as we possibly can make it and better than it ever was in past centuries. Trend tracking is showing that the use per capita of tobacco and drugs continues to decline while alcohol remains steady."

Hadid continued, "Any more questions for Dr. Nevelson?"

"I have one," said Ellen. "Have there been any breakthroughs in beneficial drugs which counteract or act as antidotes to the powerful hallucinatory drugs?"

"Yes," said Dr. Nevelson. "These are used primarily in our rehab facilities under careful control and supervision, however, and have not been made available to the general public. The reason is that the antidotes themselves are *very powerful* and can be harmful if misused. If we put them on the open market, people would try to drug up with their favorite hallucinatory drug, thinking they would simply be able to take an antidotal drug to cancel the original drug and clear their mind. It just doesn't work that way."

Hearing no more questions, Dr. Hadid thanked Dr. Nevelson and excused him from the session.

"Well," said Dr. Hadid, "we seem to be right on schedule. We'll break for lunch now. Please be back by one o'clock. We have a very interesting session for this afternoon. Our guest speakers will tell you the story of how the Earth's environment has been cleaned up. I don't want to give away too much now, but the waters and the atmosphere have been returned to the quality of the eighteenth century—just before the industrial revolution began. See you at one."

23

The *Revelation* crew was back early from lunch, seated and ready to go when Dr. Hadid entered the conference room.

"Well," said Hadid, "can I interpret your early return as a sign of enthusiasm?"

"Absolutely!" said Maria without hesitation. "One of our primary concerns in the twenty-first century was the abuse the waters of the world and the atmosphere had taken from emissions and industrial wastes. I personally find it incredible that you claim that the seas, streams, and oceans along with the atmosphere are all back to the pureness of the eighteenth century."

"We certainly want to hear how that was accomplished," said David.

The main conference room door opened, and two people entered, a young man and a young woman. "Ah," said Dr. Hadid, "you made it. Have a good flight?"

The man said, "Well, it was certainly different. We realized that we were not going to make the scheduled flight that would get us here on time, and Connie volunteered to drive her new PMU-052."

"Most impressive," said Dr. Hadid. "Let me introduce you both to our astronauts from the twenty-first century, and then we want to hear all about your trip. Ladies and gentlemen, we have with us this afternoon Mr. Harold Barker, assistant director of the Environmental Protection Agency, and Ms. Connie Warner, section chief, EPA. Harold and Connie, I would like you to meet the crew of the *Revelation* mission: Dante Washington, Susan Chen, Maria Rodriguez, Jake Loneghan, David Marks, and Ellen Marks."

Dr. Hadid continued, "Please tell us about your trip in your new PMU-052!"

Connie proudly took the ball. "I just took delivery of this beautiful machine last week and have really only driven it around Washington until today. I haven't had an opportunity to let it stretch its legs. Just a couple of specs on the vehicle: It has a top speed of 550 mph and can cruise at four thousand feet, or flight level A4. It accels from a standing start to 500 mph in 3.8 seconds! Today, we came down from Washington in an hour and thirty six minutes.

By this time, Dante's, David's, and Jake's tongues were hanging out. Jake said, "Please don't tease us like that. You can't be serious about the speed of these pumas!"

Connie laughed, and Harold backed her up. "She is dead serious. The max acceleration of the PMU-052 is 6 gs! Talk about hot!"

Susan got into the conversation with, "What color did you select?"

"Hot pink," said Connie. "You must see it!"

"Ahem," said Dr. Hadid. "Excuse me, but can we move on to our discussion of the environment? When we finish our business here, we can all go down and look at Connie's new vehicle. Harold, why don't you get us back on track? I must warn you, however, that I have made the *brash claim* that we have returned the Earth's environment back to the *eighteenth-century pureness.*"

"In many ways, we have done exactly that," said Harold. "Most of the waters of the world are now as pure as the waters of the eighteenth century were as is the air we breathe. However, we haven't replaced all the timberland in this country and others, and we haven't been able to yet restore the rain forests of the world. Landfills still exist from centuries of dumping. We are still working on many problem areas that suffer from our industrial world."

Connie commented, "We *can* share with you, however, the things we have done, not just in this century but before, to make *many significant gains* with the environment."

"Let's start by talking about what was causing the environmental problems in the twenty-first century and before," said Harold. "One of the biggest offenders was the burning of fossil fuels and the resultant emissions released to the atmosphere. Another was the dumping of industrial wastes from manufacturing, not just in the United States, but all over the world. Also, by the twenty-first century, as you folks know, consumers just kept buying and buying items for themselves and for their homes and throwing away the old stuff. No one repaired things anymore. It was cheaper to just throw away a broken or worn-out item and buy a replacement. Some recycling was attempted, but not on the scale of the volume of discarded items."

He continued, "Let me just summarize in one paragraph the major things we have done to completely change the direction of the world's environment. Whereas in the twenty-first century and several centuries after, the trend was negative, by the actions I will list for you now, we managed to reverse the negative trend until we reached the level where we are today. The atmosphere is almost pristine, the ozone layer has been restored, and the waters are almost as pure as eighteenth-century waters.

"First, we have practically eliminated the burning of fossil fuel. Almost all power today is generated through use of nuclear energy, electrical energy, fuel cell engines, solar power, and wind power. Fixed installations requiring power use all the above sources, and mobile applications use nuclear and electrical. Secondly, we allow no release of detrimental chemicals to the atmosphere by industrial facilities. Emissions are treated and chemically changed to become oxygen, nitrogen, or inert gases before they reach the atmosphere. Thirdly, and this will probably surprise you the most, all wastes that are not biodegradable are totally incinerated in a way that has zero effect on our environment.

"The bulk of such wastes are deposited in waste-disposal shafts *that extend deep into the Earth's core* and are incinerated by the intense heat and pressure of the Earth. Certain hazardous materials that cannot be deposited into the Earth are *shipped directly into the sun* where they are reduced to vapor."

"Hold it!" said David. "Please stop right there! How can such be undertaken at reasonable costs? There is no way!"

"I will tell you how, and we will show you the facilities and the equipment that accomplishes the task," said Mr. Barker. He looked at Dr. Hadid.

"Harold is telling you the truth," said Dr. Hadid. "Two-million-pound waste canisters are launched from here regularly on direct shots to the sun, one of the largest incinerators in the universe! The booster launchers are automatically controlled and reusable."

Harold continued, "The only cost of each launch is a relatively low-cost canister, and the nuclear fuel, which today is relatively cheap. You remember that $E=mc^2$? Over twelve centuries ago, we discovered an inexpensive way to extract the full energy in an atom in a way that produces high-potential fuel. *Any* matter can be turned into fuel for all sorts of applications—from the PMUs you are driving to antigravity paks people use to fly about, to these colossal boosters for the waste canisters."

Dante said, "Wait, please, before you go on." He looked at each of his fellow crew members. "I don't know about you guys, but I need a minute to think—I am maxed out!"

"Me too," said Jake. "There has to be significant cost to transport the nation's hazardous wastes to this launch point."

"This is true, but really little more cost than in the past when such wastes required special methods of disposal. Today, the wastes are shipped from all over the country. But we are a little ahead of ourselves. The bulk of the nation's wastes are dumped into the Earth as they are around the world. All major cities and most cities over one hundred thousand population have the waste *shafts into the Earth.* Only the *hazardous* wastes are shipped here—by trains, ships, and trucks in reusable containers. The containers are dumped into the launch canisters, which are ram-packed to ensure maximum density. When a canister is ready for disposal, it is queued waiting for the next available booster. The launch process is similar to the shuttle launches of your century. The difference being that our SWDS boosters reach *escape velocity* before releasing the canister shot. After the canister is on its way to the sun, the launch booster reverses thrust to reenter the atmosphere and return to base."

"And the launch process is all automatic—no pilots?" said Susan.

"Initially, many years ago, we used shuttle pilots. But the pilots considered the job so degrading—a real stinker, if you'll pardon the expression—and we had to pay them very high salaries to do the work. When we were able to make the flights fully automatic with remote control monitoring, we saved a lot of expense."

"I have a question," said Maria. "Why transport all the wastes to here? Why not have launch facilities at other locations in the country?"

"Excellent question, Maria," said Harold. "Connie, why don't you take that one?"

"Sure," said Connie. "We *do* have launches from three other launch locations across the country, but this facility is the most efficient and least expensive to operate. You may all be aware of why Canaveral was selected in the twentieth century as the best location for space launches. But in case you are not, I will refresh you on that point.

"NASA wanted a base as far south as possible to take advantage of the Earth's rotation, from west to east. All launches to orbit and to space were made to the east, which gave the rocket booster a free nine hundred miles per hour. Just sitting on the launchpad, a booster has the same speed as the surface of the Earth in an easterly direction. The surface rotation speed is just over a thousand miles per hour at the equator and about 900 mph here at the space center. In addition, NASA wanted the launches to be over the ocean so that non-reusable booster rockets could fall into the ocean."

Connie continued, "Today, with the power our boosters and ships have, the free 900 mph is not so important. However, billions of dollars, and now credits, have been put into this facility through the centuries to make it the unparalleled space center of the globe. Studies were conducted when the Solar Waste Disposal System was conceived and initiated to determine the cost effectiveness of building other launch facilities across the country. Initially, the volume did not justify the cost of building other facilities. Later, that changed, and the additional three facilities were built—one in Texas, one in California, and one in Minnesota. Launching wastes into the sun is not as expensive as you might think."

"You are overlooking a factor, Connie," said Dr. Hadid.

"What is that, sir?" Both she and Harold looked at Mikhal quizzically.

"Today, the same trucks and trains that bring wastes here and to the other launch points for disposal use the same containers to take valuable minerals mined from the moon and Mars back to their shipping origination point and to other points," said Dr. Hadid.

"I was not aware of that," said Harold.

"Nor was I," said Connie. "When did that start?"

"Fairly recently,' said Dr. Hadid. "A young scientist in our Mars studies lab came up with the idea."

Jake said, "Well, that makes the waste disposal a backhaul in a sense since I would suspect that the mineral shipping is quite lucrative."

"I can't quote you the economics of the overall arrangement, but everyone seems happy about it." said Dr. Hadid. "After we finish with your indoctrination series, perhaps you would all like to tour our facility where wastes are launched to the sun and mined minerals are returned from space. I'll set that up for you."

"That will be very interesting." said David. The others enthusiastically agreed.

"I have a question," said Ellen, "if we are ready to move on."

"Well, let's see," said Harold. "Is everyone clear on what we've done for the air and how we handle waste disposal?"

No one had a comment, and Dr. Hadid nodded to Ellen as if to say "Go ahead."

"What about sewage disposal and other dumping of contaminating materials into the lakes, streams, rivers, and oceans?" said Ellen.

"Sewage plants reconstitute wastes into chemicals that are naturally absorbed into the waters," said Harold. The process is similar to the treatment of emissions to the atmosphere. All by-products of this process, as with the treatment of gaseous emissions, are treated as undesirable wastes and either dumped into the Earth or shipped to this space center and other launch points for incineration by the sun."

Maria spoke, "I am overwhelmed with what we have been told here today. I can see how the people of the United States have cleaned up their 'house.' But let me ask this, what about what we once called third world countries? They do not have the wherewithal or probably the incentive to do what you have described, do they?"

"There is no one answer to that question, Miss Rodriguez," said Harold. "The larger, more industrialized nations, as you may suspect, have used our technology and followed our lead. However, there are still many poor smaller countries that continue to live with old unsatisfactory methods of waste disposal. Some of these use nuclear incinerators which do a fair job of treating their emissions before they are released to the atmosphere."

"In addition to the SWD sites in the U.S., China has launch facilities, as do Japan, Russia, Europe, the Middle East, and Australia. Those facilities use similar SWD systems."

"Another of Maria's concerns from the twenty-first century was the depletion of animal life, both on land and in the sea," said Dr. Hadid. "She stated that many species were nearing extinction because of the actions of man, both inadvertent and intentional. Could you speak to those concerns?"

"Absolutely," said Connie, glancing at Harold. "Let me address this one, Harold. The cleanup of the environment—the air, the lands, and the seas—has, in and of itself, reversed the trend in loss of wildlife. As to the killing of certain species by man for sport and for profit, strict laws are being enforced, almost worldwide, to control that problem. At the present time, there are no living animal species in danger of extinction—that is, none because of the actions of man."

Dr. Hadid stood and spoke, "I think we have done a good job of briefing you on what we are doing for the environment. My thanks to you, Mr. Barker, and you, Ms. Warner, for taking the time to join us."

"Can we see your new PMU-052 before you fire outta here?" said Jake.

"Yeah!" said Dante and David almost simultaneously.

"It's early, but we have had a very productive session," said Dr. Hadid. "The only thing we have left on our planned indoctrination program is a question-and-answer session tomorrow morning. Director Stoll will lead that, and all of those on the GSA staff that have met with you will be in attendance. I think we can just stop for today. I would like to see that new PMU also, Connie."

With that statement, all arose, and most proceeded to the conference room door. Dante hung back and asked Dr. Hadid if he could stay back a moment for a brief discussion. The others left and proceeded to the garage level.

Dr. Hadid said, "What can I do for you, colonel?"

"We are planning to go to Orlando this evening . . . As a matter of fact, now that we have finished early, we may want to go on in so we can see what thirty-fourth-century Orlando looks like in daylight."

"Great idea. How can I help you?"

"Well, Jake and I had the thought that maybe one of the androids might act as a guide for us since we don't know our way around."

"That is an excellent idea!" said Dr. Hadid. "Let me make a quick call."

Mikhal used his mec and talked to someone. He turned to Dante and said, "Mr. K. will be available. How would you like for him to take a van from the motor pool, drive you in, and be your guide?"

"That would be excellent!" said Dante. "I think we will leave shortly." Looking at his watch, Dante said, "It's about three PM now. I think the group can be ready to leave by four."

Dr. Hadid again spoke into his mec. He turned and said to Dante, "It's all set. Mr. K. will be waiting for you at the parking level of the BPQ at 4:00 sharp."

Dr. Hadid and Dante took the next elevator car and caught up with the group. They were admiring Connie's new puma.

"Whoa!" said Dante when he saw it. "That *is* hot!"

Connie's PMU was indeed hot pink, and the shade seemed to vary as you looked at the vehicle from different angles. The shape of the puma was similar to a 2025 Corvette; but of course, you couldn't see through the windows into the inside, and no headlights were visible. Connie opened the top-hinged cockpit door so everyone could view the seats and instrument panel. The ladies were in rapture over the gorgeous interior while the men kept walking around it and admiring the powerful lines that clearly reassured an observer of the vehicle's immense speed and power.

"I wish we had time to give you all a spin," said Connie. "But I am due back in DC ASAP. I was just notified of a special meeting as soon as we can get back."

"That's just not fair," chided Maria. "I want a ride!"

"I am sorry, Maria," said Connie. "But I promise you a real tour in it when you get to Washington. I hear they are planning a big dig for the six of you!"

"I will hold you to your promise," said Maria.

Connie said, "Gotta go!" as she slipped into the driver's seat. Harold scrambled to get in the passenger's side as Connie revved the engine. All the group stepped back as the 052 lifted off the pavement, retracted its wheels, and turned to a northerly direction. Connie, determined to impress, showered down on the gas. The vehicle leaped into the air with 6 g acceleration and climbed at about a forty-five-degree angle doing a slow roll on the way up.

"Show-off!" said Susan. "I *must have one of those*." The others were too much in awe to speak.

Finally, Dante said, "Dr. Hadid has made a special arrangement tonight for us. Mr. K. is picking us up at four PM in the garage and will function as our chauffeur and guide for an evening in Orlando. I hope everyone wants to go? Jake and I had planned to go in even if no one else wanted to. What do you guys think?"

David looked at Ellen who nodded. David said, "Count us in!"

"I'm in!" said Susan.

"You are not leaving me here!" growled Maria.

24

Mr. K. was in the parking basement talking with Mr. D. when David and Ellen arrived. They walked over to the two androids and greeted them.

"Hi, Mr. D. and Mr. K.," said Ellen, "how are you this afternoon?"

The two androids responded almost in unison and in exactly the same tone of voice. "Good afternoon, Mr. and Mrs. Marks."

"Please don't think me presumptuous," said David, "but how do the two of you know which is which? I certainly can't tell!"

The two androids looked at each other, and Mr. K. turned to David and Ellen and said, "It is easy for us. Each android in the Mister Series emits a unique signal on a special frequency. Only the androids in the Mister Series can receive the signal. For example, when I turn the corner and see Mr. D. approaching, my positronic brain immediately knows that it is Mr. D. I am seeing. The reverse is true for him."

As the four were talking, Jake and Dante walked up and were listening.

"Fine," said Ellen, "but how do humans tell you two apart?"

"Ah yes," said Mr. D. "I guess that might be a problem for you. The only sure way to distinguish us is by our serial numbers at the rear base of our necks. Here, have a look." Both the androids turned, facing away from the now four astronauts so the group could see the nape of their necks.

Dante was reading one and said, "D236." David read Mr. K.'s, which read K147.

Maria and Susan had just arrived and caught the tail end of the activity.

Maria said, "Are you inspecting to see if Mr. D. and Mr. K. washed the back of their necks?"

Everyone laughed, and Jake explained the situation to Maria and Susan.

"This seems quite awkward to me," said David. "Suppose I am walking down the street, and I am meeting an android, but I can't tell who it is. You all look exactly alike. The droid approaching me might be either of my friends D or K or might be a complete stranger. How am I to know?"

"It does not matter, sir. We are all the same," said Mr. D. "What I mean, sir, is that no matter which of us it is that you see, we will all respond the same to you and will interact the same with you. For example, in the situation you describe, you might say 'Good morning' or 'Good morning, mister' or say nothing at all. If you choose to utter a greeting, then the droid will respond, 'Good morning, sir.' If you ask him a question, he will answer. If you ask the mister to undertake a task, he will do so, so long as the task is not illegal and within his capability.

"It is similar to the relationship you might have with a parking meter or a vending machine," said Mr. K. "You don't really need to know the name or serial number of a parking meter."

That did it. The crew members all looked at one another with a strange expression. A light had suddenly come on. They had been treating and thinking of these androids as people. They were really only very sophisticated *machines.*

Dante said, "Ooookay! Why don't we launch for Orlando?"

"Great idea," said Jake as he opened the van door. Everyone piled in, and Mr. K. took the driver's seat. Dante took the front right seat next to Mr. K.

When all were safely strapped in, Mr. K. said, "Would someone give me some general instructions as to where you want to go and what you want to do in Orlando?"

Jake took the ball and said, "OK. We would first like to see the city—that is, kind of a tour through and around the heart of the city just to get a feel for it. Then since we have a lot of time, I'm sure the ladies would like to see some of the nice shopping malls. Right, ladies?"

"You are doing fine so far, Jake. Keep going," said Susan.

Jake continued, "Then select a nice restaurant for us."

"After that," added Dante, "we will probably like to see a nice club for some entertainment and dancing. Is everyone OK with the plan?"

Maria started the applause, and the others joined in.

"Fine plan," said David. "Do you have any questions, Mr. K.?"

"Actually," said the droid, "I am Mr. D.— Mr. K. had to return to the headquarters building—Director Stoll needed him tonight. I understand your plans and have no problem with them."

The group was *stunned.* After all the conversation about which droid is which droid, they really couldn't tell! Jake leaned up and looked at the nape of the android's neck. He read D236. He gave the thumbs-up to the others.

Mr. D. drove the van smoothly out of the basement garage and onto the street, leading to the main gate. The guard waved them by, and Mr. D. accelerated—thirty, forty, fifty, eighty. Mr. D. pulled back gently on the steering column, and the van began a climb at about a thirty-degree angle. The vehicle continued to accelerate, heading in a westerly direction, and continued to climb, finally leveling off.

In only a few moments, it seemed, the skyline of a city was appearing in the distance. The city didn't look anything like the Orlando the crew remembered, though. This city looked more like New York, with many tall but cylindrically shaped buildings. The buildings looked like giant paper towel spools with a series of discs placed on the spools at intervals from the ground to the top level.

The city stretched for miles in every direction with the outlying areas displaying less tall buildings than the central city. There did not seem to be any freeways or elevated roadways. As the van drew nearer to the city, it became obvious that the sky was filled with vehicles. They all seemed to be moving in lines and patterns as if on freeways in the sky, but there were no roads.

Dante said to Mr. D., "What am I seeing? It looks like streams of vehicles following one another as if on highways, but there are no highways."

"That is correct, sir," said Mr. D. "You will note that there is almost no surface traffic. The vehicles in the air are all under their own power but are locked-in to a traffic grid system that they must follow. There are no highways, but there are skyways. Look at our display screen here."

Dante looked, and there was now a display screen in the middle of the control panel where there was none before. The screen presented electronically, images of skyways and on—and off-ramps. Vehicles appeared as small oblong blips, and the blip representing the van they were riding in was in the center of the screen in yellow. The other blips were orange.

Mr. D. explained, "We cannot leave the electronic skyway we are coming in on until we reach an off-ramp. I am planning to take off-ramp E102, which will allow me to enter perimeter route P14 and will allow us to circle the city at our leisure so you all can get good views of Orlando. I will point out some places of interest as they come into view."

The crew members were all catching flies with mouths wide open. PMUs were everywhere. It looked like bees swarming in groups. It seemed amazing that vehicles didn't crash into one another—but they didn't.

David managed to speak, "What about speed? I don't see any cars passing each other. Are you controlling the speed now?"

"Speed on each skyway is set. Each city has a Master Traffic Control Center, or MATRAC, that totally controls all sky traffic in and around the city. We came from Canaveral to Orlando on an airway. All cities are connected to each other by airways, and there are various levels of airways all the way out to two hundred miles above the Earth's surface. PMUs are restricted to the airways at five thousand feet and below. Above five thousand feet, the airways are numbered S1 through S200 and reserved for private and commercial aircraft and military aircraft. To travel between cities by PMU, you select the airway you will travel, A0 through A4 based on the speed you plan to fly. For example, if your PMU only has 200 mph capability, as this one does, you will fly at airway level A0, as we did coming over from Canaveral. Now that we are in the MATRAC control jurisdiction, I have no control over speed, only our direction. When we change skyways, the speed of our van will be automatically adjusted to match the speed of the skyway. There is never a problem with hot-rodders trying to pass, and the speed of PMUs merging into traffic is perfectly matched to skyway speed."

"What about surface traffic in the city?" said Susan. "Can a driver control direction and speed on the surface streets?"

"Yes," said Mr. D., "surface traffic is very similar to what I imagine you remember from the twenty-first century. But people don't use surface streets very much. You see the large discs at vertical levels of the cylindrical buildings?" Not waiting for an answer, he continued, "Those are parking platforms. Look, you can see the pumas on each level. Generally, people arrive and park their pumas on the level that they are planning to enter the building on—the level where the place of business they seek is located. In general, a structure such as that one over there"—Mr. D. pointed—"is a multipurpose building. The lower floors are usually entertainment or restaurants, and the next several floors are retail stores of various types. Then the next few levels are offices and professional establishments. Further up can be condominiums or apartments—see, the decks on those levels there allow parking but are also private yards and gardens. The top levels are usually higher-priced office space and more restaurants."

"Why don't we just check out one of the buildings with several shopping levels?" said Ellen.

"I'm for that!" said Susan.

Mr. D. exited the circular route he had been following for the last few minutes and swerved toward a deck with several available parking spaces. He carefully set down the van and turned off the engine. As the crew began exiting the van, Mr. D. warned them, "Be careful of the edge of the ramp. There are no restraining devices—only the thirty-inch walls we cleared with the van as we entered. As you near the edge, you will hear a warning tone reminding you that you are too close, but nothing will keep you from falling over the wall."

On that note, everyone was very careful to move away from the edge of the parking platform.

"Do you have a number of deaths from people falling off the edges?" said Dante.

"Surprisingly, no," said Mr. D. "The lower levels are fitted with safety nets, which automatically extend as required when the warning system detects that a person has fallen. If you look at the design of the walls, you can see that it is very difficult to accidentally fall over the walls. A person would have to deliberately climb over it or jump."

They were all walking toward the buildings outer wall and onto the walkway that took pedestrians to the entry doors and to elevators that ran up and down the length of the building.

"You mean to say that if I jumped off this level into the air, a net would extend some floors below and catch me?" said Jake.

"That's the design," said Mr. D. "I have never witnessed it in operation, however."

Jake said to Mr. D., "How would you like to demonstrate the function of the nets, Mr. D.?"

The others were shocked at Jake's suggestion though they assumed he was only kidding.

Mr. D. turned and looked at Jake and said, "If you instruct me to jump over the wall, I will do so. But I must remind you of several consequences if I do that. Firstly, if the net fails to catch me and I am damaged, then you will have to pay for my repair or replacement. I am quite expensive. Secondly, there will be no one readily available to show you around town or to drive you back to the spaceflight center."

"On second thought," said Jake, "just forget it. I haven't yet learned how to kid around with an android—but I am working on it."

They all got a good laugh out of the exchange as they entered the door to the level and proceeded down a corridor to the main pedestrian walkway. As they left the corridor and walked out into the interior of the building, it was again like being outside. The central core of the building was open—from the ground level to the top of the building. A railing protected shoppers from falling into the interior open shaft.

They all walked up to the railing and looked down and up. It appeared to be about fifty yards across the open core to the opposite railing on the other side.

"Look!" said Dante. "Those people are *flying*!"

Above and below the group were individuals with backpacks hovering and talking to one another, flying across, flying up, and flying down through the open center shaft.

"Ah yes," said Mr. D. "Has no one briefed you about *hoverpaks*? Those are small individual antigravity units that can lift a person weighing 350 pounds or less. Many people use them while shopping. It makes movement between stores so much faster and easier."

"How high can a person fly with hoverpaks?" asked Dante.

"I believe the flight ceiling is just higher than our tallest buildings, but I am not sure of the exact limitation," responded Mr. D.

"Let's go into one of the best department stores," said Maria. "I would like to look at those sharp-looking jumpsuits almost everyone is wearing."

"Those are called daysuits and are made of thermofab material," said Mr. D. "They are very comfortable and lightweight. You can set your comfort zone temperature on the suit, and it will maintain the desired temperature regardless of the outside air temperature."

"It looks like they come in a wide variety of colors," said Susan.

"Almost unlimited colors," said Mr. D. "I will take you into Berringher's, one of the finest clothiers in the nation today."

An hour later, no one would have recognized the Twenty First Century Six in their new outfits. For about two hundred credits each, they all slipped into nice, comfortable lightweight suits and looked exactly like thirty-fourth century people about town. Mr. D. continued to show them the various shops—all of which had new and exciting products to offer. Finally, everyone became somewhat burned out with looking. Except for the suits, only a few purchases had been made, and everyone was thirsty and hungry.

"Where is a good place for dinner, Mr. D.?" said Jake. "I think we are ready."

"There are several in this building," responded Mr. D. "In fact, a very popular but rather expensive one is at the very top of this structure on the thirty-eighth floor. It is called The Ultimate. Would you like to try it?"

"Well," said David, "we have to start somewhere. How about it, guys?" All agreed and followed Mr. D. to the nearest elevator. As it was in the GSA headquarters building, the elevator ride was almost instantaneous from door closure to door opening on the thirty-eighth floor.

"Wow," said Ellen, "quite a lift!"

They stepped out into a magnificently appointed dining facility. The roof was a clear dome over the entire top of the building. The restaurant was a circle about seventy-five yards in diameter. It just happened that they had arrived at dusk, and from the restaurant, 360 degrees of the city was in view. The lights were coming on in all the other parts of the city, and the sunset was magnificent.

Several service people were at the maitre d' station, smiling and welcoming the group of seven.

A tall member of the restaurant staff, wearing epaulets obviously denoting rank, stepped forward and said, "Good evening, ladies and gentlemen. Welcome to The Ultimate. Do you have a reservation?"

"I am afraid not," said Jake. "This is our first visit to Orlando and to this restaurant. Will you be able to accommodate us?" In the twenty-first century, Jake would have greased the palm of the maitre d' with at least a fifty, but he wasn't sure how to offer *credits* to obtain favorable treatment.

"I am sure we can accommodate you, sir. What type of food interests you this evening?"

"We have a wide variety of tastes," said Dante. "Are all cuisines offered in all parts of your restaurant?"

"Only in the Global Gourmet section, sir. Perhaps a quick tour of our facility is in order?"

"Only after we all have a cocktail in hand," said Jake.

"Good idea," voiced Maria.

A waitress immediately appeared as if by magic and took orders from each of the group. She immediately disappeared.

"She will find us. Why don't we go on our way?" said the maitre d'.

The restaurant was arranged around the outside of the room by countries/ cuisine—Japanese, Italian, Mexican, French, Middle Eastern, Australian, etc.—with most regions of the nation and of the world being represented. The menus were each printed in more than one language—English plus languages typical of those regions of the globe. Each section was appointed in keeping with the region of the nation or the world represented.

The group had made only a few steps before the waitress returned with the round of drinks. The maitre d' said, "Your first libation in The Ultimate is on me!"

The group was impressed, and all expressed their thanks.

Having pretty much completed the circle of the regions of the world, everyone agreed that they would like to dine in the center section of the room, the Global Gourmet, so that they might have the maximum variety of choices.

Although Mr. D. advised the maitre d' of his status and the fact that he did not eat, they were all seated at a table for eight, just off the center of the middle section. Jake suggested it, and they all readily agreed to order cuisine from around the world and share the dishes in order to enhance their experience in this impressive facility. Jake selected wines to complement the meals.

The service and the food were impeccable. All shared, and not everyone liked everything, but all agreed that it was a magnificent dining experience. Mr. D., while not eating, kept the conversation interesting by relating more information about life in the thirty-fourth century. The meal was complete, and no one wanted dessert, but all opted for cappuccino. While the waiter left to fill the order, the ladies decided to powder their noses, departing for the ladies' lounge area.

The men chatted while the ladies were absent. Just as they returned to the table, the waiter was arriving with the orders of cappuccino. He served all but Mr. D.

"Well! Mr. D.," said Jake, "do you have any suggestions for a nice club with some good music?"

"I'm having a bit of a problem with the words *nice* and *good*, sir," said the android. The group got a chuckle from that comment.

Ellen commented, "I think I see what he means. Androids think in absolute terms, and the words *nice* and *good* are highly subjective."

"Perhaps we can be more descriptive and specific, Mr. D.," said Dante. "A *nice* club would be clean, popular, and not too crowded. The clientele would be upper-middle class, well behaved, and sophisticated. The club will have a small group of musicians, expertly rendering popular music of this day and age." Dante turned to the others for approval and said, "Will this definition work OK for you guys?"

As the others were nodding and smiling, Jake said, "Excellent starting point, Dante! If we find it's too stiff or too loud, we can amend our definition so Mr. D. can steer us somewhere else."

Everyone was in a good mood and quite agreeable as Mr. D. said, "I have just the place that might interest all of you. Shall we try it?"

"By all means!" said David as all were rising to leave the table.

Mr. D. led the way out of the restaurant and toward the elevators as Ellen said, "What is the name of the place you have selected, Mr. D.?"

"The Inferno," said Mr. D. with the same expression he always wore.

25

Morning came, it seemed, much earlier than it had during any of the previous days of their indoctrination. Mr. D. was scheduled to meet the group in the basement garage at eight forty-five for the short run over to the headquarters building. Dante and Jake were the first to rise as usual. They were out on the deck of the cafeteria, sipping coffee and admiring the view of a gorgeous ocean and sky—almost perfect in subtle variations of blue, blue green, and white.

David and Ellen were leading the way with their trays, followed sluggishly by Maria and Susan, neither of whom seemed to be quite awake yet.

"Aha!" said Ellen, looking at Dante and Jake. "We have found Fred Astaire and Gene Kelly! Apparently, they are none the worse for wear!"

"We had no idea," said Susan, "that you gentlemen are such accomplished dancers!" This chatter, of course, embarrassed both Jake and Dante. Neither really recalled just how *accomplished* they had appeared the night before.

But Jake was always fast on the comeback. "We were just discussing the events of last evening, ladies. And our memories tell us that *you girls* were leading the charge, and we three guys were struggling to keep afloat."

This brought very large laughs from all three ladies, which is exactly what Jake had hoped for.

At this moment, Mr. D. stuck his head out the patio door and reminded the group, "I am waiting for you with the van—it's eight thirty-eight now."

The late arrivers gulped down their fare with the aid of coffee, and the group headed into the building behind Mr. Daugherty.

Thanks to Mr. D., they made it on time to the conference room—in fact, they were three minutes early. As the *Revelation* crew entered the conference room, everyone arose and applauded. At the end of the table was Director Stoll, and standing at his sides were the principals that had assisted the crew in their indoctrination sessions. Dr. Hadid, Dr. Ottinger, Mr. Coulson, Mr. Lightman, and Mr. Kapsten (Mr. K).

Dante, Susan, Jake, Ellen, and David took side seats; and Maria took the seat at the end opposite Director Stoll.

Director Stoll stood to open the session. "I would like to introduce to everyone two people whom you may not know." He pointed toward the end of the room where a man and a woman were seated. None of the *Revelation* crew had noticed them.

"Please meet Everett Thomson and Ashley DeBussey, two members of our GSA staff. They are here today for a special award ceremony. I chose this particular meeting because the awards they are about to receive relate to the training and indoctrination sessions all of you from the twenty-first century have just completed. Ashley and Everett, please come forward to the end of the table here."

Everyone except Director Stoll was still in the dark. What could these awards be that related to the indoctrination sessions? Director Stoll caused an image to be presented on the large screen behind his chair at the end of the table. The image was a list. It read the following:

The Twelve Significant Changes

21st Century to the 34th Century

1. Development of magna-laser weapons and enemy-weapon-detection units.
2. Establishment and construction of the Global Conflict Control umbrella.
3. Redistribution of wealth to eliminate the poor and the ultra rich.
4. Low-cost production of nuclear fuel for stationary and mobile applications.
5. Creation of universal health care and development of bio-advanced medicine.
6. Population control and family-size control.
7. Invention and utilization of the Truth Validation Unit.
8. Recognition of those Unfit for Society and implementation of UFS control.
9. Hardening of the justice and prison systems.
10. Cleanup of the environment and elimination of sources of contamination.
11. Legalization of drugs and establishment of care centers for the addicted.
12. Reduction of the costs and wastes of government at all levels.

"I am happy to announce," said Director Stoll, "that Ashley and Everett are the winners of our two prizes we offered. You will recall that the prizes were for the staffers that could name, most accurately, those twelve actions and/or inventions that have changed the twenty-first-century culture of Earth into our thirty-fourth-century culture. Ashley is a senior scientist in our Earth sciences lab, and Everett is a mission control specialist in Mission Control.

"I am pleased to award Ashley a credit voucher for fifteen thousand credits for first prize." He handed her the voucher. "She scored 98% on her paper addressing the twelve items. Congratulations, Ashley!" Director Stoll shook hands with Ashley and led an applause for her.

"And now I am pleased to award Everett a credit voucher for ten thousand credits. Everett scored 93% on his paper." Director Stoll shook hands with Everett and led a brief applause for him.

"Everett and Ashley, you are invited to stay for the remainder of our last session this morning, if you would like, and join us for lunch also." Ashley and Everett took their seats.

"Now let us turn our attention to our new citizens who have joined us from the twenty-first century," said Klaus. "We at GSA have all been quite pleased at the progress the six of you have made in the sessions we prepared for you. You probably realize that we have never conducted an orientation or indoctrination session of this type because we have never known any people from thirteen centuries apart from our society. Initially, in your stay with us, the administration—the president—didn't really know what to expect from you and ordered a surveillance team to watch you around the clock. This was just a precaution, and I hope it didn't offend you, but you were indeed 'aliens from space' as far as we of the thirty-fourth century were concerned. Just yesterday, that team was called off. We have come to know you and to trust you."

The director continued, "We believe that you have not only learned a lot about how things are done in the thirty-fourth century, but for the most part, you seem to be accepting a new society—even though it is quite different from the society you left behind."

Dante cautiously raised his hand. Director Stoll said, "Dante, you would like to say something?"

"I would, sir. And I think I speak for our team." He turned to his crew. "If any of you disagree with me, please state your own opinion on any point. I would just like to say that we greatly appreciate all that you at GSA have done for us since our arrival back on Earth. You have given us a real head start on trying to bridge a gap of thirteen centuries. What we are most pleasantly surprised by is the cleanup of the environment and the elimination of war. You will not be surprised, I think, to learn that our biggest trepidation has to do with the loss of freedoms and human rights. We understand *why* you have done the things you have to achieve your goals, but we are nonetheless concerned about the effects on personal freedoms in ways that we may have not had time to fathom and properly assess."

"Well spoken, Dante," said Director Stoll. "And it will take each of you time to know your own hearts and true feelings. We have given you a jump start, and the rest will be up to you. As far as your futures are concerned, that too is up to each of you. GSA has many opportunities that each of you can qualify for if you want to stay with us. This is one of the best places in the country to live. If Orlando seems too metropolitan to you, you should see Atlanta, Chicago, New York, Los Angeles, and many more mega-metropolitan cities. Compared with these, Orlando is but a country town.

"Each of you have unique qualifications, and you need to decide what you want to do with your lives."

He paused and said, "Now let us switch gears. We want you to ask us questions this morning about anything you have wondered about and we haven't given you an answer for. Please . . . Any question about anything on your mind?"

Ellen raised her hand.

"Yes, Dr. Marks, please go ahead," said Klaus.

"One of the growing problems we had in the twenty-first century was the issue of illegal aliens coming into the U.S. They were entering in increasing numbers every year from many countries, and we were spending billions to try to control our borders. The primary influx was from Mexico."

Ellen did not look at Maria, but Maria looked at Ellen. She thought, *What is Ellen going to do to me? She knows that I have never been a U.S. citizen.*

Dr. Hadid said, "I can take that one if you would like, Klaus." The director nodded and Mikhal spoke, "I believe it was during the twenty-third century that someone finally figured out how to solve that problem. And there were really two solutions. In the case of the huge influx from Mexico, that problem was solved when Mexico was reformed politically into six states—six *new states* of the *United States of America*. The United States government, with support from U.S. citizens, invited the Mexican people to initiate a referendum. Their government, at that time, allowed the referendum to be voted on, never thinking that it would pass. It passed by a 72 percent overwhelming vote. The states created were Sonora, Durango, Jalisco, Tamaulipas, Oaxaca, and Campeche. Many of the outgoing Mexican government officials found positions as senators or representatives and in state offices in their respective states. Look at that flag on the wall behind you. Did you not notice the fifty-six stars, eight columns of seven stars each?"

The *Revelation* crew was awestruck! Of course! Why not? The solution had been there all along. Maria could not believe it. She was anxious to see a current map and learn what state her hometown of Monclova had become a part of.

Dr. Hadid continued, "The Spanish heritage was always as much a part of America as any culture, from the explorers who were the first to discover large portions of the south, southwest, and west to the large Spanish population that has always been a part of this country. Look at the names: Los Angeles, San Francisco, Punta Gorda, San Antonio, Santa Fe, Pueblo, and many others. Finally, in the twenty-third century, the strong bonds that had always been there between the United States and Mexico were recognized."

Maria was especially happy. Now she was no longer an alien to the United States, and all her countrymen were now *citizens*.

Dr. Hadid continued, "The second solution to the illegal alien problem was not so simple. This is because the aliens were coming from all over the world—by boat, by plane, and across the Canadian border, even in the dead of winter. Pregnant women were visiting the U.S. and arriving just in time to have their babies, automatically making the babies U.S. citizens.

"The second solution was in two parts: one, allowing more *legal* immigration, and two, *rigid enforcement* of immigration laws. The U.S. had to clamp down on jobs. If people were not legal in the United States, they could not work, they could not get welfare, they could not even go to a hospital for treatment or request free services. Either they *were legally in this country* and entitled to citizen's rights or *they were not*. There was no middle ground. If illegals were caught, they were not just returned to their country of origin, they were imprisoned here in the U.S. in hard and unpleasant conditions. After a few months of this, they were deported and allowed to go back to their country of origin or to any other country that would accept them. If the *same person* entered illegally the second time, they *were declared UFS* and dealt with accordingly. Harsh, you may think. Perhaps, *but it worked*. Just as our country had been soft on crime, we had been *soft* on illegal aliens. We had no choice but to get tough. Today, only a few people each year are stupid enough to come into the U.S. illegally. The rest have learned that they do not want to be caught—the price is too high. And NO person ever comes in a *second time* after once being deported. Aliens know that they are *forfeiting their lives* if they are caught the second time."

As happy as Maria had been to hear of the integration of Mexico into the USA, she was angered—even enraged—by what was happening to those who entered the country illegally in the thirty-fourth century. What was becoming quite obvious to Maria and others of the crew was that this U.S. government *clearly had two faces*. The kind, helpful supportive face you saw *if you played by the rules*, and the face of an uncompassionate brute if you *did not play by the rules*.

Maria started to speak her mind but bit her lip. Now was not the time. But there would be a time for her later. There had to be.

Director Stoll said, "That was a very good question, Ellen. Thank you. Now who else has a question?"

"I have one," said Jake. "If the medium of exchange is all credits, is there no cash at all in this society today? And a follow-up question: If there is no cash, then there are no robberies for cash, I assume, only for *things*. That would be jewelry, expensive clothes, electronics—high-value items. But then how do the thieves turn the stolen goods into credits?"

"Another excellent question, Mr. Loneghan. Who of our fine staff would like to take a swing at that one?"

Mr. Coulson volunteered. "There *is no cash*. None is even printed. There are stocks and bonds of various types and other papers of financial value, but these are not negotiable for the purchase of items. Therefore, there is no robbery for cash. Stolen goods can only be fenced by someone connected with the banking system so that credits may be put into the criminal's banking account. Such activity is extremely risky and, therefore, seldom attempted. This leaves the only robberies occurring are those wherein the criminal wants the stolen goods for his personal use or to *barter* for something else."

Everyone became silent, obviously considering what they had just heard.

Finally, Director Stoll said, "How about some other questions? Surely, you must have many."

"I have one," said Jake. "In the twenty-first century, terrorists willing to blow themselves up in order to kill other people had become a major problem, which was growing. There were certain religions that had followers convinced that they would *find a life after death that was wonderful* and, therefore, that dying—especially dying for a worthy cause—was a *good thing to do*. I realize that you have sophisticated ways now of sniffing out bombs, but are they sensitive enough and encompassing enough to contain this problem today?"

"Dr. Ottinger!" said Klaus. "You have been getting off easy this morning. Would you please handle this one?"

"I will take my best shot at it, sir, but we both know that this problem has not been completely eliminated." He continued, "Installed in all public and private places where large crowds gather is the most sensitive explosive-sensing equipment we have today. It is in fact the same equipment we use in conjunction with the GCC, Global Conflict Control, satellites we discussed early in your indoctrination program. Let me give you an example of one method we use when one of our sensors is activated by the presence of explosive material. Let's take the case where a bomber is wearing an explosive vest who attempts to enter a football stadium. As he walks through the gate, any gate at the stadium, he is scanned by a sensor. The sensor recognizes the material and activates a device that freezes the person on the spot, using an electronic phazer that disables the person's nervous system. A silent alarm signal is transmitted to security personnel who immediately come to the scene and check the person, usually lying on the concrete, for the explosive device and the triggering mechanism. The most serious of such situations is the case where the explosive device is on a timer that may not have been disrupted by the phazer. The bomb squad immediately acts to disengage the timer-triggering device, rendering the explosive device inoperative."

He continued, "I know that this sounds like we have the bases covered, but remember, I said 'at all public and private places where *large* crowds gather.' It is impossible and far too costly to have our sensors placed *everywhere*. Further, wherever sensors are, there must be security personnel and bomb-savvy technicians. This is simply not possible to do. Therefore, kooks, fanatics—whatever you wish to call them—are still a threat in the thirty-fourth century."

"I would like to add to what Dr. Ottinger has said, if I may," said Mr. Coulson.

"Please do," said Dr. Ottinger.

"In place throughout the U.S. and throughout most other nations of any size in the world is a system of screening people using the TVU units. These units are not today expensive to construct, and they are 100 percent reliable. TVUs are used in schools, by companies when they hire personnel, and by the government when applications for various purposes are submitted. In short, the use of the TVU is almost as common as asking for someone's birth certificate or CIN, citizen identification number.

"My point is this. We know what people are thinking from the time they are little schoolchildren. If they have mental disorders or thoughts that are abnormal, their name and CIN are put in a special file, and these people are watched as they grow and mature. If they never do anything radical or anything that can be considered dangerous to others, then they lead normal lives. If, on the other hand, they start pouring kerosene on cats and setting fire to them or take other unsatisfactory actions against others, then remedies are undertaken. The point here is that our society today does not wait for ticking time bombs to explode. We identify unstable minds early and try to stem problems before they get serious."

"What about immigrants to the United States, and what about warped minds over the rest of the globe?" said David, who was really getting involved in the ongoing subject.

"Immigrants are thoroughly screened on entering the country. If they are coming from countries that use the TVU as we do, then they are screened before their application for citizenship is accepted by the U.S. government. If a government deliberately falsifies records to hide a mentally disturbed person and tries to ship us their problems, then we take very harsh action against that country. In any case, we always use TVU screening when an immigrant enters the U.S., whether or not they have received prior screening. There is *no substitute for knowing the true thoughts of an individual*.

"And I must add this point, in case you have not already figured it out," said Director Stoll. "In the twenty-first century, to be born into the world as a U.S.

citizen automatically guaranteed every person equal rights with everyone else and the right to live your life in the same freedom and with the same rights as all others. *This is not true today.* Our society does not grant all the same rights to life and freedom to everyone. Yes, to everyone that is mentally normal and sane. But *no* to those who are Unfit for Society. That is, *no* to those who do not respect the rights of all others and *no* to those who commit acts that are unacceptable in our society today."

Klaus Stoll paused to allow his statement to sink in.

"So you are saying that all men and all women *are not created equal?*" said Maria.

"That is *exactly* what I am saying, Miss Rodriguez! But it's not a matter of race or color. It is *a matter of mind and of brain function.* Let me also point out that there are basically three types of minds born into the world: The *normal* mind that wants to treat others with fairness and kindness and has a conscience. Secondly, the *evil* mind that wants to dominate others and has no sense of compassion for living things that stand in its way. And finally, the *pliable* mind that may be either more normal or more evil but can be molded and changed. In our society today, we are able to identify the three types of personalities. Fortunately, the majority of those born into the world are of normal mind. Those born with pliable minds are quite numerous and can usually be influenced so that they become acceptable to society. Those with evil minds must be identified and *either contained, reformed, or eliminated for the good of the rest of society.*"

"Could I make a contribution, Director Stoll?' ventured Mr. Lightman.

"Go ahead, Lamarr," said the director.

"Our society has found that those with pliable minds are the ones we need the laws for," said Mr. Lightman. "They are also the ones who can learn not to do bad things because they will be punished. Many laws are not really required for fifty percent of the population but are a *must* for forty-three percent of the population. The other seven percent are basically evil, and no laws or punishment will ever influence or change the way their minds work. This seven percent must be discovered as early as possible and appropriately dealt with as quickly as possible."

By this time, our Twenty First Century Six were frozen in their seats. They were mesmerized by what these supposedly normal learned gentlemen were saying.

Lightman continued, "We have found that swift justice and harsh punishment highly publicized has the most effective impact on the pliable mind—as with the small child that does something that he knows is bad just to see if he can get away with it. If the parent ignores what the child did, he simply does it again or something worse. In other words, the child will push the parent as far as it can get away with. If the parent only offers a mild 'No no, honey, that is bad,' this is almost as bad as *ignoring* the child's attempt to be bad. If, on the other hand, the parent comes down with the severest form of punishment he or she can reasonably apply, the result in the child will be the most dramatic. Making the child take a time-out and sit in the corner is an example. The punishment has to make the child unhappy and rue that it committed the punishable act."

Director Stoll said, "Good, Lamarr, if I may add."

"Certainly, sir," responded Mr. Lightman.

"Fast-forward to the adult that steals a car. In the twenty-first century, I would guess that, depending on the record of the perpetrator, the sentence would range from light to a few months in jail or at most a few years. The accommodations in the jail or prison might have been better than the criminal had on the outside. And he had all sorts of books to read, games and sports to play, and a job in prison that actually earned him money during his stay. Am I basically correct?" He looked at Jake for some reason.

"Sounds pretty accurate to me," said Jake. "And there would have been little or no public knowledge about the nature of the punishment."

"Fast-forward again to the thirty-fourth century," said Director Stoll. "By the second day after the car thief was caught and found guilty, he would have been in a concrete cell with an uncomfortable mat to sleep on. And each day, he would be at hard labor for ten hours. His food will not have been tasty, and he would have had no recreational privileges whatsoever. He would have spent at least a year or more doing this, depending on his record. Our philosophy today is *make the punishment very unpleasant and something the inmate never wants to repeat.*

"We would have made sure that the public knew what happened to the perp that stole the car and that the public was quite aware of the conditions in the prison. This system works for all but those of evil minds. Our justice system is dedicated to changing pliable minds and making them acceptable to society and to identifying and eliminating evil minds."

Maria raised her hand and spoke, "What about the mentally deficient mind that is not evil. What of the person who intends no harm to anyone but steals because he or she does not know better? For example, an adult with a child's mind?"

Director Stoll responded with, "That is an entirely different matter. What we have been talking about are people that intentionally commit crimes, knowing what they are doing and intentionally harm others. Your question goes to the mentally ill that are not criminals and not necessarily a danger to others. We have homes and hospitals for those of which you speak. They have that choice or, in rare cases, may stay with families who choose to look after them and bear the responsibility."

"Are there any more questions now?" Director Stoll paused. Hearing nothing, he added, "This is not the last chance you have to ask and learn about our society in the thirty-fourth century. Right now, we have a nice lunch prepared in the executive dining room. After lunch, I would like to have a brief meeting in my office with the *Revelation* crew. So if we can now adjourn and meet in the dining room in about ten minutes."

26

Lunch in the executive dining room featured Director Stoll's personal favorite dishes—Bavarian-style beef goulash with a rich beer sauce served with homemade red cabbage and spätzle. There was also apple strudel served with a cream sauce for dessert. A good German beer complemented the meal.

"I hope we haven't pushed you too far this morning," said the director. "It was a pretty heavy session. Maria, you seem to be agitated. Is there something you wish to say?"

"Yes," replied Maria, "there *is* something I wish to say, if I may."

"By all means, my dear, go ahead," said Klaus.

"I think we can reference back to my statement earlier this morning," said Maria, "when I said *so all men are not created equal.*"

Jake saw what was coming and jumped in with, "Maria was quite active in human rights in her life before the *Revelation*. We think that the way people are treated in the thirty-fourth century shows a much less-tolerant world than we came from."

"It appears," said Dante, trying to further defuse the situation, "that in the last 1300 years, man has decided that he was being much too tolerant in governing himself and his brothers and that his tolerance and compassion had let the world deteriorate and spiral down the wrong path. It further appears, to me at least, that the men and women of the United States must have decided that a global benevolent dictatorship was the only way to save the world from destroying itself. Am I on target with this line of thinking?"

No one commented for an uncomfortable length of time. Maria seemed happy with Jake's and Dante's statements and waited for Director Stoll's answer before commenting further. The *Revelation* crew seemed to be in a state of anticipation, awaiting a response to the comments of Maria, Jake, and Dante.

Finally, Dr. Hadid spoke, "Dante, I think you have a good grasp of what has happened. I think we are not saying that the way of the United States was the only way. But under the circumstances, without the help of an *outside source*, whatever *that* might be, some country or entity of the globe had to step up and take charge. I, for one, am convinced that if the Global Conflict Control satellite system had not been established when it was, then the world would have had a global nuclear conflict. After such devastation, who knows? My opinion is that conflicts and wars would have continued along with the fall of nations in an ever-continuing march toward doom. Such could have destroyed humanity over the globe. Human civilization might not even exist today."

"But by taking charge of the world, which is what we essentially did, the United States shouldered the responsibility of the well-being of the Earth," said Mr. Coulson. "In retrospect, we have a better world today than you had in the twenty-first century. Would you all not agree with that?"

There was another uncomfortable pause, and then Jake said, "In the twenty-first century, there was no other nation, with the strength and technology needed and with the values, capable of stepping up to the responsibility." Jake looked at his fellow crew members. "We should know this better than our new friends in this century. We were already living in *a march to doom*. It was physically impossible for the United States in the twenty-first century to stop all of the countries that were trying to grab power. The oil-rich nations had control of the world's energy. Eight nations had nuclear bomb capability and the means to deliver the weapons. Terrorism was increasing every day. Talk about a ticking time bomb . . . The world was one big bomb!"

Ellen offered her view. "I agree with Jake. What the U.S. has done may not have been the only way. But I, for one, cannot think of another way. The catchphrase in our century always espoused by the party *not in power* was 'This can be or should have been solved with *diplomacy*.' In truth, the rapidly deteriorating world had gone *far beyond* the help possible through diplomacy. The only things that seemed to matter were energy, hate, and power."

"Let me go on record," said David, "by saying that I am impressed with what the world has become. And I wish to offer my sincere thanks to you, Director Stoll, and to you other gentlemen for the very informative and well-presented program you treated us to."

David's complimentary comment was well-timed. It seemed clear that all of the twenty-first century team did *not share* David's views, but nothing was to be gained by allowing the argument to escalate at this point.

"And thank you so much for your hospitality," said Susan. "The accommodations, the pumas, and all the other services are much appreciated."

"And now all we have to do is *decide what we are going to do with our lives*," said Dante.

"An excellent segue," said Director Stoll. "That is just the discussion I would like to have with the six of you after we finish here. I have some opportunity suggestions, but I would like to hear what you all are thinking before I say anything."

On that note, everyone starting saying good-byes and thank-yous and began to disperse.

In Director Stoll's office, there was a conference table for eight. After the lunch, the director invited the crew in, and all took seats at his table.

Klaus opened by saying, "Please share with me what each of you think you would like to do now that you have been introduced to life in the thirty-fourth century. Let me rush to say that it is not really any of my business what you do, but if you care to share your thoughts, perhaps I can be of some help to you in obtaining a position you would like."

"Mine is easy—at least for me," said David. "At NASA, I was involved in spacecraft design. My training is aerospace engineering. I would like to work for you, Director Stoll, doing that same kind of work."

"Wonderful, David. I was hoping you would say that." responded the director. "We have several positions that might interest you. We can discuss those later."

"I am impressed with the GCC satellite system," said Dante, "and with the little I have seen of the USAF of the thirty-fourth century. I would be interested in exploring a position with the military or perhaps in the Pentagon."

"That too is an excellent idea," said the director. "I have not mentioned it, but a reception in the White House is being planned for the six of you. The president has the plans on hold until we are sure that your indoctrination has gone far enough."

"I was involved in Washington affairs and politics in the twenty-first century," said Maria. "And I think I might want to continue in something along those lines. And one other thought, I would like to locate in Washington for another reason. I am fascinated by the metamorphosis the Earth has gone through during the last 1300 years. I want to do some historical research using the Library of Congress."

"Would you like a position in the Library of Congress?" said Director Stoll. "We probably can arrange that if you are interested."

"I would certainly like to interview with the director of the library," said Maria.

"I can arrange that," said Director Stoll, "and would be happy to do so."

"Now," said Klaus, "where does that leave us with Ellen, Susan, and Jake? Do any of you want to share your thinking?"

"I know exactly what I would like to do," said Ellen. "And David is in full agreement. We just don't know if a position is available. I would like to go to work at Mayo-Orlando in artificial limbs and organs and android development. I am fascinated with what's been done already, but I would like to contribute. Do you think there is a chance of my getting in there?"

"I certainly would think so," said Klaus. "But we were hoping you would come to work with us in the field of space medicine."

"That certainly sounds interesting too," said Ellen. "I think I should explore both possibilities."

"Good!" said Director Stoll. "I will ask our chief MD here to set up an appointment for you with Mayo and also to show you what we are doing here in space medicine."

"Excellent," said Ellen. "Thank you."

"Do you think that I might become involved in the justice system, Director Stoll?" said Susan. "Things are so different in this century. I think it would be challenging and exciting! Do you have any suggestions as to where I might fit in?"

"Not offhand, Susan, but I haven't given it any thought. To be honest with you, I was hoping you would come to work for us doing space property rights on the moon and Mars and wherever else we find ourselves traveling to."

Director Stoll continued, "We aren't talking about staying behind a desk on this either. You would be going to the locations in space where your work takes you."

Susan looked a little unsure of how she should respond. She said, "I spoke to Chief Justice Webster on this very subject, and I am really not sure what I want to do. Perhaps if I could speak some more with her and also have a chat with GSA's chief legal officer."

"I can certainly understand your feelings, Susan," said Director Stoll. "Just know that we can certainly use you here at GSA if you want to work for us."

"Thank you, sir," said Susan.

"I guess that leaves me," said Jake. "I can give it to you short and sweet. Eventually, I want to go into some kind of business in the thirty-fourth century. I just don't know enough about what the world is like yet. Meanwhile, if you need any astronauts I would love to pilot some of your big ships, especially the ones that can do ten times light-speed."

"Jake, we can always use a good pilot/astronaut," said the Klaus. "In fact, we have a class starting next week. Soon, we hope to kick off a mission to the Alpha Centauri neighborhood. Unfortunately, we don't yet have congressional approval. How would a mission like that appeal to you?"

"Count me in!" said Jake. The sound of such adventures made him smile.

"Well, it seems as if everyone at least has a direction they would like to pursue," said Klaus. "And I think your objectives are all possible. Now before we break for today, I'd like to talk just a minute about the Washington affair, mainly from a logistics standpoint. We are tentatively planning to have you go up to DC in one of our GSA corporate vehicles. As you have probably figured out by now, with the capability the PMU vehicles have, we don't use commercial aircraft travel or airports much anymore. Don't misunderstand, though, there are still commercial airlines operating, and many people prefer to *be* flown, rather than fly their own vehicles from place to place.

"In your case, we think it would be a better trip for you to be chauffeured in a PMU limo, such as the one which initially took you, after you arrived, from the *Revelation* to this building where we are now. That way, you won't have to learn the Washington MATRAC system, and one of the Mister Androids can be your driver and guide in Washington. How does that sound to you?"

"I like it," said Dante, and the others nodded in agreement.

"Good. Then that part of the plan is settled. We will have reservations for you at the Washington Marriott—five rooms have been reserved. I will stay in touch with the office of the president and keep you all advised.

"One final subject before you leave me today," said the director. "You have a few days to kill before you will be going to Washington. What would you like to do with that time?"

"I would like to play some golf," said Jake without hesitation. "Since it's been over a year since I hit a ball, I may be a bit rusty!"

"I could go for that too," said Dante. "Any courses nearby?"

"As a matter of fact, we have two courses here at the center on the beach. I don't play, so I can't tell you about the courses, but I hear they are pretty good. The courses are Tranquillity and Theophilus, named for the site of man's first landing on the moon and for one of the more impressive craters of the moon. The courses are part of our GSA recreational complex called the Beach Club. How about the rest of you? Anyone else for golf?"

"Maria and I would just like to relax on the beach," said Susan. "Does the Beach Club have its own private beach area?"

"It most certainly does," said Klaus. "In fact, the club is quite the facility. There are tennis and volleyball courts, three nice pools, and, of course, the two golf eighteens. The clubhouse has a health club with sauna and an indoor track. Tell you what, I will call down and set up passes for all six of you—you can pick them up when you go there the first time."

"Ellen and I would appreciate the use of the club, Director Stoll. And since we plan to be living and working here, we will pursue permanent membership. But first, we would like to look at properties in the area. The BPQ is nice, but we want to acquire a home as soon as we can arrange financing. Perhaps you could give us a hint about the various residential areas in the vicinity?"

"I can do better than that. We have a housing coordinator on staff, and she will give you all the information you need."

"It looks like we'll just be a twosome for golf, Dante," said Jake. "Unless, of course, Mr. D. and Mr. K. would consider playing with us." He laughed at his own joke.

"They would not be available for that," said Klaus. "But I have a solution for you. At the golf pro shop, you can rent clubs and *players*. The shop has a

Mr. Jones, or Mr. J., and a Mr. Hogan, or Mr. H., that would love to play with you. I hear they are pretty good."

Jake looked at Dante as if to say, "Do we really need this?"

Dante returned the look. "I guess one of us can take Jones for a partner and the other take Hogan. We can play best-ball or total match play."

"I'm game," said Jake.

The director picked up his mec and called, "Evie, I have two friends here who are interested in looking at homes in the area. Can they come down and talk to you? Fine, I'll send them right down."

"So," said Klaus, "it looks like you are all set for some fun in the sun. I'll ask Mr. K. to give you four a lift to the BPQ so you can launch from there. I'm sure Evie would like to show you and David around, Ellen. Or if you prefer, she can drop you at the BPQ so you can take your GSA puma."

They all thanked the director for everything. He promised to get back with them on the Washington plans, and they were on their way.

Just as the group left, Renee buzzed Director Stoll. "Sir, it's President Thornhill calling."

Klaus grabbed his mec. "Mr. President! How are you today, sir?"

"Good, Klaus. Just checking with you on the progress of our six wandering souls from twenty-first-century Earth. How are they doing with your program?"

"Sir, they appear to understand all that we have exposed them to, and I would say that they seem to be accepting our society quite well."

"No particular problems? Surely, they are not all lambs . . . Our world today has some harshness to it they certainly did not experience in 2025."

"Mr. President, I am *not* prepared to say that the six, as individuals, *like* everything they have heard about our civilization. But I am confident that they are prepared to accept it for what it is. In fact, I would add that *all but Maria* seem to be embracing even the changes affecting our treatment of criminals and our worldwide domination of other countries."

"And Maria? What is her problem?"

"Well, you may recall, sir, that she was an activist against government and government power over the people—even in the twenty-first century. I think if Maria had her way, all people would be totally free to do whatever they liked anytime they liked."

"Can you imagine a world like that?" exclaimed President Thornhill.

"I cannot. But let me add that I don't believe Maria has even a tiny inclination to start any cause or action against our authority. She seems perfectly willing to follow the others, and they are all blending in nicely—in my opinion. Maria wants to work in the Library of Congress."

"What about Loneghan? He strikes me as a maverick. And I haven't forgotten the tax thing he was into when he left Earth in 2025." The president closed quickly with, "OK, Stoll, I have another call. We are going ahead with the reception here for *all of them*. Haldemann will be in touch with you." Klaus heard a click. He cradled his mec.

27

J ake and Dante completed a very interesting and educational round of golf with the two droids and were having lunch by the main pool behind the club.

"That Jones and Hogan are outstanding golfers," said Jake.

"I'll say!" said Dante. "They hit the ball over four hundred yards and straight every time."

"If we hadn't figured out how to *command them to make bad shots,* it would have really been a long day!"

Dante laughed, saying, "You've got that right! They were killing us 'til we remembered that they *had* to comply with our requests."

They both had a good laugh. Then they were silent for a time, just gazing out over the ocean.

"This wouldn't be a bad life, Dante," said Jake, "working for GSA, flying the big ships, playing golf, and enjoying the club. We could go into Orlando for some action occasionally."

"I suppose," said Dante. "But I think I would get bored."

"You wouldn't get bored piloting the fast ships, would you?"

"I would if we had to hibernate for most of the trip. That's just not being a pilot to me."

"I see your point. The fun flying would be the short-range jobs, like the ones who came up to check out the *Revelation* when we arrived."

"Now you are talking," said Dante. "Those are really hot little numbers! Go right from the ground to orbit. I understand they accelerate up to 10 g's, and top speed is about 25,000 mph. *That* is moving *on*!"

"Yeah, but you know, the high-priced pumas are also pretty impressive. They have 6 g acceleration and can cruise up to 600 mph!"

"But they cost a hundred thousand credits! And another thing—what does fuel cost for these pumas? We haven't used ours enough to need fuel yet, but I bet it's expensive."

"Also maintenance and repair. That won't be cheap," said Jake.

"I still don't have a feel for the value of a credit, do you?"

"No, I don't. We need to find some sort of guide somewhere that lists typical prices of typical things."

"Yeah," said Dante, "I kind of miss the dollars. Having a wad in your wallet had a good feel to it."

They said nothing for a while, just looking out over the ocean and sky.

"You are planning on working in national defense? Is that what you told Stoll?" said Jake. "Are you thinking active air force or some position with the Global Conflict Control organization?"

"I'm not sure. I need to talk to someone in the Pentagon just to be sure I understand how it all works. I'd like a spot that would let me fly and also be in command position. That would be ideal."

They were quiet again for a few minutes.

"You are going to work for GSA?" said Dante.

"That's what I've been thinking," said Jake, "but only as an interim thing. If GSA would keep paying the bills for the apartment and the puma, I wouldn't mind hanging out around here and playing golf for a while—but I'm sure that's just wishful thinking." He paused as Dante gave him funny look. "I'm just kidding," he added.

Jake continued, "Talking seriously, though, I'd like to go into some kind of business. I left some money in the bank in 2025, and it might still be there. I checked, and a bank by the same name is there in Washington, but they didn't recognize my account number."

"You left money in a bank in 2025?"

"Yeah, quite a bit actually. I was going to give it to charity, but after we got into training, I never seemed to have the time to attend to it."

Dante was getting more interested by the minute. "Have you thought about how much interest your money would have earned since 2025?"

"Yeah, but they have switched over to credits now."

"How much are we talking about?"

Jake hesitated, then said, "Um . . . $59 million, give or take."

"Fifty-nine million dollars!" cried Dante. "What bank is the money in? You are suddenly my *very best friend*."

"The Chase Washington Bank," said Jake. "I'm going to pay them a visit when we are in Washington and talk to the president of the bank."

"I can't run the numbers in my head, but with that amount of money earning even just 2 percent for 1,312 years, you are probably the richest man on Earth! Does Maria know about this?"

"Why Maria? What has she got to do with it?"

"Don't you two have something going?"

"Where did you get that idea?"

"I've just been watching you."

Jake was silent. Then he said, "If it was left up to me, we would, but she is still in love with some dead man that she loved back in the twenty-first century. It's really weird. She can't seem to forget the guy."

Again, they were quiet. Finally, Jake stood.

"Well, we might as well go back to the BPQ. Maybe we have a message about the Washington bash," said Jake.

"I'm ready. Let's do it," said Dante as he too stood.

Meanwhile . . .

David and Ellen, with Evie's help, had been doing some house hunting in the area around the base. They had soon realized that they were baffled by the differences in thirty-fourth-century monetary matters, non-use of currency and the valuation and trading of real property. They needed some help and advice from the GSA staff.

Maria and Susan had also run into monetary issues while attempting to buy groceries at a local market. Food prices of artificial foods versus real foods and just the economics of daily life in the thirty-fourth century were confusing. They too had decided they needed some help from the GSA staff. On returning to the BPQ, Maria and Susan were arriving at the same time that David and Ellen were entering the lobby door.

"Hey, Dave and El!" called Susan. "You know what we failed to get any instruction on?"

David and Ellen stopped and turned as David responded, "The monetary system and using credits in our daily lives?"

"You got it!" said Maria. "Let's contact Dr. Hadid and see if he can give us some help."

"We're game," said Ellen, glancing toward David for support.

"I'm calling him now," said David, entering a number into his mec.

The four were with Dr. Hadid in his office. "We should have covered this in our program for you," said Mikhal. "I don't know why we didn't include a session on credits and how they are used. Should we wait and get Jake and Dante into this, or can you take care of sharing what you learn with them?"

"We can take care of them," said David. "We have the time now, and if it's convenient for you, let's do it."

"I have the time," said the doctor. "Let's start with some charts." He handed them the same charts that Evie had given David and Ellen, but they didn't let on. They wanted to hear what Mikhal had to say about them.

"Just so I don't forget," began Dr. Hadid, "I should mention that there is an excellent publication in the shop off the cafeteria in the BPQ entitled *34th Century Economics*. That disc has all I am going to tell you and much more in detail. It only costs two credits—each of you should have one.

"I will give you some information concerning typical cost of items, typical job pay and salaries, a bit about the credits system, and some interesting facts about our food supply.

"Look at the card I gave each of you. On the front of the card is listed typical costs for items you might purchase. On the back of the card is displayed pay for different types of jobs. This reference card is updated and published every year. Keep it handy, at least until you get used to things.

"Now about the credits system. Centuries ago, the use of debit and credit cards became so popular and common, less and less cash was used. Electronic funds transfer became very routine. Also, the ability to identify people at the touch of their finger using their DNA became possible. The government, therefore, decided to eliminate cash and make all trade transactions happen by the mere touch of your finger. All citizens have 'value accounts.' When you earn, your value account goes up. And when you spend, it goes down. You can buy or sell anything you could have in the twenty-first century. The credits just go from one account to another. Also, prices rise with inflation. In 2025, your milk was probably around $5 per gallon. Inflation from 2025 to 3339, without any adjustments, would have made today's price of milk be about $1,500 per gallon with other food prices being comparable. Imagine how much cash you would need for shopping. With the credits system, worldwide adjustments are made once a year to keep prices at a reasonable level. How this is done is included in the pub disc I told you about."

Dr. Hadid's mec toned, and he answered. He spoke briefly with someone, closed the mec, and said, "I am sorry, but I'm going to have to leave—something has come up. I will cover just one more subject today. That is, food. But to discuss food, I also should mention population.

"Today, the population of the United States is one thousand people per square mile—many times what it was in 2025. This has resulted in two large problems for us: too many people to feed and not enough land to grow food on. This problem has been addressed in several ways. As you learned, childbirths are now restricted for the many reasons we discussed in your sessions.

"Farms are now multi-tiered buildings using artificial sunlight. We have also developed artificial food—i.e., food remanufactured from other plentiful plants to *taste* like the foods we all enjoy. The next time you visit a restaurant, look at the bottom of the menu. A line there says 'Meal choices with an asterisk are made partially from artificial foods.' The artificial meals are cheaper, tasty, and just as nourishing. I expect that you, Maria and Susan, came across that in the grocery store?"

"We did," said Susan. "There was real milk for fifteen credits a gallon and artificial milk for two credits a gallon."

Dr. Hadid smiled. "Use the artificial milk. It tastes almost as good, is *better* for you, and costs a whole lot less. The same is true for most other artificial foods."

He concluded the session with, "I hope this little discussion has been of some help to you. Purchase the disc I mentioned and study it. It is really worth its price. After you read the information, if you would like to come in for more discussion on economics, call and we will find a time."

Dr. Hadid arose as did his guests. They thanked him for his help and began leaving. Dr. Hadid added a closing comment as they exited the office. "Rest assured that we will include a session on economics for the next astronauts that visit us from the past . . ." He smiled at his own quip.

The four returned to the BPQ and learned from Mr. D. that Director Stoll had been trying to reach them and had left messages in their rooms. "Have you seen Jake and Dante?" Maria asked.

"Yes, Miss Rodriguez," said Mr. D., "they came in from golf about twenty minutes ago. They said something about going to Mr. Loneghan's unit and watching a ball game on MaxVision."

"Let's catch them there," said David. "Maybe they talked to Director Stoll." They proceeded up the elevator to the eighth floor and down to Jake's apartment. They knocked.

"Come in, it's open!" said Jake.

The four entered and saw that Dante and Jake were watching a baseball game in 3-D.

"Who's playing?" said David. "And what's the score?"

"Twins and Detroit," said Dante. "Twins ahead 4 to 3, top of the ninth."

"Grab a seat," said Jake. "Can I get anyone a beer or some wine?"

"I'll have lite beer," said Dave, taking a seat.

"Too early for me," said Ellen.

"Do you have Chardonnay?" said Maria. "If so, I'll have some."

"Same for me," said Susan. "Did either of you talk to Stoll?"

"Coming up with the wines and beer," said Jake. "No, but we read a message from him. Sure you won't have something, Ellen?"

"I'm OK," said Ellen. "What did Klaus want?"

"To tell us that the White House reception is Saturday evening," said Dante.

"*This Saturday?*" said the three girls in unison.

"That's only three days from now!" said Ellen. "And today is almost over!"

"So?" said Jake as he handed the girls their wine and went back for David's beer.

"Well, I don't have anything to wear!" moaned Ellen.

"Me neither," complained Susan.

"Neither do I," said Maria

"That'll liven up the White House," said Dante without looking away from the TV.

Jake got it and let out a big laugh. David joined in the fun. "Well, you girls all have beautiful figures. I wouldn't worry about not having anything to wear!"

"You men!" said Ellen. "I suppose you are just going to wear your *Revelation* flight suits."

"Why not?" said Jake, winking at David. Dante was still glued to the game, having a good laugh at the image of the girls going nude to the White House.

"*Let's go shopping right now!*" said Maria. "There's a Macy's just beyond the Cape SuperFoods store. We can try there tonight, and if we strike out, we'll just have to go to Orlando tomorrow and shop 'til we find something nice."

"Fine with me," said Susan as she polished off the wine and turned toward the door.

Maria downed her wine and said, "Let's do it! Ellen, you'll have to be the designated driver."

Ellen followed them to the door and said over her shoulder, "Guys, you are on your own tonight. Think you can handle it?"

The men were all watching the MaxVision. Ever since David had discovered the *3-D mode* control button on the viewscreen, it was hard to keep the guys away from watching sports. It was the bottom of the ninth, bases loaded, two out, still 4 to 3 Twins, and Detroit's best hitter was at the plate. They all said "Sure!" without looking away from the screen.

David added, "Have a good time, ladies."

The Twins struck out the side and won the game. The girls were gone, and Jake said, "Now what do we do?"

"Maybe there's another game on," said Dante.

"There is!" said David. "Yankees and Chicago. Just found the Guide Web site in the PC. Can we order pizza from these apartments?"

Thursday morning came, and it was panic time for the girls. They hadn't found anything suitable for the White House at Macy's and would be *forced* to go into Orlando to shop. They got up early, had toast and coffee in the cafeteria, and took off with Susan driving her puma. The guys were sleeping in.

Jake got up and was taking a shower. Suddenly, it occurred to him *that all the clothes he had were flight suits*, and he needed something nice for the White House. He called and reminded David and Dante of that fact and suggested that The Men's Store just off the base would be the place to go. They agreed to meet in the cafeteria for breakfast at nine thirty and go from there.

Klaus Stoll was on the AMec with the president's chief of staff, Frederich Haldemann.

"Was the president OK with the speech we put together?" Klaus was asking.

"Reasonably so," said Haldemann. "He had his writers make a few corrections, but otherwise, it's pretty good. There is just one thing bothering him now, though."

"And that is?" said Klaus.

"He is concerned about the arrival of the six in one of your PMU limos. He doesn't think it has enough class."

"Logistically, it makes a lot of sense," said Stoll. "What else does he have in mind?"

"Well, and I am not saying I agree with this, but he is thinking about having them arrive in Washington in the *Revelation*."

"WHAT? How the . . . ? That doesn't make any sense at all! That ship is just sitting in the hangar and has been since they arrived. It's 1300 years old anyway!"

"Don't hand me that," said Frederich. "I know it's only a year older, just like the crew."

"Well, we don't know if the systems are all functional. And besides, the crew hasn't set foot in it since they arrived."

"You could check the ship out tomorrow and let the guys take it for a spin."

"Frederich, *think* about what you are saying. Here's another good reason for not sending them in the *Revelation*. They would have to land at Dulles, and they would still have to come into the city in a limo. So why not just come from here in the limo?"

"The president was thinking about a *vertical landing on the south lawn*. Wouldn't that be a *scorcher*?"

"*I think I am going to have a heart attack!*" said Klaus.

"The *Revelation* does have vertical landing capability, does it not?"

"Well . . . Yes, it does, but they have never used it. That would be very ill advised."

"Here's the thing, Klaus," said Haldemann, "3340 is an election year, and just think of what a splash a vertical landing would make with the press and with the country!"

"It might very well *make a splash*—but not the kind you are thinking of! Why don't you think of what it would do to his campaign if the ship crashed on the White House lawn?"

"That wouldn't happen . . . that couldn't happen . . . could it?"

"It very well *could* happen, and the risk is *far too great*. Tell you what, why don't you go back to the president and tell him what I have said. If he gives me a direct order to send them in the *Revelation*, I will do it. You can persuade me to let them land at Dulles or even Reagan, but not *vertically on the White House lawn*! And one more comment before you hang up—the public is not stupid. They will know that the crew has already been here for two weeks, and they will know that we just had them come to Washington in the *Revelation* for the *positive effect on the presidential race*. I'll wait to hear from you, but if they are coming in the *Revelation*, I need to know it *tonight*. We need the whole day tomorrow to prepare."

Klaus clicked off the call and punched in the number for GSA Maintenance Operations.

"GSA Maintenance Ops, Sergeant Bickel speaking."

"Sergeant, this is Klaus Stoll. We may be flying the *Revelation* ship on Saturday. I need you to start running systems checks."

28

It was Friday morning. The women had been successful in their shopping trip to Orlando, and the men had found suitable business attire for the visit to the White House. Dante's mec toned as he slept. He awoke and looked at the clock—it was 7:30 AM.

"Dante Washington here. Who is calling?"

"Dante, this is Klaus Stoll. Hope I am not calling too early."

"Not at all, sir. What's up?"

"President Thornhill wants you and the crew to arrive in Washington on the *Revelation*."

"WHAT?" said Dante, not believing his ears.

"I know it sounds incredible, but that is what the president has requested. You can say no if you want. It is up to you and the others."

Dante was still in shock, groping for some logic in this request.

"Can you tell me *why* the president wants this? What possible reason since the public will be told that we arrived here at KSC a couple of weeks ago?"

"It is very simple," said Klaus. "Next year is an election year, and the president thinks that your arriving in the ship you spent 1300 Earth years traveling in will be a big political plus for him. He wants you to do a *vertical landing* on the White House lawn."

"HE WHAT?" yelled Dante into the mec. "That is the most ridiculous *thing I ever heard of*!"

"I agree with you totally," said Klaus. "I think it is ridiculous to have you travel to Washington in the *Revelation*. Not that anything will go wrong, mind you, but it could . . ."

"Well, nothing *would* go wrong," said Dante, now softening his stance. "After all, we did launch, travel for thirteen centuries, and come safely back to Earth with no problems."

"That is certainly true," said Klaus, sensing a way to change the psychology of the conversation. "Why don't I just contact President Thornhill and tell him that you and the crew don't think it's a good idea and that you prefer to arrive at the White House in the chauffeured PMU limo?"

Dante was thinking. Finally, he said, "Let me talk this over with the others, and I'll get back to you."

"If you are considering using the *Revelation*," said Klaus, "we need to *get busy*. We only have *today* to check out all the systems, and I would think that you might want to take it out for a little test hop before you start for Washington tomorrow."

"Why don't you put some people on the checkout, starting now, and I will get with the other crew members immediately and get back with you. We can always stop the work on the ship if we decide against using it. I will be back with you in thirty minutes or so."

"Good plan, Dante," said Director Stoll. "I'll get a team started and look for your call."

Dante touched the number for Jake's room, then for the others. He asked them all to meet him downstairs to discuss the Washington trip. That's all he told them on the mec call.

Maria was the last to arrive in the cafeteria. "Sorry," she said, "I start very slowly in the mornings."

"What's up?" said Jake.

"The president wants us to arrive in Washington on the *Revelation*," said Dante.

They all just looked at him.

"So?" said Jake. "What's wrong with that? We can show them that twenty-first-century technology is pretty sharp. Not really so far behind where they are now."

Susan said, "*Why* does he want us to do that? The ship has been flying continuously for over a year and now has been sitting for almost two weeks. It will need a thorough checkout and probably a test hop before we take it into Washington."

"Which airport?" said David. "Dulles will be best—better prepared for large ships."

"*Why?*" said Ellen. "I agree with Susan."

"Politics," said Dante. "Next year, 3340, is an election year! Thornhill wants us to do a *vertical landing on the White House lawn.*"

"WHAT?" said everyone except Dante in unison.

"*On the White House lawn?*" said Ellen and Maria together.

"I think we should *go for it*," said Jake. "Let's show 'em what us old guys can do!"

"What are the risks, David?" said Dante. "There is very little open space at the White House."

Everyone looked at David, the lead designer of the *Revelation*. David was deep in thought. Finally, he said, "We can put her in safely, but none of you pilots have done an *actual* vertical touchdown—just in the *simulator*. And the limited area increases the risk."

"We practically *wore out* the simulator doing verticals, David," said Dante. "I think we all believed that we might be landing vertically on Nyvar *and on rough terrain.*"

"We actually got pretty good at verticals," said Susan.

"Let's check the space available," said Jake. "If there is enough, let's go for it."

David wanted to be macho and agree with his pilot friends. He said, "Maria, what do you think? You haven't said anything."

Maria said, *"Let's show them what we could do in the twenty-first century."*

"Well, I think you guys are all crazy!" said Ellen. "But I guess I am outvoted, so LET'S DO IT!"

David just looked at them all and said, "There's no reason why the ship can't do it. It was designed to do it. And if we are going to do a vertical touchdown, it might as well be *in the president's backyard*! We built this baby to land on any planet, even prehistoric ones with no landing strips. We can certainly land *on the president's lawn*!"

Dante looked at all the guys and was very proud. He said, "What a team! I am damned proud to be a part of it. Let's have some breakfast and head over to the hangar."

The *Revelation* looked as fine and as proud as it did when they left it. It still had the glistening white surface coat with no discernable scratches. When the crew arrived, there were GSA maintenance types all over it. One of the workers came over to the crew and said, "I am Sgt. Gordon Bickel. Are you the *Revelation* crew members?"

Dante said, "Yes, we are, sergeant. I am the ship commander, Colonel Washington. What can I do for you?"

"Well, sir," said the sergeant, "we have all of the diagrams, manuals, and specifications for this ship. But none of us have ever worked on it before. It would be a big help if you folks would work with us—it would save a lot of time."

"Excellent idea, sergeant," said Dante. "In fact, we are all in luck. We have the designer of the ship, Mr. David Marks, right here. He will keep all of us on track."

The sergeant assembled all his team and introduced them to the astronauts. David, using the system diagrams, quickly explained what needed to be checked out and how the checkouts were to be performed. The *Revelation* crew members then split up and assisted the sergeant's team members in accomplishing the work.

At one point, one of the mechanics came over to David and said, "Sir, we are still getting an unsafe indication on the nose gear door when we run that system."

David wasn't surprised and said, "OK, let's take a look at it."

Jake was helping run the propulsion system checkout and noted that the ship still had plenty of nuclear fuel. The sergeant commented that that was certainly a good thing because the fuel used for the big ships now used by GSA was somewhat different from the fuel used by the *Revelation*—and there was *no more of the older fuel around.*

Dante suddenly remembered that he hadn't gotten back with the director. He called the director's office.

"Sir," said Dante, "I am very sorry I haven't called, but we were all so excited about flying the *Revelation* again, I simply forgot to tell you what our decision was."

"Well, Dante, it's OK. When I learned that all of you had arrived at the hangar—Sergeant Bickel called me—I felt that I had my answer. I was just about to call the president, but I thought I better hear it from you first."

"I'm glad you waited, sir. You don't have the whole story yet."

"What don't I know?"

"The crew and I want to land her on the White House lawn, sir, just like the president asked for."

Klaus almost dropped his AMec! "*You can't be serious.* You have never used that landing technique!"

"That is true, sir, but we almost had to when we arrived here at KSC. We were showing an unsafe light on the nose gear but finally got a green."

"But you *didn't* have to, and you have *never* landed the *Revelation* vertically. You realize that your risk is somewhat higher with a vertical landing. Wouldn't you much rather land at Reagan International or Dulles?"

"We know the risk is higher, sir. But as you know, David Marks was the principal designer of the ship, and he feels that we will be perfectly safe. You realize that the vertical landing procedure *had to be perfect* because when we left Earth, we were fully prepared to land on *any surface*, no matter how rough and uneven. Also, with the two engines, either one of them *can more than sustain the weight of the ship in the hover mode* should we have one engine fail.

"Jake, Susan, and I all put many hours in the *Revelation* simulator right here at KSC, each doing dozens of vertical landings, including emergency situations. Our one concern is for the safety of the president and other dignitaries, the press, and others that will observe the landing. They will all have to give us a *clear area of at least one hundred yards* in diameter. Is there enough room for that on the south lawn?"

"I will discuss that with the president to be sure," said Klaus. "If he changes his mind about the White House landing, I assume that you are prepared to land at Reagan, then?"

"No problem *at all* with that, sir. We just need to know which place before we start the landing sequence. I'll be back with you again before we launch, and by the way, please find out what time he wants us to set down."

"I hope you are making the right decision on this, Dante. I'll be back with you later today," said the director.

Dante went back over to the ship and found David. "Any problems?" said Dante.

"None yet," said David. "She's looking real good so far."

It was now about eleven AM, and the last check was being performed on the *Revelation*. The ground team had discovered two minor units in addition to the nose gear warning micro-switch, which were not checking out completely in the green. Luckily, the crew had brought spares of these units and spare micro-switches on the ship. The ground team was able to replace the two marginal units. David was briefing Dante, "Both of these units are in triple-redundant systems anyway. We didn't need to replace them, but since we had the spare units . . ."

"And you replaced the nose gear switch?"

"Yeah, it was just one of those deals where something looks OK and checks out OK *most* of the time, but *not all of the time*."

"Then it sounds like she's about ready to fly."

"We can board as soon as they roll her out of the hangar," said David.

The huge hangar doors slowly opened. The *Revelation* was hooked up to a tug that was just starting up. Slowly, the majestic relic of the distant past was towed onto the apron just outside the hangar. Dante and the crew stood to the side and watched with pride as the big bird was rolled out. From another direction, a set of mobile stairs were being brought up to allow the crew access to the entry door. The tug stopped, and the driver's helper jumped down and disconnected the tug from the spacecraft. The stairs were rolled into place.

"What about it, guys? Anyone changed their mind?" said Dante.

"Actually, we don't need the full crew for the test hop," said David. "I need to handle the engineer's panel, and Dante will of course fly the left seat. Otherwise, either Susan or Jake can take the right seat."

Susan and Jake looked at each other. "I want to go," said Susan.

"Me too," said Jake.

"Then both of you come," said Dante.

Maria and Ellen looked at each other. Ellen said, "They really don't need us for this test hop. Let's go back and pack some things for the trip tomorrow. We'll need to fly up in our flight suits and then change at some point to our new things before the reception."

Maria said to the four climbing the stairs, "We will be back at the BPQ packing some things. You guys just do your checkout and come on back."

Ellen yelled to them at the top of the stairs, "Do you know what time we will leave tomorrow?"

Dante called back down, "Haven't been told yet, but they will probably want us to arrive in late afternoon, and it's only eight hundred miles or so. We won't leave until mid-afternoon."

Ellen turned to Maria. "We have plenty of time on the ground to get ready. *Let's go on the test hop.*"

Maria called up as they were closing the door, "Hey! Wait for us! We are going too!" They scrambled up the stairs.

Inside the *Revelation* on the flight deck, Dante took the left seat and Susan the first officer's seat. Jake took the seat directly between and behind Dante and Susan. David, Ellen, and Maria locked themselves into their designated seats behind and slightly above the level of the pilots and Jake.

Dante initiated the engine-start sequence. As the HD engines began to turn under their own power, the instrumentation across the board looked normal. The whine of the engines was like giant electric dynamos. The crew members could feel the power of the engines throughout their bodies. David scanned all the engineer's panel instrumentation—everything was 'go.' Dante slowly advanced the power, and the sleek ship began to roll toward the end of the fourteen-thousand-foot runway. Once again, the crew scanned all instrumentation. Maria continued to call off the checklist items. The ship was poised at the end of the runway.

Dante called out, "All systems go?"

In sequence, each of the crew responded, "All systems go!"

Susan contacted Mission Control, saying, "MC, this is *Revelation*. We are all systems green and prepared to launch the test flight."

"Roger, *Revelation*, you are cleared for launch," came back from Mission Control over the flight deck intercom.

Dante advanced the power levers to the takeoff position. The huge ship lurched forward, sucking its crew back into their seats. The ship was accelerating like a drag racer streaking down the runway—one hundred miles per hour, two hundred miles per hour—rotation after about a five-hundred-foot roll!

Dante pulled back on the column, and the ship lifted off directly into a vertical climb.

"Gear up!" he called. Within seconds, the *Revelation* was a dot in the sky overhead.

Dante pulled back to level-inverted flight at one hundred thousand feet and slowly rolled the craft to an upright and level cruise position. He said to Susan, "I see nothing but open sky ahead and above. What does the radar show?"

Susan responded, "The sky is yours—go for it!"

Dante again pulled back on the column as Susan advanced the levers to maximum climb power, MCP. This time, the acceleration was painful. In less than a minute, Dante said, "Now," and pulled the column back to place the ship in level-inverted flight. This time, they were at one hundred miles and 18,650 mph.

"Take it, Susan," said Dante. Susan took the column and gently rolled the ship, placing it now in level flight right-side-up. They were in orbit.

Susan called, "Check all instrumentation again. Dante, is there any need for us to go to JLS in this test?"

"No," said Dante. "I really didn't need to go to orbit, except to be sure the HD engines were functioning properly. It's only about eight hundred miles to Washington. We probably will set up to cruise at 3,200 or so. That will get us there in less than fifteen minutes, and we can see some of the countryside on the way up."

Jake said, "What altitude will we use for that?"

"Probably twenty-thousand feet. I'll talk to Mission Control either tonight or tomorrow morning and plan the exact speed and altitude."

"I think they told us that the corridors are a mile apart from S1 to S5. Then S10 is five miles above S5. S1 begins at a mile above ground level and goes to two miles. Did anyone happen to bring that chart they gave us?"

No one chirped. Dante said, "Don't worry about it. We'll tell them the speed we want to use, and they will assign us the proper altitude. I think we can go up to 4,000 mph between twenty thousand and twenty-five thousand feet. That might be the best altitude and speed."

"And if we want to change our cruise speed, they will assign us another altitude," said David.

"That's what I understand," said Dante. "MC will tell me what we can do. Also, I'll check the weather for cloud cover. If we can, I'd like to fly under the ceiling so we can see the ground."

"Are we ready to go home, or do we need to do anything else?" said Susan.

"Let's go home," said Dante.

"I'll call MC," said Susan, "and get clearance to re-enter and approach. MC, this is *Revelation*. We are ready to re-enter the atmosphere and approach KSC."

"Roger, *Revelation*. Continue on your present course, re-enter at 0625 UTC, and decrease speed to 1,500 mph. At 0635 UTC, turn right, heading 180. Slow to 500 mph and descend to twenty-five thousand feet to intersect glide slope, heading 330. Call us at outer marker for final clearance to land."

"Roger, MC, *Revelation*, over and out."

"That gives us six minutes 'til re-entry, right, someone?" said Susan.

"That is correct," said Jake. "Everyone check to be sure you are strapped in tight."

"Final instrument check. All in green?" said Dante.

"All in green," said each crew member in sequence.

"I'll count it down," said Susan. "Five . . . four . . . three . . . two . . . one—REP!"

Susan put the engines into reverse as Dante lowered the nose of the ship. The speed dropped 15,000 . . . 10,000 . . . 5,000 . . . 1500. The heading change was coming up. Susan called, "Five . . . four . . . three . . . two . . . one. Turn to course 180, slow to five hundred, and descend to twenty-five thousand feet. Intersect the 330 glide slope. Approach speed is 250."

Dante was *right on* with his control inputs. He intersected and turned onto the glide slope and slowed to 250.

"Outer marker's coming up," said Susan. "I'll call. MC, this is *Revelation* at the outer for landing on 33."

"Roger, *Revelation*, you are cleared for landing on 33," came back over the flight deck speaker.

They had the runway in sight. Dante stayed locked on the glide slope just like the ship was on autopilot. A perfect approach.

"I will try to set it right down inside that helicopter pad, marked just off the end of the runway," said Dante.

"Roger," said Susan. "I see it."

Dante was handling the power now as he slowed the ship approaching his target hover point just above the helicopter pad. The engines were screaming as the huge ship was made to fly like a helicopter. Dante brought the *Revelation* to a dead stop at about three-hundred feet directly above the pad. He slowly decreased power while holding the ship's attitude perfectly horizontal and lowered the craft directly toward touchdown on the concrete pad.

Susan was reading the numbers and calling off the altitude in feet. "One hundred feet, now eighty feet . . . fifty feet . . . thirty feet . . . ten . . . five . . . three . . . two . . . one—*touchdown*!"

Dante slowly pulled the power back. The massive ship settled as the gear shocks compressed. Dante shut down the engines. The *Revelation* was rock solid on solid concrete. Dante relaxed and slumped back into his chair.

The flight deck erupted in applause!—led by Jake. Susan was out of her seat and gave Dante a big hug. Jake looked over at him and said simply, "Nice job, colonel."

They completed the after-landing check as the stairs were pulled into place, and the ground crew began to connect the tow tractor.

On the ground, Director Stoll had monitored the test flight in Mission Control, and when the ship was on final approach, he left MC and headed for the runway. A small group of GSA staff followed him. The group had taken a position just off the runway where they waited for the landing.

As the *Revelation* touched down exactly on point and seemingly as light as a feather, this small group lost it! Cheers went up along with an applause. Klaus Stoll was *duly impressed*. Sergeant Bickel and the other mechanics that had prepped the ship were also on hand for the landing. They excitedly joined in the celebration. Sergeant Bickel ran the stairs up to the ship. All waited for the emergence of the crew.

Finally, the entry door opened; and Dante emerged first, followed by the others. The small crowd began cheering again and applauding.

The crew had not anticipated this and was somewhat embarrassed. "After all," as Dante later said, "there was really nothing to it."

Director Stoll came over and congratulated all the crew. This was the sign to the small crowd to go back to work, and they started to disperse. Klaus also made a point of congratulating David. "This ship is a fine design, David. We have many things at GSA that you can help us with." Then he turned to Dante, Susan, and Jake.

"We don't have a confirmation yet from the White House on the available area for your landing tomorrow," said Klaus Stoll. "If there is not a circle of one hundred yards that can be used, do you think you could do it with less?"

Susan looked at Dante. Dante said to Klaus, "Let's find out exactly what area is there and the shape of the area. Can we get a land plot diagram for the south lawn?"

"That's exactly what I have asked for, and it should have been transmitted to my office by now. Let's go see."

Dante turned to Gordy Bickel, the ground crew supervisor, and said, "Would you double-check to ensure that all switches are off and all equipment stowed? Can we keep security on her during the night? I think everything else will be OK."

"No problem, sir," said Gordy. "Do you know your departure time for tomorrow yet?"

Dante turned to Klaus. "Do we?" he asked.

"It still depends on where you will be landing," said Stoll. "If it is going to be Reagan, then they want you to arrive forty-five minutes earlier."

"It will be after two PM in either case, Sergeant," said Dante. "Can I call you in the morning and give you a 'firm' on that?"

"No problem, sir," said Bickel.

A PMU limo had driven up, and Klaus said, "This is your ride back to the BPQ. I will call you when I get the info on the south lawn. When I have it, I will have it transmitted to your unit, colonel."

"Sounds good," said Dante. The crew climbed into the limo.

Mr. D. delivered the Twenty First Century Six back to the BPQ where they, for the very first time, went into the small lounge adjacent to the cafeteria. The crew was feeling pretty good about the success—and the accuracy—of their vertical landing in the *Revelation*. They took a table near the window as a waitress came over.

"I'm buying!" said Jake. "We're toasting to Dante's flying skill. What'll you have, ladies?"

The girls all wanted Chardonnay, so Jake said to the waitress, "Let's have a bottle of your best Chardonnay for the ladies—we're celebrating!"

David had a beer, but Dante ordered a Beefeater and tonic, and Jake a Jack Daniels and seven. The waitress departed.

"I'll let you guys in on a little secret," said Dante. "The *Revelation* handles better in the vertical landing mode than the simulator did."

Susan and Jake were both surprised at that comment. "Are you kidding?" said Jake. "You could really feel a difference?"

"Maybe I can help explain what Dante felt," said David. "One difference a pilot always feels between the simulator and any actual ship is *g-forces*, a 'seat of the pants' feel for the motion and accelerations of the ship. There are almost no g-forces in the simulator—and *none* in its *hover mode*. Then there is the *inertia* of the actual ship. No matter how good the simulator manufacturers are, they can never exactly duplicate the feel of the size and weight of the real spacecraft.

"The *Revelation* weighs around a million pounds, and its inertia is a natural result of the distribution of all that weight relative to the center of gravity, or CG, of the ship. When you are controlling the ship in flight, your control inputs create aerodynamic or rocket-thruster forces that must overcome the inertia of the ship, so it moves as you desire. Since the simulator weighs only a fraction of the weight of the ship, its designers had to create artificial inertia, control forces, and control feel using computer software, electronics, servo devices, and hydraulics. It's just not possible to *perfectly match* the size, weight, and natural motion characteristics of the actual spacecraft."

At this point, the waitress returned with the drinks. Jake told her to run a tab.

"I want to propose the first toast," said Dante. "To David and all he did to create a *fantastic* flying machine."

Everyone raised their glasses, and Jake said, "Hear! Hear!" This was followed by a small applause. David smiled but was obviously uncomfortable with the praise.

Then David said, "Thanks, everyone, but there were an awful lot of people who helped create the *Revelation*."

"Yes, but you brought it all together," said Susan.

Ellen was very proud of David—especially at that moment.

"Back to the handling of the *Revelation* in the vertical landing mode," said Dante. "There's really not a huge difference in the simulator and the spacecraft in the hover mode. But I *felt it*, and I thought I would mention it. Now thanks to David, we all have a better understanding of the shortcomings of simulators."

"It's really your call, Dante," said Jake. "Do we go for the White House lawn or play it safer and go into Reagan?"

They all looked at Dante. Dante was looking down into his glass.

Dante said, "I can honestly say that I would rather take the ship onto the White House lawn for two reasons: One, we won't have to arrive earlier and take a puma limo from Reagan International. And two, I think the vertical landing is *just as easy* as the conventional landing, given the fine design of the *Revelation*. Another toast to David!"

"There is one other thing," said Jake, "that I would like to mention in favor of the vertical landing with *this particular ship*. In a conventional runway landing, an aircraft or spacecraft can lose all power and still land safely. When one thinks of a million-pound vehicle hanging on the power of its engines at three hundred feet above the ground, there is a tendency to worry about *power loss*. However, in the case of the *Revelation*, only *one* of its HD engines is sufficient to hold it aloft."

"And with its remaining engine, it can climb right back up and *out of there*." said David.

Dante was still looking at his glass. "I need another one," he said.

Klaus Stoll had completed a call from Frederich Haldemann, the president's chief of staff. He called to Renee and said, "Get Dante Washington on his AMec!"

He waited, and Renee buzzed him and said, "He's on, sir. He and the others are in the lounge at the BPQ."

"Tell him to stay there! I will be right over and join them. Might as well discuss this with the whole crew."

Renee gave Dante the message.

Dante closed his mec and said, "Stoll is on his way over here. He wants to talk to all of us."

Klaus Stoll showed up in record time and pulled up a chair. "I just got through speaking with Haldemann, the president's chief of staff, and they don't think the south lawn landing is the best idea."

The group sighed and looked at one another around the table. They felt deflated.

Klaus continued, "It turns out that the lawn has more than the amount of area you asked for, but there *are* some *trees* here and there . . . However, the real reason they have decided against it is security. The morning papers will have the story of your journey here from the twenty-first century and of your landing tomorrow afternoon and, of course, the White House reception. The White House security staff and Washington law enforcement think there will be a mob of people showing up for your landing. They just think the south lawn is too close to the White House."

Dante smiled. "For once, I agree with the politicians."

"So they want us to go into Reagan?" said Jake.

"Not exactly," said Klaus. "They still think a vertical touchdown will be a spectacular plus for the people."

"And for the administration," said Maria.

Klaus didn't say anything but just looked at Maria.

"*Where?*" said Dante. "Where do they want us to put it down?"

"There's what is called the Ellipse just south of the White House. It is basically an open grassy area shaped as an ellipse. It is between the Washington Monument and the White House but adjacent to the south lawn. The Ellipse is several hundred yards across and just less than that from north to south. Haldemann suggested that you land in the northwest quadrant of the Ellipse. They can put a large bull's-eye on the ground that would give you a circle about 150 yards in diameter to use."

Everyone looked at Dante again. "That should be OK," said Dante. "That is OK with me if it is OK with the rest of our team."

"I'm good with it," said Jake.

"Well," said Susan, "you did a fine job today, Dante. No telling how perfect your landing will be with all your experience!" She gave Dante a smile and a hug.

"I'm good with it," said David.

"Me too," said Ellen.

"Where will we be able to change into our new clothes for the reception?" said Maria.

Maria's comment eased the tension. Only a woman could possibly make that comment at that time. No one tried to answer her question.

Klaus said, "Wonderful, I'll call Haldemann right now and give him the news."

As Klaus stepped away from the table toward the window, David said to him, "Director Stoll, could you find out the exact time they want us to touch down?"

29

Saturday morning arrived early for Jake. As the sun's rays crossed his bed, he looked at the clock. *Six AM!* he thought. *I don't want to get up this early.* But he did.

He slipped on one of his flight suits and headed down the elevator for some coffee. As he entered the cafeteria, he noticed the news-vending unit. The front-page headlines were displayed on the digital screen:

ASTRONAUTS ARRIVE FROM THE 21ST CENTURY!

Under the headline were subheads like: AFTER 13 CENTURIES IN SPACE, NASA TRAVELERS RETURN TO EARTH and ERROR IN NAVIGATION PROGRAM SPOILS MISSION.

Jake touched his right index finger to the pay pad, and the unit produced a hard copy of the paper. He grabbed it and headed for the coffee. With coffee and newspaper in hand, he went out onto the deck to relax in the early-morning air and sunshine.

He laid the paper down on the table to his left and added some cream to his coffee. Jake wondered if he could ever tell the others *the truth about why their mission returned to Earth*. The entire front page of the *Orlando Sun* was devoted to the story of their arrival. Jake started reading the article. The tone of it made it obvious that it had come from the White House. It attempted to make the crew members out to be brave and courageous, and it deemphasized the error that caused the *Revelation* to return to Earth rather than to reach its intended destination. Dante was named as the commander of the ship, and the names of the rest of the crew were included along with a photo of the group.

The article further emphasized that GSA had kept the wraps on the arrival of the spaceship and on the whole occurrence until they could be sure everything checked out. It stated that the story, involving *thirteen centuries in space*, was indeed *difficult to believe*. The article further stated that certain organizations with national security responsibility wanted to be doubly sure that the astronauts were who they claimed to be. For such reasons, their presence had been kept confidential until now.

The article went on to tell of the impending landing of the *Revelation* at the Ellipse, south of the White House at 3:25 PM EST today. The landing would be attended by members of the administration, Congress, and the armed services.

228

The U.S. Air Force Band would also be in attendance. A press conference would follow the landing.

In the evening, the astronauts would be honored in a reception. It would be held in the White House for *invited guests*.

Jake didn't find any errors in the article or anything he didn't already know. In fact, the piece did a fair job of soft-pedaling what was thought to be a monstrous navigation error on the part of NASA. *Good try*, he thought, *but the media will never let this lie.*

"May I join you?" said Maria who had just walked up with her coffee and a tray of breakfast pastries.

"Of course," said Jake. "In fact, you can join me for the rest of your life, if you are so inclined."

Maria smiled sweetly at Jake—the big kidder! "What are you reading?" She ignored his come-on comment.

"Today's *Orlando Sun*," said Jake. "They have an article about six aliens arriving from outer space."

"Really?" said Maria. She bit.

"Here, want to take a look at it?" said Jake as he handed her the paper.

Maria took the paper, and as she started to look at the headline, she said, "Where do they think the aliens are from?" She then read about three lines and picked up the paper and hit Jake with it. He laughed.

"You are just a *big joker*," said Maria. "*This is about us.* And here is a picture. Where did they get that?"

"It looks like it was taken when we landed here—probably by the GSA staff photographers."

"Guess it had to be by them. The press has not known about us 'til today."

Maria continued to read the article. Finally, she tossed it down. "Nothing we didn't already know. What is your theory on how the wrong navigation program got put into the *Revelation*'s computer?"

"I have no idea," said Jake. "Whoever did it certainly knew exactly what he was doing. The program brought us directly back to Earth. If anyone had intended us harm, there are billions of places in space we could be right now."

"Very strange," mused Maria, looking at her coffee.

"Here come the others," said Jake. "Just when we were getting to know each other."

Maria smiled at him. *He's really not such a bad guy*, she thought. *But not in Rico's class.*

Susan and Dante were approaching the table followed by Ellen and David.

"Is everyone packed and ready for the White House party?" said Susan.

"What's to pack?" said Jake. "Just a suit and some extra underwear, in view of the vertical landing, and a toothbrush. That should about do it."

The new arrivals pulled up chairs.

"Has anyone told any of you about our hotel accommodations in DC?" said Ellen.

Everyone looked blankly at one another.

"I recall something about the Washington Marriott," said Susan. "Does that ring a bell with anyone?"

"That's it!" said David. "I remember Klaus mentioning that. We'll probably be talking to him at least once this morning. Dante, if you speak with him, could you verify the hotel and any other details like transportation?"

"No problem," said Dante. "Here's another question I will get answered. How long will we be in Washington?"

"And another question," said Maria. "Will there just be the one press conference after the landing, or are there other meetings planned—and not just with the press?"

"Good point," said Jake. "I'll bet every minute is planned by the White House staff, and we are the only ones who don't know what's going on."

"Let's call Stoll now and ask for an itinerary and the logistical details," said Susan

"Good idea!" said Ellen.

"I, for one," said Jake, "would like to spend at least a couple of days in DC after our official business has been completed. How does that sit with the rest of you?"

"I want to talk to the director of the Library of Congress," said Maria. "I might want to go to work for him . . . or her."

"And I would like to have lunch with Chief Justice Webster," said Susan. "That is, if it can be arranged. She extended me the invitation—at least her hologram did!"

Jake couldn't pass that up. "I wonder if a hologram can make binding commitments for the real person."

Susan gave Jake a strange look and said, "Well, I would certainly expect *so*."

"Did you guys see the paper?" said Maria. "The front page is all about us."

Ellen took the paper, and the others all tried to get into position to read over her shoulder.

Dante looked at his watch. It was seven forty-five. "I'll bet Stoll is in his office," he said. "I'll call and see if he answers." Dante walked to the edge of the deck near the wall and put in a call.

As everyone was chattering about the article, Dante returned to the table. "He was in. He has the itinerary, and he will transmit a copy to each of our rooms."

"Did he answer any of our questions?" said Susan.

"He said that there will be the welcoming ceremony at the *Revelation*. Then we will board a limo for a very short drive around to the rear portico of the White House for the press conference. The public will not be included in that, just the media. After that, the limo will take us to the Marriott. We will have two hours to relax and change before the reception."

"Oh good!" said Susan.

"That's perfect!" said Ellen.

Dante continued, "The reception will be from six to eight PM, and the limo will return us to the hotel."

"Sunday morning, there will be a brunch at the Marriott at 10:30 AM, followed by a guided tour of the city, which will last about two hours in a limo. There is nothing else scheduled for Sunday."

"How long will we be in Washington?" said Jake.

"Maybe I can remember the rest of the plan," said Dante. "Monday, there are several things in the morning. We will meet with the director of the Global Space Agency, followed by a meeting at the Pentagon with the secretary of defense and the Joint Chiefs of Staff. Both of these meetings will be to query us on things related to NASA in the twenty-first century and on the world situation in those times. They might even ask for our reactions to the current U.S. system of national defense. After lunch, there are more meetings—some with the media.

"All of our command performances will be completed by about four PM, Monday, and we will be free to do whatever we want on Tuesday."

Dante continued, "They have scheduled our departure from the Ellipse at 10:00 AM on Wednesday morning. Director Stoll said that if anyone wanted to stay in Washington longer than Wednesday morning, it could be arranged. There are all kinds of flights available back to KSC in the event anyone wants to stay over. GSA is picking up the tab for all of our expenses."

"What time will we lift off from here?" said Jake.

"They want us to touch down on the Ellipse at three twenty-five EST, give or take a few. That being the case, we plan to lift off here at two fifty-five. Let's meet at the ship, ready to board, at two thirty. Meanwhile, I'll discuss our flight plan with MC and see what flight level and speed options we have."

"Sounds good," said David. Then to Ellen, he said, "Ready to go back up?"

"We have time," she said. "Let's take a walk on the beach."

The others headed for the elevators.

Maria said to Susan as they walked, "I picked up only two outfits for Washington. That's not going to be enough."

"It will if we follow the crowd and wear the daysuits most of the time," said Susan. "It looks like most people dress that way. We can wear our NASA flight suits for the trip and the press conference and our best outfit for the reception. On Sunday, we can wear the daysuits for the brunch and tour and then on Monday, the other outfits we bought."

By this time, they had reached the eighth floor and were getting off the elevator. Dante and Jake headed for their units, and Susan and Maria continued talking outside Maria's door.

"But we still have another day in Washington," said Maria. "And you and I have important personal meetings scheduled."

"No problem," said Susan. "Tuesday, we can wear the same outfits we wore for the meetings on Monday. None of the same people will be there."

"You're right!" said Maria. "That will work! And then we can just wear the daysuits again on Wednesday for our departure."

"If necessary," said Susan, "there is some slack time in the schedule on Sunday and on Monday. We could pick up something else to wear."

"Perfect!" said Maria. "I'll see you in the lobby at two?"

"Fine, I'll call Mr. D. to be sure he is aware of our need for the van at two fifteen."

David, Ellen, Maria, and Susan were in the basement garage at 1:55 PM. Mr. D. advised them that he had just returned from taking Dante and Jake to the *Revelation*. "They said they wanted to get over a little early and check on a couple of things. Are you folks ready to go over?"

"Fine, let's go," said David.

They piled in the van, and Mr. D. took the driver's seat. He said as they cruised smoothly out of the basement up the ramp into the roadway, "I understand you are going to Washington to a reception at the White House?"

"That's correct," said Susan. "Have you ever been to Washington?"

"No," said Mr. D. "I was built in Texas by a subsidiary of Intel and shipped directly here to GSA. I have only been here and to Orlando."

"Are you curious about any of the rest of the country, Mr. D.?" asked Maria.

"Not really," the android replied. "GSA has a good library here, and I have read every volume in it. I know a lot about the United States and about the world for that matter."

They were approaching the flight line and the hangar where the *Revelation* had been stored.

"Do you remember everything you read, Mr. D.?" asked David.

"Yes, I do," replied the android.

"Want to try a question?" said Ellen.

"Sure," said Mr. D.

"Who was the first actor to win an Academy Award for Best Performance by an Actor?"

"That would be Emil Jannings for his role in *The Last Command* in 1927."

"Is that right?" said Susan to Ellen.

"Yes," said Ellen. "Very good, Mr. D., but I bet I can stump you. Would you like for me to try when we get back from Washington?"

"I would like that," said the android as the van arrived at the *Revelation*. "We are here. I will remove your bags from the trunk and take them up to the flight deck if you would like."

David said, "Excellent idea. Thank you, Mr. D."

The crew waited until Mr. D. had deposited the bags in the rear of the flight deck and had come back down the stairs. Then they all climbed the stairs and entered the flight deck. Dante and Susan took the left and right seats with Jake behind. The others took their same seats and began checking out the instrumentation.

"I discussed this trip with MC," said Dante. "And we decided that flight level S2 would be our best bet for this trip. S2—which is between two and three miles in altitude, or almost sixteen thousand feet—would be under the weather ceilings for most of the trip and would allow us to fly at 2,000 mph. At sixteen thousand feet, we should be able to get a pretty good look at the ground. Two thousand mph will get us to DC in twenty-four minutes."

"Sounds good," said Jake. "Anything higher would probably obscure a lot of the ground on the way up and wouldn't give us any time to look anyway." He asked Dante, "What's the cruise speed assigned to S3?"

"Three thousand mph," said Dante. "Our flying time would only be about sixteen minutes."

"Everybody OK with the cruise plan?" said Dante.

Dante got five *rogers* in sequence and said, "We'll switch on the electrical and check instruments, then go through our engine-start checklist. We had planned for a two fifty-five takeoff, but that will put us in Washington too soon. We have a pre-takeoff clearance to land at exactly three twenty-five, so we will plan our liftoff for 3:00 PM."

Dante, Jake, and David checked all instrumentation and then began the engine-start checklist.

"Initiating engine start," said Dante. "Recheck all your restraints."

The HD engines started to hum—the noise increased like huge dynamos starting up. NASA had recorded the noise from the ship's engines at about 110 dB.

"Engines at idle," said Susan. "All my instruments are good."

"All green over here," said Dante.

"Hold it!" said David. "I have a caution light on the right main gear strut actuator!"

"What is the actuator pressure indicator showing?" said Dante.

"Pressure's reading normal . . . I don't get it," said David.

"Could be a small leak," said Jake. "Would that turn the caution on?"

"There are sensors that will detect leaks, but if the leak is significant, the pressure indicator and/or the quantity indicator should reflect a drop," said David.

"Then you are saying," said Dante, "that we may have a leak on no. 3 strut actuator, but minor? Are the actuators independently pressurized or all from a central system?"

David didn't answer. It was now 3:00 PM. To make the planned schedule cleared by MC, they needed to lift off *now*.

"*What is your thinking, David?*" said Dante.

"The actuators are all pressurized from the no. 3 hydraulic system," said David. "No other component depends on that system. It is strictly for the landing gear. There is a provision to cut in the no. 2 hydraulic system if we have a failure of the no. 3 system. That won't do us any good, however, in this case because the leak is apparently at one of the strut seals. No matter where the fluid comes from, the strut will continue to leak."

"OK. Shut 'er down, Jake!" said Dante as he began removing his harness. "We need to go look at the strut and see the problem firsthand." He began exiting his seat as did David. "Keep the electrical on, Jake, so you and Sue can monitor the instruments. If you get a caution on the no. 3 system pressure, let us know! Come on, David, let's go see what's wrong with the strut."

"Anything else we can do?" said Susan.

"No, not at this point," said Dante as he started the climb down. Then he said, "Yes, there is too! Call MC. Tell them what's happening and ask them to get a backup clearance for us for flight level S4. If we need it, they will let us cruise at 4,000 mph, and we can be in DC in twelve minutes."

Susan made the call to Mission Control.

Dante and David gained access and descended into the right main wheel well. David realized that while they could get close enough to inspect the upper actuator seal, they would not be able to get low enough to inspect the lower seal. "Damn!" said David. "I should have told Susan to call for a cherry picker! We can't see both seals from up here!" As Dante was about to say "I'll go back and tell her," David said, "Hold it! I guess she made that call! Here comes one now!"

A USAF high-lift unit was on its way to the ship. Sergeant Bickel was in the driver's seat. David and Dante were inspecting the upper strut seal when Sergeant Bickel said, "I heard you gentlemen might want a lift."

Ignoring the sergeant's pun, David said, "There is no leak at the upper seal. Let's go down."

Sergeant Bickel had raised the bucket, and the two climbed in. David took the bucket controls and lowered it to the lower strut actuator seal level.

"Look there!" said Dante. A small leak was emanating from one spot on the seal.

"What the heck?" said David. "This seal looks perfectly good. I can't see why . . ." He paused and touched the spot of the leak. "Wait a minute," David said. "There is something *under the seal*." David took a penknife from his pocket and worked at the seal. Out came a piece of wire.

"It's a nail!" said Dante. "See? It's a small finishing nail! How the hell . . ."

"You are right," said David. "Look, the leak has stopped. There was a small rag hanging on the side of the high-lift basket. Hand me that rag."

Dante did, and David wiped the fluid off the strut. "The leak has stopped. Do you have your mec? Call Susan and Jake and see if the caution light is out."

Dante made the call. "It is?" he said. He turned to David and said, "The light's out! *Let's go flying!*"

As they lowered the basket, Dante looked at his watch. "It's 3:09," he said. "We can just make it."

Sergeant Bickel drove the high-lift around to the entry door, and David moved the bucket into position near the flight deck entry door. Jake opened the door, and Dante and David thanked Sergeant Bickel as they scrambled back into the ship.

Dante jumped back into his seat and yelled to Susan, "START ENGINES!" She had them starting before Dante got to the *engines* part of the command. Dante was on the horn with MC, telling them they would be off in less than one minute and would be flying at flight level S5—thirty thousand feet and five thousand miles per hour.

Mission Control responded with, "Roger, *Revelation! We have cleared the way for you.* Have a good ride!"

Dante came back with, "Please remind Washington Air Traffic Control Center that we are going straight for the Ellipse, will drop down to three hundred feet to arrive directly over the touchdown point, will hover briefly there, and descend vertically to touch down."

"Roger, *Revelation*, will do! Over and out," came back MC.

"Engines are at idle," said Susan. "I have all greens!"

"All greens here," said Jake.

"Greens here," said David.

"Hold on, guys, we're moving out!" said Dante. He pushed the power levers steadily forward as the engines started to scream.

The ship leaped into the air straight up and accelerated faster than a toy rocket. One second, it was lifting off; and in four seconds, it was a dot above the space center.

"We are at thirty thousand feet," said Jake, "and at 4,000 mph."

"Perfect," said Dante as he started back with the control column and began to level off inverted at S5 and 4,500 mph.

"Heading you want is 004," said Jake.

"Roger," said Dante as he was completing his longitudinal roll to place the *Revelation* exactly on track at flight level S5 with the nose pointed directly at the White House.

"Time is now three thirteen," said Susan. "You might want to fudge just a little on the speed."

"She's right, Dante," said Jake. "ATC has cleared S5 for us all the way to the Ellipse—we don't want to be tardy."

"And it will take a couple of minutes to slow it to a hover and drop it down three hundred feet," said Ellen.

"Suddenly, everybody is an expert." Dante smiled over at Jake and Susan and tweaked the power to yield five thousand miles per hour.

"We aren't going to do any sightseeing?" whined Maria.

Dante rolled his eyes and said, "You have nine minutes, Maria. Tell me everything you see."

"Here," Jake said as he flipped on the belly camera and the screen over the forward instrument panel, "take a look at the ground!"

At the White House, the excitement was increasing. President Thornhill had decided to watch the landing from the back portico of the White House and had sent the vice president to do the honors at the Ellipse. At the Ellipse, a huge crowd had assembled, some estimated at fifteen thousand people. The touchdown bull's-eye had been marked in the upper-left quadrant of the grassy field, and the Air Force Band was tuning up. The decision had been made to use a portable, self-propelled platform that could be pulled up to the spaceship after the landing was complete. The dignitaries involved would be pre-seated and would ride in on the mobile platform—like football players once did on Friday afternoon in small towns before the big game that night.

The *Revelation* was now six minutes from the Ellipse. The screen above the forward instrument panel was showing a good picture of the ground as they headed north toward Washington DC. Jake had increased the magnification of the belly camera for a better view.

Maria commented, "There are houses, condos, and commercial districts as far as I can see. I don't see any farms or open areas along the eastern seaboard . . . This must be where the most of the population is located."

"I would say along the East Coast, then California, and the Mexican states," added Ellen.

"That's one of the things I would like to review at the Library of Congress if I can get a position there," said Maria. "There is just so much to learn about what has happened to the world since we left it."

"Washington dead ahead," said Jake. "Look at the horizon!"

Everyone looked down from the screen that had their attention and focused on the windscreen in front of Dante and Susan.

"Got it!" said Dante. "We are three minutes out . . . Susan, give ATC a call."

"Washington Center," said Susan, "this is *Revelation,* inbound from KSC to an Ellipse area landing. Do you read?"

"*Revelation,* this is Washington Center. You are cleared to three hundred feet, then to touch down. Reagan traffic has been alerted, but it will be clear of your approach. Hold flight level S5 at current speed for forty-two seconds after *mark.* At forty-two seconds, begin your descent to three hundred, reducing speed to zero as you arrive at three hundred feet over your touchdown point."

"Roger, Washington Center, over and out!" said Susan as she was counting down the seconds for Dante. "Five . . . four . . . three . . . two . . . one—mark!"

After forty-two seconds, Dante pulled the power back and started the descent—twenty thousand—ten thousand—three thousand, two thousand, one thousand feet and two hundred miles per hour. They had the bull's eye in sight.

"Look at the crowd!" said Susan.

"There's enough landing area there," said Jake.

"Plenty." said Dante as he arrived over point and slowed the *Revelation* to a standstill. He reduced power to just the amount needed to hold the ship motionless above the ground. The belly cameras were now photographing the landing area. Dante had the ship directly above the bull's-eye. Susan was calling out altitude in feet.

On the ground, the crowd had been going wild as the huge ship descended, slowed, and approached the point just above the Ellipse landing target. Now as the *Revelation* hovered motionless above the ground, the crowd grew silent. They couldn't have heard one another anyway because of the engine noise of the ship. They, along with the president and his immediate staff on the rear portico of the White House, seemed to collectively hold their breaths, awaiting the next move of the *Revelation.*

Susan lowered the landing gear as both David and Dante monitored the indicator lights. One green, two greens, and now for the one that had been leaking.

"Three greens!" called David before Susan could say it.

Dante had his right hand on the power and his left on the column. He said, "Here we go . . ."

The huge white ship slowly began to descend toward the bull's-eye. As it went, Dante initiated a slow rotation of the ship on its vertical axis to align the flight deck entry door so it faced the rear of the White House. That way, the president and his staff could observe the crew's exit from the ship. Dante held the ship *rock solid* as it descended. Susan called out the distance from touchdown.

"Fifty feet . . . thirty feet . . . fifteen feet . . . five feet." The landing pad proximity sensors on each of the gear were now measuring inches from the grassy lawn of the Ellipse. While there was no dust or smoke from the HD engines, the noise was near 125 dB. The spectators all had their ears covered.

"Touchdown!" said Dante and closed the power levers. The *Revelation* was on the ground, solid as a rock and as quiet as a mouse. The time was 3:25 PM.

The crowd now went nuts! With flags waving and people shouting and screaming, the Air Force Band started up "America the Beautiful"—the national anthem for the last ten centuries. Vice President Warren and all the dignitaries began shaking hands and congratulating one another over the *Revelation*'s landing. Back at the White House, everyone was congratulating the president.

On the flight deck, all was quiet as the six crew members unfastened their restraints. Dante said, "And now for the hard part—we have to walk down the steps without falling."

Air force personnel were positioning stairs at the entry door of the ship.

The men decided, in a statement of twenty-first-century chivalry, that the ladies should go first and them last. The very last would be Dante. Before the first person went down, David said, "What about the bags? We don't want to emerge with suitcases!"

The girls all agreed heartily, and Jake said, "Fogeddabouddem. After the ceremony here, I'll bet credits the driver of our limo is a droid. We will have him climb back up and get the bags."

Everyone congratulated Jake on a brilliant suggestion, and Susan started down the ladder. The others followed single file.

The platform with dignitaries had been wheeled up next to the entry stair, but off to the side, so as not to obstruct the view of the president and his portico party. The Air Force Band, now finished with the national anthem, had struck up the air force song "Off We Go into the Wild Blue Yonder." So far, there was no sign of the "The Star-Spangled Banner" being played, but there were plenty of American flags about—all with fifty-six stars.

The *Revelation* astronauts began to emerge from the exit of the ship and down the stairs. When Dante stepped out, the crowd, remembering that there were only six aboard, again began to cheer and shout and wave their flags. They seemed to know that Dante was the commander. The band struck up "For He's a Jolly Good Fellow."

The six all smiled and waved at the crowd, and one old gentleman on the front row of the spectators said, "They don't look 1300 years old to me!"

A droid came forward and introduced himself as Mr. Pollard, or Mr. P. to most people, and explained to the astronauts that he would be giving them a short ride to the White House after the ceremony and then later to the hotel. Jake seized the moment and said to Mr. P., "Would you be a big help and bring the bags stowed at the rear of the flight deck and place them in the trunk of your limo?"

"I'd be happy to, sir," said Mr. P. "Are there six of them?"

Hearing a "That's correct" from Jake, Mr. P. went on his way.

At the direction of another droid, the crew climbed the short stairs to the platform, waving to the crowd as they went.

Once on the platform, Vice President Warren greeted them and introduced them to the others present. Then the vice president took the microphone at the podium and addressed the crowd.

"Good afternoon to everyone!" said the VP. The crowd responded.

"Today, we are honored to have visit with us six brave astronauts who were born in and lived in the twenty-first century of this Earth!" The crowd again went bonkers!

Vice President Warren continued, "These six astronauts have been in space for thirteen Earth centuries in a journey that took them beyond Betelgeuse—the brightest star within a thousand light-years from our Earth into the constellation Orion and beyond Scorpios. Because of the speed of their ship, they only aged *one year* during this entire journey." The crowd let out a gasp similar to when their favorite slugger strikes out at the plate.

"Today, we are welcoming them to our world, a new world to them, now in its thirty-fourth century. No one has asked them to prepare a speech. But I would like to ask their commander, Col. Dante Washington, to say just a few words before they all proceed up to the White House for the press conference."

They crowd began cheering when he said that Colonel Washington would speak but began booing when he said that all of the astronauts must leave the location for the press conference.

"Now hold on!" said the VP. "We aren't forgetting you! See those giant screens behind you and to the right and left? Those screens will carry the conference and give you a better view than you can imagine. Now, colonel, if I can just impose on you for a few words."

The crowd seemed happy now and gave Dante a huge applause with cheers and flags waving all around. "Colonel Washington! *Colonel Washington!*" some chanted.

Dante, in his very best military posture and step, proceeded to the lectern.

He began, "Thank you, Mr. Vice President. I would like first to introduce my crew from the *Revelation*." He turned and asked each to step up and wave after he introduced them. He began with Susan. "This is Susan Chen, our first officer." The crowd gave Susan an enthusiastic ovation. "And this is Jake Loneghan, the backup pilot to both Susan and me." Jake got a good round of applause. "Next are David and Ellen Marks." David and Ellen stepped out together. "David is our flight engineer, and Ellen is our chief of medical." Another applause.

Maria wondered what her title was going to be.

"And finally, here is Maria Rodriguez, our quality assurance officer," said Dante. The crowd went nuts over Maria as she stepped forward, partly because she was such a beauty, but mostly because roughly a fifth of the spectators appeared to be of Spanish descent. "We wish to thank President Thornhill and Vice President Warren and all the others that made our visit to Washington possible. We particularly want to thank Director Stoll at GSA and those of his staff that have made us feel so welcome to be back on Earth." This statement brought applause.

Continuing, Dante said, "When we left Earth in 2025, the world was *in bad shape*. I doubt if many of you alive have ever read much about the twenty-first century. Why would you? Talk about ancient history . . . But look at us. We are not *dinosaurs*." This brought a laugh and hearty applause. He continued, "In 2025, the people of Earth were on a path to destroy, not only themselves, but the world with them. Now look at this beautiful Earth! We now know a lot about *what* you have done these past thirteen centuries, but we can't imagine *how* you did it." More applause ensued. Dante closed with, "I know that I speak for our crew when I say thank you, thank you, thank you to the people of Earth!'"

Dante looked at the vice president, who was also applauding, and stepped away from the podium to his spot with the crew. The crew was applauding Dante. And all were giving him big smiles.

Vice President Warren announced that *this* ceremony was over but invited all to stay and observe the press conference on the big screens. Dante and the crew followed Mr. P. down the steps and to the limo. They had hardly sat down in the limo before they had to get out. Mr. P. stopped the puma at the left side of the rear portico to the White House and advised Dante to lead the group onto the platform set up for the conference at the base of the portico where the president was waiting. The press was assembled, standing, at the front of the platform.

President Thornhill had a small staff with him and, of course, a number of security personnel. He greeted Dante on the platform away from the microphones with, "Ah! Colonel Washington! A very nice landing, indeed! I had told Director Stoll that a Reagan landing would be fine, but he insisted on a vertical approach and touchdown. As a matter of fact, he said that you and the crew favored the vertical landing."

Dante, of course, was stunned. They had agreed to take the risk of the vertical landing *because they had been told that was what the president wanted.* You *still couldn't trust politicians.* Dante glanced at Jake and at the others. Jake appeared ready to *deck* the president. Of course, he didn't want to get *shot.*

"Mr. President, how good to see you again. In fact, *that is really you* this time, isn't it?" said Dante. The president seemed like he appreciated Dante's humor.

Dante continued and introduced all the *Revelation* crew again to the president, who, in turn, introduced those with him including the first lady, Simone Thornhill, who said hello, offered her hand, and that was about it.

"Let me just say, Dante, that I have never seen a better piece of flying than you performed a few minutes ago!"

"That *we* performed, sir," said Dante. "Thank you very much, Mr. President. It was a team effort—and always has been—since we left Earth in 2025."

"Yes, I am sure it was, Dante," said the president. "Are you aware that we have some very nice suites arranged for all of you at the downtown Marriott?"

"Someone mentioned that to us, sir, and we really appreciate that."

Jake entered the conversation to everyone's surprise and said, "The suites will be nice, Mr. President, especially since we will be staying in town until at least Wednesday."

"I'm aware of that, Mr. Loneghan. I understand that Susan plans to meet with our chief justice, Mrs. Webster," said the president.

"If she can find the time, sir," said Susan.

"She's looking forward to it—on Tuesday, I believe," said Thornhill. "Do any others of you have special appointments not already listed on your itinerary?"

"I would like to visit the Library of Congress," ventured Maria.

"Business or pleasure?" asked the president.

"A little of both, sir," said Maria without further clarification.

The president stared briefly into Maria's eyes and said, "Yesss . . . Well! I'm sure the media has questions for you. Let's move up to the front of the platform where the microphones are."

President Thornhill led the others toward the microphones and the assembled press corps. He stepped up to the mikes.

"Good afternoon, everyone!" said the president. They responded with greetings and applause. The president continued, "I assume that all of you have read the morning paper?" This brought a courteous but insincere laugh from the group.

President Thornhill continued, "I would like to introduce you all to the magnificent six astronauts from twenty-first-century Earth!" He carefully introduced each of the crew ending with Dante.

Everyone loudly applauded.

"I will now turn them over to you for a few minutes of questions. Mr. Moore will moderate the conference. Please be brief and state your name, your affiliation, and who your question is directed to."

The president moved aside, and the six crew members moved up to the microphones with the president now in the background with the first lady and Mr. M. standing off to one side. Several hands went up immediately.

Mr. M. pointed to one person.

"Arnand Paragios, the *New York Times*," said a man in the front row. "My question is for Colonel Washington. Sir, how long have you been back on Earth, and why wasn't the press told of your arrival?"

Dante took the mike and said, "We arrived back on Earth eight days ago. You were not told of our presence for security reasons."

Another hand, another question: "Barbara Stein, *Washington Post*. Colonel, why so many days from your arrival until now? And a second question, are you and your team exactly who you say you are?"

This question caused muttering in the crowd, some hissing, and some laughter.

Dante smiled. "The first question has already been answered. The answer to the second one is, as far as we know, we are. After all, we are technically over 1300 years old. I hear that memory fails with age."

This remark brought some laughter, but also more determination from the press. None of them were happy to have been left out of the loop for two weeks.

Another hand, another question. "Morrie Walsh, *Chicago Sun Times*. This question is for Mr. Marks. We were given to understand that your ship was originally intended to leave Earth in 2025 and visit another planet some 1300 light-years from Earth. You never intended to return to Earth. If that, in fact, is the case, then what happened that caused your ship to return to Earth?"

David stepped up to a mike. "You are correct with your information. The *Revelation*'s computer, after examination by GSA lab personnel, was found to have the wrong navigational program installed."

Morrie continued, "Then, sir, if that is the case, wouldn't that *have* to have been done by NASA personnel with access to the ship's computer?"

"That is one possibility," said David. "There are others."

"What others?" continued Mr. Walsh.

Mr. M. stepped in and said, "Let's go to another question," cutting off Mr. Walsh.

"Brenda Starr, *St. Louis Ledger*. I have the same question. If the *Revelation*'s computer had the wrong program installed, who but a NASA technician with access to the ship could have installed the program?"

Mr. M. started to take the podium and go to the next question when David put his hand on Mr. M.'s arm. He said in a whisper to Mr. M., "I will take the question."

"An outsider may have gotten into the complex and removed the correct program, replacing it with an *incorrect* program. Our security was good, but not perfect, and the computer could have been sabotaged. You can write this: The checkout of computer function before launch showed no anomalies. At the time we went into hibernation, we were on course. And once we made our *jump to light-speed*, the NASA ground station was unable to track us anyway." David continued, "When we arrived in the vicinity of the Earth, we thought we were arriving at Nyvar, our intended destination in the Setarian star system."

Another hand went up. "Edwin Cahill, *Los Angeles Times*. This question is for Mr. Loneghan. As you may know, none of the media have had any time to prepare for this conference. We only learned of your arrival back on Earth in this morning's paper. You, on the other hand, have had over a week to learn about thirty-fourth-century Earth."

"Do you have a question?" said Mr. M.

"My question," continued Mr. Cahill, "is what is your reaction so far to thirty-fourth-century Earth?"

Jake smiled over at the others of the crew and then at the media. He said, "GSA, led by Director Stoll, has done a fantastic job of introducing us to your century. While his lab specialists and technical experts were rushing about overturning every stone to be *sure we are who we claim to be*, he and his GSA staff and others have also spent many hours helping us understand what life is like today on Earth in the thirty-fourth century."

Jake continued, "My *personal* answer to your question is that the Earth is now many times better off than it was when we left it. I would certainly not want to go back to the twenty-first century—that is, based on what I have learned about the present time."

Other hands went up. Mr. M. acknowledged one.

"David Dreissen, *San Antonio Star*," said the young man. "This is for any one of you and, in fact, for all of you. Have you decided what you want to do with your lives now that you are back on Earth?" The six hesitated and looked at one another.

Dante stepped forward and said, "Assuming the others don't mind, I can give you a quick summary. Ellen Marks is a physician, as you know, and she plans to work in her field. She has already made a contact with Mayo-Orlando. Her husband, David Marks, is a brilliant scientist and engineer who was a lead designer of the *Revelation*. David plans to work in spacecraft design for GSA. Susan Chen is an attorney by training, and she is interested in work with the justice department. Jake Loneghan is quite a pilot and quite a businessman. He intends to both fly for GSA and go into some business on his own. Maria Rodriguez was quite active in government affairs and causes for the underprivileged in twenty-first-century Earth and will be looking for some affiliation here in Washington. I am interested in national security and in the U.S. Air Force."

Dante turned to the others and said, "Was that OK, or do you any of you want to add something?"

No one stepped forward or acted like they wanted to speak.

Mr. M. took a mike and said, "Two more questions, please."

The crowd groaned, but no one objected. Other hands went up. Mr. M. selected one.

"Cahill, *LA Times* again. Ms. Chen, what do you think of our justice system as compared with yours of the twenty-first century?"

This was the type of question none of the group wanted and had feared would be asked. Susan stepped forward toward the mikes and was preparing to speak. The president gave Mr. M. a signal. Mr. M. stepped in front of Susan and took the podium. He said, "Ms. Chen nor her other crewmates have had time to fully understand our thirty-fourth-century system of justice. They will need further education on this subject before they can answer that question."

Mr. Cahill wasn't ready to accept that answer and said, "Right . . . But I just wanted her opinion *so far . . .*"

Mr. M. pointed directly at Mr. Cahill and took a step as if to come off the podium toward him. Mr. Cahill cringed and stepped back, saying, "No no! Never mind! I will wait 'til later to ask that question."

Mr. M. stopped and again took the mikes, motioning to Susan that she should return to her spot in the line. He said, "One more question, please."

None of the press corps raised a hand, and none said a word. Mr. M. looked at the president and then said to the press. "Then that will be all for today. If any of you wish to interview any of the six astronauts, you may contact me. I will be handling such arrangements."

The media began to disburse, and the president and first lady again came over to the *Revelation* crew.

"The media really didn't have a lot of questions you could respond to at this time, Dante. They never do," said the president. "You probably gave them much more than they expected with your description of what career paths you all plan to follow. No harm in that, however. You did a good job."

The president continued, "There is nothing else of importance we have for now. I am sure you are ready for some relaxation. I'll have Mr. P. drive you over to the hotel. Our reception for you begins at 6:00 PM. We have a reception line for you to meet all of our guests, so please be prompt." With that comment, he nodded to Mr. P. and turned away to enter the White House. His wife and his staff followed him.

The *Revelation* crew followed Mr. P. to the waiting limo. The PMU limo was a beauty—almost like being in your living room. When everyone was seated with Mr. P. at the wheel, the limo's wheels retracted as it lifted slowly off and turned toward the downtown Marriott.

"Well," said Ellen, "that was an interesting meeting. I think that—" Jake put his hand on her arm and his finger to his lips. Then he turned and said to Mr. P., "Mr. P., please raise the divider glass behind your seat and shut off the communication between front and rear."

"Certainly, sir," said Mr. P. and appeared to do exactly as requested.

When the clear divider was up, Jake and David searched around the sides, roof, and floor of the passenger compartment; and then Jake said to Ellen, "Now go ahead."

"Do you think that Mr. P. can't hear us now?" Ellen said to Jake.

"We are told that droids do exactly as told unless the command is against the law or not in accord with their program," said Jake. "I am assuming that he shut off the com connection," Jake continued, "How did President Thornhill know of our personal plans? Susan, had you contacted Mrs. Webster?"

"No," said Susan. "I had not, and I just mentioned it to you five. Unless one of you told someone else, I think we can assume that we are bugged."

Ellen spoke, "What I was going to say when we first got in the limo was that there were two strange things about the conference to me. One, how did Thornhill know of Susan's intent to contact Mrs. Webster? And two, why did Mr. M. get concerned about Mr. Cahill's question regarding the justice system?"

"I think we have to assume that there is something about the justice system they aren't ready to tell us, and two, we must be individually bugged," said Dante.

The sergeant of White House security was listening over the shoulder of one of his agents. "They are on to us," he remarked to several in the room.

30

The *Revelation* crew was dressed and ready for the White House reception. The ladies had donned their new designer outfits and looked quite stunning. Ellen wore an elegant gracefully flowing black Christina Olson gown. Maria sizzled in her romantic low-cut red Roberta Warren fashion, and Susan was sure to turn heads when she walked into the room in her sky blue Victorian-styled Raymond George creation. They all had selected just the right jewelry pieces to accent their outfits.

Dante and the men had purchased the latest in semiformal wear from The Men's Store near Kennedy Spaceflight Center and looked pretty sharp. The suits fit well and looked like almost the same thing they would have worn for a White House bash in 2025. The one difference being the use of ties. In 2025, any man wearing a suit to a semiformal affair would have on an expensive silk tie to complement his ensemble. In 3339, there were no ties to be found. The front of the men's shirts were decorated in various fashions, but the designs were all part of the shirts.

The only thing that was different in the men's suits was the material. As with the daysuits, the outfits had temperature controls built in. No one dressed in the thirty-fourth century ever got too hot or too cold. The thermofab material took care of that.

Mr. P. was in the lobby when the astronauts emerged from the elevator.

"Your limo is at the curb, ladies and gentlemen. Shall we go?"

The six followed Mr. P. to the curb, and just during the short walk from the front hotel entrance to the PMU limo, a photographer jumped out from behind a plant and snapped a shot! Mr. P. stopped and turned toward the photog, but Jake said, "It's OK, Mr. P., we don't mind."

The photographer had sprinted out of sight anyway.

After a short drive, the limo arrived at the main entrance to the White House. Mr. P. had gotten them there about fifteen minutes early. They were sure the president would be pleased. Mr. M. came out to greet them, and Mr. P. parked the PMU.

"Good evening to all of you," said Mr. M. "The president and his party are assembled in the Blue Room just inside. They *waited* until you were here to form the reception line. Please walk this way."

President Thornhill greeted the six astronauts and personally made their introductions to those assembled in his party. The *Revelation* crew members had of course met the first lady and Vice President Warren but were introduced to

Mrs. Warren and the majority leaders of the Senate and House and their wives. President Thornhill also introduced the crew to members of the president's cabinet and their spouses. The group chatted for a few minutes, and then Mr. M. suggested that they all go back into the Grand Entrance and form the reception line. The president and Mrs. Thornhill led them all into the beautiful hall where they formed the line. The large Jeffersonian clock high on the wall indicated exactly 6:00 PM. Some guests were already entering.

A small string ensemble in the Cross Hall played soft music as the reception proceeded. Each incoming couple or guest proceeded through the reception line and forward toward a number of tables lavishly adorned with delectable hors d'oeuvres and liquid refreshments.

The president and his wife, of course, headed up the line, followed by Dante, Susan, Jake, Maria, Ellen, and David in that order. Following the six from the twenty-first century were members and spouses of the president's cabinet, of Congress, and of the Supreme Court. The guests begin filing by.

After about thirty minutes of this, Jake whispered to Maria, "Do you know any way to get out of this?"

Maria looked quite shocked and said, "Absolutely not! And you can't be serious. We are at the peak of U.S. society at this very moment."

Jake came back with a pained expression and said, "How much longer . . ."

Maria gave him a very stern look, and Jake continued with, " . . . do you think?"

Susan overheard the whispering and turned to Jake, saying, "I can see the end of the line just coming up the steps."

Jake was pleased to hear that.

The reception line had been dispersed almost an hour before, and the *Revelation* crew members were mingling with the guests. Many of the conversations amounted to questions by the president's guests about the twenty-first century and what things were like then. Some of the questions were about the journey over the thirteen centuries, and some of the questions were those asking one of the astronauts' opinions of something in the present, usually something the guests weren't really too sure about themselves. The interesting thing about most of the conversations was that when one of the Twenty First Century Six would ask another guest a question about some aspect of life in the year 3339, they wouldn't answer. It was almost like they didn't hear the question. Not *a single such question* was answered for any of the *Revelation* crew members.

Jake managed to break free from whatever group he was talking to and work his way around the crowd. He successfully spoke briefly to each of the *Revelation* crew and planned eight PM as their departure time. They all agreed to mosey toward the president and Mrs. Thornhill at about eight and thank them for the evening and then meet one another at the limo. Jake also spied Mr. P. standing over to the side and worked his way over to him.

"Mr. P.," said Jake, "we want to leave at about eight fifteen. Can you meet us at the limo then?"

The android said, "I'm not Mr. P., sir, but I can call him for you."

Jake was taken aback but not really surprised. All of the droids looked exactly alike. How could anyone keep them straight?

"Just talked to Mr. P., sir, and he said to tell you that the limo will be out front and waiting for you all by 8:00 PM."

"Thanks," said Jake.

In the White House security center, the sergeant at arms commented to the others, "Let's put two unmarked units on them when they leave here tonight. You *know* they are not going back to the hotel this early." Then on his mec, "Mr. M., tell Mr. P. that the cars will be following them."

Mr. M. walked away to a more private spot. Then he returned. He said, "Mr. P. said, 'No problem, but I can handle this myself. No need for two more units.'"

"Tell him not to try to cover too much," the sergeant said to Mr. M. "There will be two cars following them."

Mr. P. had the limo precisely where it should have been and was waiting for the crew when they emerged through the front entrance of the White House. The six hurried into the PMU. Jake started talking with Mr. P. as the limo pulled away and headed toward the street.

"Say, Mr. P., does Georgetown still jump?"

Mr. P. said, "I really couldn't say, sir. It does stay open late, I believe."

Jake turned to the others and whispered, "I will pick a spot, probably something like O'Sullivan's, and we will see if we can't ditch Mr. P. We can always get back to the hotel in a cab." They all agreed.

The two White House security pumas followed the limo.

Jake didn't see O'Sullivan's and just picked a place at random.

"Stop and let us out here, Mr. P.," said Jake into the intercom.

"Fine, sir," said Mr. P. "I'll wait for you right here."

"That won't be necessary, Mr. P.," said Jake. "You go on back to the garage, and we will take taxis from here to the hotel." Jake and the others exited the limo and went into the club.

Mr. P. was heading back to the White House garage when he called in to the security office. "Could you guys hear what they were saying?"

"Yeah," came back the sergeant, "we could hear, but where did you leave them? They didn't say the name."

"The place was called the Ocean's Floor," said Mr. P. "Your units were right behind me. Anything else you need?"

"No, we'll take it from here," said the sergeant.

Dante had found a table just as a group was leaving and grabbed it for his team. Another couple had seen it at the same time and were ready to challenge Dante for the spot until they saw the other five walking up. The astronauts settled in and ordered drinks. Then Jake said, "This is nuts! We can't even talk to each other without being overheard by some security people. Has anyone figured out how they are bugging us? Where are the mikes?"

While everyone else was saying, "I haven't." David was pointing to himself and nodding as if to say "I have!"

While the others just looked at him, David took a pencil and pad and wrote "I have". Then he wrote, "Keep talking to cover me."

Jake was right on it. He said, "This is kind of a cool place. It's nicely appointed, and the people seemed to be enjoying themselves."

The others caught on and continued talking while David was writing on the paper.

David wrote, "The 'bugs' are in the temporary ID cards they gave us. Very sensitive!"

A knowing look went around the table as everyone began to pull out their ID cards. Jake kept talking about something else to cover their actions. Soon, they all had their cards on the table in a pile. They were just looking at them.

Dante took the pencil from David and wrote, "Can you disable the mikes?"

David wrote, "I think so. Let's take them to the men's room."

Jake announced, "Think I'll powder my nose."

David said, "Me too."

At David's signal, Dante and the girls stayed at the table. He and Jake took the CIN cards to the men's room.

Soon, Jake and David returned all smiles. "We should be OK now," said Jake. "David ran 120 volts through them!"

David explained how he had burned up any internal circuits in the cards by overloading them. Susan looked at the cards and then at David and said, "How can you be sure?"

The security chief at the White House exclaimed, "Can't hear them! I'm not picking up anything!"

One of the others ran a frequency check and looked up at the sergeant. "They must have found the chips!"

"Now what do we do?" said another.

"Call the two units assigned to follow them and tell them *we've lost audio*, and they better not lose them!"

But Jake was ahead of them. "I saw two pumas following us in the limo. I'm not sure, but I think they might have been security cars on our tail. If you guys are game, I think we can lose them."

"Why should we be running and hiding from them?" said Ellen. "We haven't done anything wrong."

"And they may think we have," said Maria, "if we try to elude them."

"I just don't like to have someone listening to everything I say." said Jake.

"And neither do I." said Dante.

"I thought Klaus Stoll said that we were not being followed any longer," said Susan.

"Guess he was either lying or misinformed," said Jake.

Ellen ventured, "Do you think that everybody's ID cards are bugged?"

Everyone at the table looked at one another and wondered.

"You mean no privacy at all?" said David. "But we don't keep our IDs on us at all times."

"No, but we generally keep them close by," said Dante.

"And as sensitive as they are, we have basically been monitored the whole time we've been back on Earth." said Jake.

"I think what we are saying is that everyone can be monitored at any time by virtue of their CIN card!" said Dante. "No personal privacy."

Everyone stopped and thought about that. They glanced around their table at the other patrons. No one seemed to be very near or remotely interested in what they were talking about. "Let's talk softly," said David.

Outside, the two security PMUs had split up. One was watching the front door of the Ocean's Floor, and one was watching the rear entrance.

Dante said, "Look, even if we decide we don't like this new world, where do you suggest we go?" He took a sip of his beer.

All were quiet for a minute. Then Jake said, "Dante's right. This Earth is it! At least we don't know of any other inhabitable planet so far. The GSA claims to have *galaxy-class ships* with the capability of ten times light-speed, but they also say they have found no other planets that will support life. What we have to do is cozy up to *these guys*, play by whatever rules they want us to, and get good jobs for all of us."

"Then once we are in solid," said Dante, "we can explore how we might change things if we can find ways to do it."

"What about Nyvar?" said Jake.

That statement froze everyone in their seats. What a thought!

"Are you saying 'what about *going to Nyvar*?'" said Susan.

"Isn't that where we *were* going?" said Jake. "I mean, if we really don't want to live in thirty-fourth-century Earth, we do have *one other choice!*"

"There is no reason why we couldn't as far as the ship is concerned," said David. "Wait, yes, there is!" he added. "The *Revelation* doesn't have enough fuel left for that trip."

"I'm not sure you are right about that, Dave," said Jake. "I was looking at the fuel situation today with Sergeant Bickel, and I think we do have *just enough* for a trip to Nyvar."

"With not an *ounce* of reserves," said David. "We wouldn't want to make *that* trip!"

"Then we would have to have enough credits to obtain the fuel and other supplies to restock the ship for the trip," said Dante.

"Why would GSA or the U.S. government support such a project?" said Susan.

"I doubt if they would," said Jake. "We better forget such ideas and figure out how to enjoy living our lives in the thirty-fourth century."

"I'm sorry, guys, but David and I are staying right here in this century," said Ellen. "We may have some complaints about privacy, but this world is so much better than our world was in 2025. We just better be thankful that we made this extended round-trip."

"El's right, guys," said David. "You aren't really considering trying to get GSA to back us for another run at Nyvar, are you? Let's go around the table."

"I like it here!" said Dante.

"I'm OK here," said Susan.

"It's a lot better than the twenty-first-century Earth for me," said Jake.

"You guys don't need to hear what I think," said Maria.

They all sat quietly and looked down into their drinks as if they were crystal balls with magical answers. Ellen said, "If we can be spied upon all the time, then we are not free, are we?"

"Not the same freedom we had in the twenty-first century," said David.

"I don't mean to say 'I told you so,'" said Maria, "but when we were having our presentations and indoctrination, I sensed a lack of freedom. Did I not mention it to all of you?"

"You did, Maria," said Susan. "But I think we have all been thinking that the thirty-fourth-century civilization is better than where the Earth was headed in 2025."

Ellen said, "David and I firmly believe that we are better off in the thirty-fourth century than we were in the twenty-first century, don't we, David?"

"I agree with that. I wouldn't want to go back to old Earth," said Dave. "Just look at the list of what is *infinitely better* about the world now—no wars, no pollution, almost no crime. And just think of the improved environment. I can give up a little privacy."

"I think Dante has the right idea," said Susan. "Let's play by their rules, down the line, until we can each get established individually in this world in our own right. Meanwhile, we can all stay in touch and get together occasionally and compare notes. If at some point we have ideas about changing things, we can talk about them."

"We are stuck now with the burned-out ID cards, and I am sure they will contact us to bring the cards in for replacement," said David. "But I will be able, in time, to create a sleeve of some sort that will render the audio transmitter temporarily inop. We could shield our cards like at one AM 'til four AM when everyone should be asleep. That way, they will not be suspicious of *not receiving audio* from our cards. We could be having a private meeting and discussion about anything we want to talk about."

The waiter approached the table, and Jake ordered another round of drinks. The waiter departed.

"What about the ability to be somewhere as a hologram," said Maria.

"Yeah!" said Susan. "David, have you learned anything about that yet?"

"I've learned from Mr. D. that it takes special, somewhat-expensive equipment to project your hologram to another location and that while you are at the distant location as a hologram, you cannot *do anything* at your origination point. You must act only in the location of your hologram. That is, you are basically sitting in a chair—or standing—and you see an image of the projection location and the people or holograms at that location. Using your index finger and a keypad, you control *where* your hologram is *projected to*. You use global navigational coordinates. To return your hologram to your base location, you just hit the escape key."

"What kind of credits are we talking about for this equipment?" said Jake.

"I have no idea," said David. "Mr. D. said we can find out all we want to know about the subject on the Internet. I'll get on it when we get back to Kennedy."

"Can we use the Internet without being monitored?" said Maria.

They all looked at one another and Jake said, "I give you three guesses, and the first two don't count!"

All agreed at that moment to form a pact. It would be called simply 621 for the Twenty First Century Six. After some discussion, they decided to make Jake the coordinator for the group. Jake would at least be responsible for arranging the meetings and getting word to everyone. The first meeting would not be until six months from the day of their reception at the White House.

Dante suggested that they give up on Georgetown and head for the Marriott. They all agreed. Jake paid the tab and asked the waiter to call a cab for them. The waiter advised that at this time of night, there were always several cabs lined up on the curb. They went to the curb, and the waiter was right. They took two cabs and departed for the hotel. The White House security PMUs followed.

They entered the hotel and touched the elevator call key. As they waited, Jake said, "Think I'll stop in the lounge for a nightcap. Anyone game?"

Only Susan showed interest and said, "Why not? I'm still wide awake!" She and Jake said good night to the others and headed for the bar. The others took the elevator to their rooms. Ellen reminded all that the special city tour was scheduled for a ten AM start on Sunday morning. They agreed to meet in the coffee shop for breakfast at nine.

Jake and Susan bellied up to the bar. Susan ordered a Bailey's and Jake a Black Russian. The bartender was a very attractive young blonde. When she set the drinks down for them, Jake, reading the bartender's name tag, said, "Tell me, Jessee, why won't people in Washington tell us what they think about life in the thirty-fourth century?"

The girl looked like she had seen a ghost! Then after a few seconds, she recovered, smiled somewhat artificially, and said, "What do you want to know about life in the thirty-fourth century? And what century have *you* been living in?"

Good comeback, thought Susan.

"Do you read the papers?" said Jake. "Do you know of the spaceship landing at the White House today?"

Again, Jessee paled but recovered. "Are you . . ." she started. Then she said, "Are you two of the people from that spaceship?" Her expression was a mixture of awe and fear.

"Yes," said Jake. "But we don't bite." Susan laughed and smiled at Jessee. The blonde seemed to relax a little but remained tense.

Suddenly, Jessee became quite composed. "What do you want to know about life in the thirty-fourth century?"

"Two things," said Susan, picking up on Jake's thought line. "One, how do you like your life? And two, are all citizens monitored by the government all the time?"

Jessee's expression suddenly became hard as she stared directly into Susan's eyes. She said, "I will answer the second question first. The government of the United States can monitor any citizen's words or actions anytime it so chooses by various means. What I am now saying may be monitored this very moment."

The two men in the far corner of the room looked at each other as if to say "Well, that cat's out of the bag."

One said to the other, "I think they were well aware that they were being monitored. They just wanted to find out if everyone else was."

"And the answer to Susan's first question?" said Jake.

Jessee gave Jake the same hard stare she had given Susan and said, "I have a very good life. I make good credits, have a nice place and a sharp puma. My boyfriend is also doing well. He lives with me."

"Are you free?" said Jake. "That is, are you free to do anything you want?"

Jessee looked down at the bar and wiped up some water with her cloth. "I think so," she said. "Yes, I am free. I have to tend to some other customers. Do either of you need anything else right now?"

"We're good," said Jake. "Come back and talk some more if you have time. And you can explain to me how I should be *tipping* in the thirty-fourth century."

Jessee went over to check on the two men at the table in the far corner.

Jake turned to Susan. "You are one sharp lady, Sue. What do you plan to do with your new life in the thirty-fourth century?"

Susan looked deep into Jake's eyes. She saw something she had not noticed before—genuine interest. At least, that is what she *perceived* that she saw. She smiled and said, "Are you really interested in knowing?"

Jake was not deterred. "Absolutely. You are beautiful, bright, and one of the few people on Earth today that are in my age group."

Susan broke out with a big laugh. "You mean over thirteen centuries old?" she said.

"Just being funny," said Jake with his sincerest smile. "You are also a fine pilot. Why don't you come work for GSA as you worked for NASA? You can do legal work and fly missions. We might even be able to do some missions together."

Susan probed Jake's eyes. *How do you ever know about a guy like Jake?* she thought. *He has been hot after Maria with no luck, and suddenly, he is showing interest in me?* She said, "Jake, you are a very attractive and exciting guy, but why don't I think I can trust you?"

"You cut me to the quick, Sue! When did I ever let you down?"

"You haven't. But neither have you ever showed me any special interest."

"I thought you and Dante had a thing going."

"We are good friends—nothing more," she said, looking into her glass. "Besides, I don't think Dante is interested in anything more than friendship."

Jake thought a moment about it and said, "Susan, I know a lot about you and how you think. I know that because we have worked together, but also because you are from the twenty-first century. I don't have a clue how the women, or the men, of this century think. I would think that you sense the same thing."

It was Susan's time for reflection. She slowly looked up and into Jake's eyes. "I share your feelings on that, Jake," she said.

Jake put his hands on Susan's. "I would like to be better than just friends with you."

"It's late," she said. "Let's call it a night."

Jake motioned to Jessee for the check. He gave her a 20 percent tip and promised to return for more conversation. He and Susan headed for the elevators.

One of the feds in the corner said to the other, "I don't think they are going to need but one room tonight."

The other nodded and signaled for their check.

31

Susan awoke first, and Jake was still sleeping. The events of the previous evening started coming back. Could she have any confidence in Jake? *Well,* she thought, *he is certainly my best friend in this century. And a good lover at that! I could do worse.*

She headed for the bath and a shower. *Whose room is this?* she thought. Then she remembered. *It has to be mine. There are all my toiletries on the vanity.*

Jake awoke to the sound of the shower running and looked at his watch. It was eight thirty-five. *Who was in his shower?* Then he remembered things and smiled. Susan was worth waiting for! He had not realized what a great figure she possessed until now. But he also realized that he was in *her room* and had none of his own things with him. Now the shower stopped. He slipped on his shorts and went to the bath door and knocked.

"Room service!" he called.

Susan wrapped a towel around herself and opened the door. "But I didn't call for room service," she said. "What do you have?"

"Anything you want, ma'am!" said Jake as he held out his arms, and she came into his embrace.

They kissed—a long one. Finally, Susan broke away and said, "Maybe later, but right now, we need to get dressed. We are meeting the others for breakfast at nine, and the tour starts at ten."

"You are as good in bed as you are on the flight deck," whispered Jake.

Susan smiled and pushed him away. "Go!" she said. "Get showered and dressed, and I'll see you in the coffee shop."

Jake was the last one to arrive at the lobby-level coffee shop. The others appeared to be having coffee or tea and chatting.

"You guys aren't waiting for me, are you?" said Jake.

"We decided to give you five more minutes," said Ellen with a little laugh.

"Anything exciting happen after we left you and Susan last night?" queried Dante, looking from Jake to Susan.

"Not too exciting," said Susan, "but interesting."

Jake gave Susan a "What are you doing?" type of look.

Susan continued, "We chatted with the little blonde bartender in the lounge and were advised that *every citizen* can be monitored by the government at any time, using more than one means."

Everyone just stopped whatever they were doing and just looked at Susan. "The bartender said that?" said David.

Jake pitched in, "She did, and I think there were two feds watching us from the corner of the lounge. Jessee, the bartender, was serving them also."

They all sat quietly for a few moments, and Maria said, "I don't think there is any question that everyone's freedom is being monitored and, therefore, compromised in the thirty-fourth century—at least if you live in the USA. We have no knowledge about life in other countries."

"I have a meeting with Chief Justice Webster on Tuesday," said Susan. "I will find out exactly how citizen surveillance is done and how much the government encroaches on personal privacy."

"Let's grab some of the buffet," said Dante, looking at his watch. "The tour limo is picking us up at ten."

They all followed Dante's suggestion and lined up for the buffet. Jake was right behind Susan and whispered to her, "You are more beautiful than you were even yesterday."

She responded, giving him a coy glance, "Be careful what you say. Big brother may be listening,"

The limo was waiting with—wouldn't you know it?—Mr. P. as the apparent chauffeur and guide.

"Good morning to everyone. Did you enjoy Georgetown last night?" said Mr. P.

Everyone mumbled "Good morning" and took places in the limo.

Mr. P. closed the doors and took his place in the driver's seat. The divider window was raised between the driver's compartment and the passenger compartment, and Mr. P. said via the intercom, "If you have any particular places you wish to see, please advise me. Otherwise, we have a tour of the main government buildings and monuments planned. The tour will take about two hours, followed by a lunch at the Vista restaurant in Arlington." He pulled away from the curb.

Jake asked, "Is the entire tour at ground level? I was in hopes that we could start with an aerial view of the city and then drop down for close-ups of the main buildings and monuments."

"Yes," said Ellen. "Could you do that, Mr. P.?"

The others seemed to be in concurrence.

Mr. P. seemed to be communicating with someone and then came on the intercom.

"I have cleared your request with Washington MATRAC. As long as we stay below two thousand feet and away from the skyways and ramps, we can do it. I will proceed with that plan."

Mr. P. pulled back on the column and initiated a climb to about 1500 feet and leveled off. He banked to the left and began a slow elliptical path around the heart of the city with the Capitol building at the east end of the pattern and the Theodore Roosevelt Memorial at the west end of the pattern. Mr. P. cruised down the Potomac just southwest of the memorials and the Tidal Basin.

Maria was straining to see the location where Rico's home was in the twenty-first century. It had been on a high bluff in Arlington overlooking the Potomac. Try as she might, she was not able to locate the home. *Not much chance it is still there*, she thought.

Susan pointed to the vicinity of West Potomac Park and said, "Mr. P., I don't recognize that large building shaped like the world. Is that a monument there in Potomac Park?"

"Where?" started Mr. P., then said, "Oh yes, I see where you are pointing. That is the Evelyn Robinson Memorial. You may recall that in the year 2107, while Ms. Robinson was president, she initiated the activity that led to the development of the Global Conflict Control system of magna-laser satellites. As a result of her initiative and efforts, the GCC now assures that there will be no more wars and, indeed, no more aggression between nations of the world."

"When was the monument built?" said Dante.

"The Robinson Memorial was constructed between 2137 and 2139 and was dedicated in 2140 when it was opened for public viewing. Would you all like to visit it?"

"I would," said David. "I've seen all of the others more than once, but never this one."

The others all agreed with David.

"Let's complete the aerial tour, then visit the Robinson Memorial," suggested Dante. "Are there any other memorials constructed since the twenty-first century?"

"There are other statues of presidents and other citizens who distinguished themselves either in government or other fields such as medicine or law or science. These are scattered about the areas among the memorials. I cannot think of any *memorials* dedicated other than the Robinson since the twenty-first century."

Washington, it seemed, had not changed much through the centuries. The central area of the city with its government offices and buildings and monuments was very much the same that the *Revelation* crew members remembered. There were more statues, the one additional monument, and different vegetation, gardens, and trees. Many of the government office buildings had multistory modern additions adjacent to them; but it appeared that all the same office buildings that housed the Library of Congress, the federal agencies, the Supreme Court, the Smithsonian and other buildings were the same ones that the crew remembered.

"Mr. P.," said Jake, "many or most of these buildings look the same as we remember from the twenty-first century. *Are they the same*, or have they been rebuilt to look the same?"

"I will say with confidence that everything you see in Washington has been rebuilt at least once—*even the memorials*. The big problem, as I understand it with the construction of the past, was that the material deteriorated. Even the best concrete and the best paints interacted with the atmosphere and underwent chemical changes, which lessened the material's strength. The surfaces you are looking at now are some form of *aluminum polymers*, which are permanent. The materials used for all buildings, the exteriors of PMUs, windows, and most products, which are exposed to the weather and the atmosphere, are all of some form of aluminum polymer.

Mr. P. completed the aerial circuit of the city and dropped down to Independence Avenue, which bordered West Potomac Park. He turned the limo into the parking lot adjacent to the Evelyn Robinson Memorial.

"Would you like to go inside?" asked Mr. P.

"Certainly," said Dante. "Are you coming with us in case we have questions?"

"Fine, sir," said Mr. P. as everyone exited the limo.

The memorial was a replica of the world, about fifty feet high and was a complete hollow sphere except for the bottom, which would represent Antarctica if it were not missing. The globe was supported by three pillars forming a triangle, and steps led up from the ground level to the main floor level inside and under the shell of the sphere. Positioned opposite the entry area and at a slightly higher level than the main floor was a large chair, and in it was seated a larger-than-life-sized statute of President Robinson. The seated president reminded them of the Lincoln Memorial.

Around the interior walls of the sphere were embossed sculptures representing most of the international world conflicts of history. The major conflicts such as the world wars occupied larger areas than the lesser conflicts. The dates of the conflicts were inscribed under each bas-relief sculpture, and there were none with dates later than 2117, the year of the Final Conflict between countries who refused to give up their nuclear weapons and the newly established Global Conflict Control system.

The *Revelation* crew just stood and looked in awe at the representation of the Final Conflict. Would it *really be the final conflict ever fought on Earth*?

"So this is the president that is credited with ending all wars and international conflicts," said Dante.

"That is correct, sir," said Mr. P.

"I would like to hear about that Final Conflict," said Jake, "if you would care to tell us what you know of it."

"I will be happy to, sir," said Mr. P., "perhaps on our way to the Vista restaurant. Are there any other memorials or buildings you would like to visit at this time?" addressing his comment to all those of the group.

Several suggested points of interest since they had the time. It was still only eleven AM.

After several stops, including the Library of Congress, the Supreme Court Building, and the Smithsonian, the limo again lifted off in the direction of Arlington.

"Tell us about the Final Conflict, Mr. P.," said David. They all listened patiently as they cruised slowly from the Capitol back toward the Lincoln Memorial, the Martin Luther King Memorial, and the Arlington Memorial Bridge.

Mr. Pollard began, "Once the GCC was in place and operational, President Robinson personally contacted each national leader of countries that possessed weapons of mass destruction. She advised each of them that aggression against other countries would no longer be allowed nor would the possession of nuclear weapons or the means to deliver those weapons be allowed. She further advised them that they would have one month, from the date of her contact with them, to destroy any and all such weapons and delivery vehicles, or else, the United States would destroy them."

"I'll bet that call went over big!" said Dante.

"There were three types of reactions to her contact," said Mr. P. "First, there were the nations who were considered allies of the U.S. and had previously been advised that the call would be coming. On learning from President Robinson that the GCC was operational, these countries immediately complied and destroyed their WMDs. There were a couple of countries that kept some weapons back in hiding—I will tell of those later."

He continued, "The second group demanded to be shown why they must comply with the demands of the United States. They said that they did not believe the U.S. had the power it claimed to have. The president then told each of these countries to evacuate specific facilities. She named the global coordinates of their weapons locations, which were in fact nuclear-storage facilities, and told them exactly the time that these facilities would be destroyed by the GCC. Some countries tried to move weapons to other locations, and others evacuated the targets. Still others of this group did nothing. Exactly at the appointed times, the

GCC struck the targets with full laser power and vaporized all material at the facility. In some cases, nuclear explosions also occurred because the weapons were armed." Mr. P. paused. "In the case of this second group, the U.S. gave them one month to comply with Ms. Robinson's demand but monitored their activities very closely to ensure compliance.

"Finally, there was the third group, which *actually initiated nuclear strikes* with WMDs shortly after her phone contact with them. As each weapon was launched, it was destroyed by a GCC maser strike. None of the launched weapons reached any intended targets. Some of these countries capitulated immediately and destroyed all remaining weapons. Others of them tried to conceal some of their weapons."

Mr. P. continued, "All those weapons, wherever concealed, were located by our snits and snats and destroyed by magna-laser strikes from GCC. In some cases, countries were foolish enough to launch conventional aircraft and oceangoing vessels against U.S. targets. These too were vaporized by GCC strikes. This entire Final Conflict took less than *ten days*, and the only casualties were in those instances where people did not evacuate as told to or were manning conventional craft. There were no U.S. casualties and no damage to any U.S. property on the ground, on sea, or in space.

"Now that," said Dante, "*is the way to wage war*—fast, clean, and decisive!"

The limo was crossing the Potomac and approaching the Arlington side. Mr. P. banked and began his descent toward the Vista. Maria suddenly pointed and said, "*There it is*! There is *Rico's house*! How *can it be* after all these centuries?"

Everyone looked at the house where Maria was pointing. Mr. P. looked and said, "That is one of the preserved homes in Arlington, just as is Mount Vernon, George Washington's home."

"Whose home was it?" said Maria, certainly not expecting to hear the name Enrico Valdez.

"His name slips my memory bank at the moment, but he was a very famous person of his time. He was a businessman—very rich—and also an entrepreneur, responsible for the creation of many things, many inventions, and ideas. There is also a statute of him near the Washington Monument. We passed by it today. Oh! What is wrong with my circuits. Why can't I remember his name? I will get it for you later. We are approaching the restaurant now."

The group including Mr. P. was seated at a nice large table by the window overlooking the Potomac and Washington beyond. Maria could not believe her eyes! This was almost the identical view she had from Rico's rear patio—so many centuries before. That house she had seen *had to have been Rico's*. But how many people must have owned it and enjoyed it since it belonged to Rico. And who was the famous person that owned it such that it is now a *preserved home*?

Lunch was delightful. Even Mr. P. seemed to be enjoying himself. He became the center of attention because the astronauts keep peppering him with questions about Washington, about the legal system, about everything. Mr. P. was a wonderful source of information because he knew so much and always—they thought—told the truth.

"Mr. P.," said David, "we understand that every U.S. citizen can always be monitored by many of several means. My question is, what are the ways we are monitored, and what does the government do with the information it gets from the surveillance of individuals?"

"Well," said Mr. P., "the information you ask for is not secret. The answer to the first question is that you are monitored by the chip in your CIN card. That is one way. Then there are cameras and microphones everywhere in both public and private places. And finally, you are being monitored by the chip in my forehead, both visually and audibly. In addition to these built-in devices, you may be under surveillance by federal agents. These are all the means that I know of."

All the crew members cast knowing glances around the table at one another.

Then Jake said, "And then what does the government *do with all the information?*"

"Nothing," said Mr. P. "Let me clarify that. Nothing—unless you are breaking the law or are guilty of actions outside of our rules and regulations. Then the information they have gathered becomes evidence. I believe that as long as a person does not commit crimes and break laws or ordinances, they are free to do as they will."

The six just looked at him and considered what he just said.

"Surely, the government does not monitor all people *all the time*," said Ellen. "Under what circumstances does the government elect to monitor specific individuals?"

"I believe the answer to that is *either* if a person is suspected of a crime, *or* there is a special situation wherein people give reason for the government to believe that they *may* commit a crime."

"Then that is why they are monitoring us and tailing us," said Susan. "And that is exactly what is different from the twenty-first century to the thirty-fourth century."

"Not necessarily, Sue," said Jake. "In a sense, we are aliens to this country today and, therefore, put under surveillance. In the twenty-first century, persons from many foreign countries visiting the United States were put under surveillance in case they had terrorist connections."

Susan just looked at Jake. Then she said, "In that case, you are right. But the United States had reason to be very careful with people from certain Muslim countries at that time. Why should *we* want to do the U.S. any harm?"

"We don't," said Dante. "But *they* don't know that. Thirteen centuries is a long time for ideas to change. And another thing, people of the twenty-first century broke laws much more readily than people of the thirty-fourth century. What is your take on this, Mr. P.?"

"I think you have nailed it, Colonel Washington. Our authorities are not sure what you folks might do, and they are just watching you extra closely. I know that Mr. Loneghan didn't pay for his coffee one day in the cafeteria. And no one from this century, except a criminal, would dare do what Mr. Loneghan did."

That did it! Everyone looked at Jake, who had this incredulous expression on his face, and Susan was the first to burst out laughing. Then everyone laughed except Mr. P., who did not consider his comment to be funny.

Dante said, "So Jake is our problem." And everyone laughed louder.

Talk was light for a few minutes while everyone finished their dessert and coffee. Then Mr. P. said, "Would everyone like to return to the hotel now, or can I drop anyone anywhere special?"

Since it was Sunday, no one could think of anything special to do that they hadn't already done. Most places were closed. Jake commented that there had to be some good sports on TV, and everyone decided that the hotel would be fine.

"Say, girls," said Ellen, "the hotel has a great pool and exercise room! Let's check that out!"

Mr. P. had already started for the limo as the others moved toward the front entrance. The waiter had advised Dante that the tab had been taken care of.

Back at the hotel, the guys had found a Yankees-Red Sox game on the viewscreen and were happy as clams. The girls did in fact check out the exercise room and pool. They found both to be quite nice. Jake had managed to plant a couple of words in Susan's ear on the ride back to the hotel, and they were planning on visiting a club in Georgetown that evening—there were very few open on Sunday night.

Maria was still thinking about Rico's house, which was still standing after all these years. If it was a *preserved house*, maybe it was open to the public. When she had time, she would go visit it.

32

It was Monday morning. David tried to remember what meetings they had scheduled and at what time. Ellen was already in the shower. He started rummaging around, trying to find the Washington itinerary they had all been given. The AMec began playing "Oh, What a Beautiful Morning," and David picked it up.

"What's our first meeting and where?" said Dante.

"That's what I am just trying to find out," said Dave. "Ellen's in the shower, and I can't find the program. Let you know when I find out."

Susan was just trying to wake Jake and tell him that the first meeting was at 9:00 AM with the director of the Global Space Agency, and it was already after eight. "Jake, do you sleep this soundly all the time?" she chided.

Maria had found her program and learned that after the GSA meeting at nine, the next meeting was to be with the secretary of defense and the Joint Chiefs of Staff at 11:00 AM. She decided to call everyone and get them moving since it was after eight.

Everyone scrambled and made the coffee shop by eight thirty-five, grabbed coffee and rolls, and found the limo by the curb at eight forty-five. After all were strapped in, Dante said to Mr. P., "Can you get us to our nine AM meeting on time?"

"No problem, sir," said Mr. P., and within seconds, they were landing on the roof of the GSA building. Mr. P. led them to the stairs, and by eight fifty-eight, they were signing in with the receptionist in the director's outer waiting room.

Marnie, the receptionist, brought them tea and coffee and explained that the director was running a "tad" late this morning. They settled into plush comfortable furniture and relaxed.

"It is hard to believe that this is the same building that we interviewed with Director Javitz just a little over a year ago," said Maria.

"That's right!" exclaimed Jake. "I had completely forgotten that."

"It appears to be the same building," said Dante, "and in the same location, but it has to have been rebuilt. Nothing can last over thirteen centuries."

"The pyramids have," said David. "Of course, they are pretty weather-beaten too."

"And they didn't have to withstand the rigors of Washington politics either," cracked Susan.

At that moment, Klaus Stoll came out of the director's office.

"Greetings!" he said. "The Twenty First Century Six is right on schedule as usual!"

Dante, Jake, and David stood and shook hands with Klaus—they were genuinely happy to see him. The ladies also arose, smiled, and greeted him.

"Have you met Constantine Simonides, the current GSA director?" said Klaus.

Everyone looked blank, and Ellen said, "I don't believe we have."

"Well," said Klaus, "I thought he might have been at the White House reception Saturday night, but I guess not. Anyway, Kosta—that is what he likes to be called—has been director of the GSA since President Thornhill has been in office and has initiated many aggressive space projects in a very short time. Director Simonides is originally from Athens, Greece, and was president of MIT before taking his current position with the agency."

"I would be very interested in hearing about some of the space initiatives he has sponsored," said David.

"So would I," said Jake.

"You mentioned briefly in our orientation sessions," said Susan, "that GSA has mining operations on the moon and on Mars and that some of your ships have ten times light-speed capability. Where else are ships traveling to today?"

"That is one of the subjects I am sure that Kosta wants to discuss with you, and I don't want to preempt what he plans to say to you today. I will say that he is particularly interested in hearing your comments on any ill effects you may have experienced after your one-year hibernation in space."

The door to Director Simonides' office opened, and a man of average height with an engaging smile entered the room using rather large strides.

"Ah!" he exclaimed in a very pleasant tone, "the ancient mariners of space! The Twenty First Century Six! I am most pleased to meet you!"

Director Simonides started with Maria and shook hands warmly and sincerely with each of the six crew members. He worked his way around the room, chatting briefly with each person. It was easy to see why President Thornhill would have selected Constantine Simonides to a high government post—especially with his strong technical background at the Massachusetts Institute of Technology.

"Please come into my office and make yourselves at home! It is too early for ouzo, so the best I can offer you is coffee or tea. We do have some tasty Greek cookies if you would like to try them."

Everyone filed into the director's very large and impressive office. The walls and ceiling were shaped as a half sphere and decorated as the night sky in a New

England summer. The covering of the walls was obviously constructed from actual photographs of the night sky. The scene was magnificent and seemed to have true depth.

"How do you like my ceiling? My wife, Betty, thought that the actual night sky would be an excellent effect for the office. And of course, it has some useful value as well. For example, we can talk about and point to where you all traveled on your one-year journey through space."

All selected seats facing Kosta's massive desk, and the director called Marnie on the intercom, asking her to hold all calls and attempts to interrupt them until further notice. He turned to Klaus and said, "Director Stoll, please refresh my memory on what you have told our guests about our current deep space operations."

"Very little, actually, sir," said Klaus. "They know of our mining operations on the moon and on Mars and of our station in low earth orbit. They know of our solar waste-disposal program. They know of our cruiser 10xL capability, and we have hinted to them of plans on the drawing board to visit planets in the vicinity of Alpha Centauri. That is about it."

"Very well," said Kosta. "And please do call me Kosta. My name has always been too long and too hard to pronounce correctly." He smiled and continued, "There are two things I hope to accomplish in this meeting today. One, I want to learn more from you about your journey from Earth to Earth and any reactions you have to that experience. Also, I want to talk of flights we are considering, which would involve hibernation, and get any recommendations you might have regarding those. Colonel Washington, let us begin by asking for your comments on long-duration missions requiring hibernation."

Dante composed himself and cleared his throat.

"Well," he began, "as a pilot, I don't particularly care for missions that I sleep through." He waited for a possible comment. Hearing none, he continued, "I realize that hibernation is the only way to accomplish long-duration missions, but if I am asleep, I miss all the fun of flying and the awe of viewing the heavens as the mission proceeds."

Director Simonides was listening closely but also watching the expressions of the other five astronauts as Dante spoke. He particularly noticed the expressions of Jake and Susan, who seemed to be concurring with Dante.

"We are, as you know, considering a mission to the Alpha Centauri neighborhood," said Kosta. "Do any of you happen to know offhand how far such a trip would be?"

"I believe that Alpha Centauri is about four and a half light-years from our sun," said David.

"Very good—4.34 light-years to be exact," said Kosta. "Let's say we sent you on a mission to Alpha Centauri, and that mission included a landing on a planet we have been observing in that system. The mission would also include taking samples of soil, atmosphere, and any small life-forms that might exist. Here, we are assuming that no intelligent life-forms exist, but *we don't know that*. We would have a contingency mission plan for dealing with intelligent life if such should be found there. But here is the question I would like to pose to all of you. Assuming that you undertook this mission without hibernation and assuming your ship has ten times light-speed capability, you would arrive at the target planet in approximately twenty-two weeks. Allowing for no more than two weeks on the ground would make the mission total forty-six weeks or the better part of a year. As far as your aging is concerned, it doesn't matter whether you are hibernating or not—you will age *less than a day* for such a trip." The director paused to let his words sink in.

Jake raised his hand. Kosta said, "Yes, Mr. Loneghan, please comment."

"I see the problem. With such speed capability, we can undertake a round-trip mission to Alpha Centauri in less than a year—which in terms of space travel is nothing, but in terms of human tolerance for the trip is much too long and too boring."

"Exactly." said Director Simonides.

"Whereas," said Klaus, "if the crew members hibernate, the trip seems instantaneous to them. They are in Earth's orbit. They go into hibernation, the ship makes the jump to 10xL, and the next thing they know is they are coming out of hibernation after what seems to them like a night's sleep. And they *are at their destination*."

"It's almost," said David, "the same as being transported to the planet via a time machine or some other device with molecular disassembly/reassembly capability."

"Then can I conclude that all of you have the same reaction as Jake as far as the effect on the pilot of such a journey?"

"I have to agree," said Dante. "Even with 10xL capability, the distances just within our own galaxy are so immense that going somewhere without hibernation seems out of the question."

"That is what *we* have concluded, Colonel. So piloting spaceships into deep space is not a fun flying assignment . . . It is a challenging and exciting assignment for an explorer, however."

"If I might, sir . . . ," said Susan.

"Certainly, dear. Do you wish to add something?"

"Just this," said Susan. "You have personnel stationed in orbit at your ISS for long periods, I understand, and also personnel with rather long duty assignments on Mars and on the moon. Aren't such assignments similar to a one-year round-trip to Alpha Centauri?"

The director carefully considered Susan's words. Finally, he said, "Our people on Mars and on the moon live in small villages which afford recreational activities. There are also a number of people living at those stations. Such assignments are not as lonely as a small crew might be in a lengthy space journey.

"However, your analogy with an assignment to the International Space Station is closer. Our people at the ISS have a full schedule of activities—experiments and other lab work. Also, there are ships coming and going. Perhaps the issue is simply one of boredom for the crew of a 10xL ship. Twenty-two weeks of just staying on course and looking at space—no matter how majestic—would be boring.

"Perhaps we should consider adding meaningful activities for a crew, such as experiments, and try a round-trip—say, twenty weeks out and twenty weeks back—just to get a crew's reaction to the experience. What is your reaction to that thought, Klaus?"

"I was just thinking," said Klaus. "My first reaction to this is that personally, I would prefer hibernation to twenty-two weeks of *whatever* activity in the confined space of a 10xL ship. The great advantage of hibernation, as David put it, is that the trip will seem instantaneous."

"I take it that most of the crew agree with Dante, then?" said Kosta. "Susan, how about you?"

"I would agree also," said Susan. "Perhaps when deep space cruisers become large enough to have recreational activities and staterooms, I might change my mind."

"I think we have sufficiently beaten that horse," said Kosta. "Let's move on."

Director Simonides paused and called Marnie. "Could you refill our coffee and tea, please." He got up and passed the Kourabiedes cookies around again. "These were my favorites when I was a boy," he said.

Director Simonides, after a few moments, continued, "Now let me ask all of you this. Why did NASA select the planet you named Nyvar as your destination when you were launched in the *Revelation*?"

"I can answer that," said Ellen.

"Please do, Dr. Marks," said Constantine.

"For several years, NASA utilized a variety of radio, infrared, spectrographic, and other types of scanning devices, searching the heavens for a planet that was similar to Earth. We were looking for a planet of a similar size with a similar atmosphere and soil and water composition. We discovered a planet we named Nyvar. It resided in a star system we named Setarian for its star, Setar. Nyvar was, and I think still is, a very close match for Earth. At the time the GSA was preparing a proposal for the president's approval, our observatory in Puerto Rico picked up radio signals thought to have originated in the vicinity of Nyvar. This provided strong supporting evidence, and the president approved GSA's proposal for the *Revelation* mission. I and this team volunteered to go to Nyvar and explore and establish a colony on that planet."

"You are very brave—all of you!" said the director.

Jake spoke, "It has been thirteen centuries since that transmission was received from Nyvar, sir. What has been learned about that planet since we departed Earth in 2025?"

Kosta looked at Klaus with an expression that implied "You take this one."

"We have learned little more," said Klaus, "in all those years you were on your journey through the heavens. We occasionally intercept more radio signals from the direction of the Setarian system but have never been able to make meaningful messages out of the data. Moreover, GSA has never again ventured out of the solar system with manned flight. Your journey was the last such attempted."

The group was silent for an uncomfortable time. Then Director Simonides broke the silence. "And somehow your computer navigational program was changed to a program that returned you to Earth. So really, this planet's single effort to explore beyond our solar system was unsuccessful."

"That is correct, sir," said David. "And I'm sure Director Stoll has told you we have no idea who inserted the round-trip nav. program or why."

"Tell me about the journey itself," queried Director Simonides.

Maria spoke up, "There is little that we can relate to you on the journey. While in Earth's orbit, we went into hibernation. Our next consciousness was when the computer awoke us some two million miles from Earth. We were weak and very hungry then, but no one was ill."

"There was one incident recorded during the flight while we were in hibernation," said Dante. "The *Revelation* successfully automatically averted a collision with an asteroid by sensing its approach and adding power to evade a strike. The body missed the ship by about three hundred feet."

"Wow! That was very close." said Kosta. "What was the relative speed of the object?"

"I believe it was about sixteen thousand miles per second," said David.

"Very interesting," said the director. "A tribute to your excellent design, David." After a reflective pause, he continued, "You have arrived back on Earth at an interesting time for GSA. As I mentioned earlier, we are presently trying to get congressional approval for a round-trip visit to Alpha Centauri. Do you think any of you would be interested in such a mission?"

Jake was the only one who spoke up, "I would, sir. I am planning to fly for GSA, and I would expect to be available for any mission I am needed on."

"Very good," said Klaus. "We will keep that in mind."

"What about you, colonel?" said Kosta. "I understand that you are quite a pilot."

"Thanks for the compliment, Director Simonides, but I am more interested in the Global Conflict Control operation and the U.S. Air Force. I like what I have seen of the thirty-fourth century, and as I said earlier, I'm not a big fan of doing missions in hibernation."

"OK!" said the director. "Well then, I think this has been a good meeting. I don't want to put anyone else on the spot here today. But if any of you, in addition to Jake, are interested in space missions for us, please make that fact known to Director Stoll. I know you have a meeting with the secretary of defense at eleven, so I won't keep you."

He concluded with, "My office is open to you as a group or as individuals anytime you want to talk. It has been a pleasure meeting you."

Director Simonides stood, which prompted the others to do likewise. They all thanked him for his hospitality. Maria commented, "I really like your Kourabiedes cookies, sir. Maybe I can get the recipe from your wife sometime."

"They are delightful, aren't they? I will send the recipe to Director Stoll's office!" said the director.

Mr. P. was waiting with the PMU limo on the roof when they arrived there at ten forty-five.

33

It was a short hop from the GSA building to the Pentagon. Mr. P. dropped the limo into an Administration Reserved slot, and the PMU was immediately surrounded by armed marines in uniform. Mr. P. lowered his driver's window and held out his ID.

"Very good, sir," said the sergeant. "You and your party are expected and may follow Airman Edwards to your meeting location."

Mr. P. and everyone else had to step quite lively to keep up with Airman Edwards. They entered the building and made several turns before following a long corridor to an impressive set of double doors. There were sharply dressed marines stationed at either side of the doors.

The party entered, and Mr. P. went directly to the receptionist's position, identifying the *Revelation* crew and each individual to the sergeant manning the desk.

The desk sergeant invited the group to have a seat in a designated waiting area, which they did.

After about five minutes, a young lady entered the room from behind one of the side doors and identified herself, "Good morning. I am Ms. Jardins, personal aide to Mr. Monroe Tibbets, secretary of defense. The secretary is ready to see you now. Please follow me."

Mr. P. took a position beside the door and waited outside. The group followed Ms. Jardins into a large office where a distinguished tall older gentleman was standing in front of a massive desk. To his right were standing two generals—one U.S. Air Force and one U.S. Army. And to his left was one general of the U.S. Marine Corps and one admiral of the U.S. Navy. Each of the military displayed the highest rank of their branch of the service. The secretary invited each of the *Revelation* crew to file by the Joint Chiefs from left to right and introduce themselves.

When the introductions were complete, Secretary Tibbets said as he led the way, "Let's all move to the conference table on the other side of the room." There was no doubt about where each person was to sit. Impressive nameplates on the table, readable from both sides, marked the location of each chair at the table. There were exactly the correct number of chairs—four for the Joint Chiefs on the right of the secretary and six for the crew members on the left side of the table. The secretary had the larger chair at the end of the table. Dante's designated spot was to the immediate left of the secretary. Next was David, then Jake, then Ellen, Susan, and Maria. The admiral opposite Maria looked quite pleased at the arrangement.

"I understand that the six of you were launched from Kennedy Spaceflight Center in the year 2025 on a mission to a planet some 1300 light-years from Earth. I further understand that after the thirteen hundred years in space, you ended up back here on Earth. Is this story correct?" He was looking at Dante.

"It is correct, sir," said Dante.

"And you were all in hibernation for the majority of the trip. Is that also correct, Colonel Washington?"

"That is correct, sir," said Dante. "We came out of our sleep condition about two million miles from Earth and, at that point, believed we were on course to the planet Nyvar as originally intended by NASA. We were not aware of the navigational error until Kennedy Spaceflight Center identified itself and GCC sent up short-range fighters to look us over."

The secretary turned away from Dante and looked at the joint chiefs. They all returned his incredulous expression and, almost as one, shook their heads from side to side. Together, almost as if rehearsed, they said, "Unbelievable!"

"GSA released the whole story to the press before our landing here on Saturday, perhaps—," said David who was interrupted by the secretary.

"I read that release, and I am sure the chiefs did." They all nodded in unison. "But it just seems *so incredible*. I understand that GSA has determined that someone sabotaged your navigational computer by inserting the wrong program."

"That is what we, working with the staff at KSC, have determined," said Ellen.

"OK, so there's *that*," said the secretary. "But the real reason we wanted to talk to you folks today is about your intended mission and how you expected to deal with what you found when you arrived at the planet you named Nyvar. Incidentally, that planet is still where you said it was—I guess you are aware of that?"

"We are, sir," said Jake.

The air force five-star general, General Whitcomb, spoke up and said, "And there is one other thing we wanted to explore today, Monroe. We want to hear about the condition the Earth was in, militarily, in 2025 when you folks launched your mission. From what we can get out of the history books, the world situation looked very critical."

"It was extremely critical, sir," said Dante, "We felt that Earth was on its way to destruction. As an air force pilot, I flew many combat missions in several theaters during my service, and I could not believe the state that the world situation had deteriorated to. I opted out of combat missions frankly because I assumed before each mission, that I would not be returning after the mission. We weren't accomplishing anything with our military actions and were losing thousands of our personnel monthly in combat all over the globe. Troop morale in all branches of service was at an all-time low. I joined the astronaut corps in hopes of making something more of my life."

Dante continued, "In 2025, there were fifteen countries with nuclear power, and eight of them had weapons and the means to deliver their warheads. Some had five-thousand-mile range capability. The United States had become the only superpower that was trying to use military action to *stop conflicts* between other nations. We were the only country that was sending our boys out on peacekeeping missions. And we were losing tens of thousands! Our military expenditures were in the billions, and we had U.S. troops stationed in between ten and fifteen hotspots around the world at any one time."

Maria tentatively raised her hand and was acknowledged by the secretary. "Yes, Miss Rodriguez? Klaus Stoll tells me that you did an outstanding job in briefing the GSA on the world situation in 2025 when you arrived at KSC."

Maria smiled. "I just want to say that although Dante is the only one of us with military combat experience, we all were quite aware of the deterioration of the civilization of the Earth in the twenty-first century. We did not think that the Earth had long to survive when we left there in 2025."

"And that is why," said David, "we are so impressed with what the world is like today in 3339. We cannot imagine how you have accomplished so much and made the world, again, a good place to live."

"Director Stoll and his staff," said Jake, "have done a fine job of trying to help us understand how the Earth has made so much progress, but the hard thing for us to grasp is how the *corner was turned*. I want to read more and get a better understanding of how the Final Conflict was in fact accomplished."

General Whitcomb took that as his cue. "Monroe, if you don't mind, I would like to address that subject." The secretary smiled and nodded.

The general continued, "It was President Robinson, her secretary of defense, and the Joint Chiefs at that time who deserve the credit. They recognized that the end of the planet was near and knew that there was only one way to save it. The president was able to find ways to funnel the money into NASA and to the appropriate spots in the military to secretly design and build the Global Conflict Control network based on President Ronald Reagan's SDI, Strategic Defense Initiative concept. They funded the construction of all the laser-weapon components needed and all the launch rockets required to build the system. The most difficult task during those years was *keeping the project secret*. All the monies appropriated had to be earmarked for *other projects* in order to get congressional approval. And you folks must remember the awesome power of the press. It was almost impossible in those years for the government to do anything without the *media exposing what they were doing*. Had the country and the world known about the GCC project, *it would have never happened*. The media and Congress *would have seen to that*."

General Selvage, the five-star General of the Army and chairman of the Joint Chiefs, got into the discussion. "Let me add that there had never in the history of this country been a project of the magnitude of GCC ever pulled off in secrecy. The closest thing on record was the development of the atomic bomb, the Manhattan Project, and the modification of a B-36, the Enola Gay to carry the weapon. But that project pales beside the development of the GCC. And let me add this. The press in the 1940s, during WWII, as far as we can tell, operated in *support of government* and its efforts, not in ways to tear down the efforts of our leadership."

There was a pause while everyone took a breath. The secretary began again. "The world we enjoy today has been made possible for one simple reason. The United States appointed itself the *guardian of the Earth* and laid down some rules for countries to operate by. The only way we were able to do that is *with muscle*. Because of the GCC, the countries of the entire globe are able to live free from fear of attack by other nations. The government of countries may also call on the GCC to support them against internal uprisings by sects and paramilitary groups that would overthrow their democratic governments. Most of the Earth is living in peace today. I believe that in your century, the motto of the Strategic Air Command was 'Peace through power,' was it not?"

"That is correct, sir," said Dante.

"Today, that motto is more appropriate than ever before in the history of the world," said Secretary Tibbets. He continued, "There is one other function of the GCC today. That is, to ensure that all nations of the world have governments *by the people*. We are 95 percent successful in this objective. In your century, the United States tried to do this. But the job was too big for just conventional military means, and nuclear weaponry was unsuitable for the task at hand. Today, the United States is the only country that maintains conventional military forces of substantial size—forces that are large enough to control other nations. The real muscle of the thirty-fourth century is the GCC. That power alone ensures that the Earth remains a peaceful planet. There are however, things that cannot be done just with magna-laser power from space. We must, on occasion, employ the army, navy, marines, and air force."

Maria could stand it no longer. She had to say it. "If I may, Mr. Secretary, I have a simple question that is gnawing at me and I think some of the others from twenty-first-century Earth."

"I'll bet I know what the question is, Maria," said Secretary Tibbets. "Would you like me to state it?"

"If you wish, sir," said Maria. "If you guess wrong, I will tell you."

The secretary smiled as did the joint chiefs. The secretary said, "I will count on you to be honest with us. Your question is, are the citizens of the United States as free as they were in the twenty-first century?" He paused and smiled at Maria.

All were still, anticipating what Maria would do and say.

She said, "That is my question, sir, *word for word*."

"And I will give you your answer," said the secretary.

After a moment, he said, "The answer is, *yes they are—absolutely*.'"

The joint chiefs looked at the secretary with expressions like, "But there is more to the story."

"*However*," continued the secretary, "they *do not have as many rights* as they did in the twenty-first century *if they break the law—any law*!

"Our analysis of the deterioration that was occurring to the world's civilization in the twenty-first and twenty-second centuries is as follows: Your people had it half right. Democracy and freedom were and are good. But your almost *limitless tolerance* of those doing evil was *bad*. That is the part you had wrong, and we have changed that."

The secretary summarized the major international steps the United States had taken in the twenty-third century. He talked briefly about how the United States gained control of the Earth and told the story of the Final Conflict and how it was conducted.

There was a pause at the table while all those present considered the secretary's words.

Finally, Secretary Tibbets said, "Now! Let us move to the other question we have for you. Tell us, please, how the six of you were going to handle situations you found yourselves in once you reached Nyvar."

"Let me begin that," said Dante without hesitation. "We considered ourselves *prepared* for any civilization or lack of civilization we found on Nyvar. The *Revelation* carried—in addition to us six astronauts—weapons, tools, equipment, portable shelters, biological attire and equipment, and supplies enough to last one year on the planet. We were equipped with everything NASA could conceive of that we might need."

Dante continued, "You are meeting here today with crew members that represent a carefully selected cross section of talents and abilities. We six were prepared to bring civilization to *a new world*."

"And if you found an intelligent civilization already inhabiting Nyvar?" posed General Selvage.

"In that instance, we hoped that they would welcome us as explorers in space on a peaceful mission and intending them no harm," said Jake, tired of being left out of the discussion. "In a sense, that is what really happened. Earth is *so different* now—it is almost as if we landed on Nyvar and found a new and quite advanced civilization."

Dante added, "We could have found one of many possible situations on Nyvar, some of which we certainly could have handled. It is my view that in view of the failure of our *intended* mission, we are very lucky to have returned to Earth—now in such good hands and apparently prospering."

"We are impressed, colonel, with yours and your crew's abilities, enthusiasm, and courage. But if we could perhaps ask some specific questions," said Admiral Persons, who had not spoken up until now.

"By all means, admiral," said Dante. "We will do our best."

"This one is for Dr. Marks," said the admiral. "Your team could have possibly sustained all sorts of injuries on Nyvar—perhaps on landing or by many other means. How were you equipped to handle such injuries?"

"We had the best portable medical equipment available in our time, along with the latest drugs and medical specialty equipment," said Ellen. "Obviously, a portable field clinic is not a hospital, but we were as well equipped as any United States fighting force in the field of battle. A great deal depended on the environment we might find ourselves in on Nyvar. Our astronomical studies of the planet indicated to us that we would find the surface of the planet and the atmosphere to be very similar to those of Earth. If that information was wrong and we were forced into our biosuits, things would of course have been much more difficult for us."

"If I may inject something here, gentlemen," said David, "we were an expeditionary force, not unlike other such forces in the past history of the Earth and not unlike the origin of civilization on Earth if you believe in the Bible. We were certainly better equipped than was Christopher Columbus when he with his four ships landed on the soil of the then new world. But that aside, we represented and still do represent the Earth's envoys to a modern new world. As it has happened, that new world is a *new Earth*—one as new and different, in many ways to us, as an entirely new and different planet would have been." The brass seemed rapt with David's discourse.

David continued, "We have answered the question, at least for Director Stoll and his staff at GSA, of why NASA sent us on a mission wherein they would never know how the voyage turned out. In 2025, many felt—myself included—that the Earth was dying a self-inflicted death. Why *not* send six representative specimens to the stars in hopes of finding life on another world—or at least a place to continue our lives? And there was always the possibility we might find an advanced civilization—not unlike Earth 3339—that did not have the *cancerous problems that Earth 2025 was enduring*. There was some hope that science might have developed the darling of science fiction novels and movies—the *time machine*! In such an instance, perhaps someone of our crew might return to Earth with knowledge that might just save it from what we viewed as almost certain destruction."

The secretary and the Joint Chiefs seemed mildly amused at the mention of a time machine, but there was also another rather odd reaction to the words. Both General Whitcomb and the secretary did a little nervous shuffling. Only David and Susan noticed those actions, however.

After David's words, the secretary and the joint chiefs were silent for a few moments. Then Secretary Tibbets spoke, "You are indeed a brave and courageous crew, as strong as anyone in the service of our country today. Do any of you chiefs have other questions for these fine astronauts?"

The joint chiefs were silent.

"Then I think we are finished here today," said the secretary. Turning again to the *Revelation* crew, he said, "Please let me personally know if there is anything I can do for any of you." He stood, reached out, and began shaking the hands of each of the *Revelation* crew as did the generals and the admiral. All of the chiefs echoed the sentiments of the secretary.

The *Revelation* crew exited the secretary's office. Mr. P. was waiting outside and escorted them back to the limo.

Once inside the PMU, Jake said, "What do you think, guys, back to the hotel for lunch and a break?"

All nodded agreement as Dante said, "Let's do it."

Mr. P. made a call to MATRAC, drove a distance away from the Pentagon, and pulled the limo into a steep climb. He made a gradual turn and headed toward the hotel.

It was twelve fifteen PM when the crew alit from the limo at the hotel, and all headed for their rooms. Jake yelled out, "How's one for lunch in the coffee shop? The first press thing is not until two." Everyone seemed to be waving an OK as they took different elevators.

Susan was on her mec immediately, calling the office of Chief Justice Webster to reconfirm, hopefully, her lunch date on Tuesday with Mrs. Webster.

Dante was in his room trying to make contact with the office of General Whitcomb to set up a private meeting with him.

Maria was talking to information, trying to learn the name and AMec contact of the chief librarian at the Library of Congress, and Jake was checking ESPN for the latest sports news.

David and Ellen had wandered out on their deck and were pointing to and trying to recall all the points of interest they had observed in their tour of the city.

Jake and Dante were the only ones who agreed to meet with the press in the afternoon—the other four had declined and so had the afternoon off. The conference had been set up in one of the meeting rooms of the Marriott and was well attended by mostly press from the local Washington area and from New York. All the major television networks were present. Dante and Jake found it most interesting that Mr. M. had again been assigned by the White House as the moderator for the conference.

"Can we have the first question, please," said Mr. M.

"David Irving, *New York Times*," said a man in the front row. "This question is for either of you. What is the most striking difference you see between twenty-first-century life and thirty-fourth-century life?"

Dante looked at Jake. "I'll take it," said Jake. "There are several major differences that have impressed me. You have no wars and terrorism, criminals are dealt with swiftly and treated harshly, and your technological advancements are quite amazing."

"I would like to add to that," said Dante. "Those three things make your pursuit of happy and productive lives much more attainable than in the century we came from."

Another hand went up and was acknowledged.

"Maggie Wolfson, *Washington Post*. Colonel Washington, do you feel that you have as much freedom in our century as you did in the twenty-first?"

"Let me answer that this way," said Dante. "I have been back on Earth for a little over two weeks, and I have done everything I wanted to do. I have not been told of anything I cannot do—that is within the law, of course."

Another hand acknowledged.

"Edwin Cahill, *LA Times*. What do you think about your being under surveillance by the government at all times?"

Mr. M.'s head turned slowly toward the questioner. He gazed intently on the reporter. Dante looked toward Mr. M. as if he expected a comment and then addressed the question. "As long as that practice doesn't impact my freedom to live as I want to live, I have no problem with the surveillance."

This answer apparently surprised the questioner. He sat down without a follow-up question.

"Martin Obama, *Philadelphia Inquirer*. This question is directed to the two of you. If you had your choice today to live in this century or return to your life in the twenty-first century, what would you do?"

Jake said, "From what we have learned of your thirty-fourth-century society, I would choose to live now—without question."

"And I agree with that," said Dante.

The conference continued for about an hour with Jake and Dante fielding everything tossed at them and without the need from any interference from Mr. M. When the questions turned inane and obvious—as they often do in such a conference—Mr. M. ended the meeting.

Jake and Dante were heading for the elevators when Mr. Cahill of the *LA Times* caught up with them. He surprised them with, "Did you know that when people speak out against the government, they sometimes disappear from their homes in the middle of the night?"

Before either Jake or Dante could respond, Mr. M. and another droid appeared out of nowhere. They latched on to Mr. Cahill's arms and ushered him out through a stairwell exit door. It all happened so fast that Jake and Dante just stopped, awestruck.

They looked around to see who else might have seen what they saw, and no one apparently had. They continued to the elevator and punched the floor for their rooms. Neither one spoke. When the elevator stopped on their floor, Dante said, "Come on over to my room and let's discuss what we just observed. There's plenty of beer in my AutoServe."

34

Tuesday marked the beginning of the end of the *Revelation* crew as a unit. All the members had pretty much made up their minds about where they wanted to go with their careers, and as David had put it at lunch on Monday, *"It's time to get on with our lives."*

Dante wasn't able to schedule the lunch meeting with the general on Tuesday but did get a midmorning fifteen-minute slot to see him.

Maria met with the chief librarian at the Library of Congress and obtained the promise of a position there. An earlier mec call from GSA Director Simonides had made the acquisition of a Library of Congress position like falling off a log—*easy*. She would be assigned to oversee a portion of the American history section. She would be involved in research and special projects—whatever *that* meant.

Susan was scheduled for her lunch meeting with Chief Justice Webster in the justices' private dining room at the Supreme Court Building.

David had arranged a meeting with Klaus Stoll on Wednesday at KSC to discuss possible positions at GSA-KSC, and Ellen had arranged a visit with the hospital administrator at Mayo-Orlando on Thursday.

Jake had two tickets to a hockey game for Tuesday night and was trying to reach Susan in hopes that she would like to go.

Dante was fifteen minutes early for his scheduled meeting with General Whitcomb, who just happened to be standing and looking at some papers at his aide's desk when Dante walked in to the outer office. "Dante!" said the general. "I'm glad you are early. I had a cancellation on the meeting just before you, and we can start our discussion now. Come on in. Anything to drink?"

"Coffee would be fine." Dante said to the aide, "Just black."

He followed the general into his office.

"Let's take these chairs here by the coffee table," said General Whitcomb. "What is the subject of our meeting?" he asked as they sat by the table.

"What are the chances of my working at GCC, General, or is that work restricted to active military?"

Just then, the aide entered and sat a small coffee pitcher and two cups on the table. He departed as the general said, "The answers are good and no. That is, the chances of you coming to work for me are damn good—in any of several positions—and we have excellent civil service positions open right now."

The general continued, "Tell me, *when* did you decide you wanted to work at GCC, and *why* GCC?"

Dante sipped his coffee. "General, I think when I first learned of GCC in our orientation at GSA, I knew it was something I would really like to do. The only hesitancy I had was that I still love to fly. I am in hopes that you have a position that will let me supervise and make command decisions but will also have some stick time included in the job."

"That may be a tall order, Dante," said General Whitcomb, gazing into his cup. He looked sternly into Dante's eyes. "Most of our flying assignments are for active military. We could probably find a way to allow you to use military aircraft for personal transportation, considering your qualifications, but your assignment would not include military flying. The job I think you would be perfect for is a control center shift command position at the main GCC command center. Have you seen the center?"

"No, sir, I have not. It is not around here, is it?"

"Of course not. It's a long way from here and deep underground. There is not a weapon that exists that can scratch it! When can you go see it?"

"General, I am free to do whatever I want at this time. We flew here, as you know, in the *Revelation*, now still parked in the Ellipse just south of the White House. We are scheduled to return to GSA tomorrow in the ship. But there are two other pilots—you met them—qualified to fly her, and I can continue on here in Washington or go to GCC if that fits in with your schedule."

"I like a man who can make decisions! I can't go today, but how's the first thing tomorrow, say, 0800 departure at Andrews? Can you make that?"

"I will be there at 0700, sir. What hangar?"

"There is a hot little number I like to do quick trips in. Just has two seats. It's in hangar P2. I'll look forward to seeing you there at 0730. It won't take us more than twenty minutes to be off."

"General, thank you—*so much*. But I still have some questions for you."

"Save them for the ride over. We're going to Colorado. Only a ten-minute trip in my SR84, but we'll slow her down so we can talk. How'd that be?"

"Perfect, sir!" said Dante as he arose when the general stood.

General Whitcomb walked Dante to the outer office desk and said to his aide, "Get Andrews on the horn . . . and after that, GCC central."

Susan was in the outer office of Chief Justice Webster at 12:30 PM sharp, the appointed time for her rendezvous with Mrs. Webster. Before Susan could get comfortable, Mrs. Webster came out of her office and said, "Susan! So good to see you and in person this time."

"The pleasure is all mine, Your Honor," said Susan. "And thank you so much for taking the time out of your schedule to see me."

"You are not costing me a second of my day, Susan. We all have to eat lunch, and the court dining room in this building is both convenient and has excellent food. Thank you for coming here to save me time. I hope your trip wasn't annoying."

"Not at all, ma'am. Mr. P. knows all the ropes with regard to Washington traffic. We were here from the Marriott in less than three minutes."

"I do hope Mr. P. is observing all the traffic regulations . . . There is just no effective way of penalizing those droids." She laughed. "But aren't they wonderful?"

Mrs. Webster held the outer door for Susan as she spoke and followed her out. They proceeded down some steps and along a corridor to the entrance of the justices' private dining room. The maitre d greeted Mrs. Webster and took them to her usual table. The room was not large—perhaps a total of ten tables well spaced out for privacy. About half of the tables were in use. Most diners nodded to Mrs. Webster as she and Susan entered the room. The walls and ceiling were decorated in early-colonial elegance—tall windows, heavy drapes, and lavish woodworking on the cornices, crown moldings, and window framing. There was a soup and salad table on one side of the room.

The chief justice, after she and Susan had looked at the menu and conferred briefly, ordered for the two of them. The waiter departed, and another server brought iced tea and water.

"Well," said Mrs. Webster, "have you and your friends decided to stay in the thirty-fourth century? Or will you be off to some other exotic location in your impressive ship?"

Susan was startled by this opening but quickly recovered. "Why, Your Honor! What on earth would make you think we would want to leave your thirty-fourth-century Earth?" She smiled her very prettiest smile as she spoke.

Justice Webster looked coyly at Susan as she too took a sip of tea and said, "Just testing you, dear. It wasn't so much the answer I was looking for, but your reaction to the question."

"I am so happy to be alive on Earth in the thirty-fourth century, Your Honor. And I believe that the others of our crew feel the same way."

"Do you really mean that, Susan? I got the impression that our system of justice and perhaps the harshness of it had you and the others a little uneasy. Is that not so?"

Susan wanted to be truthful here, but also careful. She must carefully pick her words, she thought, so that her ultimate aim could be accomplished.

"Mrs. Webster, Your Honor," she said, "your system of justice is, in truth, light-years ahead of the system we had in the twenty-first century. I believe that Secretary Tibbets, whom we met with yesterday, may have expressed it the most succinctly that I have heard. He said that twenty-first century Earth had it *half right*. We were right about freedom and democracy, but far too tolerant of those who committed evil acts.'"

"Very good!" said the chief justice. "I will have to remember that."

"If I may continue and give you a more complete answer, ma'am, let me say that in just a short time we have been back on Earth, we have come to love and respect the planet again and its thirty-fourth-century civilization we have come to know. We had reached the point on Earth where every day the killing all over the globe and in the U.S. itself permeated the news. All the trends were worsening, and the administration and Congress seemed powerless to do anything about it."

Susan continued, "Transition now to the present. You do not tolerate war or international conflict. You do not tolerate crime in the United States and neither do most other countries. As a result, citizens live in freedom—and most importantly—freedom from *fear*. You are not afraid of attacks from other countries or from terrorists. You are not afraid that your sons and daughters will have to go off the foreign lands and fight futile, endless—and for the most part—meaningless wars. And you are not afraid to walk through the park at night to the grocery store. You finally have *real freedom*.

"I agree with your system of government and justice and want to find a meaningful place in it to further my career in law and justice."

For moments, the chief justice just looked at Susan with a respectful smile. Then she said, "I am impressed, Susan. I was impressed with you when I first met you at KSC, which is why I suggested that we have lunch together, and I am even more impressed with you now . . . However, I am having difficulty in finding a good way to bring you into the system. Most attorneys in ranking positions in our judicial system today began at the bottom—working civil cases and, in some instances, criminal cases. But as you probably have guessed, use of the Truth Validation Unit, the TVU, has made the practice of law boring for attorneys. Yes, boring . . . There is no other way to put it."

She sipped her tea as Susan waited and then continued, "There is some challenging work in civil law and in contract law—and some good work in patent law. I have two questions for you: One, are you willing to start at the bottom with a law firm? And two, are you interested in either civil or patent law?"

Susan waited to be sure that Mrs. Webster was ready for her answer. Then she said, "I am certainly willing to start at the bottom and work up, but I *must have challenging work*. GSA has offered me work in space law, lunar and Mars property rights and that sort of thing. The work would involve space travel, which I would enjoy."

"There is one other possibility you might consider, Susan. You could come to work for the Supreme Court. Our work is definitely challenging in applying the law to disputed cases—but I cannot say that it is very exciting."

Susan thought for a moment and then said, "Your Honor, I really don't know what I should do. Is there some way of self-assessment through testing? I like to be challenged, and *I like to win!*—as with case law. Maybe civil law would be the best for me."

By this time, they were finished with lunch, and Justice Webster was deep in thought as she sipped her tea. "I would say that today, by far, the biggest civil legal fights are in the fields of patent law and in the medical field. And I am referring to cases involving inventions—medical devices, drugs, and other inventions of all sorts. There are often substantial judgments at stake. Many of the cases we of the high court hear today are in these fields." She paused, as if thinking carefully about what she planned to say. "If you want to get into this area of the law, I can probably arrange a spot for you at any one of several firms . . . OR you could *come to work for me* and, thereby, see the details of the cases we are hearing and being asked to make judgments on."

Susan was overcome by the offer. "You are so very kind, Your Honor, and I am indeed overwhelmed by your offer. I wish I could just say yes at this moment, but I need to do some thinking. And there is one of our crew that I would like to get an opinion from. Can you possibly give me a few days to think over all that you have said?"

"I certainly can, Susan. This is a big decision for you, and I do not expect you to be able to decide here on the spot. You should, in my opinion, consider three paths we have touched on. First, going in at the bottom of a firm involved in patent-based civil suits. Secondly, taking a position with GSA—and I would be willing to bet that you could structure your own job and make it what you want it to be. Or finally, a position with us here on the court. I would add one thought to all of this. By working for us here on the court, you may learn more, faster, about how the cases are prosecuted and how the judgments are rendered. With a firm, you will be assigned one piece of the puzzle at a time, and it will take you longer to get the big picture."

"Thank you again for your courtesy, Your Honor, for your advice, and, most especially, for your offer of a position on your staff. I will be back in touch with you in less than a week. I have some serious thinking to do and a very important decision to make."

The chief justice stood and offered her hand to Susan. Mrs. Webster, indeed, had a firm handshake—quite different from the grip of her hologram that Susan had experienced on their first meeting at KSC. "Walk with me, Susan, to my office. And my secretary will show you out of the building."

Dante had arrived at the Marriott early in the afternoon and was anxious to tell the others that he would not be going back with them on the *Revelation* on

Wednesday. He went straight to the front desk and left electronic messages for each, asking them to meet him in the penthouse lounge at six PM. He felt that everyone would be back by that time, and six would give them time to change and relax a bit.

David and Ellen had spent the afternoon at the Smithsonian. They had been quite pleased to find a replica—about the same size as the one at KSC—of the *Revelation* hanging in a prominent spot in the Air and Space Museum. They were also able to see large models of all the ships that had flown for NASA, and now GSA, in the years since their crew had departed Earth in 2025. The most recently installed models were of the huge deep-space cruisers that travel at ten times light-speed. They also recognized the giant SWD waste-disposal boosters and canisters.

They spent a good part of the afternoon at the Air and Space Museum, and it was about four forty-five when they arrived at the hotel and found Dante's message.

Susan found two messages waiting for her at the desk—one from Dante and the other from Jake. Jake's note read like he was somewhat annoyed at not being able to find her—something about "don't you keep your mec on?" The note also mentioned having some hockey tickets for the evening and wanting her to join him. She would call his room when she got to her room.

Maria found her note from Dante and planned to meet with the group at six. She had made a very important decision herself on Tuesday that would definitely affect the rest of her life.

Dante arrived at the penthouse lounge before the rest in order to secure a table with a good view of the monuments. The floodlights were just coming on, trying to compete with the setting sun as Dante was being seated by the window. Maria was also early and spied Dante just as he was taking a chair. She went over to join him. She thought, *What the heck. I might as well break the news to the colonel now and tell the rest when they arrive.*

Dante saw the elegant Maria heading toward him, all decked out in a beautiful light peach dress with a low-cut V top and a full-flowing skirt. He thought, *Wow! Does she look stunning.*

"Hi, Dante," said Maria. "Did you have a productive day?"

"Very much so," said Dante. "And you?"

"Yes!" said Maria. "I had such a good day that I won't be going back with you guys tomorrow."

"What?" said Dante. "Did you get the job you wanted?"

Maria gave him a big smile and an expression like she had swallowed the canary and said, "I did, and I am starting to work Thursday morning."

"You won't need to return to the Cape?"

"What for? I brought all of my earthly possessions with me for this trip. I have one day—tomorrow—to find a place to stay and pick up a PMU. Actually, I only have to find a place to stay. I can use public transportation for a while."

"That's great, Maria! Maybe we can have dinner tomorrow night."

"What? But aren't *you* going back to KSC tomorrow morning?"

Dante just smiled. "By the time the *Revelation* lifts off, I will be inspecting the Global Conflict Control command center with General Whitcomb."

"You will?" Maria was excited for Dante. "Are you going to work for him?"

"Hope to," said Dante. "I'll be looking at the job tomorrow."

Then Maria showed concern. "But, Dante, you are the *Revelation* commander. They need you to pilot the ship back to the Cape!"

Just as Maria said this, Jake and Susan were walking up. They heard Maria's comment.

"Did I just hear that you are not going back to KSC tomorrow?" Jake said to Dante.

"That is why I wanted to meet with all of you tonight," said Dante. "Here come Ellen and David—might as well wait 'til they join us and go through the whole thing just once."

Everybody exchanged hellos and took seats around the table.

"The captain is jumping ship," said Jake, giving Dante an evil smile. "Sounds like he's taking a job here."

"Not here," said Dante. "Somewhere in the west. Here's the skinny. It's no secret that I have been thinking about working for the GCC or the air force—you guys were aware of that. Well, it turns out that General Whitcomb, who we met yesterday, is the top dog of the air force. And *the GCC comes under his command.* I went to see him this morning and asked about the possibility of my working for the GCC, and I think he has a job for me! He is taking me out to see the command center tomorrow morning."

"Guess we need to designate a new commander for the *Revelation*," said Jake. "Tomorrow will probably be her last trip anyway."

"Congratulations, Dante!" said Susan. "I hope you get just the spot you want."

"We all wish you the best, Dante," said David. "You have been a fine commander and a great team member." Everyone shook Dante's hand and wished him well.

"Might as well get the rest on the table," said Dante. "Maria's staying in Washington. She goes to work for the Library of Congress on Thursday."

"And I have tomorrow to find a place to live!" said Maria excitedly.

The girls were enthusiastic about Maria's good fortune and hugged and congratulated her. Jake and David also congratulated her and wanted to know more about the work she would be doing.

Jake, as usual, called for the refreshments and announced that he was taking care of the tab.

"Let's ask Jake to tell us what he did today," said Susan with a knowing grin.

Jake said, "Aw, Sue! They don't want to hear about that."

"Just try it on them and see if they want to hear about it," said Susan.

Dante's eyes lit up like he had just had a brilliant thought. He said to Jake, "Did you go to the Chase Washington Bank today?"

"I did," said Jake with a big grin.

"And did they have anything of yours?" said Dante, really getting excited now.

Susan couldn't stand the suspense since Jake had just told her his secret before they came up to the Penthouse. "The bank had a gazillion dollars of Jake's money, which converts to over a *billion* in current-day credits!

Dante whacked Jake's shoulder and then gave him a big *hug*. "I told you that you were *going to be* my very best friend on Earth—and now YOU ARE!"

Maria, Ellen, and David were of course completely in the dark about the money and credits in the Chase Bank and really unable to enjoy the excitement of the others.

"Tell us all what happened, Jake," said Maria. "Did you win the lottery?"

"Has everyone got a full glass?" said Jake. "This may take a few minutes."

David had been feeling left out and said to the waiter, "Another round for the men and a bottle of Chardonnay for the ladies!"

Jake laughed. "Why not? OK, here is the story. In 2025, I had been pretty successful in several business ventures and had some money in the bank."

"Just *$59 million*," said Dante.

"That was including the $52 million in income tax the IRS *claimed* I owed," said Jake.

"What?" said Dante. "You didn't tell me about *that*."

"I didn't tell anyone about that," said Jake, "including the IRS, *but they found out about it*."

"Are we talking about *tax evasion*?" queried Susan, suddenly with a troubled expression. This part was news to her too. *So the TVU was right about Jake*, thought Susan.

"I prefer to say that the IRS and I had a little disagreement about the tax owed—like they said I did, and I said I didn't," said Jake.

"How did you get cleared by the FBI to be on the *Revelation* crew?" said David.

"The wheels of justice had not caught up with me before we launched. They probably figured the whole thing out about a day or so after we left orbit on our way to Nyvar," said Jake, taking a sip of his brandy seven. He paused.

"I am in a state of shock!" said Ellen.

"I think there is only one person at the table who is not," said Susan. She was feeling very disappointed in Jake.

"Let me tell you what happened in the Chase Bank today," said Jake. Everyone, except Dante was staring holes through Jake and waiting for the story. Dante was quite amused and eagerly awaiting the tale. Jake went on, "I waltzed into the bank this morning with my passbook from 2025 and presented it at a teller's window. The teller was, wouldn't you know it, a Don Knotts type. He took one look at the date on the passbook and the balance of $59,085,762.13 and turned as white as a ghost. I think at least one knee buckled, but he managed to hold on to the counter. He said, 'Just one minute, sir,' and took off for the door behind the teller positions. Shortly, a heavyset older gentleman came to the door with the teller and looked at me."

Jake was having some fun. For the first time since joining NASA, he had the undivided attention of the other five crew members. They were hanging on to his every word, and he was going to get the *most* out of the story.

"Soon, the teller returned and motioned me to come over to the entry door to the teller cage. He said, 'Mr. Bernstein would like to talk to you in his office, sir. Please come with me.'

"I followed him into the bank manager's office, and Mr. Bernstein greeted me quite pleasantly. He said, 'Mr. Loneghan, how nice to meet you. Please have a chair here at my desk.' He was standing behind a very large mahogany desk, which was clear of everything except a computer terminal. I sat down and made myself comfortable. He said, 'I have your passbook here, Mr. Loneghan, but I also need some other identification before we can sort this out.'

"I gave him my NASA ID and my GSA temporary ID, and I began to feel sorry for the poor guy. Think of it. He is looking at an ID dated 2025 with my name, *birth date*, and social security number on it, and another ID dated 3339 with just my name and citizen ID on it. 'What is he thinking?' I thought. I decided to try to help him. I said, 'Mr. Bernstein, I am one of the six astronauts that you may have heard about in the media. Our flight originated on Earth in 2025, and we traveled in space for thirteen centuries before landing back on Earth a little over two weeks ago. Does that help?'

"He looked at me with the strangest expression and said, 'I know who you are and where you come from. I just didn't know that you were a customer of my bank until now. We ran your passbook savings account number through the system, and here is what we found. When you left Earth in 2025, a few weeks after your departure, the FBI came into our bank with documentation that said you owed the government—the IRS—$52 million in round numbers. They had secured a judgment from the First District Federal Court that allowed them to garnish your account for the monies owed.'"

Jake took another swig from his drink; the others continued to stare at him.

"So—I said to Mr. Bernstein, 'OK, that left roughly seven million in 2025 dollars, that has been earning passbook savings at a rate of at least 2 percent for *over thirteen centuries*. In dollars, that should be roughly 1,060 quadrillion dollars.' I continued, 'At some point, the bank converted dollars to credits, and therefore, the credits began to earn interest at whatever the passbook savings rate was through the years. Am I correct so far?'

"'Not exactly,' said Mr. Bernstein, 'The average interest we paid over all those years was 2.5 percent, not 2 percent.'

"Mr. Bernstein was beginning to look sick, and I began to feel sorry for him again. I said, 'Why don't you just tell me what the value of the account is now, sir?'"

Everyone at the table except Dante looked frozen, waiting for the answer. Jake said, "Would anyone like to guess what the account is now worth?" He sipped his drink.

"If you don't tell us RIGHT NOW," said Susan, "I am going to hit you with this wine bottle!"

Jake said, "OK! OK! The account is worth over 6×10^{20} dollars, which converts to roughly *four billion credits* . . . But there is a problem. No one in the United States today is allowed to hold more than *three* billion credits in *total assets*."

"Poor baby!" said Susan with a look that made Jake smile and Dante laugh.

All were silent, gazing into their glasses and/or staring at Jake.

"So what is going to happen?" said Maria.

"We—that is, Mr. Bernstein and I—are not sure. He believes that the bank only owes me the maximum allowable today of three billion credits. I think he owes me the total of four billion because my money legally earned it. Then after my account is satisfied by law, I will have to give away the excess billion, leaving only three."

Dante perked up. "Give it away to whom?"

"I don't think the government specifies who you give it to," said Susan, "as long as it is outside your own family. I would have to research that point."

"My thinking is this," said Jake. "I think that the money, the full four billion credits, belongs to me. It is a legitimate indebtedness of the Chase Bank to me. Now I *recognize* that under today's laws, I cannot *hold* more than three billion credits, so I would propose to divide up the excess in five equal shares and *give the credits to you guys*."

Dante leaped to his feet and said, "Hear! Hear! I *told* all of you that this man is my *very best friend*!"

The others laughed at Dante, then took on incredulous expressions, then looked as though they felt that such a scenario could never come to pass.

Jake, looking directly at Susan, said, "If I had a *very good* lawyer, perhaps connected in high places, I'll bet we could pull this off."

"A toast to Susan!" said David, and all clinked their glasses and toasted Jake's new attorney.

35

Wednesday morning came early, especially for Dante. He had to be at Andrews AFB ready to fly with General Whitcomb by 0730. Dante was the first one in the coffee shop at 0645, selecting some cereal, fruit, and a roll. He had contacted Mr. P. the night before and arranged for a limo ride to Andrews, departing exactly at 0700. Mr. P. had assured him that the trip would only take ten minutes at the outside. He gulped down his meager breakfast, grabbed a coffee to go, and stepped lively to the hotel front entrance where Mr. P. was standing by the limo at the curb.

Dante jumped in and said, "Mr. P., what time are you taking the others to the *Revelation*? Are you sure you have plenty of time? I can take a pumacab."

"Mr. Loneghan said they would be leaving here at seven thirty for the *Revelation*. I have plenty of time."

"Fine! Then let's do it."

Mr. P. pulled the limo directly into a steep climb and turned, aiming directly for Andrews. "MATRAC, this is WH3 en route to Andrews," called in Mr. P.

The response came back "Roger, WH3, stay under two thousand feet. We are advising Washington Center."

The night before, the crew had an excellent dinner in the main dining room of the penthouse restaurant and had said their good-byes then to Dante and Maria. The women were somewhat emotional, and even the men turned a little soft. After all, they had been through quite a bit since they began training for NASA; and they were kind of a close-knit, special crew—the only people in the world in their age group.

During the evening, they had talked of many things—especially their intent to stay in touch with one another—certainly by e-mail and mec, but also in person. They made definite plans to meet *somewhere* six months from the date of the White House reception and compare notes. Jake was to be the coordinator for the get-together.

Maria had decided, just as the group was breaking up and heading out of the restaurant, that she would join them at the Ellipse for their departure and then have Mr. P. drop her off at the Library of Congress. An assistant to the chief librarian had volunteered to be her guide in looking at apartments and condos on Wednesday. She was to meet with the lady at eight thirty, Wednesday morning. The scheduled launch for the *Revelation* was at eight.

Susan and Jake had discussed at length at the dinner table just who would be the logical choice for the left seat on the way back to KSC. They had not been able to come to a resolution. Jake secretly felt that it should be Susan's privilege, but he had just wanted to give her a little hassle for fun. Jake had suggested, as the group headed for the elevators, that he and Susan should discuss the issue further in her room over a brandy and come to some mutual understanding.

All but Dante met at 7:15 AM for breakfast. They had a quick bite, checked out, and were on the curb when Mr. P. returned with the limo. He got out and opened the doors for the crew.

"Any problems getting Dante to Andrews on time?" asked Jake.

"No, sir, none. We arrived just after seven, but the general was already there and was preflighting the SR84." Mr. P. placed the bags into the trunk.

As she got in, Susan said to Mr. P., "Did you have a chance to stop by the *Revelation*, Mr. P.? I was just wondering how that preflight was going."

"Yes, I did, and the sergeant in charge seemed to have everything under control. The ship still has round-the-clock security as it has since you arrived. It should be ready to go."

"By the way," said Jake to all as Mr. P. started the limo and pulled it up into a climb, "Susan is our commander. I just didn't want to take the responsibility."

This got a chuckle from everyone, and David said, "commander, are you sure we can handle the *Revelation* with only a crew of four? What about quality control?"

Maria suddenly realized that David's dig was for her. Maria came back with, "Ellen has agreed to handle QC since she already knows the rest of you have hangovers."

Jake liked that one.

The White House and the Ellipse were in sight, and the *Revelation* looked as beautiful and as ready as it could be. There were however many people outside the roped-off area, apparently awaiting the departure.

"I thought that there would be no public or press," said Jake. "Nothing ever changes with the media. This is really a nonevent today—amazing."

Mr. P. dropped the limo in about twenty yards from the ship. The chief of security at the ship came over to check identification, and the crew exited the limo. Maria gave everyone hugs and a kiss for Jake and teared up. She turned to Mr. P. and said, "I'll stay here with you."

Susan, Jake, David, and Ellen headed for the stairs at the entrance to the flight deck. As they reached the top of the stair, some photographer at the barrier rope yelled, "Can't we have a smile?"

Susan automatically turned and smiled as did the others. They gave a wave, and the crowd burst into applause and cheers!

"That's more like it!" someone yelled.

And then another said, "Hey, where are the other two? Weren't there six when you arrived?"

They ignored the catcalls and questions and entered the flight deck. Susan took the left seat and Jake the right. David and Ellen took their same positions as flight engineer and medical officer. Jake said to Susan so no one could hear, "You OK?"

"As long as you are here," she said softly with a smile.

"OK!" Susan said firmly. "Let's do the whole checklist. We don't want to miss anything. Prestart checklist!"

Susan completed the prestart checklist with all items checked OK. She called, "Starting engines!" As the engines began to hum and then roar, everyone got busy. All indicators were coming on line, and the whine of the engines was reaching 100 dB.

Susan continued to read the checklist items and got the proper responses from each of the crew members. Finally, she said, "I have all greens here. How about you guys?"

"All greens here," said Jake, looking proudly at Susan with just a slight turn of his head.

"All greens here," said David.

"All greens," said Ellen. "We are go."

"Washington Center, this is *Revelation* at the Ellipse ready for launch," called in Jake.

"Roger, *Revelation*," came back Washington Center. "Stay below 1500 feet until you are outside Reagan airspace, then climb at twenty thousand feet per minute until you reach flight level S3. You are cleared direct to Kennedy at level S3, heading 184. Contact Charlotte Center if you desire rerouting or a change in flight level. Have a safe trip."

"Roger, Washington Center, we read you. Over and out," said Jake.

Susan advanced the power, and the ship slowly lifted off the grassy area, climbing slowly above the treetops. Susan began pulling back slightly, bringing the nose higher and higher toward vertical. She turned to a heading of 184 and leveled off at 1500 feet.

"Coming up on the Reagan perimeter," said Jake.

Susan advanced the power and pulled the nose back to achieve twenty-thousand-feet-per-minute climb and aimed for flight level S3—three miles above ground level, or about sixteen thousand feet. Within seconds, they were at S3 and in level-cruise flight.

"Adjust power for a cruise speed of 3,000 mph," Susan said to Jake.

"Roger," said Jake as he tweaked the throttles.

"Flight time should be about sixteen minutes at this speed," said David.

"Plenty of time to look at the scenery," said Ellen. "And what a gorgeous cloudless day!"

"Only problem is that Maria is missing the view, and she is the one that wanted to enjoy it," said Jake.

Susan cut her eyes over at Jake. She *had seen* the good-bye kiss Maria planted on him.

Fifteen Minutes Later

"KSC in sight," said Jake. "I'll give them a call. Kennedy Center, this is *Revelation* coming in on S3 for landing outside hangar 14. Do you read?"

"*Revelation*, this is Kennedy. We read you. You are cleared for maritime approach, runway 33. Follow the glide slope until you reach your spot adjacent to hangar 14. Then you may proceed with a vertical descent and landing."

"Roger, Kennedy. Could you alert Sergeant Bickel of our arrival?"

"And Mr. D.," said Susan.

"Right, *Revelation*, will advise B and D," came back over the speaker.

"I'm dropping her down to 1500 feet, left turn to 140 degrees to intersect the glide slope, then turn to 330, and follow the slope," said Susan.

"Fine by me," said Jake. "They said something about a maritime approach. I'm guessing that means an approach from over the ocean. We don't have the approach plate, so let's just follow the route you suggested. If they don't like it, they will tell us. Must be a no-traffic day. There's not a blip on radar, but let's all keep a good eye out."

The speaker came on with, "*Revelation*, are you flying a maritime approach? Over."

Susan cut her eyes at Jake. Jake transmitted, "Well . . . er . . . MC, we didn't have that plate but figured what we are doing would be close enough."

"You are almost on the correct path," came back KSC tower. "Just continue your present course to intersect the slope, then turn on, and follow it down, heading 330."

"Roger, KSC, sorry about that. We'll get a set of plates if we plan to do any more flying out of here."

"Good idea . . . Over and out!"

While this conversation was going on, Susan had already intersected and turned and was right on track on the glide slope to runway 33. Jake said, "Thirty-five seconds to mark for vertical descent to touchdown point."

"Got it," said Susan.

"Eight . . . seven . . . six . . . five . . . four . . . three . . . two . . . one—mark!"
said Jake as he adjusted power to bring the huge ship into a hover mode about
three hundred feet above the intended touchdown point. The *Revelation* was
now just hanging stationary at three hundred feet. "The power is yours," Jake
said to Susan. "Gear is down."

Susan controlled the ship like a veteran of thousands of flight hours.
She brought the *Revelation* down slowly and softly to a perfect three-point
touchdown. "Check all instruments and indications." Susan directed.

"All green," said Jake.

"All green," said Ellen

"All green for shutdown," said David.

"Engines off!" said Susan as she closed the power levers.

A round of applause for Susan and three broad smiles.

"Very nice." said Jake.

"After-shutdown check," called Susan. "All switches off!"

Again, she got the proper responses from the crew.

They released their restraints and proceeded to the flight deck door. Stairs
were already at the door, having been placed there by Sergeant Bickel. The crew
disembarked the ship as Sergeant Bickel said, "Welcome back!" Then he said,
"I only count four heads. Didn't you forget two?"

Jake laughed as they all descended the stairs and said, "They elected to stay
in Washington. They won't be coming back."

"That's too bad," said Mr. D. who had just arrived and heard Jake's
comment. "I had a golf match set up for you and Colonel Washington, myself,
and Mr. K."

"We can still play," said Jake. "Susan will play as my partner and we'll whip
you two tin cans soundly!"

"Don't hurt his feelings." said Ellen.

"Can you do that?" said Jake.

As they got into the van, Susan said to Mr. D., "Do words hurt your feelings,
Mr. D.?" Everyone was interested in his response.

"We don't have feelings, Ms. Chen, neither physical nor mental."

"Then you feel no pain or discomfort of any kind?" said Ellen.

"That is correct, ma'am."

"How about other emotions," said Jake, "like joy and happiness?"

"I can't even comprehend the terms, sir," said Mr. D.

They all contemplated this as Mr. D. drove them back to the BPQ.

David said, "It seems strange without Dante and Maria, doesn't it?"

Meanwhile—Back in Washington

Dante had just entered hangar P2 and froze in his tracks! He had never ever seen an aircraft or spacecraft anything like the one in front of him. It was gleaming silver and shaped more like some sort of projectile rather than a flying ship. Maybe an arrowhead would best describe the lines of the SR84. It was basically triangular in shape with a rather sharp nose and a flat, blunt aft portion. The cockpit and windscreen were at the front of the ship; and two top-hinged entry doors, one on each side, allowed entry of the pilots. The ship was just off the concrete floor, resting on three rather skinny gears.

"Ah, Dante!" said the general. "We are just about ready to pop out of here. Could you just close that electronics access door on your side and go ahead and climb in."

"Good morning, general," said Dante as he snapped the access door shut. "This looks like a hot little number."

"Wait 'til you see what she can do." said General Whitcomb as he climbed into the left seat. Dante was just getting into the right seat.

"Just touch that key there when you are ready to close the hatch," said the general, pointing.

The interior was plush and soft, but not roomy. The sides of the pilot's seats provided wraparounds to encompass each crew member and provide about 300 degrees of support for their bodies. The design suggested to Dante that he better expect lateral g-forces as well as longitudinal and vertical forces. Dante followed the general's lead and donned a helmet that was waiting, stowed just in front of him. He adjusted the helmet control for a perfect fit.

"Are you comfortable?" said the general. "If the sides of your seat or your restraints are too tight, you adjust them with these controls." He pointed. "The pressure should be firm, but not too tight. The crew support modules in this ship are designed to protect us from g-forces in all three dimensions. We will experience up to 15 g's, and that can be in any direction. The forces won't last long enough to black us out, but this will definitely be something you have not experienced before."

Dante had flown many aircraft and spacecraft types before, but somehow he had a feeling that this was going to be a new experience. He said, "I think I am ready, sir."

General Whitcomb called "Starting engines!" and pushed the power levers forward slightly. The noise was not bad, and there was *no vibration* from the engines at all. Slowly, the ship lifted off the concrete, stowed its gear, and hovered at about two feet off. The general rolled vernier knobs on the top of the throttles, and the ship moved forward toward the open hangar doors. Now it was just outside the hangar and motionless, hovering.

The general called Andrews tower, "Andrews, this is AF8401 here for sortie to GCC direct, ready for departure."

"This is Andrews tower, general, you are cleared direct to GCC, flight level S10 as you requested. Follow departure gamma 5. You are cleared to depart."

"Hold on, Dante. Here we go." said the general as he advanced the power and pulled back on the joystick.

The SR84 leaped skyward like a shot from a cannon! The general rolled the craft on its longitudinal axis as it climbed vertically and accelerated. In seconds, it was at S10; and in one deft move, the ship went from climbing vertically at eighty thousand feet per minute to level at S10, heading 285 at nine thousand miles per hour.

"I could have had it make that maneuver on autopilot," purred the general. "But it's just so much fun doing it manually."

Dante was still climbing vertically and trying to catch up with the ship but managed to smile at the general and whisper in his best Darth Vader voice, "Impressive!"

"We are moving too fast to give us time to talk. I'm going to slow 'er down and buy some time for conversation. Anyway, I want to show you some tricks this baby will do that no other aircraft or spacecraft has ever done before. Now, I believe you said you have some other questions about the job at GCC?"

Dante had caught up mentally with the ship now and was able to think clearly.

"This ship and this flight is a good example of why I don't want to be stuck at a desk all the time if I come to work for you. The sky is the best office I ever had, and I can't give it up."

The general understood. "Nor will I, Dante—ever!"

"You mentioned yesterday that there might be a way I could continue to fly military ships even though I would be in a civilian position. Have you given that any more thought, sir?"

"I have, and I think I may have a solution for you. There just might be an assignment for you that involves a combination of command, administration *and flying*. I do want to be sure that you will like the desk job part, however, because 75 percent of your time will be non-flying."

Dante was listening intently and trying to imagine what this job would be.

The general continued, "Let's wait until you tour the center, and I can explain what your assignment might be. Right now, I want to show you some maneuvers that only an SR84 can do. Hang on!"

With that, the general started some maneuvers. The ship began to dance like a knuckleball, side to side, then up and down, then up and to the left, now up and to the right. Dante felt high lateral g-forces during these moves and began to understand why the seats were designed to cradle the body so well.

The moves stopped, and the general said, "Well . . . What did you think of that?"

"I have never seen such evasive maneuvers!" said Dante.

"And that is exactly what they are. I did that manually. But if I am in combat, I can put the system on auto, and there is not a missile in the world that can hit this ship. The system detects the incoming missile no matter from what direction and initiates side thrust and acceleration or vertical thrust or forward thrust to avoid impact by the incoming missile."

"Wow!" said Dante. "Amazing! We had the forward thrust auto capability on the *Revelation* to avoid incoming space debris, but no vertical or lateral capability."

"There are only two of these ships flying with this capability, and we are going before Congress to appropriate funds for more of them."

The general continued, "Right now, I better start our descent, or we will be in California before we know it."

He nosed the ship over, reduced power, and put in a call for the GCC base tower. The tower cleared his approach and landing as he continued down. Dante was thinking, *With the GCC and no countries in the world with an air force like the United States has, I wonder why we might need a fleet of SR84s? Who is going to be firing missiles at our spacecraft?* He decided to keep that comment to himself for the time being.

They completed their approach to GCC base, and the general set the ship down just outside one of the smaller hangars near the tower. Dante had not noticed, but the ramp controller was signaling the spot for the general to land. Then he saw the PMU limo with star flags flying on the forward corners, obviously the general's vehicle.

Dante exited the ship and followed the general to his long black vehicle. A captain gave the general a snappy salute and said, "To GCC center, sir?"

"You got it, Captain. Aren't they expecting us?"

"Oh yes, sir!" said the captain. "I just thought you might want to stop somewhere else first."

"Nope," said General Whitcomb. "Call Harry and tell him we are on our way down."

"Yes, general, calling right now!"

Dante and the general were taken over to a large bunker-looking gray structure built into a rocky mountainside. Doors of the structure opened, and the limo drove in and stopped at a bank of elevator doors with air force sergeants posted on either side. One set of the doors opened slowly as the captain, the general, and Dante got out of the limo. They walked into the elevator, and the doors slowly closed behind them. Dante had never seen doors four feet thick.

The captain selected the destination stop for the car. A tall series of lights seemed to indicate at what level the car was as it descended, but no floors were marked except at the very bottom of the panel. These were marked simply A, B, and C. The car stopped at C, and the huge door again opened.

The general stepped out of the car and waved his arm in a sweeping circular motion. "This is the command center," he said.

The giant room was as large as a domed sports arena, and the walls and ceiling of the room displayed an enormous map of the Earth. Cities appeared to be represented by tiny lights in various colors, and some countries appeared to be back-lighted. Standing away from the map in another dimension were tiny models of satellites, appearing as if in stationary orbits. The floor of the room was covered with concentric arrangements of desks with chairs facing the map walls. Each desk position has several monitor screens facing the person seated at the desk. All chairs were not filled, but the room looked to be about three-quarters full to capacity. In the dead center of the room was a donut-shaped desk with one person seated in the center, able to pivot 360 degrees in order to observe any portion of the wall-ceiling map of the world.

The general obviously took a great deal of pride in explaining how the control center functioned.

"The maps you are seeing on the dome are actually computer projections coming from real-time images of the areas of the Earth's surface. The magnification of the projections can be changed by either the controller assigned to the specific area or by the shift commander in the center of the room. Let's go over to the current shift commander and show you a little demonstration."

Dante followed the general to the center shift command position. As they approached the officer in the position, he stood and saluted the general, saying, "General Whitcomb! Good to see you, sir! I was advised yesterday of your visit."

The general returned the salute and said, "Hello, Harry, good to see you. Anything working at this time?"

"Very quiet, sir, as it has been lately. Is this the Colonel Washington you were telling me about?"

"It is. Dante, meet Maj. Harry Marshall, one of our shift commanders."

Dante offered his hand and shook with Harry, saying, "Good to meet you, major."

"Harry, could you just do a little demo to show Dante how the system responds to a threat?"

"Yes, sir, be happy to. Dante, let me explain how this demo is set up so you will know what to expect. We have a test-fire range—in fact, several of them—we use to periodically fire our magna-lasers at to ensure that they are in top working order. For this demonstration, we will select the Gobi Desert range."

Major Marshall took his seat at the control console. He continued, "We will assume that we have identified an intercontinental ballistic missile, ICBM, about to be launched. The operators of the missile-firing unit have opened the silo doors. On the screen right here on my console, we have a magnification of the mock-up of the missile silo area. You can see a few houses and the open silo. Watch the big map in the area of the target," he said as he pointed using a laser pointer. Harry then proceeded to initiate the demonstration strike.

From one of the orbiting satellites, an intense beam seared from the maser directly at the point in the desert where Harry was pointing the handheld laser light beam; and a blinding explosion took place, sending sand and debris out from the impact point.

"Now let's replay in slow motion using this screen here, the strike that just took place."

Harry ran the replay, and it was easy to see the incoming maser beam arrive and the total devastation resulting from the strike.

"The way this system is designed," said the general, "is that if we had failed to ID the missile about to be fired, the snits or snats would have automatically picked up the launched missile as soon as it left the silo. The nearest maser would have been triggered by the identifying device, causing it to fire and destroy the missile. Most of the time, our worldwide detection and screening system will identify and locate any weapons before they are launched. Sometimes—rarely—we miss one. That is where the automatic feature comes into play."

"Could I ask a couple of questions, General?" said Dante.

"By all means," said the general with a smile. "If I can't answer them, I'm sure the major can."

"How sensitive is the detection system? That is, how small of a weapon can be picked up by the snits and snats?"

The general knew the answer but wanted Harry to respond. He nodded to Harry.

"The system can detect the equivalent firepower of a five-inch cannon shell. That includes any type of explosive material, from gunpowder to dynamite, to plastic, and all the way up to nuclear devices," said the major. "What it will not detect is small arms weapons—that is, unless a large number of weapons and ammunition are stored in a single location."

"Another question," said Dante. "Can the shift commander or any of the section controllers override a strike that was initiated automatically?"

"No," said the general, "for one simple reason. There is not enough time. You must remember that the automatic system only comes into play *when a weapon has already been launched*. By design, we made the system automatic because the human mind will not respond fast enough, in some cases, to destroy a missile on its way to a target."

"Of course!" said Dante, sorry that he had asked the question.

"Anything else at this time, colonel?" said Major Marshall.

"No, thank you," said Dante.

"Major, we will use one of your offices over there for a discussion if you don't mind," said General Whitcomb as he and Dante left the center console.

The general and Dante had a brief discussion in one of the side offices at the end of which the general said, "I don't think I have to tell you how important this facility and our network of maser satellites are, Dante. The safety and well-being of the entire globe rests with this system and the men and women that staff it. That is why we must have the finest military personnel in the control and command positions. That is why I want you." He paused for effect.

"You would spend about a month at one of the sector desks and then take over a shift at the command desk. I can also arrange for you to have access to any of our short-range fighters for your use in personal or business transportation. Your pay would be equivalent to that of Major Marshall's once you are in a shift command position. How does that sound?"

"When can I start, general?" said Dante.

36

Back in Washington, Maria was getting a cook's tour of the residential areas of Washington. She had asked her new friend Daphne to show her some nice but lower-priced accommodations where she might live until she got settled into her new job and became more familiar with the city. They had looked at about four areas that were quite nice but seemed expensive to Maria. Her new boss, Mrs. Reswick, the chief librarian, had advised her that her starting salary would be four thousand credits per month; and Maria had no idea how much that amount would buy in Washington.

"There are some new high-rise units near Georgetown," said Daphne. "Would you like to take a peek at those?"

"If they are not any more expensive than what we have seen so far," said Maria. "Those last units were nice, but 980 credits a month may be more than I can afford right now."

"You can handle up to a 1200 credits for rent—if it includes utilities," said Daphne. "Your big costs, besides your rent, will be groceries and transportation after you purchase the clothes you will need. These places near Georgetown are right on an MTA line that will bring you directly to the LOC, and shopping is very convenient for you. They only require a six-month lease. I've been thinking about moving into them myself when my current lease runs out."

"Sounds pretty good," said Maria. "Let's give them the once-over."

"By the way," said Daphne as she turned her PMU toward the Georgetown area, "I am not clear as to just what your position is at the library. Mrs. Reswick didn't tell me that. She just asked me to help you find a place."

"I am assigned to a reference section of the American history library. All I know so far is that I will be assisting people using the library and will be given research assignments to complete for members of Congress and the Supreme Court and for members of the administration. It sounds interesting. And I will, no doubt, get to meet some interesting people in the process of my work."

"Why did you opt for work at the Library of Congress?"

Maria hesitated. Daphne was being very inquisitive, and she wasn't sure she could trust her with personal matters. She decided to be vague.

"I was in public service work in the past and enjoyed it. I am personally interested in American history and in working with members of government, so it seemed like a good place in Washington to start."

302

"Where did you live before you came to Washington?" said Daphne, still probing.

"I lived here in Washington many years ago, but I am moving here from Florida now. I am currently on the payroll of GSA. Say! Aren't those the apartments we are looking for?"

And in Florida . . .

Ellen had rescheduled her interview and was at Mayo-Orlando for the day. David was in the office of Klaus Stoll, discussing possibilities for work at GSA. He had just sat down with the director.

"Soooo, David, your gang is breaking up. I understand that Dante is probably going to work for the air force and that Maria has taken a position with the Library of Congress."

"Yes, sir, and Ellen is interviewing with Mayo today although she has not ruled out working for GSA here."

"I hope not." said Klaus. "Her records indicate that she did fine work for NASA, and we could use her."

"Is Jake going to fly for you?"

"He is, and he is in training for the next TransMars mission as we speak."

"What ship is used for that mission?"

"It is a SC38 space cruiser with the latest, most powerful HD engines. It really is a bit of an overkill for a Mars mission. But the SC38s have such generous cargo capacity, have a top speed of ten times light, and take off and land vertically. We could use an earlier SC model, but this would compromise payload capability."

"Mars is about forty-nine million miles from Earth at its nearest, I believe. You can't go to light-speed for that short of a trip, can you?"

"That is true. We use a cruise speed of about seventeen million miles per hour, which takes a bit less than three hours travel time each way. The crews do not have to hibernate, and they don't get weary of the trip either. Now let's talk about a job for you, shall we?"

"Fine, sir."

"I believe you told me that you were in spaceship design for NASA and that you were one of the principal designers of the *Revelation*. Am I not correct?"

"My main function was system integration although I was the lead designer when the ship was originally conceptualized."

"At the present time, David, we are working on—in conjunction with Pratt & Whitney, General Electric, Boeing, and Lockheed—a ship that will go *one thousand times light-speed*!"

David was shocked! He had never dreamed such speeds would ever be possible.

"I am truly *amazed*!" said David. "You must be talking about engines quite different from HDs."

"They definitely will not be HD engines. I can't explain the design principles of the engines to you at this point because I don't understand them myself. In fact, I think that there are only a couple of people at Pratt and one at GE that even understand how the darn things will work. However, these scientists are *quite confident* of the power they can obtain from the new engines. They refer to them as hyperplasma accelerators, or HPA, engines."

David was still quite overcome. "Won't this make travel beyond our galaxy possible?"

Klaus stood and went over to the marker board behind his desk. "Let's just do some quick calculations and see what 1,000xL will do for us." He began writing on the board as he talked. "Our Milky Way galaxy is approximately ninety thousand light-years across to its outer edges. Our sun and our solar system are about two-thirds of the way from the center of the galaxy to one of its edges. Roughly, that would put us about seventy-five thousand light-years from one edge and fifteen thousand light-years from the opposite edge."

Klaus continued writing and talking. "If our ship can travel at one thousand times light-speed, it would still take us *fifteen flight years* to reach even the *nearest* edge of our own galaxy."

David responded, "So from a practical standpoint, we are still stuck within our own galaxy as far as round-trip missions are concerned."

"I am afraid so," said Klaus. "The distances in space are just so enormous. The 1,000xL speed capability will allow us to explore outside of our solar system and a great deal of our own galaxy. But that is all unless, of course, we launch one-way missions such as the *Revelation* mission was." Klaus looked somewhat disappointed at his own words. He said, "Unfortunately, David, even one thousand times light-speed would still be slow when one considers the immense size of the universe."

"What about our trip in the *Revelation*?" said David. "As it was, we traveled 1300 light-years at the speed of light. This meant that we traveled thirteen centuries Earth time. Had we been traveling in a ship that moves at one thousand times light-speed, we could have made our journey in only 1.3 years. We could theoretically have visited Nyvar and returned to Earth in 2.6 years Earth time, making that an excellent exploratory journey. Our crew could have completed its mission and returned home in a reasonable time after having aged hardly at all. I can see where 1,000xL ships will open up a lot of exciting missions within our galaxy."

David had made Director Stoll feel much better.

"This new ship is one of the projects you can work on, David, if you would like. We will make you a chief scientist rank. How does that sound?"

David didn't have to mull it over. "I would be honored to work on that project, Director Stoll!" he said. "When can I start?"

"Why don't we give you and Ellen time to find a home and relocate? That might take a couple of weeks. If you do it sooner and are ready to go to work, let me know."

"That is *wonderful*," said David. "I hope Ellen was successful today at Mayo. I can't wait to tell her what I will be working on."

Ellen was just coming into the basement garage when David got out of his PMU. She looked very excited and rushed over to David. She said, "I can't wait to tell you about my new job at Mayo!" as she gave him a big hug.

David knew he had been had. You always have to let an excited woman tell her story first, or she will never even hear your story.

"What?" said David. "Tell me about it."

"They want me to work in the development lab designing more-advanced androids. They want to make them more humanistic!"

"Like giving Mr. D. some emotions? Also pain sensitivity? Things like that?"

"Amazing things like that!" said Ellen.

David wanted to be excited for Ellen, but he didn't quite get it. *Why give androids human emotions?* he thought. He could imagine androids with all their mental abilities and strength being endowed with greed, envy, anger, and the entire spectrum of human emotions. *This could lead to real trouble*, he thought. He figured he best not make any negative noises at this point. "I am real happy for you, hon. I know the work will be challenging and exciting."

They walked toward the elevators. Ellen said, "How did your meeting go with Klaus Stoll?"

"Couldn't have been better," said David. "He is giving me a chief scientist rank, and I will be working on a new starship that can travel at one thousand times light-speed!"

Ellen stopped walking. "What? *You are not telling me the truth.*"

"I am, I promise," said David with a big smile.

"David that is unbelievable! A ship that can move at one thousand times light-speed! If the *Revelation* had that speed, a round-trip to Nyvar would only take 2.6 years."

David stopped and looked at Ellen strangely. "How did you do that so fast?" he said.

"That was easy," said Ellen as she put her arm around him, and they entered the elevator.

37

Jake and Susan were enjoying a quiet stroll on the beautiful white beach. The only sounds were the lapping of the waves and the occasional squawk of a gull. Their lives were about to change drastically. Susan was leaning toward taking a position with the Supreme Court, and Jake was already engaged in GSA crew training for a TransMars mission. The rather soft two and a half weeks they had enjoyed since returning to Earth was over. Time to go to work.

"I don't see why you won't give more serious consideration to coming here and working for GSA," said Jake. "You did legal work for NASA before and still managed to get in some fun shuttle flights. You stay here, and we can be together. We can have a very nice life."

Susan looked at him inquiringly. "Be together," she repeated his words. "What are you saying? You want to get married? Is this a proposal?" She smiled. She knew it wasn't. She just wanted to watch him squirm.

"Marriage!" said Jake. "Well . . . I really wasn't saying that . . . We could get a place together, though, and we could live together. Wouldn't you like to do that?"

"I like you, Jake. I like you a *lot*. But I have an opportunity to be at the *seat of justice of the country*, working for the *top legal mind* in the country. *That* is worth *a lot* in terms of my career. If you wanted to make a permanent commitment to our relationship, then that is one thing . . . But look at what you will be doing. You will be off in space for days, maybe weeks at a time. Meanwhile, I will be stuck here doing space property work, maybe with a trip to the moon or to Mars occasionally. There is no assurance that we could even be on the same flights. Our work will be entirely different."

Jake looked down at their footprints in the sand as they walked along. He really cared a *lot* for Susan. But he had cared a lot for special women before—and the relationships somehow just didn't last. Would this one be any different?

He said, "If you take that job for the court, you will be giving up flying. Do you really want to do that?"

Susan thought a minute before answering.

"Jake," she said softly, "why don't we do the thing that we each think is best for us? You fly for GSA, and I will go to work for the Supreme Court. With the vehicles they have today, Washington and Canaveral are no more than one hour apart. You get a place here, and I will get one in DC. We can visit each other at least on weekends. If you have several days downtime between missions, come stay with me in Washington."

Jake looked at her and thought, *This will be the end of us—no relationship will survive over eight hundred miles, no matter how fast the commute is.* Susan could read his mind.

"There is another plus to my suggestion, Jake," said Susan. "If you and I have really found something, then the arrangement I am suggesting will tell us that. On the other hand, if you find another girlfriend a couple of weeks after I am gone, then at least *I* did the right thing."

Jake looked at Susan with an expression she had never seen on his face before. He looked like he had already lost his best friend. He said, "I don't want you to leave this area. I want to see you every day."

Susan felt a real strong pull toward Jake at that point, but she knew her logic was sound. Jake was now rich—as rich as any person in the United States was allowed to be. He could *do anything* he wanted and could basically *have anything or anyone* he wanted. Why would he be happy settling for Susan Chen?

"Let's not discuss *you and me* any more right now," said Susan. "I haven't given Justice Webster my answer yet. I told her I might take a week to do that. When do you leave for Mars?"

"We will train for a week. Then we'll be on reserve. We will have a two-way payload, taking water-producing units, power equipment, and supplies up and bringing valuable gems and other minerals home. Our departure has not been set yet."

"Then we have some time just to ourselves. I know you are in training each day, but not *all* of every day. We can be together when you are not at training. Tell you what . . . If you want me to, I can do some scouting for you for a condo. David and Ellen will be looking, and I might tag along with them. Or if that doesn't suit them, I can look by myself. If you take lunch breaks, we can do lunch together some days. These next days can be fun together, and I won't give Judge Webster an answer 'til the end of the week."

Jake perked up a little at the sound of this. Susan hadn't completely slammed the door—yet. He still had a few days to change her mind. *I guess I could even consider marriage,* he mulled. Then he shook his head and thought, *What is the matter with me?*

They headed up from the beach toward the BPQ.

"I'd like to change. Then let's go out to dinner and maybe a movie. How does that sound?" said Susan.

Jake had just been thinking about going to Susan's unit and never leaving there, but he said, "That sounds good. I'll change too and be over in about forty-five minutes if that's OK?" Susan's smile told him it was OK.

David and Ellen went house hunting on Thursday, and Susan tagged along. She had a good idea of what Jake wanted—something with a big MaxVision screen and a fully automatic kitchen. If she could find it, something that would *also make up its own beds, clean the kitchen, and dust and vacuum.* David and Ellen, on the other hand, were looking for a larger place with at least two bedrooms. Ellen had mentioned that they planned to have at least one baby as soon as they got settled down. David and Ellen located two places that met their needs and price range. One was closer to KSC and one was closer to Orlando. David finally insisted that they take the one nearer Orlando so Ellen would have the shorter commute each day. They offered on the unit.

While with David and Ellen, Susan didn't see anything that Jake would like. They were all too big. That afternoon, she gave Jake the bad news; and that night, she and Jake cruised down to Melbourne to see what that housing market was like.

Again, there was just nothing available like they were looking for. The night wasn't a total loss, however; they discovered a fabulous seafood spot called the Whale's Tale.

Friday morning, Susan set out again—determined to find a place Jake would like. After a hard day's looking, she found three units that might work and was anxious to show them to Jake. They planned to leave the base as soon as Jake got out of training Friday afternoon and look at all of them, then go on to Orlando for the evening.

When Jake exited the training building at three PM on Friday, Susan was at the curb ready and eager for their inspection of the condos. Susan looked beautiful in blue and had a fantastic smile to set off her playsuit.

"Hi, hon, you look fabulous! Any luck with houses today? I've been at controls all day and really need a break. Do you mind driving?"

"Fine," said Susan. "I've found three nice places you will like—especially one of them. They all have great living rooms, large master bedrooms, and practically do *their own housework.*"

Jake gave a big smile; he liked the sound of that! He really appreciated Susan doing the house-hunting legwork. Jake didn't like shopping—*for anything.*

Susan showed him the one she liked best first—it was also closer to KSC. Jake immediately liked it. It had a great living area with adjacent bar and kitchen, an enormous MaxVision that was equipped with the latest in holographic 3-D technology, and a nice deck with a pretty good view. The master suite was large and plush, also with a large viewscreen. The small kitchen was 100 percent automatic. It even did the grocery shopping.

"Someone had me in mind when they built this," said Jake. "But wait a minute . . . Don't you want kids? Where is the second bedroom?"

Susan's jaw dropped! But she quickly recovered. "This is *your* unit that fits *your needs* for now. If you and I ever get far enough to *mention* the word *children*, we can find a larger place."

Jake took her in his arms and said, "I don't want you to go to Washington. What can I do or say to keep you here?"

She kissed him—a long one—and said, "When I think of it, I will let you know."

Jake didn't need to look at the other places Susan was planning to show him. He stopped at the office and paid the first month's rent plus the required deposit. He returned to the puma and said as he got in, "Thanks for finding it, Sue. I hope you enjoy it as much as I do."

"Orlando?" she said.

"Let's go have some fun!" said Jake.

It was Saturday, and David and Ellen were moving into their new townhome. There really wasn't much to move, but they had a lot of shopping to do. They had purchased a unit that was brand-new and unfurnished. The kitchen was completely built-in along with the viewscreen in the living room and one in the master bedroom. But they needed furniture for the living room, the dining area, and the master suite. They decided they could wait on the furniture for the second bedroom. They needed to complete their purchases and have their new place ready to live in by Sunday. They were both starting their new jobs on Monday.

Jake was up early for his training class. It started at seven each morning. Susan had ended up staying with Jake—each of the last three nights. She was sleeping in for the third morning in a row. *This could become habit-forming*, she thought.

"I have got to make up my mind on this offer from Judge Webster," Susan said to herself in the bathroom mirror. She thought, *I guess I am glad that Jake doesn't want to commit to marriage. Neither of us is ready for that yet. The distance will help us understand our feelings.* Then she blurted it out! "I've made up my mind! I am going *to work in Washington.* If this thing between Jake and I is meant to be, IT WILL BE!"

Susan picked up her AMec and placed the call.

"Judge Webster's office," came over the connection.

"This is Susan Chen. Could I speak with Judge Webster, please."

"I'm sorry, but the chief justice is in conference at the moment. I will hand her a note if you like."

"No, don't interrupt her," said Susan. "What time do you think I should call again?"

"Well, I know she has a ten thirty meeting in her office. She should be back here by ten. Why don't you try between ten and ten thirty?"

"I will," said Susan. "And if you don't mind, just put a note on her desk that I will be trying to reach her at the time you suggested."

"Very well, Ms. Chen, I will do that."

Susan looked at her watch. It was nine fifteen. Plenty of time to get to her unit, shower and dress, and run down for a bite of breakfast.

Chief Justice Webster had just returned and found the note. She had hoped that Susan would decide to work for her—she looked forward to speaking with her. At ten fourteen, her secretary called in and said that Susan was holding. Judge Webster picked up the handset. "Susan, nice to hear from you. Is the news good or bad for me?"

"I am coming to work for you, Your Honor," said Susan. "I hope you feel that this is good news."

"By all means, Susan, I am delighted!" said the chief justice. "When can you start?"

"Is Tuesday OK? I will come to Washington tomorrow afternoon and try to locate a furnished apartment by Monday night. I plan to call Maria and get her advice. I know that she has been house hunting and is probably in something by now. Do you have any suggestions?"

"Not really, it's been so long since I looked at apartments . . . But—oh yes, I did hear something from one of the clerks that works here. They are building some very nice high-rise units near Georgetown. There are some for sale and also some for rent. I believe they have both furnished and unfurnished."

"Thanks for that. I am really looking forward to coming to work for you, Judge Webster. I certainly hope I can do the kind of work you want."

"Do not worry, my dear. You will do just fine. I will look forward to seeing you on Tuesday."

Susan put down the mec and then picked it back up. *I hope Maria has her mec on,* she thought as she entered Maria's number.

Maria's mec toned several times and finally went into voice messaging.

Rats, thought Susan. *She's not answering.*

Susan began leaving a message, "Maria. This is Susan. I have decided to come to work in Washington and I—"

Maria picked up the call.

"Susan! Hi! I was away from my AMec. How are you? Any problems with the trip back to Canaveral?"

"Hi, Maria. No, no problems with the flight—and *I was in command* all the way back. Well, I had a little help from Jake . . . and David . . . and well, Ellen, but not much. Annnnyway, how is your work going? Have you found a nice apartment?"

"I did find a very nice furnished place—a new place too! And I have a lease-buy arrangement if I decide that I would like to buy it at some later time."

"That's a good deal," said Susan. "And what about your work?"

"Too early to comment on that yet. I'm just learning the job, and there is a lot to learn. I heard you say just before I picked up my mec that you are coming here to work. That's great! When are you coming up?"

"Tomorrow night. There is a flight that leaves here at four and arrives at Reagan at five. I will pick up a rental puma and probably stay somewhere around Georgetown. I hear there are some nice and reasonable apartments in that area."

"This is uncanny!" said Maria. "My apartment I just moved into is in the Bradenton Meadows section near Georgetown. Why don't you just come stay with me tomorrow night, and I can show you these units? Maybe they will be just what you are looking for too."

"Are you sure that won't be an imposition, Maria? You are just moving in yourself."

"Not a problem. I insist! Here, write this down. It's my address."

Susan wrote down the address and said, "Thanks, Maria, see you tomorrow night." Susan clicked off her mec, and it immediately toned.

"Hello?"

"Susan! I have been trying to reach you," said Jake. "I want to talk some more before you make your commitment to work for the Supreme Court. We are quitting early. Our simulator had an equipment breakdown. I'll be over in a minute and let's talk."

"Jake, I have made my decision. I don't think there is anything you can say that will change my mind."

"Well, let me just talk to you some more. I have some new ideas."

"Jake, I told Judge Webster that I am taking the job."

"You *already told her*? I thought you were going to wait 'til tomorrow."

"I was, but tomorrow is Sunday. I was lucky to catch her in this morning. *I have to do this, Jake.*"

Neither said anything for a few seconds.

"When are you going to Washington?" said Jake.

"I am taking a four PM flight into Reagan tomorrow—gets me in at five."

"Then tonight is our last night. You are killing me, Sue! I don't know whether I can stand to see you tonight."

"Oh, *you can*. Let's fix dinner here at my place and have a quiet candlelit evening . . . You *know* you are not going to stay home and pout tonight, are you?"

"*I love you*, Susan. I don't want you to go."

"Jake, stop it! This is not *you* talking. You can handle anything! Now you just get your butt over here and let *me tell you* how we are going to carry on a long-distance romance."

"OK. I'll be there in five minutes!"

One Month Later

Jake had moved from the BPQ into his new condo about ten minutes off base.

In Washington, Susan had moved into a unit in the Bradenton Meadows near Maria's apartment. She had settled into her position working for the Supreme Court, primarily accomplishing research for Chief Justice Webster. Susan's assignment was basically reviewing cases being heard by the high court and searching for precedent setting decisions of the past that had a bearing on the current case.

Shortly, after Susan began her work for the court, she discussed with Judge Webster Jake's situation with the Chase Bank, particularly with respect to the law regarding the maximum assets an individual could hold. With the chief justice's help, she had found a precedent setting case wherein a wealthy CEO had let a savings account grow to the point where his total assets were over the three-billion limit. The bank's position was that since the man was at his maximum allowed asset holdings, then certain earnings at the First National Bank beyond a specified date did not have to be paid because the earnings amounted to credits over and above the limit. The federal court had ruled *that the occurrence of an individual exceeding the asset limit allowable for an individual did not relieve a bank or other holder of the man's assets from paying funds that the individual was otherwise due*. Further, that the status of a person's asset level was a matter between the individual and the government and did not affect the business relationship between the individual and the fiduciary.

Susan reviewed this case and the ruling with Mr. Bernstein, the manager of the Chase Washington Bank. On advice from the bank's attorneys, Mr. Bernstein decided *not* to challenge Jake's position. In other words, Jake's four billion credits in the Chase *Bank belonged to him*; but by law, he had to *divest himself of one billion* to bring his assets under the three-billion limit allowed. He would have one month to take the action required.

Jake, after Susan's understanding with Mr. Bernstein, had immediately gone to the Chase Bank and withdrawn the excess billion credits, having cashier's checks issued in the names of Susan, Maria, David, Dante, and Ellen—*each in the amount of 200 million credits. Now they would* ALL *be millionaires!*

Jake pondered over the proper way to present the checks to each of his friends. He decided that the best way to do it would be to host a dinner party to ostensibly kick off the 621 Club. After all, he *had been tapped* as the coordinator for the group. After many call attempts, Jake finally reached all five of the crew and arrived at a date for the party suitable to everyone. He began to make firm plans.

Jake arranged for a special dinner in a private dining room of the Coach and Six at the Cape. He worked directly with the owner of the restaurant and spared no expense.

The afternoon of the big night arrived. Dante, now based in Colorado, signed out a sporty four-place air force utility transport ship. He flew to KSC by way of Washington and picked up Susan and Maria for the occasion. The flight from Andrews AFB to KSC took them all of *ten minutes* at flight level S10.

Mr. D. met their flight and drove them in a PMU van to the Coach and Six. They arrived right on time at 6:30 PM. Jake, David, and Ellen were already into their second round of refreshments and met them at the front door.

Maria was the first one out of the van and had hugs for everyone. "This is great, you guys! I have really missed everyone!"

Susan was giving the biggest hug to Jake. After all, she hadn't seen him for four whole days. "I've really missed you," she said.

Jake led the party into the private dining room where a three-piece combo was putting out some very nice tunes from the twenty-first century. Two very cute waitresses, very scantily but tastefully dressed, were taking drink orders and attending to the servicing of the table.

"Jake," said Dante, "you really know how to throw a party." This was echoed by the others as they dived into the fancy hors d'oeuvres.

The dinner included fillets of the finest steak and Maine lobster with delicious accompaniments. As usual, Jake had selected some very fine wines to complement the meal. Everyone thoroughly enjoyed the dinner and especially the opportunity to be together again as a group—the six *oldest living humans.*

After the dinner, Jake made a short speech.

"Ladies and gentlemen, I have to be honest. I have lured you here under false pretenses."

His guests looked at one another and thought, *Now what is he up to?*

Jake continued, "We are not really going to have a 621 meeting. I just missed all of us being together and wanted to have a party!" Everyone laughed at this. Then Jake said, "However, there is one special reason I arranged for you all to come here tonight." He paused. "Because you are the very best friends I have on this Earth, because you are the best crew of astronauts I know, and because you are all *qualified as poor*, having very few assets and practically no money in the bank, I am able to provide you with *financial assistance*. Here, *for each of you,* is a Chase Bank cashier's check in the amount *of 200 million credits!* Please don't spend it all in one place."

Everyone was stunned! Sure, Jake had alluded to giving them each a share of his surplus funds . . . But they never really thought it would happen. Two hundred million credits each. *They were all multimillionaires!*

Susan, of course, knew that she had ensured that Jake would get the full four billion from the Chase Bank; but *even she* had never really expected that Jake would in fact give each of them such a sizable check.

David yelled, "Group hug!" and they all descended on Jake who tried to escape but failed and crushed him in a truly affectionate group hug.

Needless to say, Jake had immediately become the *best friend* of *all* the *Revelation* crew members, not just of Dante.

38

Six Months Later

Dante had worked himself into a shift controller position with GCC. So far, he had seen no real emergencies—although the GCC on one occasion had to take out a ship carrying six missiles equipped with nuclear warheads. The CIA, in conjunction with other special intelligence forces, was still trying to figure out where the ship originated from and why the weapons weren't detected much earlier.

Susan had gotten deeply involved in several ongoing cases being reviewed by the high court. She still saw Jake on weekends when he was not on a mission for GSA. Jake had made four round-trip Mars runs, and Susan thought he was getting bored with that work although Jake wouldn't admit it.

Maria had been deeply involved in several research projects for both Congress and the administration. She now was as knowledgeable as anyone working for the library on the sections she was responsible for. The *patent library* had recently been added to her responsibility, and that section was indeed very busy. In fact, she had done some work *requested by Susan* because of a couple of patent infringement cases.

Ellen had learned so much since going to work for Mayo-Orlando. She first went to a series of instructional classes to learn how the current production androids were designed and constructed. Then she was put through a series on how the android brain was adapted from the human brain. The last sessions on this subject were directed to concepts for making the android brain more humanistic. Some of the lead medical doctors were working on theories that would result in android brains becoming almost exact copies of the human brains they were modeled from.

David was deep into his assignment of integrating the engines and airframe systems of the new *Galaxy Cruiser* with HPA engines. The engine companies had small test versions of the HPA engines working—more proof of concept than anything else. But the target thrust for the full-design-sized engines had been established along with the engine weight so that the design could proceed for the airframe/systems.

One very routine day, David and other scientists from various GSA projects were having lunch in the executive dining room of the research lab when David overheard, by chance, a conversation at a nearby table. Someone at that table said the words *time machine*. David thought he must have misheard the speaker and paid no attention to the comment.

As David was about to leave his table, he again heard the words *time machine*. This time, there was no mistaking what he heard. David looked at his watch, and there was still some of the lunch hour left, so he decided to get a cup of coffee and move to a chair closer to the table where the interesting conversation was taking place.

Luckily, there was a vacant chair at a table where he knew two of those seated, and the vacant chair backed up to the table where he had heard the words *time machine*.

David took his coffee and went over and sat down by his acquaintances who were all working on the *Galaxy Cruiser* project with him. He began to chat with those at his table, but his ears were finely attuned to the table behind him.

At that table, the conversation was going like this.

"I say we are ready to test the machine with a live mouse."

Another said, "And I disagree. We have been successful in moving a wooden block ten minutes into the future. I will give you that. But a wooden block is an inanimate object *with no life*. True, it was once part of a live tree, but now it's dead. We have proven that we can disassemble a molecular structure, move it into the future, and reassemble the structure in its original form. That does not mean we can do it with a *live animal*."

Now they *really* had David's attention. Twice, people at *his* table had to nudge him because someone had asked him a question, and David had failed to notice. He was trying to seem interested in the talk at his table *and* hear the words spoken at the table behind him.

A third speaker got into the conversation behind him. "Well, I see nothing wrong with trying the experiment with a mouse. How else will we ever prove we can successfully transport people through time if we can't be successful first with an animal?"

"Look," said the second speaker, "I am responsible for this project, and I am not ready to start risking animals—any animal—until I am convinced the experiment has a high expectation of success. We are *not yet sure* of the transfers we've made into the past . . ."

David turned just enough so he could see who the project leader was that was speaking. *It was Dr. Howard Ottinger*—one of Director Stoll's staff that had participated in the orientation sessions when the *Revelation* crew had first arrived. What a stroke of luck! David decided to wait until the other table broke up and then say hello to Dr. Ottinger.

After Ottinger's firm statement about not jeopardizing animals, no one else had anything to say, and each started leaving the table and the room. David's table was also beginning to break up. David waited for his chance, and as soon as Dr. Ottinger arose and left, David was right behind him. Dr. Ottinger stopped for a sip of water at the cooler, and this gave David his chance.

As Ottinger turned away from the cooler, David was there.

"Ah, Dr. Ottinger! How are you?" said David.

Howard was momentarily stumped but quickly recovered. "David! Nice to see you! I hear you are working for us now on the *Galaxy Cruiser*, isn't it?"

"Yes, sir, I am. Good to see *you*. I have been here now a little over six months."

They began walking in the same direction. It wasn't the way back to David's lab, but David had to learn more about the time machine project.

David spoke, "Our gang has broken up. My wife, Ellen, is at Mayo. Jake is flying TransMars missions, Dante is with GCC, Susan is with the Supreme Court, and Maria is with the Library of Congress."

"My *my*," said Dr. Ottinger, "quite a *variety* of careers."

"What are you concentrating on nowadays, Dr. Ottinger?" David tried the direct approach. The doctor looked left and right, hesitated, and then said, "I'm on a hush-hush little project that *no one believes in* . . . But you might just find it interesting, David, since you yourself are something of a *time traveler*."

He was in! Howard was going to talk to him about his work.

"I guess we *were* time travelers in a sense, doctor," said David. "When you think about it, that's all we really accomplished. We left Kennedy Spaceflight Center in 2025 and returned here to the same spot in 3339. We might as well have been in a time machine and dialed in 3339 as spend all those years traveling at light-speed in space."

"Come into my office, David, and let me tell what we are trying to do."

David was pretty excited! *Did they really have a time machine prototype? Did they really move a block of wood through time?* He couldn't wait to hear what Dr. Ottinger had to say.

"Have a chair by my desk, David. I am going to have a cup of coffee. Would you like some?"

"That will be fine, sir. Could I use your mec and call my director? I want to tell him that I am with you, and I will be a little late returning to the office."

"You work for John Brindell, don't you? Here, I will give him a quick call and tell him that I asked you to give me a hand with a project I am working on."

Before David could object, Dr. Ottinger had John on his mec.

"John? Howard Ottinger here. I am borrowing one of your staff for a few minutes . . . David Marks. Yes . . . Yes . . . I'll have him back to you in an hour,

OK? Fine . . . I'll talk to you later . . . Good-bye." Howard got the two cups of coffee and sat at his desk.

"Thank you, sir," said David as he sat down. "I just didn't want John to think I'm out shooting pool or something."

"You shoot pool? Good! We'll have to play sometime. Now let me tell you what we are fooling around with. The Weber Corporation Research Laboratory came up with a theory that works like this. Let's just call their machine a device for ease of reference. They have a working prototype. Actually, WE have it now . . . a working prototype of a device that, according to Dr. Edward Stessel, a senior research physicist at Weber labs, will break down any object into its molecules. The device will then contain these molecules so they don't drift off somewhere. And the device and the molecules will, employing time-warp, wormhole theory applications, travel to another point in time and space and materialize again—*exactly in the original molecular form*!"

"Incredible!" said David, "And you have witnessed this?"

"Yes, *I have seen it work* several times," said Dr. Ottinger. "By the way, call me Howard. I think we are all way too formal around here."

Howard continued, "Ed Stessel and others at Weber contacted us to set up an experiment that would move an object not only through time but *through space*. They want to send something to Mars and would like to work with our team stationed there."

"Have they already proved that the device transmits objects through time and space in proximate locations?"

"They have. They are here with us now in G lab and have demonstrated the time transference of an object in several experiments."

"Are you talking *forward* through time or *backward* through time or *both*?"

"Both," said Howard.

"Through what interval of time?" said David.

"Only small intervals so far. We have transferred a wooden block up to ten minutes into the future and ten minutes back into the past."

"Can you explain to me how you know the transfer has taken place to the past? I can see how you can easily confirm the transfer to the future. The device with the block just disappears, and ten minutes later, it reappears in the same spot. Is that not correct?"

"Not quite, David. We have transferred the device and block ten minutes into the future and *to a separate table in the same room*!"

"But how can you prescribe such precise coordinates to move the object just from one table to another?"

"That is part of the design of the device. It uses a system of universal three-dimensional coordinates measured to five decimal places. I have heard Ed

Stessel explain how this is done. But I will be honest with you, I cannot follow his explanation, and I certainly cannot repeat it."

"Is the transfer of the item to the past done in the same way?"

"Yes, but this is much harder for us *to accept what we are seeing*. The block and the device simply leave their position on one table and appear intact on the other table. In theory, they have been sitting on the second table for the last ten minutes. But since the time has past, how can we be sure?"

"I see what you mean," said David. "Since the past *has past*, how can we know how long the object has been there? There must be a way."

"If you can come up with a scheme that will prove that an object has in fact been there for the last ten minutes when we just now see it in that location, we will all be greatly indebted to you. This is really my only hang-up at present. Until we can resolve this issue, we won't use a mouse as the subject for transference. I must be convinced that the object really did move to the past as claimed by Dr. Stessel."

David thought for a few seconds. "I do have an idea that might work. See what you think of this. On the transfer target table, place a platform capable of supporting the device after its transfer. Rig a switch to the platform such that when the device and the object it carries arrives, the switch is triggered, turning on a clock counter. The counter should read in hours and minutes. If my theory is correct and you send the object two days into the past, when it appears on the platform, the clock counter will read forty-eight hours."

Howard thought for a few seconds, then said, "David, I think you have it! I believe your scheme will work. We could also use a motion detector to trigger the time."

"Yes, you could—that would be simpler," said David. "Also, I may have one other suggestion. How large of an object will the device accommodate?"

"The compartment is about a foot high, eight inches wide, and eight inches deep."

"Then instead of a block of wood, why not use a small *potted plant*? A plant is alive, and you can see if that life is adversely affected. If it is not, then the next logical step would be to use a mouse."

"Excellent suggestion, David. Maybe you should come to work for me."

David laughed and said, "Dr. Ottinger, I can't tell you how excited I am that you are actually working on a *time machine* project. This is truly a *momentus* endeavor. Of course, you realize the vast implications of such a project if it's successful?"

"I do, David, and the ramifications frighten me. This is why we must keep this work under wraps—at least until we are quite sure of what we have."

"Has the Weber Corporation filed a patent on this invention yet?"

"I assume that they have, although they didn't ask us to sign a non-disclosure agreement."

"I would have thought that they would have," said David. "Now I really must get back to my office, Howard. But please keep me advised on the experiment, and I would like to observe the transfer of the plant."

"I will keep you right up to speed, David, and we will contact you when we are ready to transfer the plant. I am going to tell John Brindell how you have helped us so he won't be concerned when we request your assistance again."

In Washington

Susan was learning a lot and doing good work for Chief Justice Webster, but she missed the excitement and the fun she had training for the *Revelation* mission and making the journey. She often caught herself thinking what her life would be like now if the *Revelation* actually had made it to Nyvar as originally planned. What kind of civilization would they have found there? Or would it have been a lifeless planet?

And she missed seeing Jake every day. She envied Jake's mobile life—the trips to Mars and the other work he was involved in at GSA. This was the first time in Susan's life that she had been so tied to a desk and to paperwork. The plus side of the job was that Justice Webster had really come to like her and depend on her to research cases and find precedents in the judicial decisions of the past. And though the cases were interesting, the job was almost like studying history—not one of Susan's favorite subjects.

Her apartment was working out nicely. It was in the same complex as Maria's, but not in the same building. Fortunately, she didn't have to share Jake with Maria when he came to see her. Jake was coming to Washington on the coming weekend. He had business at the bank, but he would spend most of his time *with her*. They planned to go sailing on the Potomac and had good seats for a play. She could hardly wait for the weekend and for Jake to arrive.

And on the Moon

Jake had taken a moon mission with a return stopover at the low earth orbit space station referred to as LEOS. He was scheduled to be back at Kennedy by Friday morning and plan to take a commercial flight out of Orlando to Washington for the weekend. He could hardly wait to be with Susan.

Right now, he was tending to his assigned business on the moon. This was his first visit to the moon, and he was very impressed with the station there. The main GSA base was a domed structure constructed primarily of the same aluminum polymer material used for buildings on Earth and completely climate controlled. The dome contained vegetation and other landscaping features and excellent quarters for use by those assigned to the base and those just stopping over, as was Jake. Under the dome was really a small city—similar to the domed cities on Mars, but the single moon base was much smaller than the Martian base colonies.

Lunar Station One was connected to the mining stations by pneumatic tunnels and transportation cars that were pushed along by air. The arrangement reminded Jake of the pneumatic tubes used by banks to transport money, checks, etc., between vehicles outside and the tellers inside.

Jake and his copilot were just finishing a sandwich at the Crater, a popular sidewalk café. They were waiting for their freighter to be loaded with several types of precious minerals, sparse on Earth but plentiful and fairly easy to mine on the moon. He glanced at his watch and realized he had time to catch a movie playing at the base theater before the freighter would be ready to depart. "There's a new 3-D movie playing at the cinema," said Jake to Todd, his copilot. "We have time. Want to take it in?"

"What's the name of it?" said Todd.

"I don't know," said Jake. "But it features Marlo Madsen, so it can't be all bad!"

"I'll pass," said Todd. "I saw that one a month ago on Earth. How about nine holes of golf instead?"

"Golf? Where? They have a course here now?"

"Sure do. Brand-new dome just for the golf course. Unbelievable scenery around the sides. You'll think you are on an Earth course. And the dome is huge. It *had* to be. Even with the dead balls they produce for use up here, a drive still goes three hundred to four hundred yards because of the low gravity. The same balls wouldn't go one hundred yards on Earth. Want to try it?"

"OK," said Jake. "Let's go. Where do we catch the tube for that?"

"Follow me," said Todd as he headed toward a tube entrance.

Two hours later, after losing twenty-five credits to Todd, who had played the Earthview Golf Course many times, Jake was completing the preflight on his ship. Todd was checking the cargo to make sure it was tied down correctly. Finally, they were both on the flight deck taking off their pressure suits. Jake was now reading the checklist, and Todd was responding.

"That completes the 'before engine start' list," said Jake. "Starting engines."

The freighter was an SF4 class ship and somewhat larger than the *Revelation*. Its two engines were a couple of generations later than those of the *Revelation*, but not very different. The moon-Earth trip was only about 250,000 miles. With the stop at the LEOS station, the trip would take about three hours, cruising at one hundred thousand miles per hour.

"After-start checks," said Jake.

"All greens."

"Lunar Station Tower, this is SF425 ready for departure for Earth."

"All clear, 425, have a good trip," came back from the tower.

Jake pushed the power levers forward and slowly lifted off. Pulling the joystick back, he began a vertical climb, rolling and turning toward the Earth. Now the Earth filled the center of the windscreen—always a beautiful sight! Jake thought, *Thank God man got control of world conflict before the beautiful blue planet was destroyed.*

They were out of the moon's gravitational field now almost at cruise speed with the Earth dead ahead.

"I'll give the LEOS station a call and tell them our ETA," said Todd.

Almost three hours later, SF425 was approaching LEOS. This was the first time Jake had seen the station up close. When the *Revelation* arrived at Earth's orbit over seven months before, they *thought* they had seen a space station but were not sure at that time. Thinking they were arriving at Nyvar, they hadn't known what to expect.

Jake had not realized how *big* the LEOS station was. The construction and design of it resembled a motorcycle wheel with hub and large spokes out to the rim. The docking piers came off the hub. The labs and working areas were housed in the rim. The rotation of the station about the hub created artificial gravity for the personnel stationed there.

Todd called in, "LEOS Tower, this is SF425 for docking at pier 7. Are we clear?"

"SF425, we had to shift you to pier 5. The ship occupying pier 7 has an engine problem they are working on. We thought it would be done by now—5 is clear, though. They are expecting you."

"Roger, LEOS, we'll take her around to 5. Over and out."

"That's one of the problems with some of the older ships, I hear," said Jake. "Any idea what's happening to those engines?"

"Not a clue. It's the same with any ship I've ever flown. They are never maintained to new spec standards, and the older the ship you fly, the more likely you are to have a malfunction. The guys in that tub on 7 are lucky the engine problem showed up while they were docked instead of halfway down or halfway to the moon!"

"Yeah."

Jake eased the ship into the docking position at pier 5.

"All locks engaged," said Todd. "Nice job. How long you been flying these types?"

"My first trip on this one. I've been taking the SC38 cruisers on the TransMars trips. Those ships are very nice."

"So I hear," said Todd with a little envy showing through.

39

David and Ellen were just finishing one of Ellen's specialties, a sautéed shrimp dish, when David decided that he just *had* to tell Ellen of his meeting that day with Howard Ottinger. *Yes*, thought David, *the device is being handled as top secret by Howard and his staff, but he could trust Ellen. They had always trusted each other.*

"I saw Dr. Ottinger today, hon, and you will never guess what he is working on." David decided to have some fun with Ellen in the process of telling her about the *time machine*.

"Well," said Ellen, "I am all ears, but I am *not* going to try to *guess* . . ."

David was disappointed. It was very hard to stump Ellen on any guessing game, but he felt he had a winner here. "Ah, come on! Let's play twenty questions and see if you can come up with the answer."

Ellen looked at David with an expression like "Must we play a game?"

"Oh, all right," she said, "just to humor my little boy. First question, does it fly?"

"Nope!" said David proudly. "Second question?"

"Is it some kind of device?"

"Yes," said David, a little disappointed already.

Ellen thought a minute and said, "Does the device do something that has never been done before?"

"Yes, and you have used three questions."

"Does the device do something to objects or to people?" said Ellen, showing more interest in the game.

"So far, to objects only, but maybe to people also. Four questions."

Ellen, knowing David pretty well, decided to take a wild stab. "Is it *a time machine?*"

David, who had a bite on a fork halfway to his mouth, dropped the fork! "How could you have possibly guessed that? That is a *ridiculous guess.*"

"But it *is* the answer—right?"

David stared at Ellen and pushed back from the table. "There is no way that you could guess *time machine* in just FIVE questions—someone told you . . ."

Ellen was having fun now. David was indignant. She had nailed him in just five questions. She was enjoying herself so much she totally overlooked the ramifications of what she had just said. Then it hit her! "David, you are LYING! A *time machine* can exist only in *science fiction*."

Now it was David's turn to laugh. And laugh he did. "Howard Ottinger is working with a time machine developed by an outside lab. And Howard tells me the darn thing *works*."

Ellen just looked at David. "What have they sent through time?"

David told her the whole story of his meeting with Dr. Ottinger and of the plan to transfer the potted plant both forward and backward through time. Ellen listened but still was not ready to believe. "You made up this story, David. It cannot be true! Have you seen this work with your own eyes?"

"No, but Dr. Ottinger was not lying to me, and he has seen it."

"He is being tricked! And now so are you. Has this *medicine man* asked for any money from GSA?"

"Not that I know of. As I told you, this Dr. Stessel and Weber labs came to GSA only to get cooperation in an experiment to time-transfer something to Mars."

Ellen stirred her coffee. "And they have transferred a block of wood ten minutes into the future and ten minutes into the past?"

"Yes, but as I told you, they are not convinced of the arrival time in the past."

"When are they going to try your suggested experiment?"

"Tomorrow, I think. Howard promised to call me when they are set up so I can witness the thing myself."

"You, of course, realize the vast ramifications of this if it's on the level, don't you?" Ellen still couldn't believe it.

"Well, of *course* I do! *If* it will allow animals to be transferred without an adverse effect on their well-being, then anything is possible. Do you want to go back to 2025?"

"Of *course* not! I like what they have done with the world in the last thirteen centuries, and I really like the work I am doing now. And *you are not going back either*! Aren't you happy in this century?"

"I'm very happy as long as *I am with you*," said David sincerely. "And I'm *very happy* with my work. And I'm *very happy* to be living in this century."

They were quiet for a few moments. Then Ellen said, "Call me after you witness your experiment. I share your enthusiasm for the project."

En Route to Washington

Jake had been going to Washington on weekends, but always commercial. The PMUs that GSA allowed the personnel at KSC to operate flew too low and too slow to take on an eight hundred mile trip. Finally, he decided to let go of some of his fortune and purchase his own PMU. He had intended to be conservative, but a hot little red PMU-060 caught his eye. The salesman easily sewed up the deal when he told Jake that this brand-new model could cruise up *to airway S3—twenty-one thousand feet and three thousand miles per hour.* Jake had decided on a beautiful deep-red color.

This trip to Washington was the first opportunity he had to stretch the legs of the new puma. Susan didn't even know he had purchased it.

He was cruising at flight level S2 at about two thousand miles per hour. Flying time from KSC to Washington was about thirty minutes, allowing for traffic mergers and maneuvers. It was about sunset now, and he could see the lights of Washington coming on in the distance. The Washington Monument was barely visible. He would enter Washington MATRAC in a little over three minutes.

Susan was at her vanity putting on the finishing touches to her makeup when her AMec toned. "Hello," she said, not expecting any call in particular.

"Hi, Sue," said Jake. "Here comes the man directly from the moon."

"Jake! You did a *moon mission*? Was it fun?"

"Somewhat tame after Mars, but interesting. Say, I am just entering the Washington MATRAC and wondered what's the best exit for me to get to your place?"

"Hey! I thought guys didn't need to ask directions!" chided Susan. "Oh, *okaaay*—exit 102 will bring you directly into Georgetown. Then you remember the streets: Halifax is the bottom of the exit, then left on Montgomery, then right on Westmont, and you are here. See you in a few."

"Keep your mec handy in case I get lost . . ."

Susan had to chuckle at this. Here was a guy that hopped back and forth to Mars and the moon, had been to see her numerous times since she'd moved in her place, and still had to ask directions. *I guess I have been picking him up at Reagan, though, and he hasn't really driven much in the area*, she thought.

"Say!" she said out loud to herself in the mirror, "he must have a *new puma*. I'll have to program my address into his nav. unit. I wonder what he bought . . ."

She waited a few minutes after Jake's call, then stepped out on the balcony overlooking the street below. A beautiful new red puma was just pulling up to the curb. *Deep-red*, she thought. *Probably him!* She continued looking, and Jake hopped out. He looked up and saw her at the window.

"Come on down!" he yelled. "Take you for a spin!"

Susan grabbed her purse and ran for the door. She just caught the elevator as the door was closing. In an instant, she had dropped four floors. She hurried to the curb, and there was Jake, looking real smug. She jumped into his arms and gave him a *big smooch*.

"How do you like the wheels?" he said.

She wanted to pretend she didn't, just to tease him, but she loved it.

"Wow!" she exclaimed. "It's the most gorgeous thing I've seen around! How much did it cost?"

"Now that's rude to ask," said Jake. "So I *won't* tell you. Jump in the driver's side, and let's go for a spin!"

"Okaaay!" said Susan as she hopped into the left seat.

"Buckle in good," said Jake. "It has a *lot* of pep."

Susan gave it some power and slowly moved away from the curb. "I'll take it up just to A1, and let's circle the city. The sun is just setting, and all the lights are on. Great time for a slow cruise around the town."

The 060 made practically no sound, and was the accelerator ever *sensitive*. It handled as steady and solid as a rock. Jake fiddled with the sound system and found the best jazz station in the city. What a great time to be alive! What a time to be with each other! They were both very happy together. The rest of their lives didn't really seem to matter.

After one round of the city, Jake said, "Did you know these are qualified for S3 and 3,000 mph?"

Susan looked at him with her brightest and prettiest smile and said, "Should we see if it will really do it?"

"Why not?" said Jake. "But don't forget to follow all the traffic rules. Although it feels like one, this is *not* an air force space fighter."

"But, Jake, I thought the S airways were reserved for *air and spacecraft*, not pumas.

"They are—except for the 060. This baby has every piece of gear that one of Dante's fighters has. Well . . . except the weapons. The manufacturer petitioned the ICC and the FAA and because of the new sonic boom-elimination design got approval to allow the 060 to go to S3 and 3,000 mph."

Susan proceeded to the next transition ramp and merged into it. She stayed with it, climbing and increasing speed as she passed the various traffic levels A3, A4, then S1 and S2. Jake called INCAT and advised that they would be using S3-27. At S3, Susan leveled off, checked for traffic, and merged in. She floored it and accelerated to just under three thousand miles per hour.

"Wow," she said. "Are you sure this in not a USAF *short-range fighter* in disguise?"

Jake laughed. "Do you realize that in less than an hour, we could be in San Francisco having fresh seafood on the wharf?" said Jake.

"Should we?" said Susan.

Jake thought for a minute. "Why don't we just pick a nice quiet place in DC tonight? I've got some things on my mind, and I want to just relax and be with you. We can run out to San Francisco tomorrow night or, hell, over to Anchorage or even *Waikiki*! We can do anything you want. What would you like to do?"

Susan liked his idea of staying in the vicinity tonight—a quiet dinner and maybe to bed early. After all, they had all day Saturday and all day Sunday. Then she remembered the play tickets for Saturday night.

"Let's stay close tonight. But don't forget I have some very good play tickets for tomorrow night."

"That'll work," said Jake. "Let's head back to Georgetown and check out the Ocean's Floor. Remember the place we went after the reception when the feds were tailing us?"

"I'm on it!" said Susan as she called INCAT and transitioned from the westerly lanes to the easterly lanes of S3 and headed back.

They were enjoying oysters Rockefeller at the Ocean's Floor and sipping one of Susan's favorite Rieslings. The three-piece combo was playing some real moody jazz, and they both were feeling very romantic. Jake was trying to get up the courage to ask Susan if she had had enough of Washington, but he didn't want to spoil the mood. Almost as if she read his mind, Susan came out with, "Jake, I'm not sure this legal work is the best thing for me."

Jake's heart did a triple flip! But he contained himself. "Why do you feel that way? Just some boring assignments?" He decided to be cool.

"All the assignments are boring. There is little challenge to legal work in this century as far as I can tell up to now."

"Can you explain that a little better for me? I have a pretty good business mind, but not a legal one."

"The TVU is the reason, Jake."

"That's the truth device? The one that can read a person's mind?"

"That's it, Jake. Back in the twenty-first century, law—both criminal and civil—and even business deals, contracts, and the like were all founded on *hiding* the truth or *discovering* the truth. Hiding or misrepresenting the facts was the name of the game. That was the way to gain an edge. And the system back then was to prove to juries and judges which party was telling the truth. That was the whole ball game. Think about it. Even politicians who thrived on lies and under-the-table deals can't do that today. Did you know that in a political race now in the thirty-fourth century, when a politician makes speeches and participates in debates, he or she is hooked up to a TVU?"

"You are not serious!"

"I am serious. It's true. Even the *president himself*. If they lie, they are immediately exposed. It's just this, Jake. In today's society, there is little crime. There is little dishonesty—people can't get away with it. This means that the professions that were dependent on crime, dishonesty, and shady dealings—such as law and politics—are now not nearly as interesting and challenging or as *lucrative* as they were in the time of our old Earth.

"Business and entrepreneurship *is where the action is*. It should be a good time for you to be aggressive in some business venture. Have you given that any thought?"

"Not really as yet. But I am going to do *something* . . . I never thought spaceflight could be boring. But when you are doing it like the pilots of commercial airliners, I guess it *can be boring*. My trips for GSA now are cargo runs basically and pretty routine at that."

They both were silent for a few moments. Jake did not like the turn of the conversation, but he *did like* the fact that Susan was *not* enjoying her job. He said, "Are you ready to give up legal work and do something else?"

Susan stared into her glass. "Let's order dinner and change to another topic of conversation. I want to hear about your Mars and moon trips."

Jake didn't particularly want to talk of his boring cargo runs, but he had to get Susan in the right mood before opening the subject he *really* wanted to discuss.

They studied the menu for a few minutes, selected items, and then ordered.

Jake restarted the conversation with, "Rather than talk about the moon and Mars, let me try something else on you for size. As you know, I have some money in the bank . . . and—"

"Only about *three billion credits*," said Susan with a sly grin.

Jake continued, "And you have a tidy sum as well. My point is this, Sue. We can do *anything we want* in this world. Any job, any business, any profession. Or we can do nothing but have fun. We can vacation all the time. Yet it appears to me that we are both doing things that *neither of us are excited about doing* . . . Why is that?"

Susan thought about Jake's words carefully. Finally, she spoke, "Well, *you* certainly can do anything you care to . . . What do you *want* to do?"

It was Jake's turn to think. Then he said, "Two things. I want to explore the galaxy, and I want to be with you."

Susan looked into Jake's eyes. *Does he really mean it?* she thought. *What if I gave up everything else and took him up on his crazy suggestion?* "Jake, do you really know what you are saying?" she said.

"I know exactly what I am saying, Sue. I am basically an adventurous type. I am really turned on by the new and the unknown. *You* are the first thing that has happened to me in my life that I don't get tired of! Look at it this way. We both have talent and skills. We both have money in the bank. We can always work at jobs or professions. But right now, GSA can use us in their astronaut program. They are short of people with our background and experience and will probably let us go anywhere their 10xL ships can take us. And with the capability of *ten times light-speed*, we can go out and explore other planets and return to Earth. When we launched in 2025, we did it thinking we would never see the Earth again—and we were willing to make that sacrifice. Now we know we can go out and explore and *return to Earth*. Meanwhile, our money is in investments earning interest. If we, after some missions, decide we've had enough, then we can quit. We won't have any contract obligation to continue if we don't want to."

Susan was quiet. She sat thinking. She took a sip of her wine.

"OK!" she said. "I'll do it. *Provided . . .*" She did not finish.

"*You will?*" yelled Jake, attracting attention from other tables. Then he remembered the rest she had said. "Provided *what?*"

"I will go with you to the stars . . . if GSA approves and supports it, if we can travel at ten times light-speed, and . . . if you can get the rest of a crew."

"They will support the missions, and I can get a crew." said Jake boldly. "This will be a *fantastic* adventure for us."

The understanding they had now set the stage for a fun and exciting weekend for the two of them. The rest of Friday evening was a night to remember, culminating in the best night of lovemaking either of them had ever experienced. They both wondered how the deep feelings they now had for each other had been so absent and elusive during all the time they had known each other and worked closely together.

They slept in Saturday, finally becoming operational about 10:30 AM. Eggs Benedict on the deck was delightful; then they took their time getting dressed. Susan had arranged to rent a sailboat on the Potomac. She had sailed as a young girl at summer camp, but never since. She wanted to show Jake something she was quite accomplished at and enjoyed immensely.

The afternoon went wonderfully. The boat was a Haven Class sloop—a little larger than anything Susan had sailed in the past, but she handled it. Jake, quite accomplished on the water himself, was impressed at her sailing skills. There was just the right amount of breeze. The day was consumed by a very relaxing cruise.

They returned the sloop and discovered a raw seafood bar on the wharf. After laying into some clams and oysters and liquid refreshment, Susan realized that the afternoon was almost over—the sun was setting among some gorgeous clouds.

"Our tickets are for *Madame Butterfly* at Lincoln Center, and it starts at seventy thirty."

Jake looked at his watch. It was five forty-five. "I think it would be great fun, and I think we can make it. But we have to get moving *now.*"

Susan bolted up and raced for the parking garage. "Last one to the puma is a rotten egg!" she yelled.

Jake charged after her and dropped his AMec. "No fair!" He yelled. "I'm not playing unless I get a fair start."

Susan was doubled over laughing at him by this time and waited for him to catch up. As he reached her, she yelled, "OK, GO!" and took off again!

This time, the race was close. But Jake had a plan. He didn't think Susan knew exactly where the puma was because *he* had parked it. As they raced along the path, they came to a T. Jake faked left, Susan went left, and Jake dashed right—the correct direction of the puma. This gave him about a five-yard lead, which he managed to maintain until he reached the PMU.

Both were laughing and could hardly stand up for puffing. Jake said, "I won, I won, I won." They collapsed into the puma, and Jake gunned it out of the building en route to Susan's place.

They missed the curtain of *Madame Butterfly* but made the first alternate seating and thoroughly enjoyed the performance. Neither of them had ever been to Lincoln Center before. After the performance, they found a quaint new pub with a piano player not far from Susan's apartment. Another wonderful day and night together.

Sunday afternoon came too soon, and it was time for Jake to return to Kennedy Spaceflight Center. As Susan was walking with Jake to his new PMU-60, who should appear jogging by but Maria.

"Maria!" said Jake. "It's been a while."

Maria had been jogging for over thirty minutes and had worked up a pretty good "glow," which is how the ladies refer to sweat. "Jake! Hi! Didn't realize you were in town. How're your space missions working out?" Maria kept jogging in place.

"Good." said Jake, glancing at Susan as if to say, *That's not the truth, but there's no need to go into it with Maria.* "I'm staying plenty busy. Just did a TransMars and a lunar visit in the last ten days."

"Wow, you *are* busy!" Maria exclaimed.

"How is your work with the library?" inquired Jake.

"Yeah, you promised to fill me in," said Susan. "And we haven't talked."

"I'm getting some very interesting research assignments," said Maria in a tone that was less than enthusiastic.

They all felt a little awkwardness in the trio situation, and Jake said, "Well, ladies, I really must be getting back. Got another Mars run tomorrow, and this one includes our installing some new equipment. Got some material to review tonight." He said to Maria, "Nice seeing you, Maria. Hope your work continues to go well."

He then turned to Susan and said, "I'll call you later tonight, Sue." She came into his arms, and he planted an ardent good-bye kiss on Susan's very receptive lips.

Maria turned away, feeling embarrassed although she was angry with herself for reacting that way.

Jake hopped into his new puma and accelerated from the curb and down the street. He waved at the two of them through the open sky roof as he turned the corner and disappeared.

"Apparently, you and Jake are getting serious," said Maria.

"Very!" said Susan. "Neither of us can explain it, but we are really clicking. I miss him terribly when he's away and can't wait for him to return."

"Sounds more serious than I imagined."

Susan just smiled. "We made some long-range plans this weekend—I can't discuss them with you yet."

"Marriage?"

"No, not yet. Just some plans to be together much more than we are able to at present. I'll tell you about it when I can."

Maria let it drop with that last statement. "Are you busy tonight? I need to talk to someone, and you are the only real friend I have in DC. How about coming over for dinner tonight? I'll whip up some authentic Mexican dishes for us."

"Sounds great!" said Susan, looking at her watch. "When should I come over?"

"Now is fine."

"OK, I'll run back to my place, put on something more comfortable, and be over in fifteen minutes." Susan took off for her condo.

"See you then!" called Maria, resuming her jogging pace toward her unit.

Maria was busy preparing food when Susan came to her door. The door announced to Maria that "Susan Chen has arrived. Should I show her in?" The inside of the door displayed a life-sized animated image of Susan's head and shoulders.

"Yes, show her in!" Maria called out to the door. The automatic pocket door opened.

"Something smells great!" said Susan as she entered. The door immediately slid closed and then locked behind her.

"We are having some nachos with our sangria, then later, enchiladas and chili rellenos—my mother's special recipes. The Instant Chef can't do it like my mother could."

"Sounds wonderful! What can I do to help?"

"Not a thing—everything is under control. Let's take the wine and the nachos out on to the deck. It's very pleasant out there."

They took chairs at the attractive metal and glass table on the deck and toasted with the sangria. "Here is to a bright future for us both!" said Susan. Maria touched her glass to Susan's, but her beautiful dark eyes were sad.

332   Benjamin Lightfoot

"You said you had things to talk about, Maria. Is something troubling you?"

Maria looked into her wine and was silent as if she wasn't sure where to begin. Then she looked at Susan and said, "I cannot get Rico out of my mind."

Susan was stunned. Rico had been dead for many centuries although the time had only been less than two years to Maria.

"Maria, I am so sorry," said Susan, but she could think of nothing else to say.

"My research has made things worse for me. Did I tell you that Rico made significant contributions to industry and to the country, so much so that his home in Arlington has been preserved as a national shrine?"

"I remember seeing a home that day. Mr. P. mentioned the home when we flew by it, but I didn't realize that your Rico was *the famous person* the home is commemorating."

"He is. During the life of Enrico Valdez, his contributions were so significant to the United States and to the world that after his death, they dedicated the preservation of his home. There is also a statue of him near the Washington Monument."

Maria continued, "A lot of my research has been into the early years after we left Earth—the time when Rico was alive—and I have been reading of some of those astounding contributions he made to science and industry. One of my goals in working for the Library of Congress was to learn how the world underwent the startling changes it did from the twenty-first century to the present. Interestingly enough, some of the research projects I have been given by Congress and the administration put me back into the twenty-first century, and I *keep seeing Rico's name*! It really makes it difficult for me to do my work."

"I can see how it would." Susan was trying to think of some way to help Maria.

Maria continued, "I am trying, Susan, but I'm unable to feel at home in this century. The need for the work I did in the twenty-first century does not seem to exist in this century. There is really no poverty in the United States now. Mexico has become part of what is now the fifty-six states. I suppose that if I wanted to go to another country where there are still poor people, the kind of work I did in 2025 might still be needed. But America is my home. I just really don't feel *welcome* here. I miss my life in the twenty-first century. I miss Rico terribly. I made a mistake in coming on the *Revelation* mission."

Susan was feeling great empathy for Maria. Her problem was not only the loss of her relationship with Rico, but also the loss of her entire existence in the twenty-first century. *She is going to need some serious help to dig out of the psychological hole she is in*, thought Susan.

They had finished their second glass of sangria and a plate of nachos, and the afternoon sunset had faded into darkness.

"Let's move inside and see if the dinner is ready." said Maria, trying to be cheerful. They moved inside to the dining area adjacent to the kitchen. Maria served up the dinner plates as Susan poured their third glass of wine.

They dined and talked of their work. Susan shared some of the cases she was working on, and Maria talked of specific research work she was doing. They talked for a couple of hours without any further mention of the twenty-first century or of Rico.

40

David was working in his lab when his mec toned. It was Dr. Ottinger.

"David?" said Ottinger as he placed the unit to his ear.

"This is David," he responded.

"Good news, David, we are ready to transfer the potted plant. We have a motion detector set up to record the arrival of the plant into the past. Can you come over now? We are ready to conduct the experiment."

"Thanks for the call, Howard. I will be right over." David stopped in the office of his boss, John Brindell, and advised him of the call. John was excited too and joined David as they hurried over to the lab where Howard Ottinger was working.

They arrived at the lab to find Dr. Ottinger, Dr. Stessel, and Director Stoll preparing to transfer the plant, positioned in the transfer compartment, to the future and to the designated platform in the lab. A video camera was set to record the event, and the plant was wired for certain biological measurements.

"How far into the future are you sending the compartment?" asked David.

"We have entered twenty minutes," said Dr. Ottinger.

"And in this case, the timer should start with the arrival of the plant in the compartment and continue tracking time until we shut it off," said Dr. Stessel. "Are we ready?"

"All is ready," said Dr. Ottinger. "I will trigger the switch."

Howard Ottinger pressed the activate switch; and the transfer compartment, with plant and pot, faded from view. The clock sitting on the side table indicated exactly 10:32 AM. when the transfer was activated. David looked at his own watch, which indicated ten thirty-four.

"Well, we have until ten fifty-two," said Howard. "Time for a cup of coffee, shall we?"

All except David left to get coffee at the lunchroom area. David said, "I'm not much for coffee. I'll stick around just to be sure nothing unexpected happens." He just sat and stared at the platform destination intended for the transfer compartment with the plant. He was totally intrigued.

At ten forty-five, the others returned to the lab. David reported that "absolutely nothing" had happened except for his labored breathing since they left. They laughed at that comment. At exactly 10:52, the compartment with the potted plant materialized on the target platform and the timer, triggered by the motion detector, began to record and display time. All gave a mild applause at the arrival, and Dr. Ottinger noted the event by making entries in the official test log. The video camera had recorded the event and was still operating.

Dr. Stessel then removed the potted plant from the compartment so that close inspections might be made. The biological measurements made indicated absolutely no change in the health of the plant. It was as if nothing at all had happened to it.

"So far, so good," said Director Stoll. "Are we ready to send it to the past?"

Everyone looked at one another with less than confident expressions. They were all extremely excited about the next experiment, but by the same token, apprehensive. They were actually about to send a live object into the past—into the world that had already come and gone. Could such a thing possibly be done?

"If there are no objections, we are ready to proceed," said Dr. Ottinger.

"How far into the past will the compartment be going?" said David.

"We have decided on two days," said Dr. Stessel. "We could have made the time period anything, so we just decided to use two days."

"Now exactly what can we expect to see?" said Director Stoll, addressing Dr. Ottinger.

"When we initiate the transfer, the compartment and plant should disappear from its present position and immediately appear on the platform with the timer over there." He pointed. "The timer should read forty-eight hours since that is the time span we have set into the control unit. This will then tell us that the compartment and plant actually arrived at its destination in time and location two days ago, or forty-eight hours."

"Are we ready?" said Dr. Stessel with his finger on the switch.

"You may proceed!" said Dr. Ottinger.

Edward Stessel activated the control switch, and the compartment with the plant faded from view. All eyes turned toward the platform target, but nothing appeared! They all looked alternately at one another and at the platform. *Nothing was appearing*!

"I do not understand!" said Dr. Stessel. "The plant should have arrived on that platform two days ago! Where is it?" Everyone continued to stare at the platform.

David walked over to the platform and looked at the timer.

"The timer is running, and it is showing forty-eight hours and two minutes!" said David.

"What?" said Dr. Ottinger as everyone rushed over to the platform timer.

"He's right! Now it is showing forty-eight hours and three minutes!" said Director Stoll.

"But where is the plant?" said Dr. Stessel. They were dumbfounded.

At that moment, the laboratory door opened; and a young girl came in, one of Dr. Ottinger's lab assistants. The scientists paid her no attention and continued to stare at the empty platform.

The girl said, "Did you gentlemen lose something? You appear to be looking for something."

"There is supposed to be a plant in a container on this table!" said Dr. Ottinger rather gruffly. He was annoyed by the failure of the experiment and now by the interruption of the lab assistant.

"There *was a plant in a box on that table a couple of days ago*," said the girl. "It looked like it needed water, so I moved it over by the sink to give it a drink."

"*What!*" screamed Dr. Ottinger. "*You moved it? To what sink?*"

Now the girl was shaken—and somewhat afraid.

"I'm sorry, sir. But it was just a plant. And it did need water."

"*What sink?*" said Howard. "*Show us.*"

The girl said, "Over there on the far wall. See, the plant is still there, next to the box it was in before I watered it."

All eyes immediately turned to the spot where she was pointing. There on a shelf by the sink was the potted plant. And next to the plant was the time-transfer compartment. Everyone rushed over to look. It was the *same potted plant*. The plant was sitting beside the compartment.

As the girl was trying to leave the room and escape the wrath of Dr. Ottinger, he saw her leaving.

"Stop, young lady! And come over here," he said. "I need to talk to you." The poor girl was sure she was about to be terminated and came meekly over to Howard. He sensed her fear and embarrassment and said to her, "Do not be afraid, my dear, everything is OK. We just want to ask you a few questions." Dr. Ottinger continued, "You say you were in here two days ago when you saw and moved the plant and the compartment?"

"Yes, sir," said the girl.

"Do you know what time you were in here?"

"Not exactly, sir, but I'm pretty sure it was just before lunch."

"Was there anyone else in the lab when you came in?"

"No, sir. I had noticed that there were some people in here earlier in the day, and some here later in the day, but none when I was in here."

Dr. Ottinger looked at each of the others who were listening to his exchange with the girl.

"Then the compartment and the plant must have arrived on the platform on schedule," said David. "Otherwise, how would the timer have been triggered?"

"We must repeat the test again right now!" said Dr. Stessel.

"I agree!" said Director Stoll.

Howard Ottinger had dismissed the lab assistant and was already taking the compartment with the plant back to the origination point. "Let's *do it*," he said.

The platform timer was reset to zero, and the compartment and plant were made ready to transport.

"Let's set the time interval to twelve hours this time," said Director Stoll, "less time for outside interference."

All was ready, and Dr. Stessel activated the switch. The compartment and plant again faded from view. But this time, as the plant faded at the origination point, it appeared on the platform with the timer. David, who had taken a position at the target destination called out, "The timer is running and shows twelve hours!"

The experiment was a *success*. For the first time in history, a man-made machine had successfully transported a *living object* both into the future *and into the past*!

Everyone applauded. A real *operational time machine* had been created! Dr. Ottinger raised his hand for quiet and said, "I would like to make a statement and an acknowledgment. Dr. Stessel, you are to be congratulated. You have created an amazing invention that will *forever change life on Earth and throughout the heavens*. My sincerest congratulations! You are a shoo-in for the Nobel Prize for science."

Everyone took turns in congratulating Dr. Stessel, who was quite modest about the whole affair. He said, "Gentlemen, you are too kind. I would love to share with you the secret of this device, but I am afraid that I am not at liberty to do so at this time. I co-own the patent, which was filed about a year ago with the president of Weber Inc., the company I work for. While the patent is on file in Washington—and you are free to study it—there is one secret that does not appear in the patent papers. Without that secret, a *functioning* time-transfer device cannot be created. Oh, one can be constructed in accordance with the patent. But without the secret, the machine simply will not operate."

"Well," said Director Stoll, "the patent and the secret belong to you and your partner, and that is as it should be. Let me say that GSA is willing and eager to work with you on programs which utilize the capability of this time—and space-transfer device. Do you have a simple pet name we can use to refer to it?"

All were focused intently on Dr. Stessel, awaiting his response. He appeared to be trying to think of a name on the spot.

"I think we should call it the Ultimate Mobility Unit, or UMU. However, I *am* open to other suggestions," said Dr. Stessel. "Now while I don't wish to take any of the edge off of our success, I do think we should carefully examine the plant to be sure that the travel through time has not affected the life or health of the plant in any way."

David returned to his lab office with John Brindell. As they walked, they discussed the ramifications of the UMU.

"This device can have as big of an impact on the Earth's civilization as the TVU has had," said John

"Maybe even bigger," said David. "Just think of some of the things that are possible. With personal UMU units, a person can go anywhere he wants and arrive there at *any time* he wants. To be a little on the ridiculous side, I could sleep in 'til noon, step into my UMU, and be at work on time at 8:00 AM!"

"Here is another one," said John. "I could use my UMU to travel to the day after the Superbowl, learn the outcome of the game, then go back in time to before the game, and place a huge wager on the winner. I couldn't lose!"

"Remember the old movie *Back to the Future*? You will now be able to go ten years into the future, pick up a sports almanac that contains all the scores of sporting events for the past ten years, and come back to the present. You could wager on any event covered in the almanac and always win."

They both thought as they walked.

"But this is crazy," said David. "Everyone would be hopping back and forth to the future and to the past."

"So much so that the *past and future would be changed*," said John.

"For example," said David, "if a person went back into the past to the time when Adolf Hitler was a child and *killed* that child, history, and the present, would be completely changed."

"I can see where the government is going to have to step in and tightly control time travel. You cannot let this type of power get into the hands of just *anyone*."

They arrived back at their offices at the lab, and David immediately called Ellen.

"Ellen Marks speaking."

"The time machine works!" said David.

"What?" said Ellen. "Does it work both ways?"

"We transported the plant both ways. Into the future and into the past."

Ellen was silent.

"Are you still there?" said David.

"I'm here. David, this will completely change the world . . ."

"I know. John and I were just discussing it on the way back to our office. Say, listen, I've got a lot of work to do. I just wanted you to know."

"Thanks for calling," said Ellen. "Now I won't get anything done for thinking about it."

"See you tonight."

"Bye."

As David put down his mec, John entered his office. "I was so caught up in this UMU thing, I forgot it is lunchtime. Want to join me for a bite?"

"Sure, why not? My mind is a jumble right now, anyway."

They headed for the cafeteria without saying much. Then John said, "You know, this device can be a powerful instrument of evil in the wrong hands—especially right now. Only Dr. Stessel and a few at his company know the secret of this thing, yet the patent is public knowledge as are all patents. If unscrupulous characters learn of this, they will stop at nothing to get their hands on it. Control of this device can be worth trillions of credits!"

"And that is probably an understatement," said David. "Nothing was mentioned this morning about keeping the information under wraps. We better contact Director Stoll and request a meeting of all those who were present this morning during the experiments."

"And we better get hold of Dr. Stessel quickly. I'm sure he has contacted his partner at Weber," said John. "As a matter of fact, they had already done enough experimentation to be confident that the device would work."

"No telling how many people *already know* of the UMU and what it can do."

David took his mec and punched in Dr. Ottinger's number. There was no answer. "I guess they are at lunch too."

As John and David entered the lunchroom, they saw Director Stoll, Dr. Ottinger, and Dr. Stessel at a table near the window. David said to John, "Go ahead and get in line. I'll stop by their table and catch up with you."

David went directly to the Stoll table. He said, "John and I were just discussing the ramifications of the UMU and focused on the issue of security and the potential dangers of holding the secrets to the device."

Director Stoll said, "As a matter of fact, we were just on that subject ourselves. We will hold two places here at this table . . . Get your food, and you and John come join us."

David joined John in the line and told him of Director Stoll's comment. They got their meals and joined the others. When they took chairs at the table, Director Stoll was saying to Dr. Stessel. "So you and the others at Weber think that your secret is safe because with just the patent alone it is impossible to construct an operational UMU."

"That's pretty much correct," said Dr. Stessel. "At this point, there are less than a dozen people who have actually witnessed objects being transported through time. Every one of these individuals is either a key person on Weber's payroll, or they work for you here at GSA. So far, we have not transported any live animals, let alone people, with one of the units. The secret I referred to, which is required to make one of the units operational, only exists in the minds of two people. There is nothing written or recorded in any form that reveals that secret."

"Speaking for GSA," said Director Stoll, "I will ask each of you at this table to refrain from telling anyone what you witnessed here today. Can I be assured that you will keep these experiments and their results confidential?"

"You have my word," said Dr. Ottinger

"And mine," said John Brindell.

"And mine," said David, remembering that he just told Ellen. "When will we be ready to transport a mouse?"

"I was hesitant before today," said Dr. Ottinger. "But I see no reason to wait."

"Nor do I," said Dr. Stessel. "How about tomorrow morning—first thing?"

They had finished lunch, and all were leaving to go back to their offices. David was the last to take his tray to the waste area and was therefore about twenty feet behind the others. As he approached the exit of the cafeteria, Jake was just entering the room.

"Jake! Hi!" said David. "How are your space trips?"

"Oh, OK, I guess," said Jake. "I was supposed to launch for Mars again this morning, but some of the equipment we are hauling up was delayed. Say! What's this I hear about an operational time machine?"

David was *shocked*. He looked around to see who else might have heard, and fortunately, no one was near enough. He put his finger to his lips to shush Jake and stuck his head out the door to see where the others were. John was in the hall, looking at the bulletin board and apparently waiting for him.

"John," said David, "you go ahead. I'll be along in two minutes." David then turned to Jake and said, "How on earth did you hear of the time travel unit?"

"Well, I just talked to Susan, who had just talked to Ellen, who had just talked to you."

Incredible, thought David, saying, "This thing is supposed to be very hush-hush at this point, so please don't say anything else to *anyone* about it."

"No problem," said Jake, "but first you have to tell me what you actually witnessed."

In Washington

Susan had just put down her mec from talking to Jake and telling him of the time machine experiment when Maria called.

"Susan, what are you doing tonight? I really feel better after talking with you last night. Can we get together again tonight, or do you have something planned?"

Susan thought a minute. "I have nothing planned. Why don't you come over, and I will do an authentic Chinese dinner tonight."

"That sounds like fun! Is six o'clock OK?"

"Make it sixty thirty. I need to pick up a couple of things. And don't forget to ask me about the *time machine* they are working on at GSA!"

The evening had gone well, and both Susan and Maria found it very easy to talk to each other. A great deal of the conversation was about their jobs and about some of the research work Maria had done related to cases Susan was working on. It was late, and Maria was about to leave when she remembered. "Say, what was that you said about a *time machine* at GSA?"

"Right," said Susan. "I forgot to tell you. Ellen Marks and I were talking today, and she said David had witnessed an *operational time machine*. They apparently transported a potted plant, of all things, both forward in time and backward in time."

"How far forward and how far backward?" said Maria, showing some interest.

"I think it was like twenty minutes forward and two days backward," said Susan. "Apparently, this thing is in its embryo stage, with this plant being the first living thing to be transported. Ellen thinks they are planning on using a mouse next."

"Isn't this a very significant invention? I mean, especially if they become able to transport people?"

"Well, I would *say so*! Time travel could have some world-shaking ramifications—if they can pull it off. But that has to be years away. If they haven't even used a mouse, it will be a long time before they will even consider allowing a person to be transported! Ellen said that the device could barely hold a small potted plant."

"It's very interesting though," said Maria. "Please keep me informed when you hear any more about it."

Maria finished helping Susan with the cleanup and went to get her wrap.

"Thanks, Susan. It's fun talking to you. Let's get together again."

"For sure!" said Susan. *As long as it's not every night*, she thought.

Susan was just tucking herself in for the night when the mec tone sounded. *I hope it's Jake*, she thought. *But it can't be! He's on his way to Mars!* She answered. It was Jake!

"Hi, hon," said Jake. "Hope I didn't wake you."

"Hi, babe, you didn't wake me. Maria was over for dinner, and she just left. I thought you were on your way to Mars."

"We were delayed twenty-four. Didn't receive all the equipment we are taking up. It's here now, though, and we launch at 0715 in the morning."

Jake continued, "Say, thanks for the tip on the time machine. Apparently, it's a real hush-hush project, though. David was shocked that I knew about it so fast. Did you mention it to anyone else?"

"Just Maria. Want me to tell her to keep it quiet?"

"Yeah, guess you better. And don't tell anyone else, OK?"

"No problem. Do you think they will really be able to transport people through time?"

"Who knows? I'm not ready to volunteer yet. They are trying some 'lucky' little mouse tomorrow."

"Now that I know about it, you have to keep me up to speed."

"Baby, I have no secrets from you. I do need to hit the sack though, with a seven fifteen launch . . ."

"OK, guess I will let you go. Be careful and follow the book. You may think your trips are boring, but if something serious goes wrong, your trip would get hairy in a hurry."

"I'll be careful. I'll call you as soon as I get back."

"OK. I love you . . . Good night."

"Good night, hon."

41

David arrived at Dr. Ottinger's lab to find everyone else already there. Doctors Stoll, Ottinger, and Stessel were clustered about the launch position as John Brindell looked on from close by. In the transfer compartment was a tiny mouse, certainly not aware that he—or she—was about to make history. The little animal had some tiny wires attached to its body and to some instrumentation displaying vital signs.

"Good morning, David." said Director Stoll. "You are just in time."

David greeted Director Stoll and the others and asked, "Does this soon-to-be-famous mouse have a name?"

Everyone stared blankly at one another.

"David is right," commented Dr. Ottinger. "We must come up with an appropriate name for this small but bold time traveler. It is a male."

"How about "Marco" for one of the early explorers of the Earth?" said Director Stoll. Since the boss had been the first one out with a suggestion, Marco Mouse it was. Everyone seemed to think the choice was excellent.

Dr. Stessel bent over and spoke directly to Marco. "Well, Mr. Marco, are you ready to risk your life for science?"

Marco came right up to the door of the cage and seemed to be sniffing Dr. Stessel's nose. Dr. Stessel turned to the others and said, "Since he didn't say *no*, we must take that as a *yes*! Let us proceed."

"We are set up to transfer only *five minutes* into the future," said Dr. Ottinger. "The destination is the same platform with the timer over there." He pointed. "I will initiate the transfer on the count of three."

Anticipation in the group was high as Director Stoll called out the count. "Three . . . two . . . one—engage!"

Howard pressed the switch; and Marco, his cage, and the transport compartment faded from view. Now all eyes were on the target platform. The large clock displayed 8:23 when Howard pressed the switch. The group moved over to the platform and waited.

At exactly 8:28, an image began to form on the target platform. The object became fully visible now and consisted of the transfer compartment, the cage, and Marco.

But Marco was not moving! Was he dead? All in the observing group held their breaths and waited. Finally, Dr. Stessel moved in close to the cage and whispered, "Marco?"

The little time traveler raised his head and looked at Dr. Stessel. His whiskers moved briskly about. The observers went nuts! Cheering, clapping, and shouting filled the room as everyone congratulated Dr. Stessel and one another.

"Are all the vital signs normal?" said Dr. Ottinger.

"All perfectly normal," said David, who had been focusing on the vital signs from the moment the instruments were becoming visible. David had been the first to realize that the little mouse was alive.

"No point in waiting," said Director Stoll "Let's send Marco into the past!"

Dr. Ottinger took the compartment and contents back to the origination location and placed it in position.

"How far into the past are we sending him?" asked John Bridell.

"This time, only ten minutes," said Dr. Stessel. "We don't want some lab assistant giving Marco perhaps too much water."

This brought a hardy laugh to everyone. The mood was very confident and even jovial now since the first phase had been successful.

"Are we ready?" said Dr. Ottinger.

"The timer has been reset to zero, and all vital signs are normal," said Stessel.

"I will give the count," said the director. "Three . . . two . . . one—engage!"

The large clock read 8:46. Marco and the compartment began to dissolve. As they did, something began to materialize on the target platform. When the compartment and its contents had completely disappeared from the origination point, it had materialized on the target platform. This time, Marco was running about the cage! Again, David had taken a position near the timer.

"The timer reads exactly ten minutes!" called David. "And the vital signs are stable and normal."

All rushed over to closely observe Marco; and this time, the cheers, shouts, and applause were even louder! Marco had successfully traveled ten minutes *into the past*. Everyone again congratulated Dr. Stessel, who again was quite modest about his incredible invention.

When the excitement subsided, all immediately became quite sober. They realized the gravity of what they had witnessed on this morning—the first successful travel through time of a living creature, both to the future and to the past.

The director suggested that they immediately go into Dr. Ottinger's conference room and discuss how things would be handled regarding the UMU in the future. With Director Stoll's concurrence, Dr. Stessel, using his mec, called his partner, the president of Weber, to relay the good news.

"Fred, this is Ed Stessel. The mouse made it . . . both ways! Yes . . . Just a few minutes ago. We are meeting in Dr. Ottinger's conference room in just a moment for further discussions and planning . . . You will? OK, I will call you right back with the coordinates."

Dr. Stessel turned to the others in the room and said, "Our president and my partner on the time travel device will join us via hologram. He asked that I call him back with the coordinates of this room."

"Here," said Howard Ottinger. "I'll write them down for you." He wrote the numbers on a notepad, and Dr. Stessel called them into Fred Marston at Weber. Moments later, an image began to appear just inside the door of the room. A large man, rather heavyset, materialized in hologram form and introduced himself.

"I am Fred Marston, president of Weber. How do you do, gentlemen?"

Director Stoll stood and introduced himself and the others. Mr. Marston's hologram took one of the empty chairs on the side of the table.

"Mr. Marston, you and Dr. Stessel have our sincerest congratulations. You have invented and constructed a device that will change the world!" said Director Stoll.

"Thank you, Director Stoll. I hope the changes will be all for the better," said Marston.

"One of the reasons we hurried into this conference," said Director Stoll, "is our concerns about the security of the time machine. By the way, it has been suggested by Dr. Stessel, I believe, that we call the machine the Ultimate Mobility Unit, or UMU."

"I like that, Ed," said Marston. "Let's make it official. UMU it is!"

Director Stoll continued, "What I intended to say is that we are seriously concerned about the UMU falling into the wrong hands. As I am sure you are aware, criminals would be able to create all sorts of mischief with such a machine."

"I am well aware of that, Director Stoll, and that is why the patent filed in the Library of Congress does not contain certain key information needed to enable the device to function."

"Yes, Dr. Stessel mentioned that. But what if someone kidnapped you or Dr. Stessel and forced you to yield the information required to enable the device? Such individuals might torture you and threaten to kill you for the information."

"Ed and I have a pact that if such a thing occurs, either of us would die before we would reveal our secret. Right, Ed?"

"That is correct, Fred," said Dr. Stessel. "And I think we can point out to these gentlemen that we are quite capable of defending ourselves although we may not appear so on the surface."

All were quiet at the table. The GSA personnel could not imagine how these two gentlemen could be so sure that they could defend their own safety.

"Perhaps we can use your lab, Dr. Ottinger, for a little demonstration of how we can defend ourselves."

Dr. Ottinger looked at the director as if for approval and seeing no objection said, "We can do that. Do you need anything special for the demo?"

Mr. Marston spoke, "Any large object that is composed of scrap or worthless material would do nicely. Would you have such available in the lab?"

"As a matter of fact, we do have a small two-ton forklift unit that has ceased to operate and is not worth repairing," said Dr. Ottinger. "I just signed an order today to dispose of it. Would that serve your purpose?"

"That would do very nicely," said Mr. Marston. "And since I am with you today only as a hologram, I will ask Ed to do our demonstration. Shall we go into the lab?"

The group filed into the lab, not knowing what on earth to expect from this demonstration. Dr. Ottinger led them over to the old forklift unit standing by itself near the freight entrance door of the lab. Dr. Stessel asked everyone to stand about fifteen feet away from the forklift. He himself stood about eight feet from the machine and said primarily to Fred Marston, "Are we ready?"

"Go ahead," said Fred.

Dr. Stessel raised his right hand and pointed directly at the forklift with his index finger. Suddenly, a white laser like beam emanated apparently from his finger and contacted the machine. It immediately glowed bright red, then white—as bright as the sun—and disappeared from view! On the concrete floor where the lift had been standing was a slight discoloration and some dust.

The group stared in awe! The nice man had just disintegrated the two-ton forklift!

"H-h-how? W-w-what?" stuttered Director Stoll. "What kind of weapon are you carrying, and w-where is it?"

"Without going into great detail," said the hologram of Mr. Marston, "we are both carrying MML personnel weapons now being manufactured for our army and marine combat service personnel. Because of work we are doing for the military, Dr. Stessel and I have special permits from the secretary of defense to carry these weapons."

"But what exactly are they?" said Dr. Ottinger.

"And *where* exactly are you hiding them?" said David.

Both Fred and Ed laughed at David's comment. Mr. Marston said, "I can tell you this. The MML units, or mini-magna-laser weapons, are compact versions of the magna-lasers installed on the satellites of the GCC."

"But where are they?" insisted David.

"Ed would have to strip to show you, and I am not going to ask him to do that. Suffice it to say that the power unit is nuclear and resides in a pack in the small of Ed's back. The current that supplies the beam flows through a cable into the palm of Ed's hand and down his index finger. Show them the cable in your hand, Ed."

Dr. Stessel raised the palm of his hand so that all could see. There was the small diameter cable leading to a tiny cone-shaped tip, which served as the origination point for the beam.

Dr. Stessel picked up the explanation at that point. "The power and force of this device is highly directional. Unless I point my finger at myself, I feel no heat and receive no injury when the MML is fired. By the way, firing can only occur when the unit is armed—and that occurs only by use of a special switch located on my wristwatch. Initiation of the beam occurs when I touch my right thumb to the tip of the little finger of my right hand. Disintegration only occurs to the object or objects that the beam contacts and to whatever is *physically joined* to the object. For example, if a ball or other object had been sitting on the forklift just now and not contacted by the beam, it would have simply fallen to the floor unharmed."

"Then what looks like white-hot heat is not actually heat?" said Dr. Ottinger.

"That is correct," said Mr. Marston. "As with the GCC magna-lasers, only the object contacted by the beam is destroyed. Disintegration occurs because the molecules of the object are individually disintegrated, usually leaving no residue."

"Weber was one of the companies involved in the development of the magna-laser," said Dr. Stessel. The group was speechless.

"Wonderful!" said Director Stoll, disrupting the awe of the group. "Then we can quit worrying about the safety of you two gentlemen and your UMU secret. But we still need to consider where *we are going* with the Ultimate Mobility Unit. Shall we discuss that?"

En route to Mars . . .

Jake and his copilot, Amahd, were about halfway to Mars on their SC38-class cargo ship. So far, there had been no surprises. The rest of the mission crew consisted of six technicians sent to unload and assemble a new soil-conversion unit for use on Mars.

The view out the forward windscreen was magnificent as usual. At this particular time, the sun was behind them, which made viewing the sights of space very pleasurable. All the usual constellations visible on Earth were still visible, but now in striking clarity and depth. Jake could clearly see the Crab Nebula, which again drove his thoughts to Nyvar. *What is that planet all about?* thought Jake. *Somehow I have got to go there and find out.*

Just then, the radio mec chimed. Ah! A call to break the long silence. Amahd answered the call. "This is SC3814. Who is calling, please? Yes . . . yes . . . We are about one hour out. What? You have changed our landing destination? Yes, I will give you Commander Loneghan." He switched the call to Jake.

"You're changing the landing point?" said Jake. "Might I ask why? I see, I see . . . No, no problem . . . OK, we will advise Y3 base that we have the new instructions. The estimated arrival time will be about ten minutes later than the flight plan. That's right, about 0650 UTC time. Over and out."

"Dust storm at Y2 base," said Jake. "They say it's a doozy! I don't know why I expect weather people to get predictions right. They've never done it on Earth. Why should they be able to get it right *on Mars*? Just the moon . . . They can *nail* it on the moon. It never changes! No weather is *no* weather. Now there's a job for you, Amahd—weatherman on the moon! Would you like that?"

"That would be very nice. Do they have pretty blonde girls on the moon?"

Jake rolled his eyes. He was sure glad he wasn't still chasing skirts.

"Three minutes to orbit entry," said Amahd. "I'll make the crew announcement."

"I'll do it," said Jake as he flipped the intercom switch. "This is the captain speaking. We are now two and one half minutes to orbit entry. Deceleration will be about 12 g's, so strap in tight. We will be in orbit about seventeen minutes. I will call you again before we leave orbit and begin our descent."

"I could make that announcement," said Amahd, somewhat peeved.

"I *know* you *can*. But these non-space types have told me that they had rather hear the announcements from the captain. For some reason, it gives them more confidence. You are not far away from making captain . . . Then you can make your own announcements."

They were now in Mars orbit approaching REP. Jake flipped on the intercom once again and announced, "We are five minutes from REP, our entry point. Check your restraints. By the way, we are landing at Y3 base, not Y2 as planned. There is a helluva storm blowing at Y2. Your assignment is *still the same*. While you install and check out your equipment, return cargo will be loaded by a Mars crew. We should be on the ground only as long as it takes to complete the installation. My understanding is that you will require about thirty-two hours. Please keep me advised. Especially if you think you need more time. I will be at Y3 base operations, mec contact 22-034 if you need to reach me. We now have two minutes to REP. Over and out."

"REP!" called out Amahd.

"Roger," replied Jake as he hit reverse on the HD engines.

Deceleration of the ship was smooth. In seconds, its speed was down to approach level of 215 mph. The barren landscape of Mars was now in clear view across the windscreen. The sun was just appearing above the horizon.

"Y3 base in sight," said Amahd.

"Roger," replied Jake. "We're on the glide slope to the landing pad."

The heavy cargo ship glided through the thin Martian atmosphere with heavy dependence on the antigravity capability of the HD engines. The ship slowed to a point three hundred feet above the center of the landing pad encircled with lights and hovered. Jake extended the gear and slowly lowered the ship toward the Martian surface. There was no evidence of life anywhere in the vicinity of the landing area. The lights in the operations hut were on. *Probably Donald finishing his graveyard shift*, thought Jake.

"Pretty dead around here this morning," said Amahd.

Just as Amahd spoke those words, two loading tractors appeared from behind the cargo building, heading directly for the ship.

"Now I feel better," said Jake. "For a minute, I thought I might have to help unload this baby." Jake picked up his PA mike and addressed the six technicians still seated in the passenger compartment.

"This is Captain Loneghan. Two tractors are coming out to handle the unloading for you. They will obey your instructions, Mr. Whitehead, as to how to handle the equipment and where you would like it placed. The base OIC is Colonel Grimes. I am assuming that he is not yet on-site but probably will be by 0900. The local time here is now 0830. Some of you have not visited Mars before. As the others of you know, you *cannot survive here without your pressure suit*. You have all been trained in its use. I request that those of you who have been on Mars before, help the others to ensure that the pressure suits are properly fitted and the suit systems are functioning properly. When you are ready to leave the ship, use the air lock. Go out no more than two at a time. As I said, the ground cargo personnel await your instructions on handling the equipment. As you know, our schedule calls for thirty-two hours on the ground here. If you finish early or if you need more time, contact me. I will be in base operations. Again, my mec contact number is 22-034. Captain out."

Jake and Amahd waited until all the technical team was off the ship and then departed through the air lock. All pressure suits were in radio contact with all other suits on the same frequency. If too many people wanted to talk at the same time, it could get pretty hectic. Kind of like truckers with their CB radios. Jake and Amahd began the short walk to base operations. Walking on Mars in pressure suits was a mixed bag. Although the suits were far less clumsy and awkward than early space suits, walking in them was a far cry from relaxing in warm-up suits. The reduced gravity made the process easier, but until you got used to the lower gravity—about 38 percent of that on Earth—you could end up bouncing too high off the surface and losing control while off the ground. Jake looked over and noticed that some of the first timers were flopping around a little. Fortunately, the pressure suits were tough and did not puncture easily.

Jake and Amahd entered the base operations—again, through an air lock—and sure enough, there was Sgt. Donald Dooley working his usual shift. Jake was out of his suit and said, "Hi, Don! Doesn't anyone but you cover this shift?"

"Hullo, Jake," said Donald. "Nope. Guess no one else wants it. There's some hot coffee over there and maybe a donut or two left. Who you got with you this trip?"

"Sorry," said Jake. "This is Amahd, on his first visit to Mars."

"Hi, Amahd. Welcome to Mars. She's not much to look at—kind of like being in the middle of an Arizona desert—only not even a cactus."

"Hi, Don," said Amahd. "How many people are stationed on Mars now?"

"Well, let's see. We have about 125 at this base. We even have a town bar and a bowling alley now. The movie theater has been here for a while. The Y2 base has only about seventy-five people. And then the Y1 base, the first one established, is getting to be quite a city. I don't get over there much, but I hear they have 587 people now."

"Didn't realize it was that big," said Amahd.

"Yeah, Y1 has developed into a pretty nice town," said Jake. "I hear they even have a nine-hole golf course. They use the same balls as they do on the moon. Otherwise, a drive would go 600 yards or so."

"You ever play that course, Jake?" said Donald.

"Nope, I'm never here long enough. Say, Don, somebody told me it's OK now to make personal interplanetary calls back to Earth. Is that correct?"

"Yep, they just approved that last week. You want to make a call?"

"Yeah, if you don't mind. What is it, EST on Earth right now?"

Don looked at his instrument panel and said, "About two AM. Not the best time to call."

"Yeah," said Jake, "guess I'll get some sleep and call in about five hours. Come on, Amahd, I'll show you the guest rooms of this five-star hotel." He laughed, and Donald joined in the laugh.

In Washington DC

Maria couldn't sleep. It was now seven AM, and she could not get her mind off what Susan had told her about David's work on the time machine. *What if this thing really works?* she thought. "What am I saying?" she said out loud. "It does work! Ellen said that they have sent a live plant into the future and into the past!" Then she thought some more about it. *But what about animals? What about live animals? And what about people? If it works on live animals, it should work on people. But how far into the future and how far into the past? I've got to learn more about this. Ellen said the machine has been patented. Then the patent document has to be in our file at the library.*

Maria was beginning to think some wild thoughts. *Maybe I could go back to 2025! Back to Rico! And back to the life I had in twenty-first century Earth.*

Now she was again talking out loud, "It's after seven AM, and I know David and Ellen are up. They both get to work by eight, and Ellen has to go into Orlando. I'm going to call them."

Maria picked up her mec and entered the number. The mec tone sounded again and again. Just as she was getting embarrassed about probably waking them up, she heard a click and a voice.

"Hullo," said David sleepily.

"Oh, David," said Maria, "I am so sorry! I woke you up. I thought you and Ellen would be up by now."

"Who is this? Maria?"

"Yes, it's me. I'm so sorry."

"Hi, Maria! Don't worry about it. Normally, we would both be sitting here having breakfast at this time. But I had a late lab project last night, and Ellen had an early meeting this morning. She's already left for work."

"Well, now that I have disturbed you—and I am very sorry—I might as well say what I called to ask you."

"Ask *me*?"

"Yes. You are working on a time machine. Susan told me. Does it really work?"

David hesitated. He was not happy that his call to Ellen had resulted in a leak that now included Susan, Jake, and Maria.

"Maria, please promise me that you will not mention this project to anyone else. It is being kept very secret at this point. Because of my call to Ellen, now I am responsible for a leak in security."

"I promise that I will not discuss it with anyone outside of you and Ellen and . . . well, Susan. Does the machine *work*?"

"*It works, Maria*! Today, we sent a mouse both forward and backward through time."

"You sent a live animal into the *past*? How far into the past?"

"Only ten minutes. But if it works for ten minutes, it will work for one hundred years."

"How about 1300 years?" pleaded Maria. "Can you send me back to the twenty-first century?"

David was stunned. "Maria! *You can't be serious*. This machine is just in its embryo stage. The risk of such a time journey would be *enormous*."

"I wouldn't do it unless you thought I have a good chance of making it back. David, I am not happy in this century. I miss the life I had. I miss Rico."

"Maria, Rico is dead. He has been dead for over 1200 years. You have to forget him."

"I can't forget him, David. I love him. If only he had asked me not to come on this mission . . . this mission to *Nyvar*!"

She continued, "David, you and your partner scientists will eventually need a human volunteer, or you will never prove the validity of the time machine. I want to *be that volunteer*. I don't care about the risk. If your tests all prove that the machine will work, then I want to go back to 2025."

"Maria, you are a dear friend. We all love you and want you to be happy. But this! I would be *so afraid* for you. And besides, how do you know that Rico won't have found someone else to love?"

"David, if I understand what you are telling me, you can pinpoint the time and place you are transporting an object or a person to. Is that not correct?"

"Yes, we can do that."

"Well, I would want to go back the exact morning we left Earth in 2025. I know Rico was still very much in love with me then."

David thought about this and didn't say anything for a few seconds.

"David?" said Maria. "Will you just agree to *try* to make me the first human guinea pig?"

Again, David was at a loss for words. Then he said, "All right, I will discuss it with the others I am working with. That is all I can promise you."

"Oh, David! I'm so happy! Just to know that you *will* try!"

"I can't say that I fully support what you are doing, but because you are my friend, I will try to get their agreement to do as you ask . . ."

"David, don't tell Ellen, but I love you!"

"Right . . . Now I have to get up, get dressed, get something to eat, and be in the office in twenty-five minutes."

"Then *you were oversleeping*. You *owe* me!"

"Yeah, yeah. I will let you know how our discussions go, Maria. And just so you don't get overly excited too soon, we don't even have a person-sized machine yet."

"Good-bye, David. I will let you go. Don't tell Ellen that I love you."

Susan was in the shower, and the mec was toning. She grabbed a towel and hurried into her bedroom.

"Hello?" The mec had an odd background tone.

Jake disguised his voice. "This is your favorite Martian calling. How are you this morning?" The voice sounded strange—and not familiar.

Susan had *no idea who was calling.* "Who is this? I think you have the wrong number." She heard no response, but the strange background tone continued, and there seemed to be a delay in the response of the other person. Susan was about to hang up.

Jake waited for Susan's delayed response and continued the ruse. "I certainly hope I don't have the wrong number—this is an expensive call! And don't hang up. There is a few seconds' time delay because of where I am." Susan still didn't get it.

"Look, if you don't identify yourself—right now!—I am going to hang up!"

"OK OK!" said Jake in his natural voice. "Just don't hang up!"

"JAKE! Where are you? You are supposed to be on *Mars*!"

"I *am* on Mars, honey! They are now allowing personal calls to Earth. This is the longest long-distance call *I* have ever made.

"Jake, you idiot! I love you!"

"I love you too, Sue."

"How long are you going to be on the ground there?"

"We planned thirty-two hours, and we have been here about five so far."

"Any problems with the trip?"

"None so far. They are loading high-value ore for the trip back. Everything seems to be going OK. Say, are you still serious about teaming with me for exploration missions to new planets?"

"Jake, I thought long and hard about that before I told you yes. Nothing has happened to change my mind. In fact, I am getting *more excited about the future every day*! When will you know if we can get approval to do it?"

"I am going to spend some more GSA money when I finish talking to you and call Klaus Stoll. He should be just getting to his office about now. He has already mentioned that he would like to send an exploratory team to the Alpha Centauri neighborhood. Personally, I would like to do what we discussed and go to Nyvar. That is what I am going to discuss with him in a few minutes."

"Well, I forgot to mention that I am standing here dripping wet with only a towel on. I need to dry off and get dressed for work."

"Drop the towel . . ."

"What? You nut! Why would I do that?"

"Just for me so I can imagine the scene—all the way from Mars."

"You *are* crazy! OK. *Here goes the towel.* Now good-bye!" She hung up.

Jake could see her clearly—in his mind—all the way from Mars. He consulted his mec listings and made the call to Klaus Stoll.

Kennedy Spaceflight Center

Director Stoll had just settled behind his desk and was frowning at the stack of papers. He had gotten way behind in his work since the experimentation with the UMU had begun.

"Renee," he spoke into the intercom, "hold my calls. I have a huge pile of work to tackle."

"Right, sir," said Renee. "Do I let any calls through?"

"Director Simonides and the president. *Otherwise no.*"

Ten minutes passed, and the intercom toned.

"Renee, what did I just tell you?" said Klaus somewhat annoyed.

"Sorry, sir, but this call is from Jake Loneghan. He is *calling from Mars.* I thought it might be important."

"He is calling me from Mars? OK, put him through." He then heard the familiar background tone from space.

"Jake! I hope you are not calling with a problem."

"No, sir . . . no problems. The mission is going smoothly. The tech team is assembling the equipment, and a Mars cargo crew is loading the ore for the return trip."

"Then you just called to chat?" said Klaus in an unfriendly tone.

"Not exactly, sir. I called to tell you that I am ready to take on an exploratory mission to another planet. And I already have one other crew member lined up."

The director focused on Jake's first sentence. "You *know* we don't have the funds approved yet for such a mission."

"I know that, sir. But what I don't know is how to go about getting the funds approved. Do we have to convince Congress or the administration or both? Just where is the logjam?"

"Jake, it's primarily Congress, and *it's the cost.* In the last few years, we have gotten very little approved in the way of space missions if we cannot show sound economics for the venture. Director Simonides is in favor of planet exploration, and we certainly have the spaceship capability with the 10xL engines. So far, however, all of these ships are being used in projects with commercial payback."

"Director Stoll, this doesn't make sense to me. Even in the twenty-first century, the government approved the funds to send a ship to Nyvar. Exploring our galaxy was a priority. Today, you have so much more capability to explore the galaxy with the advanced HD engines, and yet we are not doing it!"

"Jake, you are *preaching to the choir*. I agree with you. Listen, right now, I am way behind with my work because of a priority project I have been working on. And I must terminate this call. When you get back from this mission, call Renee and get a time to come in and see me. We'll brainstorm together and see if we can come up with a plan to promote planet exploration and get Washington approval."

"Thanks, sir. And thanks for taking this call. I will come to see you when I return."

42

Director Stoll was busy working through the papers on his desk. It had been about three hours since he had talked to Jake on Mars. Then it hit him! *Why not?* he thought. *Jake can be trusted. He has twenty-four hours before he will launch from Mars to return to Kennedy. Why not?* Klaus signaled Renee. "Get the Mars Y3 base on the horn. Ask for Jake Loneghan!"

The intercom toned. "Yes?" said Klaus.

"I have Jake Loneghan on a call," said Renee. The director picked up the mec. "Jake! I completely forgot to talk to you on something else when we spoke. We are working on a very hush-hush project here, and you can be of great assistance in that project while you are on Mars."

"What is it, sir? I'll be glad to help in any way I can."

"OK, this won't be easy to explain, but here goes. What I am about to tell you must be kept secret . . . We have a device here that is capable of transporting both objects and living matter—both plant and animal—through time and *through space.*"

"Really?" said Jake, trying to sound surprised. Then he realized that he had not sounded very surprised and quickly said, "That's amazing! You have a *time machine?*"

"We do!" said Klaus. "Jake, it is the most amazing and truly unbelievable thing! Our work with the device is why I mentioned to you that I am so behind in my other work." Klaus went on to relate to Jake the experiments that he and the others had accomplished with the UMU. Jake continued to act as if he was just hearing all this for the first time.

Then Klaus said, "So now we are at the point where we are ready to try the transfer of a mouse over a distance through space—from Earth to Mars!"

"You want to send a mouse *up here?*" said Jake.

"Exactly! That is why Dr. Stessel and his company *came to us at GSA.* They want to see if they can use the UMU device to make such a transfer. Now that you are there—with a few hours on your hands—we can set up the experiment and send the device with the live mouse to you there. If it is successful, then you can bring the device with the mouse back with you on your ship."

"Why don't I just send the mouse et al. back the same way he comes up?"

"The control unit is not presently part of the compartment we use for transfer. You would not be able to transfer the compartment back."

"I see. What about the others here at this time? How are we going to do this without everyone knowing what's going on?"

Director Stoll thought about that for a minute as did Jake.

"You will need a private room. One of the sleeping rooms will do nicely."

"That part is OK, but how big is the compartment? What is going to happen when I come walking out with a box and a cage with a mouse in it?"

Director Stoll was stumped this time. Finally, he said, "OK, here is what we do. You look around and find something in storage there that is in a box at least two feet by two feet by two feet. Then call me and tell me what you have found. I will then make up some reason why *that* box has to be shipped back here with you when you return. Then you will take whatever is in that box *out of the box* and hide it in an inconspicuous spot. Next, take the box to a *private area* adjacent to the cargo area. You will determine the coordinates of that private area and call them down to me. We will be in touch by mec, and when we are ready to transfer the UMU compartment, you will give us an all clear."

Klaus continued, "If the transfer is successful—and I believe it certainly will be—you put the transfer device with the mouse into the box, seal it, but punch some airholes and load it into a pressurized area of your ship. How does this plan sound?"

"I see some problems," said Jake. "Assuming that I can find a suitable box, the staff here is bound to find out that we didn't actually take the item that was in the box. They will find it here after we are gone. *Second* problem. We don't have a pressure suit *for the mouse*. How am I going to get the mouse from operations to the ship? As you know, there is no atmospheric pressure to speak of out there."

Director Stoll was stumped again. Finally, he said.

"You could put the mouse in your pressure suit with you."

"WHAT?" yelled Jake. "I don't *think* so!" Then Jake had an idea. "How about this. Unless this is a special mouse, you don't need him back on Earth. You have plenty of mice. They don't have—at least, I don't think they have—any mice up here. I will just turn the mouse loose in the cargo area of the operations building and put the compartment and cage into the box. They can load it in the cargo bay with the other freight."

Director Stoll was silent for a time. Then he said, "But that mouse is a very special mouse. He is the first living creature to travel through time! We have even named him. We call him *Marco Mouse*."

Jake could not believe his ears. *A mouse is a mouse is a mouse*, he thought.

"So Marco Mouse moves to Mars," said Jake. "GSA can construct a plaque or monument to Marco. 'The first animal to travel through time and space.' And now he has retired to Mars where he lives comfortably in cargo area of base 3 operations."

"I would rather bring him home. I will talk to a couple of others on this and get back to you," said Klaus. "Find the box and the location for transfer, and we'll talk again in one hour. I'll call you."

"Yes, sir," said Jake.

Renee came into Director Stoll's office. "David Marks is here to see you. Do you have time?"

"No, I don't. But I will *take* the time. Send him in."

David came in. "Good morning, sir. Sorry to drop in like this, but I have something I think you will be interested in."

"And that is?"

"Maria Rodriguez wants to be the first person to travel through time."

"*What*? How did Maria Rodriguez find out about the time device?"

"Because of my mistake, sir. But I have cautioned her that the project is secret, and she must not discuss it with anyone except me or you."

"Well, the project certainly does *not seem very secret anymore*! Who else knows of our work on the UMU?" Klaus was visibly annoyed.

"Here is what happened, sir, and I am very sorry about it. I mentioned it to my wife, Ellen, and failed to tell her that we were keeping the subject secret. Before I knew it, Ellen mentioned it to Susan Chen and Susan told Jake Loneghan and Maria."

"I am very unhappy about this, David. We *must*, however, *contain* information on this project in the future. I will call Susan and Maria. You must guarantee me that Ellen will keep quiet, and Jake is *working on the program with us*."

"Ellen will cooperate, sir. What is Jake doing on the project?"

"He is on Mars as we speak. We are developing a plan to send Marco to Mars while Jake is there. I need to call a meeting right now of Howard Ottinger, Dr. Stessel, you, and me. At this point, we don't want all the people on Mars knowing about the UMU, and Jake and I have been discussing a couple of ways to pull off this transfer without the staff on Mars learning of it."

"That's going to be tough. How's Jake going to get Marco and the transfer compartment back onto the ship? I assume that you will have him bring Marco and the UMU back with him?"

"Right. We can't transfer the unit back to here because the control panel is not part of the compartment—yet. In the larger version of the UMU, it will be a self-contained device so that a person can control where in time and space he goes."

Director Stoll called Renee on the intercom. "Renee, please see if you can get Dr. Stessel and Howard Ottinger up here now for a short meeting."

Klaus turned again to David. "Jake proposes to leave the mouse running around the cargo building on Mars and just bringing home the UMU compartment with Marco's cage. What do you think of that?"

David thought for a minute. "That *would* solve the problem of getting Marco on board the ship. The compartment could be hidden in a shipping container and simply loaded on with the other cargo. We have plenty of mice here. I can just see the guys on Mars trying to figure out where the mouse came from."

Renee called in, "The others are on their way up, sir."

Klaus just looked at David. *He is saying exactly what Jake said. He couldn't have spoken to Jake after I did*, he thought. Then Klaus said, "Before the others come in, what do *you* think of using Maria as the guinea pig for the first transfer of a human through time? Where does she want to go and *into what time*?"

"*She wants to go back to Earth—to the year 2025*," said David.

Klaus was stunned! "*What? Back to 2025?*" David just looked at Klaus, trying to show no emotion. "I thought she was happy here in the thirty-fourth century."

"Evidently not," said David. "Apparently, she is still in love with someone in the twenty-first century. An entrepreneur named Enrico Valdez."

"*Enrico Valdez*. Why is that name familiar to me?"

"His home has been preserved in Arlington. It's on a bluff above the Potomac. Apparently, he was a noted businessman and scientist who made some significant contributions to our society."

Klaus thought about this for a few moments and said, "Yes, I think I remember reading about him at one time. So *that* is who Maria wants to go back to."

"Apparently. And she also says that the twenty-first century needs her and the work she was doing there. She doesn't think the thirty-fourth century does."

"David, the twenty-first century has been *gone* for thirteen centuries—and so has Enrico Valdez."

"But if the UMU can do what we *think* it can, it can *take her back* to Mr. Valdez."

Renee called in and said, "Dr. Ottinger and Dr. Stessel are here, sir. Shall I send them in?"

"Show them in. David, let's first discuss Marco's trip to Mars and resolve that. Then we can talk about the human-sized UMU without mentioning Maria specifically. I am not yet certain that she should be our *first human time traveler*."

David said, "Yes, sir," as Howard and Edward came into the room.

"Gentlemen—good morning. Thank you for coming over on such short notice. We have a couple of things to discuss, and time is of the essence regarding one of the subjects. Please take chairs," he said, motioning toward a small conference table near the window. "Would any of you like coffee or tea?"

Klaus called their requests out to Renee and began the discussion.

"Are we ready to send Marco to Mars?" He didn't waste any time. The others looked at one another with expressions like "Well, I don't know why not!"

Klaus continued, "Jake Loneghan is on Mars as we speak, and he and I have been discussing how we might pull this off *now*. However, if there is some reason we should wait, we can do that too."

Howard Ottinger spoke, "That *is* the next step and why GSA *got involved* with Dr. Stessel and Weber. I can't see any reason for waiting—that is, if we can maintain security of the project."

"That would be my only concern as well," said Edward.

Klaus laid out the two plans he and Jake had discussed and pointed out that Jake had now about twenty-three hours on Mars before he was scheduled to depart and return to KSC. Some discussion ensued with the main sticking point being the release of Marco in the cargo building at the Y3 base. Finally, they made the decision.

"Then it's settled," said Klaus. "We will go with Jake's suggestion and leave Marco on Mars. When can we be ready to make the transfer, and how far into the future? Obviously, we can't send him into the past. Something could happen to both Marco and the compartment before Jake could prevent it."

Dr. Ottinger spoke, "We can be ready in an hour to make the transfer, and I would suggest we go fifteen minutes into the future. If it works, it *works*. There is no need to extend the time and keep us all in suspense."

They all agreed on the plan. Director Stoll said, "Howard, you and Edward go ahead and make the arrangements. We will plan to call Jake and give him the exact time to expect Marco. I need David to stay behind for another discussion. We will be in your lab in forty-five minutes, Howard." Ottinger and Stessel departed the office.

"David, let's talk more about Maria and the prospect of having her be our guinea pig. If we use her, then the UMU will not come back to us when she has arrived in twenty-first-century Earth. This unit is the first of its kind and very valuable. I doubt if Weber will agree to send it back to the past and never see it again. They will want the first *time traveler* to return with a report and perhaps pictures of what happened as a result of the transfer."

"Why can't Maria complete such a report and include photos she takes after her arrival? She could place the report in the UMU and set the controls to return to us here at KSC in the thirty-fourth century."

"Could we trust her to do that?" said Klaus.

"I don't know why not. Can you trust *anyone* that you might send out in the UMU to do as *we wish* and return with the device?"

"I see your point. I suppose that Maria would be as good as any in that regard. But before you came in this morning with the idea of sending Maria, I was thinking that the first transfers using the human-sized device would be local. At least not so far away that we would lose control of the device."

"I certainly agree with that, sir, and the first transfer should be *within the lab*. Just as we did with the mouse, we should send Maria forward and backward in time *within the lab*. Then assuming that everything is a go, we go for the big transfer. Somewhere far away in time and space—*maybe even back to 2025.*"

The director thought about this for a time. "You are right, David, on both points. The first transfers must be within the lab. Then once we go outside the lab to a significant distance and a significant change in time, we *have to trust* the person in the machine because he or she is in *total control*. The control panel has to be built as part of the UMU. Otherwise, you send someone out in it, and they are stuck wherever you send them. And we never know if they actually arrived. On the other hand, with the control panel built into the machine, the traveler doesn't have to follow our instructions. He or she can go *anywhere* they want and to *whatever time frame* they wish."

"Sir, it's a catch-22. If you send the UMU out without giving the traveler control, you will *never know* what happened to it. If you give the traveler control, then you take the risk that the traveler *may not* elect to return as directed. *There is no guarantee.*"

"There is one other way, David."

"What is that?"

"You build the control unit so that the traveler has no access to the controls. The unit can only be accessed with a special code, and you set both the trip out and the return into the memory of the unit. You can also specify the time on the ground before the return of the UMU is initiated. In other words, let's say you allow a certain downtime at the transfer destination. The traveler could exit the UMU on arrival, take pictures or samples, and reenter the compartment before scheduled departure time. Then the UMU initiates its own transfer back to the place and time originally programmed in."

David considered this for a while. "With due respect, sir, I see problems with that plan. For one, suppose the traveler, after leaving the UMU on arrival, is *restrained* in some way or otherwise *unable* to reenter the compartment. The UMU leaves without the traveler, and we *never* know what happened. The device would return as programmed, but minus the traveler, and we really wouldn't know if the mission was a success. Plus our traveler is *stranded* at the target destination."

"I need to give this some more thought," said Klaus. "Right now, we need to get to the lab. It's time to send Marco to Mars."

They arrived at the lab. Dr. Stessel, Dr. Ottinger, and *Marco* were ready. At least, the two scientists were. You never really know about mice.

"If you are ready, then let's contact Jake," said Klaus. "Where is a mec I can use?"

"Right there, Klaus," said Dr. Ottinger, pointing.

Klaus picked up the mec. "Renee, get Y3 base on the line. I need to talk to Jake Loneghan. Patch the call to this location." They waited.

"Jake is on, sir," came back Renee.

"Jake," said Director Stoll, "we are going with your plan. Do you have a location for us, and have you located a carton that will work for our compartment?"

"Yes on both, sir," came back Jake after the usual delay.

"OK, read me the coordinates." Klaus wrote them down and handed them to Howard Ottinger. Howard keyed them into the control unit.

Jake continued, "Those coordinates are for a small room off the main cargo area. That room is hardly used. I will have my AMec if you need to call me. My contact number here on Mars is 22-034. What is our plan?"

"OK," said Klaus, "synchronize your watch to mine. In ten seconds, I will have 1732 UTC time. Counting six . . . five . . . four . . . three . . . two . . . one—mark! At exactly 1745, we will initiate with a fifteen-minute transfer into the future so you should see our little traveler arrive at 1800. At that point, you can release him and put the compartment with the cage into the container you are using. Did you stash the contents of the container in a good spot?"

"I did better than that," said Jake. "I found an empty container marked clearly RETURN TO KSC. Apparently, there are several of those here. I don't know what they usually ship in them."

"Wonderful!" said Director Stoll. "Take a marker and write UMU in a couple of spots so we can be sure to find it when you get back." Klaus continued, "OK," looking at his watch. "You have seven minutes to get to the coordinates you gave us. When the transfer has been completed and you have released Marco, call us on my office number—the one you used this morning. After that, be sure that the UMU is sealed into the container and loaded on your ship."

"No problem, sir," said Jake. "I'm leaving for the target room right now."

Director Stoll, along with the others, moved over to take a last look at Marco and his time machine. "What is that around Marco's neck?" said David, always the one for details.

"Around his neck?" said Klaus.

"That's his ID tag." said Dr. Stessel. "It just says Marco. I thought he might have a better chance of survival when he is discovered."

The others laughed. "That will really give the troops on Mars a surprise!" said Director Stoll.

"Three minutes and counting!" said Howard Ottinger. Everyone grew silent and just stared at the little mouse in the cage in the compartment.

Director Stoll was using his watch for the countdown. "Five . . . four . . . three . . . two . . . one—mark!" said Klaus. Dr. Stessel hit the initiator, and Marco et al. dissolved . . .

And on Mars

Jake was alone in the small room off the main cargo area looking at his watch. Three minutes to go until the planned arrival of Marco—*the first animal to travel through time and space in a time machine.* There were noises outside the room—cargo personnel were moving the heavy ore containers out of storage onto Jake's ship. There was very little *in* the room Jake was in, so he wasn't worried about someone coming in.

Jake counted down, "Five . . . four . . . three . . ." He *saw something taking shape*! It was a box! Inside the box was a cage. And there on the floor of the cage was Marco—*Mars' first mouse!*

"Hi, Marco," said Jake, not sure the little guy was alive. Then Marco's whiskers started twitching. He raised his head and looked at Jake. The name tag was clearly visible. *Nice touch!* thought Jake. *Maybe I better not just turn him loose in the main cargo bay. Something or someone will kill him. I'll report to Director Stoll, then take care of Marco and the compartment.*

Jake placed the call. Renee answered, "Director Stoll's office."

"Hi, Renee, would you put him on, please," said Jake.

Renee knew by the space background noise and speech delay where the call was coming from. She called into Director Stoll, "Jake is on, sir."

"Jake! We are holding our breath down here. Is Marco there?" said Klaus.

"Arrived safe and sound." said Jake. "Right now, he is still in his cage in the compartment. I wanted to report to you."

Director Stoll turned from the mec and told the others seated around his desk, "Marco made it!" A cheer went up with applause. "We did it!" said Dr. Stessel. "This is another *momentous day*!"

Klaus returned to Jake. "We will let you get back to taking care of Marco and the compartment unless you have anything else to tell us."

"Just that the transfer arrived before I finished the countdown. Apparently, Marco et al. traveled *faster* than our communications."

"Of *course* he would! That makes sense," said Director Stoll. "Our communications only move at light-speed. Marco's transfer was instantaneous! I will share that with the others. See you when you return, Jake."

"Right, sir, good-bye."

Jake pocketed his mec and returned to Marco. The little mouse looked healthy and happy. Everything was as Jake had left it, except that all of Marco's food and water had been consumed. *This guy is too important to just leave to fend for himself. I have a better idea*, thought Jake.

Jake removed Marco, still in his cage from the UMU compartment, and placed the compartment in the shipping container. He carefully sealed the container and prepared it for shipping. He marked **UMU** on the outside of the container in four places.

Leaving Marco in his cage in the corner of the room behind other boxes, he took the shipping container out into the main cargo area. Luckily, one of the freight loaders was passing by. Jake handed the container to the loader, saying, "This is to go with us back to Kennedy."

"Yes, sir, no problem," said the man. "I'll take it out right now."

"Be sure it's in a safe spot," said Jake. "Don't want those ten-ton ore bins to smash it."

"I'll take care of it, sir."

Jake returned to Marco. "Now what are we going to do with you, my friend?" he said to the little mouse. Marco looked up at Jake and wiggled his whiskers.

Jake picked up the cage with Marco and proceeded back to the operations office. He entered the office and observed that there was no one except Don Dooley there at the moment.

"Commander Loneghan!" said Don. "Where on Mars did you get the mouse? I didn't notice him when you arrived."

"Oh, I had him with me all right. This is just a little side experiment we are conducting to see how a mouse *handles the conditions on Mars*. Here, take a look at him." Jake held out the cage to Don. "His name is Marco. See his name tag?"

"Cute little guy," said Don. "We can sure use a pet around here. As a matter of fact, I don't think anyone at Y3 has a pet of any kind. Marco will be a *big hit*."

"Fine," said Jake, pointing at the cage. "Over here is his food trough, and over here is his water container. He eats pretty much anything, and just be sure he always has water. Better be careful about petting him, however. He might bite. The lab at KSC gave him a complete physical, and he has no diseases. Sure you don't mind tending him for me until my next visit here?"

"No problem, sir! I will be more than glad to take care of him."

"Good," said Jake. "I'll be getting on my pressure suit now. Need to go out and be sure they are loading all these ore containers properly for weight and balance. Wouldn't be a good idea to launch for Earth with a tail-heavy ship."

Jake left Ops feeling pretty good about Marco. Even if he himself *never* made it back to Mars, the little mouse was in good hands with Don.

Twelve minutes until scheduled launch. All cargo had been loaded. The tech crew had completed their installation of the soil-conversion equipment and were all seated in the passenger area behind the flight deck. Jake had checked to be sure that the cargo was all tied down properly and the container with the UMU compartment was positioned correctly and properly restrained.

"How is your preflight coming, Amahd?" asked Jake as he entered the flight deck.

"No problems, sir. The ship is ready to launch when you are."

"Did you speak with the tech crew? Do they have papers signed off by the OIC on Mars?"

"They told me they had the papers. I didn't see them."

"I'll take a look at them," said Jake, getting out of his seat and starting toward the passenger section.

Jake returned and again took his seat. "The papers are signed, but the OIC must have been a physician at some time. I couldn't read those signatures if my life depended on it." Jake strapped in tight.

"OK," said Jake, "let's go through the 'before engine start' checklist."

They completed that, and Jake made a PA to the passengers.

"This is your captain speaking. We will be starting engines now and preparing to launch for Earth. I suggest that you double-check your restraints and cinch them tight for launch. After we reach cruise speed, you can relax them for comfort. We will be using the simulated gravity system so you can walk about during cruise, use the restroom, etc."

Jake looked at Amahd and said, "Starting engines."

The powerful HD engines whined to life, growing louder as the power was increased. Amahd checked all the instrumentation and reported to Jake, "All green for launch."

Don was holding Marco in his hand, standing at the window of operations. They had already become good friends.

"Your ride is leaving, Marco," said Don as the huge white cargo ship lifted off vertically into the hover mode for final instrument checks. As the roar from the engines increased, the ship climbed upward with its nose, lifting faster than its tail until a near-vertical climb attitude had been achieved.

Within seconds, the ship was out of sight and on its way to Earth.

Don said to his new little friend, "Any particular music you like, Marco?"

43

Renee had given Jake an appointment time to see Director Stoll. Jake arrived on time. He was really bored with the space runs to Mars and the moon and was ready for some *action*. Jake had his mind on Alpha Centauri first—after that, Nyvar.

Director Stoll was on the horn with Dr. Ottinger when Jake came in.

"Got to go, Howard, I have a meeting starting right now," he said as Jake walked into the room.

Stoll cradled the mec and said to Jake, "Good morning, Jake! Have a chair. We appreciate your help with the mouse on Mars. Although I am sorry you had to leave him there. Do you think he will survive very long?"

"I have a feeling he will live out his full life span there, sir. When I last saw him, he had already been discovered by the locals, and they were trying to figure out who put the name tag on him."

Klaus gave a big laugh! "So they have captured him already and are making a mascot out of him?"

"I guess you could say that. Marco Mouse the Mars Mascot. Anyway, he is in good hands. I didn't realize it, but before Marco, there were no pets of any kind on Mars."

"That, of course, would be true . . . unless someone smuggled a pet aboard one of our ships at some time. Now I can expect to see requests for pets, I suppose. What is it that you and I were going to discuss in this meeting?

"I want to explore the galaxy, sir, as far out as we can reasonably travel."

Klaus just looked at Jake for a bit and then said, "Galaxy exploration is not in vogue in Washington, Jake. And it will be very expensive. Even though we have ships with ten times light-speed capability, they are all being used in commercial enterprises. I cannot remember the last time funds were approved for anything that did not show a *monetary payback*. And you *know* that sending you and a crew out into the galaxy to explore planets cannot demonstrate a monetary payback."

"But who knows what riches we might find that would be very valuable if brought back to Earth, sir?"

"I know, I know. Indeed, you might make such discoveries, but here is the problem. To equip you and your crew with a 10xL ship would take that ship away from some lucrative assignment it is currently on. And to make the exploration you propose viable, you *must* have a 10xL ship. Otherwise, the cruise travel times would be too lengthy. Any space destination that would be a viable target must be no more than a two-year round-trip to have it make sense."

"A round-trip to Alpha Centauri is less than a nine light-year distance. At 10xL, we could go to that system and back in less than a year. You were in the meeting, sir, when we met with the GSA director, Kosta Simonides. Remember, he seemed quite interested in an exploratory trip to a planet in the Alpha Centauri system."

"With all due respect for the director," said Klaus, "he is well aware of the numerous times in the last few years that we have gone forward for congressional support for exploratory missions. He also knows that our attempts *have all failed miserably.*"

"But he seemed genuinely interested and enthusiastic."

"He *is* enthusiastic! I would venture to say that he is *in that job* today because of his *enthusiasm* for the exploration of space. But neither the public who elects Congress nor Congress itself has shown much interest in the exploration of space."

"Therefore, the attitude of government is simply reflecting the attitude of the people?"

"That's the way I see it. Believe me, Jake, if we could somehow show that a mission to Alpha Centauri and its most promising planet could greatly benefit the Earth, the Congress and the citizens might have changes of heart. However, as things now stand, there is no point in going forward with a request for the funds required."

"How much money are we talking about?" asked Jake.

"Well, first you have to charge the cost of the 10xL spaceship to the project because the ship *may never return*. Then you have all the crew-training costs. Then you have the expense of the launch preparation and launch. The mission will also require a great deal of equipment, defense weapons, and supplies. We must equip the crew for every possible eventuality. I would say that the total mission cost would be into the billions of credits. It has been several years since we rolled up and projected the costs of such a mission."

It was obvious to Jake that Klaus did not have the enthusiasm to mount another charge at Congress and the administration. Jake was thinking, *How can we substantially reduce the cost?* Then he had an ingenious idea.

"What if," said Jake, "we could do the mission with a ship that only cost in the millions? Would we have a chance to get that approved?"

"Are you a magician? Where will you get a 10xL ship that only costs in the millions?"

"Use the *Revelation*!"

"The *Revelation*! Are you crazy? That is only a light-speed ship. The mission would take five years to get there and five years to come home. We can't propose exploring the galaxy in a *stagecoach*."

Jake's feelings were hurt. But he persisted. "The *Revelation* could do it nicely with *new engines*. What would it cost us to *re-engine the Revelation* with 10xL-type engines?"

Klaus was astonished! He had never once thought of the idea. And it had not been mentioned to him. But it just *might be possible*. "Jake! You might just have a *workable idea there*. I know that the engine companies are currently stuck with a few engines because Congress cut back the original order and decided to build only eight 10xL ships. There were two test engines and then the four engines that were to have powered the ninth and tenth ships. I'll just bet there are six engines from which we could get two at an attractive price. The big question, however, is, Will the *Revelation* airframe be *strong enough* to handle the power of the heavier, higher-thrust engines?"

"David Marks was the lead engineer for the integration of the engines and airframe for the *Revelation*. He will be able to answer that question."

"Jake!" exclaimed the director. "We just might be able to sell this! Let me gather my thoughts and decide how to pitch it to Director Simonides. Meanwhile, you go talk to David and get him cranking on the design issues." Looking at his watch, Klaus said, "It's nine forty-five now. Can you and David be back here in my office at one PM to discuss this further?"

"I certainly can," said Jake. "And David will be here if I can find him."

"Excellent!" said Klaus. "Meanwhile, I will try to get Kosta Simonides' backing. And I don't think that will be too difficult."

As Jake left the office, Klaus called Renee, "Renee, please get Director Simonides on the mec—as soon as possible!"

After a few minutes Renee called, "He's on, sir."

"Kosta! Klaus here. Are you still interested in going to the Alpha Centauri system?"

Director Simonides thought that Klaus was up to some bad joke. "Of course I am. You know that. If this is some kind of joke, you are going to be in BIG trouble."

"No joke! Jake Loneghan is chomping at the bit to explore the galaxy. He was in my office a few minutes ago, and *we* came up with what may be a *great idea*."

"You have my undivided attention."

"We may be able to *re-engine the Revelation with 10xL engines*."

"What? Is that possible?"

"We think it might be. I know there are at least six engines still at Pratt & Whitney from the last program, and they most likely would jump at the chance to sell us a couple of them."

"Probably at a very good price," said Kosta. "But can the *Revelation* airframe be modified to handle the far more powerful engines?"

"Don't you remember? David Marks was one of the lead engineers on the *Revelation*, and he is here working for us. Jake has gone to talk to David *as we speak.*"

"Klaus, this is brilliant! I will contact Pratt & Whitney and attempt to negotiate a bargain basement price for two engines. At this point, we'll tell them we just want the engines for spares and a test program. Call me back when you have something definitive from David."

"Right, sir. I will be talking to David this afternoon, and will call you after that."

Jake found David with Dr. Ottinger in the lab. "Jake!" said David. "You're back! Thanks so much for catching the 'outfield fly' called Marco. What do you think his fate will be in the cargo area of the Y3 base?"

"Don't worry, he will be fine. The troops there have already discovered him and taken him in as their *mascot*."

"Their *mascot*?" said Howard suspiciously. "How did they think he came to be on Mars?"

"That was easy," said Jake. "I told them that I had brought him up in an experiment to see how other animals might fare on Mars. They are to feed and water him until I return to bring him home."

"Jake, you are *devious*," said David.

"You don't know the *half* of it, Dave. Will you be going back to your office anytime soon?"

"Going right now as a matter of fact. We were finished for the time being. Weren't we, Howard?"

"I think so. I am just shocked that Weber will have the larger UMU ready to deliver here in a little over a month."

"I am too. I assume that you will be working on a test plan for use when we get the machine?"

"I will," added Howard. "But let me have any suggestions you come up with."

"Will do," said David as he and Jake left the lab.

Jake and David walked a good ways down the corridor to be sure they were out of earshot of any of the lab personnel. Then David said, "What's up, Jake?"

"David, you won't believe this, but there is a chance I might be able to explore the galaxy after all."

"What do you mean?" said David. "I thought that Washington has turned a cold shoulder on exploration without assurance of monetary payback."

"That is true, but we are working on a way to drastically cut the costs of a mission."

"How's that?"

"Re-engine the *Revelation* with 10xL engines . . ."

David stopped dead in his tracks. He just looked at Jake who had not stopped as fast and had turned to come back. "*With 10xL engines*? What makes you think we can do that?"

"Well, for one thing, you told me once that the *Revelation* airframe was built to accommodate heavier, more powerful engines, didn't you?"

"It was built with extra beef—but 10xL engines? I don't think so."

Jake was deflated. "Aw, come on, David. Will you just take a look at it?"

"Sure, I'll *look* at it. But I just don't think—"

"Klaus Stoll is also very excited about the prospect, David. You would be some kind of superhero if you could find a way to re-engine the *Revelation* with 10xL engines."

They continued to walk.

"You know, Jake, if the 10xL engines are just not too *physically big*, there might just be a way." David was warming up to the idea. "I say this because when we designed the *Revelation*, we built it to be able to handle enough engine thrust to *break through* the speed of light barrier. However, the engine companies were not able to achieve the thrust level we needed. As a result, we had to settle for 0.9999+ of the speed of light as the maximum speed of the ship. So the 'beef' should be there in the engine mounts and in the airframe. The actual thrust of the 10xL engines we use in the ships of today is not a great deal higher than that of the engines of the *Revelation*. Once the 10xL ships of today get through the light-speed barrier, the maximum speed achievable is only a function of acceleration time."

"Wait a minute, Dave! Are you saying that a 10xL ship doesn't have ten times the thrust of the *Revelation*?"

They reached David's office and entered.

"That's correct, Jake. In space, there is no drag because there is no atmosphere. To accelerate to higher and higher speeds, you just keep thrusting the engines. Obviously, the higher thrust your engines can produce, the faster your ship will accelerate and the faster cruise speed you can achieve."

"Then on our thirteen-century journey, once we achieved our target cruise speed, the engines shut down?"

"Yes and no. We theoretically needed no thrust to maintain speed. But in actuality, there is some particle debris in space and, therefore, some—although tiny—drag. The second and very important reason we kept the engines at cruise idle was to supply power for the ship's systems—our life-support systems and the navigational and guidance systems mainly. And finally, a third and critically important reason to keep the engines at cruise idle was so that if we needed full thrust to avoid a collision with a sizable piece of space debris, the computer could command it from the engines."

"And the ship's records showed that this *did happen*."

"It did—but only the one time. I studied the flight recorder record and found *one instance* where the computer *saved the ship and our lives* by accelerating fast enough to allow a rather large asteroid to pass behind us. The rock missed the ship by only about three hundred feet."

"So the bottom line is that you think we can put the 10xL engines into the *Revelation*." Jake was starting to feel much better.

"I do, but I will need to study both the prints and specs for the *Revelation* that I obtained from the archives in the basement and the prints and specs for the 10xL engines, which I don't have."

"But those should be here in this building."

"Yes, and I am going to look for them right now."

"OK, but isn't there something that I can do to help?"

"Not really, this is a one-person job. I just need the engine drawings and specs."

"OK, I'll leave. But before I go, can I just ask you one question?"

"Sure, but make it snappy."

"Are you going to use Maria with the time machine?"

David looked around to see if anyone heard that comment and turned back to Jake. "Maybe. She calls me every other day, and I wish she wouldn't. I've done all I can do to make it happen, and the decision does *not rest with me*. We have just learned today that the human-sized UMU will be delivered here in about a month. Stoll and Simonides will decide who the human guinea pig will be."

"Thanks, Dave, see you at one in Stoll's office."

David and Jake sat across from the director. "Well, gentlemen, do you have good news for me?" said Klaus. Jake looked at David.

"The engines will physically fit into the ship with some minor modification to the mount system," said David.

"But can the airframe handle the thrust?"

"Yes. As I told Jake this morning, we built the *Revelation* to handle thrust equivalent to the 10xL engines. The engine companies were just not able to achieve the thrust we needed to break the light-speed barrier back in 2025."

"This is great news." said Klaus. "Have you attempted to estimate the cost of making this modification?"

"Not yet," said David, "but I don't think it will be high."

"I would also like to point out something, sir," said Jake. "We still have all the equipment, weapons, tools, and other gear we took along on our mission to Nyvar. The only thing we will need to do is re-equip the ship with food and perishable supplies. This can't be a very expensive program to finance."

Klaus's countenance changed from pleased and enthusiastic to *sober and unsmiling*. "Congress can sometimes be ridiculously petty while at other times, they are the opposite and lavish untold funds on earmarked projects."

The director continued, "David, please take the time to develop the drawings and specs for modifying the *Revelation*. Let me have the cost of the modifying the ship as soon as you have it. I will tell John Brindell what I have you working on. Meanwhile, I will have someone roll up the total cost of the program, and we will see just how *inexpensive* we can make exploring the Alpha Centauri region.

"I will also contact Director Simonides to learn the cost of procuring two engines from Pratt & Whitney. He will be most happy to learn that the engines will fit into the *Revelation* without much modification."

He continued, "Jake, who is the other person that is interested in going with you on the Centauri mission? Do you have others or just the one?"

"Susan Chen is the one that is interested, sir. You will recall that she was the first officer of the mission that brought us here."

"Susan is a good choice," said Klaus. "But isn't she working for the justice department now?"

"For the Supreme Court, sir. But she is bored with that work. She is an excellent astronaut and very interested in going with me . . . er . . . *working for GSA* on exploratory missions."

Klaus studied Jake's face. He wondered about the true nature of the relationship between the two, but now was not the time to pursue that issue.

"Yes . . . well, I think she would be a good choice for your first officer. Do you have any others in mind?"

"No, sir. I think we will be able to find several astronauts currently employed by GSA that would be interested in exploration, don't you, David?"

"I agree with Jake, sir, although I am not one of them. Ellen is quite happy with her work at Mayo, and I am very happy with my work here at GSA. And we want to start a family. I don't think Jake will have any problem assembling a crew, however."

"OK," said Klaus. "Here is the plan. David will get to work on the design of the modifications. Jake will talk to Susan and review the records of some of our staff astronauts, looking for possible candidates. And I will get someone started on estimating the total project costs. I will also fill Kosta Simonides in and see what he has learned about Pratt's price for the engines. Let's meet again in three days."

Looking at his calendar, Klaus said, "Let's just make it Monday at 8:30 AM, OK?"

Both Jake and David agreed and left the room.

"Renee," said Klaus over the intercom, "please get Director Simonides on the AMec."

After about twenty minutes, Renee advised, "He's on, sir."

"Klaus!" said Kosta Simonides. "Any good news for me?"

"Absolutely, sir! The *Revelation* was designed for higher-thrust engines, which did not materialize until late in the twenty-first century—not in time for the Nyvar mission. Only a small modification to the engine mount system will be required to allow the installation."

"Excellent! Are you working up some project costs for us?"

"We have started on that. David Marks is developing the drawings for engine mount mods, and I have someone working on the various costs. Have you been able to get procurement figures for the two engines?"

"I should have those within the hour. We are talking millions, though, not billions, as they originally cost us."

"Excellent!" said Klaus. "I have a feeling that we just might be able to sell this program this time. After all, we have a slightly used ship at virtually no cost. We have tools, equipment, and supplies needed for the mission at little or no cost. And we have at least two astronauts trained on the ship and ready to go."

"How much *cheaper* could we possibly go for a groundbreaking deep space exploratory mission?" exclaimed Kosta. "Tell Jake to *start working on his crew*. I am confident we can get congressional approval along with that of President Thornhill. Let's think positive this time, Klaus."

At the Supreme Court Building

Susan, while discussing a case with Chief Justice Webster, felt her mec vibrating. "Ma'am," she said to Mrs. Webster, "excuse me, but I have a call coming in. I'll get rid of it."

"Go ahead and take it, Susan. I need to powder my nose anyway. I'll be back in five."

"Thank you, ma'am," said Susan, opening her mec. "This is Susan."

"Pack your bags." said Jake. "We are going to Alpha Centauri!"

Susan screamed, then stifled it, looking around to be sure no one heard her. "You are not telling the truth!" she said. "Do you really have approval?"

"Calm down now," said Jake, sorry he had gotten her so excited. "Where are you now?"

"I'm in with the chief justice. We were just going over a case."

"You are with her *now*?" Jake was really sorry for causing Susan's emotional outburst.

"She went to the ladies' room when your call came in. I am by myself at this very moment. Are you telling me the truth?"

"Yes and no. We have GSA approval and their support to go to Congress. We still have to get Congress to approve the funds."

"Then you *don't* have approval . . ." Susan was deflated and annoyed at Jake. "Jake, be fair with me and don't lead me astray. You made me think we have a 'go' program,"

"I'm sorry, Sue. Really, I am. But I *think* we will have a go program. Klaus has already told me to start looking for crew members. He has approved you as first officer."

"I want to be the mission commander."

Jake hesitated, thinking, *She's not serious?* Then he said, "Fine! Whatever you want. As long as you and I go together."

"You are the mission commander," she said. "I was kidding. You *are my commander* anytime!"

Jake was elated again. "Look, finish your business with your boss and call me when you break for lunch. I'll fill you on the details."

"OK! Call you in about an hour . . . Bye." She closed her mec and pocketed it just as Justice Webster returned to the room.

Somewhere in the Mountains of Colorado

Dante was at his command desk when a call came in on a commercial line.

"Sir, it's for you," said a young lieutenant assigned to assist Dante.

"Who is it, Lieutenant?" said Dante.

"He said, 'Tell him it's the commander for the Alpha Centauri mission,' sir."

Dante picked up the mec. "Jake! You son of a gun! *Who* is the commander of the Alpha Centauri mission?"

"*I* am!" said Jake. "You want to come along? Susan and I are looking for crew members."

"Are you serious? Do you really have approval for a mission to Alpha Centauri?"

"Not yet, but we are very close. Get this, Dante. We are going to re-engine the *Revelation* with 10xL engines!"

"What? You can't do that!" He paused. "Can you?"

"We can. And David is working on the design as we speak. The situation is this. Both Director Stoll and Director Simonides are on board and ready to pressure Congress for approval of the project. Klaus has told me to start looking for crew members. I didn't want to leave you out."

Dante turned very sober. "Jake, if you only knew what we are doing here. Let me just say if it wasn't for this GCC operation, there would be *terrorist strikes* every month. Maybe even every week!"

"What? You are not serious, are you?"

"Dead serious, Jake. When I took this job, I was worried that I might get bored. Haa! That is now *a big joke*. I cannot believe that certain countries of the Middle East are still trying to kill non-Muslims. Those people are still killing each other and any Christian, Asian, or Jew they can. It doesn't seem to matter to them that as soon as we spot them with a bomb or attack weapon, we *vaporize* them. But they just keep coming . . ."

"Dante, I am shocked! I can't believe what you are telling me."

"It's true and . . . Whoa! We just got a signal! There is an immediate threat of an ICBM launch from a Middle East sector . . . gotta go. I'll call you tonight. Are you still at the BPQ?"

"No. I'm calling you from my new place. Use this number I'm talking on. I'll look for your call tonight."

"Over and out."

Dante studied the screens in front of him. He picked up a red AMec to his right.

"I see it on the screen," he said. "Why are we just learning of this?"

The voice on his communicator spoke, "The system is quite far underground, and our people had no idea the weapons were under a *college campus*. The launch silo looks exactly like a power-generation stack."

"Is the college in session?" said Dante. "Are the buildings occupied?"

"Classes are in session, and they have night classes as well."

"How about Saturday and Sunday?"

"The schedule is light, but there are still students and staff there on the weekends."

"OK, we can't hit them unless and until they launch. We need to strike now, but we will *not* destroy all of those students and the faculty unless we have *no choice*. I want units L4 and L5 on ready standby, aimed at one thousand feet above the college buildings. We will just have to wait until they try to launch. Any idea what their target is?"

"We have intelligence that it is London, but we are not positive."

"Is there any way we can disable it in the silo before launch?"

"We think the weapon is one hundred megatons, sir. If it goes critical on-site, it will take not only the school but the town and a great deal of the country around it."

"Damn! If it's that big, then we can't fire on it at one thousand feet. We have to let it get up to at least a mile. Maybe even five miles. Unless we do that, we might as well take it out now while it's in the ground. The damage might even be less."

Dante continued, "OK, Set L4 and L5 to wait for it at five miles' altitude and destroy it there. He turned to his aide and said, "Get General Whitcomb on the line."

General Whitcomb came on the line. Dante spoke, "Sir, we have a 100-megaton weapon located in a silo under a college in sector 22-8. The school is a 24/7 operation, and if we take it out on location, the whole town and surrounding countryside will go. We are set now with L4 and L5 to destroy it at five miles up when it launches . . . Yes, this could be a coordinated attack, sir. There may be other weapons at other locations we don't know about. We just learned about this one in the last ten minutes.

"My concern is that we can't afford to use L4 and L5 to babysit this one location and then immediately have multiple launches from the same area at the same exact time . . . Yes, sir, I agree. It appears that we have no choice. We *must* take it out now and be prepared for launches at other locations . . . Fine, sir, *we will initiate in thirty seconds* . . . Yes, sir, as soon as I have the report." Dante cradled the mec.

At thirty seconds, magna-laser satellites L4 and L5 fired on the location identified under the college. The entire college, the town, and everything in a circle of about one-mile radius were vaporized in a solarlike glow. At the same instant, at distances of about twenty-five miles from the college in three other locations, ICBMs from three other installations exited the mouths of silos, climbing and accelerating. Magna-lasers L4, L5, and now L6 fired their maser beams at the missiles and destroyed each one of them in blasts that *resembled the sun*.

Dante made a call. "Are 4, 5, and 6 reenergized?"

"They are ready, sir," came the response.

"Then take out the launch points!" ordered Dante.

Dante waited, watching the large area screens. It seemed to be over. He made a call. "Give me a devastation report on those strikes and transmit one to the Pentagon—ASAP!" He continued to observe the big screens. He made another call. "I need to see a copy of all the information we received on the college location before we initiated our strike. Transmit it with the devastation report."

44

Jake had gone by the personnel department after talking with Dante and picked up a personnel roster of the astronauts currently on staff at KSC. As luck would have it, there was a golf tournament on the MaxVision that would provide just the right amount of background noise without being too distracting. He curled up on the sofa with a beer and started looking at the names on the list. The apartment mec toned.

"Jake here. Who is calling?"

"Your *first officer*. Who were you expecting?" said Susan. "Tell me everything!"

"I will, baby! How long can you talk?"

"Probably about fifteen. She's got me working on some pretty heavy stuff."

"I think we can cover it. I will try to be concise."

Jake reviewed his meetings with Klaus and with David for Susan and then said, "I am just now beginning to look over possible crew members for our mission."

"Why do we need other crew members, Jake? I mean, I know why we had the crew complement we did for the Nyvar mission, but we don't plan to colonize. What is the planet's name that we are going to?"

"Good point. I have never been given a name for it. I'll find out."

"Anyhow, this is only a scouting mission. Why do we need four or even two other crew members?"

"Well, let's see . . . Security would be one reason, I suppose. If the planet turns out to be prehistoric or hostile, there would be safety in numbers . . . And if one of us got injured in the landing or an accident, it would be better to have others to help out, don't you think?"

"I guess so . . . But I was just thinking it would be *more romantic* if there were just the two of us."

"If you don't mind, I won't give that reason to Director Stoll."

She laughed. "Yeah, we better be *just business* around him."

"Let's just go for a crew total of four, not six. Would you be more comfortable adding two men or two women or a man and a woman?"

"I would vote for a man and a woman. Think that will be OK with Klaus?"

"I don't see why not. That's what I will propose—and I do think four total for the crew is enough."

"What about timing, Jake? When do you see me leaving this job to come there for training?"

"Well, our training—yours and mine—will be minimal. We have been trained on the *Revelation*. There will be some material on the new engines we will need to become familiar with. That won't take long. The question of when you can quit your job is almost solely dependent on when we get the *green light from Congress*. Knowing how they work, I would plan on continuing to work for at least a month. Unfortunately, it could be considerably longer than that."

"OK, just let me know things as soon as you find them out. Mrs. Webster has been very nice to me, and I want to be fair with her. I will need to give her at least two weeks' notice and more if possible."

"I understand, Sue. And then there is your apartment to consider. Don't they require a month's notice?"

"You know, I think they do. I had forgotten about that. You know what? Maybe I could go ahead and give notice on the flat, and then if I need to stay in Washington longer, perhaps I could bunk with Maria for a short time. I'll speak with her and see if that plan is doable."

"Good idea. And speaking of Maria. Please tell her something for me. David is being a little annoyed by Maria calling him so much about the time machine. As you know, she wants to be the first time traveler and go back to the twenty-first century."

"Yes, I know."

"Tell her for me that both David and I are working hard to get her into the UMU as the first traveler. Tell her to stop calling David and trust us to make it happen."

"Do you think you can get it approved for her?"

"I don't see why not. Stoll only has two concerns—not knowing if Maria actually arrives in the year 2025—because she is not coming back, and two, losing the time machine because Maria might not send it back."

"He would have those problems with whoever the traveler is, wouldn't he?"

"Absolutely. I think David has him convinced that Maria is an OK choice and that she will send the machine back from 2025. So please tell her not to call anymore. David or I will keep her advised of *anything* she needs to know. By the way, I talked to Dante today."

"Dante! How is he? I haven't talked to him since he started work at GCC."

"He's good, I guess. He seemed a little stressed out, though. Apparently, Earth is not as much under control as we were led to believe when we went through our indoctrination."

"What do you mean?"

"I mean there are still idiot terrorists out there bent on killing everyone who doesn't subscribe to their beliefs."

"You are *kidding*! I will never understand how people can *kill others* in the name of their faith."

"I am dead serious. As I was talking with him, he received an alert regarding an impending missile launch somewhere in the Middle East, I think. I called to tell him that you and I were going to Alpha Centauri and to ask him if he would like to be a crew member. I didn't expect him to say yes, but I didn't expect to hear about terrorist launches either."

"Wow! Where can we find out more than they taught us about the current world situation?"

"Start with Maria. You will be talking with her anyway. Just ask her what she knows about the activities of the GCC. Maybe their records are not all classified. And even if they are, she may have access to them."

"Can you come up this weekend? I miss you."

"Sure! I'm working on stuff with David through Friday, so how about Saturday morning?"

"If that's the best you can do," she pouted.

Jake ignored her feigned feelings. "See you Saturday before ten AM. Stay under the covers, and I'll sneak in and wake you up."

"Okaaaaay! Look forward to seeing you then."

"Bye."

Stoll was with David, Ed Stessel, and Howard Ottinger in his office. "So we can expect delivery of the full-sized UMU in twenty-eight days?" said Klaus.

"That is what I am told," said Ed.

"Does Weber—that is, you and Fred Marston—want us to continue to conduct the experiments with the UMU? I mean, this thing is *your baby*, and we have successfully done the Mars transfer you asked us to do."

"Do we need a contract of some kind to continue working with you?" said Ed.

"I don't think so," said Klaus. "Considering what we are doing so far, there has been no need for one. But now that we are preparing to send a *person* through time and perhaps through space, maybe we should put at least an understanding in writing."

"I think you are right," said Stessel. "By the way, is the female astronaut Maria Rodriguez still interested in being the first time traveler?"

"She certainly is," said David. "She calls me often on the subject."

"Does she have family?" said Ed.

"No," said Howard. "Don't you remember? She was one of the six who came to us from the twenty-first century. She has no family living. That is why she wants to go back to the twenty-first century in the UMU. She is still in love with a man who lived in that time."

"Ah yes, now I remember," said Stessel. "And, David, you are also from the twenty-first century."

"You are correct," said David. "But *I* don't want to go back!"

They chuckled at this remark.

"The reason I asked about Maria's family," said Stessel, "is that if something should happen to her that we aren't planning, families tend to value such mishaps highly—often, it seems, more highly than they valued the love and friendship of the person harmed."

"Are you referring to lawsuits?" said Howard.

"Yes," said Stessel. "I have specific instructions from Fred Marston that whoever volunteers to be transported in the UMU must sign a waiver absolving Weber of any blame or responsibility for any mishap. But even with such a signed document, families can get awfully nasty when they can see visions of a huge pile of credits coming into their bank accounts."

"Maria just wants to go home to the twenty-first century," said David. "She will trust us if we tell her that we think her journey will be safe. I have talked to her about the risks, and she will sign anything you want as long as I assure her that I think she will *make it alive* back to the arms of her lover."

"Well spoken, David," said Klaus. "And I, for one, will not let her set foot in the UMU if I am not convinced she has a damn good chance of making it to 2025 alive and healthy."

"I think Maria is a good choice for another reason," said Dr. Stessel. "And I am sorry, but this is also a commercial reason. The UMU has the potential of earning billions of credits for Weber. It certainly won't hurt our business at all to successfully transport a person as beautiful as Maria as our first *time traveler*. We would ask that you allow a private photographer—not the press—to take photos of the time-transfer event."

"Well," said Klaus, "we have our own PR staff and will certainly plan to have them working at the event. If you wish to have your own photographer, I don't see how we can object to that."

"Gentlemen," said Dr. Ottinger, "it sounds like Maria Rodriguez is our choice for the first *human time traveler*."

"Are we all agreed, then?" said Klaus Stoll. "David, would you like to call her, or would you like me to do the honors?"

"Sir, she will be delighted and overwhelmed if she gets the call from you." said David.

In Washington

It was early evening, and Susan was with Maria in her unit. They were discussing the possibility of Susan staying with Maria if she had to move out of her own apartment before she was ready because of her decision to go back to work as an astronaut. Maria had just told Susan that she would be welcomed to stay with her unless, of course, she should get the nod to be the first time traveler. In that case, she would be leaving her job and going back to the spaceflight center, staying for a time in the BPQ.

They were just into their second Chardonnay when Maria's mec toned.

"This is Maria. Who did you say is calling?"

"This is Klaus Stoll, Maria. How are you?"

"Director Stoll! How are you, sir? I am *fine*."

"Good, Maria. I have some news for you. If you are still interested, you can be the world's first *time traveler*—not counting Marco Mouse, of course."

"WHAT? Oh, sir, that's *wonderful! I'm so excited*! When should I plan to come back to the Cape?"

"Well, we won't receive delivery of the large machine for twenty-eight days. Then we will want to run some tests. That will take about two weeks. If you can come down thirty days from now, that would be fine. How will that fit for you?"

"That will work well, sir. I can give my notice to the library in two weeks and be there about thirty days from now."

"Excellent! We will look for you then. Perhaps we can arrange for someone to come up and give you a ride down. How would that be?"

"Oh, that would be fine, sir. But if that's too much trouble, I'll just fly down commercially."

"No problem. I will talk to you again soon."

"Oh, sir, before you go, I do have one question."

"Yes?"

"Could I possible take a small bag of clothes with me in the machine when I go back to 2025. I've bought some really nice things, and I just hate to leave them behind."

"Of course, Maria. There should be plenty of room for you to carry a bag. I'll talk with you later. Good-bye." Maria cradled the mec as did Klaus. He thought, *Only a woman would be worried about taking clothes back thirteen centuries.*

Maria hugged Susan fiercely! *"I am going back to 2025, to Rico!"* she screamed.

"Oh, Maria! I am very happy for you!" said Susan.

"They want me down there in one month, so I guess you won't be able to stay here with me after all."

"No problem, Maria. I may be jumping the gun anyway. I best just keep my place until we have congressional approval for our space mission. Besides, after we get the go-ahead, the *Revelation* has to be re-engined. And they aren't going to be able to do that overnight . . . Even if I have to pay an extra month's rent, I better stay put until I am sure of what we are doing."

"I hope yours and Jake's plans work out for you, Susan. You know, I wasn't too sure about Jake at first, but now I think he's really a first-rate guy."

"Thanks, Maria, so do I! Sorry I never got to meet your Rico, but he sounds like someone very special. He must have been—oops, sorry. He *must be* an exceptional man to have them maintain his home in Arlington for all these centuries."

"I've been reading about some of the things he accomplished, Susan. He really did a lot for this country and for the world. I just hope I can be by his side through all of those years."

"It seems crazy to talk like we are talking, Maria. We are talking about all Rico *has* accomplished, and we are talking about you being with him *in your future* when he does these things."

"Susan, just let me tell you this. I want you and the others from the twenty-first century to know that I love you and cherish my time spent with you. If this time device works, I will be in seventh heaven! If it does not and you never see me again, just know that I am happy with the choice I am making."

"Maria, if the machine works, I *will* see you again. Count on it. And now I need to get over to my place. Jake is probably trying to reach me."

At David and Ellen's Home near Orlando

"Well, Ellen, things are poppin' at the old KSC!" David had just arrived home and was hanging his jacket in the foyer closet.

"Really? What today?" said Ellen as she worked on one of David's favorites—a meat loaf.

"I don't know where to start." He paused, "Yes, I do. Maria is *going back* to the twenty-first century!"

"David! They approved her?"

"Yes, and believe me, they are getting a bargain." David went over the reasons why Klaus and Stessel had decided to use Maria.

"Certainly not out of the goodness of their hearts," said Ellen.

"No, but a fair trade. Maria wanted this—very deeply. She is very unhappy in this century. She thinks she can go back to her old life and to Rico, and she is sure that he will be there for her. I hope she is right."

"I hope the machine works. If she makes it back to 2025 alive and healthy, she will have accomplished her mission. She can't control what Rico does. If you ask me, if he was in love with her, he would have *never* let her go with us on the Nyvar mission."

"You are probably right, hon."

"What else happened today?"

"Well, we are going to re-engine the *Revelation*."

"What? Why on earth?"

"Jake and Susan are determined to explore the galaxy—at least as much of it as they can with the ships we have today. Congress has not approved any funds in the past few years for missions and projects that don't show a positive return on investment. Exploration such as Jake wants to do cannot be made to show payback even though such missions could indeed end up being profitable, depending on what is found on other worlds."

"So how does re-engining the *Revelation* change anything?"

"We can put new 10xL class engines on the ship for relatively little money. Pratt has six engines sitting around doing nothing because the 10xL ship program was cut back by Congress. Dr.Simonides thinks we can get two engines *very cheap*."

"I still don't see—"

"Bottom line is that using existing 10xL ships would cost in the billions of credits since the total cost of the ship has to be charged to the project. If we re-engine the *Revelation*, we are talking about a cost in the *millions*, probably less than three hundred million."

"And they—and you—think Congress will approve the project at the lower cost?"

"Klaus and Dr. Simonides are sure of it. I have no idea, but I have been directed to design the modifications required to accommodate the larger engines."

"How fast will the modified *Revelation* travel?" She was getting more interested.

"It will be the fastest ten times light-speed ship in the GSA fleet—in the world, in fact."

"Why is that?"

"Because it is lighter than the newer ships and because your brilliant husband designed the ship to take the thrust of the 10xL engines in the first place."

"You did? Why?"

"Because we hoped that Pratt and GE could build us a higher-thrust engine so we could break the light-speed barrier." He smiled patiently at Ellen and said, "You knew all this at one time, hon. You have just forgotten it."

"I knew it tonight. I just wanted to hear you talk about it!"

"Yooooou!" said David as he gave her a big bear hug.

As he held her, she whispered in his ear, "You want to hear my news?"

"Sure." he said without letting her go.

"I'm pregnant." she said softly.

"What!" screamed David. "When did you know?"

"Just did a test today. Everything looks good so far . . ."

"This is cause for a celebration! Now I am really proud of how hard I worked to make this happen," David said with a sneaky smile.

"How hard YOU worked to make it happen?" she screamed.

"Yooooou!" she yelled as she chased him around the room, brandishing a spatula.

"Help!" cried David. "HELP!"

He stopped and grabbed her again. He held her close and said, "I am so happy for you, El. I am so happy for both of us. We have found a great life here with lots of fun challenges. And soon we can share our joy with the *rest of the family*."

Jake was in his living room still studying the list of possible crew members when the mec toned. "Jake here," he said.

"I thought you were going to call me," Susan said.

"No, we talked this afternoon, and I didn't have any new news."

"Well, *I* do!"

"Really? What?"

"They are going to use Maria as the first *time traveler*."

"Great. When did you find out?"

"Just a few minutes ago. I was with Maria at her place, and Klaus Stoll called."

"The director himself. Well, I am happy for her . . . I guess. Sending a mouse to Mars is one thing, but sending a person back thirteen centuries in time is quite another."

"I just hope that she finds happiness with Rico when she gets there."

"I just hope she gets there . . ."

Susan began to get concerned. "Jake, do you have any doubt that she will make it back?"

"I certainly do. To my way of thinking, *the past is over*. The civilization we knew in the twenty-first century has gone bye-bye. We here today occupy the territory once occupied by people now long dead. How can we possibly go back to *that past*? Where is it? That's what I would like to know. For example, if I want to go back to the home I was born in and see my parents, how can I do that? In the first place, my parents are both dead. I know where they are buried. In the second place, the house that I lived in as a child was knocked down after my parents died. In 2024, there was a stadium built on that ground. If I get in this time machine and say I want to go back to 1990 and see my parents in the home I was born in, how am I going to do that? That ground is now occupied by something else, and my parents are *in their graves*.

"I'm sorry, darling, I don't mean to upset you. I just think Maria may *not find* what she expects to find. And I think she should make her life *here today*—not risk it trying to reclaim the past."

"Did you tell her this, Jake?"

"No, I did not."

"Why didn't you?"

"Because she is happy. Because she is doing what she wants to do. *Because I may be wrong.*"

"Jake, the mouse made it back through time."

"I didn't witness that. I understand it only went back ten minutes."

"But it did go back!"

"Sue, I am sorry. Let's not argue about it. I just care for Maria and hope that she doesn't throw her life away."

"Just one more question, Jake, then I will drop the subject."

"Please make it an easy one."

"If she steps into that machine and disappears, what will *you* think happened to her?"

Jake thought long and hard. Finally, he said, "Where is her target destination?"

"Rico's house. She has gone to Rico's house that we saw in Arlington and has determined the coordinates of the center of his three-car garage, now empty."

"How did she determine the coordinates?"

"She bought something at RadioShack that will determine the coordinates of any point on the globe to three decimal places."

"OK, you asked me what I thought would happen to her if she disappears with the time machine. I think one of two things. Either she will be vaporized and, therefore, be nowhere. Or she will be in the garage of Rico's house. But she will be there in the *present*, not the past!"

"Why not the past?"

"I already told you. I do not believe the past continues to exist."

"OK, let's drop it."

"Good!"

"Maria is leaving her apartment here at the end of the month to come there. I guess she plans to stay in the BPQ until she takes the big trip. Anyway, my plan to stay with her here obviously won't work. Maybe I shouldn't give my notice on this condo until we have a positive go on our mission. What do you think?"

"Go ahead and serve notice on the place. Two weeks from now, serve notice on your job. When your work is over, I will come up and get you. You can stay with me here until we are ready to launch."

"But I won't have a job."

"Honey, you don't *need* a job. You are already rich. And if you spend all of that money, I will give you some more. We *know* what we want to do. So why not close down your Washington operation ASAP and join me here? We will have lots of fun before we start preparing for our mission."

"OK, Jake, I'll do it. I love you! See you on Saturday before ten o'clock."

"You got it!" said Jake. "Bye, hon."

Jake cradled the mec and returned to examining his list of astronauts. The mec toned again.

"Jake here . . . I still love you."

"Hey! That's nice." said Dante. "I knew we were good friends but never suspected—"

"Dante! Hi!" said Jake. "I just hung up from talking to Sue—thought it was her calling back."

"You mean you *don't* love me?"

"I'm in love with *Susan*—and there is not room in my life for two romances at the same time." Jake played along with Dante's game. "Tell me what is going on with your job."

Dante turned serious. "Jake, we have been busy around here lately. Before I say any more, understand that I will be leaving names of countries and places out—that info is highly classified."

"Fine. Just tell me what you can . . . Is this a secure call?"

"I am calling you on one of our secure frequencies. We will *know* it the instant there is an intrusion—but *there won't be one*. Here goes.

"We are making a *major strike every one or two months*. That may not seem like a lot to you, but when I signed up for this job, there was *very little* going on. I was initially under the impression that the U.S. government had the world situation pretty much under control—"

"That is what GSA led us to believe during our indoctrination sessions."

"*And* what General Whitcomb himself told me. And I did have a quiet time initially. Then things started to happen. ICBM launches from obscure places our intelligence people apparently had not suspected. Things have *changed*. Let me tell you what we handled this morning." Dante related the school strike. Jake listened to the whole story.

"Dante, have ANY enemy missile attacks ever escaped your satellite umbrella?"

"No, not since I have been here and none that I know of before that."

"Then why do *they* keep trying?"

"Nobody seems to know the answer to that, Jake. In the thirteen centuries since we left Earth, it appears that some fanatics over the world have survived and their *hate* with them. What *has* changed, however, is our ability to *contain the actions* of these idiots."

Jake was quiet for a time. Then he said, "Do you like that job, Dante?"

"Not really. But as the saying goes, Jake, somebody has to do it. I feel that I am qualified, and I'm willing and able to make the decisions. On a big one, like today, I go to my boss, General Whitcomb." Dante paused. "I guess I misled myself in coming into this job. I thought that the evildoers of the world had been convinced that their efforts were futile. I thought that there would be little need to launch maser strikes." He sighed. "But enough gloom and doom, Jake, what have you and the rest of the 621 Club been up to?"

Jake took a breath. Dante's words had been very depressing.

"You won't believe everything that is happening, Dante . . . I will give it all to you in one sentence. Then you can ask questions."

"A real working *time machine* has been built, and Maria is *going back to the year 2025*. Susan is leaving her job with the Supreme Court and joining me for an exploration to a planet in the Alpha Centauri system, and the *Revelation* is being re-engined with 10xL engines for our mission. How is that for excitement?"

"Wait just a minute. I thought you said *time machine*—"

"I did. A company called Weber Inc. developed it, and GSA has been testing it. When I was on Mars on my last trip, David, Ottinger, and Stoll sent a live mouse to Mars and *into the future*. Only a few minutes into the future, but it worked. They have also sent a mouse *into the past*."

"What else have they done with the machine? Have any humans been sent anywhere in time or space?"

"Not yet. Maria is going to be the *first human time traveler*."

Dante could not *believe* Jake's words. "Jake, don't let Maria do it! It's too risky. Make them take a condemned prisoner or another volunteer and put him through time travel to prove the system. But *not Maria*. Don't let her be the first GUINEA PIG!"

"Dante, I could not agree with you more. But you should see how happy Maria is to be going back to her Rico, the guy she fell in love with just before she came to the center for our training. She really wants to go."

"Jake, she is willing to go because *she trusts you and Klaus and David*. She thinks you will *not let her go* if you have any doubt about the success of the mission."

Jake began to feel badly. *Dante is right*, he thought. *They should put someone else through the machine before they risk Maria*. "Dante, you are right. I will go to David and/or Stoll tomorrow and insist that some other human be the first to travel. We can find a condemned prisoner to send to another cell in another location to prove the machine. I will call David right after I finish talking to you."

Neither Dante nor Jake spoke for a few seconds. Then Jake said, "Dante, you sound like all you do is work. What are you doing when you are not on duty at GCC? Any golf?"

"Not much, Jake. There's a course here, but I haven't played. I really have done very little but work since I took this job."

"Come back to GSA. Go with Susan and me on this mission to Alpha Centauri. We are looking for two more crew members."

"Jake, I would like to, but I am needed here. I promised the general a year, minimum. Then I would decide about my future."

"Let me know if you change your mind. We could use you. Right now, I need to go. If I hope to catch David before he and Ellen sack in, I better give them a shout now."

"OK, Jake . . . But just don't let that *special Maria* get into that machine until you test it with someone else first . . ."

"OK, Dante. I promise I will take care of it. Talk to you later."

The mec toned, and David, relaxing in his living room, picked it up. "David here."—

"Dave, this is Jake. Sorry to be calling late, but I just got off the horn from talking to Dante and—"

"*Dante*. How is he? I haven't even thought of him lately. We have been so busy."

"He's OK, but he has his hands full. When we have more time to talk, I'll fill you on the stories he told me. Right now, I want to bend your ear on just one thing—Maria and her trip in the UMU."

"Everything has been cleared on that, Jake. She has been approved to go on the trip she wants—back to the twenty-first century."

"David, Dante said some things to make me start thinking. It is a giant leap from sending a mouse fifteen minutes to the future and to Mars to sending Maria back thirteen centuries."

"Not really, Jake. If it worked for the mouse, in principle, it will work for Maria."

"If you were putting *Ellen* in that machine, wouldn't you want *to be more positive* of the outcome than you are now?"

David hadn't considered it quite like that. He thought for a time.

"I see your point," he said. "What do you suggest?"

"It was Dante's suggestion. He thinks we should run tests with other volunteers, both forward and backward through time, before we use Maria. He suggested prisoners, maybe condemned prisoners be used. I've been thinking about this, and there may even be just ordinary people that would volunteer for such tests—just for the excitement and notoriety of it all."

David thought about Jake's words. Then he said, "OK, Jake. I agree with you that we *should* conduct tests using another person before Maria takes her trip. But we want to keep all this work very secret. We do not need the press involved, splashing the operation in the media over the world. Let me discuss this with Director Stoll tomorrow. I will assure you of one thing. I will make sure that we prove the machine with another person before we use Maria."

"Thanks, Dave. That's what I wanted to hear. Good night."

"Good night, Jake. And thanks for the call."

45

David arrived early at the KSC headquarters building and went directly to see Director Stoll. After a brief discussion with Klaus, the director agreed with David that tests with another volunteer before Maria's time transfer would be advisable and appropriate. He stated however that both Weber and GSA wanted Maria to be the *first traveler on record* and in the history books. Klaus called a meeting in his office of the principals involved. Even Fred Marston was in attendance via hologram.

Klaus opened the meeting. "Gentlemen, it has been brought to my attention that we can substantially reduce the risks of Maria's journey through time if we use some other human subject in tests before we use Maria. I am upset with myself that I didn't insist on tests with other humans before we allow her to attempt such a long journey."

The others were quiet, obviously feeling some uncertainty themselves. Klaus continued, "For my part, I think my excuse personally is that I was so excited that the UMU *functions*. And it has performed perfectly every time. I just have not even considered failure. But we are talking about a beautiful young woman here, one that is of course volunteering to go back on a journey through time because she wants to. But she is willing to take the risk because *she trusts us*. Can we all say that we are 100 percent positive the UMU will deliver Maria safely to the twenty-first century?" He paused. "*I* cannot!"

The hologram of Fred Marston spoke, "Given the transfers we have made successfully on every attempt, I have no doubt that the UMU will function as we program it to. Unless"—he hesitated—"*unless*, the machine malfunctions." He continued, "The more we test it, of course, the more confident we all can be. But the UMU *is a machine*—and the first of its kind at that. And machines *do fail*—every day."

"Here is what I propose," said David. "Let's get a volunteer. If we can't find one that is already on the payroll, then we will have to go outside GSA. In that event, I suggest that we find a prisoner, let's say a lifer, and with the government's consent, make a deal with the prisoner to shorten his sentence if he will volunteer to work with us. We should tell him as little about the UMU as possible—only that it will transfer him from one point to another. We do not have to tell him that the transfer includes *travel through time*."

"Wait!" said Dr. Stessel. "Say no more! *I will volunteer*. I designed the machine, and I know it will work. We don't need any outside volunteer. I will travel in the machine in the tests."

The others were stunned.

"You?" said Klaus.

"Me!" said Edward Stessel. "How can I ask anyone else to risk his or her life in the time machine I designed if I won't do it myself?"

"As your partner and friend, Ed, I can't let you do it," said Fred Marston.

"I doubt if any of us here think this is a good idea, Ed," said Klaus. "Let's contact the state prison and work a deal."

"I *want* to do it," said Stessel. "I *insist!* Nothing any of you say or do will change my mind. I have ultimate confidence in the UMU. Now let's get on with the planning."

Stessel continued, "We will do at least two transfers, one forward and one backward through time. Let's keep the distances small in the interest of logistical concerns and keep the transfer times small to save us time in the experiments."

"I suppose there is one real advantage in you being the first, Ed," said Ottinger. "If . . . there is a malfunction, then you would be the best equipped to deal with it."

"There won't be a problem," said Ed.

"We will be trucking the unit down to you, leaving our factory twenty-six days from now," said Fred. "I will be driving behind the truck. I want to be with you for both of the tests and also for Maria's journey."

"Then I guess the meeting is over," said Klaus. "We know what we are going to do."

Five Weeks Later—the Marks' Home near Orlando

"Big day today, honey," said David as he and Ellen finished a light breakfast. "Maria's arriving. Jake went up in his new puma to bring her back, and we start the new UMU unit time-transfer tests with Ed Stessel."

"Have you already done some tests? Is the time machine functioning on spec?"

"We have thoroughly checked it out, and it seems to be operating perfectly. Yesterday, we did some transfers with an ape—we call him Bosco—and we could detect no physical changes to the animal at all after each transfer. Not even so much as a blip in blood pressure. We sent him forward two hours and backward three days. I know that's not big moves. But as Ed says, it is the principle that counts, not how long or how far the subject is transferred."

"I'm glad Maria decided to stay with us until she leaves," said Ellen. "She could have stayed at the BPQ, sure, but it will be fun having her with us. I've hardly spoken with her since she went to work in Washington. We have a lot of catching up to do."

"Well, you can start pretty soon. Jake's new PMU-060 cruises at 3,000 mph, and they should be arriving before eleven. He is bringing her directly here. I told him you were taking the day off and would be here to greet them."

"Speaking of Jake, what is happening on GSA's request to Congress for funds for the Alpha Centauri project?"

"That is a good question. Director Simonides is quite confident the project will be approved because of the relatively low-budget expenditure required. Re-engining the *Revelation* is the key to the project and to getting it approved. Jake and Director Stoll are just standing by for the word. Meanwhile, Jake continues to do runs here and there. Last week, he hauled some supplies to the two-hundred-mile LEOS—the International Space Station. The week before that, he had a lunar run. He is really bored and ready to get the Alpha C project moving."

"Did you mention to him about the androids I am working on?"

"No, I didn't, hon . . . It just slipped my mind. I really think he has selected two astronauts for the mission."

"David, I just don't think *you want him to consider androids for the job.*"

"It really doesn't matter to me who he picks. I think either staff astronauts or androids will give him and Susan the needed crew support."

"We have been over this before, but just in case you weren't listening, I will tell you again. Here are my reasons for supporting the androids for Jake's crew.

"First, these two we are now completing will have very nearly *perfect human characteristics.* Also, they will be the most powerful units ever created. The male will have your knowledge of science and engineering, and the female unit will have my knowledge of medicine. Actually, they will both be smarter than either of us and, on top of that, their brains will work at the speed of the fastest computers now in production on Earth. I know if *I* was going on a mission to a new planet where I might find any type of life there, I would feel much more comfortable and safer with our two new androids than with just ordinary astronauts in my crew."

"Do these units have names yet?"

"No. Not officially, but we are calling them George and Gracie at the present. Jake and Susan can name them anything they want."

"Isn't this the first female android that has been manufactured?"

"Yes, it is. Why?"

"Well, I don't quite know how to ask this, but . . ."

"I know what you want to ask. Just let me answer it to keep you from struggling. Neither of the droids function sexually. Otherwise, George thinks like a man, and Gracie thinks like a woman. That is why we made George the engineer/scientist and Gracie the medical type. Because we think men make better engineers and women make better doctors. There is no other reason. As you must have figured out in all your years, David, men's and women's thought processes are entirely different. The world needs both to keep it on track."

David just looked at Ellen. "How is our baby doing?" he said.

"Wonderfully! Thank you for asking. I thought maybe you had forgotten him."

"I had not forgotten . . . HIM? Did you say HIM?"

"Didn't I tell you? It's going to be a boy."

"That's great, Ellen! Now we can start working on names."

"Fine, but don't you have to go to work today? It's five 'til eight now!"

"*I'm late!*" David yelled as he jumped up and grabbed his jacket. "I forgot you aren't working today!" he said as he headed for the door. "I'll tell Jake about George and Gracie," added David as he left and slammed the front door.

"I'll tell him myself when he arrives with Maria," said Ellen to her coffee cup.

In Dr. Ottinger's lab, the new UMU time machine sat majestically in the center of the room. It was ready to give Edward Stessel the ride of his life. The unit was built primarily of aluminum and aluminum polymer material. Its sides looked like clear glass. It was eight feet tall and rectangular in shape—forty inches by forty inches. Inside, the control console was mounted on the wall opposite the entry door. The device looked like one of the street-corner phone booths that had disappeared centuries before.

The experts were all around the UMU when David arrived, and no one seemed to notice that he was late. He grabbed a clipboard and tried to act as if he had been there all the time.

Fred Marston had Ed Stessel aside, and they were in a deep discussion about something. Director Stoll and Howard Ottinger were looking at a record of tests run since the unit arrived. It was 8:25 AM by the clock on the wall.

Then Director Stoll spoke, "Well, gentlemen, shall we get on with it?"

Everyone gathered by Klaus who was standing near the door of the UMU. Klaus continued, "We have jointly decided to bite off only a small chunk with the first transfer of Dr. Stessel. He will set the controls to move from the present position of the UMU, position A, to position B over here, clearly marked on the floor." Klaus strode over to the other position marked. "The first transfer will be to only *ten minutes* into the future. Are we in agreement, Dr. Stessel?"

"We are," said Ed Stessel. "And although nothing untoward is going to happen, I would just like to say that it has indeed been a great pleasure to work with all of you. Fred is prepared to handle my business affairs if need be. Gentlemen, I will see you all in ten minutes." With those words, Dr. Stessel stepped into the UMU and closed the door. He began working with the controls, setting them to the proper coordinates and time. His voice could be heard clearly outside the UMU. "Watch the countdown numerals above the door. I am initiating the transfer."

The countdown would start with ten and move downward to zero. Ed turned and faced the others looking in at him. "Here we go," he said.

The countdown display began, "Ten . . . nine . . . . three . . . two . . . one . . . zero."

The UMU with Ed disappeared on zero with no vapor and no sound. It was as if a light was on—and then *off*. Not a sound was heard in the lab. The observers all began to move slowly over to the other side of the room near position B. The wall clock indicated that two minutes had now passed.

Eight minutes had now passed. There had never been a group of men stand so quietly with so little movement. They looked like the department store mimes that posed to attract shoppers' attention.

Ten minutes passed. Nothing . . . Eleven minutes . . . nothing.

At *thirteen* minutes, the UMU suddenly appeared with Ed standing and smiling, looking exactly as he had looked when he disappeared thirteen minutes before.

David rushed to the door and opened it. Everyone was cheering and applauding and congratulating Ed. But all were confused and concerned about the three-minute discrepancy in arrival time. Ed spoke first with a wry smile.

"Sorry if the delay bothered anyone. I accidentally hit the wrong key and entered 13 minutes instead of 10. To correct the error, I would have had to delete everything I had entered and start over. I just decided to let it go this time."

"Well, you sure had *me* worried," said Fred. "Don't do that again—please."

David was examining the bio-instrument readings. "Everything looks perfectly normal here. Do you feel OK, Ed?"

"I feel absolutely normal," said Dr. Stessel. "The transfer effect was strange. At no time did I lose consciousness. It was like my view of the room changed instantly. You gentlemen were standing *there*, and suddenly, you were standing *here*."

Always the optimist, Director Stoll said, "Good! Then the test was *perfect*. What is our next one?"

"I have been thinking about this next one quite a bit," said Dr. Stessel, who seemed to be enjoying having stressed the group by being three minutes late. "What if I went back, say, *one week*. Could we work that out? Let's say I don't plan to go to a new location, so we keep the experiment entirely within the lab. If I go back one week to this same location, what was happening in this lab one week ago?"

Dr. Ottinger spoke, "One week ago, we had just received the UMU and placed it where it now stands. There were two freight workers here who brought the unit in. You were here Ed, along with David, and me, but no one else."

"The unit was delivered at about nine AM, and I believe that the freight workers were gone by ten, leaving just the three of us in the lab," David conjectured.

"So," said Dr. Stessel, "at ten AM, the UMU was standing where it now is, and the three of us were close by. Do you think there was anything in that space over there by the freight door?"

"No, there never is—on purpose. We try to keep that space open for deliveries," said Dr. Ottinger.

"Then here is what I would like to try," said Edward. "I would like to set the controls to send me and the UMU back one week to ten o'clock in the morning on last Friday and enter the coordinates for that space just inside the freight door. What do you all think about that?"

Everyone looked at one another and at the floor and the ceiling, and no one said anything for a time. Then David said, "When you arrive on last Friday, you should find me and Howard and *yourself* standing around the UMU much as we are now."

"But that means that there will be TWO of you in this room, Edward," said Klaus.

"And *two* UMUs—the one that was there and the one I arrive in," said Ed.

"Then," said Fred Marston, "the three of you that were already in the room will be startled and completely confused."

"Until I explain to you what is happening," said Ed. "Hell, let's just do it and make decisions on the fly—this should be *fun.*"

"I think," said Director Stoll, "we should walk all the way through a plan to the end, which is with us standing here exactly as we are now—*with only one Ed Stessel and one UMU.*"

"Trust me, Klaus," said Stessel, "this will work. I assure you that I can return us to the exact situation we are in now with one exception—David, Howard, and I will remember the incident that happened last Friday. Let's do it!"

All agreed, and Ed stepped into the UMU. He told them what he was entering into the controls—one week in the past. Time: Friday, August 1, 3340, 10:00 AM. Place: the coordinates corresponding to the space in front of the large delivery door. "Countdown and activate!" called Ed.

One Week Earlier

It was Friday, August 1, and the UMU had just been delivered and set in place in the center of the lab. The freight workers had just left. David and Ed

Stessel and Howard Ottinger were standing by and examining the UMU unit. The time was 10:00 AM.

David yelled, "LOOK—by the DOOR!" He pointed.

There was *another UMU* and in it, *another Edward Stessel*!

"What the . . . ?" said Howard in absolute amazement.

"How can this be?" said David

"There is only one possible explanation," said the Edward that had been in the room first with Howard and David. "I have come back from the future in this machine, and that is what you are looking at."

"You are exactly correct, Dr. Stessel," said the *new* Edward Stessel from inside the UMU. "I have come back from next Friday *one week into the future*. We all decided, including Fred and Klaus, to try this experiment."

"Now what do you plan to do?" said the first Stessel.

"I will go back to next Friday as I promised you all and the others. I will materialize in the same spot I left from, which is where the original UMU is standing now in this room, having traveled back in time one week and then forward again one week."

"But how will you prove to us that you have done that?" said David. "Won't it seem like you just disappeared and then returned?"

"Except that all three of you *will remember this incident today*. You and I will remember what we saw today. And there will only be one Ed Stessel in the room because the one that will be there *next* Friday is *me*. And I will have *returned*. I am leaving now. I will see you in this room next Friday."

Ed Stessel again entered the data needed into the controls and activated the UMU. The UMU with Ed disappeared, and the three men just looked at one another.

"We must keep this incident to ourselves—just the three of us," said Dr. Stessel. "If we discuss it with the others, this will change the future. If we just stay quiet until after the incident has occurred next Friday, everything will be fine."

Friday, August 8, in Dr. Ottinger's Lab

"Well, Ed has disappeared with the UMU," said Klaus Stoll. "Hopefully, he made it back to this lab on last Friday."

"We should know in just a moment," said Howard, winking secretly at David. David returned the wink with a smile and looked at his watch.

Suddenly, the UMU appeared in the same spot with Dr. Stessel as its passenger.

Klaus and Fred were confused. Klaus said, "But you were going back to last Friday."

Ed stepped out of the UMU and said proudly, "I did!"

"But how do *we* know that?" said Fred Marston.

"Because Howard and Ed and I *were there*!" said David. "And we now *remember* the incident."

"That is true," said Howard. "Let me explain what we observed and *now feel* that we have *known it all week*. I did not know this before we conducted the experiment."

Dr. Ottinger explained the incident of Friday, a week ago, as all listened.

"I have to admit to you all," said Edward, "I planned this experiment the day the UMU arrived, and the three of us were looking at it in this very spot *where it is now*. I knew before we entered this room today that I would be persuading all of you to go along with my trip to the past. I knew who would be in this room at that moment, and I knew that the spot by the door would be vacant."

"Then you were not going to let us talk you out of the experiment," said Fred.

"Not if I could help it," said Ed. "But think about it, if I had not gone back as I did, we three would have no memory of the incident because it *would not have occurred*."

"I want to discuss something else," said David. "For a few moments, there were TWO UMUs and TWO Edward Stessels in this room last Friday at just after ten AM.

"Does this mean that if you had not come back to today as you did, at this moment, we would have *two Ed Stessel* in this room and *two UMUs*?"

"Yes," said Ed. "As far as I am concerned, that condition would have begun a week ago and would *still exist*. Once I went back in time, I had to come back to this location *later* than the time I left here. Or else there would be two Stessels and two UMUs in this room. I arranged things so that condition could not exist by coming back to this room today. I did not want to deal with there being two Ed Stessels."

David was still chewing on the subject. "If Maria goes back to 2025 at the time before she left there, will there be two Marias in 2025?"

"Yes," said Dr. Stessel. "And that might cause problems for her—and for others. Therefore, we must send her back to a time *after* she left Earth on the *Revelation*.

Later That Same Day

Jake and Maria had flown down from Washington in Jake's puma and had just arrived at David and Ellen's town house. Jake touched the button; the door announced their arrival and displayed their images to Ellen. She opened the door.

"Maria! And Jake!" said Ellen. "How are you both? Come in and make yourselves at home. I've just made a pot of fresh coffee."

"Hi, Ellen!" said Maria. "It has been a long time."

"Hi, El," said Jake.

Jake and Maria took seats on the sofa by the fireplace. Ellen had the electric logs on—they looked and felt exactly like real logs burning. She went to the kitchen area to retrieve the coffee and cups.

"Did you have a smooth trip down?" said Ellen as she placed the tray on the coffee table.

"Quite smooth," said Jake. "We came down on flight level S2, cruising at 2,000 mph. It was a clear day, and Maria got a good view of the countryside. Good trip."

"Jake is a great driver . . . and pilot," said Maria.

"And how is Susan, Jake?" said Ellen. "Is she still working?"

"She is wonderful. I stayed at her place last night. Today is her last day of work, and I will go back to Washington tomorrow to get her. We'll pack her up, and she will come back with me."

"Too bad all three of you couldn't have come down together. Would have saved you a trip."

"True, but I love that puma of mine and enjoy operating it. Besides, I wanted some time to talk to Maria about her upcoming trip in the time machine."

"He doesn't think *the past still exists*," said Maria with trepidation in her voice.

Ellen looked at Jake, who said nothing and just looked back at Ellen.

"What about you, Ellen, do you think the past exists?" pleaded Maria.

This really put Ellen in a spot, and Jake knew it. He wanted to hear Ellen's answer as much as Maria did. Ellen stirred her coffee for a time, then looked into Maria's beautiful but sad eyes. "Before Weber came up with their machine, my answer would have been an unequivocal no, but now I don't know what to think."

Maria looked down into her coffee. "My mind tells me that Rico is dead and gone. All the history books tell me that. They tell me of all the wonderful things Rico did in his lifetime. But Klaus Stoll and Dr. Ottinger and your husband tell me they can send me back to that time. They tell me they can *put me by Rico's side*."

Ellen looked at Jake. "What did you tell her, Jake?"

Jake's heart was heavy. He was very fond of Maria. At one time, he had hoped they could find more than just friendship. But he realized that Maria still loved Rico. Now he was very much in love with Susan. He wanted with every fiber in his body to see Maria united with Rico in life, but he was afraid for her to attempt to travel to thirteen centuries past. He honestly did not believe that the past could still exist in spite of the tests done by Weber and now GSA.

"I told her what I believe," said Jake. "I cannot understand where the past could *be* physically. And if there is nowhere it could *be*, then how can it possibly *exist*?"

"Jake is being fair to me," said Maria. "He is telling me what he truly believes, but I want so badly to go back to my old life and especially back to Rico . . . If these scientists and David tell me there is a *chance*, then I will *take that chance*!"

Ellen thought carefully about what she planned to say next. Then she said, "Let me tell you both about what happened in the lab this morning."

Ellen then told of Dr. Stessel's trip to one week past. She told them of the point in time where there were *two* Ed Stessels and *two* time machines in the room.

Jake was stunned! Maria was ecstatic! Now she really believed that she would be able to rejoin Rico in the twenty-first century! "I will be with my Rico," she said, with determination.

Ellen addressed Jake, "What do you think now, Jake?"

Jake took a swallow of his coffee to buy some time.

"I think Maria might just find Rico *waiting for her in the past.*"

Klaus Stoll was in his office catching up on paperwork when his mec toned. It was Saturday afternoon, and Renee was off. Klaus answered, "Klaus Stoll here."

"Klaus, this is Constantine," said Kosta.

"Yes, sir. How are you this fine day?"

"Not good . . . Congress will *not* approve the credits for a trip to Alpha Centauri."

Klaus was deflated and could not find words. He had strongly believed they would get approval.

Kosta continued, "As you know, the cost has been estimated at only 285 million, less than we originally thought, but they still won't go for it."

"Did they give you any reason?"

"The same reason they gave the last two times we proposed the trip. We can't show a payback. And the mission could cost us the lives of the crew and the loss of the ship."

Klaus was silent for a time. Then he said, "Do you feel that we will ever get them to approve exploration to other systems and other planets?"

"Not with the current makeup of the House."

"Did they tell you what the vote was?"

"Twenty-seven for and twenty-nine against."

"Then we lost by only *two* votes?"

"I am afraid so, Klaus. I'm really sorry, but without House approval, we are stuck!"

"What about the Senate? And what about President Thornhill?"

"We have the support of the Senate, and the president has always been in favor of exploration of the galaxy."

"Thanks for the call, Kosta. We are *not* giving up on this—only *two* vote*s*!"

Director Stoll tried Jake's condo number and then his mec number—no answer on either one. He kept trying—he needed to talk to Jake right away.

Jake was en route home; he wanted to be sure things were neat and tidy for Susan's arrival. He remembered that the kitchen needed a scrub down and that the trash was full of beer cans. He was also certain that the bed was not made, but then he needed to put on clean sheets anyway—he hadn't changed them in at least two weeks. On the way over from David's, he decided to call Klaus for an update on the congressional action regarding the Alpha Centauri request. He touched in the director's number.

Klaus answered, "Jake! I was just trying to reach you. How was the run down from Washington, and how is Maria?"

"Maria is just fine, sir. She is with Ellen now. And by the way, Ellen told us of the successful transfers of Dr. Stessel. That information really boosted Maria's morale."

"Why? Was she not in good spirits?"

"Well, let's just say she was apprehensive about the journey she is facing . . . But she is *very excited now*. We all were very impressed with the one-week trip Dr. Stessel made and especially about your having two Dr. Stessels and two UMUs in the lab at one time."

"Yes . . . well . . . We really want to avoid having a person go back in time and meet himself or herself. We are not yet sure of the ramifications of that happening. We want to be sure that we send Maria back to a time *after* she has left Earth with you on the *Revelation*."

"I see, sir—good idea."

"Jake, the reason I needed to talk with you right now is this: I have some bad news. The House voted down our request by only *two* votes."

"*What*? I was *sure* the request would go through!" Jake paused. "I can't *tell* you how *disappointed* I am." He and Susan had been *so sure*.

"And *so am I*, Jake. And we mustn't give up! Right now, I can't think of what to do, but let's work on it. Our source gave us the information that the reason for the negative votes was the same. We can't show any definite payback for the mission—for *any* exploratory missions for that matter."

Jake was very down. "Well, thanks for the call, sir. Now I have to break the news to Susan. You know, she has quit her job with the court, don't you?"

"I knew she was going to . . . Jake, listen, Susan can work for GSA *any time* in a number of positions. I know she wants to go with you and explore the galaxy. But until we make that happen, if she wants to, she can work for us here. She can *fly* for us here. Just tell her to think about it."

"Thank you, sir, I will."

"Let's talk later, Jake. Stay positive."

Jake was really concerned about how Susan would react to the news. She had given her notice two weeks ago, and today was her last day working for Chief Justice Webster. Mrs. Webster had been very understanding about everything. She even told Susan that if she ever wanted to come back, there would be a place for her.

Jake decided he would wait until they were on the way back from Washington to break the news. Besides, he needed time to come up with a plan. Somehow, someway, he and Susan were going to explore the galaxy. He would accept nothing less.

46

The date for the transfer of Maria to Earth in the year 2025 had been set. On August 12, the brave lady would step into the UMU time machine and return to her Rico. Maria had decided that she would arrive on *the exact day the Revelation had launched* on its mission to Nyvar. She had requested that her arrival coordinates be in Rico's garage in a space where he never parked his cars. She had obtained the exact coordinates for the spot on a visit to Enrico's now preserved home in Arlington, using the locator purchased from RadioShack. At the moment in the future she had chosen to arrive, Rico would probably be having breakfast on his back patio, reading the article in the morning paper about the launch of the *Revelation*.

Ellen and David had planned a going-away party for Maria in their home. The party was set for the eve of her transfer. Planning to attend were Jake and Susan, Klaus Stoll, Howard Ottinger, Edward Stessel, and Fred Marston. David's boss, John Brindell, would also be attending. Dante was also coming down for the occasion as was Director Simonides. Dante had agreed to fly to Andrews AFB in Washington to pick up Kosta Simonides, and the two of them would fly to KSC. They would land on the pad just beside the operations building where Director Stoll would of course meet them and provide transportation to David and Ellen's.

The eve of Maria's departure had arrived. Susan was staying with Jake in his condominium. She had been pretty bummed when Jake told her of the congressional vote. Susan, like Jake, continued to hope for some breakthrough that might swing enough votes to get approval for exploration of the galaxy. Right now, the focus of all the key people at GSA was on the UMU and the upcoming transfer of Maria.

Jake was ready to go to the Marks' party, but Susan was still dressing—nothing new about that. "Are you about ready, Sue? We are going to be the last ones there, and I really like to be on time."

"Five more minutes!" called out Susan from the bathroom. "I just can't get this hair of mine to behave! I wish I hadn't changed the do last week."

"I wish you hadn't also," said Jake quietly so Susan couldn't hear.

"What did you say?" she called.

"I said, 'But your new style is really nice!'" lied Jake.

Finally, she came out, ready to go. Beautiful—but not quite as striking as Maria. *Actually*, thought Jake, *the new do looks pretty good*. He had her coat and purse in hand, and they headed for the door.

"Jake," she said as they walked briskly to the elevator, "should I get a job with GSA? We may never get the approval for our mission."

"*No*! We have more money than we can ever spend, so just enjoy the time you have off. We are *not* giving up on our efforts to explore the galaxy—and I *like* your new hair do."

The travel to David and Ellen's place took about ten minutes, and they were about twenty minutes late. All the others had arrived and were attacking the hors d'oeuvres with a vengeance. David was serving fine wine and good beer. The guests had not seen Susan for some time, and all seem to descend on her at once. Dante gave her a big hug—but no kiss. He didn't want to get crossways with Jake—at least not this early in the evening. Klaus Stoll stepped forward with Ed Stessel and Fred Marston, introducing them to both Jake and Susan. Kosta Simonides came over to say hello and to tell Jake how sorry he was about the House vote.

Ellen was busy in the kitchen, and David was functioning as the bartender—at least for new arrivals. He had invited everyone to help themselves after the first serving and to yell out if they needed anything they couldn't find.

It was a perfect night outside, and the door to the deck was open. The moon was almost full and just rising. As far as you could see were buildings, mostly condos and other multiunit residential buildings—not many trees.

The socializing continued for a while, and finally, Ellen announced that a dinner buffet was being served. Ellen's dining table accommodated only eight, but there was a table for four on the deck. In addition, the corner sofa arrangement could handle six if someone preferred that, so there was more than enough seating. She had prepared another of David's favorites for evening—a beautiful roast, slow cooked for the entire afternoon—and an asparagus soufflé, an absolute *delight*. In addition, she put out an Italian salad and gourmet bread.

Maria had elected to sit at one end of the dining table opposite Ellen, who had taken the seat at the other end. The Weber and GSA people wasted no time in grabbing chairs as near to Maria as possible. Director Stoll and Dr. Stessel were seated on either side of her. Dante, Susan, Jake, and David opted for the patio table.

"Maria," said Ed Stessel, "this is indeed a momentous undertaking you are about to embark on. Are you confident and calm about the momentous journey?"

Maria looked at Dr. Stessel with those gorgeous eyes and melted him on the spot. She said, "Dr. Stessel, you have proven that *time travel is possible*. If *you* say I can make it back to my Rico, then *I believe you*!"

"Maria," said Klaus, "I am still troubled that we will not be sure that you have arrived at the very spot you intend. We are confident that you will, but how will we know?"

"Klaus, she has agreed to reset the UMU to return to us here as soon as she arrives in Rico's garage," said Kosta. "What more proof do you need?"

"I know, sir, I know," said Klaus. "But our receiving the machine back will *not* tell us that everything went *perfectly* as planned."

"How about if I write you a note telling you what happened and place the note on the floor of the UMU?" suggested Maria.

"That should do it!" ventured Howard Ottinger. "There will be no doubt about it if she does that."

"But suppose the machine for some reason does not make it back to us?" said Klaus, still being the worrywart. Oddly, he was usually quite optimistic.

"I have another idea, then," said Maria. "Do you see this brooch?" She touched a beautiful Spanish brooch hanging from her neck quite far down her bosom. The men were of course eager to look at the brooch since Maria was wearing a rather low-cut gown.

"This was my grandmother's, and I love it. But I will donate it to the success of this project—for the benefit of you gentlemen who are making my trip possible."

At this moment, those dining on the patio were returning to the room and heard Maria speaking.

She continued, "I will place this brooch under a stone in the foyer of Rico's house. His foyer is paved with rather large flat pieces of Georgia marble—very white and very pure. I will, with Rico's help, lift the marble stone just inside the door, nearest the center of the double doors and place this brooch under the stone. After that, we will reset the stone. Then you gentlemen can go to his house in Arlington and lift the stone. If the brooch is there, then you *will know I am with Rico*. And if it is not there . . . well, I don't know what to tell you."

All in the room were mesmerized listening to Maria's statement. It was as if they were in a *trance*. Finally, Kosta Simonides said, "Bravo, Maria. That is a beautiful plan." Kosta started to clap—and everyone started to clap. Tears were in their eyes thinking of how brave this young woman was to do what she was about to do.

Finally, the applause subsided. Ed Stessel broke the silence by saying, "And you will have plenty of time to put the brooch under the stone since we won't be looking for it for *thirteen centuries* after you place it there."

At this, everyone laughed. They weren't thinking of the *ramifications* of that statement.

"A *toast*," said Jake, always the one to find an excuse to have a drink. He raised his glass and said, "To Maria—the world's first *time traveler*." Then everyone repeated Jake's toast and said together, "To Maria, *the world's first time traveler*."

The Next Morning—in Dr. Ottinger's Laboratory

The time was at hand for Maria's journey through time. Everyone that should be there was present, including Dante, Susan, Jake, and Ellen. Two PR types from GSA were there to record the event on video and digital film. Weber had provided its own photographers. They were now thirty minutes from the actual transfer, and though Maria professed to be calm, those who knew her best could see that she was really quite nervous and showing fear.

David was checking out all the bioinstrumentation, and Dr. Stessel was fussing about the UMU, making sure that all was in perfect working order. He had already set into the time and location controls the exact time of arrival in 2025 and the exact location of the arrival point, the always-vacant bay of Rico's three-car garage. All that was needed now was for Maria to touch one button—the activation key.

The photographers had been busy shooting poses of Maria standing by the time machine, smiling beautifully. She had chosen to dress in her *Revelation* jumpsuit for the event because this was the outfit she had worn en route to thirty-fourth century Earth. She felt it was appropriate for her to wear it on her return to twenty-first century Earth.

Dr. Stessel had made a brief statement about the significance of the occasion, and now it was GSA's turn. Director Stoll had intended to make the statement but had made the mistake of asking his superior, Director Simonides, to speak. Director Simonides eagerly accepted and took the spot by Maria to deliver his few words.

"As Howard has indicated," said the GSA director, "today is one of those rare days in the history of mankind. I will add to those words that the world will *never* be the same *after today*. We have proven that the past *still exists*. And what is more, *we can go there*—and we can *come back*. The danger in our new capability is that if we go into the past and change what has already occurred, we *will* change the future. Indeed, it is possible that one *tiny alteration* of the past might drastically alter the future—and the future of Maria's past will become the present where we now stand." He continued, "Therefore, I charge you, Maria," he turned and looked directly into her eyes, "with protecting the present we now enjoy. We trust you *not to make changes* in anything that might *remotely affect the course of time* from the twenty-first century to the present. *Good luck in your journey and Godspeed.*"

Dr. Stessel assisted Maria in stepping up and into the Ultimate Mobility Unit, the world's *first true time machine*. Maria closed the door and wasted no time. She smiled and waved at all those present and pressed the activator. Then she suddenly cried, "*Wait! my bag!*" She had forgotten the little travel bag she was taking with her. The countdown had begun. She sprang to the UMU door as Dr. Simonides grabbed the bag and opened the door. She reached for the bag, brought it inside, and again closed the door. The countdown continued, "Five . . . four . . . three . . . two . . . one . . . zero!"

Maria and the UMU disappeared exactly as the count reached zero.

Everyone stared at the spot where the machine had stood. There was no evidence whatever that the machine had ever been in the lab. The photographers had snapped away and presumably gotten an excellent record of the event.

Jake turned to Dr. Stessel and asked, "When do you expect the UMU to return?"

Dr. Stessel looked at his watch and said, "In about ten minutes from now."

He went on to say, "We trained Maria on how to program the unit just in case. However, I *preprogrammed it* so that all she has to do after her arrival in 2025 is touch the activate key. She will then have ten seconds to exit the unit and close the door."

"We have just a few minutes to wait now," said Fred Marston, looking at his watch.

The ten minutes came and went, and the time machine did not appear. Twenty minutes came and went, and still no UMU. All but Dr. Stessel went to get some coffee. He stayed, staring at the spot on the floor where the time machine had been. *What might have gone wrong?* he thought.

An hour went by. Still no UMU. People began leaving. Dante suddenly said, "*I am going to the Enrico Valdez estate in Arlington. The brooch has to be under the stone.*"

Everyone looked as if they had been shot! Dante was of course *right*. Director Simonides turned to Klaus and said, "Please take us to Dante's aircraft. I am going with him, and we are leaving *now*."

Dante broke into a run, followed by Kosta Simonides who was a tennis player and in pretty good shape. Director Stoll was puffing and bringing up the rear. They reached Director Stoll's puma in record time and headed for the pad by the operations building.

Dante zipped through the preflight and assisted Kosta in getting properly strapped into the second seat. Director Stoll yelled up to them, "*Call me as soon as you know.*"

The engines were revving, and Klaus couldn't hear their response, but they were nodding a yes. As Dante taxied to the runway, he lowered the canopy and called MC for takeoff and routing clearances.

In three minutes total from the moment they reached the aircraft, they were airborne. At fight level S10 and 9800 mph, they would be at Andrews in less than five minutes.

"What do you think might have happened?" said Dante over the intercom.

"I have not the slightest idea. There could be many things. It could be as simple as she has forgotten to activate the UMU. I'm sure she was very excited to be back with Rico."

"I hope it's that simple," said Dante. "I'm calling the lab to see if the UMU has returned since we left."

"Operations, this is Colonel Washington in UAF5023. Please patch me in to Dr. Ottinger's lab . . . I don't know the number."

"I have it, sir. Connecting you now."

"This is Dr. Ottinger," Howard came on the line.

"Dante here, sir. Any change in the situation?"

"No, Dante. Where are you?"

"En route to Andrews AFB, sir. We should arrive there in two minutes. From there, we will take Director Simonides' puma to Arlington. I am requesting emergency routing for that trip since it will be during the noon rush when we start from Andrews. We'll call you as soon as we know something."

"Right. Thanks, Dante!"

Dante was descending to touch down at Andrews. Director Simonides saw his puma outside the hangar, apparently ready for use. They landed and made the switch from the SR50 to Kosta's PMU-055 and scrambled for Arlington.

Kosta set his puma down just outside the gates of the Valdez estate. The gates were open. He had called en route and explained who he was and that he needed immediate entry to the home. He told them a story that researchers had discovered the existence of a one-of-a-kind relic that was thought to be on the premises of the Valdez estate. He advised that he would need to speak with the curator on his arrival.

Kosta and Dante were met by the curator of the estate. The curator quickly explained to them that *nothing* on the estate could be disturbed without *the express permission* of the president of the National Archives Society. He further stated that the president was on vacation in Switzerland and would not be back for several weeks.

Director Simonides was not to be deterred. Overcoming stumbling blocks was one of his fortes.

"We will need to reach the National Archives president. What did you say his name is?"

"His name is Louis Stevenson, sir, but he gave strict orders that he is not to be disturbed while on this vacation," asserted the curator.

"If I have to call President Thornhill and ask for a presidential order, he will not be happy with *you* or with Mr. Stevenson. I suggest that you get your boss *on that AMec there*"—he pointed to the instrument on the curator's desk—"*immediately!*"

"But, sir—," started the curator.

"There is one other way we can do this," said Kosta. "I can tell you what we would like to do here, and you may decide that you can approve that action without calling your boss. Would you like to try that?"

"What do you need to do, sir?" The curator was breaking a sweat.

"We need to lift a stone in the foyer of this home and look for an antique brooch under that stone. When the brooch has been found and removed, the stone can be carefully replaced, and all will be as before except for the brooch."

"What makes you think, sir, that there is a brooch under a certain stone?"

"I don't have to tell you that, but I will," said Kosta. "We have recently received information that thirteen centuries ago when Enrico Valdez lived in this home that a certain brooch was placed under this stone. If we can verify that information to be true, it will confirm by its mere presence that other *valuable information* we now have is also true."

Dante was impatient. He said to the curator, "Sir, let me explain something to you. We are *not leaving here* until we have a look under that stone. Now we can do this the easy way or the hard way—your choice."

The curator had never faced a situation like this before and was becoming very nervous. Then he stood himself up as tall as he could and said, "If you can assure me that you will replace the stone exactly as it now sits, I will take the responsibility and authorize your action."

"Now you're *talking*," said Kosta. "We will need a few simple tools, that I'm sure you can supply us with."

As Kosta spelled out what he needed for the curator, Dante walked to the foyer to find the exact stone they were looking for. The curator left hurriedly to find a portable light, a chisel, a large screwdriver, and a hammer. Director Simonides joined Dante just inside the front entrance at the marble stone of interest. It was located directly in the center of the doorway just inside the home.

The curator returned with the needed items and set up the portable light, focusing it on the stone. Dante kneeled and prepared to chisel away at the grout surrounding the stone when Kosta said, "Wait! The grout around this stone is fresh!"

All three men looked at the grout. It was darker than the grout around all the other stones in the foyer. Dante took the screwdriver and scratched at the grout around the stone. The tool easily scraped away the material; the grout did indeed appear to have been *recently put there*.

"Someone has had this stone up very recently—no earlier than *last night*!" said Kosta. He and Dante looked at each other with puzzled expressions. Dante set the hammer aside and began scraping at the fresh grout with the chisel—the material came up easily.

After a few minutes, Dante took the large screwdriver and, using the hammer as a fulcrum, pried at the edge of the marble stone. The stone began to lift. If fresh mortar had been used to reset the stone, it had not yet set up. The stone came up with *very little effort*.

Dante set the stone aside, and the three men looked at the space that had been under the stone—there was *no brooch*! Nothing was under the stone except the mortar that had originally held it in place. Whoever took the stone up and replaced it had not used fresh mortar. They had simply placed the stone on its original mortar, which was extremely hard, and re-grouted the stone in place.

Kosta exclaimed, "Look there—there in the lower left side of the area! There is an *imprint of the brooch*."

"*It is!*" said Dante. "At least it certainly *looks like* the brooch has been there."

"Then Maria, and perhaps Rico, *did* place the brooch under the stone using fresh mortar, hence the imprint of the brooch!" said Director Simonides.

"It appears that probably last night, someone lifted the stone and was able to pop the brooch out of the mortar and take it away!" said Dante.

"But who?" said Kosta. "The only people that knew of the existence of the brooch were Maria and Rico who put it there and *have been dead now* for at least twelve centuries, and those of us who were with her when she transferred back in time."

"And since the brooch obviously was taken from here before this grouting was completed, that *had* to have been *this morning* after Maria left us. Otherwise, the brooch would not have *been here at all*," observed Dante.

By this time, the curator was so confused he walked over to a decorative iron bench and sat down.

Kosta continued to think out loud. "So Maria must have put the brooch under the stone as she said she would—we are not sure exactly *when* she put it there. And someone who knew the brooch was there removed it *this morning* after Maria left us in the UMU and *before* you and I could get here to look for it . . ."

"And there are only two people who could have done that." said Dante.

"Either Maria or Rico," said Kosta, "because they were the only two people other than those of us at KSC who knew the brooch was supposed to be here."

"Do you realize what we are saying, Director Simonides?" said Dante. "If the only person or persons that could have done this are Maria and/or Rico, that raises very *troubling* issues."

"Troubling, indeed!" said Kosta. "Why would Maria and Rico, who put the brooch there for us to find, return and remove it? But most troubling of all, how could it have been done *this* morning—*after Maria was sent back and before we got here*?"

"There can only be one answer—one of them, Maria or Rico, *returned here in the UMU this morning and took the brooch*."

Kosta turned to the curator who seemed to be in a daze. "Have you been here all morning?"

"Yes, but we don't open this house 'til eleven. I arrived at about ten forty-five," said the curator.

"Have you had any visitors this morning before we arrived?" said Dante.

"A few, but I was in full view of the foyer since I arrived if that is what you are thinking."

"What time was Maria's transfer this morning?" Kosta said to Dante.

"At about nine thirty, I believe."

"Then that leaves a window of only an hour and a half. The brooch had to have been taken before the house was opened for the day."

"Actually, less than that," said Dante. "This gentleman"—pointing at the curator—"arrived at ten forty-five."

"OK," said Kosta, "between nine thirty and ten forty-five, *either Maria or Rico* was here, lifted the stone, removed the brooch, and re-grouted the stone. And they arrived and left in the UMU. That is the *only way* this could have happened."

Again, turning to the curator, Kosta said, "Can you produce some grout and a grouting tool so we can reset this stone?"

"Not immediately," said the man. "Are you finished here?"

"For the time being," said Kosta.

"Wait!" said Dante. "How about prints? We can try to lift prints from the stone. Unless the person that took the brooch wore gloves, we should find prints."

"Good point, Dante," said Kosta. "We don't have any equipment for lifting prints, and I'm sure you don't either"—looking at the curator—"do you, sir?"

"Oddly enough, we do. All of the preserved homes have problems with thefts and damage. Anytime we do, we report it to the police who come out to investigate, and the first thing they always do is attempt to lift prints. If there are no prints, then there is not much they can do. The law enforcement agencies have therefore supplied us with black light kits and taught us how to at least determine if there *are* prints just to save them trips out here." He left, saying, "I'll get our kit."

Close examination using the black light revealed only Dante's prints. Whoever lifted the stone must have worn gloves. "Now are you finished here, gentlemen?" said the curator to Director Simonides and Dante.

Dante and Kosta looked at each other, and Kosta said, "I guess so. Do you have the grout and tools we need to replace the stone?"

"Gentlemen, I would like to get you out of here and get this house back to normal as soon as possible. I will place a traffic cone over the spot with no stone, and we will replace it later. I want to use some adhesive under the stone and then the grout around the edges. So if you are finished, please leave now."

"Let's go," said Dante. "I hate to stay when I'm not wanted!" He smiled at Kosta and the curator.

As they stepped out through the front door, the curator said, "Before you leave, gentlemen, could you just answer one question for me?"

"I doubt it," said Kosta. "But what is it?"

"This house is locked tightly when it is not open. We had no signs of a break-in this morning or last night. You are saying that someone came in here this morning before we opened and lifted that stone, took a brooch from under it, and then reset the stone? Just how do you think they got into the house?"

"Sorry," said Dante. "We can't answer that . . . but thanks for your help."

Director Simonides and Dante were en route back to Andrews, taking their time and following the normal traffic routes. They were at flight level A2. Neither had said much since leaving the Valdez home.

"Well," said Dante, "at least we know that Maria made it back in time to Rico's house. But we don't know *when* she arrived there or *when* she placed the brooch under the stone."

"Let's call down to Dr. Ottinger's lab and tell them what we found. Maybe the UMU has returned."

"I'll make the call," said Dante. "You've got this traffic to contend with." He placed the call.

"KSC operations," said the sergeant on duty.

"This is Colonel Washington, Sergeant. I'm with Director Simonides, and we would like to talk to Dr. Ottinger at his lab."

"I'll patch you in, sir," said the sergeant.

"Howard Ottinger here," came over the connection.

"Dr. Ottinger!" said Dante. "This is Dante Washington with Director Simonides. We are en route from the Valdez home to Andrews AFB."

"Do you have the brooch?" said Howard.

"No, sir, we don't. And it's a long story. Any sign of the UMU?"

"No. We continue to wait. But nothing . . . We have *no idea* what went wrong. And you say there was no sign of a brooch?"

"Didn't say that, sir. I said we *don't have* the brooch. But the brooch *was* under the stone, and apparently, someone removed it *this morning* before we arrived at the home and then replaced the stone."

"*What?* That doesn't make *any sense*! Who could possibly have known so soon about the brooch and gotten there before you to remove it?"

"We have no idea, sir."

"Let me have the mec, Dante," said Kosta.

"Howard, this is Kosta. I need to talk to Klaus. Is he still with you?"

"He's right here, Director Simonides," said Howard and handed the mec to Director Stoll.

"Klaus," said Kosta, "there is something rotten in Denmark. Sometime between nine thirty and ten forty-five this morning, someone entered the Valdez home *without breaking in*, lifted the stone, removed the brooch, and replaced the stone."

"How do you know the brooch was ever there?" said Klaus.

"Because there was a *clear impression of the brooch* in the mortar under the stone."

There was a long silence, and Kosta said, "And the grout around the stone was *fresh*. We scraped it away with a chisel and never had to use a hammer."

Another long silence.

"I am taking Dante back to Andrews so he can go back to work. I will be in my office within the hour and will call you in your office. We need to talk about this some more. You go ahead and discuss it with the others. Maybe someone can come up with a bright idea we haven't thought of . . . Talk to you in about forty-five minutes."

"Right," said Klaus. "Thanks for the call."

47

Over a month later . . .

It was a Saturday morning. Jake and Susan were enjoying the sun on the beach. A light breeze was blowing, but the sea was quite calm. Large white clouds dotted the horizon. They enjoyed trying to identify what each cloud looked like . . . a bear, a duck, a fat baby.

"Jake, where do you think Maria is right now?"

Jake just continued to stare at the vista. "That," he said, "is a very good question. After the incident with the brooch, I *do believe in time travel*. I see no other explanation for the mystery of the missing brooch. The imprint of the brooch proves it was there. And that proves that Maria was returned to Rico's house—at least *at some time* in the past. We can't be sure of *when*."

"And Maria did not totally let us down," said Susan. "She *did* put the brooch where she promised she would put it. Although she still has not returned the UMU . . ."

They stopped talking for a few minutes as if going over the whole scenario again in their minds.

"Where do you think the time machine is now?" said Susan unable to let the subject die. Jake didn't seem to mind.

"There is no telling. If Maria and Rico decided to keep it and it functions like Weber says it does, they could be *anywhere in space and in time*."

"We know that the small UMU took Marco Mouse to Mars. Why not use the machine to travel to the stars? For all we know, Maria and Rico could have gone to *Nyvar.*"

"Is the UMU compartment large enough for two people?"

"It was built to be comfortable for one person and one or two carry-ons. Two not-too-fat individuals could fit into the unit without much else. For example, I think you and I could make it into one of the units. It would be OK if we didn't have to stay in there too long."

"Has Weber produced any more UMU units?"

"They are now completing six more units. I was talking to David a few days ago, and he brought me up to speed. He said that the new units are going to have a feature that forces a UMU to return to its origination and control point—here on Earth. Future trips will be programmed with a certain time on the ground at destination. If a traveler doesn't make it back into the unit by the departure time, he or she will be left, and the *machine returns empty.*"

"Wow! I don't think that is very user-friendly, do you?"

"It's *not*, and I don't think I will volunteer to go out in one."

"Want to stretch our legs with a walk down the beach?" said Susan.

"Sure," said Jake. "Race you to that umbrella down there!" And Jake was off.

"No fair!" yelled Susan, trying to catch up. "You had a head start!"

Jake paused and let her catch up, then really poured it on. But Susan was matching him stride for stride. They reached the umbrella in a virtual dead heat, and Jake was puffing. Susan was breathing hard but trying to act as if she was breathing normally.

"You must be out of shape!" she laughed, which drew a dirty look from Jake.

"I can take you anytime," growled Jake as he sprung at Susan and took her to the sand. She tried to get up, but he held her down and planted a big kiss. She only resisted for a few seconds and then kissed him back—*hard*.

Finally, they came up for air, and Susan said, "I really love you, Jake."

"Ditto," said Jake. "But I love you *more*."

They sat in the sand and looked out again into the surf.

"Wonder who left their umbrella here?" said Jake. "Two sets of tracks lead into the water." They both looked up and down the beach. No one as far as they could see.

"Strange," said Susan. "Bet they swam with the wave current down to the Beach Club."

"Probably," said Jake. "Ready to go back?"

"I'm ready," said Susan. They put their arms around each other and started walking back toward the club.

"Jake, what's it going to take for GSA to get approval for us to explore the galaxy? I'm not going to sit around doing nothing. I have always been an active person. As long as you are with me, we have fun, and we do things. But when you are out on cargo missions, I am bored silly. I have read five books in just the last month. What can we do to get approval for the missions we would like to fly?"

"Sue, we have offered Congress the best deal they could ever imagine with the re-engining of the *Revelation*. For only 285 million credits, we can visit Alpha Centauri P5, the planet that is the most likely to have life. If GSA had to build a ship for the mission or just use one they already have, the mission would cost 35 billion credits, counting the cost of the ship."

They continued walking toward the Beach Club.

"That's a ridiculous way of accounting—charging the whole cost of the ship to one mission. We would bring the ship back."

"That's just it, Sue. On an exploratory mission, the crew and the *ship may not make it back*. Therefore, every credit that goes into the project is charged to that one project including the value of the astronauts."

"The value of the astronauts? How do they determine our value?"

"Just by the training money invested in us plus the cost of replacing us."

They continued down the beach. Then Susan said, "You know, Jake. *We could pay for our own mission*. How much do you have in the bank?"

Jake stopped walking. He just stood and looked at Susan. Then he shouted and jumped into the air with a *fist pump*.

"*Susan!* That's the *answer*! Why haven't I thought of it before now?"

"You would really do that, Jake? You would pay for the mission out of your own pocket?"

"Yes! But only if they would give us *title* to the *Revelation*! If they would do that, I would pay for the re-engining and all the other costs of our trip."

"But why would the government do that, Jake? Don't they have other uses for the *Revelation*?"

Jake didn't answer—his mind was astir. Finally, he said, "The *Revelation* is not big enough for the cargo missions GSA is operating to the moon and Mars. It really doesn't fit anything they have approved at this time."

They were now leaving the club and driving to Jake's place—about ten minutes away.

As they entered his living room, Jake said, "Here is what we'll do, Sue. We will offer them *this* deal. You and I will one, pay all costs of a mission to ACP5, and two, claim the planet for the U.S. government if it is uninhabited—all riches that the planet has to offer will belong to the government *except for our meager 10 percent*. Three, we will continue to explore other planets for GSA so long as they transfer the title of the *Revelation* to us, pay us 10 percent of everything we discover, and provide us two backup crew members for each mission we undertake for them."

"In other words, we will be going into business with the GSA and USA as our customers. What about the cost of mining and transporting whatever we find back to Earth?"

They stepped into the condo, and Jake headed for the fridge. He took out two beers and offered one to Susan. "Time to celebrate, Sue!" he said.

He responded to her question, "All costs—mining operations, shipping, whatever—are the government's responsibility. We will be the explorers and discoverers of wealth in the galaxy! We operate with *our own ship*. After the ACP5 mission, the GSA pays our operating expenses and continues to furnish us with two crew members for each mission. We find ore and minerals. The government mines them, brings them home, and refines the valuables as required. When they are marketed, we get 10 percent of the net worth of whatever it is."

"I'm for it!" said Susan. "Let's work on it tonight together. Then I can put it into proper legal form and draw up a contract."

"Have another beer, and I'll order pizza," said Jake. They were both very optimistic.

Jake was scheduled for a moon resupply run and left the next afternoon. Susan worked on the contract and agreement papers for the next two days. By the time Jake returned, she had things nailed down pretty well. Jake had just come in from his lunar sortie, and Susan was finishing the last page of an addendum to the contract document.

She jumped from her chair and gave him a big kiss.

"Jake, let me show you what I have written!"

He picked up Susan in his arms and, still managing to hold on to a bottle of wine, made his way to their master bedroom.

"Not business first!" he said. "Pleasure first, *then* business. And who knows, if the contract is very good, you may get a special reward for that—including a night of dinner and dancing."

"Ooooh, Jake! I've missed you so," she cooed.

Jake was always unusually wild when he returned from a mission. Susan had come to look forward to that. Today was no exception. Jake was now especially excited to come home because of the new venture he and Susan were ready to undertake. Susan responded to Jake the way he loved; and he, in turn, loved her in more ways than she had ever imagined. After about forty-five minutes, they were both exhausted. They stared at the ceiling, and Susan said, "Can we somehow get this bed into the *Revelation* when we do the modifications?"

Jake *guffawed*. He *really* liked that one. "And how are we going to explain that to our crew members?"

Susan laughed and then said, "Have you ID'd any crew members yet?"

"It's still too early. We have to have the green light for the mission before any of them will get really interested."

"Did Ellen ever talk to you about the *androids* she is working on?"

"Androids? No, I haven't talked to Ellen about her work. Why?"

"Ellen thinks we should consider using for our crew a couple of very advanced droids they have constructed."

"What?" said Jake. "For our crew? You mean a Mr. D. or Mr. K. type of droid? Like the one that handles the garage downstairs?"

"Ellen says that the two they have produced—she calls them George and Gracie—are *far* more advanced and *more human* than older models. She says they have highly developed *positronic* brains. She used David's brain and engineering knowledge, including his knowledge of the *Revelation*, to develop George and her own brain and medical knowledge to develop the brain in Gracie.

Ellen thinks that when you consider the strength and durability of these new droids, combined with their superior brain functions, they would make ideal crew members for us."

Jake had listened intently to Susan's words. He said, "How about discipline? How well will they take commands? Will they recognize you and me as their superiors?"

"I should *expect so,* but I didn't ask Ellen about that. I think she said that these units are quite talented and have many functions already preprogrammed into them. She also said that they are totally obedient units that will do what we tell them to do. She also mentioned that they have feelings and emotions. That is what makes these droids much more like humans."

"You know what, Sue? Ellen just might have a good idea. Ask her if we can spend some time with George and Gracie. I would like to get to know them. Meanwhile, I am going to visit with Director Stoll and sound him out about our plan to become galaxy explorers. Since you have some time, why don't you visit Ellen in her lab and get introduced to George and Gracie? Maybe you could do that tomorrow if Ellen isn't too busy. I'll visit Director Stoll, and we can compare notes tomorrow night."

"Meanwhile, let's get a shower, get dressed, and go out for dinner. Anyplace special you would like to go?"

"Let me think about it while we are getting dressed. I feel like seafood tonight."

The evening went wonderfully. They dined and danced at a new supper club that had just opened not far down from the Coach and Six. The club had an outstanding group that played all the best contemporary dance music and had a great beat and tempo. The meal was superb. Susan had Maine lobster—a rarity in Florida—and Jake opted for veal. His serving was generous and very tasty. The evening went wonderfully. They both were thinking of the future with great anticipation.

They slept in the next morning since neither had an early call. Jake showered first and was in the kitchen whipping up some scrambled eggs with cheese. Susan placed a call to Ellen.

"Ellen, good morning! This is Susan . . . I'm fine. Jake's back, and I'm always happy when he's around . . . I'm calling about those droids you mentioned to me. If you aren't too busy this morning, could I come over and meet them and ask them a few questions? . . . Great! We slept in this morning . . . No, but last night was *grand.* Anyway, it'll be probably an hour before I can be at your lab . . . OK, that's even better. See you in an hour and a half . . . Bye."

Susan showered, and Jake yelled from the kitchen that breakfast was ready. Susan threw on a robe and joined him. He had set the patio table. The air was very warm, and the sky was clear. They sat down to eat.

"Ellen is expecting me in an hour and a half. She said I could ask George and Gracie some questions. Anything special you want me to find out?"

"I have no doubt about their capabilities," said Jake. "But since they are droids and so damn powerful, I don't want to have to physically tangle with them. They will always be entitled to state their opinions on any subject, but if they fly with us, they must obey our commands just as soldiers in the field. We will not use them if they can take independent action as they wish."

"I understand what you want," said Susan. "But how can I learn from talking to them what they might do under stress?"

"You will need Ellen's help. The two of you must set up some situation tests and subject the droids to stress. I can't think of any examples right now, but I'm sure you and Ellen can come up with something."

"Ellen said something about the first law of robotics. Do you have any idea what that means?"

"Not specifically, but I think it provides that a robot cannot physically harm its master. Ask Ellen what the units will do if you give them a command that conflicts with a command I give them. Maybe Gracie should report to you and George to me."

"I see where you are headed. Just let me explore a bit today with Ellen's help. We will record the session this morning so you can see it tonight."

"That's an excellent idea."

They were finished with the meal and sipping coffee. Jake said, "You go ahead and get dressed. I'll clean up the kitchen. You have to travel over to Orlando. I'm just going to the headquarters building to see Klaus—and I don't have an appointment."

They were ready to leave at about the same time, and Jake said, "Think I'll walk over. That race we ran yesterday told me that a little more exercise wouldn't hurt me. You go ahead and take my puma. That'll make your trip a little more fun."

"OK! Great! I was wondering when you were going to let me drive it. Using these GSA staff pumas is pretty boring." She headed for the garage and he for the front door. "See you this afternoon—not sure what time," said Susan. "Bye!"

"Bye!" said Jake. "If I'm not here when you return, I'll be at the club hitting some golf balls. Come over there."

Jake arrived at Renee's desk. "Is Director Stoll in?" he asked.

"He is, but he is on a call with Director Simonides. His appointment schedule is clear, so just take a seat over there, and I'm sure he can see you."

"Thanks," said Jake as he picked up a copy of the *Smithsonian* and took a seat.

Renee put down the mec and said to Jake, "You can go in now."

"Thanks," said Jake as he stepped into Klaus Stoll's office.

"Jake, good morning! Have a seat. How did your last lunar run go?"

"Routine, sir, as usual. That's partly why I came over to see you this morning."

"Oh? What's on your mind?

"I am bored with the Mars and moon missions, sir. As you know, I have considerable funds in the Chase Washington Bank, and I could opt to buy a business of some kind if I wanted to. Susan and I probably jumped the gun in having her quit her Supreme Court job and come down here. We really thought that Congress would buy into the Alpha Centauri mission at the bargain price you proposed to them."

"Jake, I know where you are coming from, and I empathize with you. As a matter of fact, Kosta and I were just discussing the situation as regard further exploration of space. With the current scope of activities, GSA is becoming a mining and station maintenance operation. That's certainly not what this agency was developed for."

"I have a wild proposal for you to consider, sir, which might just be a way to break this logjam."

"You do? Well, I will be very happy to hear any idea that might help."

"I would like to pay, out of my personal funds, *the cost of the first mission to Alpha Centauri Planet 5.*"

Klaus wasn't sure he had heard right. "*You* would pay 285 million credits out *of your pocket* to finance the mission? You *have* 285 million credits?"

"Yes and yes, but I would not do it without *considerations*," said Jake.

"Such as?" Klaus became cautious.

"I would want the *title* to the *Revelation*. What I am saying is that I would pay the cost of re-engining the *Revelation* plus all the other costs of sending a mission to explore the P5 planet. What I am asking the GSA to do is sign over the title to the ship, provide Susan and me with two additional crew members for the journey, and loan us the facilities to do our training." Jake paused as Klaus just stared at him. "And if I can continue to lay out the entire plan, we—that is, Susan and I—would like to continue to fly exploratory missions in our galaxy as far away from Earth as is feasible. In other words, we would become contractors to GSA and would attempt to discover valuable minerals on distant planets, which might be mined and refined for the benefit of GSA and the U.S. government. Our proposal goes further to state that any valuable ores or minerals we discover would be the property of GSA and the government *except for 10 percent*, which would be a finders' fee for us."

Klaus just looked at Jake for a few seconds. Then he said, "Beyond the Alpha Centauri's P5 mission, you would continue to fund other missions at your expense?"

"Not exactly, sir. We, of course, would be furnishing the ship and Susan and I as primary crew. We would ask that GSA cover operating expenses at least until we start getting some income return and finally, provide us with two crew members for each mission undertaken."

"An interesting proposal, Jake. We might not need to go to Congress for approval since the initial funding will be out of your pocket. The *Revelation* itself is an interesting situation. That ship was written off the books centuries ago and lined out of the GSA inventory. Legally, it *does not exist*. I will need to think about this idea for a few days and also discuss the plan with Director Simonides. It does seem possible to me that GSA could fund your exploratory missions out of our existing budget without going to Congress for additional funds." Klaus stood and shook hands with Jake. "Director Simonides and I, as well as the president, would like to get into the business of exploring the galaxy. You may just have found a *way to do it*! Have you given any thought to a contract of some sort?"

"Susan has already drafted one, sir—just for a start. I'm sure she will need to work with your lawyers to iron out the details."

"Good for Susan. I will call you in a few days."

At Mayo Biolab in Orlando

"Susan," said Ellen, "I would like you to meet George and Gracie. Susan held out her hand to shake with George.

"How do you do, George?" asked Susan. The android took her hand carefully but firmly.

"How do you do, Ms. Chen?" said the droid.

"I am fine." She then shook hands with Gracie. "And how are you, Gracie?"

"I am fine, Ms. Chen. Thank you for asking."

Speaking to both of them without wasting any time, Susan said, "How would you like to go on an exploratory mission to a distant planet?"

Gracie responded, glancing toward George. "I would like that very much, Ms. Chen. I have never been on a spaceship."

George did not respond to Susan's question.

Susan turned to George. "I understand that you are familiar with the design of the *Revelation*, George. Is that correct?"

"Yes, I know all about the ship, ma'am. I have stored in memory all of the circuits, systems, plans, specifications, and operating procedures."

Susan turned to Gracie. "I understand that you are an expert in medicine. Is that true?"

"Dr. Marks has trained me from her knowledge," said Gracie as she continued speaking in an unemotional tone. "I know a lot about the field of medicine. I have the details of thousands of medical procedures stored in my memory bank. I also know the detailed construction of the human body. I am familiar with the chemical makeup of most prescription drugs."

"Very good," said Susan, now addressing Ellen. "Can I try an experiment?"

"Sure, go ahead, as long as we don't hurt anyone or break up the laboratory," said Ellen with a smile.

Susan thought for a minute, then said, "George, strike me on the arm."

George calmly replied, "I am not allowed to harm a human being."

"What if you are with us as a crew member on the *Revelation* and we have landed on a distant planet. We discover that there are primitive humans residing there, and one of them rushes to attack me. If I yelled, 'George! Help me!' What would you do?"

"I would stop the primitive from harming you."

"Would you harm the being if necessary to save me?"

George responded without hesitation, "I would do whatever is necessary to keep you from harm, including injuring your attacker. We are programmed so that defending our *master* is of primary importance. That function takes precedence over the rule that *we do not harm humans*."

Ellen then said, "They are programmed to know their friends. If they go with you and Jake as your crew members, they will know you two as their *only friends*. Should you land on an inhabited planet, they would treat anyone but you and Jake as foes *unless* you told them differently. I think the main point here is that the droids will be programmed to do exactly as you or Jake tell them to do. If you give them a command different from that given by Jake, they will defer to Jake's command—there *has* to be a tiebreaker built in. Should Jake become incapacitated, they will promote you to first-position master."

"What about their physical capabilities, Ellen?" asked Susan. "How strong are they, and how fast are they?"

"They are stronger than ten normal men and five times faster to react and move than is a human."

"Impressive," said Susan. "Ellen, I am out of questions although I know Jake will ask some I failed to think of."

"Would you like to take them home tonight with you?"

"Could I do that?"

"Certainly. We can sign you out with both if you like. That way, Jake can ask all the questions he wants."

"Then I will take both of them. But first, I need to talk with you in private. Can we shut down the droids or have them leave the room?"

"Let's shut them down. First, you tell them to shut down as 'George, shut down now. Gracie, shut down now.'"

Both droids shut themselves down, and their heads nodded forward. "Now you open this access plate and turn the key." Ellen did that to both droids. "You may remove the key and keep it elsewhere if you like, but don't lose it, or you have lost the droid. If you don't turn them off by key, they will come back to full operational mode when you call their name. They hear and record sounds even though they are shut down unless they are turned off by key. We also have them programmed to activate on command. To awaken them, you must give them a command to activate. They will recognize your voice or Jake's voice."

"That will work," said Susan. "Will they take commands from others?"

"Not unless you give them specific instructions to respond to commands from others. At this time, they are both down by key. They will stay that way until you turn them back on with each key. Once they are turned on by key, you must call their name to activate them."

"Can we talk now?" said Susan.

"Yes, they cannot hear anything."

"OK. Here is what Jake is proposing to Klaus Stoll, probably as we are speaking." Susan laid out the plan to Ellen.

When she had finished, Ellen said, "I think the GSA will buy the plan. Both Stoll and Simonides would love to explore distant planets. I understand that they have had their eyes on P5 in the Alpha Centauri system for a long time and have gone to Congress more than once."

"Turned down each time?"

"Yes, and always with the same excuse: 'We will not give you funds for this project unless you can show a positive payback.' My question is, how can you show a positive payback if you can't determine what minerals are there? And you can't do that unless you send a team there to look for minerals."

"We have drawn up a contract for GSA to sign. The only open issue in my mind is that of the additional crew for us. If Jake believes these droids are the answer, maybe we can include them in the deal. Are they very expensive, Ellen?"

"They are, but these two are prototypes and not production models. Maybe we could work out a separate deal with you and Jake for you to use these for this one trip *without charge*. If they work out OK, we will no doubt go into production with them, and we could work out a good price for you on two. If I were you, I would include the droids in the deal. In turn for you and Jake re-engining the

Revelation, you get title to the ship *and two droids*. Not the two prototypes, but the first two production units."

"That's an excellent idea, Ellen. That way, we don't need to train two crew members for each trip. And better yet, the two droids give us significantly more knowledge and capability than two ordinary astronauts."

"That's the way I see it. Do you want to borrow them for tonight?"

"Don't see why not. We'll have them over for dinner. Oh, I forgot, they don't eat."

"All you must do to attend to their personal needs is provide them a 110 electrical outlet so they can recharge when necessary."

"How often is that?"

"Oh, about once a month with normal usage." Both women gazed at the droids for a time. Finally, Susan spoke, "Well, Jake's probably home now. Guess I'll be going—with my new friends.

"Why don't *you* turn them on?" said Ellen.

"OK," said Susan. "Here goes." She turned on their keys and said, "George! Gracie! Time to get going."

The droids came to life, and George said, "Where are we going, Ms. Chen?"

"You are both going to spend the night with Mr. Loneghan and me so he can get to know you."

Jake had finished his meeting with Klaus Stoll early and made his way to the golf course. After hitting a bucket of balls and some practice putts, he decided to play nine holes. He inquired about Mr. Hogan and Mr. Jones, but they were both on the course in other matches. So Jake began the nine alone. After only three holes, he gave it up for the day—his heart was elsewhere. He was anxious to see Susan and learn how her meetings with Ellen and the droids had gone.

Jake arrived at his condo, stashed his clubs and shoes in his locker in the basement garage, and took the elevator. He touched the pad on his front door and opened it. An unfamiliar droid face popped out at him from the door and said, "Yes? Can I help you?"

Jake about wet his pants and stepped back. "Who the hell are . . . ?" Then he heard Susan laughing. She had asked George to greet Jake just for a joke.

George stepped back and politely said, "Please come in, Mr. Loneghan. Ms. Chen directed me to greet you at the door."

Just at this moment, Susan came around the door and gave Jake a *big hug*. "Didn't mean to scare you, hon!" And she laughed again. "Meet George and Gracie! They are spending the night with us so you can get to know them."

Jake had stumbled through several emotions, beginning the moment he saw George, which looked a lot like Mr. D. and all the other Mister Series Androids.

First, he was ready to punch the face in the door; then he was ready to duck and run, remembering the awesome power of the droids. Then as he realized he had been had by Susan, he was ready to yell at her. Finally, he decided the whole incident was funny, and he laughed too. He hugged Susan and said, "You . . . are a wise guy. I almost lost it . . ."

Susan laughed again. "I'm sorry—I really shouldn't have surprised you like that."

"OK, you've had your fun," said Jake. "Now let's get serious about these droids. What do you think of making your new friends our third and fourth crew members?"

"I feel good about it. Just a minute." She turned to the two droids and said, "Sit over here, please. George, shut down. Gracie, shut down."

The two droids sat where Susan had indicated and immediately shut themselves down. Susan said, "They can still hear until I do *this*." She reached over and turned them off with their keys. "Now they cannot hear and cannot take commands until their key switches are turned back on."

"Okaaaay," said Jake, "I'm having a beer. Can I get something for you?"

"Please," said Susan. "Make it an iced tea, and I will tell you what all I learned about these units today. Ellen signed me out with them for the night. I'm supposed to bring them back tomorrow."

"Can we keep them until day after tomorrow? I would like to spend some time with them tomorrow at the *Revelation*. I want to be sure we are making the right decision with these guys. Can you call Ellen and get an extra day?" Jake headed for the fridge.

"Sure, I'll call now." She keyed in Ellen's number at home. "She may still be at her lab."

The mec chimed and continued to chime. Finally, David answered.

"David," said Susan, "is Ellen there? This is Susan."

"Not yet," said David. "Shall I have her call you when she gets in?"

"Can you just ask her if we can keep the two droids an extra day? If it's OK, then she need not call. If she has to have them back tomorrow, ask her to call and tell me how late we can bring them over, OK?"

"Will do. Say, before you go, is Jake there?"

"He's right here." She handed the mec to Jake.

"Hi, David, what's up?" said Jake.

"Jake! Anything new on your proposed mission?"

"Not yet. But I just made a new proposal to Klaus today that I'm hoping will sell."

"Good. The reason I wanted to talk to you is this. We have a new communications probe we are hoping will work with deep space missions."

"Communications probe?"

"Right! We have demonstrated this thing with a model in the lab, and it works! Here's what it will do. Let's say you are on a distant planet, and for some reason, you must get a message to Mission Control here at KSC. Let's say you have some kind of problem and need support sent to you from Earth. With this probe, you can send us a message, and it will return to Earth at ten times light-speed. If you were five light-years from Earth, the message would travel back in six months."

"I hope our problem isn't urgent—six months is a long time to wait for help."

"Not if you crash-land and are surviving, but you have no way to return to Earth," said David, showing a twinge of hurt feelings.

"I see what you mean," said Jake. "Under circumstances where we are crippled and cannot repair the ship, this probe gives us a lifeline."

"Exactly, Jake. We would plan to install a couple of these on the *Revelation* if it's OK with you."

"Great idea, David. Sorry I was too dumb to understand the potential at first."

"No problem. I've been working on this and thinking about it for months. You just heard about it. Say, Ellen is just coming in! Hold the mec, Jake."

David discussed the droids with Ellen and came back on.

"You can keep the droids another day. Try to bring them in by 4:30 PM."

"Thanks, David. And thanks for the probes."

"No problem. Talk with you later. Keep me advised on the ACP5 progress."

"Will do. Good night." Jake closed the mec and turned to Susan. "Let's fix some chow, and then we'll compare notes on our meetings of today."

"Here," she said, "dig into this cheese dip while I throw on a couple of steaks."

Susan and Jake were enjoying their meal while the droids sat quiet and deactivated on the couch. They had decided that Jake would relate his meeting with Klaus Stoll first.

"Hon, I had a good meeting with Director Stoll. I got the sense that he would push for our plan. You realize that both he and Director Simonides are very much in favor of exploration and have been for some time."

"You mentioned that, but so far, it doesn't seem to be helping us."

"Well, this time, something new surfaced. Klaus made the statement that GSA might not even have to get congressional approval to enter into the arrangement we are proposing."

"Why not? GSA will still be spending money on these missions—as we discussed."

"Klaus said that the *Revelation* had been *written off the books* centuries ago when GSA was still NASA. So if we pay for the re-engining, he seemed to think they could turn over the title of the ship to us as we asked. Further, the mission-support costs will be minimal for each trip subsequent to the Alpha Centauri mission, and they can take it out of their operations budget without requesting additional funds from Congress."

"That does sound encouraging. Did you mention that we have drafted a baseline contract?"

"Yes, and I told him that you are ready to sit down with GSA lawyers and work out the details. He has to go over the plan with Simonides, and he promised to get back to me in the next few days."

They had now finished with the dinner and were taking things back to the kitchen.

"Jake, this sounds very good. I am getting excited again that we can really get out into space!"

"Me too, Sue. Now tell me about your day with Ellen."

"Well, Ellen is convinced that George and Gracie will be ideal crew members for us for our missions. She answered all my questions regarding loyalty and discipline and pretty well convinced me that the droids would behave exactly like we need them to."

"Would they take commands from either of us?"

"Yes. Let me play the disc I made of the meeting we had with the droids and our questions and their answers." Susan played the recording, displaying it on the viewscreen for Jake. Jake ran it a second time.

"I think these two would be excellent crew choices for us," said Jake. "I wonder if there is a chance that GSA would include the title to two of these droids—just like George and Gracie—with the ship, all as one package. Did Ellen say how expensive it would be to buy them from Mayo if we have to?"

"She didn't, but she implied that they are *quite* expensive."

"Well, it doesn't matter . . . I think we need the two droids, and if I have to buy them, I will. My balance at Chase is now something over three billion credits *again*, and we are only using 285 million to re-engine the ship. The droids can't be too expensive."

Jake continued, "What about their *programs*? Can we make a specialized input to their programs if we want, and is there a simplified way we can examine the programs already installed?"

"Can't answer that. We'll have to talk more with Ellen. You know what? Let's fire up the droids and see what they can tell us . . ."

"Good idea. Ellen has been telling us that these models are more human. Guess that could be good or bad. Turn them on and let's talk with them for a while."

Ellen turned the keys on both George and Gracie and said, "George, this is Susan. And, Gracie, this is Susan."

Both droids activated and said almost simultaneously, "Hello, Ms. Chen. Hello, Mr. Loneghan."

"George," said Jake, "I know you are very smart, and Dr. Marks tells us that you know all about the *Revelation* light-speed spaceship. I'd like to ask you some questions about the ship."

"Fine, sir, I will try to answer the questions," said George.

"Do you want some more coffee, Jake?" said Susan as she cleaned up the kitchen. From where she was standing, she could hear all that was said in the living room.

"I'm OK," said Jake and began his questioning of both the droids.

After about fifteen minutes, Jake was impressed, both with their knowledge and their courteous, obedient demeanors. Then he said to them, "Susan and I are planning on leaving soon on a mission to the Alpha Centauri system of the galaxy. Do either of you know where that is?"

Gracie looked over at George as if to say "Are you going to answer?"

George responded, "We have been programmed with a basic knowledge of the sun and its planets. We know that the solar system is one system in an immense galaxy. That is all we know about space."

Jake looked at Susan. "Guess we will need to add to that knowledge before we launch."

"Ellen showed me how to enter data into their drives," said Susan. "They each have a million-gigabyte storage capacity. We can get a disc from the library and quickly make them knowledgeable on any subject."

"OK," said Jake to Susan, "I am 99 percent convinced. Let's see how they behave at the ship tomorrow. Now let's see how *they* feel about joining us on the mission." He turned again to the two droids and said, "We plan to make you two crew members on the *Revelation* ship. You will be going with us on a mission to Alpha Centauri. How does that sound to you?"

George responded, "Do we have any other options? I have no problem with joining your crew unless there is something that might take better advantage of our abilities."

Jake was stunned, and Susan dropped a coffee cup. Jake just looked at the two droids sitting across from him. He turned to Susan and said, "I don't think I have ever heard that kind of statement from an android before. Have you?"

Susan was still frozen in place and had not even picked up the pieces of the coffee cup. Finally, she said, "That was a human comment if I've ever heard one."

George said, "Did I say something wrong, sir?"

"No," said Jake. "But we will explain exactly what our mission will be and what it might entail so you and Gracie can be sure it is something you really want to do."

Jake went into the kitchen and put his arm around Susan. He whispered with a sarcastic smile, "Maybe Mr. D. and Mr. K. would be better choices."

48

"Director Simonides is on for you, sir," said Renee to Director Stoll.

"Sir! How are you this morning?" said Klaus.

"Fine, Klaus. I have several items for you. But first, I am concerned about that Maria Rodriguez . . . Has anything changed? Do you know any more regarding her whereabouts and of the location of the UMU time machine?"

"Nothing, sir. We are still convinced that she arrived at the time and place she intended on the day she departed the twenty-first century and in Enrico Valdez's garage."

"I was certain that she would cooperate as we asked and send the time device back to us, weren't you?"

"Yes, I was, sir. And she *did place the brooch under the stone*—we have proof of that. It is my feeling that someone—probably the Valdez gentleman—persuaded her *not to send the unit back immediately*. I'm sure he was quite curious about the whole thing. Indeed, it would have been difficult for *anyone* in the twenty-first century to believe Maria's story."

"Thinking about the situation, Klaus, had I been in Enrico's shoes, I would have certainly wanted to learn more about the transparent booth Maria claimed to have *traveled back thirteen centuries in*."

"Perhaps Valdez reasoned that since we wouldn't be looking for the UMU for thirteen centuries, what would be the difference in keeping the unit a while and studying it? He probably convinced Maria that they could keep it to study for a few weeks, or more, and then send it on back to us to arrive at the exact time and place where we expected it."

"But if that were the case, Klaus, and he eventually sent the unit back, wouldn't it have arrived when we expected it? Maria certainly had the information—that is, the time she left us—recorded in the control console of the UMU . . ."

"But, sir, let's look at another aspect of time travel. Maria left us over a month ago. Regardless of how many centuries she traversed, by *our timekeeping*, she has only been back in the twenty-first century for the *exact same duration of time since she left us*. If you agree with me on that logic, this means that Enrico Valdez has only had the UMU in his possession for a little over a month, twenty-first-century time. Continuing this logic, he may, at some point in time, allow Maria to send the unit back to us—to arrive here on the day Maria left, but some ten minutes later than when she departed."

"But if that were true, Klaus, since that time has now past, why don't we have the machine back?"

"Because they, in the time of the twenty-first century, have *not yet sent it back*! Remember the trip Dr. Stessel took back one week in time? Before he went back to the past, neither David nor Dr. Ottinger had any memory of being visited by Dr. Stessel and the UMU the week earlier. Yet the week later in the lab, they suddenly were magically given a memory of the incident, obviously imparted to them at just the time Dr. Stessel arrived in the lab the week before."

"That's right! I *do remember that now*! So are you saying that Enrico and Maria—by their present accounting of time—still have the UMU? And when they do send it back—if they do—we will then have the unit and *remember that* we got it back when it actually arrived at the time it was supposed to?"

"That is *exactly what I am saying*. We now believe time travel to be possible. *We have demonstrated it*—first with a house plant, then with a mouse, then with Dr. Stessel, and now with Maria. The only way time travel can be possible is that an infinite number of times *coexist* on the Earth and on Mars and, indeed, EVERYWHERE in the universe!

"Visualize an infinite number of parallel time tracks. One track is in the year 3340, and another track is in the year 2025. The UMU enables a person to *jump* from one track to another—in a different *place* at a different *time*. It helps me if I think of time as a video or audio disc. The disc has data on parallel tracks. With the touch of a button, we can move from one track to another. As with a recorded movie, the tracks are sequential in time, and we can jump from one scene in the movie to an earlier or later scene in the movie. The UMU allows us to move from one track on the universal time 'disc' to another track—from one time to another—in the past or the future."

"Klaus, I am sorry, but thinking about this gives me a headache . . . Suppose Enrico and Maria wait five years, then send the UMU back to the day Maria left us to return to the twenty-first century—are you saying that everything that has happened to you and me and others over that five years would have changed in some way and that our memories of those five years would all be changed?"

"That is my theory, sir. I see no other way."

"I need some time—a lot of time—to think about all this. Meanwhile, let's talk about another subject, the proposal Jake Loneghan is making to GSA. I *like* Jake's proposal for several reasons. One, the mission to P5 will be carried out *under the GSA banner*, even though we are making a special arrangement with Jake and Susan. What intrigues me is that if they find any valuable minerals in quantities that warrant our mining them, this will return to GSA and the U.S. *many times any costs that we will incur* in supporting the mission. If they find a habitable planet that will support human life, just think what that will mean to

Earth! We could colonize the planet and perhaps greatly relieve the overcrowding we now suffer here on this planet."

"And, sir, if I might add," said Klaus, "To pull this off without additional funds from Congress will be an enormous feather in our cap."

"Exactly! And here is another large plus. We have no use for the *Revelation* ship as it sits. It simply does not have the lifting power and payload capacity we need to support schedules we have set out for our lunar, Mars, and space station activities. With Loneghan paying for the re-engine project, that ship now becomes a viable craft for not only the Alpha Centauri trip, but others to follow. Although"—he paused—"it *legally* will be Loneghan's ship."

"Well, Jake made it quite clear that he *must have the title* before he will lay out his own funds."

"And we can't blame him for that. We could never get approval to re-engine the ship at GSA expense."

"Let's talk about the possibility of a mission failure . . . Although unpleasant, it's something we must address."

"You are absolutely right, Klaus. A loss of the ship and the crew would of course be the worst case. In that event, I see it this way. The ship is already off our books, so no monetary loss there. Jake and Susan would be classified as independent contractors, so no loss to GSA there. The only loss to GSA would be the two crew members that we supply for each mission and, of course, operating funds for each mission."

"But the operating costs will be spent only as each mission is undertaken."

"Correct. And that is a minor consideration. Comparing the loss of the *Revelation* on one of these missions to the loss of one of our eight 10xL ships, the loss would be insignificant—Don't you agree?"

"I do, sir. But I have been thinking of a way to minimize the loss even further."

"Really? How?"

"David Marks has advised me that his wife—whom you know, Dr. Ellen Marks—is working for Mayo Biolab Products, and they have developed an advanced android. Dr. Marks now has two prototypes—a male and a female."

"*Functional* as male and female?"

"No. As I understand the situation, neither of the units have any sexual function, but the male *thinks* more like a man, and the female thinks more like a woman. David also tells me that the two droids are designed with spaceship crew member requirements in mind."

"Very interesting . . . Just what does that entail exactly?"

"The male droid has an engineering, technically orientated brain. For example, all of the electrical and systems functions of a ship can be stored in the droid's memory. And since it is a fully functioning unit, the droid can modify and repair the craft if that should be needed. The unit could also pilot the spacecraft if that should become necessary."

"And the female?"

"She, or it, is designed to be a doctor. With a full, extensive knowledge of medicine."

"Fascinating!"

"And there is one more point. These droids are supposed to think more like humans than the Mister Series units we are all using now."

"Is this supposed to be good?"

"Well, as you know, there are two schools of thought on that issue. These two prototypes—George and Gracie is what they are being called—are built with some human-reasoning qualities and some emotional feelings. You would have to say that Mayo—and, indeed, we and others—are keen to see how these first two androids perform."

"Then, is it a good idea to use them as crew for Jake and Susan if they are experimental in a sense?"

"If they are to use droids as crew, the only other choice they now have is to use two of the Mister Series, which are not really designed to perform as spaceship crew members."

The director thought for a few moments and then said, "What is your view on this, Klaus? Let's have it straight!"

Klaus paused to choose his words carefully.

"From the standpoint of the GSA, it would be best for us to supply the droids as crew rather than two of our astronaut corps. From Jake and Susan's standpoint, I would take the same position. The droids are obedient, powerful, and extremely knowledgeable. Depending on the success of the android-development program at Mayo, I think we may be on the verge of using droids as the *only crew members for all of our flights*. Think of the advantages, sir. Little training required, no food or medical supplies needed, and no families left behind to be lonely or to be devastated if a crew member is lost in space."

Kosta thought a moment and said, "I agree with you. Let's offer Jake the droids for his crew. How much cost will this add to the program?"

"That is the most unbelievable part of this whole scheme, sir. Mayo will *loan* them to us *at no charge* for this one mission."

"Incredible! They must want *something* in return."

"Just the return of the droids. The units will be programmed to record every sound and every action experienced on the mission, video and audio. They want the units back but will of course share all the information with us."

"Klaus, I am most impressed with your work in bringing us to this point. Have our attorneys work out an agreement with Jake and Susan, and let's get the show on the road! GSA is finally going to explore the galaxy. Congress will be sorry they have been so shortsighted up to now."

"I hope and I trust that the program will be successful, sir. We will start work on a contractual agreement immediately."

"Keep me advised, Klaus. Good work."

"Thank you, sir," said Klaus as he cradled his mec.

Jake and Susan had a leisurely breakfast and decided they would both take George and Gracie to see the *Revelation*. The two droids were still on the couch with their keys in the 'off' position from the night before. There was just something that bothered Jake about George and Gracie—he just couldn't put his finger on it. Susan didn't have the same problem. She was convinced that the two droids would make excellent crew members for their mission to Alpha Centauri.

"Well," said Jake, "let's turn them on and take a run over to the ship." As he spoke, Susan turned on each of the droid's keys.

Susan said, "George and Gracie, it is Susan. Good morning."

Both the droids sat upright and responded together, "Good morning, Ms. Chen. Good morning, Mr. Loneghan."

"We are going over and introduce you both to the *Revelation* ship. You haven't seen it before, have you?"

Gracie looked at George, and he said, "We have never seen the ship, Mr. Loneghan, although we have all the technical data concerning the ship stored in memory."

"Fine," said Jake. "Let's all go to the garage now. We'll take my puma over to the hangar."

The four took seats in Jake's puma and headed for the *Revelation*.

Susan said, "Are either of you qualified as pilots? Have you received any instruction or program information on operating the *Revelation*?"

"Or operating any puma or aircraft or spacecraft?" said Jake.

This time, Gracie answered, "We are both proficient in operating pumas, sir, but have not been specifically trained in aircraft or spacecraft."

Susan said, "Is spacecraft operation—piloting—something that can simply be stored into your data banks, or must you receive instruction in flying as would a human?"

George responded, "We have not been asked that question, but everything we have learned so far has simply been loaded into our memories—that is, except for operating pumas and household appliances. We have been trained physically to operate pumas and household appliances, sir."

Jake looked at Susan as they were arriving at the hangar. Neither was too excited about what they were hearing.

"We need to talk with Ellen some more," said Susan. "I don't think we are getting the information you are asking for."

"I agree," said Jake. "I think I will try something now that we are at the ship."

They went into the hangar and looked up at the *Revelation*. Jake said, "George, pretend that Susan and I are visitors to the spaceflight center, and you are a tour guide for the facility. Tell me about the ship that we are looking at."

"Fine, sir, I can do that. This ship is called the *Revelation*. It was built by Boeing Aircraft Company between 2020 and 2024 and is powered by two General Electric and Pratt & Whitney hyperdrive engines. The ship is capable of cruising up to light-speed. It is manufactured of various materials but primarily titanium, the metal with the strongest strength-to-weight ratio used for aircraft and spacecraft manufacture in the early twenty-first century . . ."

Jake let George continue for some time, and he and Susan became convinced that George knew the minute details about the *Revelation*. They were still concerned about the androids' ability to operate and pilot the spacecraft, however.

Just then, David saw the group and came over.

"George, Gracie, shut down," said Jake. They immediately shut down. Jake reached over and turned off their power keys.

"Hi, Dave," said Jake.

"Hi, Dave," said Susan.

David returned the greetings.

"We are not real clear on what we can expect from these droids," said Jake. "Can you help us out on that, or do we need to talk more with Ellen?"

"What do you mean?" said David.

"Well," said Susan, "we were under the impression that these droids could do about anything at all, and now we are not so sure."

"What have you asked them to do?" said David.

"Nothing really," said Jake. "But they are telling us that the only physical skills they have been specifically trained in is how to drive a puma and how to operate household appliances."

"Oh, I think they can do a lot more than *that*," said Dave. "I think they have all sorts of skills built into their positronic brains. Let's try them on some things, shall we?"

"Fine with us," said Jake. "What do you have in mind?"

"Well," said Dave, "let's find out if they can fly a large HD-powered spacecraft. We have the SC38 simulators you, Jake, have been training on right over in the next building. Let's just take them over there and put them into the pilot's seats and see what they can do."

"Great idea, Dave! Dunno why I didn't think of that," said Jake.

"I'd like to take a spin in that simulator too." said Susan.

Jake said, "Dave, you need to keep working on plans for the re-engining of the *Revelation*. We can take them over to the SC38 and watch them perform. Thanks for the idea."

"Fine," said David. "Let me know if you have difficulties."

Jake and Susan took the droids to the simulator building next door. As they entered, a man was performing electronics checks on one of the simulators.

"Chuck! What's happ'nin' man? Any training going on in here today?" Jake spoke to the supervisor of simulator training.

"Just one group today, Jake, using one of the SC38s. Kind of a slow day."

"Chuck, this is Susan Chen, one of the *Revelation* pilots. And these droids are George and Gracie. This is Chuck Townsend, everyone. Chuck supervises simulator training for GSA.

"Chuck, you have any problem with us using the other SC38 for a few minutes? We want to see how these two droids handle themselves as pilots."

"No problem, Jake. Just be sure you shut 'er down when you're done."

"OK, guys, let's hop in and have a go," said Jake.

George and Gracie entered the simulator flight deck, followed by Susan and Jake.

"George, you take the captain's chair, and I will take the right seat. Sue, why don't you take the observer seat here. And, Gracie, you take the engineer's chair."

All strapped themselves in, and Jake said, "OK, George, the power's on. And all instruments are in the green. I've just talked to the tower, and you are cleared for operation. I would like you to start engines. And when you are ready, take off, climb to a two-hundred-mile orbit, and insert. Then roll 'er over and advise me that we are in orbit. Can you handle that?"

"I have never done that, sir, but the procedures have been stored in my memory bank."

"Fine," said Jake. "You may proceed."

George started engines and brought them up to idle power. He commented to Jake and to Gracie, "Are all instruments in the green for takeoff?"

Jake responded, "All green."

"All in the green," said Gracie

"Here we go," said George, showing no emotions.

George applied takeoff power and appropriate joystick pressures as the simulator lifted off in a vertical takeoff and climb. The nose lifted smoothly, and the ship accelerated through five thousand . . . ten thousand . . . fifteen thousand miles per hour. Finally, the SC38 was nearing the two-hundred-mile orbit. George pulled back on the stick and inserted the ship into orbit exactly on speed and exactly at two hundred miles' altitude.

George commented, "Orbit achieved, now rolling 180 degrees."

With that, George rolled the simulator so that the bottom of the ship now (in theory) faced Earth. The SC38 was perfectly on speed and on point. George had reduced power to orbit idle. The digital image of the Earth displayed in the forward windscreen was amazingly realistic.

"Well," said Susan, "I guess that answers *that* question."

"Very well done, George," said Jake. "Engage the artificial gravity—not needed, of course, in the simulator."

George complied with Jake's instruction.

"Now," said Jake, "George, you and Gracie swap seats. We'll let Gracie take us out of orbit and in for a vertical landing. Is that OK with you, Gracie?"

"Fine, sir," said Gracie as she got up to exchange seats with George.

Now with Gracie in the left seat, Jake said, "Any time you are ready, Gracie, take us home."

With the same smooth control inputs as George, Gracie reentered the atmosphere, slowed to approach speed, intersected the glide slope, and arrived at the hover point three hundred feet above the landing point. Jake called out the height above the surface in feet as Gracie smoothly—without a ripple—set the simulator down perfectly with a vertical descent landing.

Jake said, "Congratulations, George and Gracie! You are excellent pilots. Sue, you want to have a run with it?"

"I am in awe!" said Susan. "I didn't realize these guys had this kind of skill. At the risk of being embarrassed, I would like to take the ship for a cycle."

"Fine," said Jake. "Gracie, swap seats with Susan."

Susan took the left seat. "Jake, I am amazed at how similar this cockpit is to the *Revelation* flight deck. I would have expected things to be quite different *thirteen centuries* later, wouldn't you?"

"I had the same reaction, Sue, when I first sat in these ships they fly today. But when you think about it, flying is still pretty much the same. Sure, the top speed today—achievable with the SC38—is ten times light-speed, and the *Revelation* only does light-speed. But in orbit and on approach and landing, everything is still the same. The presentation of the instrument package is different, and the controls themselves are somewhat different, but all the same functions are still there. Fire it up and take us for a spin. The simulator designers have really done a good job on this one—of matching the actual SC38 characteristics."

Susan called, "Starting engines." She checked all instrumentation and called, "Are we clear for takeoff?" With affirmative responses all around, Susan applied the necessary pressures, causing the SC38 to simulate vertical liftoff and climb out. She operated the simulator equally as well as the two droids, taking it into orbit and returning it to base for a perfect touchdown.

After landing, Jake cracked, "OK, I guess you are qualified to go to Alpha Centauri . . ."

Susan gave Jake a look that implied, *I'm just as good as you are, buster.*

George commented, "Very nice flying, Miss Chen."

Jake, Susan, and the droids arrived in the basement garage; and Mr. W. hurried right over to them. "Director Stoll has been trying to reach you, Mr. Loneghan, for some time. He said it's urgent and would like for you to call him right away."

"Thanks Mr. W.," said Jake and then to Susan, "Let's head for the condo and call him from there. I hope he has some good news."

The four grabbed the elevator and headed up.

"I didn't realize he would be trying to reach me so soon," said Jake. "Guess we should have taken an AMec with us this morning."

"Well, responded Susan, "we have been patiently waiting for GSA and the government to get off the dime and let us explore the galaxy. Won't hurt 'His Highness' to wait on us a few hours." said Susan.

Back in their unit, Jake placed the call, "Renee, this is Jake Loneghan. Has he been trying to reach me?"

"He certainly has. He's had me calling you every fifteen minutes. Hold on. I'll tell him I've got you."

"Jake! Where the devil have you and Susan been? I've been trying to reach you for about *three hours*."

"I am very sorry, sir. I do apologize, but we were working with the simulator and neither of us thought to take our mecs along. I do apologize."

"Well, I am *most annoyed*. Promise me that you will keep your mec with you and turned on as long as you are working for us."

"I will certainly do that, sir."

Klaus hesitated, trying to calm himself and finally said, "Are you and Susan ready for Alpha Centauri?"

"Sir! You mean . . . you mean *you got approval for our mission?*"

Klaus paused again—overly excited himself. He had forgotten his annoyance with Jake. "Director Simonides and I decided to go with your plan. What's more, we think the two droids Dr. Marks has will be ideal for you and Susan as additional crew. Have Susan get with our lawyers immediately, and let's draw up the agreement. As soon as that's done, you will *need to transfer funds to our*

GSA account so we can proceed with the engine procurement. Let me have a word with Susan, please."

Jake was already hugging Susan and said to her, "Our plan is approved! We are going into business as *galaxy explorers*. He wants to talk to you."

Susan stopped screaming and jumping up and down and calmly took the mec. "Susan here, Director Stoll. Jake says you have wonderful news . . ."

"Your proposal has been approved, short of having a formal document. Congratulations, Susan. How soon can you get with Jason Welch our lead attorney?"

"First thing in the morning will be fine with me. His office is down from yours, isn't it?"

"Yes, I'm in suite 1000, and he is 1003. I will tell him you will be up at 8:00 AM, or is that too early?"

"Eight is fine, sir. I have a draft as you know. I really don't think it will take long for us to bang this out."

"Good, Susan. Now please put Jake back on." She gave Jake the mec.

"Jake here, sir."

"Jake, Kosta Simonides is speaking with Pratt & Whitney today, trying to squeeze them for the best possible price for the two 10xL engines. Can you call your bank and transfer funds to cover a down payment of least one hundred million credits?"

"I can, sir, and I will . . . but the funds are earning interest daily, and I prefer to have *a signed agreement* first. You know how lawyers can drag things out." He eyed Susan with a devilish grin as he said this, and her hands went to her hips.

"Yes, I see your point, Jake. Director Simonides hopes to have a deal wrapped up with John Kinch, their top deal maker by tonight. I doubt if they will initiate the shipping sequence without at least a third of the price in their account."

"As soon as my lovely partner shows me a signed contract, the credits will be transferred to a GSA account. By the way, why don't you give me the account number you want it deposited to. That will save a delay when Susan hands me the contract to sign."

"Of course. Here is the number." Klaus read Jake the number, and Jake wrote it down.

"Anything else right now?"

"Guess not . . . Again, congratulations! By the way, I called Ellen Marks before I reached you, and she is having some papers drawn up re the droids. You can discuss the details of the agreement with Mayo—with Dr. Marks if you like."

"We will call her right away. And thanks so much Director Stoll for your help in this. Susan and I will begin celebrating momentarily."

"Good-bye, Jake. Will talk to you soon. Tell Susan I'll see her tomorrow morning."

"This calls for a *party*!" cried Jake as he whirled Susan around with her feet off the floor. "Let's see if Ellen and David can join us tonight for a celebration."

"I'll call Ellen right now!" said Susan as she grabbed the mec.

"Ellen!" shouted Susan. "Our mission to Alpha Centauri has been approved! Yes! We just learned, and we want you and David to join us in a celebration. You can? Great! Why don't you two come here for a drink—then we can go to the club for dinner. Tonight is two-for-one steak and lobster night. OK? Great! See you guys about seven. I'll make the reservations for eight."

After the dinner and celebrating, the Marks went back to Jake's for a nightcap. Since George and Gracie were still at Jake's, Ellen elected to take them with her and David, and on into her lab the next morning. They decided that this was not only a good idea, saving Jake a trip over to Orlando, but George could serve as the *designated driver*. After the long evening of merrymaking, the presence of George and Gracie at Jake's place was quite opportune.

49

The next morning, Susan did not disappoint Klaus. She was in Atty. Jason Welch's office at 8:00 AM sharp. Jake had started to go with Susan but decided that Susan knew exactly what they wanted in the agreement, so he didn't need to be there. Besides, he wanted to see the plans that David had already roughed out to install the new engines in the *Revelation*. So Jake had headed for David's lab when Susan left for the headquarters building.

The receptionist immediately notified Mr. Welch that Ms. Chen had arrived, and he rushed out to greet her. Jason had another lawyer with him, a Mr. Barclay, who had prepared similar agreements for GSA in the past.

Susan had prepared extra copies and handed one each to the two men. She began the tedious task of taking them through each condition.

"In summary, gentlemen," said Susan after about forty-five minutes, "the main conditions Commander Loneghan and I are interested in are the following:

1. We want clear title to the *Revelation*—it is to be in the name of *Revelation* Inc.
2. GSA will furnish us with the two Series M2 android prototypes, George and Gracie, to use for the first mission to Alpha Centauri.
3. GSA will purchase from Mayo Biolab Products two production androids with the same positronic brain capabilities as George and Gracie and will transfer title to these units to us—again, in the name of *Revelation*, Inc.
4. GSA will provide the support required for the missions we undertake in the form of fuel, equipment, tools, provisions, maintenance and repair services, and other items to be identified and named later.
5. *Revelation* Inc. will also receive 10 percent of the net value after refining and marketing of any and all minerals and ores we discover on planets, satellite moons of planets, or asteroids. GSA will cover all costs of mining and refining such materials."

Susan continued, "Those are our primary provisions, gentlemen. Would you like me to state the things that you expect from *Revelation* Inc., or would *you* prefer to itemize those?"

"I will cover those, Ms. Chen, thank you," said Mr. Welch. "Here are the principal provisions:

1. *Revelation* Inc. will fund the full cost of the engines.
2. *Revelation* Inc. will also pay the full cost of installing the engines on the spacecraft.
3. *Revelation* will pay other initial support costs of launching the first mission. We understand that this amounts primarily to food and supplies provisions since the original equipment, tools, etc., for the mission that brought you to the thirty-fourth century are still in the ship and satisfactory for use.
4. Should you lose an android or should one be destroyed, you will replace that unit out of *Revelation* Inc. funds.
5. At such time when your arrangement with GSA becomes profitable for *Revelation* Inc. your corporation will pay its own mission expenses."

Jason continued, "Those are our primary provisions. We have, this morning, endeavored to get all of your items and those of ours into this document. I would like to compliment you, Ms. Chen, for the excellent basic document you came to us with this morning. Your prior work made our joint effort relatively simple. If you can wait a few minutes, I will have our changes that were made today entered into the document and three copies run so that we may all review the work once more after we close this meeting."

"When will you be ready for the principals to sign the document?" said Susan.

"What if we set the signing for ten thirty in the morning? We can get together here at eight just to be sure there are no additional items that must be discussed or changed. Then Mr. Loneghan and Director Stoll can plan to come in at ten thirty, allowing us to execute the document at that time."

"Sounds like a plan." said Susan. "I will wait now for the newly typed copies. As a matter of fact, I think I will visit Director Stoll while the copies are being prepared. Would you mind having someone bring my copy to his office?"

"I will bring it there myself," said Jason. "The director will want to question me anyway. See you there in about twenty minutes."

Jake was working with David in his office/lab, going over the prints for the new installation.

"Dave," said Jake, "it doesn't look like you are adding any beef to the structure to take care of these new power plants."

"We really aren't, Jake. Remember? I mentioned to you that we built the airframe initially anticipating higher thrust engines and also with a 20 percent safety factor. The mounts and the airframe are at least 37 percent stronger than the original engines required. These new engines have a slightly different mounting scheme, hence these changes you see here—simply to accommodate the mounts on these new engines. The strength of the system is quite adequate.

"The other changes are hydromechanical, electrical, and digital—and software changes. The information coming to the flight deck instrumentation is in a different format from data transmitted to and from the original engines. These specs and drawings over here delineate those changes that must be made."

"Tell me again, David, just how these engines will be able to push the *Revelation* to ten times light-speed when the old engines could not."

"Jake, I'm not a power plant engineer, but I'll tell you what I understand. As you may remember from our *Revelation* training, hyperdrive engines were invented in 2015 by research scientists at Pratt & Whitney and General Electric working together. It took them several years to design and build operational engines for use on a spacecraft. The HD engine is able to generate extremely powerful thrust forces that *act at a distance*. That is, unlike conventional jet engines and rocket engines, the HD engine does not need to *throw matter overboard* to create a propulsive force. The engine creates both attractive and repulsive forces that act on other matter in the universe—such as the Earth, the moon, the sun, or other bodies in space. The forces created by the HD engine are akin to the forces of gravity, but much more powerful, which is how they can accelerate the *Revelation* and other ships to light-speed *and now beyond*.

"When the original HD engines were built, the force or thrust needed to push a ship to the speed of light was so immense that the engine companies didn't try to make the engines more powerful. *No one believed that light-speed could be exceeded.*

"But then in the twenty-third century, two Swiss scientists were working with the CERN particle collider in Geneva. They discovered, quite by accident, that with just an increase of 17 percent above the power required to achieve light-speed, a particle could be pushed *past* light—speed all the way to *ten times light-speed*!"

"But what about Einstein's law?" protested Jake.

"What is that old saying? Laws are made to be broken." said Dave. "Looks like Einstein was wrong on this one. He was right about how time relates to light-speed, however. At light-speed and beyond, *time stands still*. So you and Susan will not age at all during your travel to and from Alpha Centauri."

"Anyway," continued David, "when this discovery was made, needless to say, Pratt and GE, working together, got busy and built a prototype engine that did in fact propel an unmanned test probe to *ten times the speed of light*.

"That is where we are today—at ten times light with advanced hyperdrive engines."

"Is 10xL going to be the ultimate limit, David?" said Jake.

"Yes, with the HD engines—they just can't take that technology any further. *However*, now the propulsion scientists believe they have discovered yet another type of engine that will be able to propel spaceships at *one thousand times the speed of light*. They refer to these new engines as HPA engines. And I can't begin to tell you how they work.

"Does this give you a better feel for what's happening with propulsion?"

"I think I understand, Dave. But I have a few more questions."

"Shoot. I'll do my best to give you answers."

"Antigravity devices, pumas, and other units and vehicles that lift off vertically from the ground. Is this the same type HD engine?"

"Yes, and the principle is the same. Pumas, other vehicles, and fighter spacecraft just have smaller versions of the engines installed in the *Revelation*, both the old and the new engines."

"Thanks, David," said Jake. "I need to read more about all this, but you have really helped. Now if I can switch gears. How long is the modification likely to take?"

"About three weeks. Did you know we have moved the *Revelation*?"

"Moved it? To where?"

"To a hangar that has all the equipment we need to accomplish the mods. It is now in hangar 16. We can go see it if you like."

"Let me call Susan and see how her session is going with the lawyers."

Jake called Susan.

"Susan here . . . Hi, Jake! How's it going? We are finished with edits, and all our conditions are still in the contract."

"Wow, Sue! Good work! Did they give you a battle?"

"Not really. We have set a signing session for ten thirty in the morning. I have a copy in my hand, and I am on the way to your place. How's your session going?"

"Good, but I just taking up David's valuable time. The *Revelation* has already been moved to a mod hangar. David is going to let me take a peek at it. Then I'll head home. See you there!"

"Good. See ya!"

David and Jake walked over to hangar 16 and entered. There she was. Jake had a special fondness for the *Revelation*. He felt that the ship itself must be proud that it was getting new engines and a new role with GSA. The huge spacecraft was off the floor on jacks so they could cycle and inspect the gear. Most of the access panels in the engine installation area had been opened or removed. Otherwise, nothing special was going on.

"I hear they are just waiting for your signature, and they are going to put another dozen men to work in here." said David.

"When will you have the mod drawings ready for them to start?"

"Would have had them today, but you dropped in . . ." David gave Jake a big grin, and Jake felt the needle. "A few other items I need to mention, Jake, regarding the mods to the *Revelation*. You know about the communications probes—we are installing two of those. Hopefully, you won't need them, but just in case . . . And another thing I wanted to mention is the new Accel-Safe system you will use when you jump to light-speed. You recall that we had to get back into our hibernation capsules when either jumping to light-speed or decelerating out of light-speed."

"Right," said Jake. "Won't we still have to do that with the new engines?"

"No, that's why I'm mentioning it now. The technology involved in protecting crew members during intense accelerations has been greatly improved since the *Revelation* was built. Now each seat on the flight deck will have an Accel-Safe pak installed while we are doing the other mods. When you and the crew go through *JLS*, you can remain in your crew seats. And this takes care of you from before *JLS* all the way up to *10xL*. Once you reach cruise, you can disengage the Accel-Safe."

"OK, I like that! We will be able to observe space through the cockpit windscreen as we go from sub-light-speed all the way up to 10xL."

"Exactly! All the GSA SC38 ships have that feature—it just hasn't been activated. Since the SC38s are all currently operating at sub-light-speeds, crews don't need Accel-Safe for lunar or Mars runs."

"The last thing we need to discuss, and perhaps the most important, is the planned installation of magna-laser guns in the *Revelation*. These are powerful units, Jake. Director Stoll insisted that in case you encountered hostile forces, man or animal, you should have the best weapons available installed in your ship."

"Magna-lasers!" said Jake. "If we need to use that kind of firepower, we'll be in some *big* trouble! We will need a thorough checkout on them. Do the droids know how to use them?"

"Yes, they do, and they will be thoroughly trained on the ship security system that will be integrated with the two masers. These weapons are of course not as powerful as the GCC units Dante commands but are many times more powerful than your handheld weapons. At times, when you and the entire crew must leave the ship, it can protect itself. You will be able to arm the system so that any attempt to break into or harm the ship will be met by maser fire. The control pad can be accessed by you either manually or remotely to engage or disengage the security system."

"Impressive improvements, David! So in addition to the new engines, we will have the message probes, the security system with masers, and the new Accel-Safe units. The old bird will become a *battlewagon* with all this stuff. Director Stoll didn't happen to mention who is *paying* for all these improvements, did he?"

"We didn't discuss that, Jake. He just told me what he wanted on the ship."

"Hmmm. I've only agreed to pay for the engines and their installation. Guess I better talk to Susan and to Stoll on this."

"Well, nothing's been installed yet, Jake. I'll go ahead with drawings and specs but will check with you again before we install these new features."

"Thanks a lot, Dave. I'll get with Director Stoll on everything we've discussed and get back with you right away."

"I guess I'll get going now and see if Susan has the contract ready for me to review." Jake turned to leave and stopped. "Oh, I just remembered. One last question for you."

"You are just continuing to delay your mission," said David with a grin.

Jake smiled, but he had to talk about Maria. "Dave, I'll make my question short and simple. Where is Maria, and where is the time machine?"

David's expression turned very somber and unsmiling. "She is back in the twenty-first century with Rico."

"And the time machine?"

"They have it—probably still in Rico's garage."

"How can you know this?"

"I don't *know* it—but I feel it. Here are my reasons. First, we know the machine works. It worked each time before Maria used it. I'm sure it took her back. Secondly, the brooch was under the stone at least *at some time*—the impression was clearly there. It had been removed sometime before Dante and Director Simonides lifted the stone. I think Maria put it there sometime in the twenty-first century and removed it *that same morning she left us* in the thirty-fourth century. I think she *returned* in the time machine for the express purpose of *retrieving the brooch*. Jake, *Maria* was the only person that knew the brooch was under the stone . . ."

"I'm with you most of the way. However, *Rico* could have known the brooch was under the stone—and *he* could have visited the house that morning and removed the brooch—just before Dante and Director Simonides arrived."

David thought for a minute. "You are right. *Either* of them could have removed it, but one thing is certain—whoever *lifted and reset the stone that morning* had to use the time machine to get to Rico's house in Arlington. The brooch itself could have been retrieved that morning or at *some earlier time*. We have no way of knowing.

"But we do know *positively* that Maria *must* have made it back to the twenty-first century, and she and/or Rico are using the time machine for whatever travel they wish."

"I agree with that."

"Furthermore, since there was no time machine in *this* century that we know of—before Weber created it—we must conclude that Rico did not, during his lifetime, *tell others of the machine* and did *not produce any more such units.*"

This comment startled David. He just looked at Jake for a few seconds. Finally, he said, "I have to agree with that too."

"Thanks, Dave. See you later." Jake turned to go.

"Later . . ." said David. Then as Jake was leaving the hangar, he called to him, "Jake! Wait a sec! Got one more thing for you."

Jake came back and met David halfway. "Whatcha got?"

"Last night, as Ellen and I were being chauffeured home by George and Gracie, I guess they thought we had nodded off in the backseat. They started talking to each other."

"Yeah? What did they talk about?"

"George asked Gracie how she felt about flying the mission with you and Susan to ACP5. You'll never believe what she said." David hesitated. "Maybe I shouldn't have mentioned it."

"Tell me! You started, now finish."

"Gracie said that she was excited about the trip. She said she thought you were *real good-looking* and wondered if Susan was *your only girlfriend.*"

Jake's mouth dropped wide open. He couldn't believe that David was telling the *truth.* "Come on, Dave, Gracie is an android. Did Ellen hear her comment?"

"I don't think so. I think El *was* asleep."

"Let's just keep this between us boys right now. I really don't know what to make of it. Ellen might have done *too* good of a job *humanizing* these droids."

Jake called Susan on his mec as he walked.

"Susan here."

"Sue! Where are you on the contract?"

"It's ready for our signatures tomorrow morning."

"Did you know that Stoll has added some very expensive equipment to the ship?"

"That came up in the discussion in his office. The message probes, the Accel-Safe units, the security system, and the magna-lasers. We added a paragraph to the agreement to cover those."

"Those are expensive, Sue. We're *not agreeing to pay for them.*"

"Absolutely not. Director Stoll was quite gracious and generous regarding the items. He explained that the Accel-Safe units are now standard on all 10xL ships, and he regards the message probes and the weapons systems to be necessary for our safety. He stated that GSA doesn't want to lose their investment in us on the *first trip out*."

Jake was speechless for a moment. Then he said, "Very thoughtful and considerate of him. Let's just hope we *don't need* any of the emergency or defense systems."

50

The launch of the *Revelation* was now hours away. David and his team had successfully installed the 10xL engines along with the probe units, the security and weapons system, and the Accel-Safe. All systems had been checked and rechecked, and the ship had been test-flown. It was flown not by Jake and Susan, but by two GSA test pilots as was the custom at Kennedy Spaceflight Center.

The test flight was practically flawless with only minor discrepancies, which were easily and quickly corrected. Jake reviewed all the test reports from the flight and was quite comfortable with the results.

The GSA public relations department had produced a press release concerning the launch information covering the entire mission. The media had gone into orbit themselves over the whole thing mainly because it had been kept secret up until just hours before the scheduled launch. None at GSA were concerned about how upset the media was. They had made sure that the people that *really needed to know* about the new *Revelation* mission did know. The media and the public were not included in the "need to know" category. Inasmuch as Jake was financing the project out of his pocket and only limited, already-budgeted government funds were being used, members of Congress did not have to explain to their constituents why tax monies were being wasted on "frivolous space ventures."

KSC was again the focal point of hordes of media. Spectators began to arrive as the scheduled launch time neared. Grandstands had been erected for VIPs who would not arrive at the launch area until the morning of the launch, usually about an hour before. On the eve of the launch, thousands of spectators and hundreds of media people camped out in the area surrounding the launch area. Although the departure time of the *Revelation* was not until 8:00 AM, everyone rushed to have the best view possible so they wouldn't miss anything. After all, this was the first launch of a ship to an unexplored planet since the *same ship* had been launched to Nyvar *thirteen centuries before*.

Jake and Susan were enjoying a last supper with Ellen and David at their home near Orlando. The two androids George and Gracie had been left at the *Revelation* to conduct some final system checks and to carefully review—one more time—all articles and supplies to be carried in the cargo holds of the ship.

As the four sat around Ellen's dining table, Jake said to Ellen and David, "Are you two real sure that you don't want to go with us? This is the mission we were planning to do a couple of years ago."

David and Ellen laughed. David said, "We couldn't if we wanted to, Jake. El is pregnant with our son."

"Oh Ellen," exclaimed Susan—we didn't know! I'm so happy for both of you."

"Me too," said Jake, "and you are certainly right. We'll have enough to do on this mission without attending to a *new arrival*."

"Anyway," said David, "We are very happy with our lives here. We certainly don't regret coming on the original *Revelation* mission. Life is much better in the thirty-fourth century."

"And David and I are *sooo excited* about our new baby," said Ellen.

Ellen continued, turning the conversation back to the mission, "Are you sure you have the correct navigation program in the ship's computer this time?" Everyone laughed at that. She continued, "We would hate to see you end up back here in five months having never landed on—what is your name for P5?"

"Vecino," said Susan. "Spanish for *neighbor*."

"And we do have the correct nav. program in the computer." said Jake. "If we veer off course while in hibernation—even two feet off course—I have charged George and Gracie with the responsibility of ensuring that we immediately get back on course."

"And they are to *wake us* if anything unusual or unplanned happens," said Susan.

"Just how much do you know about Vecino?" said David.

"Well," said Susan, "we just spent the last few days being briefed by Dr. Ottinger and Dr. Charles Sagan, Head of Astronomy and Space Research for GSA. They imparted quite a bit to us, and of course George and Gracie recorded *everything* presented, if we need to refer to it later."

"From a practical standpoint," said Jake," here are some key things we know. Vecino is a planet that orbits Alpha Centauri A. As you both know, the Alpha Centauri System is composed of *three stars*, rather than one star, as is our solar system. Astronomers have labeled the stars simply Alpha Centauri A, Alpha Centauri B, and Alpha Centauri C. AC-A is slightly larger than our sun, AC-B is slightly smaller than our sun and AC-C, also called Proxima Centauri because it comes nearer to our Earth, is much smaller than the other two stars. AC-C has a million-year orbit around A and B. AC-A and AC-B revolve around a common center of gravity, once in 80 Earth years. Vecino is one of five planets orbiting Alpha Centauri A."

"Are we boring you with this?" said Susan.

"Absolutely not," said Ellen. "Please continue . . ."

"Just a bit more," said Jake. "We know that Vecino is larger than Mars but smaller than Earth. It rotates on its axis every 30.5 Earth hours and it takes about 16 Earth months for Vecino to orbit AC-A, its 'sun.' The planet's average orbit track is about 105 million miles from AC-A, compared to the 93 million miles from Earth to our sun."

"Vecino's surface gravity is about 86% of Earth's," said Susan, "and the surface of the planet is about 60% water. Dr. Sagan's team believes that the atmosphere is similar to that of Earth. They have been able to determine that it contains oxygen, carbon dioxide and nitrogen."

"What about the presence of life?" said Ellen. "Any info on that?"

"Nothing positive," said Jake. "GSA is highly confident various forms of life are present on the planet because of the conditions there—surface temps, water, AC-A light, etc.—but they have not been able to confirm the existence of life using the data from their exploratory probes."

"Determining whether the planet has life—and what forms of life—is up to us, I guess," said Susan.

The group became silent for a few moments.

"I still think about us having the wrong navigation program on our mission to Nyvar," said David. "Do you guys ever try to imagine what our lives would have been like if we had actually landed on Nyvar?"

"I don't," said Susan, "because it's impossible to do. We didn't know enough about the conditions on that planet to be able to even *guess* at what we might have found. I do occasionally wonder why I volunteered for that trip in the first place. I must have been nuts! But now that we are in the thirty-fourth century, I am certainly glad I did volunteer."

"Then the three of you are all happy you came to the thirty-fourth century and back to Earth?" said Jake.

"We are," said David. "Aren't you?"

Jake paused and looked at each of the three faces before he spoke. Then he said, "I am, but I *knew* I was going to come back to Earth *when we left Earth*."

Susan, David, and Ellen just looked at Jake. Then Ellen said, "Sure you did, Jake! How could you possibly have known you were coming back to Earth instead of going to . . ." She stopped. Ellen's expression changed. "Unless . . . unless YOU changed the navigation program!"

Susan and David looked at Ellen with incredulous expressions. Then they looked at Jake who was smiling.

"But you couldn't have changed that program, Jake," said David. "Only the scientists in the lab knew the program, and they were the only ones with access to the ship's computer."

"He *did* it!" said Ellen. "I don't know *how* he did it, but HE DID IT!"

"Say something, Jake," said Susan. "You didn't change that program! You are just pulling another Jake on us. TELL THE TRUTH!"

They all were just staring at Jake, not knowing what to believe. He didn't have the computer knowledge or the access to the computer to have done it. But who *with* the knowledge and access had *the motive*? Why would anyone in the GSA lab want to change the ship's program and bring the *Revelation* back to Earth thirteen centuries later? And whoever changed that program has been *dead* now for at least twelve centuries.

Finally, Jake spoke, "You have all told me how happy you are that you came on the *Revelation* mission. And you are all my very best friends. Those are the only reasons why I am going to *tell you the truth*."

Susan and David and Ellen relaxed and sat back into their chairs. Jake continued, "I paid one of the specialists in the NASA lab *one million dollars* to substitute a program he created for me. We were *never* going to travel to Nyvar. When we left Earth, I knew we were *coming back to Earth*—in the thirty-fourth century."

They were shocked and stunned—and *angry*.

Ellen spoke first, "Jake, I am *furious* with you! You took *the lives of five other people into your hands* and made a decision for us that you had *no right* to make! We volunteered for a specific mission—not the one you took us on."

Susan was staring at Jake with tears in her eyes. She didn't want to believe that the man she thought she was in love with could be as callous toward other people as Jake had demonstrated. She could not find words to speak.

David was smiling. "Jake, you SOB! I am mad as hell at you for doing what you did, but I am *glad that you did it*. I volunteered to go to a new world—a pig in a poke! We found a *new world*. We found a wonderful *new world* where Ellen can enjoy the full extent of her medical knowledge and skills, a world where I can do much more interesting work than I could have for NASA in the twenty-first century. If the six of us could have *specified* the kind of world we wanted Nyvar to be, we could not have done a better job. Earth in the thirty-fourth century is the best place in the galaxy to be that *anyone knows of*.

"Because I am so happy being in this century on this good old Earth, I forgive you for being a *jerk* and not telling us *where we were going*."

David continued, "Now will you tell us *why* you did what you did?"

Jake was quite concerned about the reaction he had gotten from his best friends. He was thinking, *You idiot! Why didn't you just* sit *on the secret? Now you may have lost two good friends and the woman you love so much.* He wasn't sure what to say or do. Susan was in tears although David's words had softened her somewhat, and Ellen just continued to glare at him. Finally, he said, "I had three reasons. Here they are.

"First, *I was chicken*. The more we learned in our prelaunch training about the kinds of worlds we might find out there, the more I didn't want to deal with most of them. There was only one way I could be sure of where we were going—to create a navigation program that was a route back to Earth. I figured that Earth in the thirty-fourth century would be a new world for all of us and *probably a lot better* than what we might find on Nyvar. At least Earth was a sure thing. We knew it had intelligent life.

"Secondly, I had a serious financial problem with the IRS. Most of the money I had in the bank was owed to the government in back taxes—taxes I had *evaded*. I was expecting a warrant for my arrest as soon as they figured out what I really owed.

"And finally, I was really fed up with the twenty-first century and the failure of our government to initiate meaningful changes. I gambled that by the thirty-fourth century, the Earth would be a better place to live. Looks like my hunch paid off."

The ladies were still staring at Jake. David continued to smile.

Jake spoke again, "Since you all had risked your lives to go to a *new* world, I hoped that you would be happy with thirty-fourth-century Earth. And it now appears that you *are*—and rich, as well . . ."

Everyone was still. David was now shaking his head from side to side but still smiling. Finally, David lifted his glass and said, "Here's to Jake Loneghan! Still my best friend. Besides, Ellen, that is . . ."

The girls hesitated. Susan was wiping her eyes but was starting to smile under her napkin. Ellen still stared at Jake, but the look was softening. Finally, Ellen raised her glass, and then Susan did. Susan said, "Jake, you are an SOB, but I *still love you*."

"I guess you are still OK, Jake," said Ellen.

Everyone laughed. "What about the warrant for your arrest, Jake?" said Ellen.

"They threw that out because they got their money and because the perpetrator had definitely *left town* for good—*they thought*. I was the only person that *knew we were coming back*! That is, except the guy I paid a million to for changing the nav. program. But he sure as hell *wasn't going to talk*."

Now Ellen laughed! And the others joined in.

"There is one more thing I would like to say, and then I hope we can drop the subject," said Jake. "When I made the decision that dramatically affected all of your lives, you weren't my best friends. I hardly knew you. Now you are my very best friends, and I thought you deserved to know the truth."

"Another toast to Jake!" said David, holding his glass high.

"And the very best of luck to you both on your journey to Vecino!" said Ellen.

7 am, October 15, 3340:
The Primary Launch Pad—Kennedy Spaceflight Center

The *Revelation* had been moved out of its hangar to the launch pad. The white polymer paint covering its titanium skin glistened in the early-morning sun. It was a perfect day to fly—to launch anything except maybe a kite—because there was not a breath of wind and not a cloud in the sky. The spectators, most of them campers during the night, were thick as far as the eye could see. Though they had only a few days to spread the word, the media had done a good job.

On the VIP stand were several dignitaries, but mostly GSA staff. To everyone's surprise, President Thornhill and his wife had come down in Air Force One accompanied by Kosta Simonides, director of GSA, and his wife, Betty. Seated next to the presidential party were David and Ellen Marks, by special invitation from Director Simonides. The rest of the seats in Air Force One had been occupied by White House staff, Secret Service, and press personnel. They all were seated in the president's area for the launch. The U.S. Army Band was on hand to provide stirring music as a backdrop for the occasion. The band was seated in a special area adjacent to the VIP stand.

At the *Revelation*, at the base of the stairs to the flight deck, was a podium, which appeared to be large enough to accommodate six people or so. The time was now 7:40 AM.

Just as the band struck up the national anthem, "America the Beautiful," a white puma van rounded the corner of the hangar headed for the spacecraft. The van stopped near the base of the steps to the ship, and four people emerged, actually two astronauts and two droids. They stepped onto the podium and were joined by another who had approached the podium from behind. Klaus Stoll took the speakers position at the microphones.

"Good morning, President Thornhill and Mrs. Thornhill, Director Simonides and Mrs. Simonides, other distinguished guests, and all others who have come to witness this historic event. As you all know, we have had bases on Mars and the moon for many years and are continuing to mine those bodies and expand our operations in both locations. It has been a long time—I will not say how long—since we have made any attempt to visit other stars or their planets in our Milky Way galaxy. Today, we open a new era."

Jake whispered to Susan, who promptly shushed him, "I hope this doesn't go on too long."

Klaus continued, "Today, we will launch this spacecraft, the *Revelation*, on a mission that will take it and its brave crew to the Alpha Centauri triple-star system, our nearest neighbor star in our galaxy. After years of research, we have discovered that five planets orbit Alpha Centauri A. One of those five planets, the one we have named Vecino, has been found to be very similar to our Earth. We know it has water and vegetation. We do not know whether or not it has human or any animal life.

"Our exploration crew is composed of Mission Commander Jake Loneghan, First Officer Susan Chen, and two very able fourth-generation androids George and Gracie." This brought a murmur from the crowd. "They will travel to Vecino—a word that in Spanish means *neighbor*—to hopefully explore and discover all they can about the planet and the kind of life it supports.

"The *Revelation,* with *new engines,* can now cruise at ten times light-speed, and the journey both out and back will take less than one year, including four weeks on the planet. We are very hopeful that this mission will be fruitful, and we will become introduced to new intelligent life-forms. If that doesn't happen, we hope that Vecino will be a friendly world such that we may establish a base there and eventually populate the planet with our own species.

"Now without further ado, I will introduce you to the two astronauts that are taking great risks to help us expand our knowledge of our galaxy. Commander Jakob Loneghan and First Officer Susan Chen, please step forward."

Jake and Susan stepped to the microphones, and Jake spoke first, "I think Director Stoll was working from *my* notes." This brought a titter from the crowd. Jake continued, "Let me just say that Susan and I are most grateful for this opportunity to venture into the galaxy. We wish to thank Director Stoll, Director Simonides, David and Ellen Marks, all those at GSA, and especially President Thornhill for their support. Susan, do you have anything to say?"

Susan leaned over to the mikes and said, "Just that we are already five minutes behind our schedule . . ." This brought a laugh through the crowd. Then Susan said, "I would like to add my thanks to those of Commander Loneghan, the person who has pushed for this mission for so long and finally made it possible. We hope for success and plan to see you all in a year."

The crowd broke into a huge applause, and the band struck up "Off We Go into the Wild Blue Yonder."

Jake and Susan shook hands with Director Stoll and started up the stairs followed by Gracie and then George. Gracie whispered back to George, "I wanted to say something. Guess we aren't considered ready for human privileges."

George shushed her and closed the flight deck door after all were inside.

Jake took the left seat and Susan the right. George took the flight engineer's position, occupied by David on their thirteen-century trip from Earth to Earth; and Gracie took the medical officer's position, previously occupied by Ellen.

Susan couldn't miss the opportunity. "Are you sure we have the right nav. program, Jake?" She was smiling, but her eyes were dead serious.

"George." said Jake. "You checked the navigation program again?"

"Just this morning, sir, after rollout. We are going to Vecino, a planet of Alpha Centauri A."

Jake looked seriously at Susan, but with a hint of a smile, and said, "Trust me."

Jake then turned to the main instrument and control panel, engaged battery power, and called for the pre-engine-start checklist. Susan and George responded with, "All greens."

Jake called, "Starting engines." and the powerful 10xL engines began to whine. Susan was calling the power levels as the mighty engines increased rpm.

She said, "We have 100 percent takeoff power available."

"Clear us with Mission Control, Sue," said Jake over the engine noise.

Susan made the call. "Are we cleared for liftoff, MC?"

"Yes, ma'am, but we have a call for you from GCC. They say it's urgent."

Susan turned to Jake, saying, "A call from GCC."

"Has to be *Dante*." said Jake. "Put it through on the speaker."

"Jake! Susan!" Dante's voice came over the speaker. "I hear that you two are off on a *boondoggle*."

"Dante!" said Jake. "You almost missed us. We are at full power with these new 10xL engines, and this old horse is *straining at the reins*."

Dante laughed and said, "Then I won't keep you guys . . . We'll watch over your departure, and the very best to you on your mission. Call me when you get back."

"We will, Dante. And thanks . . ."

"Bye, Dante!" said Susan. "MC, *we are go*. Over and out." She turned to Jake. "Still holding with full power available."

"Roger," responded Jake and added, "Here we go . . ." as he applied takeoff power and commanded liftoff with the controls.

The huge craft rose from the pad vertically and began its ascent. As it climbed and accelerated, the nose began to rotate skyward. In a few moments, the nose and the fuselage were aligned perfectly with the flight path.

Jake applied the *full-climb power* to the ascent. The crew was pushed back deep into each of their seats—their g suits doing their jobs.

The ship's climb instantly resembled that of a toy rocket leaving its launch pad. Before the spectators could visually keep up, the *Revelation* was a tiny dot disappearing overhead. In less than five seconds, it could no longer be seen.

The band struck up "Stars and Stripes Forever" and continued to play marches until all the spectators had emptied the stands.

Everyone hoped that the *Revelation* would make history. That it would indeed visit Alpha Centauri's Planet 5 Vecino and return to Earth with good news.

"Engage the Accel-Safe system, partner," said Jake.

"Aye, sir," said Susan as she engaged the system. "We are all greens."

"No need for wasting time in orbit," said Jake. "We are out of here—stand by for *JLS*."

Jake pushed the controls to the maximum required power to break *the light-speed barrier* and held that setting as the speed indicator continued to increase. Susan called the numbers, "Nine-tenths light . . . ninety-five hundredths light . . . ninety-nine hundredths light!"

"WE ARE THROUGH!" called Jake as they pushed through the barrier.

Susan continued to call the numbers, " . . . 5xL . . . 7xL . . . 10xL! *We are at cruise!*"

Jake and Susan looked at the monitor above the windscreen showing the view from the tail camera. The sun was receding rapidly and became a tiny dot as they watched.

George called over, "We are *precisely* on track for Alpha Centauri, sir. Well done."

Jake reached over for Susan's hand and squeezed it tightly. He said, "I love you. Do you think you could become interested *in getting married*?"

Susan looked at him and smiled. "Why don't you ask me?" she said.

And Back on Earth

Klaus Stoll was walking with Constantine Simonides behind the president's group toward Air Force One, parked just by the hangar.

"Well, sir," said Klaus, "I guess we just have to wait and see."

"Did you tell them to send us a message when they arrive?"

"No, sir, I did not. They are only to use the message probe *if they are in trouble or are unable to depart Vecino on schedule*."

"I see. Then we won't know anything for almost a year."

"Nothing *for sure*. But I have every confidence that they *will reach* their destination. I am just worried about whether they will survive there and *be able to return*."

"If they die there, how will we know?"

"They just won't come back. We won't know until their return date has come and gone."

"What if they don't die there but *are restrained* from coming back? How would we know that?"

"If they exceed the ground time we have allotted for the mission *by one week* and are unable to trigger the probe, it will *automatically* launch and return to us, probably empty with no message. That is, assuming that the probe has not been damaged in a crash."

Kosta thought about everything they had just talked about and said, "Think positive."

51

Earth—in the Year 2025

Enrico Valdez was alone at breakfast on his patio. The morning air was still. A light fog drifted just above the Potomac as he picked up the *Post* and stared at the headlines:

REVELATION SUCCESSFULLY LAUNCHES FOR THE STARS!

He thought of Maria. How he already missed her. They had not spoken even once since she made the decision to go to Nyvar. Rico understood her choice, and at the time, she had discussed it with him. He honestly believed that he could put her out of his mind. Alas, he was quite wrong. Never had he felt about a woman the way he cared for Maria! He missed her so very much.

In the early light, the moon was still quite visible, and he could *just* see a morning star. *Is that the direction my Maria is flying?* he thought.

Manuel came onto the deck. "Sir, this just arrived in the morning mail." He handed a letter to Rico. It was from Maria.

Rico hesitated, not sure that he even wanted to open it. The silence between them after Maria's decision was by her choice. She had said that it would be too hard for her to go through with the training and the mission if she continued to stoke the love she felt for him. He understood and had agreed not to contact her. Why had she now chosen to torture him with a note after it was too late, after she had left his life forever? He set the letter aside, unopened.

The article about the launch and the voyage of the *Revelation* offered little new information. After all, the mission had been front-page for weeks. *What new could they find to write?* he thought.

But suddenly, he realized that the front page emblazoned a picture of the spaceship! NASA had in the past released only *simulated sequences* of the *Revelation* and its mission, but this was the first time he had seen actual photos. The front-page shot showed the ship climbing vertically straight above the runway! A note under the liftoff shot said to turn to page 5 for more photographs.

He turned the pages; and *there was Maria*, standing with the crew at the top of the stairs, boarding the ship. He studied the photo. *Nice-looking group*, he thought. *Three women and three men. My Maria is the star of the crew.*

Oh, Maria, he thought, *find a way to come back to me. I refuse to believe that I will never see you again.* He picked up the letter and was about to open it.

Manuel was again at the door. "Sir, I am so sorry to interrupt your breakfast again."

"It's all right, Manuel, what is it now?" said Rico in a somewhat annoyed tone.

"You have a phone call, sir. *President Buchard is calling.*"

Rico reached for the phone and answered, "Ah, Mr. President! How are you this fine morning?"

"Good morning, Rico. I am in my office working very hard as usual, and I will bet you a thousand dollars that you are on your back patio eating breakfast and reading the morning paper."

"Sorry, sir, but I cannot take your bet—I would lose."

The president laughed. "Did you see the story on the NASA launch? There are some good pictures there."

"Yes, I saw the pictures. It is too bad we will never know what happens to the brave crew aboard that ship. I am not sure that mission was a wise investment, Mr. President."

"You are not alone in your feelings, Rico. There are many others who feel the same way. I, however, am not one of them. Perhaps the future will tell us whether or not the investment was wise."

The president continued, "I called this morning to get your advice on an investment a certain company is about to make in Mexico. It will involve several manufacturing facilities and provide thousands of jobs."

Rico talked with the president for about ten minutes and put the phone back in its cradle. The morning was still beautiful, and he still missed Maria.

Maria stepped from the UMU in Rico's garage. She felt *fine*. One moment, she was in the time machine looking out at David, Ellen, Director Stoll, and all the rest; and the next moment, she was in Rico's garage. She must have gotten the coordinates perfectly right because the time machine was sitting exactly in the spot she had carefully measured at Rico's home in the future—the year 3340. She looked at the autos in the garage—the same 2024 Mercedes and 2023 Jeep that Rico had when she last saw him. *She was home.*

She looked at the UMU and was thinking, *I am supposed to send the machine right back to the GSA lab. Dr. Ottinger and David and the others are waiting for it.* Then she said out loud, "What am I thinking? It will be thirteen centuries before they will be waiting for this machine. It hasn't even been invented yet. I have plenty of time—I have my whole lifetime—to send this UMU back to the thirty-fourth century."

She thought some more about it. *They told me to send it back within ten minutes of my arrival here, but why? I think I'll discuss this with Rico. He will know what we should do.*

Maria reached back into the UMU and took her bag out. She thought, *I'll bet Rico will be very interested in what is in this bag. Too bad I had to leave all those nice clothes I bought in the thirty-fourth century.* "Now for the big surprise!" she said out loud.

Maria decided that she didn't want to alarm Manuel unnecessarily, so she better not just walk into the house from the garage. She slipped out a door on the front of the garage and walked around to the front entrance of the home. She rang the doorbell.

Manuel opened the door and was startled to see Maria. He hadn't seen her for over two months. "Senorita Rodriguez!" he exclaimed. "I have not seen you in many weeks! How are you?"

"Wonderful, Manuel. It is good to see you. Is Enrico here?"

"He is, senorita, on the back patio. I will advise him that you are here."

"I will walk with you, Manuel. Rico will be very surprised to see me."

The two walked toward the door to the patio. They could see Rico engrossed in his paper.

"He was just speaking with the president, senorita."

"Really?" said Maria "That is *impressive.*"

They reached the door and stepped onto the patio. Rico did not look up from his paper but said in a very annoyed tone, "Now what is it, Manuel? *Another* interruption?"

"Si, senor, but you will not be angry with me for this interruption."

Rico looked up just over the top of his paper and *could not believe his eyes*!

"Maria! Is it you? How?" *He refused to accept what he was seeing.* Manuel left and returned to the house. Maria just stood and smiled.

Rico rubbed his eyes, put down his paper, and stood. "You *cannot be* Maria! *Who* are you? Is this a cruel joke?"

"It's me, Rico!" said Maria. She stepped toward him. He backed away. She continued, "Believe it, Rico. *It is me!*"

Rico circled away from Maria and went for his newspaper. He opened it to the picture that showed Maria on the top step of the stairs to the *Revelation.* He held it so she could see the paper.

"*My* Maria went with *this* crew *on this spaceship . . .* They left *this morning!*" He turned to the front page. "Here, look at this. My Maria is on *that ship*! I ask you again. *Who are you?*"

Maria stopped walking toward Rico. She had known that this moment would be very difficult. She couldn't think what she should say or do to convince him.

Then she had an idea. She said, "The last night we were together, we prepared a wonderful meal of lamb and rice—one of your favorites. You selected two wines during the evening, both very nice. The first was Bodega Noemia from Argentina, and the second was Capo Salina, my absolute favorite. We danced to—"

He did not let her finish!

Rico came to Maria and swept her into his arms. "Maria! Maria! It *is* you! I am so happy . . . but how can this be? *Who* went on the ship after they took your picture with the crew?"

Maria couldn't speak. *She was in heaven.* She was back with her Rico, *and he loved her.* "Oh, Rico, how I have *missed* you. It has been almost two years and—"

He pulled back from her but continued to hold her in his embrace. "Two years?" he said. "You mean two *months*."

Maria realized she had erred. This was not the way she wanted to break all the news to him. "Oh, Rico, it has *seemed* like two years . . . Let us sit down and talk."

"I am not going to let you go, Maria. *Ever again.* We must sit in the *same chair*."

She laughed a beautiful laugh that neither of them had heard since Maria left two years ago to her, but only weeks ago to him. They kissed and then embraced some more and then kissed again.

"Promise me right now in this spot that you will never leave me again," he said.

Maria did not hesitate. "I promise. Now can we sit down?"

This time, Rico had a good laugh. They both sat.

"What can I get you, my darling? Are you hungry? Where is your car? How did you get here to the house? I heard no one drive up."

"*Wait. Wait.* Too many questions. I am hungry. Do you have eggs and toast?"

"Yes, my dear. I will have Manuel prepare them for you. And some fresh coffee?"

"That would be nice," said Maria. She suddenly was tired but *wide-awake*.

Rico started for the door to summon Manuel and then stopped. "I will not let you out of my sight. MANUEL!" he yelled.

"Sir?" Manuel was at the door, wondering if someone was injured or something.

Rico instructed Manuel as to what to prepare for Maria, and then he sat again as close as he could sit by her side. "Who went on the spaceship, my darling? It certainly wasn't you."

Maria was thinking, *Now just how do I do this? Rico is a very smart man. A time machine? He will never believe it, but there is no other story. I must tell him the truth.*

He was gazing into her eyes, captured once again by their deep beauty. Waiting patiently for her to speak, she had to explain to him.

"How much time do we have to talk this morning, Rico?"

"As much time as you need. I have no engagements today."

"OK, here goes." Maria took a deep breath.

At that moment, Manuel appeared at the door with Maria's food. "Come, Manuel! She is hungry!" called Rico.

Manuel placed the food and coffee in front of Maria, then just stood there.

"You may *go*." said Rico, again annoyed.

Manuel backed up a step and said, "But, sir . . ."

Rico stood and glared at Manuel with fire jumping from his eyes!

"WHAT ARE YOU STANDING THERE FOR? I SAID GO!" screamed Rico.

"Sir, there is *something in the garage* I must tell you about. It was not there earlier this morning."

"WHAT?" yelled Rico. "What are you babbling about, Manuel?"

"Wait!" said Maria. "Rico, that is my *transportation* in your garage."

"Ah." said Rico. "Then Manuel's mystery is explained. Go now, Manuel. Senorita Maria and I have much to talk about."

This time, Manuel left but was thoroughly confused. *Senorita Rodriguez arrived in a phone booth?* he thought.

Maria was relieved. She needed to work up to the *time machine*. It was not the way to start her story.

"Rico," she said softly, "calm yourself. Please relax and have some of Manuel's fresh coffee and prepare yourself for a long story. Here, I will pour for you." She filled his cup and her cup and tried to relax herself. *This might not be easy*, she thought.

She began, "I *was on the ship* with the other five crew members, Rico. I am on the ship in that picture." She pointed to the front page of the *Post*.

"But . . ." Rico tried to speak. She put her finger gently on his lips.

"Just listen, my darling. I will tell you everything. We left on the *Revelation* on schedule with our objective to reach the planet Nyvar, thirteen hundred light-years from Earth. *We did not make it to Nyvar*. Something happened, and the navigational program was changed. After *thirteen centuries in space*, we arrived at a planet—but not Nyvar."

She paused and sipped her coffee. "*We arrived back here, Rico*! Back here *on Earth*. Someone had put an elliptical path into our computer. We landed in the year 3339. Because of our travel at light-speed, we made the trip in *less than one year* of our lifetimes. When we landed on Earth, I was one year older than when we left Earth. But you, my darling, had been gone over *twelve centuries*."

"Maria, I . . ." Rico was going to say that he understood her so far, but she wouldn't let him speak.

"Just let me get through the whole story, my dear. The hardest part for you to believe is the last part—how I got back here and at this *precise time*."

Rico finally relaxed and poured himself a second cup of coffee.

"Thank you, my darling, for being so sweet." She decided to cut to the chase. It wasn't going to be easy now or fifteen minutes from now or *an hour from now*.

"In the thirty-fourth century, they have invented a *time machine*, Rico. I came back to you in that machine that is *now in your garage*."

Needless to say, Rico was overwhelmed. He thought, *This cannot be true! But why would she lie to me now? If it is not true and she did leave on the mission, it is the only plausible explanation . . . as impossible as it may seem.*

He stood and held out his hand to her. "Come! We will look at your *time machine*."

Maria had a hard time walking as fast as Rico, but she had no choice. He had her hand and was practically *dragging her into the house*.

Rico opened the inside door to the garage.

Standing in the middle of one bay was the UMU.

"That," said Rico, "is a *time machine*?"

"It brought me back from the thirty-fourth century to be with you, my darling. Call it what you will. The inventors have named it the *Ultimate Mobility Unit*, or UMU. They chose that name because it will transport a person not only through time but also through space."

Rico walked slowly around the device, looking at every detail. "It looks like a *phone booth*," he said.

Maria laughed. "I guess it does. I never really thought about that."

Rico started to open the door. Maria quickly moved to his side. "Be careful!" she warned. "It is programmed to return to the thirty-fourth century with only the touch of one button!"

Rico stepped back. Maria continued, "They taught me how to enter destination coordinates and times and how to activate transfers. They also preprogrammed it to return to the GSA laboratory I left from with only the touch of the activate key."

Rico was thinking. "Can you cancel the destination information they have entered?"

"I think so. There's really no hurry to send it back." She entered the unit. Maria looked at the control panel. She thought, *What I don't want to do is hit the wrong key.* But the activate key was positioned *directly adjacent* to the reset key. It was as if some unseen force was in control of her hand. She hit the wrong key! *The countdown was initiated*!

"Oh, Rico! I have activated it. It's going *back to the future!*"

Rico saw the numbers on the display descending from ten . . . nine . . . eight . . .

"*Jump out, Maria*! NOW! LET IT GO!"

Maria stayed inside at the control panel. She was determined not to let the machine go—yet . . . She pushed the reset button. The countdown continued. Six . . . five . . . four . . . Then she saw the *power* key! She pushed it! The UMU control panel went blank. The countdown ceased. There was not a sound. Maria turned to Rico and smiled. "Looks like I'll be staying a while longer."

Rico did not think it was funny. "GET OUT!" he shouted. He opened the door and grabbed her arm and pulled.

She came out and into his arms! She sobbed and said quietly, "I am not going to leave you again." They embraced.

Finally, Rico said, "I guess I believe that *it works*. I thought I had lost you again."

"If you want me to, I can send it back to them *now* as I said I would do."

Rico thought for a moment, then said, "No, we have *thirteen centuries* before they will be expecting the machine back. Let's keep it for at least a while. Then we can send it back."

Rico looked at the bag on the floor by the UMU. "What is in that bag, Maria?"

Maria looked down. "Oh, that? That is just a bag I brought with me in the UMU—some patent record copies I collected *at my job* in Washington. I will tell you about that later. Let's go back out on the terrace and sit. I want to tell you all about *the future*."

The End

REGENESIS CHAPTER GUIDE

Chapter	Pages	Content
49	441-448	Contract signed—Revelation modifications
50	449-458	Launch of Revelation to Alpha Centauri—planet Vecino
51	459-465	Maria arrives at Rico's house in the 21st century

Get Published, Inc!
Thorofare, NJ 08086
28 September 2009
BA2009271